ENTHRALLING

Perfect and white against the amber sky, like a cloud set on a carpet of emerald green, the Castle stood just as Mary always remembered it. Often she had gone back to it in her mind. Now, at last, she was again to be its guest—at the invitation of Vivian, her dearest friend.

But Vivian had gone to London. And neither Lord and Lady Clareham, her parents, nor Edmond, her brother, were prepared for the unexpected guest.

HAUNTING

"Vivian asked you to visit her here at Castle Cloud," Edmond asked, "without telling us anything about it, then left when you are expected? You must have been mistaken about her intent."

"No, she begged me to come," Mary protested. "I must see Vivian. Where near London is she staying?"

"I am afraid it is too late. . ." Lady Clareham began. She paused for a brief interruption, then resumed.

"I am afraid it is too late for you to go anywhere today, Mary, so you will stay the night here with us."

CASTLE CLOUD

ELIZABETH NORMAN
CASTLE CLOUD

AVON
PUBLISHERS OF BARD, CAMELOT AND DISCUS BOOKS

CASTLE CLOUD is an original publication of Avon Books. This work has never before appeared in book form.

AVON BOOKS
A division of
The Hearst Corporation
959 Eighth Avenue
New York, New York 10019

First Avon Printing, June, 1977

AVON TRADEMARK REG. U.S. PAT. OFF. AND IN
OTHER COUNTRIES, MARCA REGISTRADA,
HECHO EN U.S.A.

Printed in the U.S.A.

AUTHOR's NOTE

AMONG THE MIDDLE AND UPPER CLASSES in England in Victorian times, only the members of one's family, his oldest and closest friends, or his betrothed would ever address him by his first name. Such familiarity implied only the greatest intimacy and deepest affection.

But today, of course, first names are widely and casually used. So much so, that the extreme formality of the Victorians in this respect would at times, I think, not only seem ridiculous to us but might often be misinterpreted.

So where I have felt there was a danger of this in CASTLE CLOUD, I have allowed my characters to address one another somewhat less formally than they actually would have in 1856.

Otherwise I have tried to portray accurately the manners and customs of the time.

E. N.

🜲 Chapter One 🜲

"YOU WILL NOT BE WANTED up there, so you may as well save yourself the walk up the hill." Then he said: "Pity! What a charming girl you are—such pretty eyes."

"Thank you, Edmond," I said.

My answer seemed to bewilder him. He sat on his horse staring down at me.

"I am Mary Thorpe, Vivian's friend. She must have told you I would be coming."

"No." Still he couldn't place me. Suddenly he remembered. "You looked like a servant in search of employment. Who else would come walking up the hill out of nowhere? And you certainly couldn't expect me to recognize you after all this time. We met only twice, and that was five years ago. You must realize that an enormous number of things happen in five years' time."

"Yes, I realize that. It is good to see you again, Edmond. It was four years ago, actually. I hope you have been well."

"Where on earth have you come from? Vivian is not at home."

"But she will return, surely. And Lord and Lady Clareham? Are they not at home?"

"I will ride on ahead and tell Mother you are coming."

And without another word, he shot up the drive at a gallop, sending pebbles rattling back across the ground toward me. Then all was still.

My story really begins there—begins with my peculiar reception at Castle Cloud.

I had known Vivian, Edmond's sister, at school and had come to visit her. Castle Cloud was her father's seat near the coastal town of Barnstaple in Devonshire. I arrived on Wednesday, June 25, 1856.

1

The Devonshire countryside lay shimmering in the sun on that golden afternoon as I walked toward the Castle. The leaves hung still on the trees, and a few milk-white clouds stood unmoving in the sky. Only the bees and the flies moved, buzzing among the buttercups and marguerite and foxglove which bloomed at the base of the hedgerows bordering the drive. Long before Castle Cloud had been dreamed of, the drive had been a country lane, and the hedgerows had, most probably, been planted when it began. They stood too high to see over—even when riding in a carriage—and prevented me from looking into the meadow beyond, but I knew that milfoil bloomed there. It perfumed the air.

As I walked, I remembered the delightful week I had spent at the Castle when I visited Vivian four years before and how Castle Cloud and its grounds had captivated me. I had fantasized then that the most wonderful thing in all the world would be to be mistress of the Castle. And many times since then, when I was unhappy, I had gone back to Castle Cloud in my mind and been comforted. No other place had ever affected me that way.

So I was eager to see it again. But I would not see it until I had climbed the drive which half circled the hill and reached a wide, grassy plateau near the top of it where the hedgerows ended.

I was not to climb there alone, however. To my right, beyond a hole in the wall, I heard leaves rustle and a twig snap, and then a black, bearded head appeared from a thicket of elm saplings. It belonged to a thin, scraggly, part-terrier, little mongrel dog. The dog stared at me, excited yet cautious. Then she crept from her cover and plodded warily toward me, sniffing.

"Sarah!" I called, and I held out my palm for her to smell. "Hello! Good dog. Hello, Sarah."

Sarah was Vivian's dog. She seemed to remember me. Her tail wagged furiously as she wriggled against my shins. I bent and scratched her behind the ears. Panting and slobbering, she looked up at me adoringly.

"Sarah, you are all wet. Look what you have done to my skirt. Have you been swimming? In the river? Well! And where has your mistress gone this afternoon, leaving you all alone?"

As if in answer, Sarah danced and pranced back and

forth in front of me, and then loped ahead toward the house, sniffing the ground as she went. Periodically, she stopped to look back and wait for me before she ran on. We climbed the drive together this way.

Finally the hedgerows ended, and the white dome of Castle Cloud rose like a white cloud against the sky. I had never come upon the Castle this way before, and I wondered if this were how it had gotten its name. Then the entire building rose into view, standing on its flat, emerald carpet, gleaming white in the sun. It looked as if it had been carved from an enormous sugar cube.

Castle Cloud was not a castle at all, but a Palladian-style country house—a very famous architectural masterpiece. It was designed by Colen Campbell and built, I believe Vivian had said, about 1730. It was one of Campbell's two near-replicas of the Italian architect Palladio's Rotunda at Vicenza, in Italy. It was a square, flat-sided, two-and-a-half-story block of stones, with an identical two-story, columned portico topped with a triangular pediment standing against each of its four sides. Above this, gently sloped a slate roof capped by an enormous white-tile dome. From the summit of the dome rose a lantern in which Vivian and I had often sat together looking out over the countryside.

The house was of white Beer stone, the same material used for Exeter Cathedral, and it was flanked at some distance by smaller twin pavilions of the same stone with porticos of their own. These housed the servants and stablemen.

The buildings had lost none of their magic, and I would have loved to sit on the grass and admire them until I had had my fill. But Sarah was waiting for me and so, I was sure, were Lord and Lady Clareham. So I walked on up the drive toward the house.

A flock of sheep grazed in the park in front of the house. Several of them stood in the drive blocking our path and looking belligerently at us, but Sarah herded them aside for me.

She and I parted at the base of the stairway to the entrance front, as she was not allowed in the house. She sat down next to Edmond's horse, Cinnamon, and looked wistfully after me. Cinnamon glistened with sweat. He should be curried, I thought, as I walked up the steps to the portico.

The steps, I noticed, were in rather bad repair. Mortar was missing from between many of the stones. And ivy had been allowed to climb up over the staircase. It had even been allowed to begin to climb one of the columns. And neither the landing halfway up the stairs nor the floor of the portico had been recently swept. Last winter's leaves lay where the wind had blown them and the rain had tamped them down.

Heightening the feeling of neglect, the entrance door stood open and unattended. I walked through it into the vestibule and found it empty and also unattended. Then I crossed the vestibule and passed through a doorway into the rotunda, the center hall of Castle Cloud. I stood for several moments, looking up at the inside of the dome which floated more than three stories above me. Then I glanced about the gallery that circled the hall on the second floor. It was deserted too.

"Do you wish to see her ladyship on business?"

"Oh, good afternoon, Mitchell," I said to the butler. He had appeared out of nowhere and startled me, but I tried not to show it. "I am the Baroness Beauford. I believe her ladyship is expecting me."

"I beg your pardon, my lady," Mitchell said.

But there had been no note of apology in his voice. He did not so much as bow his head, but stared insolently at me and my clothes before turning and walking toward the doors to the drawing room.

I followed him.

He swung the drawing room doors open and announced: "The Baroness Beauford, my lady."

Lady Clareham and Edmond stood together on the far side of the room, near the windows. Was it my imagination, or had they been quarreling? I couldn't be sure, but I did not imagine Lady Clareham's expression. As I entered the room, she turned toward me and stood for an instant with her arms extended slightly, an expression of submission or surrender on her face. Then, almost at once, the look vanished. But surrender to what? I wondered. I did not understand it.

"Mary, my dear! How nice," she called.

She crossed the room toward me, holding out her hand.

She was nervous. Her mouth twitched into a smile.

As she approached, I had a moment to study her, and I was shocked by what I saw. Lady Clareham was about fifty-five and beautiful. She was one of those women with perfect bones who had always been beautiful and would always be beautiful, even if she lived to be a hundred. She was tall and carried herself like a queen, but her hair had turned white since I had last seen her. And how gaunt she had become, and how dreadfully pale! She is ill, I thought. How dark her illness has stained the hollows around her eyes. And I noted that she was dressed entirely in black.

Behind her, Edmond stood still, watching us intently.

"This is a surprise," Lady Clareham said.

I took her cold hand in mine. Her eyebrows rose to question me, but she waited for me to speak.

Then Edmond began to cross the room toward us, saying, "That will be all, Mitchell."

"Very good, my lord."

Mitchell left the drawing room, closing the doors behind him, and the three of us were left alone.

"It is so good to be back at Castle Cloud again," I said, more to Lady Clareham than to Edmond. "I thought I would never get here. The train seemed to take forever. How have you been, Lady Clareham? It is so good to see you again. And how are Lord Clareham and James? Are they at home? When will Vivian return?"

"We don't know," Edmond said.

"You don't know?"

"Vivian has gone to stay with friends. She left Castle Cloud the day after James's funeral."

"James has—passed away? Oh, I am so sorry!" I turned to Lady Clareham. "I didn't know—I am so dreadfully sorry, Lady Clareham."

She did not speak, but the look of grief and despair on her face told me more about her misery than I wanted to know.

"When did Vivian leave?" I asked Edmond.

"About three weeks ago."

"But . . ."

"She was distraught over her brother's death," he continued. "She was almost out of her mind with grief, and she felt she had to get away. We thought it best, too. I am sorry you have made the trip for nothing, but I am sure that next time you come she will have returned."

"Next time?" I said. "But I have come all the way from Holland to see her. You are jesting!" I paused, looking from Edmond to his mother. "There will not be a next time. I—I was barely able to get here this time. I don't understand. Vivian asked me to come—she practically pleaded with me to come to England to visit her, and here I am. Where has she gone? When will she return? Surely if she knows I am here—" I tried to think clearly. Lady Clareham looked completely mystified. "Didn't Vivian tell you I was coming to visit her?"

"No, my dear," Lady Clareham said.

"Where is she?"

"I told you. She is visiting friends," Edmond said.

"Where?"

"Near London."

"Then I shall go to her there. I must see her. Will you give me her address?"

"Certainly. I have it written down somewhere. Now, we shall sit down like civilized human beings, and perhaps you will tell us what this is all about. Perhaps we can help, but we cannot be expected to help if we do not know what we must do, now can we? After all, we are not mind readers, you know." He flashed me a brilliant smile.

Edmond led the way to two sofas facing each other on either side of a fireplace, and we sat down. He and his mother faced me. I could tell that they had known nothing about my impending visit to Castle Cloud. Vivian had obviously not told them about it. They were surprised to see me.

"Vivian asked you to visit her here at Castle Cloud," Edmond said, "without telling us anything about it, and then left when you are expected? You must have been mistaken about her intent."

"No, she begged me to come. You see, Papa died last August," I said. "He died in The Hague. The estates had been sold. Papa had spent everything. There was nothing left. Mother was alone then, of course, so after a time she remarried—a Dutchman, a farmer—and I went to live on the farm with them, between Schiedam and Delft.

"Vivian and I had kept up our correspondence, and last January she invited me to come to stay with her here at

Castle Cloud. I didn't think I should and wrote and told her so, but she insisted that I come. In letter after letter she *insisted*."

Then I reached into my reticule and took out a letter.

"This is one of her last letters to me. Let me read a paragraph, and you will see how insistent she was." I read:

". . . so you see you really *must* come. There is nothing, *nothing* to keep you on that dirty old farm and certainly no future for you in Holland. You must remember the wonderful, wonderful week we spent here at Castle Cloud in 1852—you said it was one of the *happiest* you ever had. It will be like that again and for more than a week. Come and stay as long as you like. Mamma and Papa will *love* to have you. It is so grim here—I am quite terribly lonely, and I need my friend by my side. Your future is in our lovely England. It has *always* been here. Who knows what wonderful, *wonderful* things we could arrange for you here? So come to me. I simply *will not* take no for an answer."

I handed the letter to Lady Clareham who looked at the handwriting and handed it to Edmond. He looked it over and then handed it back to me.

"Finally I said I would come," I continued, "but I did not know exactly how soon I could arrange it. Vivian said that that didn't matter—that she would be here anyway: to let her know if I could, but if I could not, to just come. So here I am."

At that moment one of the doors opened, and Cecile, Lady Clareham's maid, slipped into the room.

"Oh, I did not know your ladyship had a visitor," she said.

"That is quite all right, Cecile," Lady Clareham said. "Would you wait for me in my room, please? I shall not be long."

"Oui, my lady," she replied. Then she left us.

"But how on earth did you get here from Braunton?" Edmond asked.

"I walked from the station," I said.

"You *walked?*"

"Yes. It is not far, and I like to walk. And I did not

want to spend the money to hire a carriage. I must see Vivian. Where near London is she staying?" I asked.

"I am afraid it is too late. . ." Lady Clareham began.

But she was interrupted by Ahmad (I would not have thought I would remember his name), who entered the room and walked over to Lady Clareham without making a sound. He and Lady Clareham spoke briefly in Hindustani. Then Ahmad salaamed to her, bending his body and head very low and touching first his forehead with the inside of his fingers and then the floor with the back of them. He backed out of the room and silently closed the door behind him.

"That was Ahmad, my husband's valet," Lady Clareham said. "But you must remember him."

"Father wants to know who is here, I suppose," Edmond said. "I do not know why you don't make that black devil speak English. This is an English-speaking country, after all, and it is extremely rude to speak in a foreign language, especially in front of guests."

"Yes," Lady Clareham said, without looking at her son. "I am afraid it is too late for you to go anywhere today, Mary, so you will stay the night here with us."

"Of course she will, Mother," Edmond said.

"My bags—" I said.

"Your bags are obviously at the railway station." Edmond walked to the bellpull and rang.

"Yes, my lord?" Mitchell asked from the doorway.

"Mitchell, go out to the stables and ask Colen to collect Lady Beauford's bags at the station in Braunton," Edmond said. "I suppose the stationmaster knows which ones they are, Mary?"

"Yes, thank you, Edmond."

"And, Mitchell, ask Colen to look after Cinnamon. I left him at the entrance front."

"Yes, my lord."

"Mitchell announced you as the baroness Beauford," Edmond said, when the butler had gone.

"Yes, by writ," I said. "My father was the last marquess of Penbroke, but the barony is mine in my own right."

While I was saying this, Ahmad returned and stood waiting just inside the doorway. When I finished, he and Lady Clareham spoke in Hindustani.

"My husband would like to see you, Mary," she said, "if

you would be so kind as to go up to him. Ahmad will take you. I will go and see about your room, and then I must lie down awhile before dinner."

"Of course, Lady Clareham. Thank you," I said.

"And, Mary, he has been ill. You will find him greatly changed since the last time you saw him. Try not to show your surprise."

"I will go along with her, Mother," Edmond said.

Then I stood, walked across the room to Ahmad, and followed him out. Edmond stayed behind to speak to his mother.

Something mysterious and even sinister seemed to emanate from the Indian servant who walked so silently ahead of me. He wore a knee-length, white-cotton garment over his trousers and stood well over six feet tall. He was thin to the point of emaciation. His mahogany-colored skin made the whites of his eyes look bright and his decaying teeth whiter than they were. His hair and beard hung lank and greasy. But it was his eyes that terrified me. They glared at one omnisciently, hypnotically, and I imagined them capable of casting evil spells.

I had seen this strange man before, but only occasionally and at a distance. Now I followed him into the rotunda, across it, up a spiral staircase, and out onto the second floor gallery. There, I glanced over the railing just in time to see Edmond leave the drawing room and hurry across the hall below toward the stairway we had just climbed.

Then he disappeared into the stairwell as Ahmad and I walked on around the gallery toward the northwest corner room which was Lord Clareham's. And as we walked, I tried to remember the famous man as I had last seen him, standing on the west portico waving good-by to Vivian and me, four years before. He had been of only medium height and portly, but had borne himself commandingly nevertheless. And his skin had been very pink. It was Lord Clareham's hair, however, that I remembered most. It had turned silver white, he had kept it all, and it lay in long, perfect, wavy ridges. He had been sixty years old at the time. He was the second son of the sixth earl of Clareham, had attended Harrow and Cambridge, then pursued a distinguished civil service career in India, become governor of Madras, then governor-general of India, and later, advisor to Lord Dalhousie. He had known everyone—Palmerston, Pell, Russell, the duke of Wellington, Disraeli, Albert, the Queen. He had awed me.

When we arrived at his door, I waited nervously while Ahmad knocked. A voice from the other side of it called something in reply. Ahmad opened the door for me, and I passed through it into the sour, rancid air of a sickroom.

Propped into a half-sitting position on the bed against the windows lay a frail figure crowned by a mass of white, wavy hair. His head lay back on the pillows and his huge, black eyes stared at me. If it had not been for his hair, I would never have recognized Lord Clareham—he had changed so much. As I looked at him, I was barely able to stifle a gasp.

"Mary, come here my child," he said, "and sit in this chair near me, where I can see you." His voice was surprisingly strong, but his pronounciation was slurred and difficult to understand.

"Good afternoon, Lord Clareham," I smiled. I walked to his bedside and sat down. "How lovely to see you again, but I am sorry you have been ill."

It looked as though he had had a stroke. One corner of his mouth was drawn strangely down and to the side of his face, and his right arm lay lifelessly across the bedclothes. He must be half-paralyzed, I thought.

"Thank you, Mary, but I am getting better. I was able to move a toe in my right foot this morning. Yes, I am sure I was able to move it. I am certain of it.

"Now, what brings you to Castle Cloud, my dear, after these four long years? I saw you walk up the drive down there." He pointed with his left hand to two enormous mirrors. One, a full-length standing mirror, stood at the foot of his bed. The other had been hung from the ceiling above his bed by ropes. Both were tilted at the proper angles for him to see out of the window—in two different directions—to the ground below. "They do not quite add to the decor, do they? But they allow me to see what is happening out there. What brings you to Castle Cloud, my dear?"

"She came to see Vivian, Father," Edmond said from behind me.

"I don't suppose it would ever occur to you to knock,

would it? Just because I have been ill does not give you the right to come marching in here whenever you please without even a knock on my door.

"Vivian?" Lord Clareham's eyes returned to me. "Why do you want to see Vivian?"

As his father spoke, Edmond walked to the foot of the bed, to my right, and stood looking down at him. "And I don't suppose it ever occurred to you, Father," he said, "that if we were to adhere to such formalities and you should have another attack and be suffering helplessly in here all alone, we might find ourselves standing indefinitely outside your door waiting for permission to enter. When one is a sick man, he is simply not treated as if he were well. I should think that would be apparent, and I think it would be most unwise for him to insist upon these formalities. After all we have done for you during these months, I should think a small show of gratitude to the members of your family. . ."

"Edmond!" Lord Clareham interrupted, shaking his finger at his son. "Please be kind enough to remember to whom you are speaking. I am not accustomed to being lectured to."

I was uncomfortable sitting there in the midst of that quarrel, but I am ashamed to say that I was fascinated by the confrontation. And it gave me time to examine Edmond. He stood looming above us—tall, sallow, and overweight. In spite of his height, his head seemed rather too large for his body. His face was long and thin with a heavy chin and beaked nose. He must be twenty-six years old, I thought—only five years older than I am—but he looks thirty-six. His eyes fascinated me. Edmond's eyes were of a very pale blue (if one were lucky enough to see them) under heavy, pink-edged lids. He seldom looked at one directly, and when he did, it was as though he failed to find anything of interest there.

"It is very easy," he was saying, "for one who is ill to lose perspective. . ."

"Why have you come to see Vivian, my dear?" Lord Clareham said to me, ignoring Edmond.

"Because she invited me to come for a visit, Lord Clareham," I replied.

"Evidently, Vivian had written many letters to Mary," Edmond said, "asking her to come for a prolonged visit.

We cannot imagine why she never mentioned it to us. Since Vivian is not here, Mary has decided to go to her. Mary's father is dead, she has little money, and she does not wish to go back to Holland where her mother lives. I have, somewhere, the address of the friends Vivian is staying with. I shall have to find it and give it to Mary later. She is, of course, staying the night at the Castle."

"Welcome to Castle Cloud, Mary," Lord Clareham said. "It is delightful to have you here with us again, but you must be tired after your long journey, and we have no right to keep you from retiring to your room to refresh yourself. See that Mary finds her way, Edmond, and then return here to me. I have some things I wish to say to you. Good afternoon, Mary. We will see each other again later. God bless you, my dear."

"Thank you, Lord Clareham," I said, rising from my chair.

Then I followed Edmond out of the room, and Ahmad closed the door behind us.

Outside, the gallery was brilliantly lit—the late-afternoon sun shown through two of the oval windows at the base of the dome above us and splashed on the wall directly across the rotunda.

When we had walked far enough away from his father's door so that we could not be heard, I asked, "Was it a stroke, Edmond?"

"Yes. His right side is paralyzed," Edmond said. "He is really quite helpless—never leaves his bed. But he insists on carrying on an enormous correspondence, even though he cannot write a word of it himself. Mother is forced to spend most of her time in there writing his letters for him."

"When did it happen?"

"October last. The doctor said it would be a matter of only a few days, perhaps a week, and here it is more than six months later and no change. His disposition is impossible, he is wearing Mother out, and there he lies waiting to die.

"We will go downstairs now, see if we can find Mother, and see what room she wishes you to have."

We turned onto one of the landings and began to descend the stairs—a different staircase than the one we had come up. Castle Cloud boasted four staircases leading to the second floor—one corresponding to each of the four corners of the building. But when we were halfway down, a young maid in a printed-chintz uniform and cap climbed around the bend of the stairs toward us.

"Oh, Jane, do you know which room Mother has chosen for her ladyship?" Edmond asked.

"Yes, my lord," Jane said. "She is to have the mauve bedroom. Mrs. Foley is up there now preparing it for her."

"Will you show her ladyship to her room then, Jane?"

"I don't know as that is up to me, my lord, as Mrs. Foley will tell you, that not being part of my duties."

"Do as I say, Jane!"

"Oh! Yes, my lord." She brushed past us then, with her nose held high in the air, and ran up the stairs.

"Jane will show you to your room," Edmond said.

"Thank you, Edmond," I replied.

Then I turned and retraced my steps to the second-floor landing where Jane waited for me.

"Will you follow me, then," she said. "We are sure you will like the mauve bedroom. It is very sunny and cheerful in the afternoon, and there is a lovely view of the bay from the windows. It is one of the nicest rooms at Castle Cloud. We are very proud of the Persian rug and the paintings."

As she walked ahead of me around the gallery, I could not help noticing that Jane Spence (as I later learned her name was) had a beautiful figure. I must admit I was a trifle envious of her tiny waist and her superb, creamy-smooth skin.

"Here we are," she said, as she opened the door.

It was the same bedroom I had had during my last visit. Mrs. Foley was smoothing the bedspread.

"You may take the dustcovers there down to the laundry rooms, Jane," she said, "and put the duster and cloths in the closet on your way."

Jane picked up the duster, cloths, and covers and left the room without a word, leaving Mrs. Foley and me alone.

Mrs. Foley, a tiny, nervous lady, was the housekeeper at Castle Cloud. I remembered her well. Her face seemed to be all one huge, pointed nose upon which she wore a pince-nez. One hardly noticed her mouth or her tiny inquisitive eyes.

"Good afternoon, Mrs. Foley," I said. "You probably do not remember me—I am Lady Beauford. I was Lady Mary Thorpe when I visited Lady Vivian four years ago. Thank you for fixing my room for me."

"Yes, I remember you," Mrs. Foley said. "Now, if you will excuse me, my lady."

She took a folded blanket from the foot of the bed and carried it past me and out of the room, shutting the door behind her.

A rather abrupt departure, I thought, but I was too delighted to have the mauve bedroom again to think much about it. It was a lovely room. Its woodwork was painted white and trimmed with gold, but the walls were painted a pale mauve color, thus the room's name. These were hung with paintings in gold frames—all were landscapes except for a portrait by Romney, painted in 1775, of Lady Rachel Ramsay, Lord Clareham's great aunt, which hung over the chimney piece. The mauve bedroom had been hers. It was an enormous room, and the mauve of the walls had been repeated in the furnishings, together with lavenders and purples. My bed wore a canopy of white Chinese silk embroidered with purple iris. Chairs of the same material, and little tables, stood about the room, and a sofa upholstered in lavender silk, flanked by easy chairs, faced the white-marble chimney piece.

But the huge red, blue, and purple Persian rug was the most beautiful thing in the room and one of the Castle's treasures. It had been the holy carpet of the mosque at Abdelril, Vivian had told me, and had been purchased by Lord Clareham in Calcutta in 1844, shortly before he left India the second time to return to England.

I stood for more than a minute admiring it. Then I crossed to the window, opened it (the air was stale—the room had not been aired), and looked out across the park which swept to the edge of the slope that I had climbed earlier. Below it, the river Tay half circled Castle Cloud Hill and emptied into Bideford Bay. From the window, I could see down the entire length of the bay—past the villages of Instow and Appledore and all the way to Bideford and the hazy hills beyond it. And I could see the channel, which cleaved a narrow ridge of land to my right, joining the bay and the ocean. Through it, followed by a cloud of gulls, three tiny fishing boats sailed home from the sea.

The view entranced me, and I stood for a long while looking out at the bay and the patchwork fields and the villages that bordered it, while the fishing boats sailed through the channel and slid toward Barnstaple.

And as I watched them go, I wondered where I would go the following day. Where would I sleep the following night? In London? Near Vivian? What would she say when I suddenly appeared? What would her friends think of my unexpected arrival?

"Well—and what should I do now?" I thought aloud.

I suppose I could wash, I thought, and then I might lie down and rest, though I know I won't sleep. But when I looked, I found no water in either jug on the wash-hand-stand, nor any soap in the dish. And I noticed that Mrs. Foley had left me only one tiny towel. I was sure, however, that she would return with the things I would need or send someone with them.

"She is an absolute marvel," Vivian had said. "She does half the work at Castle Cloud all by herself, and she seems to do it in several places all at the same time and to perfection. She is more like a woman of forty than seventy-five."

This reminded me of the day Vivian and I had sat at the edge of a still pool where one of the brooks empties into the Tay, and she had pointed to a long-legged black bug that skated frantically this way and that upon the water.

"Whom does that remind you of?" she had asked.

"Mrs. Foley," I had answered, and we had both cried with laughter.

Mrs. Foley was, however, the most unemotional person I had ever met. I do not believe she had ever laughed or shed a tear. Vivian had always been a little afraid of her. Vivian had said that she was sure Mrs. Foley was not quite human.

But I was becoming impatient to wash, and I wanted to know what time dinner would be served, so I went to the bellpull and pulled it. If I rang, someone would come, and I would ask for water and soap. The house remained silent, however, and after waiting for ten minutes or so, I flicked open the cover of my watch. (My father had given it to me in Paris, and I wore it on a ribbon around my neck.) It said six-thirty. The clock that stood on the table beside my bed said twelve-thirty. I crossed the room and wound and set it.

Still no one came. It seemed that instead of their coming up to me, I must go downstairs to them. I left my room and descended the stairs to the hall. I found no one there or in the vestibule, not even a footman, and when I looked into the drawing room, I found no one there either. Nor did I see my bags anywhere. But as I stood in the rotunda looking about and wondering what to do, a swishing sound drew my attention to the open doorway of the dining room. Mitchell walked to the dining table carrying a handful of silver. He had come out of his pantry—the door was still swinging—and was about to set the table for dinner.

"What time is dinner served, Mitchell?" I asked from the doorway.

"At half-past seven, my lady," Mitchell replied.

As he answered me, he straightened up and faced me. His shrewd little eyes stared at me from under extraordinarily long eyebrows. He combed these long hairs upward at his temples and curled them back toward the center of his forehead, giving him a Mephistophelian look.

"Haven't my bags come from the station yet?" I asked.

"No, my lady. If they had, I should have carried them to your room."

"Where is her ladyship?"

"I believe her ladyship is lying down in her room, my lady. She often does before dinner."

"And his young lordship?" Edmond would help me.

"Dressing for dinner, I should imagine, my lady."

"Thank you, Mitchell."

I left the doorway and retreated across the hall. Mitchell, I thought, was just a shade less than insolent. I disliked him intensely. It was almost as though he delighted in making me uncomfortable. He certainly was not trying to be helpful. How did he dare behave so rudely?

I walked toward a stairway which I knew descended to the kitchens and the servants' hall. And as I did so, Jane Spence came out of the hall chamber and hurried toward me.

"Jane, have you seen Mrs. Foley?" I asked.

"She is usually in her rooms at this hour, my lady," she said.

"Would you go and ask her if she would send some hot water and soap and towels to my room, please?"

"Them are not my duties, my lady," she said.

She sailed past me then and ran down the steps toward the servants' hall.

"Faith, if you don't watch where you're going, you might end up there," someone said. Feet shuffled on the stairs, and then the woman to whom the voice belonged rose into view. She was portly with a shiny, red face and blond, braided hair. "Up there, ja?" she said to me, pointing to the ceiling. "Ha, ha, ha. Hee-hee."

I could not help smiling. I pointed to the ceiling too and said: "I am afraid *I* need a little help up there, and I don't know how to go about getting it."

"No," the woman said, pointing to the floor, "it's down there that you'll be needing help. In more ways than one, it's there that you'll be needing it, ja? Ha, ha, ha. Hee, hee, hee. Can I help you at all, my lady? It's Mrs. Muldoon that's at your service."

Her inflections rose at the end of her sentences, and she pronounced her *w*'s as *v*'s and her *t*'s as *d*'s. She is Scandinavian I thought, but surely "Muldoon" is an Irish name.

"I am afraid I have been forgotten, Mrs. Muldoon. I would like to wash before dinner, but I have no hot water or soap."

"Sure and I'll see what I can do. Go up to your room, my lady, and it's up I'll come in just a bit."

I went back upstairs then, and in ten minutes, Mrs. Muldoon knocked on my bedroom door. She carried two cans of water—one hot and one cold.

"There you are, my lady," she said, as she filled the jugs on the wash-hand-stand with cold water. "It's the hot water I'll leave here, and this can I'll take downstairs. Och! It's soap and towels you'll be needing from the linen closet." She stalked out of the room and returned with soap and some face and bath towels which she tucked into the rack on the stand. "Is there anything else, my lady? I'll be leaving here at seven."

"No, Mrs. Muldoon. Thank you so much," I said.

"Well now, that's quite all right, my lady, and I hope you'll have a good night."

When she had gone, I stepped out of my dress and brushed the dust off the skirt as best I could. Since I had nothing else to wear, I could hardly change for dinner, so I washed, put on the dress again, combed my hair, and went downstairs.

In the hall I heard voices coming from the drawing room, and I walked in that direction.

"It is the only thing we can do under the circumstances," Edmond was saying. "I should think that would be self-evident. It will not do her any harm, and anyway, what else can she do except pray for a miracle?"

In answer, Lady Clareham murmured something which I could not hear. And then I reached the open drawing room doorway.

Edmond saw me at once and said: "Good evening, Mary. Come sit with us."

I walked to them and sat down on the sofa next to Lady Clareham, who gave me a wan smile of greeting. "Good evening, my dear," she whispered.

"I must apologize for not changing for dinner," I said, "but my bags have not arrived. I am sure that either Mitchell or one of the footmen would have brought them up if they had. Did you find Vivian's address, Edmond?"

"Of course," he said, flashing me a brilliant smile. Then he reached into his pocket, drew out a slip of paper, and handed it to me.

I unfolded it and read,

> Vivian's address:
> Care of
> Miss Nancy Ackerman
> 39 King Street
> Greenwich

"Thank you, Edmond," I said, still looking at Vivian's address. "Now I shall have to arrange to get from the railway station to Greenwich. Is there a train from London out to Greenwich, do you know?"

"Mary, I have been thinking that . . ."

But he was interrupted by Mitchell from the doorway. "Dinner is served, my lady," he said.

We stood then. Edmond took his mother in to dinner,

and I followed them out of the drawing room, across the rotunda, and through the double doorway of the dining room.

The dining room seemed changed since I had seen it last. It was still a large, oblong room papered in dark red-and-gold-figured paper and hung with family portraits. But it looked even larger than I remembered it because the dining table, now without leaves in it, had shrunk so and was surrounded by so much empty space. And now the table looked even smaller than it actually was because the silver candelabra which stood upon it were so monumental. Their candles lit the room, as the curtains had been drawn against the evening light outside. Each candle flame glowed and flickered inside its own little pink-paper shade.

Finally when we were seated, Edmond said: "Our guest senses a change at Castle Cloud."

"I was wondering where . . ."

"The footmen are? Arthur and Robert were discharged two years ago." He paused dramatically. "Along with Drummond, the head coachman, and Gaspar and Ambrose; Wiley, the head gardener, and his men; four housemaids; a sewing maid; two laundry maids and various kitchen, stillroom, and scullery maids—not to mention pantry, lamp, and steward's room boys and etcetera."

I wanted to know what had happened, but I did not think I should ask. I was not, however, to be left wondering.

"How many did we count, Mother?" Edmond continued. "Twenty-six servants discharged in six months' time? And that did not include the men on the farm. We are left now with a grand total of nine—that includes Ahmad, Herbert, and Mrs. Foley. All because of one man's raging extravagance and another's complete indifference.

"You see, by two years ago, the estates had fallen into such indebtedness that our creditors placed the management of them in the hands of trustees who now condescend to dole out a pittance for us to live upon. If my esteemed uncle, the seventh earl, had thought of one other thing besides how he could spend more money, and if my own father had given one thought to something besides his beloved India, we would find ourselves living as luxuriously as the Ramsays have always lived, instead of at starvation level.

"However, that will be changed. *I* shall infuse the estates with the necessary moneys to restore them to their former magnificence, and once again we shall have footmen serving at the table. Their livery will, I have decided, be changed. Instead of that ghastly shade of green, they shall wear lavender and gold. We shall repair the glasshouses, and again orchids and pineapples will grow in them. And the gardens will be beautiful again."

As he spoke, I glanced at Lady Clareham. She sat with her head bent, her eyes closed, and the fingers of one hand to her forehead.

"God only knows," Edmond continued, "what would have happened if James had inherited. Why, Castle Cloud would have fallen to ruin while he was off digging . . . ."

"Edmond!" Lady Clareham cried. "Stop it! I will not have you talk about James like that. How *you* of all people could criticize him. Oh, my boy—my poor sweet boy." She began to sob into her black-edged handkerchief.

After that, we did not speak until Mitchell had removed the soup plates.

Then Edmond asked, "Mitchell, why have her ladyship's bags not arrived?"

Mitchell paused in his carving at the sideboard to glare at Edmond. "I couldn't say, my lord," he replied.

"Well, find out then," Edmond demanded.

"Pork cutlets or roast lamb, my lady?" Mitchell asked Lady Clareham.

Later, after Mitchell had finished serving the entree, Lady Clareham turned to me and asked, "You knew James, didn't you, Mary? He was such a handsome boy—a scholar. He told me that he had deciphered the mystery of the hut circles on Dartmoor, but now it may never be known."

"Yes, Lady Clareham," I said. "He was a charming man. I can understand why he and Vivian were so close and why she was so distressed when he passed away."

"It was hideous," she said. "He had been ill for more than a month—just an upset stomach, nothing important—but it kept getting worse. . ."

"Valvular disease of the heart, complicated by epidemic diarrhea," Edmond said, interrupting her.

"I am so sorry," I said. "I wish I had known. I—I have

been admiring the miniature of James you are wearing, Lady Clareham. It is lovely."

"James is on one side and Vivian is on the other—my two sweet children," she said. Tears sprang to her eyes again as she held the pendant away from her chest and twirled it slowly, rolling the chain between her fingers, so that I could see how the two miniature paintings had been mounted back to back. "I wear it always. You know, it is strange how James died completely—he is so dreadfully in the past. But Vivian's presence is everywhere."

"She is a very vital person, Mother," Edmond said. "When one is so alive, her presence lingers like good perfume."

Then Edmond turned to me and said, "About Vivian, Mary. I have been thinking that you should write to her in Greenwich, and that you should stay here with us until you receive her answer. Now wait, let me finish. We have not the vaguest idea what her plans are and neither have you. Suppose you left Castle Cloud tomorrow and arrived in Greenwich tomorrow night and found that Vivian and Nancy had gone to visit friends for a few days or a week? Then what would you do? Or suppose they have gone to Scotland? Vivian said she would like to travel a bit to clear her mind—not far, but she did mention Scotland. On the other hand, suppose you found that Vivian had left Greenwich to return home, and your paths had crossed. What then? No, there is no point in your traveling farther to no avail, especially when you say you are short of funds. You are, I am sure, intelligent enough to realize that this is the surest approach to the problem—the *only* way of being sure of what you are doing. You must write to Vivian tonight, and when she answers you and you know her plans, *then* go to her. Don't you agree? She may be planning to return to Castle Cloud shortly. She may be on her way. Certainly she will return home when she knows you have arrived."

"I would feel as though I were imposing," I said. "But yes, I think you are right. It would certainly be prudent. . ."

"Of course," Edmond gave me his widest smile. "And you are not imposing. You are a *friend* of Vivian's—her best friend. And when she returns, you will be with us for some time, as it was planned. We shall consider it decided then, and you must be grateful that you need not travel farther."

"Oh, I am! I shall write to Vivian, then. Thank you so much, Edmond and Lady Clareham."

As we talked, I noticed that Mitchell had been listening intently to every word that was said.

During the salad, Edmond looked several times at his watch, noisily flicking open the cover and shutting it again. He had become nervous, impatient. During the dessert, he took out his watch again, opened it, and snapped the cover shut.

"We are late!" he said. "My coffee please, Mitchell." Mitchell poured his coffee. He sipped it. "Simply because we have a guest is no reason why dinner cannot be served on time. It can hardly take longer to prepare food for three people than for two, can it? And even if it did, one would think that preparation could have begun a little earlier. Couldn't it? Or isn't Laval able to reason to that extent?" He gulped down the rest of his coffee. "Now if you ladies will excuse me—" He wiped his mouth with his napkin, got up, and left the room.

"It is eight-thirty," Lady Clareham said, in answer to my unspoken question. "Edmond must have his cigar on the portico at eight-thirty and no later. He must be awakened precisely at seven o'clock. He must breakfast precisely at nine. At exactly ten, he departs for the bathing pavilion for his swim, and he returns at precisely noon. We must lunch precisely at one, and dinner must begin at exactly seven-thirty, so that he may have his cigar at precisely eight-thirty on the entrance portico. Absurd! He has an obsession with time. One would think he was part clock.

"Shall we have our coffee in the drawing room now?"

Afterward, when we had finished our coffee, Lady Clareham sat in front of her embroidery and worked on it listlessly, and I sat opposite her. I sensed, though, that she would rather be alone. Since I was tired, I said good night and left her.

I will unpack and hang up my dresses, I thought, as I climbed the stairs, and then go to bed. I cannot wait to lie down in that big, comfortable bed and sleep, and sleep, and sleep. And tomorrow I needn't go away. I will be staying at Castle Cloud! I will be staying here for days, and then, after Vivian comes, possibly for weeks, even months. Lovely! Simply lovely!

But when I opened the door of my room, I could see at once that my trunk had not arrived, and that no one had bothered to light a lamp for me. It would not be dark outside for half an hour yet, but it was dark enough inside my room for a lamp to be lit. So after looking about, I found a box of matches lying on the chimney piece and carried it to the table by my bed to light the lamp on it, but when I held the match to the wick, it merely sputtered and smoked. It would not light because the lamp had not been filled. One of the other lamps, however, did have oil in it, and I lit it. Then I stood looking out of the window, watching the darkness gradually snuff out the view. Even after it had gone out I stood there, gazing at the twinkling lights of the towns and farmhouses far below me. A green light moved through the darkness—a boat sailed across the bay toward the sea.

Finally I closed the curtains, and, carrying a lighted candle, I left my room and walked downstairs. The ground floor of the house lay dark and silent except for a night light that glowed in the vestibule. There, just inside the entrance door of the house, stood my trunk and bag.

The trunk would have to spend the night there, but I carried the bag to my room. Then I turned down the bed without removing the spread, undressed, put on my nightgown, blew out the lights, and climbed into bed hoping that I would be warm enough during the night: only one thin blanket and the spread covered me.

❦ Chapter Two ❦

"GOOD MORNING! Good morning, my lady," someone shouted above the sound of curtains being drawn. Then the room was filled with light, and a big shape bustled back and forth. It was Mrs. Muldoon. "It's your water I've brought, my lady," she said as she left the room. But almost at once she returned carrying a sheet and a bath, which she arranged on the floor. Then she placed the can of hot water in the bath and covered it with a bath towel.

"Thank you ever so much, Mrs. Muldoon," I said.

"Sure, since it was not about to be done by anybody else," she replied, "I thought it might as well be done by me, if you don't mind, my lady."

"On the contrary, I am very grateful. You are early at the Castle this morning."

"It's eight o'clock, my lady, and it's an hour I've been here already. Do you know, my lady, what Lady Twittingham asked the maid she was about to engage?"

"Not knowing Lady Twittingham, I haven't the faintest idea."

"She said: 'Do you need to be called in the morning, Nancy?' And Nancy says: 'Oh, no, my lady, not unless you needs me.' Ha, ha, ha. Hee, hee, hee. 'Not unless you needs me,' she says. Ah, ha, ha, ha."

I found myself laughing. It was not Mrs. Muldoon's story so much, but the way her eyes popped more and more as her story progressed that amused me, and her laughter was infectious.

My laughter, of course, delighted her. "Ja, it's good to find somebody at the Castle that knows how to laugh," she said. "Blessed saints! It's cold you must have been in the night to have put your robe over you like that. It's an extra blanket I'll put on your bed later and tuck one up on the shelf there too, in case you'll be needing it."

I thanked Mrs. Muldoon again, and when she had left me, I poured my bath and lay back in it for a few minutes, dreaming in the hot water. I must write to Vivian after breakfast, I thought. How soon will I get a reply from Greenwich? I wonder.

And as I looked about, I noticed that my trunk stood just inside the door. It must have been carried up earlier, and Mrs. Muldoon must have dragged it in. I took my dresses out of it after my bath and hung them up. Then I finished dressing, combed my hair, and went down to breakfast.

It was eight forty-five then.

But though it was almost Edmond's breakfast time, I saw no one when I reached the ground floor. The rotunda was deserted. So I walked to the hall chamber door, opened it, and walked through the little room to the breakfast room beyond. When I opened the breakfast room door, however, I saw that the room was no longer used. Dustcovers had been thrown over the table and chairs, and the chandelier had been wrapped in tissue paper.

On the way toward the hall, I paused to admire a carved wooden screen in the corner of the room. I had thought of it many times since I had last seen it. The screen had once been part of the palace at Tanjore, and Lord Clareham had brought it home from India with him. Its perforated wooden panels were carved in a lacework of flowers, figures, and animals—all inlaid with ivory and gold.

Hanging on the wall beside the screen, I noticed a little painting which I did not remember having seen before. This was not surprising, since Castle Cloud held so many treasures that one might almost *never* see them all! The painting was round and about six inches wide. It was a portrait of a boy with light-brown hair wearing a fur-trimmed coat. The background was of a most intense and luminous blue. I was sure it was a painting of Edward IV as prince of Wales, and I was equally sure that no one but Holbein himself could have painted it.

I must remember to ask Lady Clareham about it sometime, I thought, as I returned to the dining room. I found Edmond seated at the table, having already begun his breakfast.

"Have you taken the *Times* up to his lordship, Mitchell?" he asked. "You know perfectly well that he can see Colen ride up from the village and knows when he has returned. So there is no point in making him angry by neglecting to take it up to him.

"Ah, Mary. There you are. Have you written to Vivian? Give me the letter, and I will take it myself to the village and mail it for you."

"Good morning, Edmond," I said. "I have not written it yet. I thought I would do it right after breakfast."

"Excellent!" he said. "Have some of these little sausages. They are really quite good. Mitchell, hand her ladyship some of those sausages."

"Oh, no, thank you. I really couldn't. A soft-cooked egg, if you please, Mitchell, and some toast and coffee." Then I turned back to Edmond. "I heard you talking about the *Times*. Does it come on the train with the mail? What time does the mail arrive?"

"On the early train, almost always in time for breakfast," Edmond said. "When you come down in the morning, you will find that Mitchell has put the mail on the brass tray on the table next to the door there. Are you expecting something?"

"No, nothing."

"The *Times* and his letters go at once to my father. We, of course, must wait until much later to see it. He cannot wait to get his hands on the *Times* to see if there is anything in it about India. There he lies, an invalid in his bed in the south of England, with his mind five thousand miles away. He cares nothing about Castle Cloud or his family. All he can think about are those black heathens out there in that filthy country. It is not sensible. He is no longer governor-general. He has nothing to do with it anymore. That is all in the past. Why not leave it there? But no, when he is not dissecting the *Times* for word about that disgusting place, he is writing letters to people there. If not that, he has his nose in those Persian books of his. It is abnormal. He is as much responsible for the state of things here as anyone. Look what I shall inherit—a wreck. A decayed old wreck, that's what it is.

"Some more of those sausages, Mitchell, and another scone, I think. Have one of those scones, Mary, and try that honey. You will not taste the like anywhere else. Grandmamma brought it over from Lewis House."

"No, thank you, Edmond, really," I said.

We ate in silence then, and after a while Edmond said, "Tell me about yourself, Mary. Surely your situation cannot be as precipitous as you have led us to believe. Your father was a very wealthy man. And Lady Penbroke—surely your mother's family could provide assistance."

"Only my mother's mother is alive. She is weak-minded from age. She lives with a niece in a cottage not far from Gunderbury Hall.

"You know about Mother, of course."

"Humm?"

"That she was a parlor maid at Gunderbury Hall before she married my father?"

"My dear Mary, that must have happened when I was a child. Needless to say, I was not interested in—that sort of thing at the time."

"It is still talked about, I believe."

"Yes. Well, go on. You were saying—"

"She married Papa after his first wife died. They were very much in love, Papa told me. Mother was twenty-three, and he must have been forty at the time. He loved my mother until he died. They were very happy with one another all their lives. Mother was a good wife to him, though she could never fit into his world socially. Naturally the first Lady Penbroke's friends and my father's friends, as well, did not welcome Mother into county society in Kent. So Papa closed Gunderbury Hall, and they lived in the London house on Portman Square, spending much of their time abroad. We moved to London in 1837 when I was two.

"So it is not surprising that I do not remember Gunderbury Hall. I have not seen it since that time, and now that it has been sold, I do not wish to. Well, my father thought that he and my mother would be happier living permanently abroad, and the rest I have told you. He spent furiously and left me nothing. I do not blame him for that. His life was a difficult one, and he and Mother needed all the joy they could buy. Oh, I have a few pieces of jewelry which cannot be worth so very much, but I would never sell them anyway because he gave them to me.

"It seems that both our families have seen more prosperous times, doesn't it? Anyway, Vivian wants to help me, and I am sure she will."

"And she cannot help you," Edmond said, "if you do

not write and tell her you are here, now, can she? Come with me, and I will see that you have paper and ink and everything you need. Do not write a long letter. Simply tell her you are here, and that you want to know what her plans are. Ask whether you should go to Greenwich. You can tell her everything else when you see her. Come with me, and we will see what we can devise. You must get right to it."

"Isn't Lady Clareham coming down to breakfast?" I asked.

"No. She seldom does. Cecile almost always takes her breakfast to her on a tray. Come into the drawing room. Mother and I write our letters on the table in front of the east window. The writing room has been closed. When there is such a lack of help, one's only alternative is to close all unnecessary rooms. That is why you will find that most of the ground-floor rooms are no longer used."

I followed Edmond out of the dining room, into the drawing room, and down the length of it to a long table with a green, inlaid-leather top. A black cat slept in the sun that poured in the window, warming the table. Then Edmond motioned me to a chair and helped me to be seated.

"There are paper and envelopes and stamps there in the drawer for you whenever you need them, and pens and ink," he said. "Here, let me help you."

He reached down in front of me, pulled out a drawer, and took out a crystal inkwell and pens and some envelopes and stamps.

"Blast it!" he said, quickly opening and shutting the other drawers in the table. "I will go and get some more paper. There must be some somewhere."

During all this, the cat had not moved. Its eyes looked closed, but they were not, quite. And I could see that it watched me. "What is your name?" I asked, as I reached over and stroked the back of its head. The cat opened huge, green eyes wide, stared at me for a moment, and then leapt to the floor, stretched, and walked away.

I watched it until it had walked into the rotunda, and then I let my eyes wander, wondering why anyone would build a room as large as this one. The drawing room was the largest room at Castle Cloud. It was rather narrow, but it ran the entire length of the north front of the build-

ing—perhaps eighty feet or more. Yet in spite of its size
and the light from the north windows, it was not at all
cold or austere. On the contrary, it was warm and almost
cozy. This was because on clear days, sunshine flooded the
room from the east or west windows and because nests of
sofas and chairs in yellows and golds and tables were
grouped invitingly down its length. It was as though
several rooms existed there with invisible walls between
them. And the room was filled with beautiful things:
paintings and tapestries covered the walls, and Indian cabi-
nets and chests, vases, and ivory and brass curios were
scattered about among priceless English and French por-
celains, crystal, bronze statuettes, urns, ornamental boxes
and *objets d'art* of almost every description. Sitting there,
in that room, gave me intense pleasure, and for a few moments I was content.

"Here we are at last," Edmond called, waving some
sheets of writing paper in the air as he strode in from the
hall. "Now you can go to work, and I will leave you in
peace. When you are finished, give it to me. I will be going down to the village later, and I will post it for you. I
suggest you hurry, though. It is clouding up out there, and
it will rain before long."

He left me then, and I gazed out of the window across
the park for a long time, watching the sun splash intermit-
tently on the grass from between threatening clouds and
trying to decide what to write. I hated writing letters—
mine always seemed so inadequate.

Finally after several unsuccessful beginnings, I wrote:

June 26, 1856

My dearest Vivian,

I arrived at Castle Cloud yesterday, only to learn
of James's passing. I know how you must grieve for
him, and believe me, I share in your bereavement.
Truly I do.

I long to see you, and I hope that I can comfort
you. Will you be returning to Castle Cloud soon, or
shall I come to you in Greenwich?

Of course, I will do whatever you wish, but please,
if you possibly can, come home now so that we can
be together here at the Castle as we had planned.

Please write and tell me when you will arrive.
How can I wait to see you again?

Ever
Yours
Affectionately,
Mary

When I had finished the letter, I sat reading it over and over—not happy with it, but not knowing what else to write.

"What? Not finished yet?" Edmond said, smiling down at me. I had not heard him come into the room. "What is all this? How many letters have you decided to write? Or have you decided to write a novelette?"

"Oh, Edmond, I don't know," I said. "It seems such a hard letter to write. I suppose this will have to do. I could sit here all day and not do any better. Let me address the envelope, and then you may take it."

After I had sealed the envelope and handed it to him, he said: "Excellent. Now it shall be on its way, and we will see what Vivian has to say in reply. I will take it directly after luncheon." He looked at his watch. "I say, it is ten-thirty. I must be off." Then he hurried out of the room.

It showered during the afternoon, so I stayed in the house and wandered from place to place, sitting here and there, looking out of the windows at the rain, and worrying about the letter. The house might as well have been deserted. I saw no one—not even Edmond or Lady Clareham. She had not come down to luncheon. I had not seen her since the evening before. It was a long, lonely, silent, gray afternoon, and I was glad when it was over and glad to see Mrs. Muldoon when she came to my room at half-past six.

"Is there anything you'll be needing, my lady, before I leave?" she asked.

"Thank you, Mrs. Muldoon. You seem to have thought of everything. It was you, wasn't it?" I asked.

"Ja, my lady. Sure, it was, and if it wasn't, it wouldn't have been done at all. 'She'll be staying a while,' Mrs. Foley says, early this afternoon. 'Who'll be taking care of her room then?' I asks her. 'I don't know who'll be taking care of her room,' she snaps back at me. 'Och, I'll just have to do it myself then,' I says, right to her face. 'If you can fit it in, you're welcome,' she says to me. So I fit it in, my lady, and I hope your ladyship has everything she needs. I filled your lamps and laid a fire there in case you should be wanting it."

"Thank you, Mrs. Muldoon. I am very grateful, but I am afraid I am making a great deal of extra work for you." I was so glad to have someone to talk to after such a dull afternoon that I wanted to keep her there a while longer, so I added, "You were not here four years ago when I visited Lady Vivian, were you, Mrs. Muldoon?"

"No, my lady. It was in Mevagissey I was living at the time, down in Cornwall. My poor husband was lost in the great southwester we had three years ago, so his brother, Sean, asks me to come up here to Milton Penderton to look after him, and so I did. It's a cobbler he was, until he got too old to work. We was having a little dram down there together the other night, my lady, ha, ha, ha. So I says to him, I says, 'The good dies young, so here's to your old age.' Ha, ha, ha. You should have seen him look at me, my lady. 'The good dies young,' I says. Ha, ha, ha."

"And do all Swedish people have a sense of humor like you do, Mrs. Muldoon?" I asked.

"Och, I shouldn't think so, my lady, but us Norwegians does, some of us. I was born Helga Svendsen, my lady. And so I was until Patrick sails his boat in during a storm, with a broken rudder, and carries me off with him. It's my father that ran the yard there, you see. In comes Patrick on Monday, and away he sails on Thursday with me aboard, and I never so much as regretted a moment of it except for the crossing of the channel. Holy saints! Many's the time during the crossing that it's wishing I was that I'd never set eyes on him. After that it was on the shore I stayed, a happy woman. 'Twas the sea that brought him, and 'twas the sea that took him away, and I can't be blaming it, for it brought me thirty years of happy life in between.

"Och! I must be leaving, my lady. My brother-in-law will be wanting his supper. He gets just as hungry in his old age, he does. Ha, ha, ha."

I was barely able to hear the last of what she said because by that time, she had left the room and closed the door behind her.

We finished dinner early that evening. Lady Clareham had spoken little during the meal. She had come down to it but she seemed preoccupied and was very quiet. I was able to think of little to say, either to her or to Edmond. Edmond, on the other hand, was loquacious. He described in great detail his plans for the estates. If they all came to pass, Castle Cloud would indeed be a showplace once again. I couldn't help wondering where he would get the money to do it all, but of course I did not ask.

Afterward, while Lady Clareham and I were drinking our coffee in the drawing room, the light in the park turned orange and pink, and I went to the window to look at the sky.

"It is a beautiful sunset, Lady Clareham," I said. "Come out onto the portico and watch it with me."

"You go, my dear," she said. "I am much too tired this evening. I am not feeling quite well. I think I shall go up to my room now."

Then she got up from her chair and, giving me a hint of a smile, walked out into the hall.

When she had gone, I pushed open one of the long windows and walked through it onto the portico and into a world stained tangerine by the setting sun. It had fallen behind a wood that screened the west front of Castle Cloud from the river in the valley, so I could not see it, but the clouds above the trees were hyacinth-colored, and magenta, and amethyst, and mulberry-edged with flame.

How good it was to see sunlight and color again after such a gray afternoon. All during it I had felt imprisoned by the rain, and now I wanted exercise and fresh air. So, since the long Devonshire twilight would last an hour yet, I decided to walk up the hill to the Horse Monument where I could look down on Milton Penderton and see the view beyond the village.

But I could not descend to the park from the north portico where I stood. Neither the north nor the south porticos had steps leading to the ground. They served merely as balconies for the drawing and dining room. One left or entered Castle Cloud by the steps to the east and west porticos. But even if I had been able to descend immediately to the park, I would not have done so. First I wished to change my clothes and fetch a shawl.

I ran to my room, changed into an old skirt and an old pair of shoes (the grass would still be wet), threw a shawl around my shoulders, and in five minutes I was running down the steps from the east portico.

Sarah met me at the base of the stairs. She ran up to me, her tail wagging with joy, and smelled me. I reached down, patted her head, and asked, "How did you know I was coming? Would you like to go walking with me?" She pranced with delight, shook herself all over, and bounded off to the left. "No, Sarah, this way," I called, pointing ahead. At this, she swung around and headed in the right direction. Such an intelligent creature, I thought. How she must miss Vivian. She is just a mongrel dog, yet how Vivian adores her. "She is a doggy dog," Vivian had said. "Oh, you may have your 'veddy fawncy' breeds, but for intelligence and *love,* give me a doggy dog like Sarah."

Sarah had run so far ahead of me that now she sat down to wait, her tongue hanging.

And as I walked toward her, the white stone of the Castle's two pavilions on either side of me glowed in the twilight. The twin buildings stood some distance from the house and were connected to it by a circular drive. The circle of grass within the drive's circumference had been a perfect lawn when I had last seen it. Vivian and I played croquet there. Now the grass grew in tufts where the sheep had not cropped it, and I felt how lumpy the ground had become as I walked across it toward the garden. To my left, the servants' pavilion was dark, but a light shone in the stablemen's building to my right. I supposed the groom whose name was Colen had those rooms all to himself now, but there was a time when several coachmen and grooms lived there.

Straight ahead of me, at the far side of the grass circle, the drive branched to the left and to the right. To the left, it led around the house to the entrance front. And to the right, it led into the stable yard which lay behind the stablemen's pavilion.

I crossed the drive here, where it branched, and walked down a flight of steps into a walled rose garden, where I paused for a moment to look about. Then I proceeded down a gravel walk, past the fountain in the garden's center (its basin now cracked and empty of water), through an archway in the far wall, and up more steps to a sloping meadow beyond. Here began the path which would take me through a fringe of trees to the Horse Monument on the top of the hill.

The Horse Monument was a folly built by Lord Clareham's grandfather as a tomb for one of his horses.

As I walked along, the word "folly" reminded me of a quarrel I had had about follies with Abigail Comstock, an American girl who had attended Mrs. Romilly's School at the same time Vivian and I had.

"All Englishmen have a streak of madness in them," she had said. "Just look at the fake ruins, the Greek temples, and towers, and arches, and obelisks, and all the other strange, pointless structures they build in their parks and gardens. They're all crazy!"

"Crazy we may be," I had told her, "but we derive an enormous amount of pleasure from it." And Vivian had laughed and laughed.

After that, between ourselves, Vivian and I had called Abigail "Follies Comstock."

The Horse Monument was the largest of the follies at Castle Cloud—larger than Diana's Temple or the bathing pavilion. It was a slender stone pyramid about thirty-five feet high with arched openings in all four sides leading to the chamber containing the tomb. The monument was a landmark in the county. It could be seen from miles away in the countryside as well as from the sea. Sailors sometimes used it to navigate by. And the view from it was superb.

Vivian had told me the story behind the monument. The sixth Lord Clareham's horse had saved his life by jumping a very wide crevasse while hunting one day. So, after its death, he had built the pyramid as a monument to its courage and buried the horse in the central tomb-chamber.

I vividly remembered her telling me that story as I walked up the hill through the gray lavender meadow flecked with buttercups and fireflies. The color had left the sky by then and, as I approached the monument, I wondered if I would have time to walk back down the hill and to the house before dark.

"So you've come back!"

A man stepped out from behind a low yew that grew beside the path not ten feet in front of me and shouted this at me. Then he stood there, straddling the path—barring my way.

"Why the devil didn't you tell me you were going?" he cried.

I was too stunned to speak.

He stalked toward me then, but almost at once he stopped. "I—I thought you were someone else. I am sorry," he said in a much softer voice.

Sarah had wandered off on a detour of her own, but at the sound of his voice, she came loping toward us, swept past me, and jumped upon him, wagging her tail and licking his hand in a frenzied greeting.

"Down, Sarah! Get down, dog," he said, as he ruffled the hair on her head. Then he looked at me. "I thought you were Vivian Ramsay. I am most awfully sorry. I hope I didn't frighten you."

"Well, you did, rather," I said.

"You looked so much like Vivian—at a distance. I assumed you were she. Are you staying at the Castle?"

"Yes."

"Have you—have they heard from her? When will she be coming home? Do they know?"

"No, I don't think they have, and they do not know when she will be coming home."

We stood looking at each other for several moments.

Finally he said, "I am sorry I disturbed you. Will you be able to get back all right?"

"Yes, thank you."

"Well, good evening, then."

With that, he strode off toward a horse, which waited against the dark trees, took its reigns, swung himself into the saddle, and galloped off down the slope toward the village with a brief wave toward me. I walked the few remaining steps to the hilltop and watched him go until he had vanished into a wood. Then, though I could no longer see him, I listened to his horse's hoofs pummeling the ground until the sound of them died away and the evening was still except for Sarah's panting.

Of course I wondered who he was. He was young—in his middle twenties. And though not tall, perhaps just under six feet, he was powerfully built with a straight body, broad shoulders, thick neck and wrists, and big hands.

Meeting him like that had been a most unsettling experience, and I sat down to calm myself. Sarah and I sat there together for some time watching the lights appear in the village houses and the stars come out in the sky.

At last we rose and started down the slope toward the Castle. I picked out the path ahead of me without much thought. My mind strayed continually back to the young man I had met. Who was he, and what would Vivian have to tell me about him?

In the drawing room the following morning after breakfast, I discovered several copies of *Ladies Own Journal and Miscellany* and sat down to thumb through them, losing myself completely in the woman's fashion sections.

After awhile, I heard what sounded like Edmond's footsteps in the hall, coming toward the vestibule. In a few moments, I glanced out the window. Edmond threaded his way through the neglected garden below the drawing room windows toward the hedged walk, a walk which led to the bathing pavilion down by the river. This caused me to glance at my watch and smile: it was just after ten-thirty.

By that time the grass looked dry of dew, and since it was stuffy in the drawing room, I decided to take my magazine outside into the rose garden where I could sit in the fresh air.

So I left the house and stepped out onto the east portico. From there I saw Lady Clareham standing in the rose garden. I hurried down the steps and across the grass circle toward her.

In daylight the garden seemed even more neglected than it had appeared in twilight the evening before. It had been allowed to go wild: the roses had not been pruned in years, and a great deal of dead growth remained on the bushes. The beds were choked with weeds, speckled here and there with wild flowers.

Beyond a clump of yellow ox-eye daisies at the northwest corner of the garden, Lady Clareham stood watching me. She had picked a bouquet which she held in one hand. A pair of scissors flashed in the other.

"Good morning, Lady Clareham," I called, as I walked toward her. "Isn't it a lovely morning?"

"Good morning, Mary," she said, when I had reached her.

"What a pretty bouquet."

"Thank you, my dear." She looked into my eyes, wondering, I supposed, what I was thinking. "It is quite changed since you were here, isn't it?" She waved the scissors in an arc to encompass the garden. "Do you remember how beautiful it used to be? How perfect Wiley kept it? He had a passion for roses. You could have stretched a cord down the edges of the beds, they were so straight. Now . . . And it was Vivian's favorite place."

"Was, Lady Clareham?"

"When she was a child. She used to love to play here. She would spend hours here chasing the butterflies, and I can still see Wiley's face as she rolled her hoop down the walk. He knew it would crash into a rose bush. How many times did I ask her not to play with it in the rose garden?" Tears shone in her eyes, and she turned her head away from me.

"I think it is still lovely. There are still a lot of roses blooming."

"I tried to keep it up," Lady Clareham said, "but it would have been an impossible amount of work for one man, let alone for one woman, and then my husband became ill. He requires a great deal of my time."

"But you have kept this corner of it beautifully. You've planted a lovely border there—it is like a picture. Umm, I love the smell of pinks, and the delphiniums are spectacular. And that bed of roses—you have kept it perfectly. They are gorgeous!"

Lady Clareham resumed her picking, cutting some yellow roses for her bouquet. I watched while she tucked them among the other flowers.

"I hope you have everything you need here, Mary," she murmured, almost as if she were thinking out loud. As she spoke, she crossed the walk to the border and had bent to clip some long-stemmed sweet peas.

"Yes, I—I don't know what I would do if it weren't for Mrs. Muldoon. She has done everything for me. I know that Mrs. Foley and Jane Spence and Mitchell and whoever else is left are terribly busy. I know I should not say it, but I think they actively dislike having me here—which is natural, I suppose. I only make more work for them, of course, but I feel. . . . That first night when I thought I would be leaving the Castle the next day, Mrs. Foley took the dustcovers off things in my room and dusted a bit and then forgot all about me. The lamps were not filled, no water was brought, no soap, no towels, no blankets. I had to go looking for someone to bring me water so I could wash before dinner. I am sorry—I am not complaining, really I am not. It is just that I feel a—resentment!"

"It must be your imagination, my dear. We are short-handed, and you must not blame Mrs. Foley. She is getting on in years. Her rooms here at Castle Cloud are her home—everything she has is here. She has no relatives, no friends that I know of. She has given her life to this house. We must be a little tolerant, I am afraid."

"Of course," I said. "I should not have mentioned it."

Then Lady Clareham stepped to a bench behind us where some sheets of newspaper lay, with her gloves resting on top of them. "Would you take these for me, Mary?" she asked, handing me the scissors. Then she wrapped her bouquet in the newspapers, set the paper cone down on the bench, picked up her gloves, and began to put them on. "Take the scissors back to the house with you when you go, and put them on the little table in the vestibule just as you go in, would you, my dear?"

"Are you going somewhere?"

"I am going to take these flowers to James—in the churchyard in the village." Tears filled her eyes again as she looked at me.

"Is there anything I can do?" I asked.

"No, my dear. There is nothing anyone can do." She turned from me and, taking the flowers with her, walked off down the garden path toward the ruined fountain.

When she had passed through the opening in the wall, I sat down on the bench and leafed through the magazines I had brought, but I did not see the words or the drawings on the pages. And in a few minutes, I glanced up at the meadow below the Horse Monument. Lady Clareham climbed the path—the same path I had taken the night before. Beyond the monument, the path must lead down the hillside to the village, I decided.

Somehow, as I watched her go, I was uneasy and no longer felt like looking at magazines. Instead, I decided to go for a walk and, after I had returned the scissors and the magazines to the house, I set out down the drive in the opposite direction from the village, toward the stone bridge. It lay at the bottom of the hill, below the house, and together with the gates and the deserted lodge just beyond it marked the beginning of the Castle Cloud grounds. As I walked along, I thought about that brief, tense conversation that Edmond and I had had after I crossed it on my way to the Castle, three days before.

I had not stopped to enjoy the view that day. I had been in a hurry to reach the Castle. But there was no hurry now and when I reached the bridge, I leaned against its stone railing, gazed down into the Tay River, and followed the swirling water out into Bideford Bay. Trying to decide where the bay and the river met, I then looked out across the glassy water to the town of Bideford, lying clothed in pearly mist far down the Bay from me.

After a few moments, the sound of an approaching carriage drew my eyes to the lane beyond the open gateway and, as I watched, a gig appeared and drew to a stop on the bridge beside me. It was driven by a middle-aged woman with rouged cheeks wearing a vivid yellow dress. She was alone.

"Pardon, mademoiselle, is this the way to Castle Cloud?" she asked. She spoke with a heavy French accent.

"Yes," I replied. "The house is at the top of this hill."

"And Lord Clareham? How is the famous man?"

"He has been ill, but he is better now."

"I am so glad. You live there, perhaps?"

"No, I . . ."

"No matter. I am on holiday, and I must see the house of that famous man."

"Étes-vous Française, madame?"

"Ah, you speak French," she said, in French, "and beautifully too. But I must not tarry. Good afternoon." Then the carriage leaped forward, and she called back, "Thank you."

I watched her vanish between the hedgerows as she climbed the hill and wondered how, being a stranger, the woman could possibly drive up to the house and look at it. She must have done so, however, because it was not until almost five minutes later that she reappeared—the woman, horse, and gig flying back down the hill, past me, and across the bridge. But why, I wondered, had she drawn her veil down over her face, and how could she see through it to drive?

"James's grotto?" I asked Lady Clareham.

She had come down to luncheon late. Edmond had insisted that we sit down and begin eating before she arrived and, when she eventually did, he was annoyed with her. Her excuse had been that she had gone to look at James's grotto on the way home from the village and the walk had taken longer than she had anticipated.

"Why in the world did you go all the way in there?" Edmond said. "I hope you didn't go inside it." Then he turned to me and said, "It is not ancient and hardly a discovery. It is simply a neglected folly which was part of the grounds of the old house. It is nothing more than a dreary hole in the side of the hill with a lead statue in it. I am not surprised that it was closed up and forgotten."

"I think that is rather exciting," I said. "I would love to see it. Will you show it to me?"

"It is not worth seeing. Why should you be interested in a hole in the ground? Certainly I will show it to you, if you are interested, but not this afternoon. I have some rather important letters to write. But wait—I suppose we could go today. It would not take very long, and I would rather like a walk. I can do my letters afterward. Shall we go directly after luncheon?"

"I would love to," I replied.

We set out for James's grotto and as Edmond and I crossed the grass circle, Sarah came bounding over. She gave me her usual greeting—rubbing against my skirt, wagging her tail, and looked up at me adoringly.

"Go away!" Edmond shouted at Sarah. "Scat!"

Sarah cowered at my side, growling and bristling at Edmond. Then Edmond sent his foot flying at her in a vicious kick.

"Edmond, don't!" I cried.

But he did not strike her. Sarah had been too quick for him. She dodged the blow, leapt out of range, and crouched a few yards distant, snarling at Edmond. This further angered him, and he picked up a stone and flung it at her, hitting her in the side. Sarah howled with pain and fled toward the stables.

"Edmond, how could you?" I asked.

"Nasty cur," he said. "Disgusting, worthless animal. Vivian's dog. God only knows what is in it, or where it came from. I should shoot it, but it isn't worth bothering with."

He led me through the rose garden, then through the opening in the wall at the south side of it. I had not come this way since I had visited the Castle four years before. We climbed the steps, and proceeded along the walk to "Diana's Temple," a small circular building with a colonnaded portico encircling it. From there, one could look down a steep, grassy slope to the shore of Bideford Bay. And off to the right, one could see the stone bridge and the lower part of the drive leading to the house.

We walked toward the building by ourselves. Sarah had not followed us. We had not spoken since Edmond's outburst.

At last I asked, "What is inside 'Diana's Temple'?"

"Nothing. It's just a dark room with an earthen floor. Sometimes such places had statues in them, but they were really built for decoration—to be seen from the outside. The inside of this one was probably used as a storeroom of some sort. It was part of the grounds of the old house." As he spoke, we skirted the temple and crossed the lawn to the left of it. "This used to be a walk leading to the grotto. It is not hard to see where the grotto was."

Then we walked on, quiet once more. Edmond appeared preoccupied. Several times he seemed about to speak, but didn't.

Again I broke the silence. "How long do you think it will be before I hear from Vivian?"

"Tomorrow, perhaps. She should receive your letter today. I have no way of knowing how soon she will answer it, of course, but if she answered it at once and mailed it, you could receive an answer tomorrow. But I rather think it will be on Monday or perhaps on Tuesday. Do you have any idea what she will say?"

"I don't know, Edmond. I have not seen her in four years, you know, and I have no idea how much she was affected by James's death. I wish I knew."

"Why *did* she ask you to come to England? What exactly was the reason?"

"I don't know that either. She never said specifically.

She was very general about the future, but she gave me the impression that she had an idea that would help me to make a future for myself in England. She made it sound as though after I came to Castle Cloud, doors would swing open wide for me—like magic almost. She seemed sure that something wonderful would happen to me here, but she did not explain what."

"Do you think she had anything specific in mind?"

"Well—yes, I think so."

"But what could she have done for you?"

"I don't know. I suppose we will just have to ask her."

"Are you sure you want to go all the way in there?" he asked.

"Is it far? Yes, I would love to see it. Surely you have not brought me all this way for nothing."

"Of course not. I thought you might be tired, that is all. Mind this branch."

After we passed the edge of the wood the undergrowth disappeared, and the ruined walk was quite easy to follow. In five minutes' time, it led us to the grotto. The grotto was a disappointment. As Edmond had said, it was literally a hole dug into the side of the hill—a cave with an arched opening of stones and a stone roof inside. The stones at the entrance had fallen or been toppled to close the opening. But some of these had been pushed aside to provide a space large enough for a person to squeeze through. Before we passed through it, Edmond paused to light the stub of a candle. Then he led the way in, and I followed.

The cave was cold and empty except for a life-size statue of a man draped in a toga. It stood against the wall. He had been painted white, but now the paint peeled from his leaden skin and robes. Was this Pluto, god of the underworld? I wondered. If so, it was an appropriate choice for this desolate place where only the leaves that covered the ground around the edges of the cave kept him company. They had blown in from the forest long ago and lay covered with a film of dust from the mortar which had fallen from between the stones of the roof above us.

"Now doesn't this live up to your mysterious and romantic expectations?" Edmond asked.

"No, it is rather unpleasant. You were quite right—it is nothing very much to see. Has someone been digging there?" I asked, gesturing to the earthen floor in the center of the cave.

"James, of course. I believe he unearthed that piece of crockery," Edmond replied. He pointed to a brown earthenware jar, lying on the ground among the leaves. "He must have thought he was in Persepolis or Thebes. Ha! What could he expect to find in a hundred-year-old, man-made hole in the side of a hill?"

"I don't know, but I should not have troubled you to bring me all this way."

"James said the statue was by Van Nost, as if there were something wonderful in that. It has no real value," Edmond said, as he led the way back to the entrance.

"Poor James," I thought aloud. We had picked our way out of the grotto, and now walked side by side back toward the house. "How did he die? I know you told me it was his heart and some sort of complication, but was he ill long—did he suffer?"

"Yes, he was in pain much of the time, poor fellow. He was ill almost a month. He took to his bed with aches and pains and fever, and the following day he began to vomit. The vomiting continued, diarrhea, heart pain, weakness, loss of weight. The doctor prescribed pills and medicines, all to no avail. The night he died, he was taken with violent chest pains, vomiting, and convulsions. He never regained conciousness after that. He was a mere shadow of himself."

"How horrible. You must miss him terribly."

"It was appalling, of course, but we were never close. He was four years older than I, and—well, we were never friends. It was simply that James was a fool, and stupid to boot. It would be ridiculous not to admit it, and the fact that he is dead does not change it.

"I shall never forget the first time I realized how dumb he was. It was at Harrow. He had been there long before I arrived. He was prefect of our house. Now, you would think that, being my brother, he would look out for me a bit. But, no. He caught me throwing a stone at the headmaster's window one night—actually I hadn't thrown one, but I was about to. You have no idea of the dictatorial oppression of the headmasters in our schools. No intelligent boy could endure it. It is an absolute necessity to revolt against it. I tried to explain this to James but he was too dense to understand it. He gave me a caning instead. He caned his own brother! I swore I would get even with him someday. We never liked each other after that.

"He had that disgusting stutter, you know, and all he ever thought of was digging. 'Unearthing lost civilizations,' as he grandly put it, was all he cared about—as if that meant anything. If he found an old jug or knife, he was in ecstasy. Idiot! When I think that he would have inherited all this, and I would have been forced to go begging, well—"

But he didn't finish the thought. We had come out of the woods by that time, and I was glad when he said, "Mary, if you will excuse me, I shall go on ahead. I have a great deal to do this afternoon, and this has taken longer than I thought it would."

Then, without waiting for a reply, he hurried away toward the house. I did not follow him. Instead I sat down on the steps of the temple, and it was not long before Sarah joined me. We sat there together for a long time, looking out across Bideford Bay, and then we walked slowly back to the house together.

Vivian's horse was a beautiful bay mare named Chocolate. I wanted to see her again so I walked to the stables through the warm, clear air on Saturday morning after breakfast. (It was one of those rare days in Devonshire when the bowl of the sky lay bare of clouds.) As I entered the stable yard, a man came out of a doorway carrying a pail in each hand. But he set them down when he saw me, and walked over to me.

"Good morning," I said. "You must be Colen."

"Yes, my lady. Is there something I can do for you?"

"No, thank you, Colen. I came to say hello to Chocolate. Is she still here?"

"Yes, my lady. She's in the first box there. I'll show you, my lady. She has become restless lately, what with not getting the right exercise, and she misses her ladyship. I know she does. There she is, my lady."

We had walked through the open door of the stable by then, and it took me a moment to get used to the dim light after the bright sunshine outside. But then I saw that Chocolate had come to the front of her box. She whickered at me.

I went over to her and said, "Hello, Chocolate." She pushed her great nose at me with coaxing nudges, and I reached up and stroked it. "Beautiful lady. I wish I had something for you, but I haven't a thing."

"Have this piece of carrot, my lady," Colen said from behind me.

"Thank you, Colen. There you are, my beauty." As I spoke, Chocolate took the carrot daintily from my palm.

"Such a lovely animal," I said, as I turned and began to walk back toward the doorway. Colen walked along beside me. "I don't see Coconut. Is she here?"

"I don't know any horse by that name, my lady. She must have been here before I came. There's Chocolate, and Chestnut, his late young lordship's horse, down there, and Cinnamon, his young lordship's horse, in the box next to him. Then there's the four carriage horses, and that's all, my lady."

"Well, thank you for showing me Chocolate, and thank you for fetching my bags for me on Wednesday night. I am sorry to have caused you so much trouble."

"It wasn't any trouble, my lady. Stationmaster Chute showed me your bags, and I brought them back with me."

"It must have taken hours."

"About thirty minutes, my lady."

"Oh? I am really very grateful, and thank you again."

Then I left him. I could not bear to go back into the house. It was such a heavenly day. And I was very lonely for Vivian. How I wished she were there with me that morning. I had hoped her letter would be waiting for me at breakfast, but it had not arrived. What would she and I do together if she were here? I wondered. Visit the home-farm? Explore the shore of the bay? Walk down the hedged walk and then follow the brook and watch it empty into the Tay? We might have done any of these things four years ago.

But that day I could not decide what to do, and I found myself walking aimlessly with no specific destination in mind. As I did so I looked about, half expecting to see Sarah running toward me. She was not in sight, however, and I proceeded to walk alone to the northwest corner of the garden, then past Lady Clareham's flower beds, around to the arched opening in the north wall, up the steps, and across the drive that led to the home-farm and eventually, round about, to the village. Before me stood the glasshouses—two long, low hothouses extending from either side of an enormous central building of glass with a glass-domed roof.

I walked across to the door of the central building, pushed it open, and stepped inside. Four years ago, palms and tree-ferns had grown here in the humid aid. Philodendrons, orchids of every description, bananas, begonias, caladiums, and strange, tropical-foliage plants that I had never seen before had grown in profusion. They were all still there, but they were no longer alive. Leaves still clung to the trees and plants, but the dense, green tangle had shriveled to a brittle, dun lacework.

The sun blazed through the dried leaves above me, scorching the air. It smelled parched and acrid. And the dead leaves which had fallen to the ground crackled under my feet. The gardeners must simply have left the greenhouse one day, and it looked as though no one had touched it since.

The rear door opened onto a terrace overlooking the lily pond. When I stepped out, I saw that the lilies had disappeared—choked away by bulrushes and water hyacinths that shouldered each other aside, searching for more room to grow in.

I do not know what made me go to the hedged walk from there on that particular morning. It was some force that I've often wondered about—a force that draws us to a place, sometimes, at the very moment that something that affects us happens there. Of course I was not thinking about this then. I thought, merely, that the walk was near, and that there was time before luncheon to explore it.

The hedged walk was a narrow, stone-flagged walk which began across the drive from the knot garden, below the north front of the house, and descended in steps down the hill to the bathing pavilion. The walk was edged on both sides with a dense yew hedge, which once had been beautifully clipped, but which now formed an irregular, shaggy wall. Halfway down the hill was a stream which meandered through fields and woods toward the glasshouses, filled the lily pond, and then splashed down the hillside in a series of waterfalls to empty, eventually, into the Tay.

I could not hear the stream when I entered the walk.

The air was still. The steps of the walk, carpeted with several years' thickness of pine needles, muffled my footsteps. But then, as I descended, I began to hear the stream's water music. I walked along, trying to picture in my mind the view of the waterfalls from the bridge below me, just around the curve in the walk. At that point, however, my thoughts were interrupted by what I thought was a girl's voice laughing or crying out from somewhere down there. I could not be sure, though, because of the noise of the water. Then I glanced to my right and met the eyes of a man who was standing half-concealed among the branches of the hedge. He could not have heard me coming for he drew back with a start when he saw me. After staring at me for a moment, he stepped back into the bushes and was gone. It all happened so quickly that I had time to notice only that his hair was very long and uncombed, and that he wore a long full beard and, I believe, a coat that fell to below his knees.

Before I could recover from my surprise, Edmond came into view around the bend in the walk.

"Hello. Did I startle you?" he asked. "What on earth are you doing here, anyway?"

"It was the man who was startled," I said.

"Man?"

"You didn't see him? There was a man standing in the hedge, just there. I suppose he could see straight down to the pavilion. He was looking in that direction. And then when he saw me, he vanished behind the hedge. Who was he?"

"Since I did not see him, I certainly would not be able to say for sure. McComb, more than likely. Watching the bathing pavilion, you say? What on earth for? He knows perfectly well what goes on down there. I swim down there every morning. Stupid ass!"

"Who is McComb? I know you swim there every morning, Edmond. Please do not think *I* would have disturbed you. I planned to turn off onto the path that follows the stream, on the other side of the bridge."

"Estate agent—manages the estates for the trustees." He took out his watch and looked at it. "Well, are you coming up to the house? We cannot stand here chatting. It is eleven fifty-five. We are late."

"Late for what?"

"Behind schedule," he said, as he hurried along ahead of me. "One must always watch time, Mary. Guard it. Plan for it. Time is a thing that can run away from you if you don't watch it carefully. If you don't watch it, you may find that it has all escaped from you and there is none left. Little by little it goes—you have no idea how stealthily. People do not realize it until it is too late. Especially young people like yourself, Mary. To you, it seems that there is all the time in the world, but there is only a certain amount. So watch it very carefully, and do not complain to me—do not say I didn't warn you when someday you find that all the things you wanted to do were never done. You have been warned. You are one of the lucky people. Most people find, all of a sudden, that it is all gone, and that it is too late."

Since Edmond had left Castle Cloud on business shortly after luncheon, Lady Clareham and I dined alone that Saturday evening. No one told me where Edmond had gone. I would love to have known, but I did not think I should ask. Lady Clareham did not mention his journey at dinner. As a matter of fact, there was very little conversation at all.

After the meal, after we had had our coffee, I excused myself and walked out onto the east portico to see what the evening was like. The sky remained cloudless, and the sun had not quite set behind the trees. There would be plenty of time to walk up the hill before its light vanished entirely. I could not see the monument from where I stood because trees hid it from view, but it was very much on my mind. I wanted to go there very badly, so I did.

A fresh east wind blew as I stood beside the monument looking down on Milton Penderton, and I pulled my shawl snugly about my shoulders. I saw no one approaching nor anyone in the village below or in the fields or about the farmhouses or cottages that studded the countryside around it. I searched the meadows and woods and finally saw a figure driving a cart along a distant lane. Then, in the village below me, a woman left her cottage to feed her chickens. They were too far away for their cackling to reach me. I felt terribly isolated, so far away from everyone, and I almost wished I had not come to the hilltop.

But I could not leave. Instead, I strolled to the doorway

of the monument and stepped inside, out of the wind. There, beneath the vaulted roof of its single chamber, the square tomb stood. It was unadorned except for the horse's epitaph carved into a marble slab. It read, "Under this stone lies the body of King Charles. Born 1776—Died 1791. A true and loyal friend whose courage and fearless devotion. . ." The slab was cracked across the center, and across the crack lay three yellow roses. How sad it was to see those withered flowers lying there, slowly dying in that dismal place.

Then I heard a horse approaching, and I ran out to the edge of the hill where I could look down upon the village. At the outskirts of it, just below me, a rider galloped his horse across a sloping meadow. They scrambled up the hill directly toward me. The man on the horse was the same man I had met two nights before. When he reached the hilltop he dismounted, left his horse to graze, and walked toward me.

"Hello," he said. "I came here last night hoping to see you, but you did not come."

"No, I didn't know that I was supposed to," I answered. I could not help smiling.

"Well, you weren't *supposed* to, but I hoped you would. I see you didn't bring Sarah along."

"No, I have not seen her all day."

"Off hunting somewhere, no doubt. I have been wanting to apologize for the other night. I am sorry I frightened you. I didn't mean to. After I mistook you for Vivian, I am afraid I lost my manners. I might at least have introduced myself. I am David Field, and I live at Oakland Park, the house beyond the trees there."

He pointed to what must have been an enormous house on a rise about a mile beyond Milton Penderton. It was almost hidden by the trees. I could see little more than its roof.

"And I am Mary Elizabeth Thorpe."

"Vivian has spoken of me, of course," he said.

"But what were you doing up here the night before last?"

"I was out for a ride, and there was just a chance that I might catch sight of William Reade from up here."

"Who is William Reade?"

"He is our local professional poacher—out of both necessity and the pure perverse enjoyment of it. He should be caught."

"Why?" I asked.

"Because he is a nuisance in the neighborhood, and he has been getting a little too cocky lately. Everyone knows all about him and his poaching. But he is a wily one. He is famous in this part of the county because he knows everything there is to know about animals and he has never been caught. Why, you can see him walking home at daybreak with his coat bulging with hares when *we* have not been able to find one for days. He has a fantastic rapport with animals. I wish I had it, I can tell you. If only it was put to good use instead of being wasted so." He paused, looking directly into my eyes. "He has been seen coming down from here quite often these past few weeks."

"What does he look like? What would you do if you caught him?"

"He looks like he is all hair. It would be hard to see him after dark with all that hair on him—long hair and a long, dark beard. He is dirty and poor, poor devil. I wouldn't do *anything* to him except warn him to stay away from Oakland Park. Just having caught him poaching would be enough, I think. Are you cold?"

"No, not really," I said. "So you thought I was Vivian. I am not surprised. She and I are the same size. We always used to wear each other's clothes at school. Are you angry with her?"

"Certainly! Come to the other side of the monument, out of the wind." As he spoke, he began to walk that way so I walked beside him. "She left without even saying good-by to anybody. I know she is impetuous, but you don't go off like that."

"When was the last time you saw her?"

"Three days before James died. She was terribly worried about her brother. Well, any sister as fond of her brother as she was of James would have been, naturally. After he died, she was too ill with grief even to come to the funeral. And then the following day, Edmond rode over to Oakland Park to tell my father that she had gone to visit friends, that she needed to travel to recover herself. But to go off like that—"

We had reached the other side of the monument by then and were out of the wind where it was much warmer. I sat down on one of a dozen or so stone building blocks (probably leftover stone from the pyramid) which lay scattered about, half buried in the grass, and David sat down on another block facing me.

"She *is* impetuous," I said. "I have known her to be very sorry for some of the things she did without thinking. That is possibly her only fault. Otherwise she is quite perfect. I think I can understand her leaving like that."

"You must know her well," he said.

"I suppose so. We were best friends at school together for four years—Mrs. Romilly's in Windsor. But then when Lord Clareham returned from India in 1852, he said she might finish the school year, but that she would not be returning to school after that. I spent the Easter holidays visiting her here at Castle Cloud that year. Then, after school ended, she returned here and I went to join my father, who was living in Paris at the time. We might have met four years ago, but I don't remember Vivian mentioning the Fields."

"She didn't know us then. My father bought Oakland Park in 1850, but he didn't come to live here until 1852. But that was in the autumn, after you had left."

"I was in Paris by that time, then. Do you like it here?"

"Yes. I came to live at Oakland Park that autumn, after my father retired from the bank in favor of my brother, William. He . . ."

"Are you a banker too?" I asked, smiling at him.

"I was. I came with Father to help him get settled in, and I never went back to the bank. I belong in the country. Father helped by introducing me to Lord Shaftesbury, and they arranged for me to spend nine months at his country house, Wimborne St. Giles. And then I spent five months working at Rothamsted, Sir John Lawes's farm, and then three months at Windsor Farm."

"Why did you do that?" I asked.

"To learn farming. I had never known the country, really, before I came here. I was back at Oakland Park by spring 1854. I helped to manage the estates then, and now I am in charge of them—all sixty thousand acres and the home-farm."

"What an enormous responsibility."

"Not as much as it sounds. The farmers manage their farms. We make sure they pay their rents each half-year, and we keep the accounts. We are making improvements in the land, naturally—drainage, etcetera—but we must do more. If we help the farmers, we help ourselves and the country. England is changing. It is becoming industrial. The population is growing. In the future, we will need to use the land more productively if we are going to remain fed. And that is what I want to do. I am making the home-farm at Oakland Park an example of what a farm can be, but there is still a lot to be done. We have all the latest farm machinery—steam-threshing and winnowing machines, chaff-cutters and turnip-slicers. You have no idea what the steam engine means, not only to transportation but to *farming*. I am using everything I learned at Wimborne, Rothamsted, and Windsor, and everything I can learn from the Royal Agricultural Society. I get every new book that is published on farming and I have a lot of ideas of my own that I am trying out. I want the farmers to *see* what we do here and to encourage them to do the same—*help* them to do it."

"You love it, don't you?" I asked.

"Yes."

"When did you meet Vivian, then?"

"In the latter part of August, two years ago," he answered.

I waited for a moment, thinking he would say more, but he didn't. He merely sat, his forearms on his knees, his big hands clasped, looking at me in the most peculiarly intent way.

"It will soon be dark, Mr. Field," I said. "I have enjoyed our conversation very much, but I really must be starting back toward the house. I will tell Vivian that you were asking about her. Perhaps we will see each other when she returns to Castle Cloud. I am expecting a letter from her any day now."

"I will see you part of the way," he said, as we stood and began to walk toward the hill path.

"Oh, no. Thank you, but please don't bother. It is still light enough, and I will be able to find my way easily. Good night."

Then, after he had said good night and I had started down the hill, I heard his horse gallop off in the opposite direction, toward Oakland Park.

❧ Chapter Three ❧

"ARE YOU GOING to the church in Milton Penderton this morning?" I asked Lady Clareham.

"Yes, my dear," she replied.

"May I come along?"

"Certainly, if you wish," she had said.

It had not been the most cordial invitation, and if I had not chanced upon her in the gallery after breakfast that Sunday morning, I would probably not have known she was going to church at all. It was not because of the service itself that I wanted to go, although I enjoyed the music and the warmth that comes from people sharing the experience together, but it was a drizzly morning—not one for a walk—and I was bored and wanted something to do.

So it was arranged that I would accompany her, and when we were ready to depart, we walked out onto the east portico together. Below us, Colen sat on the box of the cabriolet, waiting for us. And at that moment, Sarah came running up the steps to greet me.

"Sarah!" Colen called. "Come away, girl. Sarah, come here!"

"It is all right, Colen," I shouted. "Sarah, good girl, but don't brush up against me." I shook a finger at her and then reached over and patted her head. "I hope your hunting was successful yesterday." She looked up at me mischievously and seemed to grin.

"Hunting?" Lady Clareham asked.

"Sarah and I have become friends. She likes to go walking with me. But I did not see her at all yesterday, and I assumed that she was off on a hunting expedition somewhere."

"Get away, Sarah. Shoo!" Colen said, as he helped us into the carriage a few moments later. But then, as we started off around the grass circle, Sarah began to bark

54

and run after us. "Go home!" Colen cried, pointing to the stables.

This did no good at all, however, and Sarah continued to run after the carriage until she got tired. I looked back at her as she stood in the drive gazing after us, her head tilted, wondering why we had not taken her along.

"Poor Sarah," I said. "I feel so sorry for animals when they cannot understand and we cannot explain to them."

"Yes, poor Sarah," Lady Clareham said. "I remember the first time I saw her. It was one day a year or two before we returned to India for the last time. Vivian came into my room holding the tiniest, dirtiest, scraggliest little puppy with the sweetest, dearest little face. It had just wandered in one day. 'Can we keep it, Mamma?' she said. And of course I said we could." Lady Clareham had begun to cry. "She was the sweetest little thing," she sobbed into her handkerchief.

"She is a dear dog. Does she live with Colen?"

"Yes, Cleopatra would not have her in the house." Lady Clareham glanced at me, attempting a smile.

After that we drove along in silence toward the home-farm.

At length I said, "It was rather sweet of you to leave the roses for King Charles."

"King Charles? Oh, you found them? No, I did not leave them for the horse. I did not leave them for anybody. I was rather tired when I reached the top of the hill. It was the day before yesterday, wasn't it, that I went to the churchyard? Well, when I got to the top of the hill, I was hot and tired and went into the pyramid, out of the sun to rest a bit. And then, when I looked at James's bouquet, I decided that I did not like the yellow roses in it after all, so I removed them and left them there."

"Well, I am sure that King Charles appreciated it anyway."

Lady Clareham did not reply. She sat looking away from me into the hedgerows which ended shortly, disclosing the home-farm beyond its narrow meadow. A dozen geese crossed the road near the farm as we approached it. They blustered out of our way but remained at the roadside to honk angrily at us as we passed by.

Beyond the farm, the drive swung into a lane which followed the bank of the Tay for a quarter of a mile and then left it to wind through the village, beneath a green canopy of beech and elm trees.

Milton Penderton was a cluster of perhaps twenty whitewashed, thatched, cob cottages and three or four two-story, granite houses. Most of the houses were blanketed with climbing roses, and roses bloomed in their gardens—roses seemed to bloom everywhere. The houses surrounded the church, which was set in the midst of a mossy churchyard. It was of granite, in the perpendicular style, with a lofty, square tower and gothic windows.

Lady Clareham and I arrived, and Colen helped us down. We went inside, where I noticed that James's mourning had not yet been removed. I glanced at the congregation as we walked to the Ramsay pew, but I knew no one there except Mrs. Foley. She sat with a girl whom I was later to learn was May Brooke, the kitchen maid at the Castle. They walked to church together every Sunday morning.

Soon the service began. It was a long one, and I found that I was not in the mood for church after all and was impatient for it to be over. When it finally was, and we had spoken briefly with Reverend Anderson, I told Lady Clareham that if she wished to visit James's grave, I would wait for her in the carriage, and that she was not to hurry on my account. So she left me and walked to the Clareham tomb-house, a square, battlemented, granite building which dominated the churchyard. After some ten minutes she returned to the carriage, and we were driven back to Castle Cloud.

After luncheon, which was always an hour later than usual on Sunday to give the servants time to go to church, I visited Lord Clareham.

"Am I disturbing you?" I asked him.

"Not at all, my dear. So very kind of you to come. Come in, come in. As a matter of fact, this is most fortunate. I wonder if I may ask a little favor of you? Julia has one of her headaches, and I did want to get a most important letter off in tomorrow's mail. Would you be kind enough to write it down for me?"

"Of course, Lord Clareham, I would be delighted to. Actually, that is why I came—to see if there were anything I could do for you."

"Very kind of you, very kind indeed. Sit down at the desk there. Is there paper and ink? Yes? Good! Now, quiet while I get my thoughts together."

While I waited for his dictation to begin, I was able to examine the room. It looked more like a library than a bedroom because of the enormous bookcases, stuffed with books, that lined all four walls. They were separated only by the two doors of the room, one to the gallery and one leading into Lady Clareham's bedroom next door, and by the windows. Lord Clareham's bed had been pushed as close to one of the windows as the bookcases, which flanked it, would allow. The bed wore a heavily carved and gilded canopy and hangings of dark-green and gold damask. It had, I learned later, come from Whitehall Palace. Over it, one of Lord Clareham's mirrors hung while the other stood at his bedside. But it was the bronze Buddha that faced the bed, sitting on its pedestal on the Turkish carpet, which fascinated me. It was so large that I did not understand how it could have been gotten into the room. The massive figure must have been six feet tall. It sat cross-legged, of course, its hands folded limply in its lap, bathing the room in serenity.

"June 29, 1856," Lord Clareham began, breaking the silence. "This is to Lord Dalhousie, Government House, Calcutta, but we will take care of the address later. Start it: Dear James. My health is better, thank you. I now have feeling in my right side and will soon be writing you with my own hand, I feel sure. New paragraph. In answer to your letter, I fear for the future. I must emphasize again and again that changes too swiftly imposed, no matter how they may improve the natives' lot, cannot but be resisted. . . ."

When he had finished dictating the five-page letter (he seemed to feel that a revolt of some kind was imminent in India), I addressed the envelope and then carried the letter to him to examine.

"Very good, my dear," he said. "Underline the words 'never understood' in the last paragraph. Underline them twice, and then hold it for me to sign."

When he had done so, I placed the letter in its envelope, sealed it, and gave it to Ahmad to take to Mitchell. When Ahmad had gone, Lord Clareham seemed to relax a little. His spotted left hand rested, still on his chest.

"There is going to be trouble out there," he said. "The army is Indian—Indian soldiers, mind you, not British. I do not like the look of it. James goes too fast. If only I were there."

He fell silent, then, his mind in Calcutta, I supposed. I wondered if I should leave him. But I thought I had better wait until Ahmad returned so I asked, gesturing to the open book lying on his bed: "What are you reading?"

"The *Bhagavad Gita*. It is one of the greatest poems— one of the greatest religious poems—ever written. The Lord Krishna was a very wise man, Mary. He does not demand perfection. If you are weak, he says, bring me your weakness. Quite different from saying that thou shalt not do this, or that thou shalt not do that, isn't it?

"Thank God for my friends and for their wisdom." He gestured to the books that surrounded him. "There is so much wisdom, my dear, and so few men wise enough to take advantage of it. But perhaps we expect too much, eh?

"Edmond tells me that you have written to Vivian."

"Yes," I said. "I had hoped to hear from her yesterday—but perhaps tomorrow." I paused. "I want to thank you for your hospitality, Lord Clareham."

"Pleasure, great pleasure, my dear. Tell me, what were you and Edmond discussing so seriously yesterday as you emerged from the hedged walk? Argument?"

"Oh, no. We weren't arguing. I think Edmond was telling me his philosophy of time. You saw us?"

"In my mirrors. I always look for Edmond at twelve noon. I could set my watch by him. If he is not coming out of the hedged walk at twelve o'clock, he is not at Castle Cloud."

"Well, I am afraid we almost made him late yesterday."

"We? Someone else was down there? You don't mean you went to the bathing pavilion?"

"No. I am talking about William Reade, the poacher. At least I have come to think, from what I have heard about him, that it was William Reade. He was—he seemed to be all hair, and he wore a long coat."

"Yes."

"He was down there. Well, he was halfway down the path, standing in the hedge, watching the pavilion, I suppose, or Edmond, or both. Why should he do that?"

"Why indeed?" Lord Clareham said. If you take my advice, you will stay away from there. It is not a place for nice young ladies. I have not the vaguest idea what William Reade was watching. I should not think he would go in for that kind of thing. What did Edmond do?"

"Edmond didn't see him. He vanished just as Edmond came round the bend in the path. It was my explanation that held us up."

"Well, if you see Reade again, come and tell me. He is harmless enough, but we do not want him roaming about the grounds. And come and tell me what Vivian has to say when you receive her letter. I don't suppose she would think of writing to us."

"Ah, there is Ahmad. Thank you for helping me with the letter, Mary. Now, if you don't mind, I should like to take a little nap before dinner."

I left him.

"There is a letter for you," Edmond said, as I entered the dining room before breakfast the following morning.

"Good morning. Did you have a pleasant trip?" I asked.

I had seen the letter on the tray as soon as I entered the room and had started toward it even before Edmond spoke. I could see at once that the letter was not from Vivian: the address was not in her handwriting. I picked it up and carried it to my place at the table where Mitchell helped me to be seated.

"It is not from Vivian," I said, as I glanced at the envelope. "If it were, I would recognize— But—"

Then I saw that Vivian's name was written above the return address. Quickly, I slit open the envelope, withdrew the letter, unfolded it, and immediately looked for the signature.

"It *is* from Vivian!" I cried.

The letter was dated June 27, 1856 and had been written at 39 King Street, Greenwich. It read:

My dearest Mary,

Nancy is writing this letter for me because I fell and injured my hand. I cannot use my fingers—it is too painful. The doctor says that my hand will be all right, but that I must not use it any more than necessary.

"Her friend wrote the letter because Vivian hurt her hand," I said.

The letter continued:

I am glad you arrived at Castle Cloud safely, and I am sorry that I cannot be there with you. Nancy and I are leaving tomorrow to visit some friends of hers in Scotland. I do not know how long we will be gone. They are nice people and have asked us to stay with them until I have recovered my spirits. I feel such terrible grief for James that it makes me ill at times. I am not myself.

"But she is not coming home. She is going to Scotland tomorrow. She is ill," I said, glancing at Edmond.

Then I continued to read:

Do not worry, Edmond can help you even more than I could have. I know he will be happy to do this for me and for you. He is a very kind and good brother. He knows more people in the county than I do and will find a position which will make you happy. Trust him and rely on him. A position as governess or companion in one of our good county families would be just the thing, and Edmond can arrange it as well as I could have.

I do not know what fate has in store for me or when I will see you again—I am too ill with grief to care. But I do wish you a happy future.

Ever
Yours
Affectionately,
Vivian

When I had finished reading the letter, I read it again, skimming over the first two paragraphs. Then I reread the third paragraph and then the last sentence of that paragraph again very slowly. I must have read that same sentence several more times before I could tear my eyes away from it.

"Is something wrong?" Edmond asked.

I reexamined the letter, the stationery, the handwriting, the address, and Vivian's signature, which was barely recognizable. Then, once again, my eye was drawn back to that sentence: ". . . as governess or companion in one of our good county families. . . ."

"No!" I murmured aloud.

"Well, I am glad to hear that," Edmond said. "The way you looked, one would think it was the end of the world or something."

"I will not do it. Vivian would not expect me to do it. She did not write this letter. She would not suggest such a thing."

"Do what? Something is wrong. How can you expect me to understand such irrational talk? What is it? Can I help you, Mary?"

"She wants me to take a position as a governess or companion. A *governess* or *companion*, can you imagine? She is ill. She would never suggest such a thing if she were well. Why, it is unthinkable."

I sat there clenching the letter and, I am afraid, glaring at Edmond across the table.

"Do you wish to tell me what else Vivian said in her letter? You are obviously upset, Mary, and I would like to help you if I can, but I cannot very well do that if I do not know what is upsetting you, can I?"

I handed Vivian's letter to Edmond, who took it and read it.

"I think she is absolutely right," he said, when he had finished reading it.

"*Right?*" I cried.

"Yes, my dear. I rather imagined that that was what Vivian had in mind after our conversation the other day. Well, what else could she have had in mind? Can you think of any other thing she might have had in mind?"

"Yes. Marriage, for one thing."

"*Marriage?* Marriage to whom?" he asked. "Oh, I understand. You were to meet an enormously wealthy nobleman who would also be extraordinarily handsome and who would demand that you marry him. He would threaten to take his own life if you refused him, I suppose?"

"Edmond! How can you?" I demanded.

"To show you how foolish it is, Mary. If you had a fortune, or even a substantial dowry, or forgive me, I do not mean to hurt your feelings, if you were a great beauty, it could be arranged. But, my dear—"

I sat still, staring across the table at him.

"Mary," he continued, "how we fantasize, how we dream, how loath we are to face reality. Be practical, be realistic. Now, you can either stay in England or return to Holland. Do you agree? If you return to Holland, what would you do? I do not know the country or customs, but I suppose you would need a dowry of some kind even to marry a prosperous farmer or tradesman. Am I right?"

"Yes."

"If you stay in England, you face the same problem. Well, don't you? To marry into the nobility or even the gentry without money or beauty, well—"

"I have my title. My husband's son will, at the least, be a baron," I said.

"My dear, I thought we were going to be realistic, practical. Titles do not buy land, they do not buy anything. A squire, or a prosperous professional man or a manufacturer would certainly wish to marry his son to the daughter of a noble family, if he could, for the social and business advantages the association with that family could provide. Can your family provide these advantages? And then of course a substantial dowry would come to that young man after the marriage, to help his material and social advancement in the world, but as we have said, you have no dowry. But you know all this.

"Could you expect to meet a young man of good family who would marry you for love and nothing more? Would you like to find a man who would marry you for the title that would go to his son? What kind of man would he be, and what would your life be like if you found such a man? Society does *not* approve of a lady who marries a man in trade. Perhaps you expect to find a wealthy young man of good family who would marry you for love and title and nothing more. Well, nothing is impossible, of course. It would not be impossible to find a needle in a haystack, but it would be enormously difficult, and it would take a long, long time."

"And I do not have the time?" I asked.

"Well?"

"So I have the choice of marrying a tradesman. . ."

"If you could find one who would marry you. . ."

"Without a dowry. Oh, Edmond," I said.

"I am sure you could, if you think you could bear it."

"So the alternative is to take a position as a governess or companion."

"Or returning to the farm in Holland."

"No."

"Or becoming a nurse. I understand Miss Nightingale. . ."

"No."

"Well then?" he asked.

I could not answer him. Suddenly, I was too exhausted to think anymore.

"I know how you feel, Mary," he said. "Believe me, I know. But consider carefully, and I am sure you will see that Vivian and I are right. You have no alternative. If we had the money, well— But there is no point of even thinking about that. But we can help you find a position with a good, kind family in pleasant surroundings. Why, you will live in luxury, and your duties will be light. There is no reason why you should not enjoy them. Children are delightful. You will become fond of them and be quite happy."

"Edmond, you may be right. I may have no choice but to take a position. But let us not be hypocrites. Such a future could hold nothing but misery for me."

"You are upset. I will leave you to think in peace," he said, glancing at his watch. "You will realize that both Vivian and I have spoken wisely, and I know you will be grateful for our help."

He rose from the table then, and left the room.

"My lady?" Mitchell demanded.

"Coffee please, Mitchell. Nothing more."

I gulped my coffee, left the room, and then fled from the house. Outside, Sarah ran to meet me as I descended the staircase of the east portico, and we walked together across the grass circle.

"Would you like to walk to the top of the hill with me?" I asked her. "We could pay our respects to King Charles."

Sarah bounced with joy and then went scampering off toward the rose garden.

I followed her, glad to be in the fresh air and alone. I needed solitude to think about Vivian and her letter. She is not coming home, I thought. Why has she asked me to come here? I wish I hadn't come. No, that is not true. Things would not be any better for me in Holland. If I must work, I would much rather do it here in England than there—here among my own people. But it will not happen today or tomorrow. I have a few days' time to think. It is not going to happen at once. I will not think about it until I get to the monument, where I can sit down and be at peace. But of course I thought about my situation continually as I walked to the top of the hill.

My shoes and the hem of my dress were soon wet, but I did not care, nor did I notice the day or the view. A governess, I thought. Unthinkable! But were Edmond and Vivian right? Was this what I must do?

When I reached the hilltop, I crossed to the building blocks. They were dry enough, so I sat down where I had sat on Saturday evening and, for a moment, I imagined David Field sitting on the block opposite me as he had then.

"What else can I do, David," I asked aloud. "What else can I do? Edmond was right. I have no money. I am not a great beauty. I am not a beauty at all. Who would marry me? Would you marry me?"

Then I could no longer see him because my eyes had filled with tears, and when I had gotten control of myself, his image was gone and Sarah was loping toward me, wagging her tail. She licked my hand and then sat down at my feet and looked up at me as if to say, "Come and play with me."

"Was this why Vivian asked me to come to Castle Cloud?" I asked Sarah. "I know she was unhappy, and she needed a shoulder to cry on. But when her tears had been shed, would she have rid herself of me by finding me employment?" I tried to think exactly what she had said in her letters, but she had been so vague about her plans for me and her promises that I could not remember any specific words.

Again I read her latest letter. Poor Vivian. How miserable she must be, I thought. If only I could help her somehow. I would love to see her, be with her, but now I shan't. I have counted so much on our being together. How could she go off like this and leave me? But then, her plans had been made well before she received my letter. And she *is* ill. I can tell from the sound of her letter.

I stood then, and walked back down to the house. There I found Mitchell in the dining room preparing for luncheon.

"Mitchell," I called, "would you kindly tell Lady Clareham and his lordship that I have a headache and I will not be down to luncheon?"

"Yes, my lady," he answered. He smiled a smile of undisguised triumph as he said it. He might have added that we were now almost equals. Of course he didn't, but I had no doubt that that was what he had been thinking. Was my future, then, to be spent as something little better than a servant? *Was* this what Vivian had had in mind all along?

Perhaps the solution lay upstairs in my room. I climbed the stairs to it and closed the door behind me. Even if I had had no specific purpose there, I could not have borne the thought of making conversation with Lady Clareham and Edmond at luncheon. He, no doubt, would wish to discuss my problems further, but I did not wish to discuss them with anyone until I had discussed them thoroughly with myself. He and his mother wanted to help, which was very kind of them, but I was not ready for kindness.

Instead, I wanted to reread some of Vivian's letters. I had saved them all. They lay in my trunk with a few things I had decided not to unpack. And two of the most recent letters, including the one I had partly read to Edmond and Lady Clareham, were still in my reticule. So, when I had changed into dry clothes and gotten all the letters together, I drew a chair up to a table beside the window and sat down to read them. Perhaps I had never read them carefully enough. Perhaps they held the secret of what Vivian really had in mind for me.

It took a few minutes to remove the letters from their envelopes and to arrange them in chronological order. When I had done this, I counted twenty-one letters in all. The first was dated August 12, 1852. Then three letters had been written in the autumn of that year, six had been written in 1853, four in 1854, only three in 1855, and four in 1856. But only six of the letters interested me that afternoon. These were the most recent ones.

I began with the February, 1855 letter. In it Vivian mentioned David Field. It began:

> February 3, 1855
>
> My dearest Mary,
>
> I was *delighted* to receive your letter from Marienbad. I am sending this to the address you gave me in Bern. I *do* hope after all these months, you will still be there to receive it. You *do* jump from place to place on the continent so. . . .

And then she went into a long explanation of a trip to the continent which she and her mother had planned and which had had to be postponed indefinitely, and a trip to London which she had made. This part of the letter I skimmed over and then I read,

> Life here is as always—in a way, dull, but pleasant. Mamma and Papa are well and as usual. We *do* have a pleasant society here in Devonshire. There is *always* something to look forward to—a dinner, or a ball (rather more *seldom* than I would wish). As a matter of fact, one is to be held next Tuesday evening, a subscription ball at the Assembly Rooms, and we shall all go. I *do* enjoy them and of course my program is always filled, *thank goodness.* David will be there, I expect. He is quite a nice young man who has recently moved into Oakland Park to stay with his father. No, no romance. He is just pleasant company to ride out with in the afternoons occasionally. Mamma and Papa do *not* approve—his father is a banker. He is hardly a dream prince. Do you think a dream prince *will* come for me? I do so long for *love*—the way I know it can be. And you, Mary? Have you met a handsome mountaineer in Switzerland? You must tell me all about him.
>
> Ever
> Yours
> Affectionately,
> Vivian

Vivian's letter of May 29, 1855, was short and spoke of

more parties, balls, dinners, and riding out—the not-un-usual, pleasant life of a pretty, popular girl in the country. But her last letter of that year and the following ones were the letters I wanted to study. They were responsible for my having come to Castle Cloud.

The November letter read:

November 20, 1855

My dearest Mary,

Thank you for your letter of last July. I am dread-fully, *dreadfully* ashamed of waiting so long to an-swer it. The time has gone by so *terribly* fast, and I do treasure our friendship so *very* much, and I know that if I waited another day to answer your sweet let-ter, I would never forgive myself. And I have news, dearest, *dearest* Mary. Please do not laugh—this is *very* serious. I am in *love* with the most wonderful, beautiful man.

Shall I tell you about him? Dearest Mary, my dream prince has come. He is tall, and dark, and strong, and most *handsomely* Irish. And he is so terri-bly good and so terribly kind and *he loves me!* His name is John O'Connor. He is of a very, *very* ancient and noble Irish family—descended from the very *first* Christian king of Connaught! His family has no money, but that does not make a particle of differ-ence. But I am afraid that Mamma and Papa would *not* approve. Just because John has to work for his living, he is the new groom here at Castle Cloud, *doesn't mean a thing,* does it? But they would never, *never* understand: so we are keeping our love a deep, dark secret. I told James, of course, and he said that all he wants is for me to be happy, and that he would try to find a way. He is *such* a dear! Sweet, *sweet* James. What would I *do* without my dearest, darling brother. . . .

The rest of this letter was happy small talk of no partic-ular interest to me. But then I found myself holding the tragic letter of January 20, 1856. It read:

January 20, 1856

My dearest Mary,

Something *dreadful* has happened. My dearest, *dearest* friend, if only you were here to comfort me. Only now can I *bring* myself to tell you about it and I need so terribly badly to confide in someone who will *understand*. James has been so attentive and kind, and I love him dearly, but he is a man and only another woman could *really* understand.

John and I are separated—my life is *over*. I shall never, *never* be happy again. And it could have been so terribly wonderful. Such bliss was so very nearly mine. I cannot *bear* to think of it. You see, John and I decided to flee England and make our life together in America where there are no stupid class barriers between *human beings*. We would have been so *marvelously, wonderfully* happy, I know we would. James, my dearest, darling brother borrowed the money and lent it to us. We fled to London! Oh, such happiness. But then we found that we had been found out and pursued by Edmond. Oh, how I hate him! Oh, how I *loathe* him! He threatened to have John thrown into *prison* and all kinds of *unmentionable* things if I did not immediately return to Castle Cloud. It was horrible, dreadful—you will never know the *anguish!* I had no choice but to return.

John has gone to America. He said that he would send for me. That I must wait for him, and I will. I *will!* I will wait *forever* for him. I cannot think of anyone else. He is always, *always* on my mind.

My dearest friend, could you think of coming to Castle Cloud for a visit? I would be so grateful for the blessed, *blessed* comfort you could give me. Please come. Write and tell me that you will. I cannot write more now.

Ever
Yours
Affectionately,
Vivian

Vivian's next letter began:

February 29, 1856

My dearest Mary,

   How can you be so terribly *cruel?* Why will you
not come to me? What have I *done* that you would
desert me when I need you? You must, *you must*
reconsider. . . .

It continued in a very emotional tone to urge me to
come to England to be with her in order to comfort her.

But it was her last two letters to me, while I was still in
Holland, that I read over and over that afternoon. They
read as follows:

March 29, 1856

My Dearest Mary,

   Your letter made me so *unhappy.* How can you
say you will not come to me? I need you terribly, *terribly,* as you know. I am ill with despair. I have not
heard a single word from America. Why doesn't John
write? Tell me he *will* write. When I think that he
may not, that I may never hear from him again, I am
too frightened. I will not think of it!

   But think of yourself, Mary. What has Holland to
offer you? Think of *our* position here in society.
Think how we could help you. If you do not think of
me, my dearest friend, think of *yourself.* So you see
you really *must* come. There is nothing, *nothing* to
keep you on that dirty old farm and certainly no *future* for you in Holland. You must remember the
wonderful, *wonderful* week we spent here at Castle
Cloud in 1852. You said it was one of the *happiest*
you ever had. It will be like that again and for more
than a week. Come and stay as long as you like.
Mamma and Papa will *love* to have you. It is so grim
here. I am quite terribly lonely, and I need my friend
by my side. Your future is in our lovely England: it
has *always* been here. Who knows what wonderful,
wonderful things we could arrange for you here? So
come to me. I simply will not take no for an answer.

   You will change your mind, you *must.* Please write

and say that you have, and tell me when you plan to arrive at Castle Cloud.

Ever
Yours
Affectionately,
Vivian

May 2, 1856

My dearest Mary,

Thank heaven you are coming. Your letter has made me so very, *very* glad. I *knew* you would change your mind. Mamma and Papa will be so *very* delighted, I know. And I have plans for your future. Plans that will insure your comfort and great happiness forever. You have no idea what joy awaits you in England, I am sure of it, *sure of it,* Mary. Comfort and luxury will surround you as it should. You deserve to be happy and I promise you, *promise you,* you will be. We have the connections and you have the *title*. Prepare for happiness, my dearest, *dearest* friend. Now doesn't that make you want more than ever to fly to me? Have I ever *lied* to you? Have I ever *disappointed* you? You will see that it will all come true like a lovely dream. It is too perfect to be true.

It doesn't matter if you cannot let me know when you will arrive. Let me know if you can, but if you cannot, just *come!* I will be here. But come *soon*. I need you so terribly.

John has not written. I shall die if he does not. I die little by little each day that I do not hear from him. If I cannot be by his side, I do not want to live. I *cannot* live without him.

But I will tell you *all* when I see you, and knowing that I *will* see you soon makes me feel so much better. The future grows a little brighter.

Ever
Yours
Affectionately,
Vivian

In this last letter, Vivian had spoken of plans for my future: "great happiness forever" and "joy." She had said that it would be like "a lovely dream." "We have the connections and you have the title," she had written. She could not have been talking about a position as governess or companion, of that I was sure.

Then I read the letter I had received that morning. How different it sounded from Vivian's other letters. I could not help but think that she had not dictated it. The signature, however, was hers—at least if she had sprained or cut her hand it could look like that. And she was emotionally distressed. Was it that I did not want to believe she had dictated it? Did not want to have my dreams destroyed? Did not want to face reality? Was marrying a man I loved, then bearing his children and being happy with him a dream that would not come true for me? Was reality working for my living, and had I better face up to it? No! I will not accept that, I thought. I cannot. And yet, if I do not accept it, what will I do? What choice do I have?

I sat there for perhaps an hour thinking these things, holding Vivian's letters, staring, unseeing, out of the window, and thinking: but I need not work as a governess because I shall find the man I love and he will take care of me. That is not a dream. But that *is* a dream. That is not reality. I shall have to work as a governess. But I need not work as a governess because I shall find the man I love. . . .

My mind went round and round in circles like that until finally I took off my shoes, lay down on the bed, and slept.

I knew that the dowager countess Clareham had arrived on the afternoon train that day and had spent the late afternoon with her son in his room. Mrs. Muldoon told me that, after she had wakened me to ask if I needed anything before she returned to the village.

So I was not surprised, when I entered the drawing room that evening before dinner, to see the dowager countess sitting on a sofa facing Lady Clareham and Edmond. She saw me as soon as I entered the room and examined me quickly, and rather as a child might examine a very special dessert that had just been brought to the table.

"Mary, come in," Edmond said as he stood. "My grandmamma has been longing to meet you."

"'I hope your headache has vanished, my dear," the

dowager countess said. Her black, shoe-button eyes sparkled as she smiled at me.

"Yes, thank you," I said, "It has."

She must be at least eighty-five, I thought. How extraordinarily alert she is. The dowager lady Clareham was portly and short. She could not have been five feet tall. She sat on the sofa, ramrod straight, in a black dress with the long sleeves, high waist, and narrow skirt of an earlier era. The dress was trimmed with white lace and matched a lace-ruffled bonnet which framed her round face and met at her chin in a satin bow.

"I am delighted to meet you, Lady Clareham," I continued. "Vivian has spoken of you often."

"Thank you, my dear. Yes, I remember—you were Vivian's friend at Mrs. Romilly's School in Windsor. . . ."

"Grandmamma visited the Queen at Windsor Castle, didn't you Grandmamma?" Edmond interrupted.

"Yes. Edmond knows how proud I am of having been a guest there and how I delight in telling about it," the dowager countess said to me. "And when you begin to treat me like this, my dear boy," she said to Edmond, "I believe you will soon be asking for something. He is my favorite of all the Ramsays," she said, again turning to me. "And no wonder! He is the most gifted and by far the most intelligent. I cannot resist him and he knows it."

"But how thrilling to have known the Queen," I said. "Won't you tell me about it?"

"Sit down here, next to me, my child, and I will do just that, with pleasure. It was Lord Melbourne, an old friend of my husband's, who was responsible for the invitation. We arrived at Windsor Castle in the early evening of May 2, 1837. That was long before you were there at school, wasn't it? Well, at half-past eight the Queen arrived from Buckingham Palace, looking fresh as a flower, and a few minutes later she summoned us all to dinner. I had not even unpacked, and there was no time to dress, so down we went in our traveling clothes. . . ."

"Dinner is served, my lady," Mitchell interrupted from the doorway.

We stood then, and Edmond held out his arm for the dowager countess, who took it as she whispered to Lady Clareham, "That man is rude, Julia. I cannot think why you keep him."

"Now, Grandmamma—" Edmond began patting his grandmother's arm as he piloted her out of the room.

Lady Clareham and I followed them to the dining room, and when we were seated and had begun to sip our soup, the dowager countess continued her story.

At length she concluded, ". . . and so we left Windsor the following morning. We had stayed four days, and were exhausted. Such energy the Queen has. She tired us out completely. It was only after a week of rest that I was myself again."

"What a charming story," I said. "I should love to know her."

"She is quite changed now that she has married Prince Albert, I understand," the dowager countess said. Then, after a pause, she continued, "Edmond tells me that you have received word from Vivian, which is more than the rest of us have. I have not heard a word from her and neither have Edmond or his parents. There is something strange . . ."

"We received a note from her," Edmond said, "shortly after she left—from Greenwich—don't you remember, Grandmamma?"

"I don't remember that. Did you tell me about it? I still think there was something strange about it all. Vivian would not leave on the spur of the moment like that and not tell *anyone* good-by. I know her well enough to know that much. And then not coming to James's funeral. Why she idolized that boy. She loved her brother too much, if you ask me. Oh, I am not suggesting there was anything wrong there—there cannot be enough love in the world—but then not to attend the funeral? Why Vivian would have crawled to James's funeral on her hands and knees if she had to, but she would have gone."

"You are quite right, Grandmamma," Edmond said. "She would have if she could have, but she could not go anywhere in her condition. One cannot very well go to a funeral if every time one stands one faints dead away. Vivian had grieved herself into a very weak state. She had eaten nothing for days. She could not control herself. You know what she was like."

"How could I know if she would not have me near her—her own grandmother," said the dowager countess.

"You were here then?" I asked the dowager lady Clareham.

"I was here for James's funeral, of course, but I was obliged to leave that same evening. Vivian would not let me see her. She could not bear seeing her own grandmother. But you are right, Edmond, my dear—you always are. If she was that bad, well—"

"She was almost out of her mind, Grandmamma, and so weak. Why I practically had to carry her out to the carriage the morning she left. I begged her to let me see her safely to London, but she insisted that it was unnecessary—that her friend, Nancy, would meet her at Paddington, which she did."

"But to invite this dear child to Castle Cloud," the dowager countess said, "all the way from Holland, and then not to be here to entertain her."

"No doubt Vivian had made her plans some time before I arrived," I said. "And she did not know when I was coming. I did not know myself. She sounded very distressed in her letter—very unlike herself."

"Oh, I am sure of that," the dowager countess replied. "Should she have gone, Edmond? She would be so much better off at home."

"You know Vivian, Grandmamma," Edmond said. "Who can stop her from doing anything once one of her moods takes hold? If she decided to go to Nancy, all of a sudden, then she *would* go. But you have not told us what you were doing traipsing all over London by yourself. A secret love affair, no doubt. Who is he? Where does he live—Grosvenor Square, Hanover, Cavindish? Come now, out with it."

"Edmond! You naughty boy," the dowager countess cried. She had burst into laughter: she was delighted. "At my age? Ha, ha, ha. Oh, you are impossible! But do not think that if I wanted a man, I could not have one. Ha, ha, ha. Mary will think we are both quite mad."

"Not at all," I said, unable to keep from smiling.

"As a matter of fact, I went to Kew, and Delphine went with me."

"Kew?" I asked.

"Kew Gardens," she said. "I have known Sir William for years. Sir William Hooker? He is the director there. He had some seeds for me, and I wanted to see the Arboretum, and I took him a cutting of my new Ramsay Rose. And then I needed some netting for a new bee bonnet I am making, which I could not get in Bude. So you see my dear, it was all very proper indeed."

She smiled at me. It was a very infectious smile, and I could not help smiling back.

"I will be returning to Lewis House in the morning, Mary," she said. "I have a friend living nearby—well, not a close friend, an acquaintance—who has been looking for a companion. She is Lavinia, Viscountess Hob, and she lives alone, with the servants of course, in a splendid house, though rather isolated. Shall I ask if the position is still open?"

"I don't know," I replied. "You see all this is so new ... I am afraid I cannot face—"

"Of course you must ask her," Edmond interrupted. "That would be splendid. I know, Mary, that anyone Grandmamma recommends would be perfect."

"Now, Edmond," the dowager countess said, "we all want to help Mary, but don't you think it should be her decision? I shall ask, and then write to Edmond telling him what I find out, my dear," she said to me. "If the position is open, and you decide you wish to look into it, I would love you to spend a few days with me so that you can meet Lady Hob. I can make you quite comfortable. Mind you, she may have engaged someone or her plans may have changed, and this may all be to no avail, but there is no harm in asking."

"Well, that is very kind of you, Lady Clareham," I said. "Where does Lady Hob live?"

"On the coast just north of Bude. Her house is on the cliffs—overlooking a really quite beautiful view."

"Did Edmond tell you all about my predicament and Vivian's letter?"

"Well, of course . . ." Edmond began.

"Yes, my dear," the dowager countess interrupted, as she held up her hand to silence Edmond. "We have no secrets from each other. Edmond has explained it to me and asked my help on your behalf, and I never refuse him anything that it is in my power to give him.

"I am sure that things will work out for you, Mary. We will all help you if we can, and do not forget Providence: He acts in strange ways. We never know what unexpected things will happen. I remember when my husband, Edward, died—I was only forty-six—I was obliged to leave Castle Cloud, which had been my home for ten years, I think. John had married eight or nine years before that. I thought life was over for me. . . ."

The dowager countess had begun a story meant to lift my spirits, I was sure, but I am afraid I was not able to give her my full attention. My mind had started on its roundelay: I needn't work as a companion because I shall find the man I love. . . .

And it went round and round like that, until dinner and coffee were over and I was able to escape to my room.

I was not able to fall asleep that night. Before I finally did, the darkness began to lighten perceptibly. When Mrs. Muldoon knocked on my door at eight o'clock, I was sound asleep. It was only after she had drawn the blinds that I realized it was at long last morning.

"Good morning, my lady," she called. Then she bustled out of the room, humming what sounded like a dance tune of some kind, and returned with my bath things, humming louder than ever. "Good morning, my lady. Sure, it's a lovely, beautiful morning, ja?"

"You seem in high spirits this morning, Mrs. Muldoon," I said. "Do I detect a little extra merriment this morning?"

"Ha, ha. It's not to be fooled you are, my lady. Faith, it's no more than he deserved. Ha, ha, ha. If you could have seen his face, my lady."

"Could have seen whose face?"

"Och, Mr. Mitchell's. Always putting on airs he is— thinks he's too good for the likes of us in the servants' hall. Thinks he's too good for the master himself, if you're asking me. He says to me a while ago, 'Where are you going?' So I says, 'I'm going to take Lady Beauford's water to her,' I says. 'I am going to take Lady Beauford's water to her, *Mr.* Mitchell,' he says 'Oh, *Mr.* Mitchell,' I says, giving him a deep curtsy, like I'd do the Queen, 'I'm going to take Lady Beauford's water to her, *Mr.* Mitchell, *sir*,' I says. Sure, you should have heard them all laugh. Ha, ha, ha."

"Aren't you afraid he will have you sacked?"

"No, Mrs. Foley wouldn't do that, my lady. For it's only herself and me that does any work at Castle Cloud at all. And where could she find anyone that would work like I do? That Jane Spence isn't good for anything at all." Mrs. Muldoon came to my bedside and whispered, "It's showing herself off before his lordship, Lord Althrop, is all she does, and he notices it too, as everyone knows." As she said this, Mrs. Muldoon's eyes popped at me. Then she turned to fetch a towel from the rack. "It's only May Brooke, and she helps Monsieur Laval in the kitchen, that's left. That's all there is in the house except Ida, but it's only the laundry she does and she's not right in her head, and then there's Ahmad and Madame Cerceau, but it's his lordship and her ladyship they take care of.

"Do you know what *Mr.* Mitchell says to me the other Wednesday? He says, 'I'm going to my bank in Exeter,' he says, very grand like, 'where I shall withdraw the necessary funds for the purchase of some property which I've had my eye on for some time. I shall sign the papers today.' 'Och, Mr. Mitchell, how *lovely* for you,' I says. 'Yes,' he says, 'it's a farm near Cadbury,' he says. 'It's costing me £3,000," he says. Mother of Moses! Where would the likes of *him* get £3,000? I ask you, my lady, where would the likes of him get £3,000? And he talks like there's more where that came from. Och, it's gentry he fancies himself. Sure, gentry will never see the likes of him, my lady.

There was a fishmonger named Bentry
Who fancied himself of the gentry.
Attending the Queen's ball,
He was smelled in the hall,
And out he was thrown by the sentry.
Ha, ha, ha."

"Did you make that up?" I asked, laughing.

"Well now, my lady— Och! I must be off. There's the dowager lady Clareham's room to tidy, and I want to have a word with Madame Breguet—that's her ladyship's maid. A very nice woman she is, and we always have a talk alone when she comes. Her ladyship has already gone down to breakfast. It's an early breakfast for her, and I suppose that's why *Mr.* Mitchell was so uppity. Sure, a little extra work will do him good, if you're asking me."

By that time, she had sailed out onto the gallery. Then after she had closed the door behind her, I bathed quickly, dressed, and went down to breakfast.

"Well, I shall ask him, then," I heard the dowager

countess say, as I crossed the rotunda toward the dining room.

And when I reached the doorway, the dowager countess hurried toward me.

"Good morning, Lady Clareham," I said.

"Good morning, Mary," she said. "You will forgive me for not waiting to have breakfast with you, won't you, my dear, but there are matters I wish to discuss with George. And since I shall be leaving Castle Cloud right after luncheon, and since I do not get over here very often, I want to be sure that I have plenty of time to talk with him. I shall see you at luncheon, I hope."

"Yes, Lady Clareham."

"That's a good girl. We can chat a little then, my dear." She laid a hand on my arm for an instant and then sped off toward the stairs.

"Good morning, Edmond," I said.

"Good morning, Mary." When I was seated opposite him, he continued, "Try the trout. It was swimming in one of our streams yesterday—delicious.

"Mother said you went to church with her on Sunday," he continued. "We are very proud of our little church there. Really quite a good screen—exquisitely carved, don't you think?"

"Yes. A soft-cooked egg, and some toast, and coffee, please, Mitchell."

"I am so glad you were able to see it, my dear," Edmond said. "And Milton Penderton is a pretty village. Did you meet anyone there?"

"Only Reverend Anderson. Why?"

"There has been something we have been meaning to talk to you about. It is a rather delicate matter, but you are an intelligent and sensitive girl. We know you will understand and comply with our wishes in the matter."

"Of course. Is something wrong? Can I help in any way?"

Mitchell was puttering needlessly at the sideboard. By that time, he had brought me my breakfast, and I hoped he would leave the room, but he had obviously decided to remain and listen to our conversation.

"After James's funeral," Edmond said, "and after receiving the necessary calls of condolence, which were a great trial for my mother—we began, of course, a period of deep mourning, a complete withdrawal from society, a time of meditation and prayer in our bereavement, a time of quiet and peace after the ordeal of death."

Now, Mitchell had stopped his fiddling and was listening openly. I caught his glance, but he ignored my disapproval.

"Now, we know that if you had known about James's death, you would not have come to Castle Cloud at this time. We know that you would not knowingly or willingly impose yourself—"

I found myself glaring openly at Mitchell who ignored me. Then I tried to draw Edmond's attention to him with my eyes.

"Is something wrong, my dear?" Edmond asked me. "Why do you keep twitching your eyes from place to place like that?"

"Perhaps, Edmond, we could talk privately about this some other time," I said.

"Why? I do not understand. Because Mitchell is in the room? Oh, my dear Mary, I know that Mitchell is in the room. He has been with us for more than eight years. He is the epitome of discretion. I am far better able to judge what may be said and what should not be said in front of the servants than you are, my dear. I know them so much better than you do."

He gave me his most brilliant smile.

"We know you have problems," he continued, "and we already feel a deep regard for you because you are Vivian's closest friend and she cannot be here to help you herself. We know you will want to repay this sacrifice. . . ."

"Are you speaking for yourself, Edmond," I asked, "or for your parents too? What do you want me to do? Do you want me to leave Castle Cloud?"

"No, no, my dear, but if you could limit your devotions to our chapel here at Castle Cloud and refrain from any—expeditions that might bring you into contact with the neighbors or the villagers."

"You wish to keep my presence here a secret?" I asked.

"It is not that we want to hide you from anyone or that we are ashamed of you because of your future vocation or anything of that nature. Oh, and by the way, we feel that you will be more successful in finding a position if you drop any reference to your title—after all, no one would wish to hire a baroness for fear she would not fit into her situation. No, no, that has nothing to do with it. Mary, if it became known that we were entertaining a houseguest, our neighbors would be obliged to call and welcome you. This would be a great hardship on my mother and father—on us all. And then it would be difficult to explain why Vivian is not here to entertain you. They would never understand, and this would not reflect well on my sister.

"All we ask is that you help us reestablish in all respects the atmosphere of private mourning and of peace which was so appropriate, so perfectly realized at Castle Cloud before, forgive me, your intrusion into it. Believe me, my dear, this is not meant as a personal criticism in any way. We know you will understand and, in your gratitude, help us all you can."

"Certainly," I said. "I shall make my presence here as inconspicuous as possible, if that is what you want. I shall become invisible."

My irony seemed to have been wasted on him, I am glad to say, for he continued, "Regretfully, you will only be with us for a short time. Meanwhile, if there is anything you need from the village, just ask me about it. I will see that you have what you need. Bless you, my dear. Now, if you will excuse me, I have things to do."

Edmond had humiliated me thoroughly in front of Mitchell. I was sure that he had not done it on purpose—he had merely been thoughtless. Nevertheless, I was determined not to show Mitchell that I minded. So I dawdled, and when he asked me if there was anything else that I required, I demanded more coffee. And I am afraid I did not hurry with that either.

Finally I got up from the table and sauntered out of the dining room, across the rotunda, and into the drawing room. There, Cleopatra slept in the sun on the table by the window. I stroked her head, but she ignored me. Then, after leafing through a magazine, I walked out onto the entrance-front portico, wondering, idly, how to spend the rest of the morning. It was a clear one, but mare's-tail clouds swept their long feathers across the sky, forecasting a change in the weather. They seemed to say, "Walk today. Tomorrow the sun may have gone away."

So, heeding their warning, I descended the staircase to the drive and began to stroll down it, away from the house and toward the stone bridge. But then I changed my mind, turned, retraced my steps, and proceeded to the hedged walk.

I do not suppose I would have admitted to anyone that I was curious about what went on at the end of it, in the 'forbidden' bathing pavilion, but I did remember that from the path which began just beyond the wooden Chinese bridge, one could easily see the pavilion through the trees without intruding upon anyone who might be there. Beyond the bridge and the pavilion, the path followed the stream to where it emptied into the Tay, and then followed the river to the stone bridge. This was the path that I had intended to take on the day I saw William Reade hiding in the hedge.

I examined the hedges carefully on both sides of me as I walked down the hedged walk, in case he should be hiding in them. But William Reade was not standing there that day. The walk was deserted, and when I reached the Chinese bridge, I paused to look about. I saw no one. Then I watched the stream tumble down the rocky hillside for a few minutes before I left the bridge and took the path.

The path sloped gently downhill beside the bank of the brook toward the Tay, and in a few moments I reached a place from which I could see the pavilion through the trees. It sat at the edge of the river beyond a narrow meadow and the fringe of trees that screened me from it. It was a tiny, square stone building with a flat battlemented roof. From the front of it, which faced me, two gothic windows flanking a gothic door smiled at me. And from each corner of the roof rose a delicately carved gothic minaret. The building might have been the ornament from the top of a gigantic cake or a playhouse belonging to a giant's child. In that bright still morning it dozed by the Tay.

But as I stood admiring it, the quiet was disturbed by a girl who danced around the corner of the building from the direction of the river. She stopped and peeped back in the direction she had come. Then, just before Edmond turned the corner in pursuit, she giggled and dashed into the building. Edmond vanished after her, and I heard a burst of laughter. Then all was still. Both the girl and Edmond had been wet and naked.

"It is not a place for nice young ladies," I could hear Lord Clareham saying, as I hurried along the path away from the pavilion. And then I remembered Edmond saying at breakfast: "... a time of meditation and prayer in our bereavement ... the atmosphere of private mourning ... so perfectly realized before, forgive me, your intrusion into it."

"Well, Edmond's idea of mourning," I whispered to myself, "is quite different from mine! I would not dream of intruding."

☙ Chapter Four ☙

WHEN I REACHED THE STONE BRIDGE, I leaned against its parapet and gazed across Bideford Bay. Its water gently shaded from cornflower blue to hyacinth, to sapphire, to navy at the far shore. A freshly painted ketch, a brigantine, and two schooners, anchored off the yards in Appledore, shown dazzlingly white against the blue water. As I watched, a boat slid down the ways of one of the yards. It threw a swash of white water and a cloud of startled gulls into the air as it plunged into the bay. Then, almost at once, it settled docilely on the water. Did this boat have a life of its own, as sailors believe? I wondered. If so, I must have witnessed a birth. Where would it sail in its lifetime? Would it be kind and guard the lives of those it carried, or would it provoke and destroy?

My reverie was shattered by Sarah, who came scrambling across the pebbly shore toward me, and by the sound of an approaching horse. Sarah was first to arrive.

"I hope you have enjoyed your swim, Sarah," I laughed, holding her wet body at arm's length. "But no, no—please do not dry yourself on me."

Then I turned to watch the rider approach. After rounding the bend in the lane and passing between the gatehouses, David Field slowed his horse and walked him toward me.

"Good morning," he shouted.

"Good morning, Mr. Field," I greeted as he reined to a halt.

He dismounted then and, leading his horse, came to stand before me. "Have you heard from Vivian?" he asked.

"Is that why you came to Castle Cloud this morning, Mr. Field?" I asked.

"Yes, I came to see if you had news of her. You said you expected a letter."

He smiled and shook a thick lock of straight hair away from his face as he said it. His teeth and the whites of his eyes were very white against his deeply tanned skin. The eyes that looked into mine wore heavy black lashes, but it was the color of the irises that astonished me. I imagined that at times they would look brown, but in the sunlight they were deep orange yellow.

"I received it yesterday," I said. "She has gone to visit friends in Scotland."

"Is she well? When is she coming home? Did she say anything else?"

"Yes, I suppose she is well. No, she did not say anything else, really. I don't know— Mr. Field, I am sorry but I do not think I should be seen talking to you. I have been asked to avoid people. Castle Cloud is in mourning for James."

"That is ridiculous," he said. "Avoid people? Why? Everyone knows that Lord and Lady Clareham and Edmond are in mourning. We respect that."

"Nevertheless, that is what I have been asked to do, and I *am* a guest here. Please, Mr. Field."

"Very well, Miss Thorpe," he said. Then he stepped back and immediately flung himself into the saddle. "Walk up to the Horse Monument tonight at sunset. I will meet you there."

Before I could object, his horse turned and galloped away.

A clandestine meeting at the Horse Monument with David Field was out of the question. I was a guest at Castle Cloud. Edmond and his parents had taken me in and now wanted to help me. I could not disregard their wishes, particularly because I had agreed not to.

Luncheon that day was largely a dialogue between the dowager countess and Edmond. He seemed fascinated by everything she said and did. He fawned on her, and she basked in his attention.

At one point, she said to him, "Edmond, something is living in my garden—in the ground, in a rather odious looking hole under my peonies. Tell me what it is. It eats my flowers at night."

"Hedgehog," Edmond replied. "Nasty creatures."

"But what can I *do* about it?"

"Fill up its hole with rocks and stones. That will drive it away."

"Yes! Thank you my dear. Why didn't *I* think of that?" Then she turned to me and said, "He knows *everything*. Edmond is a walking encyclopedia. He never ceases to amaze me."

I knew that hedgehogs ate insects, not plants, and that they did not live in the ground, but I said nothing.

Then, shortly after luncheon, the dowager countess left to catch her train for Holsworthy. Edmond accompanied her to the railway station. Lady Clareham and I waved them good-by from the portico.

After that, I spent the afternoon convincing myself that meeting David Field at the Horse Monument was unthinkable—it would constitute a betrayal of trust. But in the end, of course, I met him.

I found him waiting for me when I arrived at the hilltop that evening. He stood, straddling the path, in a pose which I was to recognize as characteristic of him—his legs spread apart, his pelvis thrust forward, his arms hanging loosely at his sides. He appeared confident, in perfect control, and ready to handle anything.

"Hello," he said, as I approached. "I was beginning to think you would not come."

"I nearly didn't, Mr. Field," I said.

"There is nothing wrong in it, Miss Thorpe, if that is what you were thinking."

"That *was* what I was thinking."

"You are not harming anyone, and I had no sinister motives in asking you to meet me here, I assure you. Would you like to sit down on the stones over there? And then will you tell me about Vivian's letter?"

We began to walk toward the building blocks, and as we did so, I remember thinking how charmed I was by David's way of moving. He was capable of quick action (the way he leaped to his horse that morning demonstrated this), but one felt that when he raised an arm, took a step, or performed any movement, that it had been carefully planned in advance, and that he had executed it to perfection.

When we had sat down—I on the same building block I

had used before, he on his—I took Vivian's letter out of my bag and read the first two paragraphs to him.

"Then she speaks briefly about a personal matter," I said, when I had finished reading them. "And she ends the letter with, 'I do not know what fate has in store for me or when I will see you again—I am too ill with grief to care. But I do wish you a happy future. Ever yours affectionately, Vivian.'"

David Field sat opposite me, his forearms on his knees, his hands clasped, as he had sat the last evening we were together.

He shook the lock of hair away from his face and said, "Strange. That does not sound like Vivian. I cannot imagine her leaving you here and going off to Scotland. I should think she would postpone her trip and come home. She must, as she says, be too distressed to care."

"That is what I thought. I think the signature is hers. Oh, it is from Vivian, but a different Vivian."

"I am afraid so," he said. "What will you do now? I suppose, now that Vivian is off to Scotland, you will be going home? What a pity you had to come for nothing. Didn't you know she would not be here? Why did you come to Castle Cloud when you knew she wouldn't be here?"

"I *didn't* know she was not going to be here. She had asked me to come, but I did not know how soon a friend of my stepfather's would be sailing to Devonport so I could not tell her when I would arrive. She said to come anyway—that she would be here. That was before James died."

"Sail from where?"

"Schiedam."

"Then you will be going back to Holland."

"No."

"Where then?" he asked.

"I don't know, Mr. Field. I am looking for employment."

"What kind of employment?"

"Oh, as a governess or companion to an elderly or ill lady, I suppose. Since Vivian is not here, Edmond and his parents are going to help me find something, so I will be here until I do."

"You *must* work for a living?"

"Yes." I was not going to say more, but then I found myself continuing—I could not stop. "I have no money and no family except my mother. You see, my father lived rather lavishly on the continent. He spent all his money and died leaving Mother about £50—that was all. He left me nothing. Mother used the £50 as her dowry when she married my stepfather. His name is Pieter van der Grooft. He is a farmer. The farm is halfway between Schiedam and Delft."

"Go on," David said.

As we talked, he looked into my eyes in a most disturbing way. It was as if he could not understand English well and must use his eyes to tell him what the language could not.

"Well," I continued, "I went to live on the farm with my stepfather and three stepbrothers. They were beastly to me. It was a dirty place—run in a slovenly manner. I was miserable there.

"So, when Vivian began to urge me to visit her here at the Castle, it sounded like heaven. I was tempted and finally she persuaded me to come."

"To find you a situation as a governess?" he asked.

"She did not say so, in so many words, but I suppose that was what she had in mind. I thought she had some magical plan—oh, I don't know what I thought. I did not think of working for my living, yet I don't know what else I expected. It was all a jumbled misunderstanding.

"My stepfather knows a Mr. Hanson who is a herring fisherman living in Schiedam, who has a sister living in Devonport. There was something to do with a will and an estate and he had to see her. Mr. Hanson agreed to take me across the channel with him, when he could get away. I was to be ready to leave at a moment's notice.

"And that is the end of my story. I arrived in Devonport a week ago today with a small bag, a trunk, five pounds, and a few pieces of not-very-valuable jewelry which my father gave me and which I would not part with for anything. And I took the train here."

"Was it about being a governess that you did not read to me?" David asked.

"Yes. Would you like to see it?" I said, as I handed him the letter I had been holding in my hand.

He read it (there was just enough twilight left for that) and then handed it back to me.

"Now that you know my life's history, Mr. Field," I said, "would it be wrong to ask if you know of anyone needing a governess or companion?" I smiled at him. I should be feeling depressed, I thought, but I do not—on the contrary, I feel almost gay.

"The dowager countess arrived last night," I said, "and left this afternoon. Do you know her? She thinks there might be a situation open as a companion to an elderly lady near her. She is going to find out about it for me."

"I do not know of anyone, but I will be glad to ask—very discreetly of course."

"Oh, it must be very discreet, Mr. Field. You must not bring the wrath of the house of Clareham down on my head, you know." Again I smiled.

And he grinned in return. "I know Vivian would want you to call me David. There would be no harm to anyone in that either."

"Thank you, David. Call me Mary, then."

"Vivian would want me to help you too, you know. If I do hear of something, Mary, how can I tell you about it? Shall I ride up to Castle Cloud and ask for you?"

"No! Perish the thought." I laughed, thinking about Edmond's liaison at the bathing pavilion and contrasting it with the shock he would feel at my meeting David alone on the hilltop. "I am sure I shall find something before long, David, but in the meantime, on a clear evening, I shall most probably walk in this direction after dinner. The view from here is lovely and sunset is my favorite time of the day. If you do hear of something, you could come and tell me. Would there be anything wrong in that?"

"Nothing," he said.

"Now I must be getting back." We stood then and I gave him my hand. "Thank you, David, for listening to all that and for wanting to help."

"Good night. I will keep my ears open for you."

Then I walked quickly away from him toward the path, and when I reached it, I turned and smiled back at him and waved. He stood, legs apart, feet firmly planted, staring after me.

It was raining when Mrs. Muldoon woke me the following morning. For the next three days, packs of heavy clouds were to lumber in from the sea and smother us as they slid eastward across Devonshire, and it was to rain almost constantly.

Because of the rain, I could not go for a walk after breakfast, so I wandered about with nothing to do. I had seen all the magazines in the drawing room, and the library at Castle Cloud had been closed—the furniture was shrouded in dustcovers, the books locked away behind the glass doors of their cases. I supposed I could ask for the key. Who would have it? Mitchell? No, Mrs. Foley, more than likely, but after her extraordinarily cold manner toward me the afternoon I arrived, I did not wish to ask her for it. I would ask her if I became desperate, of course, but I thought that first, after luncheon, I would ask Lord Clareham if he had anything to read which might interest me.

But the morning passed quickly after all, thanks to several boxes of cards which I discovered in the drawer of the card table in the drawing room. I sat by the north window playing patience for most of the morning and looking out into the rain. At twelve o'clock, I saw Edmond come out of the hedged walk. He was huddled in a black cloak under an umbrella, and I wondered what he could possibly have been doing down there on a day like this? Were there some books there? Had he arranged a kind of study for himself in the pavilion? Or had his young lady friend met him there?

I would have loved to ask him at luncheon. I am very curious by nature. Papa said that I was the most curious person he had ever met and that I must surely be part cat. But of course I did not ask him. The meal passed almost entirely without conversation, as a matter of fact. And when we had finished eating, I went to my room and lay down. It was a delicious afternoon for a nap, especially since I had not slept very well the night before.

It was, therefore, about three o'clock when I knocked on Lord Clareham's door and Ahmad opened it for me. Lord Clareham was dictating a letter to his wife.

"I am sorry, I did not mean to interrupt you," I said.

"No, no. Come in, Mary," Lord Clareham said. "Sit down there. This will be done in a minute.

"So, my dear Lord Clemment," he continued dictating, "I trust you will seriously consider what I have said, not only for the sake of our own interests, but in the interests of the natives as well. The Punjab, until now, has been most loyal. . . ."

Then, after a minute or so, he concluded, "Do not hesitate to call on me at any time. And finish it up as usual, my dear," he said to Lady Clareham. "No, I do not need to read it. I am certain it is perfect. Just let me sign it, and then I want to talk to this child for a bit."

"I have disturbed you, haven't I?" I said to Lady Clareham, as she prepared to leave the room with the letter.

"No, my dear, not at all," she said. "I am glad you came. I have some things to do, and now I know that my husband will have company. I will leave you two together."

When she had gone, I said to Lord Clareham, "I hoped you might have something interesting for me to read, Lord Clareham. I seem to have more time on my hands than I know what to do with."

"Certainly, my dear," he said. "Let me think. Yes! Go to the bookcase there, yes. Now, do you see the fat, red book on the fourth shelf from the bottom? Well, next to it on the right, either the second or third book, I believe, is a book entitled *Travels 1777-1781* by Alex Macintosh. A fascinating book. . . ."

Three minutes later, I held four books which I had been directed to read and which Lord Clareham assured me I would find engrossing. *Extracts From the Correspondence of Sir Thomas Munroe* was one of them, and another was called *Voyage into Uttar* by someone whose name was Raw Sanmohuari.

Then Lord Clareham said: "Sit down. Sit down, my dear child and tell me about yourself." As he spoke he motioned to the chair beside his bed.

I sat down, and while I was making myself comfortable, Ahmad said something in Hindustani, and Lord Clareham answered him. Then I turned to Ahmad just in time to see him salaam three times (such a mysterious, exotic gesture) and leave the room.

"Edmond tells me that you have received Vivian's letter," Lord Clareham said, "and that you have decided to seek a position as a governess or companion—very wise. Perhaps Lady Hob will want you to be with her."

"Do you know her?"

"We knew Lord and Lady Hob in the old days—not very well. Lord Hob was about Mother's age and Lady Hob was perhaps ten years younger. She was one of the most energetic women I have ever seen. Of course I have no idea what she is like now—that was forty years ago. She may have changed some, eh?"

"Yes, I suppose so."

"Father died a month after Lord Hob, in 1825. Mother was forty-six, John was thirty-three, and I was twenty-nine. It was something of a help for Mother, having Lady Hob living so near Bude. They still see each other once in a while, I believe."

"Is your brother John's wife still alive?" I asked.

"Andrea? Oh, my, yes. She remarried and lives in Leith, near Edinburgh. Seems to be happy. We do not hear much of her."

Just then the door was flung open, and Edmond marched into the room. Ahmad sat on his chair beside the door. He had returned without making a sound, having no doubt made his salaams, but I do not remember Lord Clareham's acknowledging them.

"Knock!" Lord Clareham cried. "I told you to knock, young man."

"This place smells like a pigsty," Edmond said. "Can't you at least open a window once in a while and air the place out?"

"And catch pneumonia? Don't be stupid."

"Stupid? Look who lies here calling me stupid. I shouldn't think spending one's life coddling a bunch of filthy, ignorant natives in a God-forsaken hole five thousand miles away from England *and* neglecting your estates, which you are not even allowed to manage anymore, *and* Castle Cloud, which is falling into ruins around your head, was so brilliant."

"Young man! Do you realize to whom you are speaking? You had better mind your manners and show some *respect* or—you—will—never—come—*into*—the—ruins. I promise you that!"

"Thank you for the books, Lord Clareham," I said, getting up from my chair. "I must be going. I must be getting ready for dinner."

I could not have sat there a moment longer listening to Edmond excite his father like that. I was terrified that Lord Clareham would have another attack. How could Edmond be so thoughtless? But I was not the only one who was concerned. Ahmad sat staring at Edmond, a hatred blazing from his eyes that sent a chill through me.

I lifted the books from the table and turned to face Edmond. "Your father was good enough to lend me some books to read, Edmond," I said. "Rainy days are long when one hasn't anything to do. I found that the library had been closed, so I came to ask your father if he had something to read which might interest me, and he has lent me these books which I am sure I will enjoy. This one especially. *Voyage into Uttar*," I read from the binding, "by San—mo—huari. Do you know it?"

"Pagan savages in the wilderness, no doubt," Edmond answered. "I am sure you will be enthralled. Try and persuade my father to get some breathable air in here. Filthy air cannot be healthful." With that, he marched out of the room without speaking again to his father.

"Can I get you anything, Lord Clareham?" I asked. "Are you comfortable? Here, let me fluff those pillows for you."

"Ahmad will do it, thank you, Mary," he said. "Now leave me to rest."

Lord Clareham's books about India did not interest me. I spent the following morning, Thursday morning, in my room trying to read first one, then another—dreaming over them, reading page after page without having the least idea what I had read. Finally, just before luncheon, I gave up entirely.

After luncheon, I wandered into the drawing room and then out into the rotunda again, where I noticed that the door to the chapel was ajar. The chapel at Castle Cloud was a miniature replica of the interior of Sir Christopher Wren's church, St. Lawrence Jewry, in London. It was a square, pilastered chamber of white plaster decorated with gold. All its colored-glass windows, set into alcoves, were painted imitations except for two windows flanking the altar—they were real and faced east to receive the morning sun. Two rows of twelve pews faced the altar. When I looked into the room, I saw that Lady Clareham knelt in the front pew, in prayer.

I did not disturb her, but wandered across to the southeast stair, climbed it, and walked around the gallery toward my room. Approaching it from that direction led me past Vivian's room, and as I was about to pass her door, I stopped. It had occurred to me that she might have been reading a novel or two before she left, and if she had and had left them lying about, she would not mind my borrowing them. Her door was unlocked, and I opened it and stepped inside.

A flock of memories struck me as I stood there looking about. I remembered the pink-flowered wallpaper as if I had seen it yesterday (how hard I had tried, one rainy afternoon which Vivian and I spent there together, to find where the pattern repeated itself), and the canopied bed of pink satin, where we had lain together talking about, among other things, how handsome and nice her brother, James, was, and the little pink-fringed lamp shades and the Chinese Temple Pattern on the porcelain wash-hand-stand things which had made us want to go to China.

But then I saw three books lying on one of the bedside tables and walked over to them. They were slim volumes of poetry—Shakespeare's *Sonnets*, Tennyson's *The Princess*, and, I was amused to find, Tupper's *Proverbial Philosophy*. But I was not in the mood for poetry that day so I went around to the table on the other side of her bed where two larger books lay, picked up the top one, and opened it to the title page. It read:

THE BOOK OF MURDER
or
100 Cruel and Inhuman Murders Explained
and Described in Detail
by
S. Rupert-Hamilford
with thirty-five illustrations

How odd, I thought, as I turned to the contents page. It told me that the first chapter was entitled: "STRANGU-LATION," and it began on Page 1. Under this was listed: "The Earliest Known Recorded Crime of Stangulation In

England - The Strange Case of Malcome the Hail - The Brutal Murder of Jane Simpson. . . ." The next chapter was entitled, "SUFFOCATION, Page 30." Then followed: "SHOOTING, Page 51; DROWNING, Page 60; POISONING, Page 72; THROAT CUTTING, Page 80." Then came: "KNIFING, BURNING, CLUBBING, STARVING, FALLING. . . ."

"What a ghastly book," I thought aloud. "I certainly cannot imagine Vivian reading it, in bed or at any other time, for that matter, and it is certainly not for me."

I closed it and was about to put it aside when I noticed a card protruding from between the pages. I flipped open the book to pages seventy-three and seventy-four, which it marked. The card was not a bookmark, but a piece of white pasteboard about the size of a calling card. On it was printed the following, "Note: The house is insured against all legal interruptions, and players are guaranteed to be free from officious interruptions as they are at their own homes."

It meant nothing to me. I replaced the card between the pages, closed the book, and reached for the one that had lain beneath it. This was *Vanity Fair,* which I had never had the time to read. And on a shelf under the table I found a novel called *Antonia or The Fall of Rome, A Romance of the Fifth Century* by someone whose name was Wilkie Collins. I tucked the two novels under my arm and left Vivian's room.

I had been delighted to find Mr. Thackery's novel, and as soon as I got back to my room, I began it—escaping from Castle Cloud, and the rain, and from myself. This was what I had wanted to do all day. I felt that perhaps when I came back to being me, I could give my predicament a fresh look and decide better what to do. Little did I know that I was about to meet a well-educated girl who would begin her adult life as a governess. Becky's problems and Amelia's, too, were like my problems, but I could never have acted as Becky or Amelia did. What would I have done in their situations? I began to think that if I had been Becky Sharp, I would have been more like Amelia, and if I had been Amelia Sedley, I would have been more like Becky.

I became fascinated by the contrasting characters of the two girls and continued to read until it was time to get ready to go downstairs. After dinner I returned to *Vanity Fair* and Becky, and Amelia, and Jos, and Rawdon, and all my new acquaintances. I sat reading by the window, occasionally pausing to look out across the bay, contrasting my situation with Becky's and thinking that if either that disgusting old man, Sir Pitt, or his son had asked me to marry him, I would have refused at once.

Then, when there was no longer enough daylight left to read by, I lit the lamps on either side of the sofa, sat down in the corner of it, pulled one of the lamps closer, and decided that I would read ten pages more. And when I had finished those ten pages, I would stop, no matter what was happening, and go to bed. But the tenth page was the beginning of chapter twenty-two. Would George actually marry Amelia? I could not stop there. I would continue to the end of that chapter.

But I could not stop reading there either, so I read on and on until my thoughts were finally interrupted by a sound from outside on the gallery. Was it someone laughing softly? Again I heard it. It *was* someone laughing. But the clock on the mantle said twelve forty-five.

I put down my book at once, ran to the door, opened it a crack, and looked out across the rotunda. There I saw a sliver of light narrow and then disappear as Edmond's bedroom door closed. Then Jane Spence walked away from it, around the gallery toward me, and vanished into the alcove at the top of the southwest stairway. The light from her candle shone on the wall for a moment, then dimmed, and finally disappeared.

While she descended the stairs, I slipped out of my room and, in the darkness, stole across to the railing of the gallery where I could look down into the hall below. I was just in time to see Jane come out of the stairwell, cross the hall, and descend the stairs to the servants' hall. She was not wearing her chintz uniform or her black Sunday one. Instead, she wore an emerald-green dress, cut very low at the bosom, which even by candlelight, showed off her creamy skin to perfection.

Friday, the third day of rain, was unusually cool. The thermometer could not have risen above the low sixties. Inside, the house felt damp and cold. And I was grateful to Mrs. Muldoon for bringing a full scuttle of coal to my room in the morning and lighting the fire before she put my bath things in front of the fireplace.

That day I spent alone in my room, in one of the arm-chairs drawn up close to the flame, reading. And by dinner time I felt so lonely that I looked forward to talking with Lady Clareham and Edmond.

I joined them in the drawing room just before Mitchell announced dinner.

"How is Lord Clareham today, Lady Clareham?" I asked, as we walked across the rotunda to the dining room. "I thought of visiting him this afternoon, but I do not know if my visits tire him, and I do not like to intrude."

"I should not worry about tiring him," Edmond said. "Just because his one side is paralyzed does not mean the other side is not functioning perfectly well."

"He does tire, my dear," Lady Clareham said to me, "but I think your visits do him good. He is so terribly isolated and alone up there. But perhaps it is just as well you did not go in today. He is not at his best in this weather."

"Isolated, my foot," Edmond said. "Why, he knows more about what goes on at Castle Cloud than anyone, thanks to that black bastard. . . ."

"Edmond!" Lady Clareham cried.

"And those ridiculous mirrors of his," Edmond continued. "Did you ever see the like of it, Mary? You would think, in his condition, that he would have better things to concern his mind with than who is walking in the park and when Colen brings the *Times* up from the village. He has ordered Colen to go the long way around just so he can see when he returns with the mail, how do you like that? Anyway, I shouldn't wonder if he suffocates soon in that disgusting air. Why don't you air the place out, Mother?"

By this time we were seated at the dining table.

"You know fresh air is bad for invalids, Edmond," Lady Clareham answered. "Why do you keep insisting that we throw open his windows? Do you want him to have another attack? You *want* him to have another attack and leave us, don't you? All you can think of is inheriting, inheriting, inheriting. You are a young man. You have plenty of time. Can't you leave him with us awhile? Must you take everything away from me?" Her last words were barely audible because her voice was muffled by the napkin she held to her face.

"Mother, do you know what you are saying? Hysterical talk! You know perfectly well that is not true. I am not God, you know. *I* will have nothing to do with how long Father remains with us or how soon he passes on. Dr. Norton is a good man, when he is sober, and that heathen savage of his is devotion itself—never leaves his side—never eats or sleeps, I suppose. Father will last as long as our Father in heaven has decided he will last. In the meantime, the least we can do is give him some proper air to breathe. It is absurd to think that fresh air is good for people who are well, but not for those who are ill. People should use their heads once in a while."

"Lord Clareham has been feeling some sensation in his right side," I said. "The feeling *does* come back sometimes. He may be out of his bed completely before long."

"Imagination!" Edmond said. "He only thinks he feels it because he *wants* to feel it. He will never use that side again. He has been feeling that for months."

As Edmond spoke I glanced at Mitchell, who was carving at the sideboard. I could tell he was listening to every word.

Then, after a moment, Mitchell asked Lady Clareham: "Breast of chicken or roast lamb, my lady?"

"Chicken, please," Lady Clareham murmured. "I do not think it is his imagination, Edmond. I pray that it is not."

"Did you enjoy your geography lesson, Mary?" Edmond asked me, ignoring his mother.

"Geography lesson? Oh, you mean the books Lord Clareham lent me? Then you have read them," I answered.

"Certainly not, but they are obviously about some Godforsaken place or other in India. What else would they be about, coming from my father's room? If I am going to read, I can certainly find something more valuable to read than that."

"I began to read them, but I found they did not suit my mood. They shall wait until another time."

"Humph! You mean you were bored to death by them. I told you you would be."

"As a matter of fact, I have been reading *Vanity Fair*. It is most interesting—about a governess, you know."

"Where did you find that?" Edmond asked.

"I borrowed it from Vivian."

"From Vivian? Do you mean you went into her room and took some of her books?"

"I am sure she would not mind. I will return them when I am finished with them."

"Did you take anything else from Vivian's room?"

"No, just *Vanity Fair* and another novel by a Mr. Collins."

"My dear Mary, it is not a question of whether she would mind or not. I am sure she wouldn't. But to go into someone else's room and disturb her things without permission— But never mind, I am sure you did not think."

"Perhaps I should have asked. I am sorry, Edmond. There *is* something I have been wanting to ask, though, and I certainly would not do it without your permission. I wondered if I might borrow one of Vivian's habits. I want to ride again so badly, and Colen said that Chocolate is not getting enough exercise. I would be very careful of her habit—nothing would happen to it, I promise you. I haven't a habit of my own anymore, and of course I can not possibly ride without one."

"My dear, if the habit were mine, I would certainly say yes, but it is not. How can I give you permission to wear Vivian's clothes? They are not mine, and therefore the permission is not mine to give. Besides, it would hardly be proper for you to be seen galloping over the hills. We are in mourning. Please remember our conversation of the other day. Don't you agree, Mother?"

"Yes, of course. I am sorry, Mary," Lady Clareham said, without looking at me. Then she turned to the butler. "Mitchell, why have you not gotten out the Kandler bowl, as I have asked you to do?"

"I am sorry, my lady," Mitchell replied. "The key to the silver chest has been lost. It may take some time to arrange for a locksmith to come and fix it, my lady."

"It was always a favorite of Vivian's," Lady Clareham said, glancing up at me. It has the loveliest frieze in relief around it—cupids and grapevines and things. It would be perfect for the fruit. I am getting tired of seeing the same old things on the table."

"That hideous fake, mother?" Edmond said. "I cannot imagine why you want it. Anyone with half an eye could tell that it is not genuine—the workmanship shouts it. Shoddy!"

"That is not true, Edmond. It is beautifully done. That bowl was given to your father and me by Lord and Lady Wallis. *They* would never give anything but the best."

"A bit more port, I think, Mitchell," Edmond said. "Mary, have some more port with the fondu—perfect together. What is it, Mitchell?"

"Vila de Montemoravo '29, my lord."

"Quite good, really, but we have better, much better. If you like to visit underground places, Mary, a visit to the cellars of Castle Cloud *would* be worth the trip. And thank God for them—practically the only decent thing left here. There are valuable bottles down there, Mary, hundreds of them. Uncle John was a connoisseur, and he did not spare the expense. I shall take you down to see it one day.

"Did it ever occur to you," Edmond continued, turning back to his mother, "that Lord and Lady Wallis were fooled by the bowl? Had that thought ever entered your mind? Obviously they were no better judges of workmanship than you are. It is a shoddy fake and should be locked away. It may be plate for all I know. I do not want to see the disgusting thing again."

"You have no idea what you are talking about," Lady Clareham said. "And I think you have had enough wine for one meal. After James, I do not see how you can touch it."

"Just because wine was prescribed for your darling James is no reason for *me* to cease drinking it. Is it?"

Then Lady Clareham began to weep, and almost at once she rose from the table, pushing back her chair as she did so, and stumbled from the room, holding her napkin to her mouth. "Cecile, Cecile," I heard her sob from the hall.

"Lady Clareham," I cried, getting up.

"Stay where you are, Mary. Cecile will take care of her. She can help Mother more than you can. She knows exactly what to do."

"Oh, Edmond, your poor mother."

"Poor Mother! Poor Mother! How much can one stand? Weeping and slobbering, and slobbering and weeping day after day. You would think she would get over it. It isn't

normal. Other mothers lose their sons and *control* themselves. . . ."

"Edmond, if you will excuse me, I must know that she
has found Cecile. She must not be left alone in that condition."

I left the table, and when I had reached the hall, I could
see that Lady Clareham was not there. Then I glanced up
at the gallery where I saw Cecile running toward the
stairs. And in a moment, Lady Clareham, weeping and
supported by her maid, emerged from the stairwell and
walked around the gallery to her room.

After that I stepped back into the dining room and told
Edmond that I would wait in the drawing room for
Mitchell to bring my coffee. He glared at me over the rim
of his wine glass, but he did not speak.

"Mary!" Edmond cried, as I entered the dining room
the following morning for breakfast. "I have wonderful
news for you. Come sit down so I can tell you about it."

Then, when I was seated, he continued, "Grandmamma
has written. The position with Lady Hob is still open. Isn't
that marvelous? Here, let me read to you what she says. It
is dated July 2nd, that was Wednesday."

He read:

My dear Edmond,
    Directly after luncheon, Ralph drove me out to see
Lavinia. She was delighted to hear about Mary. She is
still looking for a companion and would love to meet
her if she wishes to call.
    As I told Mary, Cliff House is quite far out in the
country, but it would have to be to have the location
it has. I could stand forever in front of it and look up
and down the coast. It is a simply heavenly view, and
I know she will love it. The house is furnished beautifully. Mary would have her own room, of course, and
would be most comfortable. Lavinia has more than
enough help, as well as a perfect lady's maid who has
been with her forever. So Mary would have little to
do except sit with Lavinia and go driving with her
when she goes out, write a letter or two, perhaps, and
read to her occasionally.
    The position would pay £60 a year, which I think

is generous, especially since Mary would have no expenses and could save almost all of it.

We have just gotten back from our visit, and I had to sit down at once and write the good news to you, my dear boy.

If Mary wishes to come, I suggest she do so without delay. There is no point in putting off an interview which could lead to such an advantageous situation for her. So, I suggest that you and she leave on the two forty-five train from Barnstaple—the one I always take in the afternoon—on Monday the 7th. This will bring you into Holsworthy at five. It will be so wonderful to have you at Lewis House again after all these years. I hate to think how long it has been since you paid your old grandmamma a visit. I *am* looking forward to it. I will meet you at the station in Holsworthy. We could then drive out to see Lavinia on Tuesday, and you could return to Barnstaple on Wednesday or stay longer. Oh, how I would love for you both to stay longer if you could. But of course it is what *you* want to do, my dear boy. But if for any reason you cannot come on Monday, telegraph me so I will know in time.

"Then she goes on and talks about other things. Isn't that superb? The old girl never lets me down. I have a feeling, Mary, that this is just the thing we have been hoping for. You don't look very pleased. Aren't you delighted?"

"How can I be pleased, Edmond? The prospect of becoming a companion to an old lady neither pleases nor delights me. How could it? My father was the marquess of Penbroke. He was a very wealthy man. His friends were some of the most important people on the continent—people at the French court. In Paris, the King's sister came to dine with us. I have always had everything I wanted. I am accustomed to giving orders, not taking them. How could I be delighted?"

"And what about the servants on your stepfather's farm in Holland. He must have had a great many servants for you to give orders to."

"There weren't any, of course," I replied.

"My dear Mary, this is not the end of the world. You

must realize that. In the first place you will not be a servant. . . ."

"Servant or companion, there is very little difference, Edmond."

"Pride is a dangerous and wicked thing, Mary. No, permit me to continue. It is only your pride that rebels against taking this position. Pride could destroy you, Mary. You are a poor girl without a family—except for a mother who has married a poor farmer. Accept this! Do not be proud. The time has come when you must work for a living. If you do not do that now, you may find that your pride has led you into tragic circumstances indeed."

"There is a difference, Edmond, between pride and dignity. I am fully resigned to meeting Lady Hob. I shall be ready when it is time for us to leave for the station on Monday."

"Excellent!" Edmond said. "As I was saying this is *not* the end of the world, my dear. Be more cheerful. Lady Hob is a wealthy woman. What of her family whom you will meet? What of her friends whom you will come to meet, and their families? Who knows whom you will come to know and how these people may change your life. Why, it is the beginning for you. Surely you must realize that."

"Wasn't it you, Edmond, who said that nothing is impossible? What time shall we leave? I suppose directly after luncheon, just as your grandmother did when she left? When *do* you plan to return to Castle Cloud?"

"I'll be returning, probably, in the late afternoon on Wednesday. You can tell me at dinner when you plan to take up your duties at Cliff House. I shall be very anxious to know what arrangements you have made. No, I am not going to Lewis House with you. I have business elsewhere. I cannot imagine what gave Grandmamma the idea that *I* would be coming. It is only a short ride and you are perfectly capable of making the journey alone. If you traveled all the way from Holland alone, you certainly can manage Holsworthy—though I will see you to the station with pleasure."

We had little more to say to each other. Edmond had almost finished eating when I arrived, so it was only a few minutes before he excused himself and I was left to finish my breakfast alone.

As I ate, I began to decide what I would take to Lewis

House with me and to plan what I need do in preparation for the trip. Underthings and petticoats and handkerchiefs needed ironing, two dresses needed to be pressed, there was mending to do, and I needed a new pair of stockings, though perhaps I could make do with the ones I had. . . .

After breakfast, I hurried to my room, went immediately to the wardrobe, and brought out my brown-poplin walking dress and Napoleon-blue visiting dress. I would travel in the poplin. A coffee-with-cream-colored dress with a flounced skirt, it was trimmed with broad crossway bands of pink and moss-green plaid. I would wear the blue taffeta visiting dress during my interview with Lady Hob. It had been made by Madame Camile, who at that time was by appointment to the grand duchess of Baden. It was one of several dresses I had bought on that last trip Papa and I had made to Paris. Its sleeves were divided into three large puffs, and both the sleeves and bodice were cut away in lozenge-shaped openings, which exposed the under-sleeves and chemisette. The dress was beautiful and expensive, but it was two years old and no longer quite in fashion, even in that remote part of England. Perhaps Lady Hob would think it had been given to me by a former owner. Well, if she did, so much the better, I thought.

And to travel in, over the poplin, I would wear my beige cashmere shawl. I placed it on the sofa beside the walking dress. And I would wear my fringed navy mantle to the interview. This I folded and placed next to the blue dress which I had laid on the bed. Then I brought out my plain beige bonnet to travel in, and, for the interview, one trimmed with pale blue and white flowers. Then followed an examination of my gloves and handkerchiefs. One pair of gloves needed washing. Handkerchiefs and petticoats needed washing too. The dresses were fresh, but needed to be pressed.

"Oh, my lady," said Mrs. Muldoon from the doorway. "Sure, I didn't expect you'd be here at this hour, my lady. I just cleaned this out and came to slip it under your bed."

"It is all right, Mrs. Muldoon. Come in," I said. "Perhaps you can help me."

"Ja?" she asked.

"My underthings and stockings that you have taken to have washed—I suppose Ida has done them?"

"Ja, my lady."

"Could she wash those petticoats, and starch and iron them, and wash and iron these things and have them all ready by Monday noon, do you think? I know it is short notice, but I have just learned that the dowager countess has invited me to spend a few days with her, and I shall be leaving on the early afternoon train, Monday."

"Oh, Ja, my lady. It's plenty of time, it is," Mrs. Muldoon replied. "Sure, I'll take them down to her right now."

"And one other thing. Would she mind if I pressed these two dresses myself?"

"Press them yourself, my lady?"

"Well, they are very special to me. My father gave them to me, and I do not want to risk anything happening to them. You said she—was not quite right, and I could not risk having them scorched."

Clearly this was the last thing Mrs. Muldoon expected. She seemed torn between admiration that I knew *how* to iron them and disapproval that I should wish to. She tried not to show her surprise, however, and said, "Faith if it's ironing you're going to do, you'd best come along with me and meet Ida so she can show you where the things are, and these things I'll take along at the same time."

"Now?" I asked.

"As I've always said, my lady, when a thing needs to be done, it's never too soon. A father once says to his naughty son, 'Son,' he says (Mrs. Muldoon's eyes began to bulge), 'for that I'm going to give you a whipping, but I'll let you choose your own time for it.' So do you know what the little boy says? He looks up at his father and says, 'Papa, I think I'll have it yesterday.' Ha, ha, ha. Yes, it's down we go now, if it's convenient for you, my lady."

"I could do one dress before luncheon then, and the other this afternoon. That would be perfect, Mrs. Muldoon."

So we left my room, and as we crossed the rotunda toward the stairs to the servants' hall, she said, "No, she's not quite right in the head. It's things she imagines and it's daydreams she has, my lady. But she does the washing and ironing as good as anybody, I expect. It's six brothers and four sisters she has—all working on the farms, they are. And her father is dead, but her mother lives in the village. Ida lives here in the servants' pavilion. She doesn't live at home with her mother—no room for her, more than likely. The way they all live crowded together in that little cottage is a shame, it is."

By that time we were passing the servants' hall on our way to the laundry rooms, which were in the northeast corner of the basement level of the Castle, in the opposite direction from the banging of pots and voices from the kitchens. Finally Mrs. Muldoon threw open a door and we stepped into a tiny, brightly lit room. There was a large table in the center of it and the walls were lined with open shelves. This was the folding room. To the right of it was the ironing room and off to the left the wash rooms, filled with steamy air from kettles that boiled on a stove. Mrs. Muldoon walked into one of the wash rooms and called Ida's name, but no one answered. Then she tossed my soiled clothes into a basket on a table, crossed the room, and opened an outside door. This led to the areaway and a flight of stairs descending to ground level. This, I supposed, was the way Ida carried the washed clothes to the drying yard beyond the servants' pavilion.

"Here she comes," Mrs. Muldoon called. "She'll be here in just a minute." Shortly I heard her say, "Ida, it's Lady Beauford. She's come down to do a little special ironing of her own. Will you show her where things are and give her anything she might be needing?"

Then a girl came through the doorway, set a clothes basket down on the floor beside the washtubs, and walked toward me. She was almost six feet tall and built like a bull, with huge arms and a thick neck. She had an extraordinarily large mouth and jaw which reminded me of a St. Bernard dog, but her eyes were not sad like a St. Bernard's—they were walleyed and dull.

As she approached, she brushed a strand of tangled hair away from her eyes. Then she curtsied to me, and said, "I found a little baby bird—all cuddly and warm, it was—and I picked him up, my lady, and held him high over my head so his mamma could see where he was, but she didn't come for him. If I was lost when I was a little baby, my mamma would have come for me. Why didn't the little bird's mamma come?"

"If there's nothing more you'll be needing, my lady—" Mrs. Muldoon said.

"No, I don't think so. Thank you, Mrs. Muldoon," I said.

When she was gone, Ida said, "How I should love to fly like a bird—high in the sky, up above the clouds, up to the blue. Then I would find out what the blue is made of. Did you ever think about that? Most people have never thought about that, you know."

"Good morning, Ida," I said. "No, I have never thought about that. Will I be in your way if I press my dress?"

"There's the irons," she said, running into the ironing room, "and there's the sprinkler bottles, and there's the cloths, and there's the starch, and there's the forms." She darted to each thing and pointed to it as she said its name. I had once seen a ballerina run to each member of the corps de ballet and tap her on the shoulder. Ida was an ungainly reminder of that performance.

Then Ida ran from the room singing.

It is of a rich merchant I am going to tell
    Who had for a daughter an unkimmon nice gal.
    Her name it was Dinah just sixteen years old. . . .

While she finished her song (I could tell she had begun the washing as she did so), I looked about the ironing room. The sun shown through high windows and reflected on the white walls, making the room very light indeed. Tables, covered with white pads, lined the room and in the center of the room a fire glowed inside a round stove. A dozen irons clasped in metal brackets ringed the outside of it, their faces held tightly against the hot metal, warming. It was really a most convenient arrangement—one had only to grasp the handle of an iron, lift it out of its bracket, iron with it until it became too cool to use, replace it in its holder, lift the next iron out of its bracket, and continue ironing.

I had everything I needed there and went right to work. Later, when I had finished pressing the bodice of my dress and had almost finished the skirt, I sensed that someone was watching me. It was Ida. I had forgotten about her. I supposed she had been washing and had made several trips to the clothesline while I had worked on my dress.

She stood, leaning against the doorjamb, watching me. Then she crossed to the stove, threw a shovelful of coal on the fire, and said, "My mamma would have come to find me, but my daddy couldn't."

"Oh, why not, Ida?" I asked.

"Because he's gone to heaven, and he's walking with the angels."

"I am sorry," I said.

"Sleeping like a lamb, he was. Oh, I remember it. Proper grand burying it was, too. Wine and cakes to eat. One coffin he had—only one. Some people has more than one, you know. How many coffins are you having, my lady? I'm having three.

"No one has more than one, Ida."

"His lordship had two, he did."

"Oh, I don't think so."

"Two undertakers come with two coffins, they did. I seen 'em. Oh, they did it proper grand for him, they did. Birds don't have coffins. Did you ever think of that, my lady? Most people don't think of that, you know. When they die, who puts them in the ground, miss? And lambs don't have coffins, and goats don't have. . ."

"Ida! Get on with your work now, like a good girl," Mrs. Foley said. She had appeared without a sound. "There are some more sheets to be washed and hung out, and we want to get them in before the dew gets on them."

"Oh, yes, mum," Ida said, as she scurried away.

"Good morning, Mrs. Foley," I said. "I hope I am not creating a problem for you."

"Good morning, my lady," she said. "We are not accustomed to visits from their lord and ladyship's guests. I find it is always a problem when ladies of quality sink beneath their level." Immediately, without another word, Mrs. Foley whirled about and left the room.

"How dare she say a thing like that to me?" I thought aloud. Why does she dislike me so much, I wondered. I almost believe she hates me. Her expression had been rather frightening. What have I ever done to Mrs. Foley? Why, I scarcely know her. There was a double meaning in her remark. I am sure there was. That was because Mitchell has most likely recounted all the conversations he has heard in the dining room to her and to all the wide-eyed servants in the servants' hall. By now, everyone at Castle Cloud must know all about my problems and future plans.

That evening after dinner, Sarah and I hurried to the top of the hill and stood next to each other near the Horse Monument, looking for David. I did not really think he would come, but he might have heard of a position for me. And I had told him that I would most probably walk up the hill after dinner on clear nights. But it was not for news of a position that I hoped he would come. I wanted to see him again, and I wanted him to want to see me. I wanted him to ride to the monument just to see me again, which is exactly what he did.

I saw him ride from a grove of trees into a field beyond and to the right of the village. He was too far off, then, to recognize, but I knew it was he. His horse jumped a gate in a wall and then galloped across a meadow to an opening in a hedgerow which led to a lane. The lane ended in front of a cottage at the far edge of the field, beyond the wood, at the base of the hill. In a few minutes, David had galloped across the field and vanished into the wood. Then he shot out of the trees and scrambled up the hill toward me. He had a magnificent seat: one would have thought he had been brought up in the saddle. It was thrilling to watch him ride.

"Hello," he shouted, as he reached the hilltop. And in an instant he was out of the saddle and striding toward me. "How are you, Mary? So you kept your word. Good dog, Sarah. Good dog."

"About walking up here in the evening?" I asked. "That is not difficult. This is one of the loveliest views I think I have ever seen. Did you ride all the way up here to see me?"

"Yes."

He and Sarah finished their greetings, then, and Sarah loped off looking for a scent to follow.

"You have news of a situation for me then?" I asked.

"No. I came just to see you. Well, there is no harm in that, you know. I wanted to be sure that you were all right. I think Vivian would want me to keep my eye on you since she cannot be here, herself. And I wondered if you had heard from Vivian's grandmother."

"We received a letter this morning," I said. "She wrote that Lady Hob is still looking for a companion and said I should come to Cornwall on Monday to meet her."

"Cornwall? Are you going?"

"Just across the border, near Bude. Yes. She will meet me at the station in Holsworthy tomorrow evening."

"And when will you return?"

"On Wednesday afternoon."

"Will you come up here Wednesday evening and tell me what happened?"

"Well, yes, if you want me to. Look at the ship out there. How lavender its sails are in this light, and how deep blue the sea is. Isn't it lovely? It is like being on top of the world."

"It is very beautiful," he said, looking deep into my eyes. "Very beautiful, Mary."

Soon after that David and I sat on our stone blocks, and talked until it was dark. He told me about the superintending and draining of some fields and pointed out where they lay. That led to a description of some Southdown and Wiltshire sheep he had bought, and that led, somehow, to the problems with a new hay barn he was building. He talked almost entirely about his work, which did not interest me, but I was thrilled with his interest in it. It was marvelous to talk to someone like David who was excited about what he was doing.

And then he asked about me. He was interested in the places I had lived on the continent and wanted to know about them. And as I answered his questions and described some aspects of my life there, he sat looking into my eyes in that intensely serious way of his, which frequently made a thrill go up my spine.

But our time together went too swiftly. One moment the sun was just setting and the next moment, it seemed, it was quite dark and I had to leave him. So at last, reluctantly, I bade him good night and walked down the path. Nearing the bend, I turned and waved to him.

He called in return to remind me that we would meet there on Wednesday evening.

✠ Chapter Five ✠

BEFORE GOING DOWN to luncheon on Monday, I made the final preparations for my trip to Lewis House. I packed my brushes, comb, and toilet things in my bag. I folded my blue dress and laid it on top of my extra petticoats, underwear, and nightgown, which were already packed. I placed my bonnet on top of the dress, closed my bag, and placed the bag on the floor next to the door for Mitchell to fetch. Aside from that, everything was done. The shawl, bonnet, and gloves that I would wear to travel in lay on the bed, ready, and I wore my brown traveling dress. We would be leaving immediately after luncheon. Since I could think of nothing I had left undone, I went down to the drawing room to join Edmond and his mother for luncheon.

During the meal, I remarked how convenient the railway to Barnstaple made traveling. The last time I had visited Castle Cloud, Vivian and I were met at the station in Exeter with a carriage. Edmond, who was in excellent spirits, spent most of the time during luncheon telling me about the opening day of the railway in Barnstaple two years before, about the dignitaries present, the triumphal arches decorating the streets, the arrival of the first train, the addresses, the ablutions, the prayers, the band music, the processions, the crowds, the dinner, the bazaar, and the ball. That July day must have been a happy one because Lady Clareham seemed to forget some of her sadness while reminiscing about the celebration and how her whole family and their guests had taken part in it.

So the meal passed quickly, and when we had finished eating, I dashed to my room to put on my bonnet, shawl, and gloves.

And when I returned to the hall to join Edmond, Mitchell held the entrance door open. Through it, I saw

Colen waiting with the cabriolet at the base of the steps to the entrance portico. But, though it was a beautiful, sunny day, the carriage top was up. Castle Cloud's guest was to be hidden under it on her way to the station.

Beside the carriage, Sarah sat waiting to be taken along. But as we descended the steps toward her, she crept under it and cowered there growling at Edmond.

"Stay away from me," Edmond shouted at her, as Mitchell helped me into the carriage. "Nasty cur," he mumbled, when he had stepped up and was seated beside me.

"Oh, Edmond, why do you hate that poor little dog so much?" I asked.

"Disgusting creature," he said.

Then Mitchell shut the door for us and swung my bag up on the box beside Colen. Colen called Sarah out from under the carriage and we drove off. Lady Clareham had not come out to wave good-by to us from the portico, but I suppose I should not have expected it. I had, however, waved to Lord Clareham's window before climbing into the carriage. I had been sure that he would be watching.

"The train from Braunton does not go to Holsworthy?" I asked, after we had crossed the stone bridge and turned right onto the road which wound back toward Barnstaple. "It would have taken so much less of your time if we could have driven to the station there."

"No, it goes to Exeter, where you would change for London. Besides, there is only one train a day that goes through Barnstaple to Braunton and then to Ilfracombe, and one train back again."

"Did you take Vivian to Braunton, then?"

"Yes, as a matter of fact I did. The longer drive to Barnstaple would have been too uncomfortable for her in her condition."

"I suppose Lady Clareham went to the station with you and Vivian."

"Mother? No. She was too ill with grief to drive out. She still is, except for going to church and to her charities in the village. I suppose one must take care of one's own, though I don't know how she can bring herself to enter some of those filthy hovels. She is still sick with grief. She will always be sick with grief. It is more than a man can bear. Always sobbing and sniffling at any mention of

James and—and now Vivian, now that she is away. Why, one would think she was dead, the way Mother carries on. She will never get over it. One would think she would think a little bit about *me,* but no. *They* were her favorites, *they* were her darlings. She never liked me very much, you know. Never approved of anything I ever did. And Father is the same way—poor, helpless invalid. It won't be long before he is in the tomb-house. Well, he cannot live very much longer, and really, Mary, one hates to see him suffer. And then Mother will be off to her dower-house where she can suffer in peace, and *that* will cost the estates a pretty penny.

"But never mind. I shall soon have the money to restore Castle Cloud *and* I have decided to buy a house in London. The Ramsays have always had one there, you know, and they shall have one there again. And *then* you will see the parties and the balls and all the beautiful women in their beautiful gowns and jewels. Oh, the times we shall have. Ha, ha, the times we shall have."

As we drove along he began to hum a dance tune and tap his knee with his fingers in time to it.

"I wish you could have come along with me, Edmond," I said, half thinking aloud, after we had driven along a mile or so. "Not for me, but your grandmother will be so disappointed. I know she is looking forward so much to your visit. She is devoted to you—anyone could see that."

"Oh, she won't mind. Why should I sink myself in the middle of nowhere for several days? To take the guided tour of her garden? To watch her go bouncing off to her bees under that net affair she wears over her head? Ha, ha. You have never *seen* the like. It is one of the funniest things I have ever seen—almost worth the trip. Ha, ha, ha."

"Bees?" I asked.

"Her hobby is bees—raising *bees.* Can you imagine an eighty-five-year-old-woman beekeeper? The one and only beekeeper of the English nobility. Can you imagine? And those cats of hers—well, one can always open a window.

"And while you are at Lewis House, just remember that my dear Grandmamma's jointure is paid out of the estates—a pretty penny it costs too. Widows can drain an estate until it collapses about one's ears. Well, that cannot go on much longer, either. Dum, dum, diddley um dumm," he sang under his breath.

"She is so full of life and so happy," I said. "How pleased you must be for her."

Edmond did not reply. He hummed a few more bars and then we finished our journey in silence. It was less than five miles from Castle Cloud to Barnstaple, but it had seemed twenty.

When at last we drove up to the station, I saw that the train stood waiting for its passengers. Edmond helped me out of the carriage and carried my bag to the train where he found me an empty compartment. Then, when I was seated and he had put my bag in the rack above me, he went into the station, bought a ticket for me, returned with it, and handed it to me through the window.

"Thank you very much, Edmond," I said. "I do appreciate your helping me like this. I should love to have you wait and see me off, but if you wish to hurry back to Castle Cloud, please do. I feel that I have taken far too much of your time already."

"Think nothing of it," he replied. "But if you will excuse me then, I do have some things to do. You know, it just occurred to me, Mary, that if Lady Hob wishes you to start immediately, I can have Jane pack your trunk, and I could send it to you. It would save you a trip. You could telegraph and tell me."

"Thank you, Edmond, but I should certainly want a few days before starting, and I am sure Lady Hob would too."

"Yes—Well, I will see you on Wednesday." He turned then, whistling softly to himself, and walked to the carriage, got in, and drove off without looking back.

"Thank you for wishing me a safe and pleasant journey, Edmond," I whispered to myself, as I watched the carriage disappear down the street. I was relieved that he was gone. I felt such mixed emotions about him: I *was* grateful for his help—for his wanting to find me a position, and for paying for my railway ticket—but I had hated to hear him talk like that about his parents and grandmother.

Why, I wondered, did he wish me to stay at Castle Cloud? I had not been made welcome. I felt that I was not wanted there. Why had he not suggested that I leave Castle Cloud, once he had found that Vivian was not coming home? After all, I am not his or his parents responsibility (and I felt that he spoke for his parents). Why, then, had not Edmond and his parents simply suggested that I leave? Instead, they want to see me employed as a companion to Lady Hob. Why? Not because they care about *me*. Edmond is not interested in my welfare. I don't believe he even likes me. Why is he so concerned about me then? Because of Vivian? No, because of himself. Edmond does not think of anyone but himself. But how could my being employed by Lady Hob possibly benefit Edmond?

I sat thinking about these things, half expecting that someone would enter the compartment and occupy it with me, but no one did. Shortly the conductor came for my ticket, and then the train began to move. And as we followed the river gradually uphill, past Chulmleigh toward Dartmoor, I thought about leaving Castle Cloud. I had looked forward for months to visiting the house, but I do not believe I had thought once about leaving it. My stay at the Castle could hardly have been called merry. But it was still the most beautiful place in the world—my favorite place—and David was nearby. Would I repeat this train journey, I wondered, in a week or two, never to return to Castle Cloud? I could not bear the thought. I had left it today, but I would return on Wednesday.

At length the train stopped at Okehampton Station, and from the window I could see the square keep of Okehampton Castle, about a half mile beyond the town. To the left, Yes Tor thrust itself into the sky above the purple moors.

There, I was joined by my only traveling companions of the trip—a prosperously dressed, portly man and an elderly parson. From their conversation, the portly man was a clothier on his way to the Tuesday market in Tavistock. He was to spend the night in Bratton Clovelly and he got off there. The parson was going to visit a niece in Northlew. He appeared nervous traveling.

The parson left the train at Northlew, and I traveled the rest of the way to Holsworthy alone. Fields spotted with sheep slipped past my window. Each field was a different size, a different shape, and a different color green. And each was sewn to its neighbor by a bordering hedgerow, making a gigantic quilt that covered all the land with its billowy folds.

Just before five o'clock we pulled into Holsworthy, where the dowager countess and a gray-haired man stood on the platform waiting for me. As soon as the train had stopped, I opened the door of the compartment and stepped onto the platform, waving to her as I did so.

"Where is Edmond?" Lady Clareham cried, as she hurried toward me. "Kenton, fetch Lady Beauford's bags."

"I have just one, Kenton," I said, "the brown one above the seat nearest the window, there. Thank you." Then I turned to Lady Clareham. "He could not come, Lady Clareham. He is terribly sorry, but some urgent business came up at the last minute which called him away from Castle Cloud." The expression in her eyes when I told her wrung my heart. I had been right: Edmond's visit had become very important to her.

"Well, I have you, my child, and that is delightful," she said, quickly disguising her disappointment.

"Thank you, Lady Clareham. It is lovely to see you again."

She came to me then and put her arm through mine, patting it at the same time with her other hand. Arm in arm, we walked toward her carriage.

"He has probably gone to see about a living," she said. "I do wish he could find one. I don't know why George doesn't give him the one in Milton Penderton. But he keeps saying it would not be right for Edmond, that he was never meant for the church—such nonsense. Why it would be perfect for him. Here we are, my dear."

Lady Clareham's carriage was an ancient, dark-red barouche, trimmed in gold, with the Clareham crest in gold on the door. I wondered if it had originally come from Castle Cloud. I supposed that was Ralph, her coachman, waiting for us on the box. Kenton opened the carriage door, helped us in, put my bag on the forward seat, took his place beside Ralph, and we drove off.

"Have you been well, Lady Clareham?" I asked. "Did you have a pleasant journey back from Castle Cloud?"

"Yes, my dear," she replied, "very pleasant, though uneventful." She gave me a wan smile.

"I must thank you immediately for going to all the trouble of arranging this interview with Lady Hob. It really was terribly nice of you. What is she like? Do you think I will like her?"

"She is about ten years younger, I should say, than I am, my dear—very likely, even though she has great difficulty walking. You will meet her tomorrow, and I think it might be better if I did not say very much more about her. I might give you a misleading impression."

She said no more, and we drove along in silence for a few minutes. I could tell by her expression and the way she spoke that Lady Clareham was fighting back her disappointment that Edmond had not come to visit her. She looked out at the passing landscape so sadly that I wanted to say something to distract her. Perhaps talking about him would help.

"Edmond has been so kind," I said. "I appreciate his trying to help me. You know, I had almost forgotten that Edmond had been ordained. I cannot think of him as anything but an army officer."

"Yes," she said, "that was after Oxford. Nothing would do but that he go into the army, and where do you suppose he was to get the money to purchase a commission?" She smiled at me then.

"From you?" I asked, returning her smile.

"Half from me—the other half from his father. The army was not for Edmond, and I knew it. But he would have been miserably unhappy if he could not have gotten in, so I had to help him. How dashing he looked in uniform! I suppose all the girls were agog, but I did not like it. He is too sensitive, too vulnerable for a military life."

"Yes, I remember him at Windsor. He was stationed there when Vivian and I were at Mrs. Romilly's. He was a lieutenant in the Horse Guards, I think, wasn't it? Well, anyway, I remember Vivian pointing him out to me on the street several times. He was always riding or walking along in a desperate hurry to get somewhere. No sooner would we catch a glimpse of him than he would be gone. I finally met him during that Easter week I spent with Vivian at the Castle. He was home for only two or three days while I was there, and even then we did not see very much of him."

"From Arford St. Mary," Lady Clareham said. "He had come from Arford St. Mary. He had the living there at that time. A sweet little church. I visited him shortly after he moved into the rectory. I think that was one of the proudest moments of my life—sitting in that church listening to Edmond's first sermon there. He is a born preacher, you know. We all used our influence with the bishop to get his permission—George and I, and Lord and Lady Spree. Hill House, that is Lord Spree's seat, is just above Arford St. Mary, and he had endowed the living, which was vacant at the time. Edmond had to serve under the rector of St. Antholin, in London, first, but that was only for three or four months. I was *so* glad when he sold his commission and decided to go into the church."

"What happened to his living at Arford St. Mary?" I asked.

"It simply wasn't right for him, somehow. He had doubts about the ministry. Lord Spree began to interfere and make it uncomfortable. I remember Edmond saying to me, 'Grandmamma, the Lord came to me in prayer, and He told me to leave Arford St. Mary.' Well, he left and came back to Castle Cloud. He was so unhappy then, my heart ached for the poor boy."

"And he has been there ever since? Has he thought of taking another living, then?"

"He thought he would go into business after that—into trade. Of course I would not have it. George and Julia were shocked. The trustees had just taken over at the time, and Edmond said that it would only be for a short time, that he could make a fantastic profit in a short time— more than enough to pay the debts of the estates. George was terribly upset about the situation at the Castle, naturally, and well. . . In the end, I lent Edmond the money—£10,000. He lost it. It was not his fault, I know that. He has too brilliant a mind. It was merely bad luck. It was nobody's fault, I imagine. You know how business is. I really did not have the heart to ask him very much about it. He was so unhappy about it all. I hadn't any more money to give him, so there was nothing I could do but watch him suffer over it."

"I am so sorry, Lady Clareham," I said.

"But now I know he is looking for another living. That is what he does when he goes off like this, but he doesn't tell anybody for fear of disappointing them. I know that when he gets a church and is able to give of himself again, he will find himself. God works in strange ways, my dear. It will be all right—I know it will." She rested her tiny gloved hand on my arm to reassure me.

"Here we are," she continued, "and we have talked about nothing but Edmond all the way. And nothing about you. Well, we will remedy that and get to know each other soon enough."

We turned off the lane then, passed through the gateway of a high, brick wall, rolled past a miniature gatehouse, and swung to the right on a circular drive in front of Lewis House.

"It is charming! It is a delight!" I said.

"Thank you, my dear. I have come to love it. It was built in the fifteenth century. Once it was a hospital for the monks of Stratton Abbey, which is now a ruin."

Lewis House was a small, four-gabled, half-timbered house of two stories. It looked like four small, pitched-roofed, joined houses when viewed from the gable end. And it was covered with ivy and clematis in bloom.

After we had stepped inside the house, Kenton, carrying my bag, showed me to my room. It had been freshly aired and I found everything there that I needed—water, soap, and towels. I washed then, and unpacked my things. Since I did not feel like lying down, I went out into the garden by the side of the house. There I sat on a bench under an ancient yew tree until it was almost dinner time, gazing at the well-kept garden.

When I returned to the house, Kenton met me at the door and said: "Her ladyship is in the drawing room—through the hall to your left, my lady, and up the stairs under the gallery."

I stepped into the banqueting hall then, where we were to have dinner (the table was set for it), and marvelled at the room. It comprised all of the interior of one of the four houses I had imagined pasted together, and was open all the way up to the roof—one could see its beams, two-and-a-half stories above the floor.

I walked to the end of the hall, climbed the stair under the minstrel's gallery, turned to the right, and stepped into the drawing room, where I was greeted by Lady Clareham.

"Good evening, Mary," she smiled. "I saw you out in the garden. I hope you did not go into the rose garden because I want to show you that myself after dinner—that and my hives.

"This is Cleopatra II. You have met her mother at

Castle Cloud. And over there are Anthony and Demetrius, and in the easy chair are Oberon and Titania."

We talked about her cats until it it was time for dinner. During the meal, which was served by Kenton, Lady Clareham told me about her charities in the village. It was interesting that, at that time, both she and her daughter-in-law had a poor, unwed, mother-to-be to look after.

After we had drunk our coffee, Lady Clareham showed me her rose garden where she pointed out, with great pride, her new creation, the Ramsay Rose. By then, it was beginning to grow in Kew Gardens for all England to see. It was spectacular—an enormous head of huge, luminous, apricot-pink petals.

"It is gorgeous!" I said. "How ever did you create it?"

"Cross-pollination, my dear. By trial and error, really. I have been working for years, hoping to come upon a really special rose. But the work will go on, of course. Who knows what more I shall find? Come and see my bees."

"I don't want to get stung," I said.

"No, no. My bees are very gentle—they wouldn't think of doing a thing like that. There," she said, when we reached a square, grassy yard beyond the rose garden.

"Where are the bees?" I asked. "Where are the hives? What are those square, white boxes?"

"Those square, white boxes *are* the hives, my dear."

"But I thought beehives were dome-shaped and made of straw."

"They are, but one day they will all be replaced with this kind. These are very new in the bee world. The lids lift off, and there is a separate chamber, above the colony, for the combs. The combs must be removed at the right time and enough honey must always be left for the bees."

"How on earth did you ever learn about bees, and why?"

"From two wonderful books, my dear, by the Reverend Langstroth and an American whose name is Moses Quimby. Why? I was never afraid of bees. No one who works in a garden is. And a gardener knows their value. I loved watching them, was curious about them, and decided to learn about them. And now I have these hives. I love to work with bees. Of course I protect myself with veil and gloves, and my smoker makes them quite docile. They are my families. I feel responsible for them. No matter what happens, I will always have my bees and my flowers."

"How do you do it all—the gardens, the roses, the bees, your charities—and at. . ." I blushed and stopped.

"At my age, my dear? Oh, I don't mind. I will soon be eighty-six, you know, and I am young. As long as one has things to do, she is young. It is when one has nothing to do that she sits about and waits for death, and death is most obliging.

"Come along, it is time for bed. You have had a long day and a tiring one, and we should get an early start in the morning."

We walked back to the house then, and I went to my room. There, the curtains had been drawn, the lamps lit, the bed turned down, and my nightgown laid out for me. I undressed at once and put it on, blew out the lamps, climbed into bed, and fell asleep. But toward morning, I was awakened by rain pounding the roof, and I got up and closed the windows. Then I went back to bed, but it was a long time before I slept again.

The following morning, I was awakened by a knock on the door. "Good morning, my lady," said a pink-cheeked maid. She entered the room and curtsied, expertly balancing the tray she held. "I'm Violet, my lady. Her ladyship thought you might like tea before your bath, my lady."

"Thank you, Violet," I said. "Set the tray here on the bed beside me."

I sipped my tea while Violet bustled about, opening the curtains and preparing my bath.

"Shall I light the fire, my lady?" she asked.

"No, no, Violet, thank you. Don't bother. I don't think it is cool enough for that, and I shall be going down directly."

"Very good, my lady. If you should need anything, please ring with the pull, there."

When she was gone I bathed, combed and brushed my hair, dressed for the coming interview, and went downstairs to join Lady Clareham for breakfast. She was already in the tiny breakfast room having her coffee.

"Good morning, Mary. Did you sleep well, my dear?" she asked.

"Yes, thank you, Lady Clareham," I said, as Kenton helped me to be seated. "May I have two soft-cooked eggs,

Kenton, please? And a hot scone and coffee, I think." Then I turned back to the dowager countess and said, "I was very comfortable. It is a beautiful room. I love the pink clematis peeping in the window from the vines outside. I went straight to sleep, but the rain woke me, and I had trouble getting back to sleep again. I kept thinking about today."

"Don't you worry about today, my dear, Lady Hob will love you—how could she help it?"

"This is all so strange—so repellent to me, somehow. Edmond said it was pride, but it is not. It is not that I am too proud to take a position, it is that I know I will not be happy. But it must be done, I suppose. Oh, it probably won't be as bad as I think. Strange things are apt to seem worse than they really are, don't you think so?" I smiled across at Lady Clareham.

"That's my girl," she said, smiling back. "Edmond is right. It is the sensible thing to do, and you must remember that you are not going into slavery. You can leave a post anytime you choose, if you are too unhappy there. As I said, who knows what will happen in the future—whom you will meet? Save your money, and one day perhaps you may wish to open a school of your own.

"Edmond suggested that you be *Miss* Thorpe. You will always have your title, whether you mention it or not, you know, and you can always use it when it is to your advantage, but this is not the time. Do you agree? Good. Now, Lady Hob has some unusual hobbies, or an unusual hobby."

"Oh, what is that?" I asked. "Now I will have some of your honey. What a lovely golden color." Lady Clareham waited for me to spread my scone with honey and taste it. "Umm—delicious! This is something I shall not forget, truly."

"I am so pleased you like it. You must have a pot of it when you go to stay with Lavinia. Oh, I don't think I should say anything about it after all. I might put the wrong complexion on it. We will let her tell you about it herself. But rest assured, Lavinia needs someone to help her, and she is a kind and gentle soul. If she weren't, I would not have suggested this in the first place."

Soon after we had finished breakfast, we set out for Cliff House, in the barouche. Kenton rode on the box beside Ralph. Since they rode out in the open, they were dressed in weatherproof cloaks in case of rain. Lady Clareham and I sat beneath the carriage top. We drove in the opposite direction from Holsworthy, turning to the left after we had passed through the gateway, twisting through country lanes toward Stratton. Beyond Stratton, we climbed up and up through a wood for several miles until, at last, we emerged onto a grassy moor, which sloped upward still. We wound our way across it, following the lane (which had become a mere cart track) until we reached the hilltop, where Ralph stopped to rest the horses.

Our carriage had stopped on the highest point of a grassy headland above the sea. I had known for some time that we were approaching the sea because I had smelled it, but I was totally unprepared for what I saw about me. On three sides of us, short-cropped grass sloped away to a cliff edge, two hundred feet above the water. Beyond this, both to the right and left along the coast, point after point of land stretched into the ocean like fingers of monstrous hands. Between us and each headland, the sea had drawn a veil of mist—until finally, seen through many misty curtains, the farthest points were just deeper tones of the same lead-gray color, both sea and sky.

Off to our right, our track wound from promontory to promontory, leading, finally, to a square, stone house.

"That is Cliff House, Mary," Lady Clareham said, nodding to the distant building. "You should see this view on a clear day. It is glorious."

I pulled my mantle more snugly around my shoulders. "It is so open and empty," I said. "There is not a tree, and I don't see any birds. The mist seems to have cut us off from everything, except the sheep on the hillocks over there. Are there no other houses nearby? We must be five miles from Stratton, don't you think?"

"I suppose so. Shall we have our luncheon here, my dear? I don't think we should stop any closer to the house, do you? I had hoped we could picnic on the grass, but it is quite wet from the mist. I am afraid we shall have to eat here in the carriage."

Then she asked Kenton to get out the lunch baskets. He handed us ours and threw back the lid for us, and we ate where we had been sitting. Kenton and Ralph had a lunch basket of their own and ate on the box. When we had finished the meal, we drove on toward the house.

And as we drove along, I had time to study it. Cliff House sat alone on the grass above the sea, with no tree or bush or flower to embellish it. It was a two story, square, granite house, totally without ornamentation, with nine windows across the front of the first story, and eight on the main floor, with an arched doorway in the center. The stables and outbuildings were of granite also, but they huddled in a little valley some two-hundred yards inland from the house.

"What is that structure being built by the cliff's edge?" I asked.

"The mausoleum. Lavinia has been building that for years, but it never seems to get finished. As soon as it is close to finished, she changes the plans and has it pulled down. One year it is Baroque, the next Romanesque, the next perpendicular. She is enormously wealthy and can afford to do it, and if it makes her happy, well. . . Lavinia is the only child of the duke of Mountrose, so she inherited the estates. The title went to some poor relative who was never heard of again. She outlived her husband, so the inheritance is hers to do with as she pleases. She lets Hashamshire Hall, her father's seat in Kent, and lives here."

We drove up to Cliff House, and then Kenton went to be sure that Lady Hob was at home. We walked to the door, which was held open for us by a footman in purple and black livery, stepped into the hall, removed our wraps, and after giving the butler my name, followed him down a hall. Near the end of it, he swung open a pair of doors and announced: "Lady Clareham and Miss Thorpe."

"Felicity!" cried Lady Hob. "You kept your word. And this is Miss Thorpe. How good of you to come, my dear."

"Lavinia," Lady Clareham said, as she strode across the room to Lady Hob. Then she bent over her friend and kissed her cheek.

"Good afternoon, Lady Hob," I said.

"That will be all, Claudine," Lady Hob said to a woman, almost her own age, who stood behind her wheelchair.

"Very good, my lady," her maid said. Claudine left us

then, moving softly out of the room, and closed the doors behind her without a sound.

"Sit down here next to me, my dears," Lady Hob said, gesturing to a sofa next to her chair. "Did Edmond come with you, Felicity?"

While Lady Clareham explained Edmond's absence, I was able to examine Lady Hob. She was, perhaps, seventy years old, with an oily complexion that made the skin stretched across her cheekbones shine. She wore a beautifully made violet-silk dress trimmed with lace of the same color. Her hair, in gray ringlets, peeped out from under a turbanlike lavender bonnet. Her eyes were enormous and flashed with excitement.

"Oh, well, that is a pity. Perhaps next time," she said to Lady Clareham. Then she turned to me. "Miss Thorpe, thank you for coming to see me. As a friend of the family and Julia's daughter's best friend and schoolmate, you are most welcome. I know how very lucky I am that you should consider coming to be with me, and I knew how charming you would be, too."

"Thank you, Lady Hob," I said, smiling at her.

"There are, however, some qualities that would be of enormous help to me, which Felicity and I have not discussed. Do you play the piano and sing?"

"Yes, I do, Lady Hob. Would you like me to play for you?"

"We should be delighted, Miss Thorpe."

I went to the piano, sat down, and played and sang Mendelssohn's *Spring Song*. This, I realized, was why we had been received in the music room.

"Lovely, truly lovely, my dear," Lady Hob cried. "You have a charming voice." She clapped her hands for me as she said this, and then Lady Clareham joined in. "Now— No, please stay seated there. I shall come to you. Felicity, wheel me over beside Miss Thorpe." Then, as she moved beside me, she said: "Now, if I were to sing a little melody like this, 'ta ta, ta, ta, te te te, te dum,' could you repeat it on the piano?"

I repeated the notes on the piano.

"Again, please?" she asked.

I repeated them again, and then once again.

"Excellent! Now, could you add an accompaniment to those notes? Arrange them, so to speak?"

I improvised a simple arrangement of the melody for two hands and then varied it as I repeated it. "I am afraid that is not very good," I said, "but it is not easy to do at a moment's notice. With a little time. . . ."

"But that was superb, superb. Wasn't it Felicity? But not as dance music, as a hymn—as sacred music."

This was easier for me, and my arrangement this time was more successful.

"Oh, brava! Brava! *Yes*, my dear. I suppose you could write it down so that someone else could play it? Yes? *How* I envy you. I could never play, no matter how hard I tried."

"Yes, I could write it down, Lady Hob, but I think a professional musician or composer would. . ."

"No, no! It is for only one hymn that I am writing, and I know *you* could do the music if I hummed it for you. And, having composed the music, so to speak, you would have no difficulty singing it *a cappella?*"

"But why *a cappella?*"

"Because it would be more like an angel singing, and there is no piano in my bedroom. Even if there were, perish the thought, it would be most inappropriate. No, no—only the pure voice could express the joy of the event."

"Event? May I ask what event you refer to, Lady Hob?"

"My death, my dear. The joyous, glorious moment of death."

"Of. . ."

"I know! I can tell by the expression on your face that you think something is terribly wrong, but, my dear, you *do not* understand—most people don't. If they thought, really thought about it, they would begin to realize that all along they have been thinking about it incorrectly."

"Thinking about what?"

"Death, my dear. People say that death is horrible, terrifying, the end of life. 'I don't want to die and put an end to all this, to leave it,' they say. Ah, but *what* is too marvelous, too wonderful to leave? *What?* To satisfy hunger, only to hunger again? To satisfy love, only to need more of it? To acquire the thing we want, only to find that it does not bring satisfaction but only a longing for something else? To find that happiness does not exist? To find that we cannot love another more than we love ourselves?

To watch our children drift away and finally desert us? To see our loved ones and friends suffer illness and pain and then leave us one by one? To watch our young bodies grow old and wrinkle and wither before our very eyes, and to find that all of our knowledge, all our abilities—so dearly won—must ultimately be destroyed?"

She smiled at me, and continued: *"What* can't we leave that is so marvelous? Death, my child, is the proof of life's failure. Life is the penalty, the ordeal. Death is the release, the true birth."

"And the event?" I asked.

"I have it all planned, and you, my dear, will fit in to perfection. At the moment when I am about to be reborn, you will stand at the foot of my bed and sing my 'Hymn of Joy':

> Come, ye tired and weary-hearted,
> With glad smile and radiant brow.
> Life's long shadows have departed—
> All thy woes are over now.

"Then, when I live anew, Reverend Harwich will say the prayers which we have arranged.

"But there is so *much* to be done, and you will help me. The mausoleum must be completed. I have decided on Cathedral Gothic to express the joy. We shall have to have a conference with the builder. My coffin must be perfect. I have had an ebony one made which I will show you, but I do not think the handles are quite right, and I do not like the engraving on the plate. We shall have to talk to the undertaker—perhaps a bronze casket would be better. Then there is the embalming, which must be the *latest* thing. I must talk to Reverend Harwich about the service and change the hymns. Now, we—why, you could sing my 'Hymn of Joy' in the church. Then there is the procession from the church, and the flowers to be specified, and the design and duration of the mourning, and the draping of the mausoleum, and the perpetual care to be arranged. There is so much to do. It has taken so long already, and it is barely begun."

Then Lady Hob pressed the back of her hand to her forehead and said, "It will be soon. I know it will be soon and there is so much to be done."

"The Reverend Quincy Harwich," the butler announced from the doorway.

"Oh, Rector," Lady Hob exclaimed. "Come in, come in and meet my delightful guests. I believe you already know Lady Clareham and *this* is Miss Thorpe. Miss Thorpe is coming to Cliff House as my companion, and she is going to arrange the music for my 'Hymn of Joy' for piano and voice, and we will have it published, and she will write my letters. Come, come sit here with us. Now, if Felicity and Miss Thorpe will forgive us for discussing it for a moment, the hymns for my funeral service must be changed. 'Come Spread the Joy and Glory' has a last verse which is inappropriate, so we shall have to find another. . . ."

They discussed the hymns and the design for her memorial window, which Lady Hob had decided to give to the church. The rector did not think it would be a suitable design to show Lady Hob ascending into heaven from her tomb, so they agreed to think of possible compromises. Then Lady Hob showed us the new design for her mausoleum in some pencil sketches she had had made. They were done, she said, after an engraving of Eaton Hall, Cheshire. Then, while the butler and a footman served cake and wine, she described some books by a Reverend Horace Canker or Canther, which she had recently discovered, whose beliefs about death were essentially her own. How she looked forward to my reading them aloud to her, she said—especially one entitled *When God Throws Open the Doors of Gladness.*

Then the Reverend Harwich left Cliff House. And after that, we were taken to see Lady Hob's coffin. Claudine was summoned to push her chair to the chapel where it was on display. We were asked our opinions of the hardware and the engraving on the plate.

Finally, Lady Clareham having asked for our carriage to be brought around, the butler announced that it was up, and Lady Hob was wheeled along beside us to the entrance hall.

"Now, when will you arrive, Miss Thorpe?" Lady Hob asked. "The sooner the better, my dear, as we have much to do."

"May I write and let you know, Lady Hob? I must be perfectly frank with you. This is my first position. It is important to me, and I don't believe in doing anything important without first considering it thoroughly, even if I feel sure at once that it is the right thing to do. I know you will understand that."

"Well—I don't see why. . ."

"She is right, Lavinia," Lady Clareham said. "Give the child a little time. Don't hurry it. I am sure everything will be all right. Good-by, my dear. We must be off. We have a long drive ahead."

I said good-by to Lady Hob, and then we stepped out to the carriage. Kenton helped us in, and we drove off, waving to Lady Hob who sat in the open doorway waving in return.

"You won't accept it?" Edmond said. "May I know why?"

Edmond was pale and looked drawn—as if he had not eaten or slept for days. It had been seven-forty, on Wednesday evening, before he joined us in the drawing room at Castle Cloud and we had been able to go into dinner. It was unusual for him to be late for a meal.

I had dreaded telling Edmond that I would not take the position with Lady Hob. I had made up my mind to that long before we had left Cliff House the previous afternoon. During a good part of the night and during the train journey back to Barnstaple, where Colen had met me, I had been able to think of little else but telling Edmond. I dreaded his reaction.

"How could I?" I answered Edmond. "Lady Hob thinks of only one thing—death. All her time and thoughts are spent planning for it—building her mausoleum, planning the funeral services, the flowers, the mourning, everything. She has even planned the *moment* of her death—how I would stand at the foot of her bed and sing a hymn she has written for the occasion. She even showed us her coffin. And Cliff House is miles from anywhere. I could not live like that."

"Well, haughty, haughty," Edmond growled. "What if she does think about death? That is natural. Most people do, at one time or another. What does that have to do with you? At least she would feed and house you, which is more than you can expect us to do indefinitely."

For a moment I was stunned by his reply and the

viciousness in his voice. If he had slapped my face, I would not have been more shocked.

Then I said, looking directly at him, "Edmond, I will not accept it. That is all."

He sat across the table glowering back at me, and we stared at each other for several seconds, until he finally looked down at his plate and began to eat. What had happened to him, I wondered? He had been in such a happy mood when he had driven to the station with me two days before. Now, he was acting like a savage. And how could he expect me to be Lady Hob's companion? How *could* he?

Neither he, his mother, nor I spoke another word until the end of the meal. My food tasted like cotton wool, but I was determined to eat it. Finally, long after I had choked down as much of it as I could, Lady Clareham rose from her chair as a signal that it was time for us to leave Edmond and withdraw to the drawing room for our coffee.

At that moment, Edmond looked up at me and said, "I will join you in a few minutes, Mary. I think we should discuss this further."

"There is nothing to discuss, Edmond," I said, "and I am tired from my journey. I should like a breath of evening air, and then I should like to retire to my room."

"And so you shall," he said, giving me an oily smile. "Surely you can spare a few moments. We want to *help* you. Our only concern is for your *welfare*. Surely you must know that. Let us at least talk a little bit about it. There must be gratitude enough to grant that small request."

"I am sorry, Edmond. Of course—whenever you are ready," I said, forcing a smile in return.

Ten minutes later, before we had even finished our coffee, Edmond came into the drawing room followed by Mitchell. He sat down on the couch opposite me, next to his mother.

"Would you like a glass of brandy, Mother, Mary?" he asked. "Another cup of coffee?"

"No thank you, Edmond," his mother said.

"I don't think so, Edmond, thank you," I said.

"A glass of brandy and another cup of coffee for me

then, Mitchell, please. Grandmamma was well?" Edmond asked me.

"Yes, very well. She was disappointed that you did not come with me," I answered.

"Yes, it was a pity I could not go. Tell me about Cliff House, my dear. I understand Lady Hob has furnished it quite sumptuously."

"Yes, everything is very expensively done—it is luxurious."

"Was she pleasant to you?"

"Yes, very. She could not have been more gracious. She was most pleasant."

'Did you meet her personal maid, Claudia?"

"Claudine. Yes."

"And the rest of the servants?"

"We saw only the butler and a footman, though I am sure there was a more than adequate staff. I think Lady Hob would not need to scrimp on servants."

"Grandmamma says the view from the house is breathtaking."

"I suppose so. One can see up and down the coast for miles, but it is terribly isolated."

"More isolated than Castle Cloud?"

"Well, Milton Penderton is just over the hill—Stratton must be five miles from Cliff House. Edmond, I know. . ."

"But surely the servants would go to Stratton for you," Edmond interrupted, "as Colen goes to the village for us. Thank you, Mitchell. How often would you need to go into the village and for what? You said that Lady Hob expected you to sing to her as she was dying. Is her health so poor?"

"She cannot walk very well, according to your grandmother. She was in a wheelchair when we visited her but, other than that, she seemed in good health, though she said at one point that it would not be long. Your grandmother said she would live forever with all that energy and her unflagging interest in her hobby. Her hobby is dying. That is all she talks about—all she thinks about."

"What else would your duties include?"

"Well, writing letters for her, reading to her, being a kind of secretary, musical arranger, and advisor. She seemed to like to get other people's opinions on things, though I do not think she would take their advice very often. She has too definite a mind of her own."

"You have not definitely refused the position, have you?"

"No. . . ."

"Mary, my dear girl, it sounds as if you have been offered a challenging and interesting position with a very good and kind woman in beautiful and luxurious surroundings. Is that not so? No, wait a moment. But Lady Hob has an eccentricity. She is preoccupied with death. Well, my dear, I do not see anything so terrible about that. Many older people think a good deal about it. It is quite natural, you know."

"No doubt in your ministry at Arford St. Mary you saw more of death than most people, Edmond," I said. "And perhaps you have become somewhat hardened to it. A parish priest would look upon death quite differently from a lay person. I have only known it once, when my father died. It was horrible, and I do not want to be reminded of it."

"One can never become hardened to death, Mary, but on the other hand, it is not healthy to suppress thoughts of it. Death is not awesome and terrifying if one has faith in the Lord. It can be a release, a mercy, a kindness, even a blessing, you know."

"Edmond!" Lady Clareham cried. "If you will excuse me, I—" She rushed from the room. She had begun to cry.

"Have you thought of Lady Hob?" Edmond continued. "How much your company would mean to her? How much you could help her? Or have you been thinking only of yourself? You know, Mary, the Lord said, 'It is more blessed to give than to receive.' "

"No—I could not do it, Edmond. I cannot!" I said.

"Think about it very seriously, Mary. We have found you a position that is challenging and interesting, amidst beauty and luxury, where servants will wait on you day and night, which will pay you £60 a year—almost all of which you could save—and, above all, you could help a lonely old woman enormously. I know that would give more satisfaction and joy than you can imagine. When you have thought it over, I know you will see how lucky you are and accept it gladly.

"I will leave you now, and I shall pray for you, Mary—that you may receive God's guidance and enlightenment. Good night, my child."

That evening, Edmond was fifteen minutes late for his cigar.

As soon as he had left me, I walked out onto the east portico and hurried down the steps, across the grass circle, and into the rose garden. David will think I am not coming, I thought. "Make him wait, please make him wait," I whispered, as I ran past the ruined fountain. "I need him. I must talk to him. Please make him wait for me." I ran through the archway in the far wall and up the steps that led to the meadow where the hill path began. A figure stood in the path barring my way.

"Hello."

"David! What are you doing here," I cried.

"I was worried that something might have happened, so I came down to see if I could see anything from here. Are you all right?"

"Oh, David, yes. Thank you for coming," I said. I gave him both my hands which he took in his. "Edmond wanted to talk to me, and I was so afraid you would not wait."

"Well, I did. Now, catch your breath." He stood there looking down into my eyes as if to extract all their secrets from them. He did not release my hands.

"There, that's better," I said in a few moments. Shall we walk up to the top of the hill? I do not think we should stay here. Someone may come into the garden."

I took my hands from his and began to walk up the path. David walked beside me in the grass.

"What about the position in Cornwall?" he asked. "Are you going to take it?"

"No. Oh, I don't know, David," I said. "I don't want to. I don't see how I can, but Edmond thinks I should—that it would be an excellent opportunity for me. It pays £60 a year, and Lady Hob is a very wealthy woman. It would be luxurious—" A shiver ran down my spine. "No, I couldn't."

"Well then, don't," David said.

"Edmond said that I should not think so much of myself, that I could help a lonely old woman enormously—which is true. Am I being selfish? How much do we owe others and how much do we owe ourselves? Where does one responsibility stop and the other begin?"

"I don't know. We cannot damage ourselves, I know that much. If doing something for someone else were to do us *harm*, then I think we should not do it—unless it was for someone we love very much. But it is hard to say. Each case is different, of course. That is not an easy question."

"I don't know if it would do me harm. I don't know how strong I am, David. I don't think I have ever been tested. You see, Lady Hob has what Edmond calls an eccentricity—planning her death."

"What?" David exclaimed.

"She spends all her time and thoughts planning her death. She thinks that life is unhappy—a chain of miserable, unrewarding events—and that death is the beginning of joy. She has written a hymn, called 'Hymn of Joy,' which I would sing while she dies."

"*What?*"

"Well, it is true. She is building a mausoleum for herself which she constantly changes. She has planned the burial service, the hymns, the prayers, the flowers, the mourning, even the embalming. She showed us her casket. Evidently she has been working on this for years. It is her hobby. Don't laugh. I am serious!"

David had burst into uncontrollable laughter, and then, to my amazement, so did I.

"Mad, raving mad," he said, when he could finally control himself. "Stay away from her, Mary. Don't go near her. I won't permit it. Who knows what she might do. You could not live like that. It is *unthinkable!* Edmond must be out of his mind. Seriously, Mary, God only knows what would happen to you if you stayed in that atmosphere very long. It is not for you. Don't do it."

"We should not laugh," I said. "I know it seems funny when I describe it like that, but it really isn't. Lady Hob takes it all very seriously, and she is really very nice. I feel sorry for her in a way, but I shouldn't—she is quite happy, actually. You are right, though. It is out of the question."

"Are you sure there is no money left? Your father must have had a solicitor. Have you contacted him?"

"Mr. Schraw? No, but if there had been anything, he

would have contacted me. He was practically my godfather. Strange, I have not thought of him in years. When Papa and Mother went abroad, he took care of me—well, he kept an eye on me—until I was seven. That was when I was living with Miss Hartong, my governess, in the house on Portman Square. Then, in 1842, when my father bought the house on the Boulevard des Italiens in Paris and gave up the house on Portman Square, Mr. Schraw saw to my schooling—first at Mrs. Turner's in London, and then in 1845 he came and took me to Windsor to Mrs. Romilly's. That was the last time I saw him. He sent me a short letter on my birthday that year, and that is the last time I heard from him. I know he handled Papa's legal affairs until his death, but I have not heard from him since."

"Don't you think you should have a talk with him?" David asked.

"Perhaps, but I am sure there is nothing left. Papa would have told me. He knew it was all gone. You have no idea how we lived. Why, the house on the Boulevard des Italiens was enormous, and he entertained lavishly. The dinners and balls were—like fairyland. Members of the court came. Madame Adelaide, the King's sister, was frequently there. I shall never forget the enormous bonnets she wore—ostrich feathers out to here."

"What about the revolution?"

"We fled to Brussels, and then I returned to Mrs. Romilly's where I met Vivian. But I was back with Papa in 1852. We lived in Vienna, Prague, Rome, Marienbad, and Bern for various lengths of time and in Vienna for a year, as I think I told you. Papa spent a fortune on the houses and the servants and on entertaining. It is no wonder there is nothing left. If there had been, we would not have lived so quietly for the last six months in The Hague. But why am I boring you with all this?"

"You're not. Shall we sit down?" he asked. We had reached the top of the hill, and he led the way to the blocks where we sat down. "Are you cold? Why didn't you bring your shawl?"

"No, I am fine, thank you, David."

"I have to go away for a few days. I wish I didn't. There are some rents that are due which have not been paid, and I shall have to go and find out why they haven't.

Don't let Edmond talk you into taking that position, Mary."

"How long will you be gone?" I asked.

"I don't know. I hope to be back by Monday. Will you meet me here on Monday night, and if I should not be here, would you come again on Tuesday?"

"Yes," I said. I sat smiling at him for a moment. I loved his open honesty and directness. I trusted him and felt, somehow, secure when I was with him. I did not want our time together to end, so I said, "I am surprised you did not go into the bank, David. Had you thought of that?"

"I did," he said. "I went into the bank as a junior clerk in—1851, to learn the business. I was not very good at it because I hated it, or I hated it because I wasn't very good at it—I don't know which. I got into some rather bad habits in those days, trying to escape the responsibility and the boredom, I suppose. Nothing serious.

"When Father retired, my older brother, William, became governor of the bank. He is a natural banker. He loves it. At thirty-five he was recognized as an authority—outstanding—all over England. He did not want me in the bank, and he was right. I was a liability. Well, since Father would be spending most of his time here, at Oakland Park, he decided to give the big house in Hanover Square to William. It would suit his position. Cecilea, his wife, had always had her eye on it. And Father could stay there the few times he would be in London.

"I know now that Father was worried about me and asked me to come down here on the pretext of helping him move in, but he really wanted to talk to me and find out what was wrong. I will always be grateful to him for that."

"And you fell in love with Oakland Park," I said.

"Yes, as I told you. Wait till you see the house! The bricks are an orange-pink color and, strangely enough, it is in the Dutch style. Father had had the gardens redone before he moved in—they are beautiful. I had learned to ride at school, and I was soon riding out with Hodson, the estate manager, and reading the books on the estates. And you know the rest. Father and I had a difficult time talking—really talking—at first, but we soon got to know each other quite well and got to like each other quite well, too. He is delighted with the way it has turned out. I think he has always wanted to establish a line of landed gentry. I guess I fit right into his plans.

"But it is the farm that fascinates me. Take manure—if you had told me five years ago that the principals of manuring, Lowe's and Gilbert's principals, would be one of the most exciting things, I would have said you were out of your mind. Do they manure in Holland?"

"I don't know, David. I am afraid I did not care much for the farm. It was hot and smelly in the summer and muddy, cold, and steamy in the winter. I didn't. . ."

"Oh, well, Oakland Park Farm is not like that. Could you come and see it? We could ride over together, and I will show you what we have been doing."

"I wish I could, but I have no habit. I asked Edmond if I could borrow one of Vivian's, but he was horrified, and since they are in mourning, I would not be allowed to ride out anyway. So I am afraid I must remain a prisoner at Castle Cloud. And if anyone should look for me and find that I am not down there now, they would be horrified too. I must be going back. Thank you again, David."

I stood then and David stood too.

"For what?" he asked, as he reached over and took both my hands in his.

"For putting my mind at rest and for making me feel that I am not completely alone. Good night, David."

I pulled away from him then, and walked to the path and down it a few steps, then looked back at him and waved.

He stood looking after me, waving in return.

✠ Chapter Six ✠

"EDMOND," I said, at breakfast the following morning, "I have definitely decided not to take the position with Lady Hob. I have thought about what you said very carefully, but I do not know what staying in that atmosphere for very long would do to me, and I cannot risk it."

"What do you intend to do then?" he asked.

"Well—surely that is not the only position that is available. There must be someone else somewhere who wants a companion or governess."

"And how are you going to find this person?"

"Well, you said you wanted to help me. Do you? Perhaps I should go to London and wait for Vivian to return. I have intruded upon you and your parents. . ."

"Nonsense! Of course we want to help you. I simply meant that positions for young ladies—positions with the right kind of people, that would be right for you—do not grow on trees. They are not to be found everywhere, you know. You seem to be a normal, strong, healthy young lady. Lady Hob's atmosphere, as you put it, would, I assure you, have no effect whatsoever. But, if you persist in this attitude, we shall have to find you something else. Something that is perfect—that has not the slightest blemish of inconvenience or displeasure about it."

"Edmond, please! I will not be difficult to satisfy. I do not expect too much."

"Very well, we will ask about," he said. Then he got up from the table and strode from the room.

After breakfast I strolled into the hall and then into the hall chamber. I loved the little room with its sixteenth-century paneling (which had been saved from the old house) and its pale-blue and peach silk draperies and chair coverings. It was the only other room on the main floor of Castle Cloud that was open, besides the drawing room and the dining room and the Chapel. Yet no one seemed to use it. I was standing there, admiring the carved Indian screen again, when I heard voices in the hall.

"It is too much, my lady. You cannot carry all that all the way to the village." It was Mrs. Foley's voice.

I walked to the doorway, then, just in time to see Lady Clareham take a gray metal pitcher, like a dairy pitcher, from Mrs. Foley.

"I can manage it perfectly well, Mrs. Foley. It is not a very long walk, and I can stop and rest if I need to."

"Very good, my lady, but I think you should wait until Colen can drive you there."

Then Mrs. Foley turned and walked toward the stairway to the servants' hall. At the same time, Lady Clareham must have sensed that someone was watching because she turned to see me standing in the doorway.

"Good morning, Mary," she called.

"Good morning, Lady Clareham," I said, hurrying to her side. "I could not help overhearing. You are not going to *walk* to the village carrying all that? Can't Colen take you?"

"He thinks one of the horses may have blackleg. He has isolated her and does not want to leave her, at least not today if he can help it. He is quite right, of course."

"Then you must let me help you. Let me carry the basket."

"No, Mary. I can manage, my dear."

"But I have nothing to do this morning. I have nothing to do at any time. I would *like* to help you. Please!"

"Very well, my dear. That is very good of you. Would you carry the milk for me then?"

"Milk? With pleasure, Lady Clareham. But where are you taking milk?"

She handed me the pitcher and I took it from her. It was not very heavy and it was easy to carry. It hung from a wire handle, rather like a small pail, and its narrow neck was fitted with a hinged top, so there was no danger of the milk spilling.

"It is for a poor child in the village," Lady Clareham said. "She lives in the very first cottage one comes to as one walks down the path from the Horse Monument. I do not think Edmond would mind. She is on the outskirts of the village, and we are not likely to meet anyone. Then you could bring the pitcher home while I go to the church-yard with these, if you would."

"I would love to! I feel so useless. I—I wish I could do more. They are lovely," I said, peeping into her paper cone of flowers.

"I picked them last night. They seem to last better if they have stood in a bucket of cold water overnight."

As we talked we began walking toward the door to the east portico. Mitchell must have known that Lady Clare-ham was going out because he stood at the door waiting to open it for us. Usually, he might or might not be found in the hall, and I could not help wondering if anyone had called recently and found that there was no one to answer the door.

Then as we descended the staircase outside, I asked, "Has the little girl no mother?"

Just then, Sarah came bounding toward us.

"Oh, Sarah," Lady Clareham said, "you cannot come with us. There is Colen, thank goodness. Colen! Colen, call Sarah. She cannot come with us today."

Colen called Sarah several times, and finally after we had patted her, she obeyed.

"There is a dog where we are going, and I would not want there to be a fight, though they probably know each other already," Lady Clareham said. "No, the girl's mother died giving birth to a younger brother twelve years ago. That was shortly after we returned from India at the end of my husband's term as governor-general. I did not know the villagers yet, at that time. The poor child is not married and is going to have a baby."

"The dowager countess mentioned her, then," I said. "She said that you were both looking after unwed moth-ers-to-be."

"Yes. The Reades are terribly poor, and she does not get the proper food. Her father is a wastrel who would spend anything he could get his hands on in the village pub. Her little brother, Stanley, works on Arthur Colehill's farm when there is work for him, but he cannot bring home more than four shillings a week, if that, and a few potatoes. Mr. Colehill is always threatening to take back the cottage, but I will not allow it—trustees or no trustees. He could not get anyone to live there anyway, and he knows it. I do not see how they survive. Of course, they always have meat or fish to eat."

"Her father is William Reade, the poacher?"

"Yes."

"Edmond mentioned him."

"Oh. Well, I do what I can, which is not much, of course. I have been taking her milk to drink, and I have butter and a loaf of fresh bread and a jar of Mrs. Foley's preserves in the basket, and an old mantelet of mine which I am sure she can use in the evenings. Then when I go, I give her a few shillings to buy sugar and flour and such at the store, and I have asked Dr. Norton to look in once in a while. The baby must be due at any time now."

"The poor girl," I said.

"Yes. This whole thing has upset her terribly, but she won't say who the father is. She is very unhappy."

When we reached the top of the hill, I suggested we stop to rest for a few minutes in the shade of the Horse Monument because I thought Lady Clareham looked tired, but she said she would rather continue down the hill and rest in the wood near the bottom of it. There, we sat on a crumbling stone wall in the shade, neither of us wishing to speak until a soft melodious call, rather flutelike, floated down to us from the hillside above.

"What is that?" I asked. "Lovely, isn't it?"

"A curlew," she said. "It is called the bird with the silver throat."

"It is a beautiful sound. I think Castle Cloud is the loveliest place on earth. I hope Edmond does not spoil it with his restorations."

"Restorations! Huh. I am afraid he is a dreamer, and not a very intelligent dreamer. James, on the other hand, was. He had a brilliant, enquiring mind. He wanted to know—to understand. And poor Vivian—well, there is not very much point—"

"Vivian will soon be home," I said, when I realized she would not continue. "The Scottish air and scenery would restore anyone. And then you will feel better. You must miss her terribly."

"Yes, my dear, terribly, but this will not help Alice Reade, nor will it get me to the churchyard and back before luncheon." As she spoke, she stood, and I could tell that she fought to keep from crying.

Then, without speaking further, we walked through the wood to the field beyond it. Here the path widened gradually to become a grassy track which led to the Reades' cottage and, beyond it, became one of the village lanes.

The Reades' cottage was of cob, that mixture of clay and straw so typical of cottages in that part of Devonshire. It was one story high with a loft under a sloping thatched roof. The building had been whitewashed at one time and stood behind seven or eight feet of garden, a tangle of matted grasses growing between pieces of rusty iron and rotting wooden planks. The cottage glowered at us as we left the track, crossed its garden, and knocked on its door.

But our knock was not answered. Then Lady Clareham knocked again, and when there was still no answer, she pressed the latch, opened the door, and we entered the house just in time to see a small gray shape scurry across the dirt floor and vanish behind a chest beneath the rear window.

Inside, the cottage was a single large room with a ladder leading to a sleeping loft. On one side of the room's simple fireplace stood a pine cupboard, and on the other side of it, pots and pans hung on the wall below a shelved niche holding dishes, bowls, and crocks. Besides the chest and cupboard, the room was furnished with an oak table, which stood in the center of the room, several wooden, rush-bottomed chairs, and a bed. The bed was unmade and had been placed in the corner of the room, having been brought down for Alice, I supposed, from the loft. The room smelled of damp woolens and spoiled food. There was no one there.

"Alice," Lady Clareham called. She set her basket on the table and then took the pitcher from me and placed it beside the basket. "Alice?" No one answered. Then she walked to the niche, looked into the crocks, and finding one empty, she lifted it to her nose. "Phew!" she said. We will leave the pitcher, and I can collect it the next time I come."

As she spoke, I noticed that the rear door of the cottage stood ajar, and I went over to it, pushed it open, and stepped outside to breathe the fresh air. There I saw a shed, a woodshed I supposed, at the rear of what had probably been a vegetable garden, but was now a weed patch. And then, against the rear wall of the cottage, I saw

Alice sitting on a bench in the sun, staring off into space. I knew it was Alice Reade because she was very large with child, but I was shocked at her age. She could not have been sixteen yet. She was a blond-haired girl with enormous brown eyes and skin like a pale-pink rose petal.

"Hello," I said to her.

"Alice?" Lady Clareham cried, as soon as she heard me speak. "Oh, there you are. I was afraid something had happened to you. How are you feeling today?"

"All right," Alice murmured.

Then Lady Clareham sat down on the bench beside the girl, but I remained standing a few feet away from them. "I brought you some milk, and butter, and bread, and some lovely strawberry preserves," Lady Clareham said. "I have left them on the table for you."

Alice did not reply. She looked straight ahead of her into the field beyond the garden.

"And I want you to take these," Lady Clareham continued, "in case there is anything you need." She reached into her purse which was in the basket, drew out several coins, and held them out to Alice. When Alice did not move, Lady Clareham took Alice's hand, put the coins in the palm, closed the fingers on them, and then let the closed fist fall back into her lap.

Still Alice gazed at the field beyond the garden.

"And I have brought you this mantelet," Lady Clareham said, "to keep you warm." As she said this, she draped the mantelet across Alice's lap.

At that moment, Alice turned her head and looked into Lady Clareham's face. Tears flooded the girl's eyes and crept down her cheeks. But she said nothing, and after ten seconds or so, she looked away. During that time, Alice had not smiled. I had seen not even a hint of a smile on her tiny, sullen mouth. If I had, I would have known that the look she had given Lady Clareham was one of gratitude. But it had not been gratitude. It was as though Lady Clareham somehow intensified Alice's anguish.

We left the girl immediately after that, and when Lady Clareham and I reached the front of the cottage, we parted. She walked toward the churchyard and I walked back to the path and up the hill to the Horse Monument. It was eleven twenty-five when I reached the hilltop, and I decided to sit down on my building block to enjoy the view. Perhaps, I thought, I shall wait here for Lady Clareham. She should not be long in the churchyard, and then we can walk down the hill together.

As I sat there, a gentle breeze wandered in from the sea and brushed me. The ocean stretched calm and empty from Monte Bay to Hartland Point, its horizon unbroken by mast or sail. Above, flocks of woolly clouds slept in the sky. And beyond the village, farm laborers in a long meadow loaded a wagon with hay as the wagon inched along.

"Peace," I remember saying to myself. "How peaceful it is. Everything will be all right. How can God, or whatever has created all this beauty, be planning something ugly or unpleasant for me?"

To my left, Castle Cloud and its pavilions lay hidden behind a border of trees which, with the narrow hillside meadow beyond, formed a backdrop for the rose garden. Only the very top of the Castle's dome and the lantern which crowned it showed above the trees. But from where I sat, I could see the greenhouse and its flanking glasshouse extensions and the drive in front of them. They lay below like an enormous rock crystal, its facets flashing here and there in the sun.

Did something move inside the near greenhouse? For a moment I thought I had seen a dark object pass from the glasshouse into the central building, but I could not be sure because of the sparkling glass and the towering, dried palm and fern leaves which hid anything under them from view. Then, as I stared, I *did* see something move. In a moment, a glass door opened and a man stepped out into the sunlight. It was Edmond. He looked about, and then he closed the door behind him, walked down the narrow pebbled walk, and disappeared behind the trees.

What in the world had Edmond been doing there? It was natural to wonder, and I decided to walk down to the greenhouse and see if I could tell. I need not take the path that led through the trees. I could descend in a direct line down through the grass. And I would have plenty of time to explore before luncheon.

So I walked down the hill, and when I reached the building I paused and looked about to see if anyone was watching—just as Edmond had done. I had no reason to be furtive, but if someone should ask what I was doing there, what would I say? I saw no one, however, and I stepped inside, closing the door behind me. The interior was as I had last seen it. Dead foliage hung motionless above me. The air was torrid and bitter-smelling, and there was no sound except for my footsteps. Then I walked to the open doorway which separated the conservatory from the easternmost greenhouse (where I had first seen Edmond), and into the long, low structure. Benches of about table height edged the greenhouse and also formed a long, wide island in its center. Here seeds had been sown and slips had been planted in flats, and when the plants had grown large enough, they had been transplanted into pots of various sizes to be planted in the gardens when they were ready.

Now the pots and flats sat where they had been placed years before, still holding their dried plants and seedlings. Dusty spiderwebs hung in the darkness beneath them. A veneer of dust covered everything—it covered the potting bench in the corner, and the pots, and trowels, and boxes, and sieves, and cans, and bottles, and *all* the gardener's paraphernalia. It covered the curled, yellow brown newspaper clippings, and magazine pages, and coils of wire, and the shelf of books fastened to the wall above it. All the dead plants and benches were dusty. But nowhere could I see that the dust had been disturbed.

Had Edmond come to stand where I stood only to look about? Perhaps. Perhaps he had been looking toward his future restorations, but I did not think so. If that had been the case, would he have left the place in so furtive a manner?

I retraced my steps then, and left the conservatory. My visit had accomplished nothing.

Friday, July 11th, the day after I had seen Edmond in the glasshouses, began gray and overcast. After breakfast, I walked to the stables to visit the horses and then, as I hurried back to the house under a steady rain, I saw something which puzzled me. I decided to go straight up to visit my host and ask him about what I had seen.

The ever-present Ahmad opened Lord Clareham's door, and I stepped into the room.

"Mary, my child, come in," Lord Clareham cried. "You

have been neglecting me. Why have you not come to see me? Sit here."

"I wanted to come," I said, "but I heard you were not feeling well, and I did not want to tire you."

"I am better, much better. There was feeling in my right foot yesterday—it is coming back, you know. Edmond tells me you have declined to accept the position with Lavinia. You should reconsider. A splendid opportunity, my dear."

"I could not live in that atmosphere, Lord Clareham," I said.

"Humm."

"I could not live with her constant preoccupation with—death."

"Humm. You are quite positive about that?"

"Quite positive."

"Well, we shall have to find something else for you then."

"That is very kind of you, Lord Clareham."

"We want to see you settled in pleasant surroundings with a future—with some money coming in that you can put in the bank against your old age. I often think if *I* had thought about that—perhaps if I had done it all differently . . . One thinks about these things when one is old, you know."

"But how can you say that?" I asked. "Your contribution to England and the empire has been incalculable. Why, India would have fallen to pieces if it had not been for you, and then where would we be?"

"Thank you, my dear. That is very kind of you, very kind indeed. Would have remained in pieces, my dear. Yes—one India. But it could all fall apart again. Perhaps it will, and if it does, I shall have spent my life for nothing—neglected my properties, my son's inheritance—for nothing. But, Mary, if you could see those people—the disease and the poverty on one side, and the religious fanaticism on the other. It would be worth anything to help them." For a few moments, Lord Clareham lay silently staring at the ceiling, and then at last he turned his head to look at me, and smiled. "Well—" he sighed.

I returned his smile, and then to break the silence that followed, I said, "I saw something rather odd a while ago, Lord Clareham. At least I think it was odd."

"Yes, my dear?" he asked.

"After breakfast, I went to the stables to visit the horses, and as I was returning to the house, I happened to look into one of the main floor windows of the building where the grooms and coachmen lived. A man was standing at the window looking out, but when he realized that I had seen him, he quickly stepped aside, out of sight. He had very red hair and a red mustache, and I think he held a riding crop in his hand. It was the window nearest the house. Don't you think that was odd? Does he work here?"

"McComb," said Lord Clareham. "Estate agent for the trustees. No more honest than Alsrich or Griffith, agents for me while I was in India—spent more time stealing than managing. Well, there wasn't much left anyway. John was a spendthrift—jewels, and furniture, and paintings, and horses, and carriages, and gardeners with plants from the four corners of the world, and balls, and parties. And borrow, borrow, borrow, mortgage, mortgage. So now the trustees handle it all to try to pay it back, giving us a pittance as they go, and Douglas McComb manages the estates for them.

"That room is the agent's office. Not McComb's office—he has a house in the village and does his work there. That was the agent's office while we were in control. It is not used anymore. He has some dealings with Edmond. *What* dealings, I cannot imagine, but I would like to know."

"Well," I said, "I am glad it was not a robber or a fugitive. Of course I immediately thought of the convict that escaped from Dartmoor the last time I was here. Vivian was petrified. Do you remember? Everytime we went out walking in the evening, she was sure he lurked behind every bush or tree."

"Yes, I believe he was caught in Exmouth or Sidmouth—in quite the opposite direction."

Then we reminisced a bit about that happy week. Lord Clareham seemed to remember every detail of it. In a few minutes Lady Clareham joined us, and then I left them alone together and went to my room.

Since the hem on my gray marino dress needed mending, and since there would be time to repair it before luncheon, I carried the skirt and my sewing things to the chair by the window in my room, sat down, and began to sew. Outside, the bay below me lay like a great plate of polished steel in the gray light. How somber and almost forbidding it looked under the gray sky.

Everything had seemed a little more somber and gray since my visit to Alice Reade. I began to think of her again, as I had many times since our visit two days before. That poor girl—how crushed and utterly without hope she had seemed. I thought of her lovely, still-childish face, and the defeat I had seen there. If only I could help her, I thought. If only there were something I could say to make it a little easier. Did she have any friends, I wondered? Her father, whom I had seen that day in the hedged walk, looked rather like an animal. Was he kind to her? Did she need someone to talk to perhaps—someone nearer her own age? There could not have been more than six years difference in our ages, and if she did, perhaps I could help. So I decided that if the weather cleared in the afternoon, I would go down to the Reades' cottage and try.

The weather did clear after luncheon—the sun came out and the clouds parted to reveal a cool blue sky. It had become a lovely day for a walk, and as I walked up the hill toward the monument, I hoped that Sarah would not want to come along. I loved the little dog's company, but I remembered Lady Clareham saying that the Reades had a dog and that it was no place to take Sarah. Fortunately, she did not appear, and in fifteen minutes my solitary walk to the hilltop and down to the valley beyond ended at the Reades' cottage door. I knocked.

"Ay?" a voice roared.

I waited a moment and then knocked again.

"Ay? Who be it?"

Then I heard someone moving across the floor inside, and then the door was flung open by William Reade. He stood there for a moment gaping at me. He wore a dirty, gray, woolen undershirt and a pair of pants, but no shoes or stockings. I knew he had been eating because what looked like wet gravy clung to his beard and he still held a spoon in his hand.

"Ay?" he asked.

"Mr. Reade?" I said. "Good afternoon. I am—Miss Thorpe. I came to see Alice. Is she at home?"

"Ay, her's at home. Come in, miss." He stepped back

into the room and shouted toward the bed in the corner: "Alice, get up. You got a visitor from the big house. *Alice!*" Then he turned back to me and said, "It be pitiful, pitiful. All her does is lay there all day long. Her never say a word, never work, never cook. It be pitiful—my poor girl."

As he spoke, Alice sat up on the edge of the bed and stared at me while she brushed the hair out of her face. I don't blame her for being surprised, I thought. I wondered if she even remembered me.

Then Mr. Reade went back to the table, sat down, and resumed eating what I supposed was some kind of stew. A pot simmered over the fire in the fireplace. It smelled bitter and gamey.

"Fetch that chair for the lady, and put it over here," he bellowed at his daughter, as he directed her with his spoon.

Alice brought the chair, placed it on the other side of the table from her father, and then sat down in a chair against the wall behind him and gazed at the floor.

I sat down, thinking that this was very different from what I had expected. I had imagined a quiet, confidential talk with Alice on the bench in the rear garden. And I wondered frantically what I should do next. But I need not have worried. William Reade had decided to take charge.

"Why be you up at the big house, miss? You be staying there long?" he asked between sips from a metal cup. It contained whisky. I could smell it.

"Well—I came to visit my friend, Lady Vivian," I said, "who, unfortunately, has gone traveling."

"Gone traveling, has her? Well, well."

"I visited Alice the other day with Lady Clareham, and I thought I would stop by to see if there is anything I can do."

"Aw, my poor girl. My poor little girl. Ay, there be much that can be done. Much that can be done, and her not married with no husband to keep her and the baby when it comes. There be the medicine, and the doctor, and the special food, and clothes for the baby. It cost a lot to have a baby, miss. It cost a lot. A very costly thing it be. And us being so poor—without a shilling to our name.

Without a shilling, miss." He waved his spoon back and forth like an upside-down pendulum as he spoke.

"Yes, I suppose it is," I said.

"Not a shilling to our name, and how us pay for the baby is what worry me, miss. Don't want nothing to happen to my little Alice or her baby, do us, miss?"

Alice looked up at me warily.

"Mr. Reade, I am afraid I do not have any money to give you—I do not have any, but if there is anything else I can do. . . ."

"What else, miss?" He emptied the cup in a gulp, spilling some of the whiskey down his beard and undershirt. "What else?" Then after scrutinizing me for a moment, his eyes narrowed, and he said, "Us don't want nothing to happen to my little Alice. There be no better girl in Devonshire than my Alice, nor no prettier one, neither. Ask them up at the big house if there be a prettier girl in the county than my. . ."

"Papa!" Alice cried.

"I know what go on hereabout," William Reade said. "I know the whereabout of every hare in this parish, the field where her lay, the rushes what be her form, and every smoot and gate where her pass. You think I don't know what the gentry do? I know *everything* you be doing.

"I know a rabbit run from a hare run—the rabbit hop, the hare gallop. And I know where the gentry walk, and when, and why he walk there.

"I watch a hen pheasant take care of her young. Her fight off a stoat for her young. What do the gentry do? Him don't take care of his young. Him don't even know his young."

"Papa!" Alice cried.

As she spoke, her father swept his cup off the table. It bounced across the floor and landed near a silent mongrel dog, part sheep dog and part greyhound, which lay by the foot of the bed staring at me.

"I know," William Reade continued, "where the pheasants sleep in the grass at night with their tails tucked together, and I can come up to a covey of them, with the wind in my face, and touch them before them know I be there. And I can do the same to a gentleman from the big house—him never know I be there.

"I know where the partridge feed in the morning and

what time. I know what a pheasant like on the plate of her trap, and I know why the shrew lie dead along the lane. I know how the stoat get the wood pigeon, and how she kill a rabbit or a rat, and how the weasel kill a partridge. I know a weasel from a miniver—ay, there be a difference—and how the owl get her. The gentry own the land and own the animal on it, but them don't know about the animal or the land. And when somebody *know* the animal and *know* the land, take care if he get mad."

Then William Reade got up from the table, pulled on a pair of boots, took a jacket from a peg on the wall and put it on, grabbed the pair of heavy leather gloves which had been lying on the table in front of me, strode to the door, opened it, and walked out into the daylight. The silent dog followed him.

I watched him disappear and then turned to Alice. She was staring at me—wondering, I supposed, what I was thinking. "Alice," I said, "what did your father mean? Why has he been spying on us up at the Castle? I saw him one day looking down at the little building we call the bathing pavilion. What did he want?"

"Don't know," Alice whispered.

"He would not have told me if I had asked him, would he?"

Alice shook her head slowly in reply.

"Don't be afraid," I said. "No one is going to hurt you. You remember me, don't you? I came to see you the other day with Lady Clareham."

"You mustn't mind Papa, miss," she said. "He don't know what he's saying when he drinks."

"Won't you call me Mary? I had hoped we could be friends. Could we be friends do you think?"

Alice nodded her head.

"How are you feeling today?"

"All right." Again she gazed down at the floor.

"Your baby must be coming soon, now. What does Doctor Norton say?" She did not answer. "Aren't you happy about having your baby, Alice? Just think how beautiful it will be. Will it be a boy or a girl, do you think?"

She looked up at me then with tears in her eyes, and even in the gloom of the cottage, I recognized the look of intense anguish that I had seen on her face two days before. I got up and carried my chair across to her and sat down.

"Alice," I said, "tell me why it hurts so much."

Alice turned her head away from me and looked back at the floor. It was almost as if she watched something there.

"I should think it would be lovely to have a baby," I said, "and to bathe him, and feed him, and watch him grow. To watch him take his first step and say his first word. Of course it might be a little girl. I think *I* would love a little girl, but then I would not mind if it were a little boy. Alice?" She did not move. She did not look up at me. "Is it the baby's father? Does he know?"

Alice nodded. It was a barely perceptible movement.

"And he doesn't care?"

Alice shook her head ever so slightly.

"Oh, my dear, I am so sorry. But wait until you have had your baby. He will want to see his child, surely. And a girl is always prettiest after she has had her baby—that is *true*. Your baby will be pretty too. And when he sees his own child, and sees how pretty you are—well, it might be very different then."

I sat there for a long minute hoping that Alice would say something or look at me, but she continued to study that same spot of floor. Then she got up and, without looking back, walked slowly to the bed and flung herself down on her side with her face to the wall.

Finally, after I had watched her lie there for a few moments, I got up and walked across to the bed. "Alice," I said, "I will come to see you again in a few days. If you need anything in the meantime, send your brother to the Castle for me. Bless you." Then I left the cottage, closing the door quietly behind me. I could not think of anything else to do.

I felt so defeated as I walked away from the cottage. I have not helped, I thought. I have probably made things worse, instead. How can we know when to try to help someone and when to stay out of it? Had I been a busybody—sticking my nose where it did not belong, only making things worse? What else could I have said to her? I felt so inadequate, and, somehow, humiliated. I wished I had not come.

*   *   *

That evening, Lady Clareham sat opposite me in the drawing room of Castle Cloud. We were drinking our coffee, and I had just finished telling her about my visit to Alice that afternoon and how defeated I felt by it. I had not mentioned the curious things Mr. Reade had said because, since I did not understand them, I did not think I could tell her about them properly.

She had not objected to my visit. Instead, she had seemed rather pleased. And finally after we had sat silently for some time, she said, "I will leave you now, Mary. Do not ever feel bad about being kind to someone, no matter how it turns out." She put down her cup and saucer and stood. "Good night, my dear." Then she left the room.

After that, I dawdled over my coffee for a few minutes, thinking about the events of the day and about David. If only he were at Oakland Park, I thought; I wished I could walk up to the Horse Monument and know that he would meet me there. Sunday—Sunday he would be home. Only two more days. On Sunday I would walk up there and see.

I hated meeting him in secret, but what else could I do? Edmond's ultimatum that I avoid contact with the neighbors was absurd. Openly defying him, however, would serve no purpose—it would only anger him needlessly. So, if I were going to meet David occasionally at the Horse Monument, I supposed it would be prudent to walk in the opposite direction—down to the stone bridge.

When I had finished my coffee, I left the drawing room and sauntered out onto the west portico. Edmond stood there smoking his cigar. To be polite, I asked him if he cared to walk down to the bridge with me, but to my relief, he declined. Then I descended the steps and walked down the drive away from him, knowing that he would rather I were not there. Perhaps that was what he was thinking at that very moment as he watched me walk away from him. This thought made me impatient to escape his sight. I rounded the bend in the drive. It was there that Sarah joined me, and she kept me company all the way to the river and back.

When we reached the bridge, that lavender, velvety evening, I leaned against the stone parapet and looked out across the bay to where a man rowed his small boat from one of the yards in Appledore to a schooner riding at anchor, just offshore. He lit the schooner's riding light and then rowed to the next boat and then to the next, until the lights of six lamps danced across the water toward me and it was time to go back to the house.

As I walked up the hill, I thought about my letters to Lady Hob and the dowager countess Clareham that remained to be written. I had procrastinated about them long enough, and I decided to write them that evening so that Colen could mail them first thing in the morning. So, when I reached the house, I walked around to the stable yard, instead of going directly inside, and asked Colen if he would take the letters and mail them when he went for the post in the morning. I said that I would leave them on the tray in the dining room. I was glad that I had done this because I would not have been able to tell Mitchell about the letters. He had disappeared when I entered the house, and I did not see him again until morning.

Then I took paper, envelopes, pen and ink, and two stamps from the desk in the drawing room and carried them to my bedroom. (I would return the pen, ink, and paper I had not used, in the morning.) And as I lit the lamp for myself, I could not help remembering how my room at Lewis House had been prepared for me after dinner. It had been the same here at Castle Cloud when I visited four years ago—the lamps had been lit for me, the bed had been turned down, the curtains had been drawn, and my nightdress had been laid out. I had never done any of these things for myself, except at school. Well, I thought, I suppose I had better get used to doing them.

Finally, when I got down to the letters, I found that they were difficult to write. It is not easy to refuse generosity and help. But by eleven o'clock they were done, and then I addressed the envelopes, tucked the letters inside them, stamped them, lit a candle, and carried the letters to the dining room.

But then, as I was about to leave the dining room, I saw Edmond's bedroom door, on the gallery above me, fly open and Jane Spence flounce out of it. Immediately she whirled around again to face the lighted room.

"Why?" she gasped. "What have I done? What have I done?" She stood there weeping hysterically for perhaps ten seconds until, suddenly tense and more controlled, she cried, "Don't you ever speak to me like that again, do you hear? Don't you ever dare!" Then she stamped off toward the stairway, and Edmond closed his door. I blew out my candle. I could think of no good coming from a meeting with Jane Spence at that time of night in her present mood.

Shortly, she emerged from the stairwell shielding her candle and swept across the rotunda to the stairs of the servants' hall. I could see her tear-streaked face quite plainly. Reflecting the candlelight, Jane's eyes flashed with anger.

As usual, Edmond was seated at the table when I entered the dining room the following morning. "Good morning, Edmond," I said, as I waited for Mitchell to help me be seated. How reluctantly he held the chair for me. I could feel his aversion.

"Good morning, Mary," Edmond said.

"Thank you, Mitchell," I said. "I will have the usual, I think."

"You slept late this morning, Mary," Edmond said, looking at his watch.

"I don't think any later than usual, Edmond," I replied.

"My dear, Mitchell has the breakfast ready at nine o'clock. There are only you and me to serve, and Mitchell has a great deal to attend to during the morning in the absence of anyone to help him."

"Yes, of course. I am sorry, Edmond. I will try to be a little more prompt."

"It is so easy to forget that other people function in the same sphere that we do, Mary, and that the things we do affect the things they do. We must constantly think of others in order not to affect them adversely. Oh, I know, selfishness is only too human, but one finds that consideration for others is a very easy habit to acquire if one will only try. The Lord said, 'help one another, be considerate of one another, be kind to one another.' A blessed man, Mary, is one who thinks more of others than he does of himself. He will surely inherit the kingdom of heaven. We must strive for that quality of selflessness."

"Some more coffee, and another scone please, Mitchell," he concluded.

During the lecture, I busied myself with my egg and

toast, and when he had finished, I said, "The pulpit has lost an eloquent preacher, Edmond. Really, you must find another living. You deprive so many of such wisdom."

He did not reply, but sat across from me moodily eating and drinking his coffee.

At length I said, "Have you been asking about on my behalf Edmond? How is your search for my position coming?"

"Certainly," he said. "Well enough. As I said, the kind of position you require does not grow on trees. If one is to be particular, one must be patient, my dear." He finished with an unctuous smile.

"I am so glad. May I ask a favor of you, Edmond? Would you ask Mrs. Foley for the keys to the library cases for me? If I am to be patient, I must have some way to occupy my time, and time goes quickly for me if I have a book to read. Mrs. Foley dislikes me so, and I am sorry to say she has been rather rude. I would rather not ask her myself."

"Mary, I hardly have time to take care of my own responsibilities here at Castle Cloud. I am the only man able to see to them, not to mention the heir to the estates. I simply do not have time to take on the additional duties of the housekeeper. I am sure you are imagining things. Simply ask Mrs. Foley for the keys and she will give them to you. Now, if you will excuse me, I have some things to attend to." He got up then, and left the room.

But it was not until the next day that I as much as caught sight of Mrs. Foley. I must admit that I had not tried to find her. I felt that any encounter with her would be unpleasant, and I wished to avoid it. On Sunday morning, however, as I wandered from the drawing room into the rotunda, I heard her voice.

The door to the hall chamber had been closed, but it opened as I looked toward it, and then I heard Mrs. Foley say, "We cannot go on like this, my lady. She is impossible. You would think she was, if you will forgive me for saying so, my lady, mistress of the Castle." It was Mrs. Foley, who had opened the door for Lady Clareham.

"I know, Mrs. Foley," Lady Clareham said, as she passed through it, "but there is nothing we can do about it. I will speak to his young lordship. In the meantime, I am afraid you must do the best you can."

In a moment we met in the center of the rotunda. "Good morning, Mary," Lady Clareham said.

"Good morning, Lady Clareham and Mrs. Foley," I said. This was my opportunity to ask Mrs. Foley for the library keys while Lady Clareham was present. "Mrs. Foley, I have been meaning to ask you if you would be good enough. . ."

"Excuse me, my dear," Lady Clareham interrupted. "I must rush if I am to be ready in time for church." Immediately she darted to the stairway nearest her room, and I was left alone with the housekeeper.

"Would you be so good as to give me the keys to the bookcases in the library," I continued. "I know that Vivian is fond of reading, and I am sure that most of her books will be there. His young lordship said you would give me the keys."

"His young lordship is a fool," Mrs. Foley said, looking up directly into my eyes. Then she turned her back on me and began to walk away.

"Mrs. Foley! Shall I tell his lordship that you will not give me the keys?"

She stopped walking then and turned slowly around to face me. "I do not have the keys to the cases in the library to give you, my lady," she said. "They are kept in the top drawer of the table in the library, to the left of the library door." Then she turned around and walked away.

I went at once into the library, found the ring of keys in the drawer of the table, and unlocked first one bookcase and then another. On the shelves in the cases stood a great many ecclesiastical books, and histories, and books of political essays, but at last I found a case with some novels in it. I decided upon *Hide and Seek*, another novel by Mr. Collins, and *North and South* by Elizabeth Gaskell. And all the time I kept wondering what I could possibly have done to make Mrs. Foley dislike me so much. She was so rude to me, and I felt so humiliated at being treated like that by someone little better than a servant. At last I decided that I had done nothing to her, and if she chose to act that way, well, I would try to ignore it.

After that, the day dragged by. I spent most of it sitting on a bench under an arbor in one corner of the rose garden where the dense leaves of a climbing rose shaded me from the sun. There, I read and sat idly waiting until dinner time. Then, after dinner, I hurried to the hilltop where I hoped David would come to meet me.

I arrived there earlier than I ever had before because dinner had finished more quickly than usual. And as I waited for David, I paced back and forth through the grass, scanning the valley and the hillsides beyond for a rider on horseback. Then I sat on my marble block for awhile, imagining that David sat opposite me looking at me in that curiously intent way of his. I walked around the pyramid and then stepped inside the monument and paused to read again the horse's epitaph. Then, outside, I counted the boats in the ocean and in the bay, and then the building blocks in the grass. I wondered if Vivian had ever met David there on the hill. The thought chilled me. But no, she had said that they were merely friends.

It began to grow dark, and still David did not come. Then I knew that he would not, and I walked slowly to the path and down it, into the rose garden where I met Sarah.

"He didn't come, Sarah," I said. "I waited until it was almost dark, but he didn't come. I hadn't even you to keep me company."

Sarah danced with joy, as she always did when we met, and let me pat her head. Her eyes flashed, and she seemed to smile and say, "Let us play." But I was in no mood to play, so we simply walked across the garden together, across the drive and the grass circle, to the steps of the portico. Sarah stopped and crouched, growling.

"Go home now, Sarah," I said, and she turned and ran off toward the stables, while I climbed the stairs toward Edmond, who stood at the top waiting for me.

"Mary," he demanded, "where have you been? It is almost dark."

"To the rose garden," I said. "I have lost—a letter. I—it was in one of the books I was reading in the garden this afternoon, and I thought it might have dropped on the ground."

"And did you find it?" he asked.

"No."

"I wish you would not stay out so late, Mary. You might trip and fall in the darkness and hurt yourself."

"Thank you, Edmond. Good night."

Even as I hurried into the house, leaving him standing

there, I wondered why I had made up such an elaborate lie. I hated lying. It made me feel degraded and unclean. And there was no necessity for this one. I should simply have said I was out for a walk. The lie was unimportant and had done no harm, but I was annoyed with myself because of it. It was some time before I was able to sleep.

On Monday morning, a letter waited for me on the tray in the dining room. I knew at once that it was from Mother in Holland. I carried it to my place at the table and laid it beside my plate.

"It is from Mother," I said to Edmond.

"So I gathered," he said. "Well, I saw it when I looked for my own letters."

"Naturally, Edmond," I replied. "May I have a muffin with my egg this morning please, Mitchell?"

Then Edmond pointed to the newspaper on the table next to him and said, "And Mitchell, when you have served her ladyship, take the *Times* up to Father. He must be livid about it by now." He smiled across the table at me. "Mary, I think I have good news for you. I have learned that Lady Withering is looking for a companion."

"Oh? Do you know her?" I asked.

"Well, no, not personally, but they are well known in Devonshire and Somerset. Sir Alexander was awarded his knighthood in the forties for his work on the Thames Tunnel. He was a celebrated civil engineer. He later made a fortune in railways."

"Does she live near here?"

"Just this side of Simonsbath—perhaps fifteen or twenty miles east of here. Just across the Somerset border. I shall write a note to her after luncheon to arrange an interview, and we shall see when it will be convenient for her to see us."

"Do you plan to go with me?"

"Well, of course, Mary. You could not very well appear all alone—how would it look? And, after all, we are as good a reference as you could find. You are very lucky about that, you know. I will tell you as soon as I have received an answer when we will call on her."

Later, after breakfast, I strolled into the hall with Mother's letter and sat down in an armchair near the window to read it. Her letter was a brief note enclosing a letter from Vivian. She wrote:

Dearest Mary.

The letter which I enclose came two days after you left for England. I know I should have forwarded it at once, and I meant to, but somehow it simply did not get done.

Everything is the same here, and there is little news. . . .

I did not read further then, but tore open the envelope of Vivian's letter and read it. It said:

June 4, 1856

My dearest Mary,

Do not come. Do not come to Castle Cloud. I am ill. Something terrible is happening here. How could he be such a *beast*. He is *mad*. Oh . . . I cannot tell you now. I am too ill—later, later my friend—but do not come, do not—please! I must go—

Ever
Vivian

I read the letter over several times, and then walked quickly to the stairway, climbed it, hurried to my room, and closed the door behind me. I went to my trunk and took out Vivian's other letters. Her last one, the one from Greenwich, was on top of the packet—it was the letter I wanted to see. I carried it, still holding the letter that I had just received, to the window, and read it. Then I read Vivian's June 4th letter and then the June 27th letter from Greenwich again. And when I had read enough, I sat there, looking out at the sky and the bay without seeing them, thinking about the letters. I must show these to David, I thought. But it is such a long time until tonight.

And it *was* a long time. It was even a long time till luncheon. It was a dreary meal with little conversation—three people with little to say to each other had once again been placed together through necessity. After it was over, I could not concentrate on my reading so I walked to Diana's Temple, played patience in the drawing room, and twice walked out onto the east portico feeling, somehow, nearer to David there. And so the afternoon dragged on and on. It was almost as though Castle Cloud held itself on the brink of . . . I did not know what. Then at last it was dinner time. In its atmosphere, the meal was a repetition of luncheon.

Afterward, I drank my coffee rather too quickly and then excused myself, telling Lady Clareham that I needed some fresh air and would go for a walk on the grounds. Then I dashed to my room for my shawl, put the letters in my reticule, and carried it with me.

I was glad I had brought my shawl—the evening was chilly. The sky still held a wash of cold pink, shading to aquamarine and then to Prussian blue. And as I reached the hilltop, I noticed that the evening star had arrived. Had David arrived back at Oakland Park, or was I to be disappointed again? I wondered. But then I saw his horse grazing, and he came hurrying toward me, reaching out his hands for mine.

"Hello," he said.

"David, I am so glad," I said, putting my hands into his. "I came here last night, but I suppose you had not returned to Oakland Park yet."

"No, I got back this afternoon."

"David, I have a letter from Vivian. It arrived this morning. She sent it to me in Holland, and Mother mailed it to me here. It was written over a month ago, but Mother delayed sending it." I disengaged myself and reached into my bag for the letter. "Here," I said, handing it to him.

"Come and sit down first," he said. Then when we were seated, he took the letter out of its envelope, held it to the light, and read it. He read it through several times, just as I had, and then looked up at me. "I wish you had brought the last letter as well."

"I did. Here." I handed him Vivian's June 27th letter.

David read it, then the June 4th letter again. I watched him read a sentence or two in the Greenwich letter several times. He looked up at me then, and I knew that he was thinking what I had been thinking all afternoon.

"This is hers?" he asked, holding out the June 4th letter for me to see.

"Yes! But do you notice how strange it is—even the writing? She wrote it in a terrible hurry. Some of the letters are hardly formed, and the punctuation in places is sloppy. Even the conclusion is short—she never ended a letter with only 'ever' before."

"It is hysterical," David said, looking again at the letter. "She *was* ill. Certainly emotionally unstrung, and from the handwriting, I would say physically ill too, wouldn't you?"

"Yes."

Then after a pause he said, "You know, June 4th was the day James died."

"Oh, dear. Who is the 'he' do you think? Is it as strange as I think it is, or am I imagining things?"

"I wonder if she wrote this before or after James died. She certainly was not talking about James, she was talking about someone else."

"Who?"

"I don't know."

We looked into each other's eyes as we sat there, almost as if it would be easier to read each other's thoughts than to put them into words.

"And the letter from Greenwich," he said. "I don't know which one is stranger."

"Yes," I said, "the Greenwich letter sounds almost as if she had completely forgotten writing to me on June 4th. First she frantically writes 'do not come, do not,' and then she calmly says in her next letter how glad she is that I have arrived."

" 'I am glad you arrived at Castle Cloud safely,' " David read, " 'and I am sorry that I cannot be there with you.' When she wrote that, she was not at all surprised that you had come after her warning you not to. No, it is very strange, all right, and you are not imagining anything. *Both* these letters are very unlike Vivian."

"Could she have forgotten the existence of the June 4th letter—perhaps blotted out of her mind *all* the things that happened on that terrible day?"

"Perhaps," he said, "but I still cannot imagine her leaving you alone here and going off to Scotland."

"No."

He looked off toward the sea, then. He was thinking very hard. We did not speak for several minutes.

At last I said, "What do you think I should do?"

Then he turned his head slowly toward me and said, "I think you should get in touch with Vivian."

"But she is in Scotland."

"Write in care of her friend, Nancy, in Greenwich, and put 'please forward' on the envelope. Ask Vivian for an explanation."

"Yes, all right. I am terribly worried about her—about her mind going."

"Wait and see what she answers before you start imagining all kinds of things. She may just have been upset."

"You don't really think she was just upset."

"I don't know, Mary. Wait and see how she answers your letter. If she does not answer it, I think we should go to Greenwich and talk to Nancy's parents."

"Yes. I will write to her tonight, then."

"And you? You have been well?" he asked. "What did Edmond say when you told him you would not accept the position in Cornwall?"

I told David about my conversation with Edmond on Thursday morning and also about the possibility of an interview with Lady Withering. David had heard the name but did not know anything about her. And I asked about his trip, and he told me that it had been successful, but that he was glad to be back at the farm. One of his prize sheep was having a lamb which was to be a crossbreed of some kind. I did not understand what it was all about, but he was excited about it.

"David, I must go," I said at last. I stood and so did he. "Edmond saw me coming in from the rose garden last night and asked where I had been, and said that I should not stay out after dark. I feel so like a prisoner, but I do not want to make him angry. I do not think I can come up here every night. He might become suspicious. I wish I did not have to sneak off like this."

"You are not sneaking," David said.

"Well, I don't like it."

"Very well, then I shall come to Castle Cloud and call on you there," he said, grasping my hands again and smiling down at me.

"No, David, not yet. Perhaps later. There is nothing to be gained by making Edmond angry."

"All right, let a couple of nights go by then. Meet me here on Thursday night, or Friday if it should rain. Will you do that?"

"Yes, David. Thank you so much. I am so glad—" I

stopped speaking because he had begun to draw me closer to him. It was only the briefest pull on my arms—lasting only an instant—and then he stopped. He let go of my hands.

"Good night," I said, and then I walked toward the path and down it, turning to wave back at him, as had become my habit. Then I hurried down to the house.

But instead of going directly inside, I walked to the stable yard to ask Colen if he would take the letter that I would write to Vivian that evening to the village in the morning and mail it for me. Everything was peaceful in the yard. The horses were quiet. Sarah was not there. But Colen was not there either, and no lights shone from any of the windows in the groom's pavilion. This probably meant that he had gone out for the evening, or perhaps had retired early.

So I left the stable yard, crossed the lawn, and entered the house. Edmond was not waiting for me there that evening, but inside, to my surprise, I met Mitchell coming from the direction of the entrance vestibule, where he had probably lit the night-light.

"Mitchell," I said, "would you please light the lamp on the table in the drawing room for me? I am going to write a letter tonight and will leave it on the tray in the dining room. Will you give it to Colen when he leaves for the village in the morning and ask him to mail it for me?"

"Very good, my lady," Mitchell replied.

"Thank you, Mitchell," I said, after he had lit the lamp. "I will turn it out when I have finished. Good night."

It almost amused me that he did not deign to wish me good night in return.

Then I sat down and wrote the following:

July 14, 1856

My dearest Vivian,

Thank you for your letter from Greenwich. I would have answered it sooner, but I thought you would probably rather not feel obliged to write an answer to a letter while visiting and resting in the country. Actually, I felt that you might wish to be let alone, which is understandable, my dear. I have felt that way myself—especially after Papa died.

How are you feeling? To be quite honest, I am writing this because I am a little worried about you. Mother forwarded your June 4th letter to me—I received it from her only today. Do you remember writing it to me? It was so short and written so hurriedly, and you were so obviously in distress that I think you might have forgotten writing it. You said you were ill and for me not to come to England. Do you remember? "Do not come, do not—please," you said. And you said, "How could he be such a beast? He is mad." Whom did you mean? And why shouldn't I have come? And what made you so ill? That is all you said, and everything about it is a complete mystery to me.

However, I am glad I did not receive your letter while I was still in Holland—if I had stayed two days longer, I would have. Why, I would not even have known that James had passed away. I know how much he meant to you, and I wish I could help, but all I can do is send my love to you.

If you do not remember writing that letter—if it was just part of that horrible, mixed-up nightmare of losing someone we love very much (and I do know about that, you know), then do not give it another thought. I will understand. But if there *is* something that I should know, staying here at Castle Cloud, please tell me.

Edmond is very kind and is helping me to find a situation. It was a shock at first, but I realize now that you are right and that it is the thing to do. He is arranging an interview with Lady Withering who lives near Simonsbath. I believe that is the name of the town. She is looking for a companion, and I will write and tell you what happens.

Please write as *soon* as you can in answer to this, and set my mind at rest. I think of you often and hope and pray that you have recovered.

> Ever
> Yours
> Affectionately,
> Mary

⚜ Chapter Seven ⚜

THE FOLLOWING MORNING I entered the dining room as the hall clock struck nine. I had been able to see the clock from the stairwell, and since it had said two minutes before nine and I had not wished to be a moment early, I had waited there a minute and a half before walking across the rotunda to the doorway. It was a needless bit of mockery and, as is so often the case with derision, utterly unrewarding. Edmond had not even noticed the time, I am sure, and that had served me right. He was deep in conversation with Mitchell when I entered the room, but when he saw me, he stopped talking, and we sat down. Breakfast began. Edmond seemed preoccupied, perhaps worried. He hardly noticed me and barely excused himself when he had finished his eggs and coffee. He had eaten very little and seemed anxious to be off.

After breakfast I wandered into the hall, as had become my custom, to look out the west window and across the bay, deciding what I would do during the morning. It was the same view that I had from the west window of my bedroom, just above the unused breakfast room at the corner of the building. I never tired of this view. Outside, a sun-pierced mist forecast a lovely day.

I decided that since Mrs. Gaskell's novel did not interest me, I would look for another book in the library while the sun dried the drive, and then I would walk perhaps as far as the home-farm and back, and then take my book into the rose garden until luncheon.

I turned from the window to say good morning to the Holbein little prince, but he was not there. Someone had removed the Holbein from the wall, leaving in its place a small circle of slightly lighter-colored wood paneling than the rest.

I had come to love the little painting and could not help

wondering what had happened to it, but my opportunity to ask about it did not come until I had finished my walk to the home-farm. As I approached the house on my return, I saw Lady Clareham working in her garden, and I walked down into it.

"Good morning, Lady Clareham," I said, as I approached her side. "I must tell you that your delphiniums are simply breathtaking."

"Thank you, Mary. Yes, they are lovely, but much too large for a bouquet, I am afraid. James would have loved them. Well, where have you been? Off for a walk?"

"Yes. Hasn't it turned into a gorgeous morning? I walked to the home-farm and back. You will have some marvelous goose for the table, by the look of them, though I hate the thought. I love to watch them walk and wiggle their tails.

"It is no wonder your garden grows so beautifully with all this moisture. Gardens are always lovely by the sea. Even the wild flowers grow more luxuriantly here, don't they? This morning must have been wonderful for it. It was terribly misty after breakfast. I could hardly see the bay from the hall windows. Oh, by the way, I was so sorry that the little Holbein has been removed. Where has it been hung?"

"Oh, no," Lady Clareham said.

"You did not know that it had been taken down?"

"No."

"What has happened to it?"

"Things go from time to time, Mary." Lady Clareham looked off into space. It was almost as though she had begun to think aloud, as if she were alone. "It really does not matter—the beautiful things that George and I have come to love. . . Well, they will all be his anyway—soon. If only he had the decency to wait. I am sorry, Mary." She seemed to come to herself, then, and took a handkerchief from her sleeve to daub at her eyes, but then she broke down completely and wept. "These things upset me so. Sometimes I think I don't want to live anymore." She had turned away from me and, as she said the last sentence, she hurried down the garden path toward the house. I stood there, helpless, and watched her go.

It was odd that later, on that very same morning, I should discover that yet another of Castle Cloud's treasures, a malachite and gold box, had disappeared and that Edmond had evidently not taken it.

I discovered this shortly after I had left my bench in the rose garden, at about eleven-thirty, and had returned to the house to comb my hair and wash before luncheon. I had climbed the southeast stairway, and as I walked around the gallery to my room, past Vivian's bedroom door, I heard footsteps on the marble floor of the hall below. They were Edmond's. He had come from the direction of the servants' hall, and I looked down in time to see him stride toward the dining room. He stopped in front of the dining room doorway beneath me, but he did not sense my presence overhead.

"Mitchell!" he shouted.

"Yes, my lord?" Mitchell answered from inside the dining room.

"Come here!"

"Yes, my lord?" Mitchell asked, walking toward the doorway.

"The Rastrelini box," Edmond said. "The malachite and gold box."

"The Rastrelini box, my lord?"

"What have you done with it?" Edmond demanded. He was in a rage.

"I have not done anything with it, my lord. Is it not on the table in the drawing room, my lord?"

"You know perfectly well it is not. Mrs. Foley saw it there yesterday, but she has not seen it since. Jane Spence has not seen it. It is not there now. What have you done with it? I want it back."

"My lord! One would think you were accusing me of having stolen it."

"Precisely."

"But, my lord, how could you think such a thing? If I may say so, if the box is missing, I should think your lordship might know where it has gone."

"What do you mean?" Edmond said.

"Simply that everyone at Castle Cloud knows your—er—rather desperate need for money at certain times, my lord, and your reduced circumstances. And we are all perfectly well aware of your method of raising those necessary moneys, my lord—we have been for some time. We all know—Jane Spence, May Brooke, Monsieur Laval, even Mrs. Glover—all the servants, and Mrs. Foley, who has doubtless informed her ladyship. We all know what has happened to the large cameo, the Russian icon, the gold horse, the jeweled cup, and several other *objets d'art*. The little painting in the hall chamber, for example. Is it valuable, my lord?"

"What about the painting?" Edmond said.

"Simply that I myself saw you take it down off the wall and carry it away this morning. I had gone into the breakfast room to look for another cream pitcher, which I believed to be in a cupboard there. You must have thought I would be busy in the dining room at that hour, my lord. If you wish to remove objects without being seen, the middle of the night might be a more appropriate time—if I may say so, my lord."

"The painting, the Egyptian cameo, the icon, and the horse are none of your affair," Edmond said. "They were my property—or they would have been shortly, which is the same thing. I may do as I please with them without being accused by a butler who not only does not know his place, but is a common thief as well. You had better watch your step, Mitchell. Now go and get the box and give it to me."

"My lord, I have no intention of returning the box. Well, how could I when I have not the faintest notion where it could be? Of course your lordship must realize that since he has disposed of so many *objets d'art* in the past—to everyone's knowledge—that everyone will be quite sure the—the Ras—tel—i box has been disposed of in the same fashion. That is, unless you have proof to the contrary, my lord. It is such a pity it has disappeared. How much could it have brought if you had been able to sell it? Fifty pounds? One hundred pounds?"

"Pig!" Edmond cried. "Do not go too far, Mitchell, I warn you, and if you steal another thing—"

"You will do what, my lord?" Mitchell interrupted. "Have the constable come and take me away? Nonsense. And if you should consider some other way of being rid of me, I can assure you that this time it will not be so easy. Now, if you will excuse me, I must resume my preparations for luncheon or we shall not dine on time."

Edmond did not reply. He walked back to the drawing

room doorway, stepped inside the room, and closed the doors quietly behind him.

I hurried to my room. I had a great deal to think about while I prepared for luncheon. I was very glad I had been on the gallery to hear the extraordinary conversation between Edmond and Mitchell, but I dreaded facing Edmond at luncheon. I knew he would be in a foul temper.

But I was wrong. When I entered the drawing room he came toward me smiling and said, "Ah, Mary, how lovely you look. Our English air has revived the—ah—wilted flower."

He held a glass, and I remembered the whiskey cabinet.

"My dear," he continued, "I am off directly after luncheon. I have some business that will take me away from Castle Cloud for a day or so—it is impossible to say exactly."

"I hope you have a pleasant trip, Edmond," I said.

"Thank you, thank you my dear. You are so kind. Now remember, no fraternizing with the neighbors while I am gone. I must confess, my dear, that—ha, ha, ha—you would not like them anyway. Stodgy. Dreadful bores—all of them. Most unpleasant. So you see, we are saving you from some dreadfully dreary experiences. Oh, my dear girl, you have no idea. And no riding over the hills on the horses. All must be very solemn and very quiet in memory of our dear departed."

"Certainly, Edmond," I said.

"Good girl. You *are* a very good girl, Mary. We will find a situation where you can have a time. Ha, ha. You will have a time, I can assure you."

"Isn't Lady Clareham coming down?" I asked.

"No. Sent word by Cecile. Sour pickle, that Cecile. Sent word that she has another headache. I don't care if she has a hundred headaches—keep her out of the way, they. . ."

"Luncheon is served, my lord," Mitchell announced from the doorway.

"Oh, capital! Capital!" Edmond said, taking out his watch. "And right on time too. Ha, ha. And then we are off. This will make it all come true. I feel it in my bones. Lady Luck smiles, and all will be well with the world."

But after we were seated in the dining room, Edmond fell silent. He remained in a happy mood and ate an enormous meal, but he spoke little. His mind seemed far away in pleasant dreams which I did not disturb.

When the meal was over, I went to my room to watch him leave for the station. Colen had the carriage waiting, and Edmond skipped down the steps and climbed into it. Mitchell followed, carrying Edmond's bag. Edmond had carried something wrapped in newspaper under his arm. I was sure it was the Holbein portrait.

*　　　*　　　*

"Good morning, Colen," I said. "Is something wrong with Chocolate?"

I asked because that morning, I saw him leading the horse along the drive toward the stable yard. I descended the steps, then, and went to meet him on the far side of the grass circle.

"Good morning, my lady," Colen replied. "No, she lost a shoe, is all. I took her out for some exercise, and she lost it down by the farm. I will take her to the smithy in the village and have it looked after, but it will have to wait until this afternoon."

"Oh? Doesn't the blacksmith come to Castle Cloud? Is there no smithy here?"

"Yes, my lady, but it would not be worth the trouble to get the forge going. In the old days, he must have come one day a week regularly, or there may have been a smith here all the time. But there are not enough horses anymore for that."

"Yes, of course. Hello, Chocolate," I said, as I stroked her nose. "Did you enjoy your run? I am sorry you lost your shoe, but it will be all right." Then I turned back to Colen and said, "What a lovely animal. How Vivian must miss her. I wish I could ride her."

"I wish you could too, my lady. Perhaps just around the grounds would not do any harm? It would be good for the horse—and good for me too."

"And good for me," I said, laughing. "Well, we will see. Don't let me detain you, Colen. I know you have much to do. I was on my way to the stables to look for Sarah. It is such a glorious day, I thought I would go for a walk in the meadow, and I hoped she would go with me. Have you seen her?"

As we talked, we began to walk toward the stable yard together.

"She might be anywhere, my lady, but the best place to look for her would be in the yard, I suppose."

"Well, there is only one way to find out," I said. "Oh, and, Colen, thank you for mailing my letters for me."

"It was a pleasure, my lady."

We walked along for a few moments in silence, and then I asked, "Did you drive his lordship to Barnstaple yesterday, or to Braunton? Did he say when he would be back or where he was going, Colen?"

"To Braunton, my lady. No, he said to meet the noon train on Thursday, and if he was not on that, to meet the noon train on Friday. He did not say where he was going, but it was the train that goes to Exeter. Maybe he went to London—or sometimes he goes to Southampton, or so it's said."

"That is the train that Lady Vivian took, then."

"Yes, my lady."

"Did you drive her to the station that day, Colen? How was she? Was she ill?"

"No, my lady, I did not drive her there. His lordship took her himself in the gig."

"Then you did not see her."

"Oh, yes, my lady. I brought the carriage around and held the horse while his lordship helped her down the stairs and into the carriage. Her ladyship was very sick, my lady. She was very upset over her brother's death, you know, and she was all dressed in mourning, of course. Well, she could hardly walk down the stairs. She kept leaning up against his lordship—he almost had to carry her down—and she was crying. I almost cried myself, I felt so sorry for her poor ladyship. She was sick, very sick, I'm afraid. I said to Mrs. Muldoon, that very afternoon, that she should not have been allowed to go off like that, but Mrs. Muldoon said that if she had a mind to go, she would go. And I suppose that's so, my lady."

"I am very worried about her," I said.

"The family would not let anything happen to her, my lady," he said. "And I have heard she is feeling better now."

At that moment I saw Sarah. She had come to the open

doorway of one of the stable buildings to look out, and when she saw us, she ran to me, prancing with joy.

"Would you like to go walking with me, Sarah?" I asked her.

She seemed impatient to be off. So I thanked Colen again for mailing the letters, and Sarah and I left him to explore the field beyond the temple.

At the end of the field, I found a marble bench and sat down on it. It was in a delightful, isolated spot. I remember thinking that if ever I needed solitude, that would be the place to go. But then, before I knew it, it was almost time for luncheon, and I hurried back to the house.

During the meal, Lady Clareham was relaxed and more cheerful than I had seen her since I had arrived at Castle Cloud three weeks before. I did not think she would ever recover completely from the tragedy of James's death, but I knew that time would eventually lessen the pain. It was, of course, much too soon to expect that this was beginning to happen, but the fact that she made conversation during luncheon was an encouraging sign. The meal passed quickly and pleasantly.

Afterward, Lady Clareham said that she was going upstairs to lie down, and I wandered into the drawing room to write a note to Mother, thanking her for her letter and for forwarding Vivian's.

I disliked writing letters—they seemed such a poor substitute for being with a person, and my words lying on paper seemed so vulnerable. I hated the thought that they might be read over and over and examined and questioned and perhaps be interpreted to mean things I had never intended.

Nevertheless, the note had to be written. So I sat down at the table and began it. But when I had gotten just a few lines down, I heard a carriage drive up to the house.

Naturally, I wanted to see who was in it, so I got up and hurried to the opposite end of the room where I could look out at the drive before the entrance front. The carriage was a dark-green barouche with a crest of red and gold on the door. In it sat a girl of about my own age, perhaps a year or two younger, and a woman dressed in black who might have been thirty years old. As I watched, a footman in dark-green livery climbed down from the carriage, walked toward the house, and began to climb the steps to the portico.

The doorbell rang. I ran as quickly as I could to the drawing room doorway and peeked out into the hall just in time to see Mitchell enter the vestibule. I heard him open the door.

"Is Lady Clareham at home?" I heard the footman ask.

"Not at home," Mitchell replied. Then I heard the door shut and he returned to the hall.

And I ran back to the window. By that time the girl in the carriage was speaking to the footman who stood on the drive near her. Then the footman walked again to the stairs and climbed them. Again the doorbell rang. Mitchell crossed the hall to the vestibule, and by the time I had again reached the drawing room doorway, he had opened the entrance door.

"My mistress wishes to know if the lady who is Lord and Lady Clareham's guest is at home," the footman said.

"Not at home," Mitchell replied.

Then I heard the door shut again.

"But I *am* at home, Mitchell," I cried, as I ran out into the rotunda. "I did *not* say that I would not be at home." I ran past him toward the front door. "How dare you not ask me?"

"But his lordship. . ."

I did not hear what else he said because I had already opened the door and run out onto the portico. The footman had climbed up on the box beside the coachman and the carriage had begun to move away.

But fortunately, the girl in the carriage had looked around and seen me come out of the house.

"Marsden, stop!" she cried.

The carriage stopped, and then as I began to walk down the stairs, the coachman backed the horses until the carriage stood in front of me. Before I reached the level of the drive, the footman jumped down from the box and opened the carriage door. I waited at the base of the steps until he had helped the girl down onto the drive, and then I went to meet her.

She was tall and thin, and her pale skin had broken out in red blotches and pimples about her mouth and chin. Beneath a wide-brimmed hat her brown hair had been pulled severely back and arranged in a bun behind her head. She was plain. Her gray muslin dress was plain also—it had never tried to be anything else.

"Good afternoon," I said to her. "I am Lady Beauford, Lord and Lady Clareham's guest. I cannot imagine why Mitchell said that I was not at home. I gave no such order."

"Good afternoon, Lady Beauford," she said. "I am Flora Stratton. My father is the viscount Wilton. I heard that you had come to visit, and of course, I wished to welcome you."

"How very good of you. Will you come into the house?"

"Thank you, but I would feel as though I were intruding. I know how Lord and Lady Clareham mourn for dear James, and I would not want to intrude on their quiet. It is such a heavenly day. Could we not walk in the park for a little?"

"I should love to," I said.

"I shall not be long, Marsden, Emma," she said to her coachman and her maid.

"Shall we go this way?" I said. And we began to stroll across the grass away from the house. "Do you know, I think we have met?"

"Have we? Where?"

"Right here, unless I am mistaken. Four years ago, I visited Lady Vivian during Easter week. She and I had become friends at school. And I think you came with your parents to call one afternoon. Didn't you?"

"I—I am afraid I really don't remember."

"Your parents were in the house visiting with Lord and Lady Clareham, and we were out here running across the lawn. I think Vivian was chasing Sarah, and we were running after Vivian when you fell and hurt your knee."

"Yes! I remember that. And I cried and there was such a to-do about bathing my knee. I can remember how everyone crowded around and how the water stung. I am afraid I was not very ladylike about it all."

"I think you behaved beautifully, Miss Stratton. It was an ugly gash, as I remember it, and must have been very painful. I remember you were wearing a pink dress."

"Then we are old friends," she said. "You must call me Flora. I feel as if we have known one another for ages. I am very intuitive about such things, and I know we are going to be *close* friends—ah—"

"Mary."

"Mary. Yes, of course, I remember. But I do not remember Beauford."

"I was Lady Penbroke then. My father was the marquess of Penbroke. He passed away two years ago. I am the baroness Beauford now, in my own right."

"Your father was living in Paris at the time. I remember very well. I remember thinking how romantic it must be to have a father living in Paris."

"Did you really?" I asked. I could not help smiling. "And I would have given anything if Papa had been living in Devonshire."

"My dear," Flora said, grasping my arm, "we are *never* satisfied, are we? But how delightful to have found you again."

We reminisced about what we had done that week, even though we had seen each other only that one time during it, and then she asked if I had often visited my father in Paris, and when I told her that I had lived there, she wanted to know all about it.

She was fascinated by my description of the city and my life there. As we chatted, we strolled slowly in a wide arc across the park.

Finally she said, "You know, when you came out of the house, I thought you were Vivian. Oh, just for an instant. And I thought Vivian had returned."

"Oh, really?" I asked.

"Yes. Vivian and I have become such friends in the last year. Of course our families have known each other forever—I was born at Hawthorn Hill, you know, and I have lived there all my life. But in the last year Vivian and I have become *very* close. And then she left and I have not heard a word." She gestured to the house. "Have they heard? She was so upset by James's death, but to go off like that without saying good-by to *anyone* and then not to write a single *word*."

"She is in Scotland visiting friends," I said. "I am sure she will be better there—the air, you know."

"And she will return more beautiful than ever," Flora said. "She is *so* beautiful. You know, I suppose I should not tell you this, but it is all I can do not to be jealous of her. It is not just her looks, it is that—ah—quality—that Vivian has about her. Do you know? All she has to do is walk into a room and there is something in the air that you can *feel*."

"Yes," I said. "She is like a diamond, almost—all beauty and fire. It would be perfectly natural to resent it, I suppose, if Vivian were not so good. But she is an angel, and one cannot help loving angels, can one?"

"Of course not," Flora said. "She is the sweetest. *And* such a talented actress. She always has the leading role in our theatricals. She is simply marvelous—it is as though it were all actually happening to her."

"Yes, I know. She loves the theatre. She was constantly reading plays at school."

"Well, anyone who was born in India would have a special magic about her."

"She almost was, but not quite," I said. "She was born on shipboard on the way to India, which I suppose is almost the same thing, and she lived in India for eight years. I used to tell her that she was special because of it, and she would say not to be silly—that she had had an English governess there, just as she would have done here, and saw only English people.

"But if it had not been for India, I would never have known her. It was because her mother and father returned to India, when she was twelve, that she came to Mrs. Romilly's School, where we met."

"Yes. That was fortunate for you, wasn't it? But the poor dear was so upset about James's death. It was a terrible ordeal—my heart simply broke for her. She really looked terrible toward the end of his illness. She spent a good deal of her time nursing him. They were *so* close, you know. Almost more like—well, like lovers than brother and sister. So no wonder she was upset. Everybody remarked about it."

"Yes, I know," I said. "She loved him very much. Well, if you hadn't met your brother until you were eight, because you had been in India and he was here at Harrow, and you had never had any of the usual children's quarrels and petty jealousies, and then you had begun to know one another when you were nearly a young lady and he was a handsome man of eighteen—you would have fallen in love with him too. And his stutter would not have made any difference when he was so handsome, and broad shouldered, and so strong and kind and considerate. You know, I don't think he ever in his life hurt anyone's feelings. *I* fell in love with him at once. Vivian and I would sit by the hour telling each other how wonderful he was, but there was never anything but a brother and sister relationship between them, I assure you."

"Oh, I know that. Goodness *no!* It is just that they were so extraordinarily close—it was so unusual." Then, after a pause she asked, "Do you like Edmond as much?"

"No!" I cried. "There is no comparison. I could have fallen in love with James—oh, you know, a schoolgirl crush is what I mean—but not with Edmond. He has been *very* kind, but heavens, no!"

"They *were* different," Flora said. "Goodness! We must start back toward the carriage."

As we returned to the drive, she continued, "James was physically attractive, which is not really important, but he was so—antisocial, so silent and withdrawn. I could never get *close* to him. He was always either reading in his room or riding off to those cliffs near Appledore. He had discovered some caves of Mesithic men or something. He would never take me to see them, no matter how many times I asked him to. And he would never *talk* to me. If he had *talked* to me, I would have understood. That is really what a man requires, you know, understanding."

I could think of no reply, so we walked in silence for a few moments.

Then she said, "Papa gave me a marvelous season in London a year ago last spring—at least he spent a fortune on it. But I was so bored by all those artificial, superficial people—and Papa had given me a lovely dowry, too. Well, it was when we came back to the country that Vivian and I really began to get to know each other, but James was always so aloof."

"He *was* serious," I said, "at least I thought so four years ago, but I never really knew him."

"Now, Edmond is different, don't you think?" Flora said.

"How do you mean?" I asked.

"Well, he seems to want to enjoy life more—he is not so serious or withdrawn. Mary, I am having a party next

Monday, the twenty-first, and you must come and bring him."

"Thank you, Flora, but Edmond and his parents are very much in mourning and will not go out, and they have forbidden me to, also."

"But that is nonsense. Come without him, then. I shall be quite desolate if you don't. That is no way to treat an old friend. Just because they are in mourning is no reason for *you* to be. You just said you hardly knew James. Goodness! Do you mean you have not seen anybody? You have spent all your time here alone with Edmond and his parents? You poor dear. How terrible for you. You must be longing for company—for *people*.

"They cannot *forbid* you anything—you are a guest in their house. You are imagining it. They will be delighted that *you* will have a pleasant evening. And there will be such delightful people. Everyone who is not in the city will be there. And we are having several guests down from London. My brother, Lewis, is bringing some of his friends, too. He is in the army, very handsome, and my dear," again she grasped my arm, "unmarried! Will you come?"

"Yes. It seems I must," I said, laughing. "One cannot offend an old friend, can one? Thank you so much, Flora."

"That is lovely, but do try to persuade Edmond to come with you. It is to be after dinner, at ten o'clock next Monday night. There will be a musician—so we will have some dancing—and refreshments, and I suppose some cards."

By that time we had reached the carriage. The footman opened the door for Flora and helped her in.

"Mary, this has been delightful," she said, as she settled herself next to her maid. "Until next Monday night, then, bye-bye." And she blew me a kiss as they began to move.

"Until Monday then, Flora," I cried above the noise of the horses and carriage.

I stood there and watched them drive away. Flora turned around and waved and I waved back. Then I climbed the steps and went into the house to finish my letter. But before I reached the portico, I saw Mitchell watching me from the hall chamber window. He had not, however, bothered to open the door for me, and when I stepped inside the house, he was nowhere to be seen.

* * *

But Mitchell was always very attentive when Lady Clareham was present. That evening, she was late coming down to dinner, and he hovered about anxiously until she entered the drawing room. Then he announced that the meal was served.

"You had a visitor, Mary?" Lady Clareham asked as soon as we were seated in the dining room and had begun to sip our soup.

"Yes. But of course, Lord Clareham must have seen her in his mirrors. It was Miss Stratton. Flora and I met when I visited Vivian four years ago. Do you remember when she fell and cut her knee? You must—there was such a to-do."

"Yes, I remember," Lady Clareham said.

"Well, she called to welcome me and to invite me to an at-home that she is giving next Monday night. It is to begin at ten o'clock. She insisted so, that it would have been rude to refuse."

"Oh, dear. What will Edmond say?" Lady Clareham murmured.

"I told Flora that the family might object to my going, but she said that that was nonsense—that you, of course, were in mourning for James, but that you would be delighted that *I* would have a pleasant evening with friends. It was so kind of her to ask me. I accepted of course."

"I see," was all she said.

Later, after dinner and coffee were over, I walked to the Horse Monument. I thought that perhaps David would be somewhere in the valley below or across on one of the hillsides, and see me standing there, and ride over to be with me. But he did not come.

I did want to talk to him, and Thursday evening seemed so far away, even though it was only the following day. I wanted to tell him about meeting Flora. He must know her, I thought. I wondered if she had invited him to her party.

It had been so easy for me to accept her invitation. I knew I had done so against Edmond's wishes, and I knew I had broken my promise to him again. My conscience bothered me—it had not been the right thing to do. But then it had not been right for me to make such an absurd promise in the first place, and it was certainly not right for Edmond to have extracted it from me.

I wondered then, if my visit to Castle Cloud and my present circumstances were changing me. Because my future was to be less privileged, was my integrity to become less exacting? Was I losing my principles? No. But on the other hand, right was right all the time, not only when one wanted it to be. I had always known this. And here I was, doing something that I considered wrong. I wanted desperately to ask David about it.

So I was disappointed that I had not seen him, and in a rather wretched mood, I walked down the hill to the house.

I slept restlessly that night and was glad when morning came.

Mrs. Muldoon was in a happier frame of mind than usual that Thursday morning. I knew she had a funny story to tell me, but when she told it to me, I did not feel much like laughing. So I told her that I had not slept well and was feeling depressed, and that not even one of her stories could lift the gloom. This seemed to mollify her.

Nor did Vivian's answer to my last letter help my spirits. I found it waiting for me on the tray in the dining room before breakfast. But I did not wish to read it at the table in front of Mitchell. He seemed to be watching me more closely than usual, so I placed it beside my plate and left it there during breakfast.

When I had finished, Mitchell asked, "Will there be anything else, my lady."

"Yes, Mitchell," I said. "In the future, if someone should call and ask for me, I shall be at home unless I particularly specify that I am not. That will be all, thank you."

"Yes, my lady," he replied, in a tone that he might have used to describe spoiled food.

Then I left the dining room carrying Vivian's letter, and sat by the hall window to read it.

Greenwich
July 16, 1856

My dearest Mary,
  My hand is still not well. Nancy is writing this for me. By the time you receive this letter, I shall be on my

way to America. John O'Connor, the man I love, is there, and he has sent for me. His letter, enclosing a ticket, was forwarded to me in Scotland. I set sail on the *Royal George* early tomorrow morning.

I have told no one where I shall be in America, not even Nancy. I cannot run the risk of Father or Edmond sending someone to bring me home against my will.

This is good-by, Mary. God bless you and watch over you and give you peace.

Ever
Yours
Affectionately,
Vivian

P.S. I did not want you to come to England because I knew that James would die. It was God that I called a beast, but He has forgiven me.

I read the letter over several times and then got up and walked back into the dining room, where Mitchell was still clearing away the remnants of breakfast.

"Mitchell," I said, "I received a letter from Lady Vivian in the post this morning. Did a letter also come from her for his lordship or her ladyship?"

"I could not say, my lady," he said.

"But surely you must distribute the mail after Colen brings it from the village. Did any letters come for his lordship or her ladyship from London this morning?"

"I could not say, my lady. Colen often gives her ladyship's letters directly to Madame Cerceau and his lordship's letters directly to Ahmad, my lady."

"Thank you, Mitchell."

I strolled across the hall to the drawing room doorway and wandered inside, thinking, Vivian *must* have written to her parents, but if she did not, and she expected me to tell them, they should know without delay. So I retraced my steps into the rotunda and climbed the stairway nearest Lord Clareham's room.

When I reached his door, Ahmad opened it for me. Inside, Lady Clareham sat by her husband's bedside.

"Good morning. May I come in?" I called.

"Certainly, Mary. Come in, come in," Lord Clareham said. Then he said something in Hindustani, and Ahmad brought a chair for me and placed it before the bed near Lady Clareham's.

"I must be going, my dear," Lady Clareham said to her husband. "I will leave you with Mary."

"No, please don't go, Lady Clareham," I said. "I must speak with you both. Something has happened. Did you receive a letter from Vivian this morning?"

"No," Lady Clareham said. She seemed mystified by my question and immediately looked at Lord Clareham, silently seeking guidance.

"Did you, Lord Clareham?" I asked.

"Why no, my dear," Lord Clareham answered. "We have not heard from Vivian for ages. She is traveling in Scotland with a friend. But you received the last letter from her. You know that."

"I received another letter from her this morning. She said good-by! She has gone to America. And she said she was not telling anyone where she would be for fear Edmond might try to bring her back."

As I said this, I glanced at Lady Clareham. Her eyes went to her husband's face and remained riveted there. Lord Clareham stared at his wife—it was a look that controlled and ordered in a language that I could not understand.

"Without any warning," he said to her. "We might at least have been told in advance." Then, after a pause, he looked at me and said, "Well, this is a surprise. We should have been told. Is that her letter that you hold in your hand?"

"Yes."

"Would you care to read it to us?" he asked.

"Of course. She wrote it yesterday morning in Greenwich. . . ."

I read the letter aloud, and when I had finished, there was a long silence. Lord Clareham looked at the ceiling and Lady Clareham stared at her husband.

"I see," Lord Clareham said at last. "Vivian is a very headstrong girl. She has chosen her future. I hope she will be happy. Thank you for telling us, Mary. Now, I would rather not discuss it any further."

"I thought you should know at once," I said.

"Quite right, quite right. Thank you for telling us, my dear."

"Well—are you going to try to find out where she has gone?" I asked.

"No, my dear. If Vivian wishes us to know, she will tell us. Now, I would rather not discuss it any further."

"Of course, Lord Clareham. I really should leave you now. I—I have some things to do. If you will excuse me, I—I hope I have not upset you. I just wanted you to know."

"Quite right, my dear. Good-by until later, then," he said.

Lady Clareham was dry-eyed and perfectly calm as she nodded her good-by to me.

I left them and walked around the gallery to my own room where I found Mrs. Muldoon making my bed. "Go right ahead, Mrs. Muldoon," I said. "Don't let me interrupt you. I just want to put this letter in my trunk. It is from Lady Vivian. Everyone will know about it soon enough, Mrs. Muldoon, so you may as well be the first. She has gone to America to meet John O'Connor. I suppose she will marry him. She is not coming back—at least not for a long time. Did you know John O'Connor?"

"Is she now?" Mrs. Muldoon said, as she straightened up and put both hands on her hips. "A fine lad he is in spite of all his talk about coming from the old Irish royalty. Faith, it's only a tiny bit of what an Irishman says that you can believe, my lady. Sure, I ought to know, for wasn't I married to one for thirty years?

"And an Irishman is an Irishman, no matter where he is. Full of fib and fight they are. Why, once in a pub in Dublin there was an Irishman, and he says to one and all, he says, 'I can lick any man in this pub. Better still, I can lick any man in Dublin. Better still, I can lick any man in all of Ireland,' he says. Well, my lady, when they picks him up off the floor and it's back to consciousness he comes, he says, 'It's too much territory I've covered, I think.' Ha, ha, ha. 'It's too much territory I've covered,' he says."

"Oh, Mrs. Muldoon, please—I am so worried about Lady Vivian."

"Now don't you fret, my lady," she said. "It's John O'Connor her ladyship's gone off with once before, which we all know, and it's all the way to America she's gone to be with him now, which means that it's in love with him she is. She's a fine girl, her ladyship is, and it's a fine lad he is—honest, and hardworking, and smart. And it's the will of the Irish that's in him, it is. Why, if there's something that lad says he'll do, he'll do it—you can bet your life on it, my lady. If John O'Connor says he'll do something, he'll do it. Sure, that's the way he is.

"They'll be all right and it's their own way they'll be doing things. And good for them, I says."

"Yes, I suppose you are right," I said, as I placed Vivian's letter with the others in my trunk.

Then I closed it and left the room, and I would have collided with Mrs. Foley if I had stepped out onto the gallery a moment sooner. She was in a hurry, as always. Was there even more urgency than usual in her movement as she approached Lord Clareham's door? I wondered.

Then she knocked on his door and Ahmad let her in.

But I did not wish to think about her—I felt a desperate need to get out of the house and to be alone with my thoughts. So I went downstairs and directly out onto the east portico, into the rose garden. The day lay still about me under an empty sky. No clouds floated there, and no breeze stirred the infrequent clumps of hair-tail grass. The air smelled of pinks and honeysuckle, of earth and decay. An orange-and-black butterfly poised on a field poppy, which bloomed at the base of a dead rosebush. When he had sucked the flower's nectar, he danced away through the air. Did he seek another poppy? or would any flower do, I wondered.

I would rather have thought about butterflies than about the thing that preyed upon my mind. But I could not help thinking about Castle Cloud and its inhabitants. Something strange had happened or was happening here. I felt an unrest, a seething under the placid surface of the place.

And as I sat down on the rim of the fountain, feeling the comforting warmth of stone underneath me, I wondered at Lord and Lady Clareham's reactions to Vivian's letter. It had almost been as though the news was of little importance to them. They had been mildly surprised, but not distressed. What will David think when I tell him about it, I asked myself. I wished he had been there.

But then a movement attracted my eye to the dry bottom of the fountain's basin. There, a dark-green frog sat near a wide crack in the cement. He gazed up at me, his throat throbbing, and winked.

"You are in the wrong place, my friend," I said. "There is no water here. Are you worried about that?"

The frog blinked in answer and then suddenly leaped high into the air, landing in a clump of tall grass. He had jumped in the direction of the lily pond.

I knew that Edmond had returned before he stalked into the drawing room, where I sat waiting for luncheon, because I had heard him shouting at his father only a few minutes before. He had walked out of his father's room onto the rotunda gallery as I crossed the hall below. "All right, all right," Edmond had shouted. "I said I would, isn't that enough?" And I had heard Lord Clareham shout an answer, but he was so far away that I could not understand what he said. Then I heard Lord Clareham's door shut, and then Edmond cried, "Go to hell!" But he had not shouted that very loudly, and I doubted that his father could have heard it through the closed door.

"You received a letter from Vivian," Edmond said, as he entered the room and walked to my chair. "John O'Connor was a worthless, filthy clod—a *groom*. She ran off with him last January, but I brought her back and sent her lover packing. Well, everybody in the house knows it, so you might as well know it too, for all the difference it will make."

Then he walked past me to the whiskey cabinet, poured himself a drink, returned, and slumped on the sofa opposite me.

"Stupid, ungrateful bitch," he said. "Well, that is what she was—no better than a common streetwalker. The beautiful Vivian. The magnetic Vivian. Vivian, with every man she ever met at her feet, and every woman too. The exciting, marvelous, wonderful Vivian—everybody's dear, everybody's darling. She was a common, suspicious, deceitful harlot, that is what. . ."

"No! That is not true," Lady Clareham screamed from the doorway behind him. "It is you who are common, low, and disgusting. I wish I had never—" She did not finish the sentence. As I watched, her fury crumbled to anguish. She clapped her hand over her mouth, turned from us, and stumbled back into the hall.

Then I saw Cecile hurry to Lady Clareham from the direction of the servants' hall and put an arm around her.

"My lady, my lady!" she cried, as she led her away toward the stairs. But as they went, Cecile glanced back through the doorway at Edmond. I wish I could describe the loathing I saw on her face.

At that moment, Mitchell walked past them toward the drawing room doorway, and announced that luncheon was served.

"She had no consideration," Edmond said, ignoring his mother's and Mitchell's interruptions, "for her family or her class—running off with a servant. Shall we go in?"

When we were seated at the dining table, Edmond said: "What did Flora want?"

"She came to welcome me and to invite me to an evening party she is giving next Monday."

"You would not have enjoyed it."

"I accepted her invitation, Edmond. I had to—it would have been terribly rude not to have. She invited you too, and I said I would ask you for her, but that I did not think you would come because of your being in mourning for James. I even said that you did not want me to go visiting, but she said I was imagining that—that you would be delighted that I could have a pleasant evening. She *insisted* that I come."

He sat still, glaring at me. Finally he said, "So, in spite of your promise to me, you intend to go."

"Yes."

"I forbid it!"

"But that is ridiculous! Why should you not want me to go out while I am here? It would have nothing to do with you. Why should I sit and twiddle my thumbs alone when I could have places to go and people to talk to? Very soon I shall have to work to support myself. Why should I not enjoy myself this little while? Anyway, I could not keep a promise given under such circumstances."

"What circumstances?" He spat the words at me.

How should I handle this, I thought frantically? What can I say? If we continue in direct confrontation, I will lose the battle, but if I approach him in an oblique manner, the blows may glance off me.

So I said, "Oh, Edmond, why take this so seriously? One would think it was a matter of life and death. I arrived here to visit your sister, and I was frightened and bewildered and feeling terribly alone when I found she had deserted me. That was perfectly natural. And I made an irrational promise to an unnecessary demand. You could not expect me to keep such a promise. Anyway, my going to Flora's party can do no harm. Please don't concern yourself about it. I know you have much more important things to think about."

"Unnecessary demand? How dare you judge whether it was necessary or unnecessary. You are a guest in this house, and you will abide by your host's wishes."

"You mean my hostess's wishes, don't you, Edmond? After all, it was Vivian who invited me to Castle Cloud, and I am sure she would want me to enjoy myself as much as possible, now that I am here. But let us not have an argument. I shall see to it that you and your parents' peace and quiet are not disturbed, and I am sure everyone in the neighborhood will do the same. Why, Flora would not even come into the house for fear of intruding."

"You come here out of the blue," Edmond said, "with no friends, no money, no prospects for the future, with *nothing.*" He was terribly angry, but he was trying desperately to keep his temper. "We take you in, feed you, comfort you, help you to find a situation, treat you like a member of the family, and we ask only one small thing in return—that you allow us to mourn my brother undisturbed. But you refuse us. I would have expected better of you, Mary, much better."

"You should expect a great deal, Edmond, and I trust that I shall not disappoint you. I am deeply grateful, naturally, and would do anything to repay you for your kindness. Perhaps I *will* be able to one day. Who knows? But I fail to see how my refusing to accept Flora's invitation could possibly benefit you in any way. In fact, I am sure it will be a relief to you to have your home to yourself for the evening. Guests are all very well, but one can see too much of them, and they should be considerate enough to absent themselves occasionally."

"You will not keep your promise? You intend to continue in this selfish attitude?"

"Edmond! You really are being most difficult. This is too unimportant to be considered. Why, I should think you would do anything to be sure that I have a pleasant stay. I am surprised that you do not insist that I go to Flora's party. But if this is an excuse to provoke a disagreement, Edmond, please tell me so directly, and I will leave Castle Cloud tomorrow. Oh, forgive me—that is absurd. Why should you wish to do that?

"Come with me. Surely mourning cannot help James, and you need relaxation—you look so tired. You have been working too hard."

"And what do you think you would do if you left Castle Cloud tomorrow?" he asked.

"Seriously? Well, I suppose I would go to London—I have enough money to do that, you know—and get a job teaching, perhaps even at Mrs. Romilly's in Windsor. I was an excellent student, you know. I could teach any number of things. And then I would go to the American Embassy and find out where Vivian went. I am sure it is possible to trace her somehow, and then, I think, when I had saved the money for my passage, I would go to America, to Vivian. She is my best and only friend, and I know she would help me there. Why do you ask?"

Edmond sat glaring at me for a moment, then threw his napkin on the table, stood up, kicked back his chair, and strode out of the room.

I finished my luncheon, choking down the food, and then when the meal was over fled the house to the stone bench at the end of the field beyond Diana's Temple. I sat there almost all afternoon thinking and thinking and thinking, but the more I thought, the more muddled I became. One thing, however, was clear—something strange was going on at Castle Cloud, and I knew it affected me. It was important to Edmond that I not associate with other people in the neighborhood. That was the reason he did not want me to go visiting. Why should that be important to him? Would Edmond and his parents ask me to leave Castle Cloud if I insisted on going to Flora's party? I do want very badly to go, so why not admit it? I thought. I might meet someone there who could help me—there was nothing wrong in that. I would never impose myself on or demand anything of anyone, but I certainly could use all the help I might be offered.

So I sat at the end of the field, thinking, and the afternoon dragged on. I was impatient for it to be over so that I could go to David, but I dreaded going down to dinner that evening and confronting Edmond. As is so often the case, however, I discovered when the time came that all my apprehensions had been groundless. Edmond did not dine at Castle Cloud that evening. I did not know where he had gone, and I did not care. Mitchell simply told me that Edmond had gone out and that Lady Clareham would not be coming down.

So I dined alone, rushing through the meal, and then with the packet of Vivian's letters in my bag, I hurried to the Horse Monument and David. He stood on the hilltop straddling the path, watching the place where I would come out of the trees. When I appeared, he ran to meet me and held out his hands. How comforting it was to place my hands in his and feel those big, rough fingers fold over mine.

"I thought Thursday night would never come," I said.

"So did I," he said.

"David, I have so much to tell you. I have received another letter from Vivian—in answer to the one I wrote Monday night. Here. . . ." I took my hand from his and reached into my bag for the letters. ". . . I have brought them all."

"Are you always in such a rush, Mary? Let us go up and sit first." We climbed the hill, and when we were sitting opposite each other, he said, "Now, let me see the letter."

I gave it to him, and he read it. And when he had finished, he said, "Well, that was quick." Then he studied the letter carefully. "But this is absurd. The only John O'Connor I know was a groom at the Castle last autumn, but he left early this year." He read part of the letter again. "The man I love," he read aloud. "Nonsense! This is ridiculous! She had nothing to do with John O'Connor—he was a groom in the stables."

"Do you mean you didn't know?" I asked.

"Know what?"

"No, you didn't know," I said. "She was in love with him. They ran off to London together in January, but Edmond went after them and brought Vivian back and sacked O'Connor."

"Nonsense! Who ever told you a story like that? Edmond?"

"Vivian did—in her letters. She *was* in love with him, and they did run off together."

"I don't believe it. That is impossible."

I flipped through Vivian's other letters, which I had taken out of my bag, to find the ones in which she mentioned the groom. I glanced through the November 20th letter before handing it to David. "Read this," I said. And while he read, I skimmed the January 20th letter. When he was ready, I passed it to him.

He handed them back to me when he had finished reading them and said, "These arrived in November and January in Holland?"

"Yes, a week or two after she had written them. You didn't know anything about it? They must have been very careful, very secretive. Everyone at the house knows, but I don't suppose anyone else does, or else you would have known too."

"But that is incredible. Why didn't she tell me?" he thought aloud. "Why didn't she tell me? Now I know why she was so sad, so aloof, so *changed*. Now it all makes sense. But to go on as though it had never happened—without telling me. Oh, my God!"

"Yes, it must have been an ordeal. What she must have gone through—keeping up pretenses when her heart was broken. But what was the point of telling anyone? It was all over. Talking about it could do no good—only harm. Poor Vivian, what a wretched winter and spring she must have had, what with that and James's death. Do you wonder she was so ill? She wrote three or four letters to me after that, but she had not heard from John when she wrote any of them."

David sat looking off toward the horizon. He was thinking very hard, and I did not interrupt him. Finally he said, "I cannot believe it. Well—so she has gone. Simple—just get on a boat and go. Well, that is the end of that. I hope she will be happy."

"Then you don't think it is strange?" I said.

"Of course it is! The whole damned thing is strange. I'm sorry. But then I had not known about what was going on—so it is bound to seem strange. What I really need is time to sort it all out. Maybe it is all for the best." Then he looked back into my eyes in that intent way of his. "I think it *is* all for the best. I know it is, Mary. It just comes as such a filthy shock. It changes everything."

"What?" I asked.

"Well, don't you see? We don't have to worry about

Vivian anymore. She stood between us—well, she was a mystery, a problem. Now the problem is solved. She has gone to America, which should clear her mind. Now that she can be with her—with John, she will recover, and she will be happy, at least I hope she will be. And now we can all get along with our business.

"Enough about Vivian, then," he said. "What about you? You have been well? Have you heard from Lady Withering?"

"No," I said. I folded Vivian's letters and put them in my bag. "Flora Stratton came to see me. Do you know her?"

"She came to see *you?* Why? How on earth did she know you were here?"

"I suppose I have been seen riding back and forth in the carriage to the station in spite of Edmond's attempts to hide me. And someone was bound to wonder who the young lady was who arrived at the station and walked to Castle Cloud."

"Yes." David smiled at me.

"Do you know Flora?" I asked again.

"Yes. Her family has come to tolerate my father and me socially." He smiled again.

"It turned out that we had met once," I said. Then I told David about Flora's visit. "She is having an evening party on Monday night."

"Yes, I know."

"Were you invited?"

"Yes—both my father and I."

"Are you going?"

"No, I don't think so. Father is going—it is evidently her parents' affair as well as Flora's—but I don't think I will go."

"Why not?" I asked. "There will be dancing and cards. Don't you like to dance?"

"I don't feel like parties right now. I have too many other things to think about. I have designed a new dairy, Mary, at least I have almost finished planning it, and we are going to start building it as soon as I get back from Windsor Farm. They are selling off part of their herd of purebred Jerseys. They have more than they can handle for an experimental operation, so we are going to buy two dozen of them. We should have the dairy built by October. There is room in one of the old barns till then."

"It sounds very exciting. . . . I am going."

"Where? To Flora's party? But what about Edmond? You said he has forbidden you to see anyone and that you have promised him not to."

"I am going to break my promise to Edmond, David. Is that wrong? I think it is. Somehow, I feel that I don't like the person I am turning into nearly as well as the one who arrived here."

"I shouldn't worry about that," he said. "Anyway, there is no such thing as right and wrong. Nothing is that categorized. I don't think it is a good idea to go about breaking promises, but I think that that was a ridiculous demand. If you did keep your promise now, what would it accomplish? It would only make you unhappy and do Edmond and his family no good at all. Don't be so concerned about it. It is not important."

"But Edmond was furious when I told him. I tried to make light of it all. . . ." Then I told David in detail about Edmond's and my conversation at luncheon. "You said you thought it was ridiculous—his not wanting me to see anyone. I didn't think so at first. After all, they are in mourning for James and it would be natural for them to want to be quiet and undisturbed. But this insistence—it would be different if he had simply suggested it, but I think he has other reasons for not wanting me to come in contact with people. And I want to find out what those reasons are.

"What would happen if I did talk to his friends? What would they tell me that Edmond would not want me to hear, or what would I tell them? *We* have been talking together. Has anything happened between you and me that could affect Edmond?"

"No, nothing that could affect Edmond," David said.

David's eyes suggested more than his words when he said that, and my heart skipped a beat. I think I am in love with you, David Field, I thought. I hoped my eyes did not disclose what I was thinking.

"But why should he insist, so?" I asked.

"I don't know. I don't suppose it is anything important. Having been a parish priest may make him think differently about these things. Why not wait and see what happens when you go to Flora's party? Perhaps nothing will happen at all."

"They may ask me to leave Castle Cloud," I said.

"Do you think they will?"

"I don't know, David. Vivian is not coming back. They have been kind to me. You know, they could have asked me to leave at once. They don't want me here, I know that. They were doing it for Vivian, in case she should return. Maybe they will ask me to leave now, especially if I go against their wishes."

"And nothing from Lady Withering?"

"No, Edmond has not said a word about it. Will you come to Flora's party? I would feel so much better if you were there."

"Yes, I will come. I must go up to Windsor Farm, but I will be back in time for the party on Monday night. I wish you could come and see Oakland Park Farm, before we start building the dairy...." And he began to tell me about the latest sanitary methods for processing milk.

I was not at all interested in the dairy or in milk production, but I loved being with him, no matter what he talked about. I tried to interest myself in what he was saying and resolved that I *would* be interested, but I was not very successful.

At length I said, "David, I must go. We keep getting later and later. I will see you at Flora's on Monday night then?"

"Yes. Shall I see you down?"

"No, no. I can manage. Good night, David," I said, and after waving to him from the path, I ran down the hill and to the house. I prayed I wouldn't see Edmond, and I didn't. I wanted to prolong the spell of being with David, and I did.

⚴ Chapter Eight ⚴

AFTER I WOKE the following morning, I could think of only one thing: what would Edmond have to say to me at breakfast, after having left the table so abruptly the day before?

He stood near the mail tray reading a letter, as I entered the dining room. I said good morning to him and looked to see if there was a letter for me, but the tray was empty. Then Mitchell helped me to be seated, and I told him what I would have for breakfast.

"Lady Withering is still looking for a companion," Edmond said, as he walked around the table to his place, still holding the letter. "And would be delighted to meet Miss Thorpe. 'How very kind of you to suggest Miss Thorpe,'" he read aloud. "'I shall look forward to meeting her and especially to meeting you, Lord Althrop, since my husband knew your father, and we are almost neighbors here in the country.' Almost neighbors? Why, she is at least twenty or twenty-five miles away. I shall have to ask Father about Sir Alexander. 'Unfortunately, I am going to London tomorrow to visit some friends for a week, before everyone leaves, and will not return until July 25th or 26th. But I would be so happy to receive you and Miss Thorpe on Monday afternoon, July 28th. How extraordinary to have arranged a meeting in this. . .' Well, she rattles on and on."

"It seems a long time away," I said. "That is a week next Monday, isn't it?"

"Yes, but that cannot be helped. With our recommendation, the position is yours—so that is settled. You should be able to start in a day or two after our visit to—ah—Moor House. That is an imaginative name, I must say."

"That will be lovely, then. I shall look forward to meeting her. We ate in silence for a few minutes. Then I said,

"Edmond, I am sorry about yesterday. I do not mean to be ungrateful. . . ."

"You have obviously made up your mind. I doubt that there is anything I can do to change it, so I see no reason to discuss it further. You should not go to Flora's party—you know that it is not the right thing to do. One is responsible for one's own actions, Mary, and one must live with one's self. I can only pray that you come to realize the pain you inflict upon others by being so inconsiderate."

I did not reply. There was simply nothing that seemed worth saying to him then. We finished our meal in silence.

Then, after breakfast, Sarah and I went for a long walk. I can often think best during a walk, and I had a great deal to think about.

Luncheon that day was a grim affair. Lady Clareham was even more withdrawn than usual, and Edmond had reverted to his vicious mood of the day before.

I was glad to get away from him, and after Lady Clareham and I had finished our after-luncheon coffee, I went directly upstairs to Lord Clareham's room.

"Lord Clareham," I said, when Ahmad had admitted me, "may I have a word or two with you?"

"Of course, my dear child," he said, folding over the corner of a page, closing the book he was reading, and laying it on the bed cover. "I have always hated that, but when one has only one hand to work with. . . Sit here, my dear."

"Lord Clareham, I—" I paused because I was unable to find the right words. "I do not know how to put it into words."

"You are troubled about something, aren't you, Mary? Tell me what it is in any words that come to your mind."

"I do not think I am wanted here," I blurted out. "I feel that my coming to Castle Cloud was not a happy thing, somehow, and that my staying here is causing trouble and unhappiness. There is a feeling of malaise here. I feel as though I am the cause of it, that I am intruding, and that perhaps I should leave. I would like to stay, now that Edmond has heard from Lady Withering that she wants to meet me. But that will not be for more than a week, and I have no idea what she will be like or whether, indeed, she will *want* me as a companion. I loathe this feeling—almost of being a cancer or a blight or something. I do not like being where I am not wanted."

Lord Clareham's black eyes studied me for a long time before he answered. Finally he said, "So Edmond has heard from Lady Withering? That is interesting to hear." Then, after a pause, he continued. "That may prove a perfect situation for you. Sir Alexander was very well thought of. We shall see.

"Now, let me explain something to you. You are welcome here. You—are very dear to Vivian, and you are very dear to us. I have personally given orders that you are to be made as comfortable as possible. We no longer have an adequate staff, but I have asked them all to do everything they can to make you feel at home. And we want to see you situated in a pleasant position for the future.

"I know that you have had a disagreement with Edmond about Miss Stratton's party. Lady Clareham and I would rather you did not go, but we do understand what it is like to be young and lonely, and—well, my dear, we will understand if you decide to attend."

Again he fell silent while he studied me. "I think I know what it is that you feel, my dear," he continued. "And I will tell you what it is. How often we think that we are responsible for something—ah, the human ego—when in reality it has nothing to do with us at all. No, it is not you, my dear. You have noticed that the Holbein portrait is missing from the hall chamber? *There* lies the root of the malaise that you feel in this house, Mary. Edmond has the cancer and the blight, I am afraid. An incurable addiction—the races, roulette, faro, rouge-et-noir, picquet, hazard, *et cetera*—particularly hazard. Hazard enslaves him. He dreams of gathering from the hazard tables the wealth to restore Castle Cloud and the estates. Like a happy child he goes to the tables, and when he has lost everything—and he always loses everything—he leaves like a vicious dog, attacking and destroying to retaliate for his bad luck. He is a fool, and he is possessed. I merely hope that it does not destroy him before he can marry and beget me a grandson.

"I suppose he does not mean to be cruel, but you saw him yesterday when he returned. The servants know, and God only knows how many others. It is no secret. Do not let him drive you away from us, Mary, and do not think that you are the cause of something that comes from quite another quarter."

"That is why he took the Holbein?" I said.

"And laid it on the hazard tables, so to speak."

"And you don't mind?" I asked.

"What can I do? Call the village constable? No, all this will be his anyway, someday—if he leaves any of it until then."

"But to see your beautiful things go like that. Is there nothing you can do?"

"Complain, threaten, and hope his thievery stops here. It *is* like a cancer, Mary. It grows and grows."

"But it is not only Edmond, Lord Clareham. The feeling comes from Mitchell, and Mrs. Foley, and Jane Spence, and Ahmad."

"You must pay no attention to Jane Spence," he said. "Mrs. Foley is set in her ways and has been spoiled for years. Ahmad means you no harm."

"And Mitchell?" I asked. "I feel that he loathes me. He is rude. And he is a thief. He stole the malachite and gold box, knowing that Edmond would be blamed for it."

"I do not know how you can be so sure of that," he replied. "Mitchell is another problem altogether, my dear. I am perfectly well aware of it, but it has nothing to do with you either. Do not let Edmond make you unhappy. He really does want to help you, you know, and he will. If he falls into a foul temper and says mean things, try to shrug them off. I will have a word with him."

"Thank you, Lord Clareham."

"Are you feeling better now?"

"Yes, I think so."

On impulse I turned to glance at Ahmad. He was watching us intently. How much of the conversation had he understood? I wondered.

But then I was rather surprised when Lord Clareham said, without preface, "Teaching is not for you, my dear. It is grubby work. You belong in the comfort and pleasant surroundings of a good family. Now, if you should wish to open a small school of your own someday, well, that is a very different story.

"And give up thoughts of going to America to join Vivian. I doubt that you could find her. She will marry O'Connor, and they will probably vanish without a trace.

No, we will help you find a pleasant situation, never fear. Fate works in strange ways, Mary. When one is attractive, intelligent, and good, fate is invariably kind. Be of good cheer—all will be well."

"You are very kind, Lord Clareham. Thank you."

"I should like to rest now, my dear," he said. "I am feeling very tired."

So I left him and went to my room, where, since I *was* going to Flora's party, I began to think what I would wear. I had only one evening dress which could possibly do—it had been made for me by a French dressmaker in The Hague shortly before my father died. It and my only remaining ball dress were the most stylish dresses I had. The evening dress was of Crimean-blue *satin-de-laine*. Its neckline was cut low, off the shoulders, and its skirt wore three deep flounces.

I took it out of the wardrobe and laid it on the bed. It had been made more than two years ago, but it was beautifully cut and sewn. Flounces were still very much in fashion, but somehow.... Then I remembered a dress I had seen pictured in a copy of the *Ladies Own Journal and Miscellany*. I ran down to the drawing room, found the magazine that I was looking for, and carried it to my room. As I had remembered, the dress pictured in it was similar to mine in construction, with three flounces on the skirt, but the flounces and décolletage were trimmed with wide ribbon, and the same ribbon had been used to make bows at the shoulders. If I had ribbon, my dress could look very much like the dress in the magazine.

And I did have the ribbon, or the makings of it—a length of Lyon velvet of a beautiful hyacinth-violet color. I had bought the material, just before Papa died, for a dress which was never made, and I had packed the fabric in the bottom of my trunk. I would cut it into strips to make the ribbon, turning the edges under as I sewed it on. I took the velvet from the trunk and laid it against the dress. The colors were marvelous together—imaginative and exciting. Yes, it would be superb. I would be very stylish at the party—my dress would be quite the latest. Wait until David sees me in it, I thought.

I could not completely enjoy my inspiration, however. My mind kept going back to Lord Clareham. And I kept seeing that thin, pale ruin lying on his bed and hearing the agony in his voice as he told me about his son. Why had he told me about Edmond's gambling? Did he think he could possibly connect Edmond's obsession with my discomfort at the Castle? Finally I decided that Edmond's gambling may have been responsible for Lord Clareham's malaise, but that it was not responsible for the way I had been treated at Castle Cloud or for the feeling of repulsion that existed toward me there.

How the atmosphere at the Castle had changed in four years—how much misery and enmity I found there! Would it ever be freed of this? If Edmond could think of someone besides Edmond, it would help. He might help his poor father! Lord Clareham was not well, and he needed serenity, not aggravation.

All of which (the thought of helping, I suppose) brought Alice Reade to mind. I should have gone to see her long before this, I thought. So I put the dress and velvet away, changed my shoes, and left the house.

Sarah met me outside on the grass circle. "Hello, Sarah. Good dog, good dog," I said, as I patted her head. "But you cannot go with me today, dear. Come along and stay with Colen." And she followed me to the stable yard where Colen came to meet us.

"Good afternoon, my lady," he said.

"Good afternoon, Colen. Would you keep Sarah here with you for a little while? I am going into the village where there is another dog. Sarah *will* follow me, and I would hate there to be a fight."

"Certainly, my lady. Sarah, come here."

He picked the dog up and carried her into what looked like the feed room and closed the door. Then he returned to me.

"She will be all right there for a little while," he said. "As a matter of fact, I am glad you brought her back, my lady. I have been looking for Sarah all morning so I could get a rope on her. Mr. McComb was up from the village this morning and said that a mad dog has been seen in the neighborhood. So, if you are going down there, be careful of strange dogs, my lady."

"Oh, dear," I said. "Are you sure?"

"Well, my lady, it is supposed to have been traced to several places, and to have bitten quite a few dogs. Mr. McComb heard that one of Arthur Colehill's dogs went mad yesterday, but that might be just a rumor—you know how people will talk. But I think it would be best to keep Sarah tied up here in the yard until they find the dog and the ones he's bitten or it is all over with."

"So do I. Thank you Colen. Colen, I have been invited to an evening party at Hawthorn Hill on Monday. Will you drive me there and back? I would like to arrive about ten o'clock."

"With pleasure, my lady. A cousin of mine is a gardener there, so it will give us a chance to have a visit. I will have the carriage at the entrance front at nine-thirty on Monday night then, if that would be satisfactory, my lady."

"Yes, that would be perfect. Thank you, Colen." I turned from him then, and hurried off toward the rose garden.

Twenty minutes later, as I approached the Reades' cottage, I saw Alice leaning against the doorjamb of the open doorway, watching me.

"Hello, Alice," I called. "Do you remember me? I came to see how you are feeling today."

"I was hoping it was you, miss. You said you'd come back. I saw you coming down the hill from the monument, and I was hoping it was you."

"You seem much better today," I replied.

I followed her into the cottage. The inside looked as I had last seen it—the bed unmade, the floor unswept, the dishes unwashed.

She brought a chair and set it in front of the table where she had placed it for me the last time I had visited her.

I sat down and glanced up at the entrance to the loft. "Your father is not at home?" I asked.

"No, miss, he had to go out. I could make you a cup of tea. The water is hot."

"That would be lovely, Alice."

We were silent while she got out the cups and prepared the pot. Then she leaned against the cupboard while she waited for the tea to steep. She is in better spirits, I thought, and she has made an effort to comb her hair.

"Do you really think he'll come?" she asked, examining me.

"Who, Alice?"

"The baby's father, like you said."

"Well, I should think he would want to see his child. That would be perfectly natural, don't you think?"

"Yes," she said.

She put the tea canister back on its shelf in the cupboard, and then played needlessly with the teacups until the tea was ready. When it was, she poured it, carried my cup to the table and placed it before me, brought hers, and sat down opposite me in the chair her father had used the last time I had been there. We sipped our tea in silence. I smiled at her, but I had decided to wait for her to speak.

"Will you tell him for me, miss?" she said at last. "Otherwise he wouldn't know the baby come."

"Tell whom, Alice?" I asked.

She held her cup in both hands and looked down into it. "His lordship, miss."

"His lordship?"

"Lord Althrop, miss."

I was too surprised to answer her. It was a moment before I realized that she had told me Edmond was the father of her child. And then, immediately, I wondered why I hadn't known this from the way William Reade had talked. Why hadn't I understood it at the time?

"Well, I couldn't tell Lady Clareham, could I?" Alice said, lifting her head. "After all, I couldn't tell her ladyship, could I? And you said you wanted to help me. And you don't have to come right out and say, 'I saw your son today, Lord Althrop.' You could say, like, 'I saw the sweetest baby in the village today. It belongs to Alice Reade.' You know, casual like. He said I wasn't to tell nobody or he would do terrible things to us, but he will want to see his baby, won't he, miss?"

"I should think he would, yes. Of course I will tell him, Alice. I will be happy to."

"But it wouldn't do any good if he did come, would it?" she mused. "I don't mind so much though, now."

"Oh?"

"You started me to thinking, miss."

"How, Alice?"

"I didn't want to live no more. I don't know if you could understand that, miss."

"Tell me about it. We are friends, you know. We agreed on that."

"I thought I had lost it all—that there wasn't nothing left. The mornings when we used to swim sometimes, and when we were just there in the little house by the river— well, it was part of being in heaven. I'm a poor girl, miss, and I had no learning to speak of. Oh, I can read and write. The rector had a school, and when I was little, I learned. But the mornings in the little house was part of heaven. I was gentry, miss—almost. It was nice. It was— I never felt like that before."

"Do you love him?" I asked.

"Yes, miss. Well, I suppose if he worked on a farm and lived in the village, I wouldn't love him so much, but he's a lord, miss, and he's rich. He took me up to the big house one day when they was all away, and he treated me like I was a lady. He held the doors open for me, and we sat in the drawing room, miss. It was lovely. It is fairyland up there, miss.

"And then when he found out I was going to have a baby—I didn't tell him, miss, but he guessed and then I told him. He said it was all finished, and he didn't want to see me again, and not to tell nobody or he would do terrible things to Papa and Stanley—and he *could* too."

"But now you think differently?" I asked.

"Yes, miss. I hadn't lost it *all*. I still got part of it. Part of it's in here." She drew her hand slowly across her stomach. "I thought of it after you said that he will want to see his baby. His baby is part of him, ain't it? It come from him, didn't it? So part of him is in here. Part of fairyland is in here with me. It's not *all* gone. My baby will be a little boy, miss, and he will always be a part of it. And he will always be my son, and he will always be his lordship's son. So I haven't lost it *all*, if you can understand, miss."

"Yes, I think I do."

"He's going to be a fine boy, miss. And whatever happens, there will always be a tie between his lordship and me. So I haven't lost it *all*."

"No."

"Do you really think he'll come?"

"Well, I cannot *promise*."

"He might. I was special. He said so."

"Special?"

"There was others. I know who goes to the little house with him now. Her name is Hester Glenn and she works up at Oakland Park. I seen her going through the woods to meet him." Tears had come to her eyes, and she tried to blink them away. "And he's got somebody up at the big house. She come down to the river one morning, and he made me hide in a closet. He was mad about that. And there's been Dolly Hart, and there's been others, and everybody knows it. But I was different, he told me so. He said there would never be no one like me."

Then she paused, her mind far away. At last she said, "No, he won't come. But I still got part of it and I always will. It ain't *all* gone."

I did not know what to say. So I said nothing.

"Maybe when—" She did not finish that. With a smile, she slipped back into her dream for a moment. Then she shook her head and said, "But I want him to know, miss. So just say it casual. And you won't tell nobody else will you? Promise!"

"I promise."

"Dr. Norton says it will be any day now."

"And you feel well?"

"I feel better, miss. I wasn't so good at first, but I am better now."

"Will you be all right after the baby comes?" I asked. "How will you manage?"

"Oh, we will manage. Her ladyship will help—well, it's only right, her being the grandmother and all. And then Stanley will soon be working full time, and the rector said he and his missus would help. So we will get along."

Then Alice talked about her baby, and I encouraged her.

Later, I looked at my watch and said, "I must go, Alice. I did not realize it was so late. I will barely be in time for dinner. Thank you for the tea, and don't worry, everything is going to be all right. Remember, if you need me for any reason, send Stanley for me. I will come again in a day or two. Is there anything I can bring you from the Castle?"

"No, her ladyship will take care of that," Alice said, as we walked together to the door.

There I said good-by and left her. When I reached the wood, I looked back. Alice had gone inside and shut the door, and the cottage looked as gloomy and forbidding as when I had first seen it.

That evening I had time to measure how much of the velvet "ribbon" I would need to trim my dress and how much for the shoulder bows. And I had time to cut the velvet material into strips and pin it part way along the bottom of the first flounce of the dress, but I did not have enough pins to pin it very far. I had been meaning for some time to buy more pins, and of course now that I needed them, I was furious with myself for not having done so. Fortunately, however, I had everything else I needed in my sewing bag—scissors, thimble, needles, and many kinds of thread, including thread to match the velvet, which I had bought for the dressmaker at the same time I had bought the material.

I began to sew then, but it was late, and my eyes tired rapidly in the lamplight, so I decided to wait until the next day before doing any more.

The following day was Sunday. I sewed all that morning. And when I was almost finished, Mrs. Muldoon came into my room and admired my work. I have always loved to sew, and I told her so. I love to look back at the tiny stitches I have made—each of equal length and each spaced equally far from the next.

But the sewing would have been so much easier if I had had enough pins to pin several yards of velvet at one time instead of pinning a little and sewing a little and pinning a little and sewing a little. I was also beginning to realize how much there was to do and to wonder if I would be able to finish the trimming in time. I wished I had two more days in which to do it. If only I had some help, I thought. Perhaps if I asked Lady Clareham, she would let Cecile help me for a few hours. But even if Cecile couldn't, she would let me use her pins.

So after luncheon I followed Lady Clareham into the drawing room where she sat down in front of her embroidery. I sat opposite her. "May I ask a favor, Lady Clareham?"

"What is it, Mary?" she asked.

"I have a dress which I am changing a bit after a picture I found in one of your magazines. It is of blue satin. I am edging the flounces with some violet velvet I have, and

I am going to make shoulder bows and trim the neckline with the velvet too. . . ."

"You have decided to go to Flora's at-home then, after all."

"Yes, I want to very much. Except for Flora's visit, I haven't seen— I would love to be with people my own age, that is. Soon I shall have a position, and I want to enjoy this little time. It won't intrude on you or Lord Clareham or Edmond."

"I can appreciate that, my dear, but have you thought about repaying these visits and invitations? Obviously we cannot have people calling, and a dinner party or at-home for your new friends would be out of the question. Where will you entertain them in return? It would be better not to go."

"I will just have to say that I can't. They will understand. Then after a pause I asked, "Did you mind Flora's coming? Why, she and Vivian are close friends—she told me so."

Lady Clareham did not reply, but looked at me disapprovingly.

"Would you let Cecile help me with my dress, only for a few hours, Lady Clareham?" I asked. "I am afraid that I may not be able to finish it in time, alone."

"Mary," she said, "Cecile is not as young as she used to be. When one approaches fifty, one is no longer a young girl, and she is a treasure to me. She has been with me for thirty years. She is very sensitive, and her early life was not a particularly happy one. Her mother died suddenly when she was seventeen, and it was only due to providence that an English lady was visiting her mother's employer at the time and asked her to go to England as personal maid to her daughter, who was the same age. Then when Miss Bogg left India, she abandoned her husband and Cecile. That was when she came with me, and she has been with me ever since. I could not do without her and would not risk offending her for anything.

"Her duties are to serve me and no one else. You understand—I could not *ask* her to help you, but if she wishes to of her own free will, I would not object. She has gone upstairs to bring me some yarn and should be back any moment. Ask her if you wish."

In a minute or two, Cecile came into the drawing room and gave Lady Clareham the yarn.

"Cecile," Lady Clareham said, "Her ladyship wishes to ask your help. You must understand that I have no desires in the matter one way or the other. The decision is entirely up to you"

"My lady?" Cecile asked me.

"I wondered, Cecile," I said, "if you would help me with a dress I am fixing. I am putting new trimming on it. Three or four hours of your time today or tomorrow would be such a help."

"I am very sorry, my lady. I would like to help you, but her ladyship is not well, and I must devote all my time to her."

"Yes, of course, Cecile," I said, as I stood. "May I borrow some pins for today and tomorrow, then."

"Unfortunately, my lady, I have only three or four pins left in my box. They disappear so easily, you know. I shall have to buy some more when her ladyship and I go into the village."

"I see," I said. "Well, thank you and thank you, Lady Clareham. Now I must get back to work." Then I left them.

I sewed for the rest of the afternoon and after dinner as well, until my eyes were tired. I had worked as fast as I could, and by the end of the evening I was half finished.

In the morning, Mrs. Muldoon woke me as usual.

"Mrs. Muldoon!" I said when I saw her, "what have you done to your head?"

"I got thrown a cup at," she said. "Ha, ha, ha. Oh, he was that mad, he was! You should have seen him, my lady. Oh, it was like the devil himself was inside him. Ha, ha, ha."

"Who? What happened? Your poor head—it must be cut to have a bandage like that."

"Sure, it's nothing, my lady, nothing at all. It was worth it, I can tell you. Ha, ha. Yesterday, being Sunday, I was home all day. So I thinks, it's a stew I'll make with a chicken I got. But 'twas a little different I made it, you see—that is, it's something more besides the chicken I put in it. Well, when it comes dinner time, my lady, I carries the pot to the table and we helps ourselves as we always does. 'Ah,' says Mr. Muldoon, 'It's a stew you've made,' he says. 'Never did taste a stew like this—bit different, isn't it?' ' 'Tis a bit different, Mr. Muldoon,' I says. 'What's into it?' he asks. 'It's a chicken stew, Mr. Muldoon,' I says. 'Chicken and some other things,' I says. 'What other things?' he says, as he stops eating and looks at me suspicious like. It's very particular Mr. Muldoon is about what he'll eat and what he won't eat, you see. 'What besides the chicken?' he says. 'Well,' I says, 'I don't like to say, Mr. Muldoon, for fear you won't like it,' I says. 'Like what?' he says. Ha, ha, ha. Now it's suspicious for sure he is, my lady. So I says, 'Another kind of meat, Mr. Muldoon,' I says. 'It was my mother taught me how to do it. Only the Norwegians does it so it tastes good,' I says. 'So what tastes good?' he says. 'Another kind of meat in with the chicken,' I says. ' 'Twas the chicken I saw hanging outside,' he says, 'but there ain't been no other kind of meat in the house that I seen,' he says. 'Oh, it's other meat you've seen in the house today, Mr. Muldoon,' I says. 'We trap 'em all the time at home,' I says. Ha, ha. 'No, it's no other meat I seen in this house. . . .' he says. Then you should have seen his face. Ha, ha, ha, ha. You should have seen his face. So he picks up his cup and throws it at me, he was so mad."

"But what was it?" I asked.

"Little pieces of cut-up pig sausages, my lady, but 'twas the rat that we caught in the trap in the morning that he thought it was. It's rats we caught in traps in Norway, my lady, but that doesn't mean we cook 'em. Ha, ha, ha. You should have seen his face. No matter how hard I tried, I couldn't convince him it was the sausage. He wouldn't eat no more of it—not another bite. Ha, ha, ha. Oh, it was that funny. Oh, the saints preserve us. Ha, ha, ha."

"Oh, Mrs. Muldoon," I said, but I couldn't help smiling. "How could you? How *could* you?"

"Easy, my lady. There's nothing that's so good for the soul as a laugh or two, but there's no chicken stew that Mr. Muldoon will ever eat again, I'm thinking. Ha, ha, ha. You don't think that's funny, my lady?"

"Well—"

"Something's the matter then, my lady?" she asked.

"No, it is just that I am nervous about my dress. I don't know whether I will be able to finish it before tonight or not, and if I don't finish it, I won't have anything to wear. I asked Cecile if she would help me, but she wouldn't. She would not even lend me some of her pins."

"Let me see," said Mrs. Muldoon. She walked over to the sofa where I had laid out the dress the night before. "Sure, it's going to be pretty. Why, there's papers of pins upstairs in the little room that used to be a sewing room at one time. I'll go up there right now and get them for you, and then it's back I'll come after you've had your breakfast to help you for a couple of hours, if you've no objection, my lady."

"That would be wonderful! But can you spare the time? It would be such a help if you could."

"Of course I can, and Mrs. Foley will just have to like it, my lady."

She did come to my room after breakfast, and by twelve-thirty the skirt was done. I had already finished making the bows, and I knew that I would have time to attach them and finish trimming the neckline after luncheon. So I told Mrs. Muldoon that I could finish it myself, and thanked her profusely.

By three o'clock that afternoon, the dress was finished, and I tried it on. I was delighted by what I saw in the long wardrobe mirror. The blue and violet of the dress were marvelous together, and flattered me.

With it, I thought, I will wear my white gloves, I will carry my white lace fan, and I will wear the little French silk flowers in my hair. Since I have no one to do it for me, it will be foolish to attempt anything elaborate. I will part it in the center, comb it back simply, and gather it behind my head with the flowers. But they are all white—if only I had five or six blue ones to repeat the blue in my dress. I could dye six of them blue, using ink from the drawing room diluted with a little water. Do I have the time? I must! It would make all the difference.

So I snatched a glass from the wash-hand-stand, ran down to the drawing room with it, poured a few drops of ink into it, returned to my room, poured a little water into the ink, swished the little flowers in the mixture one by one, and then placed them on a paper on the windowsill to dry. They were not quite the same blue as my dress, but that would not be noticed. They would do beautifully.

By the time I had dyed the flowers, carried my dress

down to the laundry rooms and pressed it, and returned to my room, it was six o'clock. I wished I had had time for a nap, but that was out of the question because Mrs. Muldoon had said that she would bring me water for washing my hair and my bath at six o'clock or shortly thereafter. She would not be able to do it any later than that, as she was leaving Castle Cloud early that evening.

She arrived with the water on schedule, and it was just as well that she had brought it then, because by the time I had bathed and washed and dried my hair, it was time to put on a dress and go down to dinner. After dinner I would arrange my hair for the party and change into my evening dress.

I was apprehensive about the meal. I hoped that Edmond would not launch into an interminable explanation of why I should not go to the party, and he did not. I could not believe that he had forgotten I was going, but he did not mention the subject. Instead, he and his mother manufactured conversation now and then to relieve the long period of silence. They talked about the dowager countess's long letter to her son, about the rector's cautioning his congregation in church the day before to watch out for the mad dog and to pen up any dogs found bitten, about Lord Clareham's not being able to remember meeting Sir Alexander Withering, and about Monsieur Laval's wishing to visit his niece in Rouen.

I did not contribute much to the conversation during dinner. I was too excited about going to Hawthorn Hill. The meal seemed interminable, but I was thankful that the atmosphere was placid.

Then when it was over at last, and I had finished my coffee, I ran to my room and slipped out of my dress to do my hair. It took longer to do it than I had thought it would. I could not arrange the flowers to my satisfaction, and my nervousness and apprehension about the party, about meeting so many new people at once, did not help.

But finally, satisfied with my hair, I stepped into the skirt of my dress, slipped the wide-necked bodice carefully over my head, and stood before the mirror. Yes, I like it, I thought. Then I reached for my white cashmere shawl, threw it around my shoulders, snatched my fan and gloves, and ran to the window to look down at the drive below. It was exactly nine-thirty, but Colen had not brought the carriage around yet. He would be there at any moment, though, so I hurried from my room and down to the hall below, putting on my gloves as I went.

"Good evening, my lady," Mitchell said. He stood at the doorway to the vestibule as if he had been waiting for me.

"Good evening, Mitchell," I replied.

"I have a message for you from Colen, my lady. He asked me to tell you that since his lordship required the carriage this evening, he would be unable to drive you to Hawthorn Hill."

"His lordship is using the carriage? I heard no carriage."

"His lordship departed from the east front at nine o'clock, my lady. Colen was driving."

"But he said nothing to me about using the carriage tonight," I said. "Where has he gone? When will he be back? When did he decide to do this—could he not have driven himself? He knew I was going out."

Mitchell was unable to subdue the slightest smile. He was enjoying my frustration. "I could not say, my lady," he said.

"This is monstrous! How dare he—" I was so furious for an instant that I could have struck Mitchell, and I wanted to.

But it was only for an instant. And then I knew that I would go to no party that night. If Colen did not drive me, there was no way I could get to Hawthorn Hill. In that dress and those shoes, I would not have been able to walk there, even if it were nearby. Nor could I possibly harness a horse and hitch him to a carriage to drive myself there. And I knew that Edmond had done this purposely, to prevent me from going.

So it took all my self-control to say, calmly, "I hope nothing unpleasant has happened to cause his lordship to dash off so suddenly. I shall be sorry to miss the party at Hawthorn Hill, but then, it is only a party. Thank you, Mitchell. Good night."

Then I turned my back on him and walked to the stairway and to my room.

I was dreadfully disappointed that night. I had not realized how much I had looked forward to dancing again and, of course, to seeing David. But the following morning I was able to look at things less emotionally. I was sure then, that Edmond had taken the carriage to spite me and to prevent me from going to the party. If that had not been so, if he had *had* to go out, he would have ridden or driven one of the carriages himself. No, he had done it out of spite. To have given me no warning, to have let me find out for myself at the last minute was sadistic. He wanted to hurt me for having defied him. How could he have been so unkind? It was the unkindness that I minded, not the futile anticipations and preparations for the party or even that I had missed it. I minded terribly that one person had deliberately set out to hurt another. I felt that a little of my dignity as a human being had been stripped from me because another of my own kind had been so odious. And because of this, I felt soiled and in need of cleansing myself.

And I would be having breakfast with Edmond in a little while. How would I act? I could not pretend to like him after last night, and having learned some of the things I had learned about him recently. But I would be polite and considerate, and then I would try to see as little of him as possible. To reprove Edmond would be ill-mannered and accomplish nothing, nor would discussing the events of the night before accomplish anything either. I would not mention them.

But I would not refuse any help Edmond might give me in the future. Why he wanted to place me in a position as a companion or governess, I did not know, but I was sure that he felt it would somehow be to his advantage. Well, it could be to my advantage too. It was much more advantageous than teaching. Lord Clareham was right—teaching was a grubby job. More important, since I had no vocation for it, no love of teaching, I knew I could not expect to succeed at it. As a companion or governess here in Devonshire, on the other hand, I would at least live in pleasant surroundings. I would not be completely divorced from society, and I would be somewhere near David. Perhaps the situation with Lady Withering was the thing for me, and who knew what pleasant things might happen at Moor House?

Having sorted these things out in my mind, I felt better prepared to confront Edmond, and I went down to breakfast. I think he was surprised and perhaps even disappointed that I made no accusations during the meal or even mentioned his taking the carriage the night before, and since he did not bring the subject up, breakfast passed placidly enough. We said little more to each other than our good-mornings.

As it progressed, the day seemed unable to make up its mind whether to shine the sun or to shower. One moment the inside of the house darkened almost enough to require lamplight, and the next it glowed with sunshine. So I did not go walking because I was afraid it might rain. Instead, I sat in the drawing room all morning, reading, and I returned there to my book after luncheon.

After luncheon, Flora arrived. I heard her carriage drive up and looked out the window to see who it was. Then Mitchell informed her footman that I was at home—he would not have dared to do otherwise—and shortly I heard Flora's footsteps following Mitchell's to the drawing room door.

"Miss Stratton," Mitchell announced.

"Mary!" Flora cried, as she ran toward me. "Are you all right? I have been out of my mind with worry." When she reached me, to my astonishment, she embraced me, kissed me on the cheek, and held me close for a moment, as though we were long-lost sisters. Then she held me at arm's length and examined me as she said, "When you did not come last night, I was sure something dreadful had happened. I did not sleep a wink."

"I am perfectly all right, Flora, as you can see," I said. I could not help laughing at her playacting. "Really, but how sweet of you to be so concerned."

"Concerned? I was half out of my mind. What happened? Why didn't you come?"

"I was terribly disappointed, Flora. Sit here with me while I tell you." And when we were seated on a sofa together, I continued, "I spent all of yesterday getting ready—fixing my dress and pressing it. Well, I have no one here to do things for me, so I must do for myself. I had arranged with Colen, the coachman and groom, to have the carriage at the entrance front at nine-thirty. And when I came down, all dressed, at nine-thirty, Mitchell told me that Edmond had required Colen to drive him out and that they had left at nine o'clock! You see, I had no way to get to Hawthorn Hill. So I went back upstairs and to bed. There was *nothing* else to do. I did not sleep though—I was too unhappy about it."

"Oh, my dear, how terrible, how unforgiveable of Edmond to be so thoughtless. He should have told you. He should have sent a message, and I would have sent a carriage—I should love to have. You poor dear. I shall have to have a word with him. Why that is simply shocking. Where is he?"

"Edmond? Why, I don't know. I have not seen him since luncheon. He did it on purpose, Flora, to keep me from going out."

"Nonsense, Mary, Edmond would not do a thing like that. It was just thoughtlessness on his part—truly it was. He is such a sensitive man, and his responsibilities, with his father and all, must be overwhelming. We should be understanding, Mary. He didn't think.

"But enough of that. I came to take you for a drive—that is, if you were well, which you are. You must be dying to get out a little, being cooped up here so long. I thought you would enjoy a little drive through the countryside. We could go to Croyde, and then I know a track out to Baggy Point. It is lovely there by the sea."

"I would love to, Flora, but will it rain?"

"If it rains, it will only be a shower, and we will put the top up."

I was delighted, and ran to my room for a shawl to throw over my shoulders in case it should be chilly by the ocean. In five minutes we were on our way.

It was a pretty drive through the lanes to Croyde. On either side of us the hedged fields and pastures of Devonshire lay deep in cloud shadows, splashed here and there with sunshine.

When we reached Baggy Point, Marsden stopped the carriage, and Paul, Flora's footman, let down the steps and handed us out so that we could walk a little way along the cliff path.

"It *is* lovely, Flora. Breathtaking!" I said, as we ambled along. "And the air is delicious. See how the clouds reflect in the water and how it shines where the sun strikes it. And listen to the surf down there."

"Yes," she said. "Oh, I wish we had seen Edmond, so I could have asked him along. How good this would have been for him—to get away for an afternoon of peace and beauty—it would have done him so much good. You see, I understand him. I know what he needs, Mary." She placed her hand on my arm. "He needs understanding. He needs someone to *understand* him, and stand by his side loyally, to encourage and help him. Don't you agree?"

"Yes, I suppose almost anyone needs. . ."

"Especially Edmond," she said. "Goodness, he needs someone so badly. I could give him these things. If only he *realized* it. Most men think that the physical is so important, when it is not. It is emotional security and peace that matter. Don't you agree?"

"Well, I think they are both. . ."

"I know he likes me. Oh, he doesn't wear his feelings on his sleeve, but I can tell. I can see it in his eyes when we meet. And Papa has *increased* my marriage portion, Mary, to £60,000. Isn't that marvelous? Think what that much money would mean to Castle Cloud. But I don't think Edmond knows about it, and we have got to think of some way for him to know. Now, I want to help *you*. Mamma asked me to invite you and Edmond to dinner at Hawthorn Hill on Friday night. Could you convince him to come?"

"I don't see how, Flora," I said. "He has very strong feelings about mourning."

"But it is such a little dinner party. Lewis is still down and is dying to meet you. Will *you* come? We will send Marsden with the carriage for you then, and he will bring you home, so we will not risk any repeat of last night's tragedy."

"Thank you, Flora. You are an angel. I would love to come, you know that."

"Lovely. That is settled then, but we must be getting back."

Then she linked her arm through mine and we walked, arm in arm, back to the carriage.

Later toward the end of our drive home, as we came in sight of the stone bridge and the drive to the Castle, I said, "It has been delightful, Flora. Thank you. I feel so refreshed."

"Good!" she said. "You need a friend—an old friend to keep you company. I will come and visit you often at the Castle, since you cannot very well come to me. This is just the first of so many pleasant afternoons we shall have together. We must enjoy our freedom while we have it, you know." She giggled and squeezed my arm, and then in mock solemnity said, "Soon the serious state of matrimony will be upon us."

"It may be upon you, Flora, but I think not upon me."

"Why ever not?" she asked.

"Well, I have no dowry, for one thing—for the main thing."

"But didn't your papa— He must have made some provision for you."

"He lost or spent all his money before he died."

"But he was a very rich man. Papa said he had I-don't-know-how-many-thousand acres, and Gunderbury Hall is one of the biggest houses in England."

"That may be, Flora," I said, "but I am penniless today. I know that very unwelcome fact only too well. But I will manage."

"What do you plan to do?" she asked.

"Edmond is helping me to find a position as companion or governess for the time being, and then we shall see."

"Oh, no! You couldn't *possibly*, Mary. You have your title—that will help, and you are very pretty, too."

"Oh, Flora!"

"Yes, you are. Come and meet Lewis on Friday night. He is very handsome and nice, and he has lots of friends. Oh, look! There is Edmond."

By that time we had driven across the bridge, up the hill, and around the bend in the drive. The house lay before us. There, at the base of the steps of the entrance front, Edmond stood next to a man on horseback. The man was David. They must have finished their conversation because, as we drove forward, David began to ride away from Edmond—down the drive toward us.

And as he approached, Flora cried, "Drive on, Marsden. I want to speak to Lord Althrop."

So we sped toward the house, and as we passed David, he tipped his hat and said something, but I could not hear what it was because at that moment Flora called, "Good afternoon, Mr. Field." Then we had passed him, and she turned and waved as we drove on.

We drove up to the house, and Marsden stopped the carriage in front of the steps.

"Edmond!" Flora cried. "How nice to see you."

Edmond must have seen us coming, but he had ignored us completely and had begun to climb the steps to the portico. When Flora called to him, however, he turned, descended to the drive, and walked over to the carriage.

"Good afternoon, Miss Stratton, Mary," he said.

"Edmond! Don't be so formal," Flora said. "It has always been Flora until now. Mother asked me to invite you to dinner on Friday—just a tiny dinner party, nothing elaborate at all, really. Just a few old friends. Mary is coming. Why don't you bring her?"

"Miss Stratton," Edmond replied, "your poor memory astounds me. Please let me remind you that my brother, James, died on the fourth of June. You do remember him, I hope? If you recall, he was the handsome young man—at least the ladies considered him handsome, for what reason I do not know—who lived here at Castle Cloud and was pursued so vigorously and so futilely for so long by one of our—local young ladies. The opposite will, I suppose, attract."

"I came to see Vivian. She was my closest friend."

"My sister, Vivian, was the path to James. And now that James is dead and Vivian gone, we observe a budding friendship with Mary. It is all rather revolting."

"Mary and I are old friends. We met each other four years ago through Vivian. Edmond, you have been working too hard, you look so tired. You need relaxation with friends. I know you do—I can see it. Come to dinner on Friday night and bring Mary. We will have a lovely time."

"I am pleased to say that that is one lovely time I can very well do without, thank you, and I forbid Mary to attend also." Then he turned his back on us and walked up the steps and into the house without looking back.

"Childish! Rude! Stupid!" I said, when I had recovered from shock. "How could he be so obviously nasty? Why? What could he possibly gain by it? I am so sorry, Flora."

"Mary, he didn't mean it," Flora said. "He is upset. That is a way for him to let his unhappiness out. Now, don't *you* be upset, too. We women have to understand our men. How can we help them if we don't? Edmond is very fond of me. I could see it even then in his eyes. Now he will have the ordeal of an apology to go through, which is entirely unnecessary. Poor Edmond.

"We dine at eight, so Marsden will call for you at

seven-thirty on Friday night. I will see you soon after that."

"I will be ready. Thank you, Flora."

As I said this, Paul opened the door of the carriage and handed me down. . . I stood on the steps of the house until they began to move, and then waved them good-by as they rolled away.

I had two things on my mind as we sat at dinner that evening—Edmond's attack on Flora, and David's visit to Castle Cloud. What had David wanted? What had he said to Edmond? But I decided not to mention either David or Flora at dinner. Edmond's quarrel with Flora was none of my business. And as far as David was concerned, I would walk up to the monument after dinner. I knew he would be there, and he could tell me then about his visit with Edmond.

At first, during the meal, neither Lady Clareham nor Edmond had anything to say, which was not unusual. But as we began the second course, Edmond looked up at me and said, "You are very quiet this evening, Mary. I hope you are feeling well."

"Yes, quite well, Edmond, thank you. I—simply have had nothing to say. I am sorry. This fondu is delicious."

"But you were not thinking about the fondu, were you, Mary?"

"I—hardly know what I was thinking. Nothing of any importance—the day, the drive with Flora. It was lovely."

"And my hateful remarks to her," he said.

"That is your description, Edmond, not mine."

"But that is what you were thinking, wasn't it, Mary?"

"I thought you were cruel," I said. "I do not know how you could have said those things to her."

"Flora called this afternoon," Edmond said to his mother, "and took Mary for a drive. When they returned I was, unfortunately, on the steps of the entrance front. I was accosted by Flora."

"Accosted?" Lady Clareham said. "Oh, Edmond!"

"Well, I don't know what else you would call it. I had no intention of speaking to her—of having anything to do with her. She revolts me. She is a disgusting example of the female sex."

"Edmond!" Lady Clareham reprimanded.

"Well, she is. She has no accomplishments. Can she play the piano? Can she sing? Can she sew? Can she ride? Can she dance? Can she play cards? Can she carry on an intelligent conversation? Is she attractive? Is she in the least stylish? The answers are all no. No—no, no, no, no, *no!* She is entirely without interesting or redeeming qualities. Mary says I was cruel to her. But, Mary," he looked at me then, "you do not know Flora at all, and without that knowledge you have no basis upon which to form such a conclusion. A little knowledge is a dangerous thing, and you will find that making such harsh judgments with so little of it will lead you to unwarranted opinions. It could lead to doing someone a great injustice.

"Flora," he continued, "is as determined and tenacious as a hungry wolf hunting its prey—especially when her prey is a man. We all watched her constant and futile pursuit of my brother, James, with something akin to amusement. That was cruel. She was dying to have him, and he loathed her as much as I do."

"He did not loathe her," Lady Clareham said. "He did not loathe anyone."

"Well, he certainly ran from her," Edmond said to his mother. Then he turned back to me. "*That* was cruel. Now wait, wait till I have finished. If he had told her what he thought of her, he would have spared her endless torment, but he would have had to be blunt, even brutal, or Flora would never have understood. So you see, Mary, I was being kind. I hope she was able to ascertain from my remarks that she would be wasting her time chasing after me. God only knows, I was blunt enough, but she is stupid as well as ugly and may not have grasped it after all."

"She is not ugly, Edmond," I said. "Her skin condition will vanish soon, and with the proper clothes and a becoming hair arrangement, she could be quite attractive. Actually, Edmond, I wonder you do not see the advantages of a match there."

"Ha! You sound like my mother," Edmond said.

"Well, there are the practical aspects. To a man of your superior intelligence they should be obvious. That Flora wants to marry so badly is, I think, a very good indication that she will make a good wife and mother. Further, since you wish to restore Castle Cloud to its former magnificence, why not, if you are going to marry, marry a woman with a fortune? Flora is a woman with a fortune, who is good and kind and who would make a good wife and mother. What more could you ask? You know, don't you, that her father has increased her marriage portion to £60,000. Think what £60,000 would mean to Castle Cloud."

"Who told you that?" Edmond asked.

"She did," I replied.

"Ha! And think what a man would have to go through to get it—disgusting, revolting. I don't want you to go to dinner there or in any way encourage her presence here. You will do me that kindness, please. And I have no intention of marrying. Is that clear? No intention of marrying, *whatsoever*. Now, may we talk of pleasanter things?"

"Certainly, Edmond," I said. "As I was saying, the view from Baggy Point was breathtaking. The sea was quite rough. . . ."

I made a determined effort at chitchat. Edmond was bored by it. And after a few minutes of idle talk, I stopped. We finished the meal without further conversation.

After dinner I walked up the hill to the monument, and as I neared the hilltop, I heard David's horse climbing the other side of it.

Caesar carried David to within a few yards of me. He jumped down and called, "You are all right?"

"Yes, I am fine," I answered.

"Where were you last night?" he asked, when he stood in front of me. "Why didn't you come to the party?"

"I couldn't, David. Edmond took the carriage at the last minute, and Colen had to drive him. So I had no way to get there."

"What a filthy trick," David said.

"Yes, cruel. He did not even tell me, but left a message with Mitchell." Then I told David in detail about the evening before, and how angry and disappointed I had been.

While I told my story, we walked through the grass to our seats on the building blocks and sat down, but this time David sat beside me.

"You were terribly disappointed?" he asked.

"Well, of course. I had looked forward to it and I wanted to dance with you."

"Dearest Mary," he said, looking at me in that intent way which always made my spine tingle.

"Why did you come to the Castle? I couldn't believe it was you. What did you say to Edmond?"

Then he took my face in both his big hands and said, "Did you think I would give you away? No, I was worried about you. I had to know that you were all right."

Then he kissed me.

"But—but what did you say?" I said, after a moment.

He smiled, and then released me. "Only that I was passing by," he said, "and decided to inquire whether or not they had heard from Vivian. I was very relieved to see you riding in the carriage with Flora."

"Were you?" I asked. "What was the party like?" What stupid questions, I thought. I am so confused. What should I say?

"Oh, it was very nice, I suppose. Nothing special. They had a violinist and a pianist. There was some dancing and the older people played whist. There was to be a supper of some kind later, but I left before that, when I realized you would not be coming. I could not imagine what had happened to you—I thought all kinds of things and almost stormed the Castle at midnight to find out."

He had held out his open palm to me as he spoke, and I had put my hand into it.

"You didn't enjoy it?" I asked.

"You weren't there," he said.

"Flora came by this afternoon and took me for a drive. She was worried too." Then I told David about the afternoon, about Edmond's treatment of Flora, and about the conversation at dinner.

"Are you still planning to go to Flora's dinner party?" David asked.

"Yes. Flora is sending a carriage, so I don't see how Edmond can stop me—short of restraining me bodily, and he would not do that. You are not going?"

"No. We are not asked to every function at Hawthorn Hill—not even to most of them. My father was in trade, you know, and even though he could buy and sell the lot of them and has more influence in the county than they could ever hope to have, they cannot afford to let us forget it."

"That is the kind of thing that Vivian rebelled against,

and I am glad she did, the more I think of it. I should be horrified, and in a way I am, but I am glad too. I don't know, I am all mixed-up about it, David."

"And no wonder. Things are changing so, Mary. The cities and the factories are growing, and they are making new kinds of people—factory workers and miners, organizing into unions, engineers, and scientists. Look how the railways—the steam engine—has changed our lives, and the telegraph, and now electricity. In another fifty years things are going to be very different. There may not be an aristocracy. Who knows? You have a right to be all mixed-up—a lot of people are."

"You make it sound rather frightening, David. But I must go." We stood up together, but David did not let go of my hand. Instead he took my other one in his and began to pull me closer to him. "No, don't, David, please," I said.

He smiled down at me and let go of my hands. "Mary, I am going to come to the house from now on and call on you in the normal manner. The time for clandestine meetings has past."

"No, David, not yet."

"Why not? You will be going out visiting, now, and to parties. I want to see more of you than a half-hour in the evening when I cannot even see you properly much of the time."

"David, meet me here just once more. Give me until after Friday night."

"All right, Saturday night then," he said.

"Not before?"

"I don't know if I can before, in the evening."

"Something on the farm?" I asked.

"Yes. Saturday night, and then I am off to Windsor."

"But you bought the cattle."

"Yes," he said, "that is, I made the arrangements. But now I must go and get them."

"Till Saturday night, then. I must *go*. Good night."

Then I left him.

❧ Chapter Nine ❧

THE FOLLOWING EVENING, while we waited for Mitchell to announce dinner, Lady Clareham and I sat facing each other in the drawing room, and Edmond paced restlessly from one window to another, looking out at the grounds. We had not spoken since we had said our good-evenings. Lady Clareham pretended interest in a magazine. Edmond ignored us.

The house was very quiet.

Suddenly, the silence was shattered by the sound of the doorbell. I heard it quite distinctly, and I heard Mitchell's footsteps in the hall as he left the dining room to answer it. Then I heard voices, and presently Mitchell entered the drawing room and approached my chair.

"There is a filthy boy in the vestibule," he said, loudly enough for Edmond to hear, "who insists on seeing the 'lady visitor.' I can only suppose he wishes to see your ladyship. He is quite insistent, my lady."

"Thank you, Mitchell," I said. "It must be Stanley," I explained to Lady Clareham.

"Who the devil—" Edmond said, as I hurried from the room. "Don't let this delay dinner, Mitchell. If it is ready, announce. . . ."

"Are you Stanley Reade?" I asked the boy, when I reached the vestibule. I had time to notice only how very brown his skin was and how dirty he looked—as if he had not washed for months.

"Yes, miss. It's Alice, miss. She wants you. Will you come?"

"Is there something wrong?" I asked.

"She's having her baby, miss, but the baby don't want to come. Mrs. Grundy says it should have come yesterday. Alice wants you. Can you come?"

"Yes, at once. Run on ahead and tell Alice I will be there as soon as I can."

No sooner had I said this than he flung open the door and ran out onto the portico and down the steps. I turned and dashed across the hall and into the drawing room.

"Please excuse me, Lady Clareham, Edmond," I said. "I will not be having dinner. It is Alice. She is having her baby, and there seems to be trouble. I am going to her."

"I will come with you," Lady Clareham said, getting up from her chair.

"Oh, no, stay and have your dinner. There is a Mrs. Grundy with her. . . ."

"The midwife from the village. Dr. Norton?"

"I don't know, but there would be nothing you could do."

"And what do you think *you* could do," Edmond said from across the room. "I suppose you are experienced with. . ."

"Be there," I said. "She asked for me, and I will be there. Excuse me."

I ran to my room to change my shoes, as I had decided to walk over the hill to the Reades' cottage. I could do that almost before Colen could harness a horse to a carriage. My old walking shoes, then, would get me there much quicker than the ones I was wearing.

But I did not walk most of the way—I ran. Only when I could not run anymore, did I walk, and then I ran again as soon as I could, until I came out of the wood in sight of the cottage at the end of the field. Then I walked more slowly to catch my breath, and to calm myself before entering the house.

And as I neared it, I could feel that there was something wrong there—a tenseness, a sense of urgency.

I wish it were not necessary to relate the terrible things that happened there. Moreover, I wish I could forget them myself—banish them from my memory as though they had not happened. But they are part of my story and must be told.

When I arrived at the door of the cottage, I knocked, but there was no answer. The door stood slightly ajar, so I pushed it open and slipped into the room. I noticed at once that the bed had been moved out from the corner, toward the center of the room. William Reade, a woman whom I presumed was Mrs. Grundy and Stanley stood before it, between the bed and me. They faced Alice, who lay upon it, screening her from view.

"I came as quickly as I could," I said.

The woman glanced over her shoulder at me and said, "Go on the other side and hold her under the arm."

I walked around them to get to the other side of the bed, but at the foot of it, I saw what was happening and stopped, staring at the girl who lay there.

Alice lay on her back across the width of the narrow bed. She was naked below her breasts—her nightdress had been pushed back, baring her swollen stomach and her loins and limbs. Her legs were bent double, her knees in the air, so that her heels rested on the very edge of the bed and almost touched her buttocks, which had been raised on a pillow. Mrs. Grundy stood in front of the pillow between Mr. Reade and Stanley. They had each grasped one of Alice's knees and, holding it tightly, had spread her thighs as far apart as they could go.

From the opening between Alice's legs, her baby's arm and hand reached out into the air. The tiny limb was still, the blood on it dry.

"Hold her under the arm so her don't slide off," Mrs. Grundy commanded me.

But it was a moment before I could tear my eyes away from the baby's arm. Then I took hold of myself and rushed to Alice's head, which hung down over the other side of the bed, slipped my hands under her shoulders, and held her tightly by the armpits.

She looked up at me, and I could barely hear her whisper, "Help me. My baby's not dead. Tell me my baby's not dead."

"It is all right," I said. "It is going to be all right."

Then I looked at Mrs. Grundy for further instructions. She was perspiring.

She took hold of the baby's arm and said, "I be going to push this back in, so I can reach up and turn it around and get its feet. Hold fast."

Alice held her arms straight and stiff, her fists clenched. She tensed and closed her eyes. Then Mrs. Grundy pushed, and Alice moaned in pain.

"No, no," she murmured.

At that, Mrs. Grundy let go at once, but as she did so,

Alice screamed with all the strength she had left. That scream told me something terrible had happened. And then Alice looked up at me, her eyes wide with fear, and shrieked, "Something's bust! It's broke!"

A movement drew my attention from the girl's face to her baby's arm, and as I watched, it slowly receded of its own accord back into the mother and disappeared.

Blood poured from Alice's womb in a river then, and ran out of her, over the bed, and onto the floor. And with it went her color—draining from her face and leaving a cold sweat behind. She wretched and vomited. Then I held her head in my arms and grabbed a towel from the bed and patted her face dry.

Mrs. Grundy reached for Alice's wrist, felt her pulse, and shook her head. Then she slumped and held out her palms in defeat.

Alice closed her eyes and died.

And then a dog barked outside the cottage. It was the only sound for quite some time.

"Her was wrong from the first," Mrs. Grundy said. "The child lay wrong—I knew as soon as I felt the little hand when I broke the gathering-of-the-waters. It couldn't come down. The way it lay stopped it from coming down. Then her rupture and her hemorrhage. Well, I done all I could. I delivered hundreds of them for forty years. Once in a while there be trouble, but us be not God, you know, or know His way. I been here since Monday night. I done everything. . . ."

As she spoke, William Reade walked around the bed and stood over me. Tears glistened on his cheeks. "I make him suffer worse than her done," he growled at me. "Now, go away." Then his hand gripped my shoulder, and he flung me away from Alice. "Her want to be alone with her father now."

I watched him lay Alice tenderly back lengthwise on the bed, pull down her nightdress, and fold her hands on her breast. Then he brushed the hair away from her face, sank to the floor on his knees by her side, and wept.

I turned from them and ran from the cottage. Then I walked back to Castle Cloud—into the rose garden, to Diana's Temple, and then to the far end of the field beyond it. I sat on the bench until long after it was dark and all the lights had gone out in the house.

I woke often during the night that Alice died. Over and over in my mind I heard her scream, and I heard the terror in her voice as she cried out.

I arrived late for breakfast that morning. Edmond looked at me with annoyance as I entered the dining room, but I did not care. And since I wanted only a cup of coffee, I knew that I would not interfere with Mitchell's schedule. Edmond was silent while I sipped it. He did not ask what had happened the night before—he wasn't interested.

Finally, I said, "Alice Reade and her baby died last night."

"Pity," was all he replied.

After breakfast I went to Lady Clareham's room and told her what had happened the night before, and then I left the house and walked to the stable yard. It was deserted. I looked into the stables, the feed room, and the saddle and harness rooms, but I could not find Colen. Then, as I crossed the yard to the rear of the men's pavilion, the door opened.

Colen came out of it, and as he hurried toward me he called, "Good morning, my lady. Is there something I can do for you?" Then when he stood before me, he continued, "I am sorry about Monday night, my lady. His lordship needed me to drive him, so there was nothing I could do."

"Of course not, Colen. I understand. You had to drive him. I hope it was not urgent or unpleasant business."

"No, my lady."

"Where did you drive him, Colen?" I had tried but could not resist asking the question.

Colen hesitated a moment, then answered, "I drove him to Barnstaple, my lady. We didn't stop anywhere. I just drove him there, and then we turned around and drove back."

"I see. I am going for a walk, Colen, and I thought I would take Sarah along. She must get awfully tired of being tied up here in the yard, and I would like to have her company. She would be quite safe if I took her on a rope, don't you think? Have you heard anything more about the mad dog, by the way?"

"No, my lady. But Sarah has disappeared."

"Oh?"

"Yes, my lady. I don't know what could have happened to her. I closed up last night, and then I untied Sarah and took her in with me. Then I went to bed, and Sarah lay down by my bed where she always does, and we both went to sleep. This morning she was gone. The doors were closed and the bedrooms are on the second floor, so she couldn't have jumped out the window. There wasn't a sound during the night, that I know of, and this morning she was gone. Everything was just as it was when I went to bed, but Sarah had disappeared."

"Have you looked for her?" I asked.

"Yes, my lady, I have looked everywhere. She is gone."

"But dogs do not vanish into air," I said. "There must be an explanation."

"Yes, but I can't imagine what, my lady. The only way she could have gotten out last night was if someone let her out, but I would have heard it. And nobody would do that."

"How very odd, Colen. Oh, but she will come back. When she does, tell me, will you please?"

"Yes, my lady. I am sure she will, my lady, but she didn't come back for her breakfast, and that is strange because she never misses a meal. Yes, I'll tell you when she comes back, my lady."

"Thank you, Colen," I said.

Then I retraced my steps across the yard, walked around the house and down the drive to the stone bridge, down the bank to the shore of the bay, and along it for perhaps a hundred yards where I found a rock to sit on. I missed Sarah, and I felt lonely and depressed as I sat there thinking. I must stop thinking about Alice's death, I decided, I must put it behind me. Life is full of horrors like that, and unless there is something we can do about them, we must turn our backs on them as much as we can. There is no point in thinking about those things.

I sat there for an hour looking out over the still, gray sheet of water and up at the empty gray sky, and the more I told myself I should not think about her, the more I thought about Alice. Her death had shocked me deeply. I had never witnessed anything like that before, and my mind was filled with the horror of it.

But deep beneath the horror seethed a joy: David had kissed me.

A portrait of Vivian hung to the left of one of the chimney pieces in the drawing room. It showed Vivian sitting on the rim of the fountain's basin in the rose garden. The artist had filled the basin with water, and in the picture Vivian reached down and dipped her hand into it. I stood before the painting that evening admiring it, as I had done so many times since coming to Castle Cloud. Lady Clareham entered the room.

"Good evening, Lady Clareham," I said.

"Good evening, Mary," she replied, as she sat down on the sofa near me. "I believe you have become quite fascinated by Vivian's portrait."

"Yes, it is lovely. Somehow, the artist has captured that brilliance, that excitement that Vivian has about her. I don't know what it is—the eyes perhaps. It fascinates me. When was it done?"

"A year ago last month. It was done by Watt. He painted it here. Lady Wright, an old friend of mine, knows him quite well. Vivian and I met him at her house in London a year ago last spring. He insisted on painting her, and I had a little money of my own— She was so beautiful, you see—she affected everyone who ever met her. They all wanted to be touched by her sweet, lovely spell—it was almost magic. And she was so kind and unconsciously—" Lady Clareham stopped speaking and reached for her handkerchief to daub at the tears that glistened in her eyes, but she lost control then, and wept.

I sat down on the edge of the sofa next to her and said, "Lady Clareham, you talk as though Vivian were dead. I know that America is a long way off, but I think Vivian will be happy there. She must be with the man she loves, to be happy, and the United States is a place of opportunity for her husband. She will write and then come back to visit. I know she will. I know Vivian—there is too much thoughtfulness there, too much kindness. Wait and see if she doesn't."

I meant to be soothing, but my words seemed to have the opposite effect, so I stopped speaking altogether and, after a few minutes, Lady Clareham quieted and stopped crying.

"I am sorry, Mary. I try not to do that, but I cannot help it sometimes."

"I know," I said. "I miss her too, very much. She is

wearing James's Roman-coin pin in the painting. Isn't that James's coin?"

"Yes. She insisted it be in the picture. It had become a kind of good-luck charm for her. She always wore it—many times where it couldn't be seen, but I don't think she was ever without it."

"Ever without what?" Edmond asked from behind us.

"Oh! You startled me," I said. I had not heard him come into the room. "We were talking about Vivian's portrait."

At that moment we were interrupted by Mitchell's announcement that dinner was served, and we went into the dining room.

"Did Colen tell you that Sarah has disappeared?" I asked Lady Clareham, after we had been served the soup. "Before I came in to change for dinner, I went to see if she had returned, but she hadn't."

"No, Mary. What happened?" Lady Clareham asked.

"She disappeared into thin air," I said. Then I told her the story as Colen had told it to me in the morning. "How do you think she could have vanished like that?" I concluded.

"Very simple," Edmond said.

"How?" I asked.

"She opened the door and left."

"How could she do that?" I asked.

"With her mouth, obviously," he replied. "She is a wily bitch—crafty and cunning. You cannot trust her. I have always hated that animal—common, nasty thing."

"Don't be ridiculous, Edmond," Lady Clareham said.

"What is ridiculous about that? Dogs are extraordinarily intelligent creatures. Everyone knows that. Why I have seen dogs at Vauxhall Gardens play musical instruments and even do sums. It would be nothing for the animal to turn a doorknob with its mouth and open the door, and that is what she did. She simply walked out of the building."

"Nonsense," said Lady Clareham.

"Nonsense? Look who is talking about nonsense. Why the way *you* are always running after those filthy idiots in the village with cans of milk and pots of soup. That is nonsense and it makes me sick. You cannot help those

people. Leave them be. Pots of soup indeed. Vulgar, hypocritical display."

"There is nothing hypocritical about giving a hungry
boy or girl food, and if you would think a little more
about somebody besides yourself, you would find that
people would like you more. James did and Vivian did.
They were both kind and considerate of others. I remember Vivian saying, 'Mother, if only Edmond could think of
somebody else. . . .' "

"Are you inferring that Vivian did not like me
Mother?" Edmond asked her. "Why would you possibly
want to infer that? Why?" He stared at his mother for
a moment as if daring her to answer. "You know perfectly
well that she *adored* me. She adored me even more than
James. We were extraordinarily close."

Lady Clareham looked down at her plate and began to
play with her soup. She did not reply.

A few minutes later, to break the silence, I said, "Who
are the Fields?"

"How do you know about the Fields?" Edmond asked.
"Did Vivian write to you about them?"

"I don't believe she ever said anything about them except that she knew them, once in a letter. Flora told me
that that was David Field whom you were talking to when
we drove up on Tuesday."

"One of the local families," Edmond said.

"Mr. Field is a banker, Mary, who bought Oakland
Park," Lady Clareham said.

Then, during the entree, Edmond looked at me and
asked, "I suppose you told Flora about Vivian?"

"No, Edmond, I did not," I said.

"Why not?"

"Well—the subject never came up."

"You mean she didn't ask?"

"No."

"You are going to their dinner party tomorrow night?"

"Yes, Edmond, I am. Flora is sending a carriage for
me."

"Quite right, Mary, my dear."

I looked at Edmond in astonishment.

"Yes," he said, "I have been doing some soul-searching
about this, and I have been praying for guidance about it.
I have said to myself and to the Lord, 'Mary is a good

girl, and she wants to go out a little before settling down to her position. Could we not be a little less strict, a little less rigid? Could we not stretch a point for Mary?' We think you *could* go to Flora's, Mary, without doing any harm. You would go anyway, so you may as well go with our approval." As he said the last sentence, he gave me his most brilliant smile.

"Thank you, Edmond," I smiled back at him.

"And tell Flora about Vivian," he said. "She will want to know—I know she is concerned. People will be wanting to know. We cannot hide it—it is bound to come out, so if anyone should ask, tell them about it. Tell them the truth. It will be a rather terrible scandal, I am afraid, but that will pass. And it will be best to have it over with. You should not be affected by it though—it has nothing to do with you."

"But couldn't we say that she has gone to visit someone in America?" I said. "Or why not be vague and say nothing? It could hardly benefit Vivian to. . ."

"My dear Mary, the truth is always the best. 'Thou shalt not bear false witness,' you know. I am surprised that you should consider anything else."

I did not answer him. And we spoke of nothing else of importance during dinner. In fact we spoke very little at all after that. Edmond seemed to have retreated into his own thoughts, and Lady Clareham picked at her food abstractedly.

When we had finished eating and had had our coffee, I walked out onto the west portico, briefly commented on the evening to Edmond, and then walked down the hill to the stone bridge. I thought that if Sarah were nearby, she would come to me then, but she did not appear.

As I leaned against the balustrade of the bridge, the man from the yard in Appledore began to light the riding lights of the boats at anchor offshore, and I thought about the conversation at dinner. I wondered about two things: how could Edmond say that Vivian adored him. And what had made him change his mind about my going to dinner at Hawthorn Hill?

*   *   *

The following afternoon, since it was the day of the dinner party, I lay down at about three-thirty. I did not think I would be able to sleep, but after a half-hour I did, and I slept until Mrs. Muldoon woke me. I had arranged with her to bring my hot water at five o'clock.

Then I bathed, and washed my hair, and sat before the mirror and brushed it for a long time, wondering how to arrange it. I would wear the little silk flowers, but I had more time to fix my hair that day and wished to do something more interesting with it than I had on Tuesday night. Finally I decided to part it in the center, comb it back loosely over my ears into a smooth puff behind my head, turning it under at the neck. Then I would group the flowers to come from under the puff and sweep forward and up in a three-quarter-wreath effect around my head.

So I set to work on it, but when I had finished arranging my hair and the flowers at the back and one side of my head, I discovered that I would not have enough hairpins to finish the other side. To make matters worse, it was almost seven o'clock by then—I would never have time to start all over. I had been foolish to have attempted anything so elaborate.

My only salvation would be to get more hairpins, but I was sure that Cecile would not let me borrow any of hers. Then I thought that perhaps Vivian had left some of her hairpins behind. So I threw on a robe and ran to her room to see. There, I dashed at once to her chest of drawers, and snatched a small wooden box from the top of it. When I opened the box, however, I found that it contained Vivian's jewelry. It had been a long time since I had seen Vivian's jewel box and, in my panic, I had not remembered it. But another box, an oval *papier-mâché* one, stood on a china tray next to her hairbrushes. This would contain her hairpins, I was sure, and I was about to reach for it when a flash of gold from the open jewel box in my hand caught my eye. It came from the Roman-coin pin that James had given Vivian.

The pin lay on top of a tangle of beads and bracelets and brooches. I lifted it out to examine it. I remembered it very well. James had given it to Vivian the Christmas before I had visited Castle Cloud in 1852. It was a coin that he had found on a dig in Tripoli, at the site of the city of Nineveh. He had had it polished and mounted as a pin and given it to Vivian that Christmas, and she had fallen in love with it at once. I put it back in the box and set the box on the chest.

Then I picked up the *papier-mâché* box and found that it was full to the brim with hairpins as well as little combs and hatpins—it could not have held anything more. I *was* in luck. I took what I needed, ran back to my room, and finished my hair.

I had barely time to finish it and dress. But at seven twenty-five I stood before the mirror ready to leave, examined myself, and decided that I looked very pretty. At that moment I heard a carriage on the drive, so I put on my lace bonnet, tied it under my chin, flung my shawl around my shoulders, and—carrying my fan and gloves—hurried downstairs and out onto the entrance-front portico.

Flora's cabriolet stood at the base of the steps, and when he saw me, Paul jumped down, ran around to let down the step, and opened the door for me.

"Good evening, Marsden, Paul," I said, when I reached the carriage.

"Good evening, my lady," they said, almost in unison. And then Paul handed me into the carriage.

And we were off. It had been so long since I had been to a dinner party that I felt rather like Cinderella going to the ball. But a rather odd Cinderella—it felt peculiar to be visiting and yet going off alone to a dinner party without my host or hostess.

I wish Lord and Lady Clareham were here with me, I thought, as we crossed the stone bridge. Then we swung to the right and then turned right again into a lane which was entirely new to me. Soon we followed a river, which I recognized as the Tay. We were on the other side of it from Castle Cloud, and in the distance I saw Milton Penderton for a moment through the trees. Then we swung to the left, drove up a long hill and down into a valley dominated by a gray-stone house which I thought must be Hawthorn Hill.

It was, and as we sped down the long, straight drive that led to it, I had time to examine the building. The house was a tall, rectangular, three-storied, granite structure with a central pediment. It would have seemed stark had not a graceful, horseshoe staircase, rising to the first floor, been built to soften its lines.

The carriage stopped in front of the left arm of the

staircase, Paul handed me down, I climbed to the door, which was immediately opened by a footman, and stepped into the hall.

After removing my bonnet and shawl, I followed the butler down a long hall, gave him my name, and waited while he swung open the doors of a mauve and gold room filled with paintings.

"The Baroness Beauford," he announced.

As I entered the room, all conversation ceased. Perhaps a dozen people sat or stood there, and they all turned to look at me. But it was only for a moment, and then they began talking again.

"Mary!" Flora cried, as she ran toward me. She embraced and kissed me, and then turned to a gray-haired woman who had hurried after her. "Mother, do you remember Mary?"

"Yes, I believe I do. Mary, my dear, how nice of you to come."

"How very kind of you to ask me, Lady Wilton," I said.

"Tell me, how is Lord Clareham? We all pray for him—that he will recover. Isn't it strange to think that people all over the world are doing the same? And dear Julia?"

"Lord Clareham is about the same, Lady Wilton, and Lady Clareham, too. She is so terribly broken up about James's death."

"Still? Yes, I know, my dear. And I would be too. James was such a fine boy. And Vivian? Have they heard from Vivian? I wish she would come home. It would be so good for Julia."

"Yes, we have just heard. Vivian has gone to America."

"America? Whatever for? Whom do George and Julia know in America? Where in America?"

What was I to say? I thought. After what Edmond had told me, it would have to be the truth. I certainly could not risk saying anything else and then having him contradict me. And if it was to be the truth, it would be best if it were done directly.

"She—she has gone to join her fiancé," I said. "They will be married there."

"That is impossible," Lady Wilton said.

"I did not know you had heard from Vivian," Flora said. "Why didn't you tell me?"

"I meant to, Flora," I said, "but we had so many things to talk about that I am afraid I simply didn't get to it. You see," I said to Lady Wilton, "Mr. O'Connor went to the United States last January to make arrangements and sent for Vivian only last week. She left from London on Thursday, I believe."

"Mr. O'Connor? So it is true that she. . ."

"Mother, please," Flora said. "Come and meet Lewis, Mary."

She took my hand and pulled me across the room with her, toward two young men in their middle twenties. One was tall, slim, and sensitive-looking, with a mustache. The other was short, thickset, and complacent. They stood talking to a girl about my age. Both men wore the uniforms of lieutenants in the Foot Guards.

"Lewis," Flora said to the taller man, when we reached the group, "here is Mary."

"Good evening, Lady Beauford," he said. "Please allow me to introduce Miss Pridell and Lord Charles Pomperoy. We were discussing the appalling weather in London. . . ."

But I had not forgotten Lady Wilton. She had already fallen deep into conversation with a lady who could only be Miss Pridell's mother, and Reverend and Mrs. Anderson. And as I glanced at them, they glanced in unison back across the room at me. The expression on Mrs. Pridell's face was one of horror.

The news about Vivian had begun to circulate in earnest.

"Sir Roger and Lady Molehill," the butler called from the doorway.

"Sir Roger!" Lady Wilton cried, as she rushed toward the newcomers—a frail man in his nineties with a white beard, and a lady nearly as old as he.

"Roasting!" Lewis continued. "Mr. Pridell will bear me out, won't you Phillip?" he said to a meek young man who had joined us.

"Not having been in London, how would I know?" he said.

"Have you been in London in the last week, Lady Beauford?" Lewis asked.

"No, Lieutenant Stratton," I said, "and you make me very happy that I was not."

"Eighty degrees two days in a row," Lewis said.

"Oh, I do hope it won't be that way next July," Philomena Pridell said. "Did you know, Lord Charles, that father is taking a house in London next season? He is standing for parliament—so of course we shall have to be there."

"Really?" Lord Charles said to her. Then he turned to me. "Lady Beauford, you must *stay* in the country. The city is insufferable. Stay here with us."

"Mary has no intention of going to London, Lord Charles," Flora said. "We are all staying right here, at least until after the ball."

"After all, Lord Charles," Philomena said, "with *three thousand acres,* father *ought* to be in Parliament, don't you think?"

"I don't quite see the connection, Miss Pridell," Lord Charles said. "How long will you be visiting Lord and Lady Clareham, Lady Beauford? How honored you must feel. How is Lord Clareham? Father will certainly want to know."

"About the same, I think. I don't know how long I will be staying, Lord Charles," I said.

Mrs. Pridell caught my eye, then. She was now standing between the windows telling the nasty news about Vivian to Lord Wilton, Sir Roger, and a gentleman who, I later learned, was her husband.

"But Flora says you will be here for some time," Lewis said to me.

Then Philomena left us. She walked across the room to her mother.

"Mary is coming to the ball, of course," Flora said, resting her hand on my arm. "And she will be here for some time. Mary, your invitation should arrive tomorrow morning. I *could not* send it before because I could not have known you would be going out visiting—at least I didn't know for *sure.* Forgive me, my dear. Everyone will be coming—so many people have left London early because of the heat. You *will* come?"

"But Lady Beauford *must* come," Lewis said. "A ball at Hawthorn Hill is unique—it must be experienced."

"Yes, I understand the balls here have always been unique," said Lord Charles to me. "At least that is what Lewis tells me. So we *must* see for ourselves, mustn't we?"

"Yes, I suppose we must," I said, laughing. "I would love to come, Flora. Thank you."

Then the butler announced dinner. Lady Wilton seemed to be everywhere at once arranging the procession, and we followed her into the dining room. Lewis took me in, and then I found myself seated next to him at the table.

The dining room at Hawthorn Hill was all green and gold and glitter that evening. It was a green room with an exquisite, green jasperware Wedgwood chimney piece. The room's long table wore a white cloth sprinkled, between the silver and crystal dishes upon it, with single yellow gladioli blossoms matching an enormous bouquet of gladioli in the center of it. And all the candles in two tall silver candelabra on the table were burning.

Paul and two other footmen in green Wilton livery circled the table silently, handing the soup. They were helped by another footman in red, whom I later learned Sir Roger had brought along to help out, and still another in blue and yellow.

Then, when we had begun to eat, Lewis said, "Flora tells me that you lived in France for some time."

"Yes, in Paris," I said.

"Oh? Where in Paris? Anywhere near the palace?"

"You know the city, then?"

"Only slightly. I was there on holiday once—briefly."

"Not far away—near the Theatre des Italiens." Then I found myself reminiscing about the days when I lived with my father. And Lewis encouraged me to talk about them— he seemed fascinated.

But I noticed that Lord Charles did not seem very interested in Philomena's conversation. She had been placed on the other side of Lewis, next to Lord Charles, and she talked to him constantly during dinner. But in spite of this, he leaned forward much of the time to hear what I was saying.

"Did you see the King?" Phillip Pridell asked me from across the table. He sat between Mrs. Pridell and Flora.

"Yes, many times," I said, "but I never actually met him. We were invited to the Tuileries several times and Madame Adelaide was a guest at our house, but I was never presented to her brother."

"Papist city—full of Catholics," Mrs. Pridell said in a

loud voice to Reverend Anderson. "Can you imagine living in such a place?"

"*I* can, Winifred," Lady Wilton said, "and I would spend my days on the Rue de Richelieu and Rue Vivienne shopping and my nights at the opera and theatre."

"But you can do that in London," Mrs. Pridell replied.

"Yes, but not with such style."

"Catholic or no," the rector said, "the architecture is glorious. There is a church called Sainte-Chapelle on Ile de la Cité that is simply. . ."

Then Sir Roger, who sat on my right and on Lady Wilton's left, bent close to me and whispered, "Napoleon is back in Paris, you know."

"Yes, of course," I replied.

"Most people think he is dead, but we know Bonaparte. Dangerous, very dangerous. Gathering an army. Going to attack us—he always wanted that."

This made me glance across at the rector for guidance. He winked and nodded.

"Yes, we must be vigilant," I whispered back to Sir Roger.

Then it was time for the second course. I glanced at my little menu card and decided on the Pigeons a la Dijon. The roast birds arrived lying on a bed of sauteed bread rectangles spread with chopped seasoned livers and garnished with a wine sauce. Delicious!

"Bordeaux, my lady?" Paul asked.

"Yes, please," I replied. It was a red Bordeaux Médoc and quite perfect.

". . . I was the only one out of thirty in the field," Lewis continued, "to arrive at the end. It was just luck, really, and Jasper is a fine horse. Well, the fox took refuge in a sandhole near Denton Hill and went to earth in the sand. Then the hole fell in on him and buried one of the hounds in the bargain. I was able to dig the poor dog out, but I never did find the fox."

"Not a very rewarding day for you," I replied.

"No, but I must say that today makes up for it, Lady Beauford."

"America? No!" screamed Lady Molehill, from the other end of the table. "What did you say? Speak up, Henry."

"She can't hear a thing," Philomena whispered to Lord Charles. "I don't know why Lady Wilton asks them. What did she mean by that, do you suppose?" Then after Lord Charles had whispered to her, she exclaimed: "O'Connor? Yes! He was the groom at Castle Cloud, and I heard. . ."

"Philomena," her mother cried, "tell Lord Charles about Casandra." Then she looked at me and said, "Casandra is Philomena's new riding horse. A gorgeous bay mare. Philomena is a picture on her—she should be painted."

"How lovely," I said. "She must be very happy."

"And she and Flora have a little surprise for us after dinner," Mrs. Pridell said. "No, no, I can't tell you what it is, or it would not be a surprise. Isn't that so, Georgiana?"

"Philomena and I are going to play a duet. . . ." Flora whispered as we left the dining room. It was to be a performance by the two girls of Schumann's "Arabesque in C Minor, Op. 18" in an arrangement for piano and harp. ". . . and we have been rehearsing it for ages, and I will be so glad when it is *over*. But you must play too. Mother asked me to ask you."

"I will be happy to, Flora," I answered.

Later, when the men joined us after coffee, we adjourned to the music room, where Flora and Philomena played. Heaven only knows where they got the arrangement. It held little resemblance to the original piece, being twice as long and in a terribly slow tempo. Even so, it was much too difficult for the players. It was a performance which should never have occurred—even in a music room far out in the country.

"Schumann is not only turning over in his grave," Lewis, who was sitting on one side of me, whispered, "he is wishing he could die all over again."

"No, he is wishing he had never been born," Lord Charles whispered from the other side. And when the performance was finally over, I heard him sigh, "Thank God."

Then everyone clapped politely, and Philomena left the piano to sit next to Lord Charles. But Flora remained standing and said, "And now Lady Beauford has consented to play for us."

I walked to the piano and sat down. I wanted to play something melodic and short, so I said, "I will play Chopin's 'Nocturne in D-Flat, Opus 27, No. 2.'"

I let the music take me. I did not consciously want to play well. I did not want to shame Flora's and

Philomena's performance. But my mood fit the piece, and it turned out so well that I felt embarrassed for the girls. My audience enjoyed it, judging from their applause and bravos from Lewis and Lord Charles, and nothing would do but that I play an encore. So I played Chopin's "Waltz in A-Flat, Up. 42," which they seemed to enjoy even more.

"Encore!" Lewis cried. "Just one more."

But I declined, stood, and walked back to my chair.

"Lovely! Oh, that was lovely," Flora said, embracing me before I could sit down. "I did not know you could play so well, truly."

Then Lewis and Lord Charles and Phillip and Sir Roger stood and surrounded me and complimented me on my playing. But Philomena sat still, her glances toward me filled with envy.

After that, Mrs. Pridell asked to have their carriage brought around, and shortly the butler announced that it was up.

And when the Pridells had gone, I told Flora that I should also be going. Shortly then, the butler announced that Marsden had brought the cabriolet to the entrance front for me, and I said my good-nights to Reverend and Mrs. Anderson, and Sir Roger and Lady Molehill, and thanked Lord and Lady Wilton.

"I will see you out," Flora said.

"So will I," Lewis said.

Lord Charles came too, and all three stood at the top of the stairs and waved me off.

"I will be over in a day or so," Flora called down to me.

"Good night," they all cried, as we sped down the drive.

I turned and waved to them and then sank back into the cushions and pulled my shawl close about my shoulders. The night had grown chilly. But the sky was clear, and all the stars sparkled as we drove along beneath them. I felt refreshed, not only by the night air, but because I had been with normal people again. Yet I felt strangely unfulfilled, too. Then I realized that that was because David had not been there. Cinderella's prince had not come to the ball.

"Good morning," I smiled to Edmond as I entered the dining room the following morning. Then I picked up

Flora's invitation from the mail tray and, as I walked to my seat, I tore open the envelope and read it.

But when I was seated, I noticed that Edmond had also received an invitation. Its envelope lay on the table beside his plate.

"Who was at the party?" he asked.

"Sir Roger and Lady Molehill. . . ."

"Senile," Edmond stated.

"And Mr. and Mrs. Pridell and Philomena and Phillip. . . ."

"Ah, the squire and his family. Still putting on airs? Let us hope you had the opportunity to hear Philomena play the piano—like clockwork running slow, and with as much emotion. Quite unusual."

"She and Flora played a duet," I replied.

"Oh, no. Ha, ha, ha. Not that, not all at once. Ha, ha, ha. What a delightful evening you must have had. Who else?"

"Flora's mother and father, and her brother, and a friend of his, Lord Charles Pomperoy."

"Father is the duke of Ramsbury. Never met him. Did you like him?"

"Yes, I suppose so. Why?"

"Just wondered. Well, I told you so. An ordinary evening—hardly worth the bother, but we must learn for ourselves, I suppose. Did you tell them about Vivian?"

"I told Flora and Lady Wilton who told Mrs. Pridell who told nearly everybody else. The story spread quickly. I am afraid they were all—scandalized."

"It doesn't matter in the least what they were. Does a scholar care what a moron thinks? Fetch me some more bacon and another muffin, Mitchell, and hand me the strawberry preserve, there. It is a perfect day, and I am off to the city to escape the gloom of the country. How long I shall be away, I cannot say. It may be for a day, or longer I may stay." Then he sang, "Tum, tum, te dum, dum, dum."

"But we—I have an interview with Lady Withering on Monday. Have you forgotten that?"

"No, no, my dear Mary. I have not forgotten that. No indeed. Fear not, I shall return to the country on the morning train tomorrow, like as not, and you shall behold a new man before your very eyes. Ta, ta, ta—te ta."

After breakfast I went upstairs to put Flora's invitation in my trunk with my letters. There, just outside the open door to my room, I found Mrs. Muldoon arguing with Jane Spence.

"If it's Mrs. Foley that told you to do it, do it," Mrs. Muldoon said to Jane. "And don't be trying to give orders to people when you've no right to."

Then as I approached, Jane flounced angrily off toward Lord Clareham's room.

"Faith, you'd think she was the mistress here," Mrs. Muldoon said to me in a loud voice.

Jane turned and glared at us, shrugged proudly, and then walked on.

But I was impatient to get out into the morning air. So after I had put the invitation away, I told Mrs. Muldoon to go ahead and do my room, that I was going for a walk. Then I left her and walked to the stables where I asked Colen if Sarah had returned. She hadn't. After that I walked alone in the rose garden, and by the time I returned to the house, Mrs. Muldoon had finished making my bed and tidying up.

I was still tired from the night before. It had been after one o'clock by the time we had arrived back at Castle Cloud, and I had not fallen asleep at once after getting into bed. It would have been lovely to have slept late that morning, but I had not seen any point in missing breakfast when I could lie down afterward and sleep until luncheon if I wanted to. I decided, then, to do just that, so I slipped out of my shoes and dress, lay down on top of the bed, and closed my eyes.

And I lay there thinking how pleasant the evening at Hawthorn Hill had been. How lucky Flora, and Lewis, and Philomena, and everyone there were. They could all look forward to an endless string of similar evenings, riding and visiting in the afternoons, an occasional ball—a placid life of security and comfort and even a little boredom, while I. . . What will Lady Withering be like? I wondered. And Moor House—it sounds terribly austere, somehow. Is this really why you asked me to come to England, Vivian? To see me employed as a companion to an old lady? I wish you were here. I know that if you were, things would be different. You must be nearing America, by now, in your little ship on that endless, frightening ocean. Why didn't you take your Roman-coin pin with you? And your hairbrushes? And your—

I sat up then, stood, put on my dress and shoes, left my room, walked along the gallery to Vivian's door, looked to see if anyone was watching, opened the door, and walked into her room. I closed the door quietly behind me. And then I went directly to Vivian's chest of drawers and picked up her jewel box.

Vivian's Roman-coin pin lay where I had placed it the night before. Vivian had left so much of her jewelry behind—so many bracelets and beads and chains and pins lay beneath it. There was nothing there of great value, but that was not surprising, as she was not fond of jewelry as a rule, and did not wear it often. But had she taken any of it with her? I wondered.

She had not taken her hairbrushes. They stood on the china tray on the chest of drawers. They were beautiful brushes and practically new. I could not imagine her having another pair to travel with, but perhaps she had. And certainly she had not taken many hairpins from the *papier-mâché* box—it was full.

I crossed the room to the wash-hand-stand, and noticed that Vivian had left her manicure set on the marble shelf above the top of the stand. It was obviously an expensive set—of beautifully wrought steel and ivory. And she had left her perfume. As far as I knew, Vivian wore only Guerlain's "Mimosa Fragrens." A perfume bottle stood beneath the shelf, almost full. It was "Mimosa Fragrens." Surely she would have taken it with her.

And in her wardrobe I could see no empty spaces where clothes had been removed. Her dresses, mantillas, capes, collars, and shawls occupied every space. Then I returned to her chest of drawers and looked through it. It seemed that nothing had been removed. Her underclothes, gloves, handkerchiefs, scarfs were all perfectly arranged and the drawers were full.

In the bottom drawer, under a stack of folded fichus and sleeves, I found Vivian's diary. The last entry was dated Monday, June 2, 1856. It read:

James gets worse. Cannot Dr. Norton help him? So weak, so pale. Will he be taken from me too? I am so afraid—

But I would not intrude into Vivian's privacy further. So I closed the book, returned it to its place in the drawer, looked to be sure that I had not left anything disarranged, and left the room.

Edmond left Castle Cloud after luncheon. I heard the carriage on the drive as I sat in the drawing room at the card table. I remember looking across the room and out the west windows, watching the carriage disappear down the drive. Colen had been driving.

But the card game did not interest me, and I sat for a long time gazing out the window. My mind dwelled on Vivian.

Finally, I heard Lady Clareham call, "Mary?" And then she appeared in the doorway and said, "Oh, there you are."

"Yes, Lady Clareham?" I asked.

"No, no—sit down," she said, as she walked across the room toward me.

Then, when she reached the table, she drew out the chair from under the other side of it and sat down opposite me.

"Shall we play?" I asked.

"No, I would like to ask you—something."

"Yes?"

"Some of my jewels are gone," she said. "An emerald pendant and an amethyst brooch. Have you *any* idea—what could have happened to them?"

"No, Lady Clareham. How could I? Where were they?"

"In my jewel box in my bedroom. It has been broken into."

"Lady Clareham, how could I know what happened to them? Why are you asking me?"

Tears glistened in her eyes as she looked at me. "I don't care about the brooch—it has no value, but the pendant was a wedding present from my husband. He gave it to me on the night of our marriage, and it is the only valuable thing I had left. I can never tell him that it is gone."

And she began to cry. "There could be another explanation," she sobbed. "How could he? How dare he? How could he do such a thing? If he were here, I would strike him." She broke down and wept uncontrollably then. "How could he take the one thing I prize most in all the world—the one thing I had left? First James and Vivian and all our treasures and now *this*. Where will it all end? Has he no *feelings*? Has he no *pity*? I cannot bear it.

"Oh, Mary—I am sorry, so terribly sorry."

Then she rose and rushed from the room, and I hurried after her to watch in case she should stumble and fall. But she crossed the hall, climbed the staircase, walked along the gallery above me without mishap, and vanished into her bedroom.

After that scene at the card table, I scarcely thought that Lady Clareham would be down to dinner, but we met in the drawing room as usual that evening before the meal. She was composed, but pale and tired-looking.

And as we sat waiting there for Mitchell to announce dinner, I asked, "When did Vivian leave Castle Cloud?"

"The day after James's funeral," she replied.

"Edmond said that you did not go to the station. Did you see her leave?"

"No, I was ill. She—came to my room to say good-by, and then she left. Edmond drove her to the station. Why do you ask?"

"I have been so concerned about her. I wish I had been here. I might have been able to help. How is Lord Clareham today?" I asked, and then we began to talk about other things.

But it was not until after dinner—after Mitchell had served our coffee in the drawing room and left us—that Lady Clareham mentioned our conversation about her jewels, earlier in the afternoon.

"I must apologize for my behavior this afternoon, Mary," she said.

"That is entirely unnecessary, Lady Clareham. There is nothing to apologize for. I am so sorry you were upset," I said.

"Yes, I was upset and terribly disappointed." She gave me a wan smile. "I have always hoped and always been disappointed in him. My husband told you about his gambling. When Edmond got his commission in the army, I thought that he might be all right. But that did not last long."

"What happened? Why did Edmond leave the army?"

"He was cashiered. One night in their quarters, he got into an argument with a fellow officer, a Lieutenant

Greers—they had been gambling. The argument turned into a violent fight and caused a great deal of attention. The army is very strict about that kind of thing, you know. He faced a general court-martial and was cashiered by the sale of his commission. That was in 1850. He soon gambled the money away."

"And then he went into the church?" I asked.

"Yes, briefly. But that did not last long either. At first, when he would go off on these trips, we thought he was going to see about another living—at least that is what he led us to believe—but it was to gamble, of course. It gets worse and worse. He needs more and more money— If he would only marry before it is too late."

She shook her head and went on thinking, but she ceased to speak. And for a moment she had forgotten me. Then she smiled her ghost of a smile and said, "I am so terribly tired this evening, Mary. I think I will go up and go to bed early." She stood. "Good night, my dear," she said, and then she left me.

Ten minutes later I stood next to the Horse Monument and watched David ride up the slope to the hilltop. He dismounted and led his horse over to me.

"Where is Caesar?" I asked. "And who is this?"

"In his box at Oakland Park," David said. "This is Suda. I thought you would like to see her."

"Why, she must be over seventeen hands. Beautiful— but what an oddly shaped nose. What is she?"

"A Dongola from Africa. She has beautiful manners. We have an Arab stallion at Oakland Park, and I am going to mate them."

"Will that change the nose?"

"Probably become more Roman. We will have to wait and see. Of course horses have no future on the farm, but I like them. Call it my hobby. He tossed Suda's bridle over the limb of a sapling and then asked, "How was the dinner party at Hawthorn Hill?"

"Very pleasant. I have been trying to figure out where the house lay. It must be in that direction. I know we followed the river a way. Can we see it from here?"

"No, it is behind that hill. Do you see the large triangular field off to the left of Milton Penderton? Well, that is the lane beside it that you must have taken. The house is on the other side of the hill. Who was there?"

I told David about the party, and when we had finished talking about it, he asked, "Is something wrong?"

"Why?" I asked.

"You seem preoccupied—worried. Are you?"

"Yes, David. I need your help. Could we sit down?"

He followed me to our seats and sat opposite me. "What is wrong," he said. He leaned forward and took both my hands in his. "How can I help you?"

"Something terrible has happened to Vivian."

"Good God, what?"

"I don't know," I said, taking my hands from his. "I want you to help me find out."

"But if you don't know what has happened to her, how do you know something has?"

"Because of what has happened," I said. "Her letters— we agreed they were strange at the time. Vivian did not write those letters—the two from Greenwich, I mean."

"Her friend wrote them," he said. "She hurt her hand. She said so."

"I know. I mean Vivian didn't dictate them."

"Then who did? Her friend wouldn't dream them up. She must have dictated them."

"I don't know, but she would not have expressed herself that way. They were so cold, so formal, so unlike her other letters. And then she said that Edmond was good and kind. Edmond said something at dinner the other evening—he said that Vivian adored him. That is not true. She hated him. She said in one of her other letters that she loathed him for bringing her back from London that time. And you know as well as I do that Vivian would not have gone off like that without saying good-by, without writing to anyone."

"No, you are right—not if she had been herself. But she wasn't. She wasn't herself at all. If you could have seen how worried—frantic—she was about James. But she was ill, Mary—out of her mind with grief and physically ill too, from not eating or sleeping. She was not rational. You don't expect a person who is not rational to act themselves, do you?"

"But she didn't take anything with her," I said. "I looked in her room. Her jewelry is still there. Do you remember the coin pin that James gave her? It is still in her jewel box. She didn't take her hairpins, or her hair brushes, or her perfume, or her manicure set, or any clothes that I could see. She did not even take her diary. You don't leave your diary behind. You don't leave your manicure set behind or your brushes if you are going visiting."

"Maybe she had other brushes," David said. "And she could have had another manicure set too. And another bottle of perfume. How do you know she didn't take any clothes?"

"There were no empty spaces in her wardrobe or her chest of drawers."

"Well, would you expect there to be? Jane Spence helped Vivian to dress, sometimes, and she no doubt put everything back in order after Vivian left. How could you tell if things had been taken or not?"

"Her drawers were full," I insisted.

"You mean things were not packed down. Anyway, you said that Edmond drove her to the station, so she must have taken what she wanted. If you have any doubts about that, ask Edmond."

"That does not explain the letters. I am sure Vivian did not write them."

"Of course she wrote them—but if you think that, tell Lord Clareham."

"No, I don't think so," I said.

"Why not?"

"Because I think he knows what has happened to her, and I think Edmond and Lady Clareham know too."

"Know what?" he asked.

"I don't *know*. But there is something very odd going on. Things have happened, and they all want to get rid of me before I find out *what*. That is why the servants have been so rude to me down there. That is why Edmond has lied to me about Vivian. That is why he hasn't wanted me to talk to anyone—to keep me from finding out what has happened to Vivian."

"Oh, now just a minute," David said. "I suppose that is why he wants to help you find a situation. If he wanted to get rid of you, why hasn't he asked you to leave? That would be simple.

"No, Mary. Now—we know O'Connor went to America, and he said he would send for Vivian. She was waiting and waiting to hear from him, wasn't she? What is so strange about her going? She *would* go if she wanted to, and she went. There is really nothing strange about that. The only thing that was strange was why she did not tell me about it. I don't think I can ever forgive her for that. As for the rest, the servants don't want an extra person to do for, if they can help it, especially if the Castle is under-staffed.

"Nothing has happened to Vivian," he concluded.

"Something has," I said. "I know it. You must believe me."

"You are disappointed that Vivian is not here—that it has not turned out the way you thought it would—and your imagination. . ."

"It is not my imagination. It is not my imagination about the Roman-coin pin, and it is *not* my imagination about the diary."

"But she wasn't well," he replied.

"You don't believe me."

"How can I? You have no proof. . . ."

"Well, I shall get proof, and I shall get it on my own, then. It is getting late, David, and I must go." I stood up. "Good night," I said, moving quickly out of his reach. Then I hurried across to the path and down it, and I did not pause to wave to him.

By the time I reached the bottom of the hill, I was miserable. And if I had thought he would still be there, I would have gone back to him. Why had I gotten angry with David? Because I was tired? It had been a long day, and I had gotten less sleep the night before than I re-quired. And I felt so all alone. I needed help, not hin-drance. I needed someone to believe in me. I had assumed that David would, and I felt that he had let me down. But I shouldn't have treated him like that, and I was angry with myself for having done so.

Could David be right? I wondered then, as I walked toward the house. I was too tired to try to answer my question. I would try to get some sleep, and then I would think about it again in the morning.

✠ Chapter Ten ✠

THE FOLLOWING DAY, Sunday, I asked Lady Clareham if I might go to church with her, and since she did not object, I went. I did not know when David would be leaving for Windsor. I had hoped he would come to church and leave in the afternoon, but he was not there. Lord and Lady Wilton and Flora attended the service, however, and after it was over Lady Clareham and I spoke briefly with them. Flora asked if Edmond was at home, and I told her that he had gone away but hoped to return sometime that morning.

He returned on the noon train. Colen told me so as I stood at the steps leading down into the rose garden. I had decided to stroll in the garden after church to pass the time before luncheon, and as I was about to descend into it, Colen had driven the barouche around the side of the house and stopped to tell me that he had still not seen Sarah. He was now sure that she would not come back. I asked him then if Edmond had returned, and he told me that he had just met him at the railway station and brought him back to the Castle. And Colen had gone on to say that Edmond had been furious at having been kept waiting, but that it had been necessary to drive Lady Clareham and me home from church before he could drive to the station. After all, he was employed by his Lordship, Lord Clareham, and not by any other member of the family. Poor Colen. I suppose Edmond had given him a difficult time.

But I had some thinking to do, and after Colen had driven to the stables, I welcomed my solitude and walked in the garden. I thought first of David. There was nothing I could do to repair the damage of the night before until I saw him again. Would he be at the ball on Friday? I had no idea how long it would take him to bring the cows down from Windsor Farm. Surely it would not take more than four more days. They would certainly be brought on the railway. I hoped I would see him at Hawthorn Hill on Friday night and apologize to him then.

And I thought about Vivian. I did not know what to do about her. I was convinced that something was wrong there. I knew it, but I had no proof to lay before anyone. All my reasons for thinking that something had happened to her could be explained away as David had done. I did not even know what I thought had happened. So I decided that I would have to find out more and that first I would go to Greenwich and talk to Nancy Ackerman. But then I began to wonder what I could expect to accomplish by doing that, except to spend some of the precious little money I had. Why not write to her, then? But what would I say? Whether I saw her personally or wrote to her, I could not accuse her of making up the letters from Vivian, and I did not really think she had. There was no reason to think that she would do a thing like that. Why should she? On the other hand, it was quite possible that Vivian would dictate to another person differently than she would write. It would be difficult to express things intimately with a third person, a stranger, writing it all down. At least it would be for me. And I knew nothing about the Ackermans. I had never heard Vivian speak of them. Perhaps I should try to find out about them before I did anything else.

My opportunity to do so came during luncheon.

After we had begun to eat, Lady Clareham said to Edmond, "A letter came for Vivian from Jessie Abbington. I don't know whether to open it or return it with a note."

"Who is Jessie Abbington?" Edmond growled.

"You remember—she was one of the girls that visited Vivian a year ago last autumn. The rather tall, very blond girl. You seemed quite taken with her. Vivian said that she. . ."

"Vivian! Vivian! Vivian!" Edmond shouted, banging his fist on the table as he spoke. "Must every other word in all conversations be about Vivian? Vivian is gone. She is no longer a part of our lives. Must we be haunted forever by her? I do not want to hear about Vivian anymore. I do not want to hear her name."

"Did Nancy visit Castle Cloud that autumn?" I asked, after a moment.

"Nancy who?" Edmond demanded.

"Nancy Ackerman."

"Why?"

"Edmond!" Lady Clareham reproved him.

"I was merely wondering," I said. "I never heard Vivian speak of Nancy Ackerman. She never wrote about her, but they must have been good friends."

"My dear Mary," Edmond said, "it has been four years since you were last at Castle Cloud. A great deal can happen in four years. You do not seem to realize that. Time does not stand still. Vivian met Nancy three years ago. They became good enough friends for Nancy to take her in. Why are you suddenly so interested in Nancy Ackerman? That is none of your business. Mother and Lady Ackerman are old friends. You cannot possibly imagine that we would allow Vivian to go off with just anyone. Isn't that right, Mother?"

"Lady Ackerman and I have known each other since we were children," Lady Clareham said. "But Vivian did not meet Nancy until three years ago."

"Now may we *stop* talking about Vivian and Vivian's friends?" Edmond cried.

We stopped talking altogether after that and did not say another word during the meal.

And after we had finished, I strolled out onto the east portico, wondering what to do. I remembered, then, that on the day I had walked to the home-farm, I had noticed a path that led off the drive, opposite a dense thicket of hemlock, and down a grassy slope into a wood. So I decided to explore it that afternoon. I discovered that the path descended to the bank of the stream which, further along, filled the lily pond behind the glasshouses. Here the wood had been left in a wild state. The stream bubbled and frothed over its rocky bed, splashing the ferns which lined its banks with crystal beads. Alongside it, fairy thimbles bloomed in patches of sunshine, and here and there purple loosestrife grew close to the water's edge. The path followed the stream to an enormous almond-shaped rock which jutted out into a pool beside a tiny waterfall. I sat down on it and, for perhaps half an hour, listened to the water music and watched the birds—thrushes and meadow pipits—dart through the trees.

But in spite of the beauty of the place, I began to feel even more lonely than usual, so I soon started back to the Castle. And when I came in sight of the stable yard, I saw a green and gold carriage standing there. Marsden leaned against it talking to Colen.

I hurried across the grass circle, then up the steps of the east portico, and into the house. And as I entered the hall, I heard Flora laugh. She sat, I saw from the drawing room doorway, on a sofa looking up at Edmond who stood, glass in hand, before her.

"Well you can imagine how perplexed I was," Edmond said, "until I turned around and there was the landlord, red as a beet, mopping his brow, and telling me that it wasn't my room at all—that mine was the room across the way."

Flora laughed, and then she said, "Oh, Edmond, that is priceless. I don't know when I have heard such a *funny* story."

Then Edmond saw me. "Mary, my dear, come in," he said. "I have been telling Flora about my holiday in Ireland two years ago."

"Edmond has some of the funniest stories," Flora said. "He has kept me laughing for an hour. But I must be *going,* Edmond."

"Stay and talk to Mary and me," Edmond said.

"Oh, no, I mustn't. I have already stayed far too long."

"Very well. I will go and tell Mitchell to have your carriage brought around—if I can find him." Then Edmond left us.

"Mary, come and sit," Flora said. And when I sat beside her, she covered my hand with one of hers and whispered, "He is coming to the ball. He could not have been sweeter—*so* entertaining and so *nice.* Oh, wait till I tell Mamma. What did you tell him?"

"Why, nothing—" I said with a grin, "except that I thought you would make a wonderful wife and mother, and I told him about your dowry. I hope that was all right."

"All right? You know it's all right. You *are* an angel," she said. "I owe it all to you. Lewis wanted to come, but I would not let him. You will see him at the ball. After all, one person's intrusion is enough, and I am as quiet as a mouse next to Lewis. But he did want so much to come. Mary, bring Edmond to Hawthorn Hill tomorrow for a visit—you can do it. Lewis will be at home. . . ."

"I am afraid we can't tomorrow, Flora. Tomorrow I have an interview with Lady Withering."

"What interview with Lady Withering?" Flora asked.

"I told you that Edmond is helping me to find a position as a lady's companion. Well, Lady Withering is looking for one, and Edmond has arranged an interview with her at Moor House tomorrow. Do you know her?"

"No, but I have heard stories about her. She must be dreadful. Mary you mustn't. . ."

"Mustn't what?" Edmond asked, as he walked into the room. "What are the two lovely ladies whispering about over there on the sofa?"

"Mary is my best friend, Edmond," Flora said, "and best friends have confidences which *men* would never understand. I was telling Mary about your coming to the ball."

"Well, of course," he said. "No one would think of missing a ball at Hawthorn Hill. Mary and I will come together, but of course Mother will not be coming, you understand that. She will be so sorry to miss it.

"Do you know, I have not been to a ball since—well, let me think—since Lady Spree's famous ball in London at Charlton House. That must have been five years ago."

"You knew her quite well, didn't you, Edmond?" Flora asked.

"Do you know her?" he asked.

"Mother does."

"Well, it was the ball for her daughter. Everyone knows the story. . . ." And he proceeded to tell it, much to Flora's amusement.

"Miss Stratton's carriage is up, my lord," Mitchell interrupted.

"Thank you, Mitchell," Edmond said. "Well, little did anyone, let alone her own mother, know that she had eloped with the same young man two days before."

"Oh, isn't that funny?" Flora cried, as she stood and began to walk to the hall. Edmond and I followed her. "Oh, it must have been hilarious—and to think of having *been* there."

Then we saw Flora to her carriage where she kissed me

good-by. And we stood on the steps and waved as she drove away. But afterward, neither Edmond nor I spoke as we climbed the stairs and walked into the house.

Inside, in the rotunda, Jane Spence stood waiting for us. "Oh, your lordship, may I have a word with you?" she asked. She spoke sweetly, but her eyes flashed with anger.

I ignored them both, hurried to the stairway, climbed it, and walked around the gallery toward my room. From the gallery, I chanced to look down into the hall, and I noticed that the door to the hall chamber was shut and that Edmond and Jane Spence had disappeared.

"We should have seen it by now," Edmond said. "The landlord said that we would see the house just beyond the bridge."

This was the following day, and Edmond and I were on our way to see Lady Withering. We had set out for Moor House at ten o'clock on Tuesday morning in the barouche, and between twelve-thirty and one-thirty we had lunched and rested the horses at the inn in South Molton. There the landlord had given us directions to Moor House.

And we had driven on toward it, leaving the lush, cozy lanes and patchwork fields of the lowlands for the bleak hills and tors of Exmoor where the hedgerows and woods had given way to an endless, undulating sweep of moorland. Here only moor-grass, heather, and, in the combes, gorse bushes grew.

"There it is," Edmond said, as we crept up a steep hill after crossing the Mole River.

I had seen it too. "But it is a castle," I said, "or what is left of one."

Above us, a faceless Norman keep slept on a barren hilltop. It was, simply, an enormous four-storied block of stones, slightly taller than wide, with a tiny decaying tower at one corner of the roof, rising yet another story into the air. From a distance, the structure's sheer walls seemed windowless, but as we drew nearer, I could see slits in the masonry on each of the five floors.

This keep would have been the last defense of that ancient castle. Here, in the rooms above the great hall, behind ten-foot-thick walls, the women and children would have huddled while their exhausted men fought off the attackers. I saw it all in my mind: the great oak door had given way, the enemy had surged into the great hall, and, with swords slashing, fought its way step by step up the narrow spiral stairs to the upper floors.

But as we drew still nearer, the vision dispersed. In the Norman facade, someone had remodeled the arched doorway in the English baroque style and added a graceful stairway with a lacy wrought-iron balustrade.

The combination of styles was grotesque, I decided, as I sat in front of it, looking at the building and waiting for Edmond. He had gone to ask if Lady Withering was at home. He returned to the carriage, helped me down, and we entered the castle, following the butler across a hall and up a narrow flight of stairs to a corridor on the second floor. Here the butler threw open a door and announced, "Lord Althrop and Miss Thorpe, my lady."

"Ah, Lord Althrop, how good of you to come," Lady Withering said, extending a tiny, sticky hand.

She had been eating a chocolate and had popped the last bite of it into her mouth as we entered the tiny sitting room. The room was hot—a fire blazed in the fireplace—and stuffy.

"That will be all, Stonely," she said. "You may close the door—that is, unless you think the fire can heat the entire house."

Lady Withering was an enormous, corpulent woman with bulging arms and tiny hands. She sat next to the fire, her huge bulk crammed into an overstuffed chair. She looked as though she would have to be pried out of it if she wished to stand. Beads of perspiration glistened on her brow and upper lip.

Her chair, an overstuffed sofa, and another chair filled the room.

"Please sit down, Lord Althrop and Miss Thorpe," she said, gesturing to the sofa directly in front of her chair. Then she raised a lorgnette to her eyes and studied us.

She will not be able to see very much, I thought. There is not enough light in the room for that.

"Will you have a chocolate?" she asked, after a few moments. She lifted a box of candy from the table beside her as she spoke and held it out to us at arm's length.

We declined.

"Well, how is Lord Clareham?" she asked. "My husband remembered him quite well, you know. They met at a reception for Lord Grey. That was shortly after the Negapta Mutiny. Of course *we* could not believe that it was due to any negligence on Lord Clareham's part. But then, everyone is capable of a misjudgment. It is his heart?"

"Yes, Lady Withering," Edmond said. "He had a stroke, a partial paralysis, but he seems to be recovering."

"My dear Lord Althrop, they never recover," she said, reaching for another chocolate. "It is unkind to delude ourselves. He will have another stroke before long, and that will be the end—they always do. I don't care what the doctors say. Doctors don't know anything anyway. They should all be abolished."

As she spoke, she punctuated her remarks with the halfpiece of chocolate which she held between her thumb and middle finger and which she waved in the air.

"They are all frauds," she continued. "Ah, the great men die one by one. Soon there will be no one left, and everything will fall in a heap. . . ." And she went on at length about how utterly hopeless everything had become.

"Quite right," Edmond said at last. "Things do not seem to be getting any better, do they? Have you engaged a companion, Lady Withering, or is the position still open? We have the highest regard for Miss Thorpe. She is an old friend of my sister and of the family. We are sure she will be of inestimable value, a charming. . ."

"Lord Althrop," Lady Withering interrupted, "would you be so kind as to pull the bellpull for me there? Thank you.

"You have no idea what I have been through because of that one advertisement in the *Times*. The only good to come from it was your reply. The other letters I have received have been so disappointing. Such crude, vulgar girls applying for a position with a lady. I do not think there is any refinement left."

The door opened then, and the butler said, "You rang, my lady?"

"Stonely, send John to me. This room is getting *cold*. I have asked him time after time to look after the fires."

"Yes, my lady."

"And Stonely, I cannot have my guests kept waiting outside the door downstairs."

"I am very sorry, my lady. I was in the pantry clearing away when the bell rang."

"I should have thought that you would long since have found your way from the pantry to the entrance door. Shall I draw you a diagram?"

"No, my lady."

"Be more prompt then, Stonely. And send John up to me at once. That will be all." Then she turned back to Edmond and said: "You have no idea of the grimy paper they write on, and the spelling— One ninny spelled the word education: *e d u k a s i o n*. The world is full of imbeciles who— John!"

A footman had entered the room.

"Yes, my lady," he said.

"The fire! Did anyone ever tell you that fire must be fed or it will die?"

"Yes, my lady."

"Well, feed it then—and keep it fed. That is one of the things I pay you to do."

"Yes, my lady."

"And, John—I found a smudge on the crystal, at luncheon. Smudges *dim* crystal. If I had wanted dim crystal, I would have purchased glass. Is that understood?"

"Yes, my lady."

"This house is so cold, I loathe it," Lady Withering said to Edmond, as John squeezed past us to get to the fireplace. He piled more coal on the still-blazing fire and then tip-toed out of the room. "Cold and drafty," she continued, "and bleak. I get so tired of the moors. From every window it is the same. What I wouldn't give for a *tree*. And in the winter it is beastly." She complained for some minutes about her isolation and then about her neighbors. "If my husband had not been such a fool," she concluded, "as to throw all his money into those stupid engineering schemes, I would not be here. We could have kept our house in London, and I could have lived in civilized surroundings.

"Oh!" she exclaimed, looking at her chocolate box. "Lord Althrop, could I trouble you to pull the bellpull there? Thank you."

Shortly Stonely entered the room in answer to the bell, and Lady Withering asked him to send Violet to her.

Meanwhile, Edmond had been praising Sir Alexander. "... and we shall always be indebted to him for the

Thames Tunnel and his other engineering achievements. He was a great man."

"He was a fool—look how he has left me—in a ruin, and a dirty one at that. Always digging around in filth and muck—everything covered with mud. Violet!"

"Yes, my lady?" said a maid from the doorway.

"Bring me the box of bonbons from my room."

"Yes, my lady."

"Are there any particular prerequisites that you had in mind, Lady Withering?" Edmond asked. "Any qualifications. . ."

"Not a brain in her head," Lady Withering said, as soon as her maid had left the room. "It is impossible to get decent help these days. Lady Pratt and I were discussing that very thing shortly before I left London, yesterday. I stayed with her at Hansonby House on Portman Square. Put it here Violet, and take the empty box away." She reached into the box that Violet had brought even before the maid could set it down. "Do you call this a bonbon?" she shrieked. "Never mind, Violet, it takes an enormous amount of intelligence to tell the difference between a bonbon and a caramel, and I should not ask too much of you. But if you could possibly remember that bonbons are light colored and caramels are dark colored, it might provide a clue as to the difference. There is only one other box of candy in my room, so you could not possibly bring me the wrong one this time."

"Yes, my lady," her maid said. And she hurried from the room.

"London was hot," Lady Withering continued. "Hotter than you can imagine. And smell? With all those horses and drains? We had to keep all the windows closed. We sweltered! Beastly city." And she complained about London until Violet brought her candy and set it on the table beside her. "Bonbon?" she asked, holding out the box to us.

"Lady Withering," Edmond said, "we have a long drive ahead of us, and we must be starting out shortly. About Miss Thorpe and the position. . ."

"£50 a year," Lady Withering said. "I think that is generous, don't you? Has she had experience? I presume the child is educated?"

"Oh, yes," Edmond said. "She attended the same school

as my sister. Her father lost all his money and has passed away, so Miss Thorpe finds it necessary to seek a position. We could not speak more highly of her in every way."

"Very well, that is excellent, then," Lady Withering said. "Miss Thorpe, we shall expect you to arrive and begin your duties on Friday, the first of August."

"Excellent!" Edmond said.

"That is very good of you, Lady Withering," I said, "and I appreciate your kind offer, but I should like to think it over. It is an important step for me, and I never make an important decision without careful consideration, even though I am tempted to at once."

"Hmm," Lady Withering murmured, fixing her lorgnette upon me. "If you have not come to realize by this time that opportunity knocks but once, you will probably never realize it, Miss Thorpe."

"You are quite right, Lady Withering," Edmond said, as he stood. "You may expect Miss Thorpe on Friday. I will drive her and her luggage to Moor House, personally. Now, we must be on our way. Please do not trouble—we can find our way down. Mother and Father will be so happy that we have met. Are you ready, Mary?"

I stood. "It has been delightful, Lady Withering," I said. "Good-by."

And then I followed Edmond out of the room and down the stairs where we found Stonely and asked him to have Colen bring our carriage around.

While we waited, Edmond stood, his hands clasped behind him, looking through the glass panes of the door, at the drive. I wandered into the great hall to look about, but I saw nothing. I was too angry. I was so angry with Edmond that I trembled. I must calm myself, I thought. I must be very careful what I say to him in the next few hours.

I had enough time then, to think what I would say to Edmond. When we had finally gotten into the carriage and were rolling down the drive, away from Moor House, I said, "Wasn't she dreadful, Edmond? Can you imagine working for a woman like that? Why, one would be battered and bruised in a week."

"Lady Withering is very well liked," Edmond said. "Everyone has difficult days, Mary, and she is having problems with inept servants. Who can blame her for complaining. Anyway, one can hardly judge another from a half-hour's conversation, and £ 50 is a generous wage."

"That may be, but I shall earn it somewhere else. One couldn't think of living with someone like that. Oh, don't worry—there will be other advertisements in the *Times*, Edmond. Many others, and placed by far pleasanter ladies than Lady Withering."

Neither of us spoke after that. I looked out of my side of the carriage, and he looked out of his until, more than two hours later, Edmond said to Colen, "Turn left here, Colen. We will stop at Hawthorn Hill for a few minutes."

By that time it was five o'clock by my watch.

A few minutes later, as we drove up the drive toward the house, I said, "Isn't it a little late for an afternoon call?"

"Perhaps," Edmond said, "but Flora will not mind, nor will her mother."

"I am sure she won't. As a matter of fact, she suggested that we drive to Hawthorn Hill for a visit today, so you might say that we did not want to disappoint her."

"I am quite capable of deciding for myself what to say, Mary," he replied.

Once inside the house, we followed the butler to the drawing room and were announced. Flora rushed to us as soon as we entered the room. Her mother sat in a chair by the window where she had been working on her embroidery. She and Lewis, who sat opposite her, rose and advanced a step toward us. Lord Charles, however, was not present.

"Mamma," Flora cried, "it's Mary and Edmond."

"I can see that, my dear," Lady Wilton said, extending her hand to Edmond. "Mary and Edmond, how nice. Come and sit here with us."

"But I am so surprised," Flora cried. "You said you wouldn't be able to come, Mary. This is lovely."

"I didn't think there would be time, Flora," I said, as I sat down. "I am so glad to see you again, Lady Wilton. Good afternoon, Lieutenant Stratton."

"How are you, Lady Beauford?" Lewis asked. "This *is* a pleasant surprise."

"We must apologize for calling so late in the afternoon, Lady Wilton," Edmond said, "but we thought Flora must be hoping we would call, and we did not want to disappoint her."

"Not at all, Edmond. How are your mother and father?"

"Just about the same, Lady Wilton, though Father says he is regaining some feeling in his right side, which is wonderful. I hope you and Lord Wilton have been well?"

"Yes, quite well, thank you, Edmond."

"We hoped to arrive sooner," Edmond said, "but it is a long drive from Moor House. That is Lady Withering's house, outside of Simonsbath. Mary and I called on her this afternoon. Do you know her?"

"We have met," Lady Wilton replied.

"She is looking for a companion, and since our poor Mary is destitute and compelled to seek a position as a companion, or perhaps as a governess, I arranged for Lady Withering to interview her. Mary's father left her nothing, you know. She is in quite dire poverty. The position would pay £50 a year. Think of what that would mean to someone with no money at all. And it was offered to Mary, who turned it down. I think it was foolish and irresponsible of her to do so, don't you agree? And I am really quite afraid of what may become of her with such an attitude."

I couldn't help laughing at the melodramatic implications of that last sentence. "You know perfectly well, Edmond," I said, "that nothing will become of me that you or anyone could possibly be ashamed of. As for Lady Withering, she is a monster." I took a pillow from the sofa beside me, placed it in my lap, and stroked it. "Now, you must remember that Lady Withering is *constantly* eating chocolates, and her fingers are sticky and her mouth smeared with them, and she is enormously fat. John," I mimicked, "I found a smudge on the crystal. Smudges *dim* crystal. If I had wanted dim crystal, I would have purchased glass." Lewis snickered. "And, John," I continued to mimic, "did anyone ever tell you that fires must be fed or they will die? Well, feed it!" Lady Wilton covered her mouth. "And Stonely, I will not have my guests kept waiting. Shall I draw you a diagram of how to get from the pantry to the front door?"

Lady Wilton laughed openly then, and Lewis threw back his head and guffawed. But Flora glanced uncertainly at Edmond.

"She is a beast," Lewis said, still laughing. "Everyone knows that."

"Really, Edmond," I said, forcing a smile. "How could you possibly expect me to consider her offer, let alone accept it for me? And without even consulting me. Are you so anxious to be rid of me? Dear Edmond, I am so sorry about that."

"It was for your own good, my dear," Edmond said. "We treasure your company at the Castle, you know that, but one must look to the future. I cannot imagine *why* you should refuse such a generous offer. We know it might be a bit difficult to adjust to working for someone, but you have an enormous advantage there. After all, your mother was a parlor maid at Gunderbury Hall before the first Lady Penbroke died, wasn't she?"

"Yes, but it would be ridiculous to suppose that an aptitude for domestic service could be inherited. Really, Edmond," I said, smiling broadly.

"I simply meant that since your mother was a domestic, that some of the philosophy must have communicated itself."

"But my father was the marquess of Penbroke, Edmond. Please don't forget that," I said. "And there was a very great understanding between us. We were always very close. And since you have brought up the subject of my mother, it is hardly any fault of mine that she was a parlor maid, nor any fault of hers either, for that matter. She loved my father, but she knew she would never be happy in his world. Still, she married him because she knew he needed her. And she made him very happy all his life, which pleased me enormously.

"But how boring all this must be for Lady Wilton and Lieutenant Stratton and Flora," I said to Edmond. "My job-seeking can hardly be news to them. I have told Flora all about my financial problems and asked if she knew of a position that might be available. So I am sure she has told her mother and brother, at least I hope she has. Nor can my family history be of any great news to them. I believe everyone has heard of my father's marriage.

"I am looking forward so to the ball on Friday night," I said to Lady Wilton, then. "I have not been to a ball since Princess Adelaide of Hohenlohe's ball in Baden-Baden."

"Really? What was it like?" Lady Wilton asked.

"Eugenie was there," I replied. "She was the countess of Teba then—it was before she met the emperor."

"Is she as beautiful as they say?" Lewis asked.

"Yes, definitely," I replied. "She was with her mother, and she was very proper and beautifully mannered. Yes, she is very beautiful, and she loves clothes. She has exquisite taste. I saw her many times in Baden-Baden. . . ."

And I went on to talk about society on the continent, as Lady Wilton was fascinated by it, by Baden-Baden in particular, and kept asking more and more about it. Meanwhile, Edmond sat morosely for the first few minutes, and then he began to talk to Flora. I could tell that he was trying hard to be charming.

Finally, after about forty-five minutes, we took our leave, and in the carriage on the way back to Castle Cloud, I turned to Edmond and asked, "Was that necessary?"

"Was what necessary?" he said.

"You know perfectly well what I mean."

"One would think, Mary, that you would deceive our friends," he said. "Things of this nature always come out. It is always best to admit them from the beginning. Deceit breeds distrust and dislike. A deceit is a lie, and a lie is nasty and evil and a sin. I am so happy I had the opportunity to put your relationship with our friends on an honest, truthful plain. I cannot bear deceit, or dishonesty, or foolishness, or stupidity. And I strongly urge you to reconsider Lady Withering's excellent offer."

I did not reply, but turned and looked away from him. And we said nothing further to each other during the ride back to the Castle.

I felt terribly alone during that ride, and that evening after dinner, I felt even more alone as I sat in my room looking out of the window at the bay. There had been no sunset—clouds had covered the sky in the late afternoon. And as I watched, a deep blanket of fog slid in from the sea, buried the villages of Westward Ho! and Appledore and crept across the bay toward us till, at last, everything beyond our hill lay smothered beneath its shroud.

I longed for David, then. I needed him there with

me—close. I wanted to feel his thick arms around me, to be held tightly, warmly against him, to be wrapped in his love. I felt *so* lonely. "Oh, David, David, David," I whispered, what a fool I was to act like that and spoil it all."

But if he were in love with me. . . Could he be in love with me? I wondered. Why shouldn't he be in love with me? He had kissed me, hadn't he? Yet I knew how little a kiss meant to a man—at least I had read that that was true. And as for marriage— No, he would never want to marry me.

It rained during the night, and Tuesday morning dawned dark, gray, and showery. I did not know it then, of course, but we were to see the sun only once, briefly, in all of the next four days. That first day, I spent the early part of the morning in my room mending a petticoat and a pair of stockings, thinking. By noon I had finished my sewing, and I decided to visit Lord Clareham for a few minutes before luncheon.

As I walked around the gallery toward Lord Clareham's room, Edmond came out of the stairwell on the other side of it and walked toward his room. Our eyes met and I nodded to him, but we did not speak.

Then, as Ahmad opened his master's door for me, Lord Clareham called, "Mary! How very thoughtful of you to pay the invalid a call. Sit here."

When I was seated, I said. "Everyone has been asking about you—Lord and Lady Wilton, Sir Roger and Lady Molehill, the Pridells, everyone. Oh, but am I disturbing you, Lord Clareham?"

"Not at all. Distractions are welcome to one who must remain in the same spot night and day. That was very kind of them, wasn't it?"

"But you have your mirrors, your books, your letters, and Ahmad and Lady Clareham and Edmond, and you seem to know everything that is happening at Castle Cloud. I would think there would be distractions aplenty."

"Not enough, my dear. The books? I have read them all before, and no one pays any attention to my letters, it seems, and there is nothing much to see in the mirrors."

"Did you watch Vivian leave—that last day when Edmond drove her to the station?" I asked.

"Yes. Why do you ask?"

"I have wondered about her condition."

"She was very ill and weak from grief," Lord Clareham said. "I tried to dissuade her from going until she had recovered her strength, but she insisted, and Lady Clareham has known her friend's mother since they were children. Yes, I watched Edmond help her into the carriage. I can see almost directly down in that one." He pointed to the mirror suspended from the ceiling.

"Did she take a bag along?"

"Of course. Yes, Edmond carried it for her. I remember him setting it down as he helped her into the gig."

"Was it a very large bag?" I asked.

"Medium-sized I would say. She had not planned to stay away long. Why do you want to know about that?"

"Well, I have wondered why Vivian never sent for any of her clothes. She never even wrote to you or Lady Clareham, did she?"

"She wrote to me after she arrived."

"Oh, I did not know that," I said.

"Vivian had a little money of her own," Lord Clareham explained, "not a great deal, but enough to buy new clothes. I doubt that she had anything here that would have been appropriate for Scotland, or for America either, for that matter. I would think she would want to wait and see what clothes she would need in the United States and buy them there. Any further questions?" He smiled at me.

"Yes—how are you feeling?"

"Better, better," he chuckled. "I have feeling in my right toe. And you, Mary? I understand Lady Withering has offered you a position which you have decided to refuse. Is that so?"

"Yes, I did not care for her at all. She takes pleasure in criticizing and humiliating people."

"There are many people with whom we must associate in our lives whom we do not like, Mary. It is unfortunate that we cannot like everyone we come in contact with, but we must learn to coexist with them, nevertheless. It may be too much to expect to find a position with someone you *like*."

"I am sure that I can find a position with someone I like a great deal more than I like Lady Withering," I said.

"Do not expect too much, my dear," Lord Clareham replied.

At that moment someone pounded on the door. Lord Clareham spoke to Ahmad, who had been watching us. I may have imagined it, but I thought I saw a suggestion of a smile about Ahmad's eyes. Again we heard the pounding—louder and more insistent this time. Then Lord Clareham spoke again to Ahmad who went to the door, turned the key in the lock, and opened it.

"What in blazes is going on in here?" Edmond shouted. "What do you mean by locking yourself in here like this."

"This is my room," Lord Clareham said. "If I choose to lock the door, I shall. And I shall do so in the future so that I may have a little privacy. Mind your manners. Thank you for knocking."

"Thank you for knocking," Edmond mimicked. "Suppose Ahmad fell ill, or had a stroke, or fainted, and the door was locked and you were alone—you would be in a fine mess. But I don't suppose you have thought about that. God, this room stinks!"

"There is a lady present. Watch your language," Lord Clareham commanded. His face had become flushed.

"Your father and I were discussing Lady Withering's offer, Edmond," I said. I felt I had to say something, and I had not been able to think of anything else. "Do sit down. I really don't think your father should become excited."

"It seems you have taken a great deal upon yourself," Edmond said to me. "First you refuse to accept a perfectly good position, and now you tell me how to speak to my own father. He is as strong as an ox. His illness is all in his mind. Just because they do not want him in India anymore, he has decided to take to his bed in pique. And I should think you would have more sense. This is the second perfectly good opportunity you have turned down for one reason or another. I don't think you are interested in accepting any position that is ever offered to you. You think you are too good for that. Well, let me tell you something—you will not stay here. . . ."

"Edmond! Be quiet," Lord Clareham shouted. "Don't be a fool. Now, we will be calm and sensible. Mary has every right to expect a pleasant employer. We will find her a place that she can accept and will come to like. I think she should be with children. I think she would like that. In the meantime, we are delighted to have her with us, and don't forget that."

"If you would take my advice," Edmond said, "you would tell her to take the place with Lady Withering and be done with it."

"I do not take the advice of idiots! Mary must decide these things for herself. I think you had better leave me, Edmond. You disgust me, and I am not feeling well. The only reason you come here is to find out if I am ready to die yet. Well, I am not ready to die. You will have to wait a while for that. Now leave me, please—both of you."

He gave a short command to Ahmad then, and turned his face to the wall.

"Thank you, Lord Clareham," I said.

"What stupid nonsense," Edmond shouted at his father. "You must be getting senile—"

But then Edmond saw the menacing look on Ahmad's face, and he stalked from the room. I followed him.

After luncheon, I decided to begin to press my ball dress so that it would be ready before Friday night.

Let me tell you about the dress. Papa and I took our last trip to Paris in April of 1854. We went alone, since Mother was not feeling well and preferred to stay behind in The Hague. The marquess of Alcanizes, a friend of my father's, had invited us to visit him in the city, and he was to give a ball in honor of the princess de Metternich. So, naturally, the occasion demanded a new ball dress.

I had seen sketches of dresses by a young Englishman who worked at the Maison Gagelin in Paris, a shop where I had previously bought cloaks and some materials, and I insisted that he design and make the dress for me. His name was Charles Worth, and he was, of course, to become the most famous dress designer of the century, but in 1854 he was still quite unknown.

The dress I chose from his sketches was made of rose-pink silk taffeta. It was cut low off the shoulders, and from the narrow waist of the bodice billowed a bell-shaped skirt measuring eight yards around. The skirt required six starched petticoats underneath to puff it to its proper size. Above the skirt floated a matching-pink, knee-length over-skirt of tulle edged with a wide garland of the same material, puffed and gathered by nine bouquets of pink-silk roses encircling the skirt. From these bouquets flew pink-taffeta ribbons.

When I wore the dress at the Paris ball, the princess herself asked who had made it. Everyone envied it. It was a dress that would make anyone beautiful.

This then, was the dress that I would wear to the ball at Hawthorn Hill. David must be there to see me in it, I thought, as I carried the overskirt down to the laundry rooms. The overskirt would be the most difficult part of the dress to press, so I had decided to do it first.

When I reached the ironing room, I found Ida working at one of the tables.

"Good afternoon, Ida," I said. "Would I be disturbing you if I pressed my dress over there?"

She had finished ironing, and as I entered the room, she completed folding a nightgown, placed it on a pile of freshly ironed clothes on a shelf above the table, and walked over to me.

"Oh! The pretty flowers," she said. "If you wear them in the garden the bees will get on them. Don't let the bees get on them or you will get stung. A bee can make a person die, my lady. Farmer Berner was stung in the throat by a bee and he died from it. Most people don't know that, do they, my lady?"

"No, Ida. But bees would not like these flowers," I said, "because they are not real. They are made of silk. See?" I held up the skirt to display one of the rose bouquets for her to see more clearly. "This is part of my ball dress which I will wear to the ball at Hawthorn Hill on Friday night. Isn't it pretty?" Ida looked at the mass of fabric in a strange, uncomprehending way, and I wondered if she understood what it was. "It is part of the skirt," I said, holding it at my waist so that it fell down in front of me almost as though I were wearing it.

But then Ida glanced up at someone who had come up behind me, and ran from the room.

It was Jane Spence. "Wash those sheets I brought down, you lazy thing," she called after Ida.

"Oh, you startled me, Jane," I said, as I swung around to face her. "I was showing Ida the skirt of my ball dress. She thought the roses were real, poor dear."

Jane's eyes were at once riveted to the skirt which I still held in front of me.

"Don't the roses look real, Jane?" I said. I took a step closer to her and held up the skirt so she could see one of the bouquets. "One would almost have to touch them to know they weren't—they are so beautifully made. You like pretty clothes, don't you, Jane?"

She reached out and touched one of the silk flowers as I spoke. I could see she was entranced.

"This dress was made in Paris. I wore it to a ball there. Lady Vivian has lovely dresses too, doesn't she? I am told that you helped her dress sometimes. Did you?"

"Yes," Jane said.

"I am so glad. She must have needed your help after his late young lordship died. Was she very ill?"

"Yes."

"She must have been grateful for your help then. But not too ill to come down to meals, I hope."

"I'm not paid to answer questions, my lady," Jane said. "That is not part of my duties." Then she swung around and began to walk from the room.

"Jane!" I said. She paused at the doorway and looked back at me. "Very often when one does not wish to answer questions, it is because she has something to hide. Do you have something to hide? Has something happened to Lady Vivian that you do not want me to know about?"

"Certainly not, my lady. What ever gave you that idea? What would I have to hide?"

"I can think of no other reason why you would not wish to tell me about her. She is my best friend and, naturally, I am concerned about her."

"She didn't come down to meals. She wasn't well enough for that. She had her meals in her room on a tray. I took them to her myself."

"When did she leave Castle Cloud?"

Jane leaned against the doorjamb in an insolent pose and replied, "After luncheon on Monday—the day after the funeral."

"Did you help her pack her clothes?"

"No. She wanted to do that herself."

"Did you see her leave?" I asked.

"Here, why are you asking all these questions? I can't stand here answering questions all day. I've got work to do. Yes, I saw her leave. I watched her from the window. His lordship drove her to the station. Why don't you ask him about it?"

"Thank you, Jane. It is only because I am concerned

about her. Just one other thing—did you tidy up her room after she left? She didn't take much with her, did she?"

"Yes, when I got back. She took what she wanted."

"Where did you go," I asked.

"To my mum's in the village. She was sick, and I stayed the night with her. Mrs. Foley said I could. I tidied up her ladyship's room when I got back the next day—put everything back neat like. Is that all?"

"Yes, Jane. Thank you so much."

Jane flew from the laundry rooms then, and I was left to press the skirt of my dress undisturbed.

But later, I wondered if Jane Spence had had any work to do. She seemed to have time to dally with Mitchell in the servants' hall. As I approached it, on my way back to my room, I heard Jane say, "But I told you, Mr. Mitchell, I don't want you touching me. You will please keep your hands to yourself."

Alice's funeral took place the following afternoon.

But since Colen drove Mrs. Foley and Monsieur Laval to Barnstaple on alternate Wednesday afternoons to shop and since that afternoon was their day to go, he could not very well drive us to the village, too. So Lady Clareham and I decided to walk there to the funeral.

It was a grim little affair and I do not wish to dwell upon it. Just let me say, briefly, that an undertaker from Barnstaple with a wretched set of horses and an ancient hearse was hired to carry the body to the church. The service was brief. Only Alice's father and brother, and a handful of village people, and Lady Clareham and I were present.

I had wondered if Jane Spence or May Brooke, the kitchen maid at Castle Cloud, would be there. They were both local girls, they must have known Alice, and Wednesday afternoon was their afternoon off. But they did not attend.

After the service, the sun shown dimly through the clouds as Alice and her baby were lowered into a grave in the churchyard. Half-a-dozen bouquets of home-grown flowers waited on the grass to be placed above her, after the grave diggers had finished their work.

And as soon as that ceremony was over, Lady Clareham and I came away. We had spoken to no one.

After we returned from the funeral, I wrote a letter to Lady Withering refusing the position, and then I pressed the taffeta skirt of my ball dress. I would do the bodice the following day, Thursday, which would then allow me plenty of time to rest during the morning and afternoon of the ball.

It was while I was pressing the bodice, about four o'clock the following afternoon, that Mitchell came into the laundry rooms looking for me.

"His lordship would be pleased if you could join him in the hall chamber, my lady," Mitchell said.

"Oh? Do you know what he wants, Mitchell? I have only a little more to do, and I would like to finish it now."

"I couldn't say, my lady."

"Is anyone with him?"

"Her ladyship is with him. His lordship was quite insistent that he see you at once, my lady, otherwise he would not have sent me to look for you."

"Thank you, Mitchell. Tell him I will be there in a minute."

I replaced the iron I was using in its bracket on the stove, draped the unfinished bodice on a hanger, and hung it on a rod suspended from the ceiling. Then I hurried upstairs.

Edmond and his mother sat on a sofa between the windows.

"Come in, Mary," Edmond said. "Mitchell," he called to the butler, who hovered at the door, "bring that chair and place it there in front of us." When Mitchell had done so, Edmond said, "Thank you, Mitchell. That will be all. Please close the door as you leave."

"Sit down, Mary," he commanded.

When I was seated, he stood and looked first at me and then at his mother.

"Edmond, what is all this?" Lady Clareham asked.

"I was about to tell you, Mother," he said. Then he reached into his waistcoat pocket, drew out something tiny, and handed it to me. "Do you recognize this, Mary?"

It was a stone from a piece of jewelry—an amethyst.

"No, Edmond," I said. "I don't believe I have ever seen it before."

"Are you sure?"

"Quite sure," I said. Then I handed it back to him.

"That is odd. Jane Spence found it on the floor in your room. You will recognize it, Mother." Lady Clareham reached out her hand and Edmond dropped the stone into her palm. "It is, unless I am very much mistaken, a stone from the brooch which was stolen from your jewel box."

Lady Clareham examined the jewel. Then she stood and faced her son. "Edmond, this is too much," she said. "How *could* you blame Mary?"

"I am not blaming anyone, Mother," Edmond said. "But if the stone was found in Mary's room, she must know how it got there, and I think we are entitled to an explanation."

"Don't be stupid, Edmond. Mary does not know anything about it. She does not deserve this. I will not permit it. How did you know the brooch was stolen from my jewel box? I did not tell you anything about it."

"Father told me, of course," Edmond said, with a victorious smile.

"Your father knows nothing about it. I did not tell him. How could I tell your father that you stole the pendant he gave me on our wedding night? Oh, Edmond, how could you?"

"Well, somebody told me about it, that is how I knew."

"This is horrid. Your father shall know about it now, though, Edmond. Oh, I cannot bear it," she said. She turned her back on him, hurried to the door, flung it open, and stalked across the hall to the stairs, leaving us alone.

"And Edmond," I said, "Jane Spence never goes into my room. But if she had and had found the stone there, she would most naturally have assumed it was mine and returned it to me. She certainly would not have gone rushing to you with it. I am surprised you didn't think of that."

"Not unless she had seen you steal it," he said.

"If she had seen me steal it, she would have made the biggest scene the world has ever known, and she would have made it last Saturday when the brooch disappeared. You see, your mother did not tell your father about the theft, but she told me about it. You made your mother very unhappy by taking the pendant. I wonder whether you would have stolen it if you had known how it would hurt her. And why should you want to blame me? Why have you done this, Edmond?"

Edmond looked down at me as if I were a worm, but he did not answer me.

"Very well," I said, "if you will excuse me, I must finish pressing my dress." Then I stood and left him.

That evening, Edmond did not appear for dinner, nor did Lady Clareham. Mitchell served me alone at the table. Afterward, I threw a cloak over my shoulders and walked down the hill to the stone bridge. But I did not stay there very long. A mist hung heavily over the bay and the bridge. Wet and cold, it made me long for a fire in my room.

☙ Chapter Eleven ☙

I HOPE I am not disturbing you," I said, as I entered Lord Clareham's room on Friday evening, "but I thought. . ."

"Ah!" Lord Clareham exclaimed. "The princess goes to the ball. You look positively lovely, my dear, and if I wish to tell you so, I shall."

"Thank you. I thought that since you and Lady Clareham could not go to the ball, that I would bring a little bit of the ball to you. I will be thinking of you both this evening."

"That was very sweet of you, Mary," Lady Clareham said, from her husband's bedside.

"If only Vivian were here, I would be happy," I said. "I miss her terribly. She loves a ball almost more than anything, I think."

"Yes," Lady Clareham said, "I remember the last one at Hawthorn Hill—in October. It was just before my husband was taken ill." She turned to Lord Clareham then. "We all went—James, and Vivian, and you, and I. Do you remember how excited Vivian was? She was so excited that I thought something must burst inside her head. She loved to dance, almost more than—" She had begun to cry, and she daubed at her eyes with her handkerchief.

"There, Julia, that won't do any good, you know," Lord Clareham said.

"Is that Colen with the carriage?" I asked, as I rushed to the window to look down at the drive. "Yes, it is. I must hurry. I wish you could come. We will all miss you, and I know that everyone will be asking about you. I will come and tell you all about it tomorrow. Good night."

Then Ahmad held the door open for me, and I ran from the room, down the stairs to the hall, and out onto the portico, where I threw my shawl about my shoulders and ran down the steps to the waiting carriage.

And as I ran, I thought again how pleased I was with the girl who had looked out of the mirror at me in my room, a little while before. And I saw her again in my mind. I wore little jewelry that evening—my dress was too elaborate for that. I wore only a plain gold bracelet, which my father had given me. I had parted my hair in the center, combed it back very plainly, and gathered it behind my head in a bouquet of the little white silk flowers and some pink roses—the same roses that had been used to trim my dress and which I had kept for just that purpose. My gloves and shawl were white and I carried my Japanese fan with the painted pink apple blossoms on it.

Below me, as he waited on the drive, Edmond made a great show of pacing up and down in front of the carriage and looking at the watch he held in his hands.

He and I had hardly spoken during the day. He had not mentioned the scene that had taken place the day before. He acted as though it had never occurred, and so did I.

Now, as I approached, he said, "I do wish you could be more prompt." Then he opened the door of the carriage for me and helped me up into it. "It would seem that if Colen can have the carriage here at eight-thirty and I can be here at eight-thirty, that you could be ready at eight-thirty, also."

"I am sorry, Edmond," I said, as I looked up at Lord Clareham's window and waved. "I wanted to show your father how I looked."

"Whatever for?" he asked.

"To give him a little pleasure—a little of the feeling of the ball," I said.

Then Edmond closed the carriage door, and as we began to roll down the drive, he said, "I should think, in view of your present circumstances and future prospects, that you would have dressed less elaborately this evening. When one is soon to become a companion, it would seem a trifle dishonest to dress like a duchess."

"This is the only ball dress I have, Edmond," I replied.

After that, we did not speak to each other at all during the drive to Hawthorn Hill.

Hawthorn Hill blazed with light from every window. And as we neared it, three carriages preceded us down the drive. Two others had already arrived at the sweep in front of the house and were discharging their passengers at the steps.

It was after ten o'clock then. The evening was calm, and warm, and still, except for the noise of horses and carriages. And all the night's stars glittered above the house in an indigo sky. The clouds, which had hung over us for days, had parted at sunset, turned crimson and purple, and finally flown away.

Ahead of us, a man and woman were being helped out of a brougham by their footman, and a party of ladies and gentlemen climbed the far arm of the stairway, laughing and calling to each other.

Then it was our turn to draw up before the steps. Edmond helped me down, we climbed the stairs together, and stepped into the entrance hall. It was filled with people, everyone talking at once. In a moment the men began to drift off in one direction to leave their hats, and the women in another to remove their cloaks and shawls.

And above their chatter, I heard Flora saying, "Good evening Mr. Swoop, Mrs. Swoop, Hello Dierdre and Percy. The cloakroom is there, as usual. Good evening Lord and Lady Milne. Where is Eulalia? Just follow the ladies."

Then she was rushing toward us, crying, "Mary and Edmond!" She was breathless when she reached us. "Edmond, you know where to leave your hat. Mamma is upstairs. She has been *asking* for you. Mary, I will show you where to put your things." Then she led me to a little room off the hall where two maids were stationed. They were helping several ladies with their wraps as we entered, and everyone there was laughing and talking. "Here let me take that for you," Flora said. *"Wherever* did you get that dress? It is positively ravishing."

"My hair?" I asked.

"Perfect," she said, handing my shawl and bonnet to one of the maids. "No, I did not know that, Lady Milne," she said, in answer to a remark from a long-necked woman who had come up behind us. "No, I have never heard of him. I must go up to Mother, now. Come up when you are ready. You know the way." Then she grasped my hand and began to pull me toward the doorway. "Wait till you see the long gallery."

We climbed the stairs together, and at the top we stood

for a moment in the open doorway of an enormous room, while the butler announced me.

"The Baroness Beauford," he cried.

This was the long gallery: it stretched across the entire length of the house. From the center of the ceiling to all four walls of the room, pink, yellow, and orange paper ribbons had been strung, creating a tentlike paper roof. Pink and red azaleas, cyclamens, geraniums, and tree ferns had been brought in from the glasshouses and banked in the corners. Here and there between the chairs that lined the walls of the gallery stood tables with bouquets of flowers on them.

Thirty or more people sat on the chairs and milled about the huge room talking and waiting for the dancing to begin. Men asked for dances, and women wrote in their programs. The orchestra waited, a cornetist, a violinist, and a violoncellist tuned their instruments to a piano.

And apart from everyone, reflected in the waxed and polished floor at the far end of the room, David stood watching me.

"The decorations were Lewis's idea," Flora said. "We always try to do something different. I helped him put them up, and Lord Charles helped too. We have been working on them for days. Mamma was afraid it would damage the walls until Lewis told her his idea about the wooden frame to attach the ribbons to. Old Arthur, our carpenter, built that. Isn't he clever?"

"Who, the carpenter?" I asked.

"No, silly, Lewis."

"Yes, marvelous," I said.

"Here is Mamma. Here is Mary, Mamma," she cried.

"So I see, my dear. And there is no need to shout, there is too much noise in the room already," Lady Wilton said, smiling. "Good evening, Mary. How lovely to see you. Did Edmond bring you?"

"Good evening, Lady Wilton," I said. "Yes, he is here somewhere."

"Good," she said, as she took a dance program from the pile that lay on a little table next to her, and handed it to me.

"The Marquess and Marchioness of Milne," the butler cried.

"Later, I want you to meet my cousin, Lady Mauldridge, Mary," Lady Wilton said. "But first I must attend to our guests, and they have only begun to arrive. Run along and enjoy yourselves. Introduce Mary to some of your friends, Flora."

"Georgiana!" Lady Milne cried from behind me. "What a lovely party. . . ."

"Come and meet Angela and her brother," Flora said. "Angela and John and their parents came down from London for the ball, and they are staying with us for a day or two."

But before we had walked ten steps, Lewis stood in our path. He asked me for the first dance, a quadrille, and before I had finished writing his name in my program, Phillip Pridell had asked for the second. Then Lord Charles hurried across to us and asked for a dance. Since I had decided not to dance the third, sixth, and ninth dances (the room was already too warm for comfort, and I did not want to perspire) and the fourth dance was a waltz, which I intended saving for David, I gave Lord Charles the fifth, the lancers.

Finally we crossed the room, and I met Lady Angela and her brother, Lord Houghton. He asked me for a dance at once. The seventh was the next dance open in my program, so I gave it to him.

David joined us then and asked for the first dance. He was disappointed when I told him it would have to be the fourth. I was thankful, though, that in the confusion, no one noticed that we had not had to be introduced.

After that, Lewis and Lord Charles each asked for another dance, and then David said that he had better ask for two more, before they were all gone. At that point, my first twelve dances were arranged. And then it would be time for supper.

"The Lord Parkerton, the Lady Parkerton, the Honorable Francis Graves, and the Honorable Rupert Graves," the butler cried, and then after a moment, "Sir Roger and Lady Molehill."

And then the master of ceremonies cried, "Ladies and gentlemen, please take your places for the quadrille." The introductory music began, Lewis offered me his arm, and led me out onto the floor. David followed us with Lady Angela, and Lord Charles hurried after him with a blond-haired girl, who I later learned was Lady Jessica Talbot.

The fourth couple, completing our set, was Gerald Armstrong, a friend of Lewis's, and his partner. Then Lewis led me to the post of honor, placed me on his right hand, bowed to me and then to Lady Angela, and the dance began.

But I wondered what had happened to Flora, and it wasn't until we were advancing in the L'Ete that I saw her in the far set, dancing with Edmond.

It was shortly after that, when we had returned to our places, that I heard a girl standing just behind me, say: ". . . to America. Can you imagine? Poor Mr. Field."

"Word gets around quickly," Lewis whispered to me. "I suppose *the* topic of gossip tonight will be how Lady Vivian ran off to America with the groom. It's bound to be."

"Yes, I suppose so," I said. "Aren't people awful?"

"Sometimes, but don't blame them too much," he said with a smile.

Lewis was a charming partner, but the dance had no sooner begun, it seemed, than it was over, and he led me back to the bank of ferns and flowers where we had started. And at almost the same time, Flora arrived on Edmond's arm. He bowed to her and excused himself to go in search of his partner for the next dance, and Lewis hurried away in the opposite direction searching for his. A dour young man with a beaked nose approached us, and Flora introduced him as Percy Swoop. He was to have the next dance with her.

As Flora and Percy were about to leave me, Phillip Pridell appeared and led me onto the floor for our waltz. He was most attentive, and he complimented me over and over on my piano playing. How he hoped that I would call at Crompton Manor, his home near Croyde! They had a marvelous harpsichord which I could play on for him. Could Flora bring me? How his mother and Philomena would love it if I visited them! Could he visit me at Castle Cloud? Would Lord and Lady Clareham mind? Did I ride? Would I be at Lord Preston's hunt?

"Mr. and Mrs. Stafford and Georgette Stafford," the butler called from the doorway, as the dance ended.

"Would you care for some refreshment, Lady Beauford?" Phillip asked.

"No, thank you, Mr. Pridell, but I would like to sit

down for a minute. It is terribly hot. I wish someone would open a window."

Phillip led me to a chair next to Lady Angela and her mother and, as I was about to sit down, I saw Flora and Lady Wilton hurrying across the room toward me. Phillip bowed, thanked me for the dance, and asked for the dance immediately preceding supper. I said that I was engaged for that one so he asked for the thirteenth instead, which I gave him.

Then he left me just as Lady Wilton and Flora approached.

"There, Mary," Lady Wilton said, when she reached my side, "they are the last. Now everyone is here, I think."

"I didn't know there were so many people in all Devonshire," I said.

"Neither did we," Flora said, "until we began sending out the invitations. Every time we have a ball, we invite more people. Pretty soon— Oh, good evening, Mr. Strong. Lady Beauford, allow me to introduce Mr. Strong."

"May I have the pleasure of dancing this quadrille with you, Miss Stratton?" he asked, after we had exchanged pleasantries.

"Thank you, Mr. Strong," Flora said.

The introduction to the quadrille had begun, and Mr. Strong offered his arm and led her away among the dancers scurrying to find their places.

"I want you to meet my cousin, Lady Mauldridge," Lady Wilton said, "but I don't see them." She rose on her toes, trying to see through the dancers to the other side of the room.

"Such a lovely party, Georgiana," a gray-haired woman said. "The orchestra is divine."

"Where did you find them?" her escort asked.

"We brought them down from London," Lady Wilton replied. "They played at Charlton House last April when we were there. Have you seen Lady Mauldridge? Oh, there she is. Excuse us, my dears, I want Lady Beauford to meet her."

I followed Lady Wilton. We threaded our way between the dancers on the floor and the groups of people standing and sitting along the wall, toward the end of the room. A doorway led to an adjoining chamber which now served as the refreshment room.

"Camellia!" Lady Wilton called, as she waved to a tall, gaunt woman with grayish skin who stood against the wall. Lady Mauldridge looked about forty years old and stood next to a dark man, much shorter than she, who was bald and much younger—perhaps thirty. His eyes were glued to a young girl with a swollen bosom who was dancing in front of them.

When we reached her cousin, Lady Wilton said, "Lord and Lady Mauldridge, may I present Lady Beauford."

"We are enchanted, Lady Beauford," Lord Mauldridge said.

Though he was a short man, he was brawny, with a bull neck and thick, hairy wrists. He was clean shaven, but his beard was so heavy that it stained his face gray.

His little black eyes glittered as he asked, "Has Lord Beauford come down to Devonshire with you?"

"I have never been married, Lord Mauldridge," I said. "I am a baroness in my own right."

"Oh, I beg your pardon, Lady Beauford. Well, this has been charming, but you must excuse me—it is almost time for the next dance, and I must find my partner."

No sooner had he left us than David said from behind me, "I believe we have the next dance, Lady Beauford."

"Lady Mauldridge," Lady Wilton said, "allow me to present Mr. Field."

Lady Mauldridge offered her hand, David took it and bowed, and after a minute's conversation asked if we cared for some refreshment. Lady Wilton and Lady Mauldridge declined, but I accepted David's invitation, and we left them.

As we entered the empty refreshment room, we passed Edmond and Lord Wilton. They stood deep in conversation beside the doorway.

Once inside, David brought me a lemonade, and then he said, "I thought I would never have you to myself for a moment."

"I am afraid it was only a moment, David," I said, glancing into the long gallery.

The dancers had finished the quadrille, and many of them were descending on the refreshment room. I finished my lemonade, and as they surged toward us, we squeezed our way through them—back toward the dance floor. As we did so, I heard a girl's voice say, "There he goes now.

It doesn't seem to have dampened his spirits at all, does it?" I sensed that they were talking about David, and I wondered what the girl had meant. But I forgot about it as soon as the music began, and David put his arm around me and swung me into the waltz.

"I am sorry I was angry on Saturday night," I said.

"It was my fault. You asked for my help and I didn't give it to you. We will see about that business—you could be right about it."

"But you don't think so."

"I am sorry, Mary, I don't. But if you do find out anything, tell me about it at once."

We were quiet for a moment, then I asked, "Did you get the cows down from Windsor all right?"

"Yes. All safe and sound. There was a bull which we brought along also. He was very nervous on the train, but when we changed trains at Exeter. . ."

"You dance divinely," I interrupted. "I could go on like this all night—round and round and round. You didn't learn to dance like this on a farm, David."

"No," he said, "you forget I lived in the wicked city before I moved to the country. I went dancing almost every night in London. I preferred it to banking."

"And now you prefer farming to dancing."

"I like dancing," he said.

"But not as well as farming?"

"They are two very different things. I like to dance and I like my work. There isn't any need to compare them."

"But aren't you enjoying yourself? Isn't this lovely?"

"I enjoy myself when I am with you, but—"

"But?" I asked.

"I never feel comfortable or at ease with Lord and Lady Wilton, for instance, or with any of the—aristocracy. I never have. I suppose it goes back to my school days."

Are you at home with me then, David? I thought. But I did not say it. I did not want to be serious. "How?" I asked instead.

"Boys don't bother to disguise their feelings. My father was in trade, and that was responsible for a rather bad time at Rugby. There was a lot of fagging, and I had to learn to fight and fight hard. In those days I wanted more than anything to be accepted. That is why I spent all my time playing cricket. I thought that if they admired me, they would like me."

"And did they?"

"No. They tolerated me, but they never liked me. It wasn't as bad at Oxford because I made friends with other fellows like myself, and we kept together. But I was still the best there at cricket and rowing. Forgive me if I change the subject and say that you are looking very beautiful tonight."

"Not as beautiful as Vivian," I said.

"What made you say that?"

"I don't know. Silly, wasn't it. Maybe because I have been thinking about her all evening."

"No one could be as beautiful as Vivian, but that doesn't have anything to do with anything, does it?"

"No," I said. "Let us dance and not be serious or think anymore."

The waltz was by Strauss. We became caught up in his music, and we moved almost as one person. I was happy then, and David was happy too, I felt. So there was no need to speak, and we finished the dance without saying anything more.

When it was over we went to find Lord Charles, with whom I was to have the next dance. As we approached him, Lord Charles bowed to a girl, who had seated herself next to her mother, and then stepped toward us. David thanked me for the dance, and then he turned and walked away—down the line of guests that stood and sat against the wall. But he had not gone ten feet when a girl in a beige silk dress stood and blocked his path. She was Percy Swoop's sister, the girl I had heard Flora call Dierdre. She had been sitting with Philomena Pridell and Philomena's mother. But when David approached her, she forgot them in her determination to intercept him. She was bold in her manner. I could tell that she was demanding to be taken to the refreshment room. I suppose David had no choice but to take her there, so he offered his arm and they walked away together.

Then Lord Charles led me to our place for the lancers. During the dance, I noticed that Lady Wilton and Edmond sat together, deep in conversation. Lady Wilton's eloquent hands could express as much as her words could, and as I watched, they seemed to say, "But what else could I do?

I was powerless. It really is such a pity." I was curious about this.

But I was even more curious when I heard two plain-looking girls whispering about Edmond in the ladies' cloak-room during the sixth dance. I had gone to the cloakroom because I had discovered, during the lancers, that one of the roses on my dress had come loose, and I wished to have it sewn back on. I stood before a mirror while one of the maids knelt and repaired the damage, and the two girls entered, talking.

"Flora is dancing with Lord Althrop again," said one.

"Yes, I think it is disgusting," the other girl said, "the obvious way she is throwing herself at him."

"Not disgusting, foolish."

"Foolish?"

"Ruth! You know he has slept with every servant girl between here and. . ."

"Sh-h-h! Dora!"

"Well, it is true," Ruth hissed.

I pretended not to have noticed them and not to have heard, and in a moment the maid had finished. I thanked her and returned to the second floor where I found Phillip Pridell standing at the top of the stairs. We began to talk, and I suggested that we remain on the landing until the galop was over. It was cooler there, and we could watch the dancers through the open doorway.

As we watched, someone from inside the room to the right of the doorway cried, "She has run off to San Francisco with one of the pantry boys at Castle Cloud." Then the music swelled, and the voice was lowered, and I heard no more until several sentences later ". . . he is here," the voice shouted, "and having the time of his life. You would think it had never happened."

But that was all I heard because Lewis Stratton came out onto the landing and said, "Lady Beauford, I have been looking everywhere for you. I believe we have the next dance."

"And we have the one after this one, Lady Beauford," Phillip said.

"Yes, Mr. Pridell," I said. "And I am looking forward to it."

Then Lewis led me back into the gallery. In a moment the music started and we began to waltz.

Twice, as we whirled about, Lewis had been about to say something, but then he had thought better of it. But when it happened a third time, I questioned him about it with my eyes, and he said, "I have something I wish to discuss with you, Lady Beauford. I had hoped to bring it up casually in conversation, but I have not been able to find a way to do that."

"What is it, Mr. Stratton?" I asked.

"It is my sister. She—she would—she is interested in Edmond."

"And do you approve?"

"I am afraid I do not, Lady Beauford. I am worried about it, and I would like to ask you, since you and Flora have become such good friends, to try to discourage her."

"I don't see how I can do that," I said. "If Flora is interested in Edmond, it is her business, not mine. I would have no reason to try to discourage her interest in him. I do not think we have any right to form a judgment about their relationship, or to express an opinion about it one way or the other."

"But we *do* have a right to form a judgment about them," he said. "We have an obligation to shield those we love from being hurt when we can. What kind of a husband would Edmond make?"

"I could not say. But marriage— Has the subject come up?"

"No, but that is what he wants, and that is what she wants."

"Flora *should* be married, I think," I said.

"To someone who will make her happy. You are not related to Edmond's family, Lady Beauford, so I shall speak plainly. Edmond does not want my sister, he wants her money."

"Yes, Mr. Stratton, but there have been countless marriages—most marriages, as a matter of fact—that have had financial foundations, and many have been happy ones. Castle Cloud is a beautiful house. Flora would have children. . . ."

"Would she?"

"Well, I presume she would."

"Perhaps, but Edmond would spend little time in her bed, and that would cause her great unhappiness. I am sorry, but you must know his reputation for philandering by this time. And I would hate to see her money thrown away on the hazard tables and watch her grow old in a decaying, understaffed house."

"I see. I don't know what to say, Mr. Stratton. I would hate to see that too," I said. "I will have to think about it."

Involuntarily, as we talked, I had begun to search for Edmond. I found him standing in a corner of the room with Lady Wilton, talking to Lord and Lady Mauldridge. Edmond looked intent. I could tell by his manner that the conversation had been important to him. He seemed to be explaining something and, as he talked, Lord and Lady Mauldridge became increasingly amiable.

I wondered what they had been talking about. I had no idea that it might have anything to do with me, but I soon found out that it had. I was surprised when Edmond and Lady Wilton approached me and Lady Wilton said, "Mary, we have a marvelous surprise for you."

"Lord Mauldridge has asked to speak with you," Edmond said. "Shall we go over and see him now? Flora said that you did not intend to dance this waltz."

"Don't be so mysterious, Edmond," Lady Wilton said, as we followed him through the crowd. Then she said to me, "My cousin and her husband have two darling twins, Ethelind and Eugenia, and it happens that their governess has decided to leave Flowerwick Hall on Monday without giving any notice whatsoever—completely irresponsible. As I said to Camellia, 'A person like that should not be in charge of children.' Well, Camellia was frantic, and when we told her about your dilemma, she nearly cried with joy. They want you. . ."

But by then we had reached Lord and Lady Mauldridge, and she was interrupted by Edmond. "Here she is," he said.

"Dominick," Lady Wilton said, "I have been telling Mary about your predicament. Dominick and Camellia are praying, Mary, that you will come to Flowerwick Hall to look after their daughters."

"I have been so distraught," Lady Mauldridge said to me, "ever since Miss Constantine told me she was leaving. I have been so *upset*. I have not slept. I am so *nervous*. My poor little ones. 'What ever will they do?' I have been asking myself over and over. What will. . ."

"Camellia!" Lord Mauldridge said.

"Oh, yes, Dominick. I am so sorry. . . ."

"Miss Thorpe. . ." Lord Mauldridge began.

"I have told Lord Mauldridge," Edmond interrupted, "that you wish it to be *Miss* Thorpe, in order to avoid any embarrassment."

"Quite so, Miss Thorpe," Lord Mauldridge continued. "As Georgiana has no doubt told you, we have twin daughters—age six. Their governess is leaving us. And since you are seeking a position in the country, we hope that you will consider staying with us, and that you will come to Flowerwick Hall early in the week to meet the children."

"Oh, please do, Miss Thorpe," Lady Mauldridge said. "You will find it a heavenly house—it has been in my family for hundreds of years. You will love it, and you would be such lovely company for me. It is lovely in the hills, and my little girls would. . ."

"My dear!" Lord Mauldridge said.

"Yes, I am so sorry, Dominick," Lady Mauldridge said. "I did not mean to. . ."

"Shall we say Monday afternoon, Miss Thorpe?" Lord Mauldridge asked.

"It *is* a lovely spot, Mary," Lady Wilton said. "You will fall in love with it at once. She will be quite perfect, Camellia, and I know she will love it there. And the twins, Mary, are adorable."

"Shall we say Monday afternoon, Miss Thorpe?" Lord Mauldridge repeated, as he glared at Lady Wilton.

"Yes," I said. "That would be perfect, thank you, Lord Mauldridge."

"Good," he said. "Gregory will meet the train at Bampton station. I would suggest the train that arrives at 2 P.M. Then you could make the 6 o'clock train to return. I presume you will accompany Miss Thorpe, Lord Althrop?"

"Yes, indeed," Edmond said. "What a remarkable coincidence. . . ."

"Now, my dear Miss Thorpe," Lord Mauldridge said, "we shall talk of business matters on Monday. This is a social occasion, and we must all make the most of it. May I have the pleasure of the next dance?"

I could not, of course, give it to him since I had promised every dance except the fourteenth and eighteenth. So finally we agreed to dance the fourteenth together.

Then Percy Swoop, to whom I had promised the lancers, found me and led me away from them and onto the floor. Edmond danced that dance with Percy's sister, Dierdre, but they were not in our set. Dierdre, I noticed, seemed fascinated by Edmond's conversation.

And as Edmond and Philomena danced by me during the waltz that followed, Philomena, too, seemed fascinated by Edmond's conversation. Edmond seemed to be trying very hard to be charming. And so was Lord Charles, with whom I danced. But unlike Edmond, or even Phillip Pridell, he was no conversationalist. Lord Charles was very attentive and smiled attractively, but although he tried to be entertaining, he had little to say, and I was rather glad when the dance ended.

The waltz was followed by a quadrille, which I danced with David.

"What were you and Lord and Lady Mauldridge talking about?" he whispered during it. "Whatever it was did not seem to make you very happy."

"It didn't. I will tell you about it during supper," I said.

At that point we advanced to the center, where David left me with Lewis, but presently the dance brought me back to David again, and so it went on. As we danced, I noticed that Philomena Pridell was staring at me. She sat against the wall with Dierdre Swoop, who was whispering in her ear. Ordinarily I would not have paid any attention to her (everyone who sat around the room watched the dancers most of the time), but her look was so filled with repugnance that I was startled by it. Then Dierdre followed her gaze, and I saw the same look of aversion on her face. It had all happened in an instant. Then the two girls lowered their eyelids in unison and turned to look at each other as they whispered together. They had decided to hate me. I was sure of it, and I wondered why—especially since I had never even met Dierdre. I was annoyed by the incident and continued to watch the two girls as I danced.

"What is it?" David asked.

"Dierdre Swoop and Philomena Pridell just looked at me in the strangest way—almost as though they hated me," I said.

"I will wager everyone here is envious of you," he whispered.

"Oh, David!" I said, smiling back at him.

As the dance continued, we formed two lines, changed places and partners, and cast off to the right. But I could not forget the way Dierdre and Philomena had looked at me, and I kept watching them. Shortly they stood and marched together to Flora, who sat alone. The two girls sat down on either side of her, and both began to talk to her at once. The fact that Flora was sitting alone made me look for Edmond. He was not far away. He stood talking to Lord and Lady Wilton. Lady Wilton was laughing, but Lord Wilton did not seem amused.

Shortly the quadrille ended, and it was time for supper. Most of the guests strolled, then, toward the doorway and began to descend the stairs to the dining room.

"Shall we go down now, or wait a few minutes and avoid the crush?" David asked.

"Let us wait," I said. "I am really not very hungry, but I am terribly thirsty. May I have something to drink?"

"As easily done as said," David replied, giving me his arm.

Then we walked into the refreshment room, which was deserted, and David ladled lemonade into a glass and handed it to me.

"Thank you, David," I said. "Your father did not come with you tonight?"

"No," he said, "there is some kind of banker's meeting in London, and he is to receive an award of some kind. I am ashamed to say I really didn't pay any attention to it. I must make a fuss over it when he gets back. Tell me about Lord and Lady Mauldridge."

"They are about to lose their governess. They have twin girls, six years old, and they want me to take the position. Edmond and Lady Wilton seem to have arranged it."

"In the middle of a ball?"

"I know. It doesn't seem the time for it, does it?"

"They might have waited until tomorrow," he said. "They are staying here, aren't they? Edmond could have driven you over. But don't let it spoil your evening."

"It might be pleasant at Flowerwick Hall. It is supposed to be lovely, and Lady Wilton said the twins are adorable.

We are to go and meet them on Monday. Do you know Lord and Lady Mauldridge?" I asked.

"No, not really."

"She seems quite pleasant, though terribly meek. I think I would like it better than at Lady Hob's or Lady Withering's. Still, I do wish so that I didn't have to do it."

"So do I," David said.

We finished our lemonade then, and sauntered back across the long gallery, down the stairs, and into the dining room. The supper displayed on the dining table before us was a lavish one. There were turkeys, pheasants, hams, roasts, and tongue—all carved—little sandwiches of all kinds, cold fish and fruit jellies, seafood salads in bowls of ice, blanc-mange, trifle, tipsy cake and several other kinds of cake, and raspberry, strawberry, lemon, and orange ices, among other things. The butler and footmen served champagne, Moselle, sherry, claret, pale ale, and stout.

After David had helped me to some sandwiches and salad, we walked to the doorway of the drawing room, where many of the guests sat eating. The drawing room, the library, and the salon, all connecting rooms, had been provided with extra chairs. And those who wished could dine later—during the last six dances—as the supper rooms would remain open until the end of the ball.

Flora saw David and me standing in the doorway, and got up at once, running across the room to us.

"Mary," she said, "bring Mr. Field with you and come join us. I have saved a seat for you next to me."

She had been sitting in the drawing room with her mother and father, Edmond, Lewis, Lady Angela, Sir Roger and Lady Molehill, and a gray-haired lady whom I could not identify.

And as we approached the group, I heard Edmond saying, ". . . happy coincidence that Lord and Lady Mauldridge required a governess. Hello, Mary, David," he said, as I sat down across from him, next to Flora. "I believe you know everyone. Oh, Lady Agatha Prigger, may I introduce—ah—the Baroness Beauford. I was telling Lady Agatha what a marvelous coincidence it is that Lord and Lady Mauldridge require a governess just as you are searching for a position."

"What?" Lady Molehill asked. "Who is searching for a position?"

"Lady Beauford is going. . ." Edmond started to say.

But he was interrupted by David who had stepped quickly between Edmond and Lady Molehill, bent close to the old lady, and shouted into her ear, "During a ball is hardly the time to speak of business matters, don't you agree, Lady Molehill?"

"I don't see why not," Edmond said to David. "We are very concerned about our Mary's future, and when one is in dire need, anytime is the time for true friends to step in to help her."

"One can do more harm than good under the guise of helpfulness," David said, "if one acts in a thoughtless manner."

"What does that mean?" Edmond demanded. "If you think I do not have the best interests. . ."

"I agree entirely," Lewis said. "Tonight was no time to be discussing anything of the sort."

"Lewis!" Lady Wilton cried. "There is no harm in an introduction. Mary was delighted to meet Lord and Lady Mauldridge, weren't you, Mary, and Flowerwick Hall is so lovely. Their gardens are enchanting. Have you visited Camellia at Flowerwick Hall, Agatha? Edmond, you have a treat in store. While you are there, ask Dominick to show you his gun collection, but perhaps you are not interested in guns."

"I am indeed, Lady Wilton," Edmond replied. "I understand you have a collection of your own, Lord Wilton. Perhaps you would be good enough to show it to me one day."

Then Lord Wilton began to tell Edmond about his gun collection. Lady Agatha and Lady Wilton talked about gardens. Lewis and David talked about horses, while Flora listened. And I, having managed to choke down some bits of sandwich, sat back and tried to hold on to my temper. Edmond had deliberately set out to embarrass me. I was furious with him. But David and Lewis were dears to have come to my rescue.

If only everyone were as kind and considerate as those two, I thought, but they are not. Most people are dreadful. Just look at Lord Mauldridge sitting in the salon staring at that girl next to him. She is the same girl I had seen him staring at upstairs in the gallery. He can hardly take his eyes from her bosom. Has he actually brought her to have supper with him and his wife?

And see how Dierdre leers at David. The Swoops and the Pridells all sat together on the other side of the room between the windows, where Dierdre spent half her time trying to catch David's eye, ignoring Lord Houghton who was her escort for supper. Philomena sat very close to Lord Charles on the sofa, lavishing all her attention on him and acting as though he had cast a spell upon her.

I glanced from her, back at Dierdre, and when Dierdre saw me looking at her, she turned to Lord Houghton and said something that caused the entire group to look in my direction. She had said something unpleasant about me—I could tell by their looks.

But I was determined not to show that I cared, so I forced myself to join in the conversation with David, Lewis, and Flora and to laugh and pretend I was enjoying myself. And at last it was time to return to the long gallery for the remaining dances.

"Are you all right?" David asked, as he led me toward the staircase.

"Yes, but I wish we were sitting by ourselves on the hill next to the monument," I said.

"So do I," he replied.

Then Dierdre brushed past us, pulling Lord Houghton along by the hand. "Don't forget, David," she whispered in his ear. And then in the hallway, as they began to climb the stairs, she turned and flashed a smile at David.

"I have the last dance with her," David said. Then he smiled. "It was better than risking a scene."

David stayed with me, after we had entered the gallery, until Phillip Pridell arrived. I had begun to wonder if he had forgotten that we had the quadrille together. The introductory music was almost over by the time he led me onto the floor. We were so late that we were lucky to find a place in a set. I do not believe Phillip said one word during the dance. And afterward, as soon as he possibly could, he left me. He had made me feel as though I had a contagious disease. I was mystified and a trifle hurt by his aloofness.

Lord Mauldridge was not aloof, however. The next dance was the waltz that I had promised him, and during it, he held me a little closer than was proper. And when I pulled away from him, he said, "Miss Thorpe, soon we will be seeing a great deal of each other, and we should be friends. Don't you agree?"

"Yes, of course, Lord Mauldridge," I said, "and I am sure that neither of us would ever presume upon the association."

"The word *presume* has a connotation about it which offends me. Associations must be allowed to develop freely. Don't you agree?"

"Well, yes—" I replied.

He held me a little less closely, then, but I still felt uncomfortable. And his smiling at me did not make me feel any more at ease.

So I was relieved when the waltz was over and Lewis led me onto the floor for the lancers. I enjoyed dancing with him. He was charming.

David must have noticed this because, during our waltz which followed, he said, "You seem to enjoy dancing with Lewis Stratton. He was in great spirits during the lancers."

I smiled at him and said, "No more than Dierdre Swoop will be during the country dance when you dance with her."

This made David laugh and was responsible, I thought, for a certain lightness in his step as we whirled about the floor. It was thrilling to waltz with David, and I was flushed and out of breath when it was over.

"Let me catch my breath," I said. "I must look a fright."

"I have never seen you look lovelier," David said, as we came to a stop. His huge brown eyes bore down into mine and caused that strange thrill to run up my spine.

The following dance, the galop with Lord Houghton, was as dreary as the waltz with David had been exciting. Lord Houghton was very polite and very correct, his movements and timing were perfect. But he did not smile, and he spoke no more than the minimum amount that manners dictated.

What had brought about such a change in him and in Phillip Pridell? What had Dierdre been saying to have caused it? It was hard to believe that anyone would deliberately set out to turn one person against another, but I felt that Dierdre had done so. What could she have been saying about me? She and I had never met. Could I be imagining it? I wondered. Perhaps it was simply that it was late, and we were all tired.

I was to have plenty of time to wonder about it, since no one had asked me to dance the last dance of the evening—the country dance, which followed the galop. When the galop was over, Lord Houghton led me to a chair next to Mrs. Pridell and, after bowing and thanking me in the fewest possible words, he left me.

"Good evening, Mrs. Pridell," I said. "Isn't this marvelous?"

"Yes, isn't it," she said. But she stood as she spoke, and then without looking at me, walked away.

After that I sat alone and watched the dancers. I tried not to watch David and Dierdre, but I was not successful. I watched every movement. I was fascinated by the way Dierdre was able to move and smile with just that hint of sensuality that would entice but that would not be positive enough to be objectionable. This was an achievement, I had to admit. Yes, Dierdre was far from being a stupid girl. But either she was immoral or she had a morbid imagination.

Toward the end of the dance, I went to join Edmond who stood talking to Lord and Lady Wilton. Flora stood next to them, and Lady Agatha crowded close to hear the conversation.

"Here she is now," Edmond said, as I approached. "Mary, we must be off at once. I have just the slightest pain behind the eyes, and you look exhausted. I sent a message to Colen to be at the entrance front before the country dance was over, so he will be waiting for us now. If we leave at once, we can avoid the chaos down below.

"Good night, Lord and Lady Wilton. It has been a wonderful evening. I will always remember it. Good night, Flora. It has been marvelous. Good night, Lady Agatha. Come, Mary." Then he hurried away toward the doorway to the stairs.

"Thank you, Lord and Lady Wilton," I said. "It has been heavenly. Good night, Flora. I am afraid I must rush, or I will be left behind. Good night, Lady Agatha."

Everyone said good night in return, including Lewis, who had suddenly appeared—everyone except Lady Agatha. She did not speak to me, though I am sure no one noticed it.

But as I ran after Edmond, I heard her say, "One must be so careful nowadays about invitations. . . ."

Then David stood in my path. "Good night, David," I said. "Edmond is in a panic to get away. I must hurry after him."

So I ran to the stairs and down them to the hall below, where I found Edmond waiting for me. And when I had put on my bonnet and shawl, we dashed for our carriage.

A dozen horses and their carriages jostled for position on the sweep below the steps, and others waited for space to enter the area. There was already pandemonium. But Colen had parked our carriage at the base of the stairs, in a place where we could be off at once. We hurried down to it and were quickly driven away.

"That was an abrupt departure," I said, as we sped down the drive away from the house.

"Better abrupt," Edmond said, "than to spend another minute with them. God! What a bore. What an endless, tiresome, stupid, dull, disgusting bore."

I did not reply. I did not want to talk to Edmond. I was too exhausted to. And I felt strangely unfulfilled. So I drew back into my corner and, gazing at the flickering carriage lamps against the blackness, thought about the ball. Somehow, it had not been the gay, exciting, wonderful evening that I had looked forward to. But I was too tired to figure out exactly why. I simply wanted to go to bed and to sleep.

It was after four o'clock by the time I had gotten into bed that morning. I had gone to sleep at once and did not wake until Mrs. Muldoon knocked and entered my room.

"Sure, I knew you'd want to sleep," she said, "so I didn't wake you earlier. It's a scone and some coffee I've brought you." She set the tray down on the bed beside me. "So you'd best drink it while it's hot."

"You are an angel, Mrs. Muldoon," I said. "Thank you."

"Well," she said, "You know what the little boy says when his mother told him that it wouldn't be to heaven with the angels he'd go if he didn't say his prayers."

"No, what did the little boy say?"

"He says, 'It's not to heaven with the angels I want to go—it's with you and Papa.' 'It's with you and Papa,' he says. Ha, ha, ha, ha."

I laughed too. She enjoyed her story so much, I couldn't help it. Then, after a moment, I asked, "What time is it? Oh, it is eleven o'clock. Did his lordship come down to breakfast, do you know?"

" 'Twas a half-hour later than usual that he came down, because of the ball, my lady. *Mr.* Mitchell served him his breakfast, and then off he went."

"Where did he go? Do you know?"

"Does anyone ever know, my lady? Mrs. Foley says there's nothing that's been missing lately that she knows anything about, but that don't mean anything. His lordship told him that he'd be back in time for Sunday dinner, *Mr.* Mitchell tells us. Well, if you'll excuse me, my lady, I'll go and get the water for your bath."

Later, after I had bathed and dressed, I visited Lord Clareham and told him all about the ball. Many people had asked about him the night before, and he was pleased when I told him so. But I could see that he was preoccupied, perhaps worried, and when I asked him about it, he told me that Lady Clareham had had a chill and then a fever during the night. And although the fever had abated somewhat by morning, she was still feverish and would remain in bed until the fever had passed completely.

Consequently, I dined alone at luncheon. And when the meal was over, I went into the library, found a book to read, carried it into the drawing room, and sat by the window with the book open in my lap. I gazed out at the park, thinking about David and all the things that had happened at the ball.

And as I thought about him, I saw him in the flesh, riding toward the house. I had seen him as soon as he rounded the bend of the drive at the top of the hill, and I watched Caesar carry him to the house, around it, and toward the stables. Then I ran out onto the west portico and stood there waiting for him to come out of the stable yard. And when he did, I called his name and ran to meet him.

"David, I am so glad," I said, giving him both my hands.

He took them, smiled down at me, and said, "You left so quickly last night that I didn't have time to say a proper good-night."

"So you have come to say good night?"

"Uh, huh. Good night and hello."

"Hello, David," I said, laughing.

"No after-effects from the ball?" he asked.

"None that I know of. I loved waltzing with you best of all. It was lovely. I think it is silly that one may dance only three dances with a gentleman in a whole evening. And some people think three dances is being too familiar. Who do you suppose made the rules, David?"

"I don't know, but I agree with you. I suppose it makes for a better party, though. It wouldn't do for the same people to dance every dance together. However, whatever the rules, we must be proper."

"Then you must be proper with me this afternoon."

"How?" he asked.

"We must not be alone together, not here at the house, anyway. At least we should be under the watchful eye of someone. If we walk in the park in front of the house, Lord Clareham can keep an eye on us. He has mirrors by his bed and can watch everything that happens in front of the house."

"Very well—lead on, my lady," he said.

As we walked around the house and out onto the lawn in front of it, we talked about the ball, and I asked, "What time did you leave?" As I spoke, I glanced up at Lord Clareham's window to see if I could see him watching us.

"It must have been almost four o'clock before John could bring the carriage around. What a muddle it was."

"Edmond said that the ball had been a terrible bore. I was surprised to hear him say that. He seemed to be having such a good time. Are all men bored at a ball? Is it only the ladies who have a good time?"

"I suppose that if a gentleman were in love with a lady," David said, "and the lady were not at the ball, then he would be bored. But if she were there, he would enjoy himself tremendously. I enjoyed myself very much last evening." He had looked at me in that thrilling way as he spoke. "I am uncomfortable with those people, sometimes, I told you about that. But that certainly did not spoil the evening for me. As a matter of fact, it did not have anything to do with it."

"But what about me?" I asked. "I am a baroness, so you must be uncomfortable with me."

"No," he said with a laugh. "I have known all along that you had a title, and you know I am not uncomfortable with you." He took a menacing step toward me and said, "I have kissed you once, Lady Beauford, and if you do not stop talking nonsense, I will kiss you again to prove it—right here in front of Lord Clareham."

"No, David! Please!" I cried. Then when I realized he was not serious, I asked, "You knew? How?"

"Vivian told me about you."

"And you didn't tell me?"

"You didn't ask," he said.

"When we met you called me Miss Thorpe. Why not Lady Beauford, then?"

"Because you introduced yourself as Mary Elizabeth Thorpe, and I didn't know we were going to become friends. It seemed much simpler not to get into an explanation of what Vivian told me about you."

"What did she tell you?"

"What you told me. That you had been in school together—not in any detail—and that you were friends, and that she hoped you would be coming to visit her. She never said where you would be coming from or anything about your life in Holland."

"And that I had a title?"

"She mentioned it. It was mentioned last night, too. There was some talk about you at the ball which I think you should know about."

"What?"

"That your title is not—genuine. I don't know if it makes any difference. . . ."

"That is ridiculous. Who told you that?"

"Dierdre Swoop."

"Dierdre Swoop? What did she say, David?"

"She said that you—"

"Tell me."

"That you are not the daughter of the marquess of Penbroke. That your mother was a parlor maid at Gunderbury Hall, and that you were born before your mother and fa-

ther were married. That your real father was the blacksmith there."

"What? Oh, David," I said, laughing. "Where on earth
did she get that story? What an idea."

"I don't know."

"I have never even met her. Where did she hear that?"

"I don't know. I asked her, but she wouldn't say."

"Would it make any difference if it were true?"

"To me? No. I don't care who your parents were, but it
would probably make a difference to a lot of other people.
Do you have any proof?"

"No, how could I? But my mother and father's marriage
is registered, and I suppose my birth is too. Mr. Schraw
would know.

"I knew there was talk about me last night," I continued. "I felt it and heard little bits— What an ugly thing to
do. David, why? Why should she spread such a story? I
don't suppose it really makes very much difference in my
present circumstances, but I would hate to have people
thinking I am a fraud."

"Go see Schraw about it."

"What, and run about with a piece of paper proving I
am genuine? No, David. I think I had better ignore it.
This kind of thing is beneath notice. Still, I do want to
find out where she got that story—whether she made it up
or someone told her—and why she is spreading it."

"How are you going to do that?" he asked.

"Ask her. Thank you for telling me about it, David.
How are the cows?"

"All very well," he said.

I sat down on a wooden bench then, and he sat beside
me. He understood that I did not want to talk about the
rumor anymore and began to tell me the latest about the
construction of the barn and how the stalls were to be arranged. But I couldn't concentrate on his description: I
kept thinking about Dierdre.

Soon he said he had stayed more than the proper
amount of time, and that Lord Clareham would be sending someone out after him if he did not leave. So we
walked to the stable yard together, Colen brought Caesar
out, we said good-by, and David rode away.

I saw no one except the servants until after luncheon the following day.

I had decided not to go to church that Sunday morning. If I had gone, I would have been all alone. Edmond had not returned, and Lady Clareham still had a slight fever and remained in bed.

In the afternoon, a hazy, midsummer afternoon, I retreated to the shade of the rose garden with my book.

But my reading was interrupted by the sound of horses and a carriage approaching the entrance front, on the other side of the house from me. Curious, I got up and walked across the garden toward the house, and in a moment one of the green Wilton carriages, Flora and Lewis in it, rumbled around the grass circle.

"Mitchell said you were not home," Flora called, as I walked toward the carriage.

"I am sorry, Flora, I gave no such instructions. I am very much at home."

"Oh, good! Then we can visit awhile," she said. "Help me down, Lewis."

Lewis jumped down and helped his sister to the ground. Then he said, "It is lucky we decided to turn toward Milton Penderton or we would never have known you were here. How are you, Lady Beauford?"

"Very well, Mr. Stratton," I said, giving him my hand. "Why don't you call me Mary? Flora does."

"Thank you, Mary, and you must call me Lewis."

"Is Edmond really not at home?" Flora asked.

"No, he left yesterday and told Mitchell that he would be back in time for dinner this evening. Shall we go into the house, or would you like to walk in the garden? There is an arbor with a bench in the shade there. It is quite pleasant."

"I don't want to go into the house," Flora said, as she began to saunter toward the rose garden.

Lewis and I followed her.

"Where did he go?" Flora asked.

"I don't know, Flora. I suppose off on business, somewhere."

"One could hardly call it business," Lewis said.

"How do you know?" Flora demanded of her brother.

"It is a pity that it has gone to ruin," I said. "It used to be such a beautiful garden."

We descended the steps, and as we walked toward the fountain, Flora said, "It can be restored. I think that is one of the first things I would do at Castle Cloud—plant the gardens and get the fountain working again."

"Without any gardeners?" Lewis asked. "It would be a lot of work for one woman."

"There is a great deal of money which I could bring to the Castle, or haven't you heard about that, Lewis? My dowry would bring considerable income, and we should have gardeners again."

"Your dowry would never see the Castle or a gardener," Lewis said.

Flora glared at her brother. Then she turned to me, slid her arm through mine, and we walked on together with Lewis following behind.

"Wait till you see the gardens at Flowerwick Hall, Mary," she said. "They are gorgeous. I don't know how many gardeners they have working *all* the time there."

"What are they like—Lord and Lady Mauldridge, I mean," I asked. "She seemed so—well, almost afraid of her husband."

"Oh, she is not afraid of him," Flora said. "But he *is* determined to have his way, and if everything isn't just the way he wants it, there is trouble. He is very strong-willed."

"That is putting it mildly," Lewis said from behind us. "He is a tyrant. She has lost all will of her own. He has beaten her into utter submission."

"Lewis, don't be dramatic," Flora said. "But he is not what we would have liked," she said to me. "Mother fought with Cousin Camellia not to marry him. She is about ten years older than he."

"She was in love with him?" I asked.

"Not exactly, but she wanted *desperately* to be married. . . ."

"Women should not want *desperately* to be married. It leads to trouble," Lewis said.

"She wanted *desperately* to be married," Flora continued, "and she was an heiress—all of the Quirebury fortune. She was the sole heir."

"Women should watch what they buy," came from behind us.

"Pay *no* attention, Mary," Flora said. "It really didn't

work out very well. I am afraid. Dominick seems to have an eye for every girl that passes by. . . ."

"An eye?" Lewis murmured.

Flora stopped and swung around to her brother. "Will you kindly stop making comments about my conversation with Mary, Lewis?"

"I did not know that I was excluded from the conversation, but before you banish me completely, let us put the record straight. Dominick will get into any woman's bed that he can—excepting his wife's."

"Lewis! I will tell mother."

"She already knows, but she hasn't the sense to give the same advice to a daughter that she gave to a cousin."

"Lewis! You keep out of this."

"Flora! Lewis!" I cried. "Please! It is a beautiful afternoon—don't spoil it. Shall we sit over there in the shade? What are the children like?"

"I don't know," Flora and Lewis said in unison.

"We never met them," Flora said. "We have only been to Flowerwick Hall a few times, and they were always in the nursery, but the house is lovely—so full of windows and sunshine."

Then the conversation turned from Flowerwick Hall to other country houses, to city houses, to London and the social life there during the season, then back, of course, to the ball, and to life in the country versus life in the city, and in England as compared with France.

Soon it was time for them to leave, and Lewis went off to tell Marsden to bring the carriage to the garden steps. Flora and I strolled in that direction.

"I suppose you have heard the stories about me," I said to Flora.

"Who told you?" Flora asked.

"David. David Field."

"David? Oh, it is *David* already?"

"That *is* his name. He called yesterday and told me that Dierdre Swoop told him that my title is not genuine. Is that what you heard?"

"Mary, that is only stupid gossip."

"Is that what *you* heard?" I repeated.

"Yes, but there are always stories. . . ."

"Who told you about it?"

"Dierdre," Flora said.

"Where is Lacy Farm? That is the name of their house, isn't it—the Swoop's house?"

"Yes. Why do you want to know?"

"Because I intend to pay the Swoops a call. Percy said he hoped I would call—that was during the early part of the evening, of course."

"Oh?"

"Yes," I said, "and I intend to ask Dierdre where she got that story—whether she made it up and, if so, why."

"No, I wouldn't do that. It is a nasty story, but let it lie. You don't know Dierdre: I do. I understand her. She can be very cruel sometimes. She has always been interested in Mr. Field, and now she intends to have him—or at least she thinks she will. I can satisfy you on that point. But don't confront her—just let it pass."

"I can't do that. Will you come with me?"

"Oh, no. I don't want to get into the middle. . . ."

"Flora, please. You said we were friends. I can't let this kind of talk get about. I must try to put a stop to it, but I cannot do that until I know where it came from. If Dierdre made the story up, I will ignore it, but if she did not, I want to know who told her and why. As far as you are concerned, it will merely be a friendly call. I will be very sweet and nice."

"How could you find out by being sweet and nice?"

"Please, Flora," I begged. "I have helped you. Please help me."

"All right, but I cannot do it till after tomorrow. Mamma and I are going to Exeter to shop. Oh, but you are going to Flowerwick Hall tomorrow, aren't you."

"Could we do it on Tuesday, then?" I asked. "I will arrange it with Colen. We will call for you."

"No, Marsden will drive us," Flora said. "I will say that I was taking you for a drive and wanted to show you their pretty house—or something like that. We will call for you at two o'clock on Tuesday. Is that all right? But I am doing this against my better judgment. It is only because you do so much to help me."

"Thank you, Flora," I said. "Tuesday then, at two."

By that time we had reached the steps to the drive where Marsden and Lewis waited with the carriage, and after we had said our good-bys, Lewis and Flora got into it and drove off.

✠ Chapter Twelve ✠

WE SPOKE LITTLE during the train ride the following day. As a matter of fact, Edmond and I had hardly spoken to each other at all since he had returned to Castle Cloud in time for dinner the evening before. He had been in a vindictive mood, as he always was after one of his trips, and the mood had remained with him into Monday. He stared morosely out of the window all during the journey to Bampton.

Gregory, Lord Mauldridge's coachman, and a footman met us at the railway station in Bampton in a beautiful new Landau, lacquered Chinese red and edged with gold, and drove us up into the hills toward Flowerwick Hall.

And after traveling through the hilly countryside for three-quarters of an hour, we passed through a gateway and rode down a serpentine drive for perhaps two miles, across a flat, grassy park, skirting groves of Spanish chestnut, tulip, weeping willow and copper beech, Scotch fir, and several trees besides, which I had never seen before. Then Flowerwick Hall appeared. The long, two-and-one-half-story Georgian building sat beyond a still lake and reflected in the water. As we drove around the lake and stopped in front of its columned portico, I had time to examine the structure and guessed that the Georgian front was a comparatively recent addition to a much older house.

After the carriage had stopped and Edmond had helped me out of it, the entrance door of the house was thrown open and Lord Mauldridge strode through the doorway toward us.

"Ah, this is splendid," he called. "We have been looking forward to this afternoon with great anticipation. Miss Thorpe, this is delightful. Welcome to Flowerwick Hall, and you too, Lord Althrop. Come in. Camellia has been almost as eager as I."

We followed him into the house, across the hall, past a lovely Georgian staircase, and into a large yellow drawing room that looked out upon the lake.

"Miss Thorpe and Lord Althrop," Lady Mauldridge said, rising from her chair. "How nice of you to come. You have such a perfect day. I did so want Miss Thorpe to see Flowerwick in the sunshine. I am afraid it can be rather gloomy when the mists. . ."

"My dear!" Lord Mauldridge said.

"Oh, I am so sorry, Dominick," she said.

"You are quite right, my dear," Lord Mauldridge said, "it is a glorious day, and we must take advantage of it. Since Miss Thorpe is to make her home here with us, she will most naturally wish to see as much of the house and grounds as her short visit this afternoon will allow. Will you not, Miss Thorpe?"

"Well, yes," I said, "but I am more interested in meeting the children."

"Yes indeed," Lord Mauldridge said, "Now, I shall take Miss Thorpe along with me, and we shall make a brief tour of the gardens. You must see the peacocks, Miss Thorpe, before you go. And then we shall come back into the house and see the schoolrooms, and you shall meet the children.

"Entertain Lord Althrop, my dear, while we are gone. I am sure the gardens would be of no interest to him, and you must not tire yourself. Shall we, Miss Thorpe?" he said, gesturing to the door.

I followed him across the room.

"Now, which shall I show you first," he said, as he opened the door for me, "the lily ponds or the Alpine Garden?"

I knew that he didn't expect an answer—that he had already made up his mind—so I said nothing, but allowed him to lead me across a flat lawn, to a wood, and up a hill. As we walked, he told me something of the history of the house and gardens.

Then, when we reached the top of the slope, we came out of the wood and stood at the edge of a rock garden which descended the other side of the hill before us in a series of rocky terraces.

"At one time, this was all part of the flat plateau on

which the house is built, Miss Thorpe," Lord Mauldridge said. "Ah! An alpine buttercup."

He reached down and picked a flower that looked like an ordinary buttercup to me and held it to my neck. His hand touched my skin.

"Yes, Miss Thorpe is fond of gold," he said. "Did you know that if the yellow of the alpine buttercup reflects upon the skin, the lady is fond of gold and jewelry and other pretty things? What is your favorite stone, Miss Thorpe?"

"I do not like jewels very much, but I am rather fond of pearls," I said.

"Yes, they would suit you. You must have pearls, Miss Thorpe. Now, as I was saying, this hill was constructed to form the rockery, creating the dell below where the lily ponds are located. We will descend to them through the Alpine Garden by way of these steps. They are irregular and rather treacherous, so I would advise you to take my arm so that you do not trip and fall."

"I think I can manage, thank you," I said.

"No, please. We cannot risk your hurting yourself."

"Thank you, Lord Mauldridge," I said, putting my arm through his.

As we began to descend, he held my arm snugly against his side and, after a few steps, he laid his free hand upon it.

"There is an Alpine orchid," he said. "No, no, over there." He patted my arm as if that would somehow draw my attention to it. "You will not see it anywhere else except in the mountains above Geneva. And there is a mountain rose, the tiny pink flower to the right, there," he said, pressing on my arm with his hand. "Now, isn't this lovely?"

He held me fast, and I was not able to extricate myself until we had reached the bottom of the steps, where I thanked him and said that I could walk unaided now that we were on level ground. But then, as we walked alongside a high, clipped hedge, I felt his hand on the small of my back.

"In here," he said, turning me toward a narrow opening in the hedge, "are the lily ponds which we saw from the hilltop, and you can see—Uhps!" His arm went around my waist, and he held me tightly against him. "Take care of these steps. Step down. You would have fallen if I had not caught you."

"No, I am perfectly. . ."

"There now," he interrupted me, "just relax. You did not fall. Are you all right?"

He continued to hold me, however, and as he looked into my eyes, he smiled a long, slow smile at me. We stood like that for several seconds, and for a terrible moment I thought he was going to kiss me. I knew that no one could see us behind the high hedge, and I had an uneasy feeling that no one would hear me if I called for help.

But he did not kiss me. Instead, to my immense relief, he released me and continued: "Now we will walk around the lily pond to the opening in the hedge there, which will take us to the Lime Walk where you will see the house again and the windows of your room and those of the schoolroom."

I felt much more at ease as we walked up the Lime Walk toward the house in full view of anyone who might be at the windows. But when we had climbed to the second floor of the building together, and he had ushered me into a bedroom and closed the door behind us, I began to feel uneasy again.

"This will be your room," Lord Mauldridge said. "As you can see, it is large and well appointed and very sunny and cheerful in the morning. Now, go over and look out the window."

When I reached the window, and stood looking out, he walked across to me and stood very close behind me. I could feel his breath on my neck.

"Isn't it a lovely view?" he whispered. "You will be very happy in this room, my dear."

I swung around and faced him. "Lord Mauldridge!" I said.

"Yes, Miss Thorpe? Oh, of course—you wish to meet the children. Well, I suppose they are in there with Nanny." He pointed to a second doorway which led to an adjoining room. "Shall we go and see?" he asked.

I preceded him to the door, which he opened for me, and we walked into the schoolroom. A black-haired little girl in a frilly pink dress chased an identical black-haired little girl in an identical frilly pink dress around a woman who sat in a chair in the center of the room.

The woman cried, "Ethelind! Eugenia! Stop that at once. You will get all hot and—"

Then they saw us. The nanny clapped her mouth shut and the two children stopped running and stood still, side by side, facing us.

"Good afternoon, darlings," Lord Mauldridge said.

"Good afternoon, Papa," the twins answered in unison.

"This is Miss Thorpe. She is going to be your new governess, children. And this is Nanny Thompson, Miss Thorpe."

Nanny Thompson smiled and nodded her head, but she did not speak.

"What have you to say to Miss Thorpe, children?" Lord Mauldridge asked.

"Good afternoon, Miss Thorpe," they said. "We wish you welcome to Flowerwick Hall."

"That was very nicely done, my dears," Lord Mauldridge said. "Sit down children." The girls sat down side by side on a bench beneath a blackboard on the wall. "Now, if you will excuse us, Miss Thorpe, Nanny Thompson and I will let you and the children get acquainted. They will direct you to the drawing room when you have finished your chat."

When their father and Nanny Thompson had gone, I turned the chair she had vacated to face the twins and sat down. The twins and I sat silently facing one another for perhaps a minute. They did not move or speak.

Finally, I said, "Thank you for your very nice welcome."

They did not reply.

"It is a lovely day to visit Flowerwick Hall," I said. "Your father has been showing me some of the gardens."

Still they did not speak.

"Do you like flowers?"

No reply from the bench.

"I like flowers very much, and I know the names of a great many of them. Did Miss Constantine teach you about flowers and trees?"

Still the twins did not answer.

"Did you like Miss Constantine? You must be sorry she has gone. Did she live here very long?"

The two girls sat staring at me, now making a show of pressing their lips tightly together.

"Let me see if I can guess who you are," I said. "The little girl to my right is Eugenia and to my left is Ethelind."

"You are wrong! I am Ethelind," the child on the right shouted.

"You promised!" the other girl cried. "You promised you wouldn't talk to her."

"Well, I changed my mind," Ethelind said. "We hated her."

"Oh, no! We *loved* Miss Constantine," Eugenia cried, as she jumped up and ran to a cupboard. She threw open the doors of it and drew out something which I could not see, since she stood in front of it with her back to me.

"No, no!" screamed Ethelind. "You promised!"

"If you can change your mind, so can I," Eugenia said.

Then she swung around to face me, and I could see that she held a doll in her arms. She ran toward me, but stopped a few feet away, holding out the doll for me to see. It was a blond-haired doll with a china head and hands and a stuffed cloth body. It wore no clothes at all. A pair of scissors had been thrust into the doll's chest and red ink had been smeared where it pierced the fabric. As I watched, Eugenia grasped the scissors, withdrew them from the doll's body, and plunged them back into the doll's breast; and she repeated this action again and again as she hissed: "*That* is how we loved Miss Constantine. *That* is how much we loved her."

"What are you doing?" I cried.

"Making witchcraft," Eugenia whispered.

"You promised you wouldn't—you promised you would never tell," wailed Ethelind.

"And *that* is for Miss Andrews, and *that* is for Miss Betts," Eugenia shrieked, stabbing the doll to punctuate her words. "And *that* is for Miss Hollis. *Five* weeks for Miss Constantine, *two* months for Miss Andrews, *four* days for Miss Betts. . . ."

"Three days for Miss Betts," Ethelind said.

"Four days," Eugenia corrected.

"She came on Wednesday night," Ethelind said, "and I put the powder in her bed on Saturday night, and she left on Sunday morning. That is *three* days."

"You put something in her bed?" I asked.

"Itchy powder," Ethelind said.

"Itchy powder? Where would you ever get itchy powder?" I asked.

"We get it from the plane tree," she said. "It is the seeds, you see. You take apart the ball of seeds that you see hanging from the branches in the wintertime, and you crumple them all up till it's a powder, you see. . . ."

"Eugenia!" I cried.

The child had stolen around behind me as I watched Ethelind and had almost succeeded in putting something down the neck of my dress. And she would have succeeded if Ethelind hadn't given her away with her eyes. I couldn't see what it was, but it was a pinch of something: I suspected itchy powder.

"Stop calling me Eugenia," the little girl shouted. "I am Ethelind."

"But you told me you were Eugenia," I said.

"I did not, did I, Eugenia?" she said.

"She said she was Ethelind, and you kept calling her Eugenia," the other little girl said. "And we saw you walking down there with Papa."

"Well," I said, as I stood, "this has been charming. I am so glad we have had this little talk together, but it is getting late and I must go back to the drawing room. Your mamma and papa are waiting for me. Which way do I go?"

When I had walked to the door and opened it, one of the children ran to me and pointed to the left.

"You walk that way," she said, "and keep to the left."

I followed her directions and found myself walking down a long corridor which ended in a blank wall. I retraced my steps then, found a narrow stairway, and descended it. But it was not until I had reached the first floor that I realized it led to the kitchens and that I had used the servants' stair. At this point, I was rescued by a maid who climbed toward me from below, and with her help I was able to find my way back to the drawing room.

There, we were served cake and wine, and listened to Lord Mauldridge talk about his daughters—how they were as good as gold, and how I would love to be with them and instruct them. He also spoke at some length about the delightful life they led at Flowerwick Hall, how I would become almost a member of the family, and how happy I would be with them.

"The position will pay sixty pounds a year," he continued to say, "which we feel is very generous, since you may put that in your purse and not spend a penny of it. Have you any questions, Miss Thorpe? Anything at all? Is there anything more I can tell you?"

"No, I don't think so, Lord Mauldridge," I said. "You have been very kind and I am loathe even to think of leaving, but if we are to make the six o'clock train from Bampton, should we not be leaving soon?"

"Quite right, Mary," Edmond said. "They will be expecting us for dinner, and if we are not on that train, Mother will be worried about us and upset, poor dear."

"Gregory should have brought the carriage around by now," Lord Mauldridge said. "Ah! I hear him coming. You see, Miss Thorpe, we anticipate your every desire—and so it should be."

We stood then, and began to walk toward the door.

And as we talked, Lord Mauldridge asked, "Now, when can you come to us? Thursday? Friday would perhaps be better?"

"Lord Mauldridge," I said, "you have been very kind. I know that you will understand when I say that I find Flowerwick Hall enchanting and the twins charming and that I am tempted to accept your generous offer at once, but this is a very important step for me, and I have *always* made it a rule never to take an important step without thinking about it overnight. You do understand? I know I will wish I had said yes immediately and be terrified that you will have changed your mind before you receive my letter, but I must—" I did not finish my sentence, but gave him my most helpless, pleading look.

"We understand, my dear—better than you can imagine," he said. "And we shall eagerly await word of your arrival."

We said good-by then, got into the carriage, and were driven away.

"What is the reason this time?" Edmond growled, as we rode away from the house.

"I will tell you on the train," I said, glancing toward the coachman.

And when we stood on the railway station platform in Bampton and watched the Mauldridge carriage drive away, Edmond demanded, "Well?"

"Lord Mauldridge is more interested in me personally, than professionally," I said.

"Ha!" Edmond said.

As he spoke, a horse and carriage careened around the bend in the road and raced toward the station. "We are about to be joined by other passengers on the platform, Edmond, and I do not wish to discuss my private affairs in public."

Five minutes later the train chugged into the station, belching black, sooty smoke, and we climbed aboard it. I had hoped that we would find ourselves with company during our ride to Barnstaple and thus avoid, for the time being, the argument that I knew would come sooner or later. But Edmond found us an empty compartment, and we sat alone.

"So you think Lord Mauldridge is interested in you personally," he said, when we were seated and the train had begun to move. "What are you afraid of—that he will try to seduce you?"

"Exactly," I said. "But you put it so delicately, Edmond."

"This is not a delicate matter. You are in a bad situation, and there is nothing delicate about that. And don't talk nonsense. Believe me, Lord Mauldridge is not interested in you physically. I speak as a man."

"What makes you so sure that he is not?" I demanded.

"Never mind, I can assure you he is not."

"Edmond, I am in a far better position to judge that than you are. He could hardly keep his hands off me—as a matter of fact, he did *not* keep his hands off me. I know perfectly well what Lord Mauldridge is interested in. He has a reputation for philandering—that kind of reputation, Edmond, gets abroad quickly. And I resent your implication that I am not attractive. I may not be attractive to you, but tastes differ. It would be stupid to judge everyone's likes and dislikes by one's own. Why do you enjoy suggesting that I am unattractive?"

"I do not *enjoy* the unattractive in anything, especially women. And it is *you* who are stupid to think that there is any personal danger from Lord Mauldridge—under the same roof with his own wife and children. Don't be absurd. He wouldn't dare. He is no half-wit. On the contrary, he is an intelligent, kind, and thoughtful man, and

his wife is delightful. She wants you to come to Flowerwick Hall. She wants you desperately, and so do the children. She told me so."

"The children do not want me or any other governess at
Flowerwick Hall."

"I suppose you have invented reasons for believing that
also," he said.

"The children are two little beasts. You did not even
meet them. I sat there watching while one murdered her
doll with a pair of scissors—stabbing it in the chest, over
and over. She had even painted blood on it; it was macabre. They put things in the governess's bed, and they lied
to me and tricked me. The two 'darling little children' are
monsters. Who knows what they will do next?"

"Make-believe," Edmond said. "Children's worlds are
made of make-believe. They were merely playing. Do you
know nothing about children? Their imaginations must be
encouraged and channeled. They are healthy, normal children. Discipline and channeling is all they need—all any
child needs."

"That is very easy to say, Edmond. . . ."

"And it is very easy to make excuses. Flowerwick Hall
is a beautiful place. Lord and Lady Mauldridge are delightful and very wealthy people: everything there is the
most expensive. The house is obviously well staffed, and
just look at that carriage and those horses—superb. And
they *want* you there. It is a perfect situation for you,
Mary, and you will accept it."

"I will not accept it. I will not spend my nights fighting
off a lascivious man and my days protecting myself from
his monstrous children."

"Since we are being imaginative, perhaps you are in the
mood to tell me what you will do as an alternative. You
will not remain at Castle Cloud: I can assure you of that.
So, what *will* you do? Traipse from one miserable little
girls' school to the next looking for a teaching position,
without references or experience, until your paltry few
pounds run out and you are hungry and have no place to
stay? Suppose a gentleman asked you into his house
then—for *any* reason. What would you do? What would
you do? Have you ever been really hungry and cold? I
could show you hungry, cold young women on the London streets that would go home with a man for *nothing*.

You would end up on the streets, Mary. Are you too stupid to realize when you are well off?"

"You want to be rid of me, don't you Edmond? You want to be rid of me very badly."

"Of course! You are a stranger to us. We don't know you. Just because you were a friend of Vivian's and visited the Castle once, for a week, doesn't give you the right to move in permanently. You are not going to sponge on us and make your home for the rest of your life at Castle Cloud. We don't want you prying about and asking questions about things that are none of your business. Do you think Mother and Father suddenly want a foster daughter? Do you think I suddenly want a foster sister? God! I had enough trouble with the one I had. We don't want you in our house. We want our house to ourselves."

"Are you asking me to leave?" I demanded.

"Yes!" he cried.

I did not answer him, but turned to look out the window, my mind racing. I should have avoided this, I thought. If I had been wise, I would have parried this attack instead of facing it directly. Now he has asked me to leave. If only I had more time. Time? What would I do if I had more time. David? No. Then, what shall I do now? He is right about tramping from school to school. Suppose Miss Buzzer doesn't want me or doesn't need any more teachers? I should take the position at Flowerwick Hall and save my money. But I can't. It would be unbearable. I will have to look for a teaching position, but suppose I cannot find one? I should take the position at Flowerwick ... And so my thoughts went round and round, never getting anywhere.

But when we finally approached Barnstaple, Edmond turned to me, forced a smile, and said, "We do want to help you, you know, Mary, for three reasons. First, you were Vivian's friend; second, we do not want your future on our consciences; and third, we have become genuinely fond of you. But it is difficult, when one tries to help another, to be constantly thwarted in one's efforts. At least promise me one thing."

"What is that?" I asked.

"That you will not write the letter to Lord and Lady Mauldridge at once. That you will at least think about it for two or three days."

"Very well," I replied.

"Now, shall we speak of something pleasanter, if that is possible? I plan to visit Flora and her parents at Hawthorn Hill tomorrow. I should think you might like to come with me."

"I am sorry, Edmond, but Flora and I are going visiting tomorrow afternoon."

"Oh? And whom are you and Flora going to visit tomorrow afternoon?" he said.

"We are going to visit Mr. and Mrs. Swoop and Dierdre and her brother Percy."

"I didn't know you knew the Swoops."

"I don't, but we intend to call. I hope you do not object?"

"No! Certainly not. Not at all. I hope you have a very pleasant afternoon. Perhaps I shall wait then, and call at Hawthorn Hill on Wednesday. You must tell me all about your visit."

"Thank you," I said.

"By the way, I shall not be dining at Castle Cloud this evening. I find I am in need of a more congenial atmosphere, and I am fortunate in having such an atmosphere at hand. It may not be as richly appointed as Castle Cloud, but there are other considerations."

He smiled then, as he turned away from me. And we did not speak to each other again—not even after we arrived at the Castle. I left him as soon as we had entered the house, and I did not see him again until the following afternoon.

The morning of the following day was uneventful. I did not see Edmond during it: he did not appear at breakfast. But he did appear at luncheon. It was a silent meal, for the most part, but I noticed that Edmond eyed me speculatively more than once, when he thought I wasn't looking. Lady Clareham did not join us. She was, however, much improved and was planning to come down to dinner.

But unlike the morning, that Tuesday afternoon was eventful indeed. After luncheon, Flora called for me at two o'clock as we had planned.

And as we drove away from Castle Cloud toward Lacy Farm, I asked her, "Are you afraid of Dierdre Swoop? Why don't you want me to ask her about the rumor?"

"No, of course I am not afraid of her," Flora said, "but she can be very mean and spiteful if she doesn't like you. Some people get mad and then it is all over—like an explosion—but not Dierdre. She will carry a grudge forever, and you would always have to look out for what she might do or say. It simply isn't worth it."

"What is she like?"

"Just like I said, mean and spiteful—sometimes. But she is very clever and smart and can make you laugh whenever she wants to, if she wants to. If she likes you, she can be lots of fun, but if she doesn't, she can make life miserable."

"How could she make your life miserable?"

"Oh, by always saying little things to hurt you, and criticizing, and watching for anything that would not look right to tell someone about, and generally making trouble."

"So you think she will be at home? She will receive us?"

"If she is there, she will be at home. She is not afraid of anything, but she won't like me bringing you—being on your side—and she won't tell you anything. If she thinks you want to know something, and she doesn't like you, she would not tell you if you beat her."

"I see. Well, I certainly don't intend to do that, and I will try not to get you into trouble with her. I will be gentle and sweet."

"I wish we weren't doing this," Flora murmured. "It won't do any good."

But she didn't object further, and after driving for another mile, we turned into a side lane which twisted down to the bottom of a comb. There, in the deep valley between two fingerlike hills, nestled a two-storied, slate-roofed, dormered farmhouse of white, plastered stone. And as we approached the entrance door, our horses' hoofs and carriage wheels clattered and ground on the stones of the yard.

"Well, they should certainly know we are here," I said.

I thanked Peter as he helped me down, and for a moment all was quiet. Then we heard a harpsichord being played.

"That is Dierdre—I can tell," Flora said.

We walked to the door, and Flora rang the bell. Shortly

the door was opened by a maid, who showed us into the parlor.

"Miss Swoop," the maid said, "there's some young ladies to see you."

Dierdre continued to play her music, without hurrying. After a few bars she stopped, turned her head to look at us, slowly rose from the bench, and took one step toward us.

"Good afternoon, Flora," she said.

"Good afternoon, Dierdre," Flora said. "Allow me to present the Baroness Beauford."

"Indeed?" Dierdre said, without changing her position.

"Miss Swoop," I cried.

Instantly I rushed across the room to her. And while I did so, I decided that, though I had never been a very good actress, that afternoon was to be an exception—I would be a brilliant one. I willed it so.

So, when I reached Dierdre, I held out my hand to her, and when she did not take it, I grabbed hers and exclaimed, "I have heard so many lovely things about you that I insisted Flora must bring me to meet you."

"From whom?" Dierdre demanded.

"From Lady Vivian, who is my best and oldest friend, and from Lord Althrop, and Mr. Field, who has told me—more than once—how sweet you are. He holds you in the highest esteem, Dierdre. May I call you Dierdre? And you must call me Mary. I know we are going to be the closest friends."

"Oh?" Dierdre replied, taking her hand from mine.

"Yes, and Flora has been telling me what a delightful friend you are and about your marvelous sense of humor. She says you can make anyone laugh *whenever* you wish. I wish I could do that." Then I touched my forehead. "May we sit down? I think I feel a bit faint."

"Mary! Shall we get you some water?" Flora said.

"No. No, I am all right, Flora, really," I said, as I sat down in a chair opposite the harpsichord.

Dierdre sat down on the music bench then, and Flora sat in a chair next to mine. Dierdre composed her hands in her lap and then, with raised eyebrows, looked at me, and then at Flora, and back at me again, but she did not speak.

"You play beautifully, Dierdre," I said. "Will you play something for us?"

"I am too tired," she said.

"I am so sorry. Perhaps another time. Is Mr. Swoop at home?"

"He is not at home," Dierdre said.

"What a pity. I had so hoped to see him. Well, this is charming. It is such a lovely day. Thank you so much for bringing me, Flora. And, Dierdre, I am so glad that you were at home—this has all worked out beautifully, hasn't it? I would be quite happy if—"

"Are you feeling well, Mary?" Flora asked.

"Yes, Flora. Thank you, dear. It is just that I feel so terrible about—you know. But Dierdre will help, won't you, Dierdre? A dreadful rumor is being circulated about me, and it really makes me feel quite ill. The rumor is that my title is not genuine, that my parents were not married— Oh, but you have heard it, Dierdre. It is too dreadful to repeat, and it is not true. My parents were married years before I was born: I can prove it. So we must find out who started this story and tell him or her that it is not true. Who told you about it, Dierdre?"

"I cannot imagine why you should think that anyone told me about it," Dierdre said.

"But someone must have told you about it because you told Mr. Field about it. He told me so. He thought I should know what people were saying about me, and I am sure that you do too. I know how much you all want to help. Who told you, Dierdre?"

"I don't remember," she replied.

"You know," I said, "I thought and thought about what I should do about this, and then I remembered the Comtesse de Révéler. She had the same problem. She was a very good friend of my mother and father. Comte de Révéler had a country house near a small village just outside of Tours, where we stayed sometimes. Well, a story began to circulate that she was having a liaison with the very handsome owner of the cafe in the village, which was *not* true. So, do you know what she did? She asked the person who told her about it, who had told *her*. And then she asked the person who had told that person, until she had traced the story back to a Madame Richelieu, who could not tell the comtesse *who* had told her. And then the comtesse knew that it was Madame Richelieu who had made up the story. That was how she found out who had started it. And sure enough, Madame Richelieu was in love with the cafe owner and had made up the story to create trouble between the comtesse and her husband.

"Oh, try and think, Dierdre. You must remember who told you a story like *that* about me. If it were some little thing, I could understand your forgetting, but *such* a story. You didn't make it up? No, I cannot believe that. You would not *do* such a thing. I don't believe it, and I am sure that Mr. Field will not believe it either. Why, that is. . ."

"Lord Althrop told me at the ball," Dierdre said. "But the story *is* true, *Miss Thorpe*. If Lord Althrop says something is true, people in the county will believe him regardless of anything you may say or do."

"Dierdre, it wasn't Edmond," cried Flora. "He wouldn't."

"If you don't believe me, Flora, ask him." Dierdre replied.

But I was not as shocked by the revelation as Flora was. I knew at once that it was true—somewhere in my mind the suspicion had lurked that Edmond was responsible for the story, but I had not wanted to notice it.

In any case, Flora's remark and Dierdre's reply gave me the moment I needed to collect myself and decide what to do next, which was to leave.

So I stood and said, "Thank you for telling me what I wished to know, Dierdre. This has been most enlightening. I cannot thank you enough. And thank you for a most charming visit. Shall we go, Flora?"

A few minutes later, as we drove up the hill away from the house, Flora said, "I can't believe it. Edmond would never circulate such a story."

"I am sure he did, and when you ask him why, I am sure he will be able to give you what would seem to be good reasons for having done so."

"It was your story about the countess that did it."

"Was it?"

"Who was she?"

"She never existed, of course."

"Goodness! I am so glad we are such dear friends. Oh! Lewis asked me to bring you back to Hawthorn Hill, if there was time this afternoon. Will you come?"

"I don't know if I could, Flora. This has been an awful experience. Yes, Flora, forgive me, but I will come. I cannot go back to Castle Cloud just yet, and it will give me a little time to recover."

Then, after we had driven along in silence for several minutes, Flora said, "You have not told me what happened at Flowerwick Hall. Are you going to take the position with cousin Camellia?"

"I don't think so, Flora. The children and I did not get along very well when we met. I don't think it would be good for them."

"You are sure it was the children?" she said smiling at me.

"That and perhaps one or two other things," I said, smiling back.

Later, when we reached the hilltop overlooking Hawthorn Hill, Flora cried, "Look! A carriage has pulled up to the house. It is the Pridells'. There are Philomena and her mother getting out. Philomena has come to see Lord Charles—with her mother's blessing, naturally. She is so overbearing: you would think Philomena had no mind of her own. I don't know how she stands it."

Philomena, Lewis, and Lord Charles stood near the windows when Flora led me into the drawing room a few minutes later. Mrs. Pridell sat on the sofa next to Lady Wilton.

"Here is Mary, Mamma and Lewis," Flora cried. "Good afternoon, Mrs. Pridell. Hello, Philomena, Charles."

"Mary, how nice," Lady Wilton said, without getting up. "Come and sit down. You know Mrs. Pridell and Miss Pridell."

"Yes," I said. "Good afternoon."

Mrs. Pridell did not speak, but merely nodded her head. Philomena glared at me and then turned back to Lord Charles.

"So, Mother and I got in, and the train left the station," Philomena said, continuing a story which Flora and I had interrupted, "but the gentleman kept staring at me. . . ."

"How did you like Flowerwick Hall, Mary," Lady Wilton asked. "Lady Beauford and Lord Althrop called on my cousin yesterday afternoon, Winifred."

"It is a lovely house," I said. "It was a most pleasant afternoon, but I am afraid the twins and I did not get on very well. However, I thought the gardens were lovely."

". . . Would that be all right?" Charles said to Lewis.

"Of course," Lewis repiled. "Perhaps Mary and Flora will join us. Philomena and Lord Charles have suggested a game of croquet, Mary. Will you join us? Flora never needs coaxing, but you never let her stand over the ball. It is apt to move, mysteriously, under her skirts.

"Lewis! It doesn't either," Flora cried. "Yes, Mary will join us, and we ladies will show you how the game should be played—so watch out."

"I am afraid that is quite impossible, Philomena," Mrs. Pridell said, as she stood. "We stopped by for only the briefest possible moment, Georgiana, so that once again we could say thank you for the lovely ball. . . ."

"But Mother, we only just arrived," Philomena cried, "and Lord Charles and Lewis are going back to London on Friday."

"They will, no doubt, be returning to the country, Philomena," her mother said.

"It isn't fair." Philomena glared at me. She was furious. "I know why you want to leave," she said to her mother. "It is not like a disease, you know. I couldn't catch it. *Your* diamonds would be perfectly safe if *I* played croquet for days."

"Philomena!" Mrs. Pridell cried. "That is not the point. Mind your mother. She knows what is best. No, don't trouble, Georgiana, we can find our own way out, and Ludley will have our carriage brought around for us. We will wait on the steps for it. Good-by, my dear. Good-by."

She turned and sailed out of the room then, with Philomena stomping along behind her.

"I am afraid I must be going too, Flora," I said. "I really must now."

"But you just arrived," Lewis said.

"Yes, Lewis, but I am suddenly feeling very tired."

"If you will excuse me," Lord Charles said, "I have some letters to write." He stood, bowed curtly to me, and then he also left us.

"Would you ring for Ludley, then," Flora asked her brother.

Ludley came to tell us that Marsden had the carriage at

the entrance front for us. We had just heard the Pridells' carriage on the drive. Flora and I went out, got into the carriage, and were driven off toward Castle Cloud.

"What was that about?" I asked Flora. "Other rumors? What wouldn't Philomena catch so that her mother's diamonds would be perfectly safe?"

"I was hoping you wouldn't ask," Flora said.

"You may as well tell me because now that I know there is something, I will find out what it is. I think I know already."

"Oh, some story about some jewels being stolen at Castle Cloud."

"And me being suspected?"

"Yes."

"Flora! Why didn't you tell me?"

Flora looked at me helplessly without replying.

"Only one person could have done that," I said.

"Edmond?" she asked. "No, Mary. Why would he tell such terrible stories about you? Why? You are a guest at the Castle. There must be some other explanation."

"No, no other explanation. His parents' guest, remember, and that is the point. He does not want me to be a guest any longer. He wants to be rid of me."

I wanted to talk to David so very much that evening before dinner. I needed him—to feel that somebody cared about me, that I wasn't entirely alone. I wanted to feel his arms around me, and to be held close to him, and I wanted to stay like that forever. But I knew that I couldn't be with him that night. Now that he was calling upon me at the Castle, I would have to wait until he came. Perhaps tomorrow he would come.

Earlier that afternoon, I had said good-by to Flora when she had left me at the entrance front of the Castle, and had gone to my room to rest and change for dinner. At first I had decided not to go down to the meal. I didn't want to see Edmond—didn't want to be in his company. But then I realized that I would have to see him sooner or later, and I decided not to allow him to deprive me of dinner.

So, at the very last minute, I left my room and went downstairs, where I found Edmond and his mother sitting opposite each other in the drawing room.

I was happy to see Lady Clareham and said, "It is so good to see you up, Lady Clareham. Are you feeling better?"

"Yes, much better, Mary, thank you," she said. "A bit weak still, but otherwise quite well."

"Good evening, Mary," Edmond said. "And how was your afternoon?"

"Very pleasant, thank you, Edmond," I said.

"Did you and Flora visit the Swoops?"

"Yes."

"Well, who was there?"

"Dinner is served, my lady," Mitchell announced from the doorway behind me.

"A bit late this evening, Mitchell," Edmond said.

"Yes, my lord," Mitchell replied.

After we had allowed time for Mitchell to return to the dining room, we stood and followed him.

And when we were seated at the table and Mitchell had served the soup, Edmond said to me, "Well, who was there?"

"Where, Edmond?" I asked.

"At Lacy Farm, of course. Did you have a pleasant visit?"

"Yes, thank you," I replied. "It is quite a charming farmhouse. It must be ancient."

"Was Dierdre there?" Edmond asked.

"Yes. She was playing the harpsichord when we arrived. We asked her to continue, but she refused."

"Didn't you talk?"

"Well, of course."

"What did you talk about? You are very uncommunicative this evening. During dinner one is expected to contribute to the conversation."

"We talked about the nasty story that you have been circulating about me," I said.

He smiled at me. "Nasty story?" he said. "I don't know what you mean."

"But you do, Edmond. I am sorry, Lady Clareham. I do not mean to exclude you from the conversation. We are discussing a story which Edmond spread at the ball. He told Dierdre Swoop that my title was not genuine because I was born before my mother married my father—that my real father was the blacksmith at Gunderbury Hall."

"Is this true, Edmond?" Lady Clareham asked.

"Quite true, Mother," he said. "You know, Vivian always thought it strange that Mary's father never visited her at school, and never wrote, and never seemed to want her with him. Now, wait." Edmond held up his hand. "Be that as it may, Lord and Lady Mauldridge were looking for a governess. But when Lady Wilton told them about Mary, they would not consider her because of her title. And who can blame them? A baroness for a governess? Not very likely. So I told them, Mary," he said to me, "that your title was not authentic, but something you assume to keep up appearances. That, of course, made all the difference in the world. *Then* the doors were thrown open, and you were eagerly sought for the position. Of course the story spread—all the better for you and all the more believable for Lord and Lady Mauldridge.

"This is a *local* matter, Mary," he continued. "These are *local* people. What difference does it make what they think? It is of little consequence—in a few days you will be gone. Anyway, a title now is a liability. You realize that. You realize the importance of being *Miss Thorpe*. When it comes time to use it—when a title becomes an asset—use it. That is—if you can substantiate it, of course. One cannot live a fraud. But, as I say, be that as it may. The important thing now is to be without one, to look to the immediate future and to take the position with Lord and Lady Mauldridge, and you may thank me that it has been offered to you. One might show a little gratitude."

"And the accusation that I stole your mother's jewels?" I said. "I trust you told Lord and Lady Mauldridge that story, also—that they were about to employ a thief."

"Certainly not. Don't be absurd," Edmond said.

"But you told Philomena Pridell who has, by this time, told every other *local* person about it."

"My dear Mary," Edmond said. "One would think, by the way you talk, that I was intentionally trying to harm you in some way. Ingratitude is very often the wages of favors done.

"If you would stop to think about it, you would soon realize that servants talk, and in a small community such as ours, servants' gossip is, unfortunately, one of the chief sources of entertainment. That one of the stones from Mother's brooch was found in your room by a servant was

unfortunate. Whether one believes or disbelieves your ve-
hement denial, it was, nevertheless, found there. And news
of it has most certainly reached the servants' halls at Hawthorn Hill and every other house of any consequence. It
was in your best interests that I set the story straight—that
you denied having had anything to do with the missing jewelry, and that you were unable to give an explanation as to
how the stone got into your room. It is only fair that your
denial should be known."

"Thank you for being *so* kind and helpful, Edmond," I
said.

"I think your behavior has been despicable," Lady
Clareham said to Edmond.

"You are entitled to your opinion, Mother," Edmond
said, "but I do not believe that anyone else in the neighborhood would agree with you. By the way, Mary, you
had a visitor this afternoon. Mr. Field called."

"And, Mary," Lady Clareham said, "I must ask you—
We are in mourning. This is a house of *mourning* for my
son. James has not been gone eight weeks, and already the
house is being turned into a social meeting place. I cannot
have it. I am sorry, my dear."

"One could hardly consider one call. . ." Edmond began.

"He called on Saturday, also," Lady Clareham said.

"Oh?" Edmond said.

"We want only to be left in peace with our sorrow,
Mary," Lady Clareham continued. "But even if that were
not the case, I cannot imagine your seeing a young man
without the proper chaperon. Vivian and David were
never alone together—not even after their engagement."

"Engagement?" I asked, stunned.

"But she was never chaperoned with O'Connor,"
Edmond said. "Nowadays young ladies don't want to
marry the men they are properly engaged to—elopement
seems to be the thing. Too bad you didn't keep a better
eye on her."

"Edmond! Stop it!" Lady Clareham cried. "I am not
feeling well. You must excuse me. I am afraid I must go
to my room."

She stood, and Mitchell rushed over to Lady Clareham
and drew back her chair for her.

"Vivian and David Field were engaged to be married,
Lady Clareham?" I asked.

"Certainly," she replied. "Didn't she tell you? I am sorry, but I must—"

She hurried from the room without finishing, and I watched her cross the rotunda. I was not worried about her—she seemed to walk quite steadily.

"So it is *David,* is it?" Edmond said.

"Yes," I replied, looking directly into his eyes. "Why didn't you tell me they were engaged?"

"Because at first I thought you knew about it, but then when I thought perhaps you didn't, I decided that it was best not to mention it. And you didn't ask. Shall I think of all the things you have not asked about and begin to tell you about them? Where shall I start?"

"I asked you about the Fields, and you said that they were a local family and nothing more."

"They are a local family. We were not particularly proud of the match, so the less said about them the better. Young Mr. Field has a history of—philandering—I believe that is how you would express it—and otherwise—unihibited conduct. In London, his debauched morals were famous—on every front page of every newspaper in England, in the empire. His flight, alone with the notorious Mrs. Crinnings in a balloon at night from the center of Vauxhall Gardens, no less, where he, incidently, was a fixture, together with his crowd of drunken companions, was a sensation. And the time he threw his drunken self down in a puddle for Jenny Lind to walk on, as she came out of His Majesty's Theatre, is legend. And other adventures too *delicate* for the ears of one as young and inexperienced as yourself.

"But, Vivian and David were very much in love, and nothing else would do. At least we thought they were very much in love, and the match would have been better than with a groom. Vivian, however, shortly had other ideas. This may have fanned David Field's passion for her to even greater degrees of intensity. Who knows?

"At any rate it was all too painfully obvious that he worshipped her. When were they to be married? When were they to be married? was his constant plea. He was out of his mind with love and desire."

"I don't believe you," I said.

"No? Well, my dear, Mr. Field left a message that he

would call on you, here at the Castle, tomorrow afternoon. Ask him."

Somehow, I managed to get through the rest of the meal, and when at last it was over, I told Mitchell that I did not wish to have coffee that evening and literally ran from the house.

I wanted desperately to be alone somewhere where I would not be disturbed. I walked down to the stone bridge where, cloaked in the darkness, I felt free at last to cry. And cry I did.

I cried because my dreams were dead: David would never love me, never ask me to marry him, never hold me in his arms away from loneliness and fright. He was in love with Vivian. How foolish I had been to think that he could be in love with me. How foolish I had been to think that I was attractive enough or charming enough to entrance him. Vivian was. That was why he was in love with her. How could I have thought that I was that splendid?"

"Oh, God, why didn't you make me that splendid?" I asked.

And then I cried out my hurt until the tears wouldn't come anymore.

The following morning I carried a book of poetry out to the marble bench at the end of the field beyond Diana's Temple and sat there reading some of the shorter poems and gazing out across the bay. I felt terribly alone. I didn't even have Sarah to keep me company. What solace the little dog's affection would have given me that morning. If only she had returned to Castle Cloud! And I felt bruised. The blows of the day before had left me stunned, and I had not recovered from them enough to think or plan: I wanted simply to rest and repair myself.

And then I read Elizabeth Barrett Browning's lines:

I love thee with a love I seem to lose
With my lost saints—I love thee with the breath,
Smiles, tears, of all my life!—and, if God choose,
I shall but love thee better after death.

And I wept again.

*　　　*　　　*

"Mitchell," I said, when luncheon was over, "I am not at home if Mr. Field calls this afternoon."

"Very good, my lady," Mitchell replied.

"Thank you, Mitchell," I said.

"You are not going to see Mr. Field, Mary?" Edmond asked.

"No, I am not going to see Mr. Field, Edmond," I replied. "I have letters to write."

Then I turned my back on him and swept from the room. I walked straight to the desk in the drawing room, sat down, took a sheet of paper, pen, and ink from the drawer, lifted the cover of the inkwell, and sat, still looking out of the window. What was I going to write? To whom was I going to write? I put the pen down. David was coming this afternoon, but I had no intention of seeing him: I never wanted to see him again. I must think about what I would do now. I would write to Miss Buzzer—

Yes, I will write to Miss Buzzer, I thought, and ask if there might be a position. . . . I wonder what he will think? Will he come again tomorrow? I will write to Miss Buzzer and ask if there might be a teaching position open at her school and if not, if she knows of one elsewhere. A breeze stirred the trees beyond the rose garden. Lady Clareham walked across the grass circle toward it, carrying her flower basket. How calm and peaceful and usual everything looked out there—the sun, and the flowers, and Lady Clareham—it was almost as if nothing at all had happened.

Then I saw David riding Caesar around the drive from the entrance front toward the stables, and my heart lurched. I got up from my chair and stood back from the desk, so that he would not be able to see me through the window. I knew that in a few minutes I would hear his voice from the vestibule and Mitchell saying that I was not at home. I walked to the drawing room doors, closed them (I did not want to hear his voice), and returned to the window, being careful to stand well back out of sight.

Shortly, as I watched, David walked around the corner of the stable pavilion with Edmond. When they came in sight of the house, Edmond said something to David and pointed at the window where I stood. Then Edmond returned to the stable yard, and David walked toward the house, up the steps of the east portico, and vanished from my sight into the house.

A half-minute later, the drawing room doors were thrown open. I turned to see what had happened, and David walked into the room.

"Hello, Mary," he said. "Edmond told me to come right in. Mitchell is off somewhere, I gather. Didn't he tell you I was coming?"

"Yes, he told me you were coming," I said.

I leaned back against the desk as David came across the room toward me. And in a moment he stood in front of me.

"You seem surprised to see me," he said. "How are you? I called yesterday afternoon, but you were not at home."

"Why, David?" I asked.

"Why what?"

"Why did you call yesterday afternoon?"

"To see you, of course," he said.

"Why did you want to see me?"

"Because I wanted to. Mary! What is it?"

"You are engaged to Vivian, David. I do not understand why you should wish to call on me. Further, I do not think it is proper."

"But there hasn't been any question of propriety until now. Why talk about the engagement? It is over. Vivian has gone to America."

"That has nothing to do with your being in love with her. And if you are in love with her, I think it is improper of you to call on me, or to hold my hands, or to say how happy you are to be with me, or to kiss me, or to look at me in that way you do, or to keep your engagement a secret from me."

"I wasn't keeping our engagement a secret from you," he said. "How could I? Everyone knew about it. It was no secret from anyone."

"It was from me," I said.

"You didn't know? Do you mean you just heard about it? Vivian didn't tell you?"

"No."

"Oh, my poor Mary. . . ."

"I am not your poor Mary," I spat at him. "I am not anyone's poor Mary. I can take care of myself perfectly well. It would help, however, if people were honest with me and would stop spreading lies."

"I haven't spread any lies about you, and I haven't been dishonest."

"Do you call kissing me when you are in love with Vivian and engaged to her, honest?"

"Mary, I was never in love with Vivian," he said.

"You were not in love with her? You were engaged to marry her, but you were not in love with her? Do you expect me to believe that?"

"Yes! Because it is true. Vivian and I liked each other enormously, yes. We were comfortable in each other's company. Yes. We were happy together, yes. We liked the same things. We needed not to be alone. But we were not in love. I was not in love with her and she was not in love with me. But—we found ourselves engaged. It happened. It just seemed to happen—to be taken for granted by everyone. And there it was. But we were not in love."

"I don't believe you. How can I believe you when you haven't been honest with me from the day we met—holding my hands while your bride-to-be was in Scotland, and keeping secrets from me. You never told me about Vivian. You never told me about your famous exploits in London, either. Did you enjoy your night with Mrs. Crinnings and your other nights with all the other women at Vauxhall Gardens?"

"I told you—I was unhappy then," David said. "I was in the bank, and I was miserable—I told you about that. And don't accuse me of being dishonest and lying to you. I have always been completely honest and truthful."

"I don't think you have, David. However, it doesn't matter. I am leaving Castle Cloud in a few days. . . ."

"Where are you going?" he asked.

"Since I will be gone," I said, "I don't see that it could possibly make any difference to you where I am going."

"Very well! If that is the way you want it."

I was stung by the look of hurt and anger that had flashed across David's face as he said that. Then immediately he turned away from me and, without another word, stalked out of the room.

From the window, I watched him run down the stairs and hurry across the grass circle toward the stable yard, and then in two or three minutes, I saw him gallop away—down the drive toward Milton Penderton.

For the rest of the day that scene with David tormented me. I relived it over and over—continuing to see that hurt look on his face. I had pounced on him—attacked him, insulted him, and made him hate me. He could never forgive me for being such a harridan. I had believed Edmond's account of David's relationship with Vivian, but now I began to wonder if I had been wrong in doing so. Perhaps David had not loved Vivian: it was possible.

But I hated David for making me say those things to him. I wanted to leave Castle Cloud—to get away from him and anything that reminded me of him. I wanted to forget. And all the time I kept seeing that crushed and then angry look on his face, and I wanted to hold his head in my hands and kiss that look away.

Is it any wonder, then, that I was in no mood to talk to Edmond and his mother that evening and that I asked Mrs. Muldoon to tell Mitchell that I was not feeling well and that I wouldn't be down to dinner?

So, instead of going downstairs, I sat at the window in my room and in the late afternoon watched the sun gradually stain the sky and bay, first gold and then crimson and then, later, just as gradually fade the color to blackness. And I thought about how wretchedly I had treated David and wondered why I had found it necessary to hurt him.

Then, much later, as I sat by the window still, someone knocked on my door.

"Come in," I called.

The door opened and Lady Clareham came into the room followed by Jane Spence, who carried a tray.

"Mary?" Lady Clareham said. "Are you all right? It is so dark in here. Put it on the table there, Jane, and light a lamp for her ladyship. I brought you some soup, Mary, and bread and butter and some good, hot tea."

"That is very kind of you, Lady Clareham," I said. "Thank you so much."

Then, when Jane had lighted a lamp, Lady Clareham said, "That will be all, Jane, thank you. And after she had gone and closed the door behind her, Lady Clareham said, "Where don't you feel well, Mary? Could you take a little soup?"

"I am quite all right, really," I said. "I just did not feel like eating. Yes, I will have the soup. It was very thoughtful of you to bring it."

"We will put it here on this little table in front of the couch. There you are, now come and eat it while it is hot. You are not sick?"

"No."

"Diarrhea? Stomach pain?"

"Good heavens, no! Should I?"

"No, of course not, my dear. I wanted to be sure that you were not ill, that is all. Sit down and have your soup, and I will keep you company for a few minutes."

I sat down then, and began to sip. The soup was hot and delicious, and it and Lady Clareham's attention were temporarily comforting.

"Mary——" Lady Clareham said, after she had watched me for a minute or so.

"Yes, Lady Clareham?" I asked.

"I think it is time for you to leave Castle Cloud. It is not that we don't want you. We enjoy having you here, and we have become fond of you, but——"

"But? Lady Clareham."

"I am worried. I don't like what has been happening."

"You are worried about Edmond—what he will do next."

"—Yes."

"He has asked me to leave, too, you know."

"No, I didn't know. Then you must go, Mary."

"You are afraid of him, aren't you?" I asked.

"No, my. . ."

"What are you afraid he will do? Why does Edmond want to get rid of me so badly? I shall go, of course—I shall be only too happy to. I do not want to impose myself upon you, and I am extremely grateful for what you have done for me—taking me in like this. But Edmond doesn't want to be rid of me because he is afraid I might stay on and on, indefinitely. No, there is an urgency about it. Why? Is he afraid I might discover something, Lady Clareham? What could I discover? What has been going on here? What are you afraid he might do to me?"

"Well, nothing, Mary," she said. "What could possibly have made you think that? It is simply that Edmond is a very emotional and a very foolish man, and he might create a scene—who knows what he might do. I think you had better take the position at Flowerwick Hall, Mary. Take the position and tell him so. Now I must go." She rose from her chair and added, "We will leave the tray for Mrs. Muldoon in the morning. Good night, my dear."

"Good night, Lady Clareham," I said.

She left the room then, and closed the door behind her.

I went to bed and lay there, staring up into the darkness, feeling the breeze that occasionally blew through the open window onto my face, and thinking. I fell asleep as the sky began to get light.

❧ Chapter Thirteen ❧

IN THE MORNING, Mrs. Muldoon woke me at the usual time, carried hot water into my room, and began to prepare my bath. But I asked her to leave the water in the cans, saying I wanted to sleep a little longer. I did not care if I missed breakfast. And if in an hour the water was only warm, that would be quite all right.

But I slept longer than an hour. It was after ten o'clock when I got out of bed and poured the water for a luke-warm bath. I dressed, combed my hair, left my room, and descended to the ground floor. I was longing for a cup of coffee.

As I reached the rotunda, Mrs. Foley emerged from the drawing room carrying an armful of newspapers and magazines. She had almost passed me by the time I got the courage to ask, "Mrs. Foley, do you think there might be some coffee left in the kitchens? I did not get up in time for breakfast and I would love a cup, if there is."

"There ain't no coffee at this time of the morning," she said, "and if there was, we've got better things to do than run about the house serving coffee to them that wants it at all hours of the day."

"I do not expect you or anyone else to serve me coffee at all hours of the day, Mrs. Foley. I have never asked for it before, between meals. This is an exceptional instance. Further, I can find no reason for your being rude to me. I have never done anything to inconvenience or trouble you. Why do you dislike me so much?"

Mrs. Foley looked at me, first in surprise and then with distaste. But then we saw Lady Clareham coming toward us through the hall, followed by Cecile.

"Is something wrong, Mary?" she asked.

"No, I was merely asking if there might be some coffee

335

left from breakfast. I slept badly last night and stayed in bed late this morning, so I missed breakfast."

"Certainly there is coffee, Mary. Mrs. Foley, go and tell Mitchell to bring Lady Beauford some coffee. Will you be in the drawing room, Mary?"

"Yes," I said.

"There ain't no coffee," Mrs. Foley said. "The chef will have to make it special."

"Then ask him to do so, please, Mrs. Foley," Lady Clareham said.

"No, please don't," I said. "That would be too much trouble, and I can really do quite well without it. Actually, I would like to go for a walk, and I would rather not wait while it is being made. Thank you so much for offering it, but please don't trouble. Shall I see you at luncheon? Lovely. Have a pleasant morning, then."

And without looking again at Mrs. Foley, I left them, walked out of the house to the drive, and down it toward the stone bridge. I breathed deeply as I walked along: it was a breezy morning with the clear sharpness of autumn in the air. I arrived at the stone bridge and leaned, as usual, against the balustrade and gazed out across the bay. Far across the choppy water, I could see the windows of the houses in Bideford and every tree on the hills beyond the town. The air was so clear that it magnified the landscape. The air seemed alive—almost electric—and I knew that, in that clear open place, I must decide what I would do in the immediate future.

I made up my mind almost at once: I decided to accept the position at Flowerwick Hall. The simplicity and ease of the decision surprised me. But what else could I do? Edmond had asked me to leave Castle Cloud, so I could not stay longer. His stories about me had made it impossible to visit or be entertained at any of the houses nearby. And I had very effectively destroyed my relationship with David, so I could not expect any help from him. Nor could Flora help me, and Lewis was returning to his regiment in London. So there was no reason to stay at Castle Cloud, even had I been welcome. Two avenues lay open to me, then. I could search for a position (with no money to sustain me); or I could accept the one that had been offered. I must make the best of it. It would mean fighting off Lord Mauldridge and being constantly vigilant in case the twins should try to harm me, but that was what I would have to do.

Edmond was bent on my accepting this position, and I would capitulate. He would have his way, and no doubt he would be very pleased with his success. I would have to tell him about it sooner or later, so I decided to get it over with as soon as possible. Why not tell him before luncheon, then? Would there be time to? I flicked open the lid of my watch: it was eleven forty-five. Yes, if I took the path that followed the stream to the Chinese bridge, I would probably be just in time to meet him as he walked up from the bathing pavilion. I could tell him of my decision as we returned to the house together.

I would have to hurry, however, so I left the stone bridge at once and walked quickly down the path along the river, crossed the stream, and followed its banks until I saw the pavilion through the trees.

At first I thought it was deserted, but then I saw the door open and a girl come out of it, followed by Edmond. I think it was the same girl I had seen frolicking with Edmond the last time I had been there, but this time she was clothed. He grasped her chin with one hand, turned her face up to his, kissed her on the mouth, and said something to her. As she walked away along the river-bank, he strode to the walk and vanished between the walls of yew.

I picked up my skirts then, and ran along the path to meet him. And just as I approached the walk, Edmond appeared from behind the hedge, not twenty feet ahead of me, and stepped onto the Chinese bridge. He had not looked to his right and so had not noticed me hurrying up the path toward him. I did not want to call to him, as there was no point in informing his lady friend, somewhere off to my left, that I was there. So I ran faster in order to catch up to him. By the time I had stepped onto the bridge, Edmond had crossed it. He was, however, only a few yards ahead of me, and in a moment I could overtake him.

But then, just in front of Edmond, I saw Sarah running down the walk toward us. When she reached him, Edmond swung his foot to kick her, but before he could do so, she lunged at him and snapped at his leg.

"Sarah!" I cried. "Stop it!"

Edmond shook his leg frantically, but the dog held fast to it. Finally, however, he flung Sarah from him, screaming "Get off me—you filthy cur!"

"Sarah, come here," I shouted.

As Sarah lurched toward me, I heard an explosion. She fell to the ground, quivered, and lay still.

"Sarah!" I cried, as I sprang forward and knelt before the little dog. "Sarah, sweet. . ."

"Don't touch her," someone shouted.

I looked up and saw two things at once: William Reade emerged from behind the hedge, and Edmond bolted around the bend toward the house, disappearing from sight.

"Her be sick, and I think her be dead, miss," William Reade said, as he walked toward me. "Don't touch her."

"Sick?" I asked.

I still knelt before the dog. I knew she was dead and that I could not help her. The bullet had gone through her head, just behind the eyes. But everything had happened too quickly—I was shocked and bewildered and could not move.

"Her was sick. See the froth about her mouth? Her was mad," William Reade said.

"Mad? Hydrophobia?"

"Ay."

"Oh, no!" I cried, shuddering and stumbling backward to get to my feet and away from the animal. "Oh, no! How do you know?"

"Ay, I know. It be lucky I be passing by at this time, and it be lucky I have my gun by me, miss."

"Yes. She might have bitten me. But she bit Lord Althrop, Mr. Reade. She bit him! I saw her do it. What can we do?"

"Ay. Nothing, Miss. Nothing. Don't touch her. I be going now. It be lucky for you I be passing by this way at this time, miss."

He lifted his hat, then walked past me, crossed the Chinese bridge, and descended the walk toward the river. I watched him until he reached the end of the walk, where a tall hedge hid him from sight.

No sooner had William Reade disappeared than I saw a horse approaching from the direction of the house. Douglas McComb walked his horse around the bend of the walk, and in a moment, he reined up in front of me.

"What the devil's been going on?" he said. "First I hear a shot down here, and then Lord Althrop passes me—running for the house like the devil was chasing him. I had business with him and he wouldn't even stop long enough to speak. What is going on?"

"Mr. Reade shot Sarah," I said, pointing to the dog.

"Reade?"

"He said she was mad."

Then Douglas McComb jumped down from his horse and squatted to examine Sarah. "What the devil was he doing here? Whatever it was, you are very lucky that he *was* here. The dog was mad, right enough. Why was Lord Althrop running like that?"

"She bit him."

"You are sure?" he said, looking hard into my eyes.

"No, but I think so."

"Where?" he asked.

"In the leg. It could have been just his trousers, but I don't think so."

"So," he said. Then after a pause, "Well."

"Is it hydrophobia?"

"Judging by the froth around the mouth, I would say it was almost certain. See those sores on her body? They snap at everything, when they have it, including themselves."

"But what shall we do? We can't leave her here."

"I will bury her, but there is no need to inconvenience you, my lady. I will take care of it."

"I would like to be there, Mr. McComb. She was my friend, and I would like to know where she is buried. Could you do it soon?"

"All right, but don't touch her. Don't go near her. I will go and get a shovel."

"Is it so contagious?" I asked.

"One drop of her saliva on the smallest cut or open place on your hands or anywhere, and that would be the end. There would be nothing anyone could do about it. I will get the shovel and come back as soon as I can."

I did not sit down while I waited for him. I moved a few steps away from Sarah's body and stood, trying not to look at her. I thought of some of the happy hours we had spent together. She had never done anyone any harm. She was such an appealing little animal, and now she was dead. Mercifully, she had been shot and probably spared a great deal of agony. And what would happen to Edmond? Should I go to him? But he wouldn't let me help him if I did go to him. Surely, he could take care of himself. I think I was still in a state of shock and unable to think coherently.

Five minutes after he had left, Mr. McComb walked toward me carrying a shovel and a length of rope.

"We will bury her on the other side here. I don't want to have to drag her any further than I have to," he said, pushing his way through the hedge. "Better stay there until I find a place." I heard the sound of his spade in the earth, then. "I was afraid of that—too rocky. Try up a bit." Again he dug. "No," he said. Then I heard him walking still farther up the slope on the other side of the hedge. "What the devil—" I heard him say. "Well, this is damned convenient." He dug again, and this time I could tell by the sound of his shovel that there was enough earth to dig the grave in.

Presently he emerged from the hedge at the bend above me—from about the same spot that William Reade had come. He carried a large leather sack, and he was wearing heavy leather gloves.

"Most convenient that someone should leave these up there," he said, as he reached down and picked up the dead dog. He dropped Sarah's body into the sack and said, "There now, if you will follow me, my lady, I think you will be able to get through the hedge."

Douglas McComb carried Sarah, and I followed him up the walk. But I was not able to take my eyes off the gloves he had found. I had seen them before. There had been plenty of time to examine those gloves as they lay on the table before me in the Reades' cottage while William Reade told me all about the hares and the pheasants. That had been almost three weeks before.

"Can you get through?" McComb asked, when we had reached the place in the hedge. "Here, I will hold this back—there."

I passed through the opening he had made for me, holding back some of the yew branches myself, and he followed me.

"Is this where you found the sack and gloves?" I asked.

"Right where I dug the hole," he said.

Then he lowered the sack containing Sarah's body into the grave and removed the gloves and threw them into it also.

"I don't think anyone should wear those again," he said.

It may seem odd, but I prayed for Sarah while Douglas McComb covered her with earth. And then we gathered stones and piled them on top of the grave.

"What will they do to him?"

"Lord Althrop? Put him away," McComb said. Then he looked at me and saw the look of disbelief on my face. "They go mad, you know. Poor devil. I wonder which is worse, the disease or the madhouse."

We said no more until we had finished fixing the stones, and then I thanked him, squeezed my way through the hedge, and hurried to the house.

As I walked along, I felt a bit guilty about paying more attention to Sarah than to Edmond, but it had been important to dispose of Sarah's body, and I was glad I had held my own private funeral for her as we had done so. Besides, twenty minutes time would not have affected Edmond one way or the other. There was, indeed, only one way he would be affected now. How long would it take?

"Horrible!" I whispered aloud. "What can I do?"

But it was not up to me to do anything, I thought. Lord Clareham must be told about it, if Edmond had not told him already, and whatever was to be done was his responsibility.

So, after I had entered the house, I walked toward the stairway nearest Lord Clareham's room. On the way, I saw Mitchell step into the rotunda from the servants' stair.

"Mitchell," I called, "have you seen his lordship?"

"No, my lady, I haven't seen his lordship since he went out at ten-thirty."

"I am going up to his lordship's father, Mitchell. If you see him, would you ask him to join us there, please? It is quite important."

"Certainly, my lady," Mitchell replied.

"What is so important?" Edmond called from the drawing room doorway.

I turned and walked quickly toward him. "Have you told him?" I asked Edmond.

"About the dog?" he said. "Come in and let me get you a drink. You look as though a brandy would do you good."

"Yes, I think it would."

"That was an unnerving experience," he said, and he walked toward the liquor cabinet. He set down his own glass and began to fix a brandy for me. "No, I haven't told father about it, but I will, I suppose, if I don't forget." He smiled at me. "Well, I can't very well tell him every little thing that happens at Castle Cloud, can I? I couldn't remember them all, and there wouldn't be time. . . ."

"Every little thing? Edmond! Sarah was mad! Oh, Edmond, I—I—"

"Mad? Nonsense."

"But—I think we had better tell your father about it."

"Why?" he asked, walking back toward me holding out my drink.

"Thank you, Edmond. Because he will know what to do. I am sure there is some way of—well, there must be something—"

"Mary, it is charming of you to be so concerned, but Sarah wasn't mad. What ever gave you that idea?"

"William Reade was there and shot Sarah just as you left. Did you see him?"

"I heard the shot, but I was unnerved, and naturally, I wanted to look at my leg and wash it as soon as possible."

"He said she was mad. And then Mr. McComb came along, and he said she was mad, too."

"Mary, I have lived in Devonshire as long as Reade or McComb. I am as good a judge of a mad dog as they are, and I saw Sarah up close and alive, which is more than any of you did. She was slobbering just like all dogs slobber, but she was a perfectly healthy animal. Reade wasted his bullet on her, though I can't say I am sorry. I have always said she had a nasty disposition. Anyway, rest assured. She did not bite me, if that is what you are worried about. Not even a scratch. I must admit," he said with a shaky laugh, "that I thought at first she had, but there is not a mark, though she ruined an expensive pair of trousers. So you see, there is no reason to make a fuss and scare Mother and Father out of their wits."

"Are you sure she didn't bite you?" I asked.

"Perfectly. But as I said, if she had, there would be

nothing to worry about. Sarah has always been a perfectly clean and healthy dog."

He walked back to the liquor cabinet as he said this. Then he poured himself another drink.

"Thank God," I said, leaning back in my chair. Then I took a gulp of brandy. "Oh, thank God. I was terrified." I closed my eyes then, and savored the warmth of the liquid flowing through me.

"What was Reade doing, walking about the grounds in broad daylight?" Edmond asked.

"If William Reade wants hares or pheasants from Castle Cloud," Lady Clareham said, as she walked into the room, "let him have them. They are food for him, and we can spare them." She walked to the sofa opposite me and sat down. "We don't shoot them anyway—the fields are probably overrun."

"He shot Sarah, Lady Clareham," I said. "She came back, and we thought she had bitten Edmond. Then Mr. Reade shot her."

"Sarah came back?" Lady Clareham said. "Did she bite you, Edmond?"

"No, but she ruined an expensive pair of trousers," he said.

"Then why did William Reade shoot her?"

"Because he thought she was mad," I said.

"Well, she wasn't," Edmond said, "and Reade has no business on our land shooting our pets. I will tell McComb about it and tell him to keep him off."

"He already knows," I said. "As long as you are all right, Edmond, that is all that matters. I shall not be long, but if luncheon is served, please do not wait for me."

Mitchell did announce the meal before I had finished washing and tidying my hair. And when I stepped out of my room onto the gallery, I looked down into the hall and saw Edmond and his mother entering the dining room.

"But you are sure the dog was well," I heard Lady Clareham say.

Then, when I had joined them at the table and we had begun our soup, I said to Edmond, "The reason I came to meet you at the walk was to tell you that I am leaving Castle Cloud as soon as I can arrange with Lord and Lady Mauldridge to begin my duties at Flowerwick Hall."

"Well, our little Mary has gotten some sense into her

head at last," Edmond said. He reached for his wine and drank half of it at a gulp. Then he continued, "Congratulations, little Mary. But tell me, why did it take you so long to reach this momentous decision?"

"I had hoped that I would not have to take a position, Edmond, and it took a long time for that hope to die."

"Ha! I thought it never would."

"Edmond!" Lady Clareham said. "I think you are doing the right thing, Mary, and I am sure Lord Clareham will be happy to hear it too."

"Yes, I am sure he will," I said. "I will write to Lord Mauldridge directly after luncheon and accept the position."

After luncheon was over and Lady Clareham had gone up to her room, I sat down at the table in the drawing room to write to Lord Mauldridge.

Cleopatra pretended to sleep on the tabletop before me, but I could see that her eyes were not completely closed and that she watched me.

"Well, Cleopatra," I whispered, "the final step is being taken at last."

I took paper, pen, and ink out of the drawer, dipped the pen into the ink, and wrote:

August 7, 1856

Dear Lord Mauldridge,

If you still wish me to come to Flowerwick Hall as governess to little Eugenia and Ethelind, I should like to accept the position.

I could arrive on Monday, August 11th, or any day thereafter that might be convenient.

As I paused, wondering what else to write, something outside the window caught my eye. It was David, galloping Caesar past the grass circle toward the stable yard.

I watched him vanish behind the men's pavilion, and in about two minutes he reappeared on foot, strode toward the house, and disappeared in the direction of the entrance front. In a moment he would ring the bell, and Mitchell would answer the door. Had David come to see me?

"Please, dear God, make him want to see me," I whispered.

Then I jumped out of my chair and hurried to the drawing room doorway. From there I would be able to hear what David said to Mitchell.

Shortly, David rang the doorbell. I waited, holding my breath and listening for Mitchell's footsteps. But the hall remained silent. Where *was* Mitchell? The bell tinkled again, and still I did not hear Mitchell. He must be in the servants' hall, I thought. So I ran out of the drawing room toward the vestibule to answer the door myself.

But as I entered the vestibule, David threw open the door and strode into the house. We stood facing each other.

He was out of breath. "May I speak to you?" he said.

"Yes, of course," I answered.

I turned and led the way to the hall chamber. Once inside the room, I walked to the center of it, stood, and watched David close the door behind us. Then he walked over to me and stood looking down into my eyes.

"Will you marry me?" he said.

When I had caught my breath, I examined his face to be sure that he was serious.

"Yes," I answered.

Then he slid his arms around me, pulled me to him, hugged me, and buried his face in my neck. Then he kissed me, and I threw my arms around him and held him close with all my strength.

Finally, when he had released me a little, I held his head between my hands and covered his face with kisses.

"I have wanted to do that ever since I saw the hurt on your face yesterday—I—I have wanted to kiss it away. David, I love you so much. Can you ever forgive me?"

"Anything but live without you. I could not do that. I love you too much, Mary. I didn't love Vivian. Please understand that. I didn't know what love was until I met you. Don't cry."

"I didn't think people *did* cry when they were happy—I thought that happened only in books. Oh, David, thank you so much."

I turned from him then, and took out my handkerchief to wipe my eyes, but David did not let go of me—his hands still held my waist. And in a moment, he turned me back to him, and held me close, and kissed my forehead and hair, and then my mouth again.

"David," I said. "Give me a moment to—collect myself."

So he led me by the hand to the sofa and we sat down. But he did not let go of my hand. He held it tightly, and looked into my eyes, and smiled.

"I know you didn't love Vivian," I said. Then after I had examined his face again, I asked, "David, are you sure about this? Have you told your father?"

"I couldn't tell him until you had accepted me."

"Did you think I wouldn't?" I asked.

"I had to be sure."

"I could not marry you if he didn't agree."

"He will love you," David said.

"Are you sure—about this?"

"Positive. Surer than anything I have ever done in my life. I need you, Mary. I couldn't let you get away."

Again he pulled me to him and kissed me. Then he held me tightly against him for several minutes, and I began to feel a strange, new thrill within me.

"Please, David," I said, smiling and drawing away from him a little. And after a moment's silence I asked, "What do we do now?"

"Darling," he said. Then he kissed the end of my nose and burst into laughter. "Oh, you are marvelous. I love you. I love you. I love you." He got to his feet, pulled me to him, and swung me into a waltz as he sang: "I love you . . . I love you . . . I love you . . . I love. . ."

"Mary!" Lady Clareham cried from the doorway. She had opened the door and stood just inside it, looking wide-eyed at us. Cecile gaped from over her shoulder.

We stopped dancing, but David did not take his arm from my waist.

"I am sorry if we were making too much noise, Lady Clareham," David said. "I am afraid we got carried away."

"I am afraid so, David," Lady Clareham said.

"I have asked Mary to marry me and she has consented," he said.

"Marry you?" Lady Clareham asked. "David! You don't even know each other. Don't be absurd."

"We know each other very well."

"But how can you? What does your father say? I have never heard of anything so ridiculous."

"I haven't told him yet," David said. "He will love Mary—who could help it? But if he should object, I shall marry her anyway."

"No, David," I said.

Lady Clareham drew her fingertips across her forehead. "I think we should all sit down," she said.

David and I sat on the sofa, and Lady Clareham sat in an armchair to our left.

"That will be all, Cecile, thank you," she said. "The position at Flowerwick Hall?"

"Mary will write to them and refuse it, of course," David said.

"Refuse it? Refuse what?" Edmond asked from the doorway. "Refuse what? What are you all plotting in here? The question does not arise. I told you the dog was not mad. Do you think I don't know a mad dog when I see one? She was hot and slobbery. You know how she used to slobber, David. All dogs do, but Sarah slobbered more than most—always dripping—and she had been running. Anyway, what does it matter? I have told you she didn't bite me, so there is nothing to be concerned about. You don't believe me?"

"What about Sarah?" David asked. "Has she been found?"

"We were not talking about Sarah, or about you, Edmond," I said. "Edmond was almost bitten by Sarah this morning," I said to David. "She came back. She was acting rather peculiarly and snapped at Edmond, but she only caught his trousers, and then Mr. Reade shot her, and Mr. McComb buried her. Mr. Reade and Mr. McComb said she was mad."

"She was perfectly healthy," Edmond said, "and if I see Reade on our land again, I will see him in jail."

"You will do nothing of the sort," Lady Clareham said. "Edmond, David has asked Mary to marry him."

Edmond stared at his mother for a moment, looked at David, then at me. But he did not speak. He walked to a chair opposite his mother's and sat down on the edge of it, still looking from one to the other of us.

"Why?" he asked, at last, of no one in particular.

"Because we are in love," David said.

"In love?" Edmond replied. "You don't even know each other."

"Exactly," Lady Clareham said.

"Mary and I know each other very well," David said. "We have not known each other very long, but we know each other very well. They are not, you see, necessarily the same thing. And we are going to be married."

"But what about—?" Edmond sputtered. "How can you think of marriage? What do you expect—?" Then, suddenly, Edmond seemed to understand. "Oh! I *see*," he said.

"Well, I am glad we made that clear," David said to me.

"Oh, I *see*! And you think your father will approve?" Edmond said to David. "My dear fellow, what makes you think he will? What makes you act so rashly? I cannot believe you are serious. What do you know about Mary, other than her sweet and charming nature? One cannot help being fond of her of course, but what do we know about her family? I'll tell you what we know. We know that Lord Penbroke suddenly leaves England with a parlor maid, Mary's mother, never to return. One of the largest fortunes and estates in England falls to ruin and disappears. Lord Penbroke is never seen again on English soil. Odd, don't you think? Now, now, let me finish." He held up his hand. "Be that as it may, more to the point is the fact that even Vivian always wondered about Mary's background. She may have mentioned it to you, David. . . ."

"She never mentioned it to me," I said. "She never wondered in the least about my background."

"She wondered," Edmond said, "whether she mentioned it to you or not, Mary. I don't mean this unkindly, of course, but the truth must be told in matters as serious as this. Vivian wondered about your father's total disregard for you—he never visited you, never wrote, never seemed to want you with him, never treated you as a daughter. So I cannot but believe that there is some truth in the rumors, however unpleasant they must be, about your title, Mary. Rumors do not grow from nothing, you know. I understand, David, that Mary's father was not Lord Penbroke at all, but someone working on the estate. Mary was born, you see, before her mother's marriage."

"That is not true," I said. "My father loved me very

much. And David has already heard that story, Edmond. David, Edmond started that rumor himself, at the ball—Dierdre Swoop told me so. For some reason he wishes to discredit me. Edmond, my title is genuine. I do not know why you wish to think it is not, but thinking that a thing is true does not *make* it so. You cannot believe a thing into reality. My mother and my father, Lord Penbroke, were married long before I was even thought of. Simply ask Mr. Schraw if you may see the record of their wedding."

"Who is Mr. Schraw?" Edmond asked.

"My father's solicitor in London," I replied.

"Be that as it may," Edmond continued, turning to David, "even if Mary's father was Lord Penbroke—give her the benefit of the doubt—and I say this to clarify a very important situation—to avoid a dreadful mistake for you both—even if Mary's father was Lord Penbroke, what of her mother's family? What do we know of them? There is the heredity factor to be considered. What maladies or peculiarities of behavior are inherent in that bloodline? How do we know what might crop up? The unfortunate episode of Mother's jewels, for example—who knows what kind of madness that might foreshadow."

"Someone stole some of Lady Clareham's jewels, David," I said. "Edmond claims to have found a stone from a stolen brooch in my room."

"A servant found the stone, Mary," Edmond said. "Jane Spence, to be truthful about it."

"Edmond is implying that I stole the jewelry," I said. "This is another story he told about me at the ball. I don't think you have heard that one."

"Ridiculous!" David said, looking Edmond in the eyes. "If some of Lady Clareham's jewels have been stolen, there is only one person to be suspected. Things have been disappearing from Castle Cloud since long before Mary came to visit, and that is common knowledge."

"Edmond wishes me to leave Castle Cloud, David," I said, "quite urgently, it seems. That is why he has been trying to make me uncomfortable by spreading these stories. I think there must be something here that he does not want me to find out about. I have felt that since I first arrived. What is it Edmond? Is it something to do with Vivian?"

"Mary, you are talking nonsense," Edmond said. "You

are hysterical. We only want to help you. We have become very fond of you, and we are only thinking of your welfare. We want a comfortable future for you, and we don't want to see you make a mistake. I must say, your gratitude is positively overwhelming."

He stood then and said, "Well, David, this is a serious step. Think it over very carefully—and when you find that you have made a mistake, that this would bring only misery to you and to your father as well, then admit it. Come right out and admit it, and we will understand. One should never do things on impulse—that is a lesson sometimes dearly learned."

"Edmond," David said. "Mary and I are going to be married. There is nothing you can do to prevent it."

"I don't know what you mean," Edmond said. "But since you are so cocksure of yourself, David, and since it is apparent that all sensible suggestions will be ignored, I shall ask that you excuse me. I have things to do."

He left the room then, and I watched him walk across the rotunda toward the drawing room. We sat without speaking until we could no longer hear his footsteps. Then I looked at David. He smiled and reached for my hand and held it in both of his.

"I know this has been a shock for you, Lady Clareham," he said. "I know how you mourn for James, and I apologize for intruding. I shall arrange for Mary's future, but may I ask that she stay with you here for a few days more?"

"David," Lady Clareham said, "Vivian has only—just gone. I do not think that talk of marriage is proper or advisable, and I do not think that Mary should remain at Castle Cloud any longer. I think that she should take the position with Lord and Lady Mauldridge. But if you are adamant, Mary may remain until you can make arrangements for her. After the way Edmond has acted, I think that is the least we can do.

"It is not that I do not wish you both happiness, for I do. And we *have* become genuinely fond of Mary, which is why I have spoken so frankly. Lord Clareham and I will help you both in any way we can. It is what Vivian would have wanted, I think, and what James would have wanted too."

Tears had come to her eyes as she finished speaking. Now she rose, and so did we.

"I must go up to Lord Clareham now," she said. "I think you have both acted quite improperly, and it distresses me, David."

"Yes, you are right, Lady Clareham. I hate to go, Mary, but I think I must," David said. "We will have the rest of our lives to be together. I will come again tomorrow afternoon. Meanwhile, be as happy as I am. Everything will be wonderful, I promise."

And I felt he was right. The three of us walked together into the rotunda, and David said good-by. Then Lady Clareham went upstairs, and I walked into the drawing room where I found Edmond standing before a window with a drink in his hand, looking out at the park.

He turned as I entered, and our eyes met, but he didn't speak. Instead he looked back out of the window. I ignored him after that: I walked to the desk, picked up the unfinished letter to Lord Mauldridge, and tore it into little pieces. Then I walked slowly out of the room and out onto the west portico, where I stood until David had ridden out of the stable yard.

David loves me, I thought. I am going to be his wife. But has he acted rashly? Will he be sorry that he has asked me to marry him? No, I know that he will not be. I know that he loves me as deeply as I love him. And happiness flowed through me.

"Mr. Field and the Baroness Beauford request the pleasure—" I whispered aloud, as I began to descend the steps. "Of course I will use my title—my son will be the lord Beauford—but I would so much rather it be Mrs. Field. Yes, we will be very, very happy."

But what if David's father doesn't approve? I wondered. David had said that he would still want me to marry him, but could I marry him then? And if his father does approve, where will we live? At Oakland Park, or somewhere else? Will David inherit Oakland Park, and will I be its mistress?

These and many other questions remained to be answered. I didn't know what the future would hold, but I knew that the man I loved also loved me, and that he had asked me to marry him. And that was all I needed at the moment.

Since I missed David already and wanted to feel close to him, I walked to the hilltop and stood near the Horse Monument where we used to stand together. David had made this a special day, and God must have known that he would because He had provided special weather for the occasion. The sky and the sea were especially blue, the cotton-clouds especially white, and the air especially clear that afternoon. And as I looked at its roofs and chimney stacks rising above the trees across the valley, Oakland Park seemed enormous.

Then I sat for a long time on the building block where I had sat with David, hugging my joy and dreaming of my life to come—of David and the children we would have. And then, at last, it was time to walk back to the house and change for dinner.

". . . and he asked if Mary could stay here for a few days more, until he could make arrangements for her," Lady Clareham said, in reply to Edmond.

"A few more days? I don't understand," Edmond said.

"She has to stay somewhere," Lady Clareham said, "and she cannot stay at Oakland Park—that would be *most* improper."

"Of course she can't," Edmond said. "What do you mean, 'She has to stay somewhere?' Mary will stay with us until her marriage. There is no question of her staying anywhere else."

"I have no idea what David's plans are," I said, "but I could not stay here."

"But of course you will stay here," he said. "Why ever not?"

"Because I am not wanted here, Edmond," I replied. "I have not felt wanted here from the moment I entered this house. I am very grateful for having been permitted to stay for as long as I have, but I do not like staying where I am not wanted. I shall leave as soon as possible."

"Mary!" Edmond cried. "Where on earth did you get that idea when we have become so fond of you? We love having you here with us. Why, you have brought sunlight into our lives. And it is most convenient and proper for you to stay here until you are married, and we are delighted. No, you will stay here with us. We shall consider the matter closed."

If Edmond was almost pleading with me to stay, as he seemed to be, then I had the upper hand, for a change. I could not resist using it.

So I said, "That is very kind of you, Edmond, but since Castle Cloud is so understaffed, it would be an imposition, and I would not feel comfortable. To feel at ease when one is a guest, one must be treated as a guest. You must realize that I am not complaining, but I have never had to close curtains, or turn down a bed, or light a lamp for myself, and I am accustomed to having my things laid out for me at night and my tea brought to me in the morning."

"But surely, Jane has been doing these things for you," Edmond said. "Mother?"

"I am afraid. . ." Lady Clareham began.

"Well, she will," Edmond said. "My dear Mary, I am so sorry. I assumed that you were being properly taken care of. Of course your room will be prepared for you, and you must have your tea in the morning. But I cannot read minds, you know. You must tell me when things are not satisfactory."

"And I should like to ride, Edmond," I said, "but I have no habit. And you have forbidden me to borrow any of Vivian's clothes, in spite of the fact that she will probably never use them again."

"I was just about to say, Mary, that you look a little pale, and I think you should get more exercise. Exercise is the thing for health. We have excellent horses. Of course you must ride. Borrow one of Vivian's habits and take Chocolate for a run. It will do you good. Yes, borrow her clothes. You are the same size as Vivian, aren't you? There are beautiful clothes there. You must use them, Mary.

"We want you to be happy, and we will not rest until you are married and safely ensconced as mistress of Oakland Park. You cannot deprive us of the pleasure of your company until then, now, can you?"

"Very well, Edmond," I said, "perhaps I shall stay then, if David—agrees. Thank you so much."

During the rest of the meal, Edmond seemed in excellent spirits. He talked a great deal and strove to be charming. He even joined us for a few moments in the drawing room while we were drinking our coffee, before he stepped out onto the portico for his cigar.

After we had finished our coffee, I left the house and strolled down to the stone bridge. This had become a habit with me on clear evenings. After I had reached the bridge, I leaned against the railing, thinking about David and how very happy he had made me.

But I was also apprehensive about Edmond's new attitude. Why the sudden turnabout at dinner? Until tonight he has wanted desperately to be rid of me, and now nothing will do but that I stay. It is not because he is fond of me—I know that. Then why should he insist that I remain at Castle Cloud?

I thought and thought about it, but I was no closer to an answer when, finally, I walked back up the hill.

When I reached the house, I went directly to my room. There, the curtains had been drawn, the lamps lit, my bed had been turned down, and my nightgown was laid out for me.

But it had been such a long and exhausting day that I was almost too tired to notice. I went to bed at once, and no sooner had I closed my eyes it seemed, than someone knocked on my door and it was morning.

The door opened slowly, and Jane Spence walked into the room carrying a tray. "Good morning," she said. "Isn't it a beautiful morning? Where shall I put this?"

"Put it here on the bed, Jane, thank you," I said.

"Oh, it's no trouble at all. We want you to be happy here with us. If there is anything I can do—"

"Thank you, Jane."

She stood examining me for a moment. Then she smiled and said, "You must be very excited about being mistress of Oakland Park."

"Oh, you have heard that Mr. Field has asked me to marry him."

"Yes, his lordship told me last night. You will be our neighbor, and of course you will be coming to the Castle to call. Is it hot?"

I sipped my tea. "Yes, it is delicious."

"Oh, good. Well, if there is anything I can do, please don't hesitate. Mrs. Muldoon will be along with your water shortly. Have a very pleasant morning."

"Thank you, Jane."

She left me then, closing the door behind her.

What an amazing change in her attitude, I thought, as I

munched a thin slice of bread and butter. I was too happy, however, to think very much about it. I banked my pillows behind me, leaned back into them, dawdled over my tea, and thought what a lovely day it was, and how I wished it would soon be afternoon, when David would be with me.

But as I daydreamed, something drew my eye to the door. It had opened a crack, and then, suddenly, through the opening. Cleopatra bounded into my room. Once inside, the cat stopped running and stood still for an instant, as if in a daze. Then she looked in my direction and shot straight at me. I was paralyzed and could only shriek with terror as she flew toward me. The animal was foaming at the mouth—she was mad.

Instead of jumping at me, however, Cleopatra darted under my bed. Then I heard Mrs. Muldoon laughing, and I looked up and saw her peeking merrily into my room.

"Mrs. Muldoon! Get Edmond quickly," I cried. "Cleopatra has gone mad and she is under my bed."

"Ha, ha, ha, ha. Sure, if you could have seen your face," Mrs. Muldoon cried, as she came into the room. "Oh, she gave you a proper fright she did. Ha ha, ha."

"Mrs. Muldoon! It is not funny!"

"There, there. It is just a bit of shaving lather on her mouth. Ha, ha, ha. Just a bit of shaving lather. Hee, hee, hee."

"Mrs. Muldoon! You put shaving lather on Cleopatra? You frightened me to death. I could have had a heart attack. Mrs. Muldoon!"

"Scared you half to death, didn't I. Ha, ha, ha."

"Please don't do that again. Oh!—Where on earth did you get shaving lather?"

"From his lordship's bedroom. Sure it's up and out early he is, my lady, and I always stop in there to see what's to be done before I bring your water. And there was Cleopatra sleeping in the linen closet on the gallery. So I had to do it, my lady. I just had to do it. Faith, it's the devil that's in me that makes me do these things sometimes. Och, you should have seen your face. Ha, ha, ha."

"I was terrified, Mrs. Muldoon. After yesterday, I can not find it amusing, I am afraid, though it *was* beautifully done. The poor cat must have been as terrified as I was. No wonder I thought she was mad. We must take the lather off the poor thing's face."

"She'll do it herself, my lady, and be none the worse for it. You're not angry? 'Twas no harm in it, my lady."

"No, but one of these days you will have a death on your hands if you keep it up—mark my words. You did manage it quite beautifully, however, and I am sorry that I cannot quite laugh. I take it you have heard about Sarah."

"Yes, my lady. The poor creature—that's what made me think of it."

"I suppose you have heard about my coming marriage, too."

"Oh, yes, my lady. 'Tis just wonderful, my lady. And it's happy you're bound to be. You'll have your hands full, though—Oakland Park is the grandest house in all the county. But Mrs. Reston's the housekeeper there, and a very able woman she is, they say.

"I'll get your water now. Leave Cleopatra—she'll take care of herself. Oh, I wish you could have seen your face," she said, as she left me. "Ha, ha, ha."

After breakfast, I was still a bit on edge from the incident so I walked in the rose garden for awhile, and then, when I felt more relaxed, I went to visit Lord Clareham. His door was opened for me, as usual, by Ahmad, and when Lord Clareham saw me he called, "Ah, Mary. I was hoping you would pay me a visit. Come in, come in. Sit here."

"Am I disturbing you?" I asked, as I sat down beside his bed.

"Not at all, my dear. I can read my books anytime, but it is rare that I have such charming company."

"You are feeling better?"

"Yes, much better—better every day. I shall soon be up and about. But you, Mary. What is this I hear about your marrying David Field? Surely you are not serious about this."

"Very serious, Lord Clareham. Do you mind?"

"Mind? Because of Vivian? No, not because of Vivian, but you hardly know the boy. How many times have you seen him—three, four?"

"I am not sure, Lord Clareham, that the number of times matters. Do you think it does? David says that he knows people who have been married for years and don't know each other at all."

Then I told him about meeting David on the hilltop shortly after I arrived at Castle Cloud, and about our friendship.

"Not at all proper," he said, when I had finished. "I do not approve at all. What will young people expect to do next? Meeting a young man alone at night like that is disgraceful, Mary. Shocking! Nevertheless, I wish you happiness. You know that. I think you deserve it. And I hope that you will come and see me occasionally and tell me how you are getting on."

"I would love to," I said.

"Now, I want you to tell me exactly what happened on the walk yesterday. Sarah returned? What did she look like?"

I told Lord Clareham everything that had happened including Edmond's and my conversation before luncheon—everything, that is, except about finding William Reade's gloves and the leather bag. "I did think for a while that Sarah had bitten him. Thank goodness she didn't." I concluded.

"Nasty business. Glad the dog is dead," Lord Clareham said.

"Yes," I said. Then, for some reason, I turned round to see if Ahmad was staring at me, as he usually was, but he was no longer in the room. "Where is Ahmad? I didn't hear him leave. It is positively eerie the way he moves about—rather like a shadow."

"Fixing my luncheon, no doubt. He is quite an excellent cook, you know, among other things."

"So is Monsieur Laval," I said.

"Yes, but I prefer Eastern food."

"Does Ahmad cook all your meals?"

"Everything I eat."

"Does he speak English? He seems to know everything that is going on, at least he looks as though he knows everything. He is a terrifying man—he frightens me to death."

"Ahmad is a very fine man, Mary. I could not possibly manage without him. I might not be alive if it were not for him. I imagine he does understand English, somewhat, but he would never speak it. The Indians are a strange people. They do not think like Europeans, and that is why we have made so many mistakes in dealing with them."

"How did Ahmad come to be with you? Did you buy him?"

"Good heavens, no! There are no slaves in India. No, Ahmad comes originally from the village of Karimpur. His story is an interesting one. He is an Untouchable and was the *dhobi*, or washerman, of the village. We gather, from what little we have been able to piece together, that he fell in love with a Chamar girl—also an Untouchable, but a caste below his. They ran away together, but the girl's father followed them, brought his daughter back to the village, and killed her for disgracing him."

"Horrible! Barbaric!" I said.

"They had both broken caste, you see. Ahmad was in no physical danger, but by that act he had cut himself off forever from his family and friends. So he wandered to Madras, and to Government House, where he became a servant. And to make a long story short, he attracted my attention. I needed a valet—I preferred, contrary to local custom, to have one man attend me with the smallest amount of ceremony possible—and Ahmad suited my needs perfectly. He has been with me ever since. He is devotion himself. I worry, however, about what would happen to him if I should die. I am very concerned about that."

But then Lord Clareham stopped speaking as he glanced toward the door. I heard a squeaking sound behind me and followed his gaze to see who had entered the room. It was Ahmad. He pushed a small table on wheels through the doorway and across the room to Lord Clareham's bedside.

"I had better go and let you eat in peace," I said.

"No, stay a few minutes, and see what Ahmad has prepared for me," Lord Clareham said. He spoke in Hindustani to Ahmad and then said to me, "It's a *polo*, which is one of Ahmad's specialties. You must see this."

Ahmad had brought a short-legged tray from a chest against the wall, and, after lifting Lord Clareham to a sitting position against his pillows, the Indian set the tray with cloth and silverware. Then he lifted the lid of a deep silver dish, picked up a spoon, and ate a mouthful of soup, before serving it in a plate and placing it before Lord Clareham.

And as I sat watching the meal progress, I noticed that

Ahmad ate some of everything he handed Lord Clareham—not merely a taste, but a substantial mouthful. After the soup, he served the *polo*, some small cakes or biscuits, and fruit. He had eaten some of each. He had also drunk some of Lord Clareham's wine before placing the glass on his tray.

I wanted to ask about this ritual, but I decided against it.

Instead, as Lord Clareham tasted the *polo*, I said, "It smells divine."

"Like to sample some of it?" he said.

"I would love to, but I think I had better not, thank you. It might spoil my luncheon, and I shall have to leave you or I will not be in time for it."

So I wished him a pleasant afternoon and left him to his meal.

After I had had my own luncheon, I sat by the window in the drawing room waiting for David to come. But I was too restless and impatient to sit there for long, so I walked to the stables, using a visit to Chocolate as an excuse to be where I would be with David the soonest.

I had no sooner given Chocolate a piece of carrot than I heard Caesar trotting along the drive toward the yard, and I ran out to meet David.

"Hello," he said, when he had dismounted and given Caesar's reins to Colen. "This is a lovely surprise!"

"I couldn't wait to see you," I said.

"I thought the afternoon would never come. Is everything all right?"

"Yes, David. I have never been happier. And you? Do you still—"

"Do I still want you to marry me? Idiot! Of course I do—that will never change." He held out his arm for me, I took it, and we walked toward the house. "I want you with me for the rest of my life. Now, there will be no uncertainty about that."

"Yes, David," I said in mock servility, which made him laugh. "What did your father say?"

"I didn't tell him yet. He has had one of his headaches. He has violent ones, sometimes, which last twenty-four hours or so, and he had one yesterday when I returned to Oakland Park. It was no time to tell him about us—he can barely think when his head hurts him like that."

"I am sorry," I said. "They sound terrible.'

"They are and they worry me. They are coming oftener now, and they seem to be more intense. It will be gone by this evening, most probably, and I will tell him then."

"Edmond has asked me to stay here until we are married."

"And what did you say?"

"Well, I didn't know what your plans were, but I said that I would if you approved. I refused at first, but he was insistent. He would not hear of my leaving. That puzzles me, David. Until yesterday he wanted to be rid of me in the worst possible way, and then last night he completely reversed himself."

"And Lady Clareham? She didn't seem to want you to stay either. Why was that?"

"I think she is afraid of what Edmond will do next. And that puzzles me, too. What could he do to me—spread more rumors?"

"Maybe you had better not stay then. We have one or two friends who would be pleased to have you stay with them. Perhaps the surroundings would not be as aristocratic, but they would make you welcome, I am sure."

"I am sure they would, David, and aristocratic surroundings are not important to me. But I will be all right at Castle Cloud, now that Edmond wants me to stay here."

"Well, it would be convenient and cause less talk, perhaps—not that I care about talk, especially—but there are other people to be considered. Stay then, but only if you want to."

"Oh, good! Then I will," I said.

"You love it here, don't you?"

"Yes. I love Castle Cloud. I can't explain it. Ever since the day I saw it for the first time, it has filled me with joy, somehow."

"Then we will buy it."

"Buy it?"

"For your dower house."

"But it will be Edmond's. He wouldn't sell it."

"Who knows, he might someday."

"And I don't want to think of dower houses."

"All right."

"And Edmond said that I may borrow Vivian's clothes, if I need to. I have very few of my own and no habit.

And I may ride Chocolate. I always had horses until shortly before Papa died, and I have been longing to ride. And poor Chocolate needs exercise. She seems so sad, cooped up in her box all the time. I thought I might go riding tomorrow."

"We will go riding together, tomorrow," David said.

"Lovely!"

We had climbed the steps of the east portico of the house and entered the east vestibule. Inside, David took me in his arms and kissed me, but we had only a moment alone together before I heard Lady Clareham calling to Cecile.

Then she appeared, and we went to meet her.

"Good afternoon, David," she said. "Come into the drawing room and sit down, both of you. Have you told your father about Mary? What did he say?"

David described his father's headache, as we walked across the rotunda, and said that he had not. Then we sat down together in the drawing room and talked about impersonal things. Lady Clareham worked on her embroidery, only occasionally joining in the conversation. She had evidently decided that no matter how painful it might be for her, David and I would be properly chaperoned at Castle Cloud.

"David has asked me to go riding with him tomorrow," I said, after awhile. "Could you spare Colen to ride behind?"

"Naturally, my dear," Lady Clareham said.

At that point we heard a carriage draw up to the entrance front, and I ran to the window to see who it was.

"It is Flora," I said. "Is Edmond at home, Lady Clareham?"

"Oh, dear—No, my dear," she said. "He rode out directly after luncheon. I haven't the vaguest idea where he has gone or when he will be back."

"What will we do?" I said to David. "Shall we tell her our news?"

"Of course," he said, grinning broadly at me.

"Then everyone will know."

"The sooner the better," He said. "I *want* everyone to know."

"But if your father doesn't approve—"

"It won't make any difference."

As we spoke. I returned to my chair beside David's, and we waited quietly for Mitchell to announce Flora. I had no doubt that Mitchell would answer the door: he had an uncanny knack for being on duty whenever Lady Clareham was anywhere on the main floor of the house.

And I was right—he did answer the door—and as soon as he had shown Flora in and we had said our good-afternoons, David told Flora the news. She was astonished, but she recovered quickly and came and knelt by my chair, kissed me on the cheek, and told me how pleased she was. She was a bit envious, I think, which was natural, but she was also genuinely pleased for me—I was sure of it. Flora is a sweet soul, I remember thinking, and she deserves a lot better than Edmond.

Edmond's absence disappointed Flora, but I believe she hoped that he would return if she waited for him, so she sat and talked with us. After awhile, David proposed a walk in the park. Lady Clareham did not object, since Flora would accompany David and me. When we returned to the house, both David and Flora decided it was time for them to leave. So I said good-by to David, who reminded me that we were to go riding together the following day after luncheon, and waited with Flora until her carriage had been brought around. I stood on the steps and waved to her as she drove off.

Then I went up to Vivian's room to try on one of her riding habits.

❦ Chapter Fourteen ❦

AT BREAKFAST the following morning, Edmond was excited and gay. I knew, before he told me, that he would be away from Castle Cloud that day and evening. Often of late, he had left the Castle on Saturday—sometimes directly after breakfast, sometimes after luncheon—and when he did so, he almost always returned on Sunday afternoon. I knew he went somewhere to gamble. And I wondered, idly, where he was going that Saturday and where he had gotten the money. It was, however, none of my business, and I had no great desire to find out.

I had no desire to darn stockings either, but several of mine needed repairs, and I could not put off the task any longer. My stockings were wearing out, and I would soon have none to wear if I did not buy new ones. There must be a shop in the village, I thought, where they sold stockings. One day before long I would have to go and see.

But I could make the ones I had last a little longer. I went to my room after breakfast, then, took my sewing bag and the stockings to the chair by the window, sat down, and looked out at the fog, which had slid in from the sea. I wondered if it would lift before afternoon. If it did not, David and I would have to postpone our ride together.

I had looked forward to riding out with David and was apprehensive about the weather. After half an hour the sky seemed to be lightening, and I got up and walked across to the west window to see if I could see any improvement in that direction, but as I looked out, a dense cloud of mist crept toward the entrance portico below me. A wagon or cart stood there.

But no, it was not a wagon, it was a hearse—a long, black box on wheels. I could see the sockets for its plumes quite clearly, though they were empty. Today, the hearse wore no plumes, neither did the horses.

A shiver ran through me; the hearse made me think of Lord Clareham. But nothing could have happened to him: I had breakfasted with Edmond not three quarters of an hour before, and if Lord Clareham had died, he or Mitchell would have told me about it.

Still, it is very odd, I thought, as I stood looking down at the hearse and the small boy who sat motionless on the box, holding the reins. I saw no one else, and nothing moved—not even the horses. Perhaps it has something to do with James's funeral, or perhaps Lord Clareham is making arrangements of some kind.

Whatever it was, it was no business of mine, I decided, and I went back to my mending. But the image of the hearse would not leave my mind, so a half-hour later, I got up and crossed to the window again and looked down at the drive to see if it was still there. It was. The hearse, the boy, and the horses all remained as I had first seen them—nothing seemed to have changed. And a half-hour after that, at eleven o'clock, they stood there still.

By that time, curiosity had almost consumed me, but I also felt that if something terrible had happened, I might be able to help, instead of sitting uselessly in my room. So I stepped out onto the gallery and listened: the house was silent. And I saw no one on the gallery or down in the hall. I returned to my room, took a cloak from the wardrobe, threw it over my shoulders, and hurried downstairs. The rotunda was deserted—Mitchell was nowhere to be seen. That is not surprising, I thought, as I walked quickly across the hall and through the vestibule to the door to the portico. I was about to open it when I heard a faint tapping and realized that I was not alone.

A man sat against the wall of the vestibule in one of the uncomfortable wooden chairs provided for waiting tradesmen. He was a thin, sallow-skinned man with hollow eyes, and as he sat there waiting, he tapped his foot and rolled the brim of his hat between his fingers. I recognized him at once as the undertaker who had been hired for Alice's funeral.

"Is someone taking care of you?" I asked him.

"I be waiting to see Lord Althrop, my lady," he said, as he rose from his chair, "and I don't go until I see him."

"But Lord Althrop is not at home and may not return until tomorrow. Didn't Mitchell tell you?"

"Ay, Mr. Mitchell say that, but him be lying."

"But why should he lie to you?"

"Why should him lie?" I tell you why him should lie—so his lordship don't have to pay me, that be why. Mr. So-and-so be not at home. What happen if Lord So-and-so die and his wife send for me to get the coffin and take care of the funeral, and *I* be not at home? Eh? What happen? But I be at *home.*

"Lord Althrop ride to my shop in Barnstaple, my lady, and say, 'My brother, Lord Althrop, be dead. Come at once and measure him for his coffin.' *I* be at home. I come at once and measure the deceased and have the coffin made and deliver it on time. I keep my part of the bargain. I be there when I be needed and I do my job.

"I have a wife, my lady," he continued, "and a son who can neither hear nor speak, and two young daughters who marry one day, and my wife's mother. Us must *eat,* my lady. Us must have clothes, my lady. My daughters must marry one day, my lady. Because I be an undertaker, do people think I do not eat? I be alive just as them be. I need food just as them do. But how can I feed my family when them be 'not at home'? Them must pay me my money. Pay me my money or give me back my coffin. Who pays the coffin maker? *I* pay the coffin maker. Who pays me? Nobody. Then give me back my coffin."

"But his lordship couldn't give you back the coffin," I said, "Mr.—"

"Podock. Bartholomew Podock, broker, undertaker, and sworn appraiser; buyer and seller of household goods; opposite the Bull and Gate, Barnstaple—at your service, my lady.

"He *can*! Of course he can give it back. It be here. It be here in the cellar. I put it there myself—well, me and the boy put it there. I deliver it on Saturday morning as I promise, my lady, and when I get here—when me and the boy get here—there be Hackley's hearse from Bideford, and there be Hackley already laying out the deceased. 'What be all this?' I says to his lordship. 'What be Hackley doing here?' 'It be a mistake,' he says. It be a mistake, you see, my lady. Lord Clareham order a coffin from Hackley in Bideford, and Lord Althrop order a coffin from me in

Barnstaple. When I deliver it, Hackley be already laying out the deceased in his. Then Lord Althrop says he don't need me for the services—that it be a mistake and he pay for the coffin and any trouble it cost.

"But he want the coffin and to put it in the cellar. I says, 'What do you want a coffin for? You already got a coffin from Hackley.' He says, 'We always have what we pay for. We pay for it, we have it,' he says. 'Put it in the cellar.' So I put it in the cellar—well, me and the boy put it in the cellar, my lady. And that be where it be. And I don't go until I see his lordship and I get my money or my box."

"Well, I sympathize with you, Mr. Podock," I said, "but I am afraid there is nothing I can do. And his lordship is away from the Castle and will not be back until tomorrow afternoon or evening—I am sure. That is the truth. You may believe me. I can at least save you the ordeal of sitting here for the rest of the day for nothing."

"Aw, well," he said, "if you be sure, my lady, then I be going—me and the boy be going—but I be back. Us be back, my lady. Good day then, my lady."

"Good day, Mr. Podock," I replied, as I watched him open the entrance door.

Then he left the house, and in a moment I heard the hearse and the horses pull away from the steps and retreat down the drive toward the bridge.

But I did not leave the vestibule immediately, after he had gone. I stayed there for several minutes, thinking, and then I decided to go down into the cellar. I did not know where the stairway to the cellar was, but I thought that it would probably be directly beneath the one leading down to the level of the servants' hall. So I took a candle and some matches from the shelf next to the stair, descended to the basement level of the house, and walked around behind the staircase. There, I found a heavy oak door which was unlocked and which, when I opened it, revealed a flight of stone steps leading down into blackness.

I lit my candle, descended the first two steps, closed the cellar door behind me, and then continued down the staircase into the darkness. A cold draft blew at me from below. This made the descent difficult and slow because I was obliged to shield my candle flame from it, leaving no free hand to hold onto the railing or hold up my skirts.

And the stairway seemed to extend for miles. But at last I stood on the stone floor of the cellar and looked about. I could see nothing, however, except the stair stretching back into the darkness above me and a circle of lighted stone floor at my feet, It was cold, and I shivered. I wondered if I would be able to find my way back to the staircase if I investigated farther.

But I had to know if Mr. Podock's coffin was in the cellar, and my curiosity overpowered my apprehensions. I walked slowly forward, away from the stairs, and because I knew that Castle Cloud had been built over the foundations of a much older house, I began to have visions of medieval torture machines with skeletons still shackled to them. I found nothing more dramatic, however, than an ancient brick wall with an iron door in it. I pulled the handle of the door, but it did not budge. So, since it barred my way to that direction, I followed the wall to the left and soon came to another door. This one was unlocked, and when I opened it and walked inside, my candlelight reached to all four walls of a chamber which had probably been built as a storeroom. It was empty.

I left the empty storeroom and walked along an unbroken stone wall, turned a corner to the left, and explored, one by one, three other storerooms exactly like the first I had found. Then I followed another long wall, but this wall was broken by an archway and a flight of steps leading up through it. I climbed them until I came to a landing where I saw a sliver of light above me and realized that this was an exit leading to the areaway that surrounded the basement floor of the house and provided light for its windows. Outside, from the trapdoor above me, steps led, no doubt, to ground level.

I retraced my steps then, to the cellar floor, followed the wall to its end, explored still another storeroom, and finally found myself once again at the locked iron door. The cellar, therefore, consisted of a central chamber and six storerooms, one of which was locked.

My explorations had yielded a stack of picture frames, five boxes of moldy curtains and tapestries, a pile of dusty rugs, three plaster statues, and several wooden, straight-backed chairs—but no coffin.

After that, since I knew the plan of the cellar, I was able to examine the central chamber of it, into which the stairs descended and which I had encircled, without getting lost. But I found no coffin there either.

By that time, my candle had burned almost entirely away, and I had begun to shiver in earnest. But I decided to walk across to the locked door and examine it once again before going back upstairs.

When I reached it, I heard a bolt thrown; the door swung open, and a man stood before me.

He held his lantern high to light my face—which temporarily blinded me—and asked, "Is there something you wish, my lady?" It was Mitchell.

"No, Mitchell," I said. "What are you doing down here?"

"This is the wine cellar, my lady," he said. He stepped quickly toward me, slammed the door shut, locked it, and then continued, "In England, my lady, the butler has charge of the wine cellar, and it is not unusual for him to be found there inspecting its contents to be certain that there is an adequate supply of wines and other beverages on hand for every occasion. And may I ask what your ladyship is doing wandering about alone in the cellar? Were you looking for something, my lady?"

"I have never been in the cellar of Castle Cloud, Mitchell, and I was curious to see what it looked like. Is there any reason why I should not wander about here? Is there something that I should not see?"

"Certainly not, my lady. I would have been happy to show you about myself, had you asked. This secret expedition might, however, have proved dangerous—I shudder at the thought of your falling or becoming ill alone down here by the inadequate light of a small candle."

"Your concern for my welfare is touching, Mitchell. Thank you. May I see the wine cellar?"

"I shall be happy to show it to you, but at another time, my lady. I must not neglect my duties in the dining room. I am already late in the preparations for luncheon. Allow me to light your way back up the stairs."

"Oh, this is magnificent," I exclaimed. "Could we rest awhile? Could we sit on the wall there and watch the ocean?"

"Why not?" David said.

He dismounted and then helped me down from Chocolate. Then the horses walked away and began to graze, and David and I sat down side by side on a ruined stone wall that had been part of the foundation of a house or castle on the bluff above the sea.

David and I had been able to ride out that afternoon after all. The fog had lifted after luncheon. The horse had been delighted with the exercise and had behaved beautifully. We had ridden along the shore of the bay for a quarter of a mile and, then, cut across the fields to the ocean. Then we had turned north and ridden along the cliffs toward Baggy Point. At length we had come to a stone wall and a gate, which Colen had opened for us, and had followed a track to the end of a peninsula where the ruined stone foundation lay.

"Blue and green is my favorite color combination," I said, as we sat down. "Where did Colen go? Oh, there he is. How green the grass is. It is greener in England than anywhere on the continent, I think, and the ocean is bluer here, too. Isn't it lovely? And see the patterns the water makes as it washes the rocks down there."

"Yes, it is very lovely," David said, examining my face.

"But you are not looking at the sea," I said.

"No, I have been distracted."

"David, you make a shiver go up my spine when you look at me like that."

"Why?"

"Because I love you, and because I want you, and—No, please, David, don't. Colen is over there, and we are supposed to be proper."

"All right, I will try," he said. Then he laughed, and continued, "but if I don't succeed, you will be completely responsible."

"What did your father say?" I asked then. "Was he surprised? How did he react when you told him?"

"He wasn't surprised," David answered. "He already knew."

"How? How could he know?" I asked.

"Edmond told him."

"Edmond? When?"

"Yesterday afternoon," David answered. "That is where he had gone, you see, to Oakland Park. Edmond must have been complimentary about you, at least father said he was, because in spite of Father's headache, he seems to have gotten a good impression of the whole idea. But he is a cautious man. Well, I suppose all businessmen are—especially bankers. He is not going to make up his mind at all until he gets to know you, but he seems to have an open mind and even seems to be slightly disposed toward you. I think you can thank Edmond for that."

"But why should Edmond go straight to Oakland Park and tell your father about us?" I asked. "Why? Why would he do that?"

"I don't know."

"It wasn't for the joy of spreading glad tidings, I can tell you."

"Well, Father said that Edmond said he was just passing. He mentioned it casually and said that he wanted Father to know that the family had no objections because of Vivian. Evidently he couldn't say enough good things about you."

"How odd," I said. "Very unlike Edmond. You are sure it was *he*."

"Yes. Father is anxious to meet you and hopes that you will come to Oakland Park for dinner tomorrow night. I know it is impossibly short notice, and we could make it Monday night. . . ."

"David!" I said. "And you waited until now to tell me?"

"You will come, won't you?"

"Of course. I can't wait to see Oakland Park and meet him. David, I am frightened."

"I'm not. He will love you—I promise. You are not to be frightened or nervous."

"Yes, David."

He smiled and continued, "He puts on a rather forbidding front, but he is very softhearted underneath. Remember that."

"Is he *so* forbidding?" I asked.

"Well, yes, but I think you will see through it."

"Oh, dear, I am glad it is to be tomorrow night, I don't think I could bear having to wait any longer."

As I said this, I had looked down at the gulls skimming along the water below us, and I felt David's hand cover mine.

Then I looked up into his face, and he said, "It will be all right."

"I know it will," I said, smiling back at him. "I will

make it all right, and anyhow, I know I will like him enormously. He is *your* father, isn't he?"

After that we made arrangements for the following evening: David would call for me in a carriage at seven o'clock and take me to Oakland Park and bring me back to Castle Cloud afterward.

"David," I said, when that was settled, "some things have happened at the Castle that worry me."

"What?" he asked.

"Well," I said, "you know that Sarah came back mysteriously and almost bit Edmond...." Then I told David in detail how it had happened—especially about Mr. McComb finding the gloves and the bag. "Those were Mr. Reade's gloves. I saw them in his cottage when I visited Alice, and it must have been his leather bag, also," I concluded.

"And you think he brought Sarah to the walk in the leather bag and set her on Edmond?" David said.

"Yes, and I think he stole Sarah and infected her with the hydrophobia—by putting her with a sick dog until she was bitten by it, probably."

"Good God! Why should he do that?"

"Because Edmond was the father of Alice's child. Now that she is dead, it doesn't matter if I tell you. And I think her father blames Edmond for her death."

"Good God! The man must be mad."

"With grief," I added. "The point is, should I tell Edmond about the gloves and the bag? There is no proof. The gloves *could* have been someone else's, but I am sure they were not. And anyway, Mr. Reade could have left them there at another time. It might be a pheasant run or something."

"I don't know, Mary," David said.

"Edmond wouldn't believe it," I said.

"I think I would tell him. If there is any question of Reade wanting to harm him, Edmond ought to know. Reade might try it again, and Edmond should be warned about it so he can be on guard. If he doesn't believe you, at least you have done all you can to protect him."

"Yes."

"Anything else?" he asked.

"Yes. Mr. Podock, the undertaker from Barnstaple, called this morning."

"And?"

"And he wants his coffin back." Then I told David everything that had happened that morning. "So you see, Ida was right—there *were* two coffins."

"Ida?"

"The laundry maid. Didn't I tell you? She is—rather odd. She said James had two coffins—that she had seen them. But I thought that was part of her nonsense, poor girl. There *were* two coffins, David. One was used to bury James in. What was the other for? And where is it? It is not in the cellar of the Castle, unless it is in the wine cellar."

"What do *you* think it was for?" David asked.

"I don't know, but there is obviously something strange about it. People don't make mistakes like that, and if they did, they would not keep the extra coffin. Why on earth would you want a coffin lying about the house? You wouldn't. You know, I can't help wondering if it has something to do with—"

"Vivian? Oh, Mary. . ."

"I know you don't think anything has happened to Vivian, David, but I do. I know something has happened to her. Something has happened, and everybody at Castle Cloud is trying to cover it up—but I am going to find out about it. You told me to tell you if anything else happened."

"Look in the wine cellar," David said.

"Mitchell said he would show it to me, so I am sure the coffin is not there. But that is what I will do next."

"You think Mitchell is involved then?"

"I think *everybody* is involved."

"Why? Why do you think so? What an imagination."

"David! Vivian disappears, she says good-by to no one, writes to no one except me and, possibly, Lord Clareham. The letters are completely unlike her. Then we find that she has gone off to America—gone forever. How convenient."

"But there is no proof, and she was ill."

"It is a feeling I have, and I know I am right. When I find out more, I will tell you about it. Or would you rather not hear?"

"Of course I want to hear about it—tell me. I *love* you, Mary. I don't think there is anything in the idea, but I could be wrong, I admit that, and if you are right, I will help you. I will do anything—that goes without saying."

"Thank you, David. Yes, I know you will. Forgive me. I love you so terribly much, too. Don't let me spoil it."

Then David slid his hand over mine again, and we sat there, alternately looking at each other and at the ocean until, shortly, it was time to leave.

* * *

Edmond returned on the noon train the following day in time for luncheon. He was as morose as he usually was after one of his expeditions—far too ill-tempered to talk to. Did his fortunes never change? I wondered. Would he never return as exuberant as when he had left? I wanted to tell him about William Reade's gloves, but I realized that that must wait.

By the time Flora called, late in the afternoon, Edmond seemed to have recovered his good humor. When her carriage arrived, I was reading some new magazines in the drawing room, and Lady Clareham kept me company as she worked on her embroidery. Almost as soon as Flora was announced, Edmond entered. We sat and talked together until he suggested a walk in the park. Flora was delighted with the idea. But it would have been improper for Flora and Edmond to have gone alone, so Lady Clareham and I accompanied them.

We left the house by the entrance portico, where Lady Clareham and I sat on the lower steps while Flora and Edmond strolled on the grass, arm in arm.

When they returned to us, I glanced at my watch and, seeing that it was four o'clock, excused myself saying that I was dining at Oakland Park and that it was time that I began to get ready for the evening.

I left them and walked back into the house and up the stairs to my room. And when I entered it, I was surprised to see Jane Spence standing at my window looking down at the drive.

She did not try to disguise the fact that she had been watching us. On the contrary, she admitted it by saying, "I see Miss Stratton has called again. Mrs. Muldoon will bring the water for your bath in just a minute. I know you are dining at Oakland Park this evening, and I stopped by to see if there was anything I could do to help you get ready."

"Thank you, Jane," I said. "That was very kind of you, but I can manage. Yes, Miss Stratton has called. Isn't she charming? His lordship seems to be most attentive. They make a delightful couple, don't you think?"

"She is so terribly unattractive—I shouldn't think she would appeal to him at all," Jane answered.

"She is really very sweet, and of course, she is heiress to a considerable fortune. I understand her marriage settlement will be substantial. And I think, quite confidentially, that she is drawn to his lordship. Of course there is no definite evidence that the relationship is anything more than a simple friendship, still. . ."

"You can be sure that there is nothing more to it than that," Jane snapped.

"Oh? Speaking of evidence, Jane, now that you are here, exactly where did you find the amethyst stone?"

"I—it was on the floor. On the rug. It was just over there—by the wash-hand-stand."

"How clever of you to have seen it amidst the rug's pattern—all the little leaves and flowers and curlicues."

"Yes," she said. "But that was before—that is all forgotten. Anyway, it didn't mean anything."

"No, but his lordship seems to think it was quite significant, Jane."

"Does he? Well, it didn't mean a thing—why, all it means is that the robber must have come in here to see if you had anything to steal and dropped it while he was looking."

"Yes, that must be the explanation. I wonder if he went into Lady Vivian's room. You know, his lordship has urged me to borrow any of her things that I might need. That was very kind of him, wasn't it? After all, Lady Vivian will never need any of her things again, will she?"

"What do you mean by that?" Jane asked. "That is a very odd question, I'm sure. Of course she won't need them if she has gone to America. She was very changeable, anyway. She never liked anything for more than two minutes. She had so many beautiful things, and she wouldn't wear them because she got tired of them right away."

"Was? Why, Jane, you say that almost as if she were dead."

"Well, she isn't here, is she?" Jane replied. "She has gone, ain't she? Now, if there's nothing else, I will be going. I have things to do."

"No, there is nothing else. Thank you, Jane."

Jane walked to the door then, and when she reached it, she turned back to me and, with her widest smile, said, "If there is anything you need, just ring, and have a *very* pleasant evening." Then she left the room and closed the door behind her.

Only moments after she had left, Mrs. Muldoon brought the water for my bath. I bathed, washed my hair, brushed it until it gleamed, and then arranged it with the blue and white silk flowers, as I had for Flora's party. And as I pinned the flowers in place, I thought how differently my situation had become from that heartbreaking night when Edmond had taken the carriage and forced me to remain at Castle Cloud. I had dreamed of marrying David that night and had thought it impossible, and here I was preparing to meet his father because David had proposed to me.

Yes, my thoughts were happy ones that evening. When I had finished, the clock on the mantel said six forty-five. I had beaten it for a change. All my life, whenever I had dressed, clocks had conspired to cheat me. Always they had raced ahead, depriving me of time. But that evening it was different, and I gave the mantel clock a look of triumph as I passed it and glided out of the room.

I went directly down to the drawing room and stood by the window, waiting for David. Shortly after seven o'clock, he arrived in a beautiful blue barouche, and I rushed from the room and out of the house to meet him.

By the time I had reached the portico, he had climbed halfway up the stairs. So I waited for him at the top.

"You are very punctual," I said, as I gave him my hand.

"Of course," he said. "How are you?"

"Terrified," I replied.

"Now, you are not to be terrified, remember?"

"Yes, David," I said, smiling at him.

"Come into the vestibule for a moment. I want to tell you something."

He opened the door for me then, and when we had stepped inside, he took me in his arms and kissed me, and then he held me tightly against him.

Finally I drew back a little and whispered, "Thank you for telling me, David, but what if Mitchell should come."

"Darling, I couldn't care less." David kissed the end of my nose then, and said, "But we must be off. Father is very impatient to meet you, and we should have time to get you and him acquainted before dinner."

"What is your father like?" I asked, when we were seated in the carriage and had begun to drive around the house toward the home-farm.

We went that way because David had told John, his coachman, to take the most direct way, through Milton Penderton.

"It is hard to describe him, Mary," he answered. "He is short and his hair is almost totally gray. He is seventy— Let me see, he was born in 1784—that would make him seventy-two, wouldn't it. He is very determined, very businesslike."

"Was he always a banker? Was your grandfather a banker?"

"No, Father was first a tailor—in Manchester."

"And he began to lend people money?" I asked.

"No," David said, laughing. "I don't think one becomes a banker that way. No, he was a member of a Welsh dissenting chapel in Manchester. . . ."

"You are of Welsh descent?" I interrupted.

"No, he was just a member of it. I suppose he liked the services, or perhaps it was because my mother, whose name was Emma Elliot, was a member of it. Her father, Benjamin Elliot, was a member too. I don't know which came first, the chapel or my mother. But they fell in love. Her father would never have given permission to marry, and they knew it, so they eloped. He was a cotton manufacturer and banker in Manchester—in those days that was not an unusual combination."

"But Benjamin relented afterward," I said.

"Eventually, yes. But not until he had disowned my mother—he refused to see her or have anything to do with her. But she was his only child, you see. She begged him to forgive her and eventually he did. Then he suggested that Father enter the counting-house firm, which he did—

a tailor in the family would never have done, you know—and before long, Father became a partner. That was when it was first called Elliot, Field & Co. The company's London agents were becoming difficult about the accounts at that time, and my grandfather Elliot decided that Father should go to London and establish a bank there under the same name."

"And it was successful," I added.

"Yes—remarkably. Then when my grandfather Elliot died, he left everything to my mother. So my father gained complete control of the firm and, through the years, has made it the largest of its kind. It is enormously wealthy and powerful. Not like Rothschild's—Nathan's operation depends largely on his father and his brothers on the continent—but similar in its influence.

"And now your brother has taken control?"

"William. Yes, William is now the governor, thank the Lord, and an eminent banking authority in his own right. He lives in the house on Hanover Square in London. Happily married, no children, hates the country, and rarely comes down to Oakland Park."

"What of your mother, David?"

"She died in '32—typhus."

"I am so sorry. Will William be at Oakland Park this evening?"

"No, nor Malessa either. Just Father and my aunt Honoria, and you and I, of course. I am afraid Aunt Honoria has been dragged down here at the last moment to be hostess. She is father's sister and never married."

"You have another sister. Does she like the country?"

"That question does not arise, I am afraid. Silvia is practically disowned: the family does not speak of her in front of Father."

"Why?" I asked.

"Because she decided to become a nurse. Most unladylike in Father's eyes—disreputable and disgraceful, you know. She is at Kings College Hospital in London and the only one of the family who is doing anything for anybody else, really. Someday, nursing will be an honored profession—but meanwhile, poor Silvia is almost familyless."

"But you are doing something for somebody else. All your work and experiments are for other people."

"Yes—indirectly, but yes. I am helping in a way."

We had passed through the village as we talked, and now we drove along a lane that climbed the hills beyond.

I turned then, to look behind us and said, "There is the Horse Monument and the path from it down to the village."

"Yes," David replied. "When I rode to meet you there, I would cut across this field and then down to the wood below the hill. You will see Oakland Park in a minute."

As he said this, we swung abruptly to the right, through a gateway, and onto a drive which crossed a flat, grassy park.

And as we sped along, I asked, "Where will we live, David?"

"Here," he said, gesturing to the house which, at that moment, appeared from behind a row of ancient oak trees.

Now, across its park—beyond its terraced gardens— Oakland Park rose before me, and I gasped when I saw it.

"It is enormous, David," I said. "Why should anyone ever build such an enormous house? Could we stop a minute?"

"John," David called, "stop the carriage a minute, please."

I knew that he was trying to gauge my reactions to it as I sat gazing at the house. It was an immense, flat-sided, three-storied block of orange-pink brick—trimmed and decorated with gray stone—flanked by two stone wings. Large, symmetrically arranged, closely spaced windows pierced both the brick and stone facades: I counted forty-four windows in the front wall of the central brick portion, alone. At either end of this entrance facade, arched gables rose above the roof level. These were connected by a pillared parapet of stone, and above this rose the chimney stacks, also fashioned of orange-pink brick. And on either side of this central block of the house, extending from behind it, stretched the two stone wings. They stood three stories high also, were as long as the brick front was wide, and were covered with a blanket of ivy.

"But it is so friendly," I said. "How can anything so huge be so gracious and welcoming? It is lovely. And sunset is a marvelous time to see it, don't you think? I have never seen brick of such a lovely color—the light makes it positively glow."

"You like it? It was designed by Hugh May and begun in 1660. You have recognized his triumph—that something of its size can seem so intimate. It is the opposite of monumental and austere, somehow. It is the proportions that do it, I think. May, incidentally, was Dutch."

"Yes," I said, "it has a Dutch feeling, but somehow Italian as well. It is a thrilling house, David. I love it. Is that a church behind the left wing? And the little orangery connected to the end of the house beyond—it is enchanting."

"That is our chapel, and we are very proud of it. It is very old: the tower is Norman. Beyond the right wing, there, you can see the stable block, and beyond the trees, behind it, is the farm. See the tall, gray roof? That is the new cow barn. And there is a lake behind the house. I will row you to the island in the lake some warm, sunny afternoon, but I won't let you off until you do everything I tell you to do."

"Take me there soon," I said, "but I warn you, I can swim very well."

David laughed, and then he called up to the coachman to drive on. We half circled the house as we approached it and finally stopped before the entrance front where David helped me out of the carriage and up the single step to the door. It had already been opened by a footman in blue livery.

"Thank you, Peter," David said. "Wakley, where is Father?"

Wakley, the butler, stood just inside the door and answered, "In the Red Drawing Room, Sir."

Then David lifted the cloak from my shoulders and handed it to a maid who stood behind the butler. I removed my bonnet and gave it to her, too.

"We will see a little of the house on the way," David said, giving me his arm. "This is called the Painted Hall, because of the murals, obviously."

"Who painted them?" I asked.

"I don't know much about painting and that sort of thing," David said. "The staircase leads to the long Gallery above us, which stretches across the entire length of this part of the house. Lady Bateman, the former owner, held a reception for Queen Victoria there shortly after her coronation. One day I will show you an engraving of the scene. Now, through here is the Salon. . . ."

From the Salon, with its Van Dyck, Gainsborough, Romney, and Lawrence portraits, we passed into the State Drawing Room, its wood-paneled walls clothed in tapestries—which I later learned had been woven by Mortlake in 1620, after cartoons by Rubens. Then we passed through a room called the Blue Drawing Room, named after the blue Brussels tapestries which hung there, and through the Statue Gallery, and at last into the Red Drawing Room. It was a smaller, more intimate room than the others we had passed through and took its name from the red Genoa velvet which covered its walls. There sat David's Aunt Honoria, and, beneath an enormous Raphael, David's father.

"This is my father, Mary," David said, "and Aunt Honoria."

David's father rose and said, "Lady Beauford, I am so glad you could come."

"Thank you, Mr. Field," I said. "I have looked forward to it. Good evening, Miss Field."

David's aunt nodded, smiled, and moved her mouth in reply, but she did not speak.

"Sit here with me, Mary," David said.

We sat down on a sofa opposite his father and his aunt. Mr. Field sat down also. In the silence that followed, David's father and I examined each other—or, rather, he examined me, and I found my eyes glued to his face. I wanted to say something, but I was tongue-tied—unnerved by the man who sat opposite me. I tried to remember that David had said I was not to be afraid, but that didn't do any good.

It was not Mr. Field's general appearance that upset me. He was of medium height with gray hair and a lined, slightly sallow, slightly waxy complexion. He was not unusual looking in any way except for his eyes: they unnerved me. Unlike David's, his father's eyes were dark, almost black, with small irises surrounded by very clear whites. But it was the intellect that flashed from those eyes that was so awesome. The way they blazed, one felt that the mind behind them was almost supernaturally keen.

"How is Lord Clareham, Lady Beauford?" he asked at last.

"His condition does not seem to change very much, Mr. Field," I said. "He is still bedridden and paralyzed on the right side, though he sometimes seems to feel some sensation there."

"Ah, yes. A great pity. A most remarkable man. We are in his debt, to be sure, though memories are notoriously short in Parliament. I often wonder what the world would be like if our interests had lain in other directions—but that is useless speculation. And Lady Clareham?"

"She is well, but still grieves terribly for James."

"Yes, James was a fine young man."

"Yes," I said. "I liked him very much, though I never knew him well. Poor Vivian—I feel so sorry for her."

"She was, evidently, extremely upset by her brother's death," David's father said. "Much more so than one had imagined, apparently. But then you must know all about that. You must know her very well, having been such close friends for so many years."

"Yes, I think I can understand how crushed she must have been. She adored him, you know. When I first visited Vivian here at the Castle. . ."

And then, prompted every now and then by a question or an observation from David's father, I found myself telling him all about my friendship with Vivian—our school days together and our correspondence.

I didn't mind doing so: David's father seemed to want to know about it, and it was a relief to be making conversation. I had been apprehensive about this very thing— about what we would find to talk about during the evening.

". . . one draws away from a friend in some respects," I concluded, at length, "but many aspects of a relationship seem to be strengthened by absence, I find."

"Yes, perhaps that is so," Mr. Field said. "And do you find relationships with places strengthened by absence, too? How you must miss the magnificence of the continent here in the plainness of Devonshire."

"Oh, no. I love it here. I love being near the sea. When I am away from it, I find it less easy to breathe, somehow. And the Devonshire coast is more beautiful than anyplace on the coast of France or Holland. Yesterday, David and I rode almost all the way. . ."

I told him about our ride together and how beautiful it

was. This led me to think about a picnic that Vivian and Lord and Lady Clareham and I had had one afternoon at a very beautiful place near Clovelly, in 1852, and I told David and his father and aunt about that spectacular day.

". . . no, I love it here. It is my favorite place in all the world," I said.

"You must have missed England, then," David's father said. "David tells me that you have lived for years on the continent with your father, Lord Penbroke."

"Yes, for the last four years. I lived with my father in Paris in 1847, but then I returned to England to school. I rejoined him in Marienbad in the autumn of 1852 and remained with him until his death in 1854, in The Hague."

"Dinner is served, sir," Wakley announced from the doorway.

"Your father will take Lady Beauford in," Miss Field said to David, "and you and I will follow."

As we entered the dining room, I noticed that it was done in white and gray-green to set off the silver service and the elaborate silver epergnes and candelabra. But I had more important things to think about than the decor of the room or the silver and crystal on the table.

When we were seated at the table and had begun our soup, David's father said, "You were telling us of your life abroad, Lady Beauford."

"Yes—when I rejoined my father, he had taken a house in Marienbad. . . ." Then I described our life there and in Vienna, and Prague, and Rome.

"Your father never returned to England?" Mr. Field asked, when I had finished. "I believe he had a rather large house—I can almost remember its name—and substantial estates, in Sussex was it?"

"Gunderbury Hall in Kent," I replied. "No, he and Mother were happier on the continent."

"And your mother? Is she still there?"

"Yes, my mother has since remarried. My stepfather's name is van der Grooft. He is a farmer. They live just outside of Delft."

"Then you must know something about farming. I suppose you lived with them before you came back to England?"

"Yes, but I am afraid I know very little about it, Mr. Field."

"You know, of course, that it is David's primary interest—almost his only one. He thinks of nothing else. Did you ever hear from Sir John about the corn-clover cycle?" he asked David.

"Yes, David replied, "and it is incredible. . . ."

All through the second course, his father encouraged David to talk about his experiments and the problems on the farm. I knew that Mr. Field was watching my reaction, and I tried to seem interested. But as a relief to this, I addressed a remark or two to Miss Field. She, however, barely replied. I found out later that she had been told to be silent during dinner.

While we drank our coffee together after dinner, in the Blue Drawing Room, we chatted about flowers, which were her passion, and waited for David and his father to join us.

When they did, David's father sat down opposite me, and David sat beside me on the sofa.

"Has there been any further news from Vivian?" Mr. Field asked, shortly after they had arrived.

"No, there has been no other word since she wrote to me that she was going to America."

"Life is a very strange thing, isn't it?" he said. "Things change quickly, completely—often within a seemingly impossible amount of time. Two months ago, I had expected to welcome Vivian into our family. You know that David and Vivian were engaged to be married."

"Yes."

"One never knows, does one, what fate has in store? That relationship has ended, of course. And now another delightful young lady has come to Castle Cloud." He smiled at me then.

"Yes," I said, "but fate was not kind enough to bring me here in time to see my friend."

"No. You must have been disappointed. How long have you been visiting at the Castle, now? A month?"

"Six weeks, I think. It will soon be seven."

"And now David has asked you to marry him, and you have accepted him."

"Yes."

"Father!" David said. "I did not ask Mary here to be questioned and bullied."

"It is I who have asked Lady Beauford here," his father

said. "And I do not intend to bully her, David. But you wish to marry her and you have asked for my consent. That was wise of you, but I cannot give it merely by seeing how lovely the young lady looks, or by listening to her delightful conversation. There are things one must know before consenting to something as important as this."

"Your father is right, David," I said. "I shall be happy to answer any questions he cares to ask. Yes, Mr. Field, I wish to marry David, and he wishes to marry me." Then I smiled at him.

I had wondered all evening if something like this would happen. Now it had, and there was to be no beating about the bush: his approach was to be direct. I liked that.

Mr. Field studied me for a moment. Then he said, "I am sure that you realize the seriousness of this decision and have thought about it very carefully and at some length."

"Yes."

"Forgive me, my dear, but since your father is no longer here to guide you, allow me to be presumptuous and speak like one. Do you think this is wise? Have you considered the future?"

"I know," I said, "that David and I have known each other for a short time, but I do not think that is necessarily important."

"I was not thinking about the length of time you have known my son, Lady Beauford. I was thinking of your very old and distinguished family."

"Yes, but I love David, Mr. Field."

"But there are other considerations."

"As far as I am concerned, none. I would never wish to associate with people who would find it difficult to accept David and me after our marriage, if that is what you are referring to. We will have many friends, just the same, and we will have each other."

"You are of a liberal turn of mind and an idealist as well, it would seem."

"Yes, I think so. But a marriage requires more than liberal ideas and idealism: I need the security that David can provide, and his protection."

"You speak of security—" Mr. Field said. He did not finish the sentence: he had not meant to.

"Yes. I think every woman needs to feel secure—needs to know that the man she marries will provide for her."

"You should know then, that David has nothing. He is doing valuable work for me here as my steward, for which I pay him £450 a year, but he has nothing except what I pay him and what he can save from it. Now, suppose I should decide to replace him?"

"You have no right to ask these things of Mary, Father," David said. "It isn't done."

"I am sure Lady Beauford realizes that I do not mean to be rude—rudeness is a waste of time—nor am I antagonistic toward her in any way. I have no reason to be. I have heard nothing but the most complimentary things about Lady Beauford. I was prepared to be enchanted by her, and she has not disappointed me. What is more, she is obviously an intelligent woman who is aware of the desirability of speaking, at times, quite candidly. She and I understand each other, I think, and will get on superbly. Your apprehensions, David, are quite unfounded." Then his eyes returned to my face, and he smiled at me again.

"If David were penniless, Mr. Field," I said, "with no prospect of ever having more than enough to provide a roof over our heads and food for our mouths, I would marry him. If he could not provide that, I would marry him anyway. I could not face the future without him. I certainly do not wish to marry him because of any money or property you may wish to give him. How could I? I have no knowledge of these things."

"And if I do not give my blessing?"

"I do not know, Mr. Field. I earnestly hope that you will. I have told David that if you do not give your consent that I will not marry him. I think that that was hasty, and if you do not give your consent, I will certainly reconsider. I must think what is best for David. If marrying him could possibly do him any harm, then I would not."

"And you have principles, it would seem," he said.

"Certainly," I replied. "I find it necessary to like myself, Mr. Field. Consequently my standards of behavior are high."

"Father hoped you would play and sing for us," David said, almost before I had finished.

He was unmistakably upset by his father's and my conversation, and this was an excuse to end it. His remark, I noticed, brought a glance of amused affection from his father.

"I would love to," I said.

So we adjourned to the music room where I played some Chopin and sang two of Mendelssohn's songs. And when I had finished, I got up from the piano and sat beside David.

"That was delightful. Thank you, Lady Beauford," Mr. Field said.

"Won't you call me Mary, Mr. Field?" I asked.

"Very well, Mary. I have been wondering ever since we spoke about it during dinner, why your father and mother never returned to England."

"Because my mother was never accepted socially here. You see, she had once been a parlor maid at Gunderbury Hall. She was never to become part of Papa's world, really, but they both felt more comfortable living on the continent."

"I think David told me that you are an only child."

"Yes, and I was always terribly lonely for brothers and sisters. I always envied children in big families. I would never have only one child if I could have more. I don't think it is fair to a child to be alone."

"Then you like children?" David's father asked.

"Oh, yes!"

"And I suppose you would plan a large family."

"Yes, if David wanted a large family too."

"It is getting late," David said, "and I think I had better take Mary home now." He got up and pulled the bellpull. Looking at his father, he said, "I am sure the evening has been an ordeal for her. She must be exhausted."

Soon Wakley announced that the carriage was at the entrance front, and I said my good-nights. Then David led me through the house and, after I had put on my cloak and bonnet, out to the carriage. He handed me up into it, and we drove off.

"Do you think he liked me?" I asked, as we sped down the drive, away from Oakland Park.

"Yes. Well, how could he help it?" David said, reaching for my hand. "And if possible, *I* love you all the more after tonight. You were wonderful, darling," Then he whispered: "If it weren't for John and Peter, I would kiss you right here and now."

"Don't you dare, David Field," I said, laughing.

"Mary, I had no idea he would act like that. What he put you through! It was humiliating and distressing. But parents will be parents. What can you do when it is your father? Can you ever forgive him—and me?"

"There is nothing to forgive. He acted the way I should imagine a banker would act. A son's marriage is a serious piece of business, David."

"Why did you say that?" David asked.

"Well, isn't it? Do you think he liked me?"

"Yes, I am sure of it."

"Well? When will he give his permission?"

"When he has thought it over very carefully, I imagine. He will want to see you again, probably—maybe more than once, to clear up anything he missed tonight. Who knows? He is not like most people. He is difficult to read."

"Yes, I could see that. Well, you give me hope, anyway. It must be all right, David. He *must* give his consent."

"He will. Now, don't worry. If he shouldn't, we will be married anyway—we are both of age. Now, do you think you can get along without me for a few days? I have some business to attend to."

"Oh, David. Where?"

"Camelford."

"But that is in Cornwall."

"Yes."

"Is it really necessary?"

"Mary, we have sixty thousand acres here in Devonshire and Cornwall, and I am responsible. There will be many times when I will have to go off and tend to things."

"Of course, David. I am sorry—it is just that I will miss you so much. What is the problem down there?"

"There is a dispute over a boundary between two farms, and the farmers have turned nasty about it. And there is a drainage scheme which I should see to while I am there."

"When will you be back?" I asked.

"Thursday, or Friday at the latest—as soon as I can, my love. I will miss you too, you know—perhaps more than you will miss me."

"I hope so. It will serve you right for leaving me alone and in suspense about your father's decision. Oh, look at the moon, David. Why is it so huge when it is low in the sky?"

"Because I love you so much."

"That is why the moon is huge?"

"Uh-huh."

❧ Chapter Fifteen ❧

JANE SPENCE brought my tea the following morning, and while I sipped it and waited for Mrs. Muldoon to fix my bath, I thought about the evening before. It had been a successful dinner at Oakland Park: I could not think of any mistakes or misjudgments that I had made, and I thought I had come through Mr. Field's examination with high marks.

But then I thought about the days ahead. What would I do with myself during the long, dreary days? I wondered. Monday, Tuesday, Wednesday, and perhaps even Thursday were to be gotten through before I would see David again or hear if his father had made up his mind about our marriage. I did not suspect, as I sat in bed drinking my tea, that I would have some curious things to tell David when I saw him again.

David had told me a little about his father the night before, but I wanted to know more about him. I thought that if I did, I might be better able to predict his reaction to David's and my marriage. So, after breakfast, I visited Lord Clareham to ask what he knew about David's father. He had little to tell me about Mr. Field, however, as he had not known him very long. Because of his illness, they had met only a few times. He did seem to know something about Elliot, Field & Co., though, and he seemed in awe of it.

"It is the largest and most famous of the old private banks, Mary," he said, at one point. "... immensely wealthy, with investments worldwide. Just as an example, and this I know about from personal experience, shortly before Waterloo, the East India Company had, it was thought, £800,000 worth of gold to sell. But the sum was actually £1,200,000. Eight hundred thousand pounds worth of the gold was sold to N. M. Rothschild and

Sons—that is known—but who bought the rest? Elliot, Field & Co. did—that is not generally known. Then, during the famous panic that sent consol prices plummeting, who bought at the last minute? Nathan Rothschild bought an enormous parcel of consols at a song, and at almost the same moment, so did Thomas Field. Field was only a young man at the time, and even then, you can see how astute he was. Their buying sent prices soaring. Who knows how many hundreds of thousands of pounds those two men made in that one day?

"I don't think anyone knows what the assets of Elliot, Field & Co. are. We would probably be terrified if we found out. I do not think it wise for power of that kind to be in the hands of one man or one family."

We talked about other things then, and finally I left him. But since we had talked much longer than usual, I had time for only a brief stroll in the rose garden before luncheon. And in the early afternoon, I changed into Vivian's habit and, accompanied by Colen, took Chocolate for a run, following the route which David and I had taken the Friday before. The afternoon had turned overcast, however, and the countryside and sea were not as pretty as they had been on Friday.

We returned to the Castle about five o'clock, and as I entered the house, Mitchell was crossing the rotunda from the direction of the dining room.

"Oh, Mitchell," I said, "could you take a moment to show me the wine cellar? I am terribly curious to see it—it must be fascinating, and now, before changing for dinner, would be a perfect time to do it."

"I am afraid I could not spare the time at the moment, my lady," he replied. "His lordship insists that meals be served on time. There is much to be done, and I cannot neglect my duties."

"When *would* be a convenient time for you, Mitchell?"

"It is most difficult to say, my lady. Please allow me to suggest a time in the near future. Now, if you will excuse me—"

He hurried past me then, and disappeared down the stairs to the servants' hall. I climbed to my room to change for dinner.

During dinner that evening, I decided to tell Edmond

about William Reade's bag and gloves and get it over with.

So when we were seated at the table, I said, "Edmond, there is something I have been meaning to tell you—something you should know about. I should have told you before, but I did not know whether it was connected with Sarah or not, and it may not be."

"Sarah?" he said. "What could possibly interest me about Sarah?"

"After you left, Mr. McComb and I buried her. That is, Mr. McComb buried her and I watched. Well, the only place where there was enough earth to bury Sarah in was behind the hedge where Mr. Reade had stood when he shot her. In that same place, Mr. McComb found a pair of thick leather gloves which had belonged to Mr. Reade—I had seen them in the Reade cottage when I visited Alice—and, with the gloves, he found a large leather sack. We buried Sarah in the sack, and the gloves along with her."

"I don't see that that is a very significant or even particularly interesting bit of information, Mary. No doubt there is a hare run there. I have seen them crossing the walk dozens of times. Reade had come to bag one, I suppose."

"Yes, that is possible. It is also possible, Edmond, that he brought Sarah there in the sack."

"That is absurd. Why should he do a thing like that?"

"Well, I thought you should know," I replied.

"Huh," he said.

We fell silent then. It was a heavy silence, and I was determined to break it. At last, for want of something better, I said, "Do you know that on Wednesday I will have been visiting you for seven weeks? It doesn't seem possible, does it?"

"I am glad that time goes quickly for you, Mary," Lady Clareham said. "I hope you never find the days and weeks interminable."

"You look tired this evening," I said to her.

"I am not feeling very well, my dear."

"Parliament adjourns tomorrow," Edmond said.

"And Wednesday," Mitchell said, "is the thirteenth of August, if I may say so, my lord."

"Well? What of it, Mitchell?" Edmond said.

"Well, my lord, when the thirteenth of the month falls on a Wednesday, it is said to be an extremely lucky day, if you will pardon my saying so, my lord."

"Lucky?" Edmond said.

"Just a bit of irrelevant information, if you will excuse it, my lord."

"Is that so? A lucky day, you say? Yes, I have heard that, Mitchell. As a matter of fact, I believe it is a common bit of superstition."

"Quite so, my lord."

Edmond turned to me then, and said, "I plan to leave Castle Cloud on the afternoon train tomorrow, Mary. As I was telling Mother earlier, it is a very festive night, the night Parliament adjourns. And I have friends in London who will be—ah—celebrating and whom I have not seen in some time. I shall stay with them for a few days—perhaps until Saturday or Sunday—though I suppose London will be rather dull by then. Just think: tomorrow at this time I shall be dining at White's and looking forward to an evening of theatre."

"I hope you have a lovely time, Edmond," I said.

"I always do in London, thank you," he replied.

The following day then, Tuesday, Edmond left for London, as he said he would, directly after luncheon—in the rain.

It had begun to rain about ten o'clock that morning, and the day had grown grayer and darker as it progressed. It was a perfect day to reread *Wuthering Heights*. And that is what I did, snuggled in an armchair in the drawing room with Catherine and Heathcliff, while gusts of wind slapped at the windows outside.

But by evening the storm had passed, and as I waited for Mitchell to announce dinner, the color of the park outside the windows changed from gray-green to rose—forcasting a lovely day to follow.

Lady Clareham did not come down, and when Mitchell announced dinner, I asked about her.

He replied, "Her ladyship's fever has returned, my lady. She has had dinner in her room, and Cecile has informed me that she will probably remain there for a day or two until she has recovered."

*   *   *

On Wednesday, before luncheon, I had just finished combing my hair when Mrs. Muldoon knocked on my door.

When she came into my room, she said, "If there's nothing more you'll be wanting this afternoon, my lady, Mr. Mitchell has given me the afternoon off. If it's anything you're needing this evening before dinner, Jane Spence will be back and she'll do it for you, my lady, if that would be satisfactory. And if it's anything you're needing now, I'll go and get it for you."

"Thank you Mrs. Muldoon," I said. "No, there is nothing. Have a nice afternoon."

" 'Mrs. Muldoon,' *Mr.* Mitchell says to me, 'Mrs. Muldoon, 'tis hard you've worked and well, and it's a reward you're to have. You will take the afternoon off. It's Mrs. Foley that insists upon it,' he says. 'You will leave directly after luncheon has been served, and it's not until tomorrow morning that you are to return.' Holy saints, you could have pushed me over with your little finger. Imagine *Mr.* Mitchell complimenting me on my work! What's the world coming to, I wonder."

"I am sure I don't know, Mrs. Muldoon, but we must take our pleasure when we can—run along and enjoy it."

"Which reminds me, my lady, do you know why it's pleasure that's like the medicine bill, my lady?" Mrs. Muldoon asked, her eyes twinkling.

"No, Mrs. Muldoon," I said. "Why is pleasure like the medicine bill?"

"Because—Ha, ha, ha. Because the cost of it increases the older you get. Ha, ha, ha. The cost of it increases the older you get. Ha, ha, ha."

I didn't understand what was so funny, but Mrs. Muldoon did not stay long enough to notice that. She had hurried away even while she was still laughing.

Soon after Mrs. Muldoon had left me, I went down to luncheon where I sat alone at the table. Mitchell served me, as usual, but there seemed to be a hint of deference in his manner. I thought at first that I must be mistaken about it. I had done nothing that could possibly change his attitude toward me.

But a little later, I believed I was correct when he said, "It is a very pleasant day, my lady."

"Yes, Mitchell, it is quite lovely," I replied.

"A perfect day to be out-of-doors, I should say, my lady."

"Yes, Mitchell. As a matter of fact, I plan to walk to the village after luncheon," I said. "Is there a shop in the village that might have handkerchiefs and bits of ribbon and the like?"

"Oh yes, my lady, adjoining the post office in the stone house down the lane from the church. Just walk along past the church and around the bend in the road, and you will see it, my lady."

So after luncheon, I changed into a pair of walking shoes, put on a bonnet, threw a light shawl about my shoulders and, taking my gloves and reticule, set out for the village to buy a pair of stockings.

The sun shone through a thin haze, and a light breeze brushed my face as I strolled across the grass circle and ambled through the rose garden toward the path that led over the hill past the Horse Monument. But it was not until I had walked through the fringe of trees at the base of the hill that a thought struck me with a jolt. Suddenly I remembered that I had never written to Lord Mauldridge. On Thursday, after David had proposed to me, I had torn up the letter I had begun writing to him, and I had never written another! I wondered how I could have forgotten to do so, so completely. It was extremely ill-mannered of me, and I decided to return to the house immediately, write the letter—which could be very brief—carry it to the village, and post it that afternoon so that Lord Mauldridge could have my decision without further delay. It was still early, and I would have plenty of time to do this before it was time to dress for dinner.

I hurried back to the house then, and began to write the letter. Shortly, I heard a horse and carriage approaching the east front and looked out of the window to see whose it was. It was not a carriage, however, but a wagon, and Mitchell was driving it. The wagon was drawn by one of the docile old carriage horses from the castle's stables, and as I watched, it lumbered around the grass circle and stopped before the steps to the east portico. Then I saw Mitchell jump down from the seat, but I did not see him climb the steps to the house. I could see only part of the stairway from the window, though, and I supposed he had, and that I would hear him enter the vestibule in a moment. But though I listened, I did not hear a door open or close, nor did I hear footsteps.

I did not think any more about it then, and returned to my letter. But after a few sentences, I became curious about the wagon and got up from the table, walked across the library, and through it into a tiny study. Here, a window to the right of the east portico, corresponded to the drawing room window to the left of the portico, where I had been sitting. From here I would have a better view of the wagon.

It was not the wagon, however, that interested me as I peeked through a crack in the curtains, but what was happening on a narrow flight of steps beside the staircase to the east portico. I had never noticed this flight of steps before. They descended from the ground level to the areaway which surrounded the basement of the house. Up these steps staggered Mitchell carrying a basket of bottles. Then I realized that the stairway I had found in the cellar, during my explorations there, led up to the areaway where it passed beneath the east portico, and that Mitchell must have carried his basket up that stairway, along the areaway beneath the portico, and now lugged it up these narrow steps to the drive where the wagon stood.

The bottles he carried, I was sure, came from the wine cellar. And then, all at once, I thought that if there were other baskets of them to be carried up to the wagon, I might, if I rushed down to the cellar, catch Mitchell there during one of his trips and demand that he show me the wine cellar.

I watched him hoist the basket into the wagon, descend the steps, walk along the areaway, and vanish beneath the east portico. Then I ran into the hall, took a candle from its shelf by the stairs, and descended to the oak door which led down into the cellar. It was unlocked, and I opened it: but this time, after I had lit my candle and had begun to descend the stairs, I left the door open to help light my way.

This descent was easier because Mitchell had placed lighted lanterns on the cellar floor below, and they helped me to see the way down. But when I reached the bottom of the stairs, I found the cellar deserted. Mitchell had evidently made a trip to the wagon and had not yet returned.

In front of me, the wine cellar door stood open, and just inside it, a lighted lantern hung by a peg in the wall.

I saw no reason to stand in front of the open door waiting for Mitchell to return, so I walked into the wine cellar, took the lantern from its peg, and held it above my head. I examined the room. On the floor, immediately inside the doorway, sat eight baskets of empty bottles neatly arranged in a line, waiting for Mitchell to carry them away. Beyond them, lining all four walls of the room and standing free in the center of it, stood several wine racks. I walked between them all, but found nothing unusual. The racks held hundreds of bottles of wine and seemed neatly arranged. The coffin, however, was not there.

Having finished my exploration, I hung the lantern on its peg and was about to leave the room when I noticed bits of straw protruding through the sides of the baskets on the floor, catching the light. The bottles had been packed between layers of straw. Wasn't it odd to be so careful of empty bottles? Suppose a few did break in transit, would that be such a loss? Then the thought flashed through my mind: suppose the bottles are not empty. Quickly I stopped and lifted three of the empty bottles from the nearest basket. The bottles lying beneath them were still corked.

Then I heard footsteps. Mitchell was returning. I barely had time to replace the empty bottles and straighten up before he appeared.

"Well, this is a surprise, my lady," he said. "I was under the impression that you were on your way to the village."

"I was, Mitchell," I answered, "but I found that I had forgotten something and returned to the house. It will not be necessary for you to show me the wine cellar: I have already seen it. I am afraid it did not live up to my romantic expectations. I found it dusty and uninteresting. I am sorry to have disturbed you. I will leave you, now, to your work."

Then I left the room and, without looking back, walked past him to the stairs I had used, and began to climb them. I had left my candle on the floor beside the wine cellar door, but I did not go back for it. Instead, I continued to climb through the darkness, keeping my eyes on the lighted oblong of the open doorway above, and finally emerged safely into the basement hall.

From there, I climbed to the second floor of the house, hurried to Lord Clareham's room, and knocked on his door. Ahmad opened it a crack, and as he stared at me, put his finger to his lips and shook his head.

"But I must see him," I said. "It is important, Ahmad."

I do not know whether he understood my words or simply the urgency in my tone, but he held up his hand, signaling me to wait, and closed the door. When he opened it a few moments later, Lord Clareham was awake and propped up in bed on his pillows.

"Is something wrong?" he asked.

"I am sorry to disturb you, Lord Clareham, but something is happening which I think you should know about."

"Sit here," he said. "What is it?"

"It is really none of my business, but Edmond is away, and this is the Wednesday that Colen takes Mrs. Foley and Monsieur Laval to Barnstaple to shop, and you know that Jane Spence and May Brooke have Wednesday afternoons off, and today Mitchell insisted that Mrs. Muldoon take the afternoon off too. And Lady Clareham is in bed. So there is no one here to tell you that Mitchell is stealing your wine."

"What?" Lord Clareham exclaimed.

"Well, he is carrying baskets of wine bottles out of the cellar and loading them onto a wagon right now. I thought they were merely empty bottles until I discovered the ones below the top layer are still corked.

"Are you sure? He let you examine the baskets?"

Then I told Lord Clareham exactly how I had made the discovery. "So you see," I concluded, "I thought you should know about it."

"I will have a word with him," Lord Clareham said.

"But by then it will be too late. The wine will be gone and you won't even know which bottles he has taken. Edmond said some of the bottles down there are quite valuable and. . ."

"I will talk with Mitchell *later,* Mary."

"Yes, of course," I replied. Then, after a moment, I looked at Lord Clareham and said, "The reason I wanted to see the wine cellar was to see if the other coffin was there. I searched the rest of the cellar last Saturday, but I did not find it."

Lord Clareham stared at me, but he did not speak.

"Mr. Podock said that he had carried it there himself," I said.

"My dear," Lord Clareham said, "I don't know what you are talking about. What other coffin?"

"Mr. Podock said that both you and Edmond ordered coffins for James, and that Edmond had insisted on keeping the extra one."

"That is nonsense, Mary. There was a slight mix-up, but it was straightened out at once. Podock is imaginative in the extreme, to put it kindly. In his line of work, it is not surprising. He will be paid for his inconvenience, but there was only one coffin for James. What would we want with a coffin in the cellar?"

"I see," I said. "Well, I am glad to know that it was just a story. Now, I will let you get on with your nap, and I have a letter to write. I am so sorry to have disturbed you."

Then I left him, but I did not go down to the drawing room. Instead, I climbed the stairs to the floor above where, under the sloping roof, were the schoolroom, sewing room, nursery, nurse's, governess's, and nanny's rooms, and storage rooms were located. But I did not find the coffin there either. Then I thought of the dome above me and the lantern that topped it. And I wondered if the coffin might be wedged between the massive beams which held up the structure.

To find out, I needed only climb the narrow stairway which rose to the cupola between the inner and outer shells of the dome, and look. The stairway was odd in that it began almost immediately behind the door in the corridor. Only the tiniest triangular landing lay in front of the first step, and if I had not remembered to step up almost as soon as I had passed through the doorway, I would surely have stumbled in the gloom. And it was a steep, winding stair, but I climbed it without mishap, looking among the beams as I went. I did not find the coffin there, however. Nor did I find it in the lantern itself when I reached the top.

"There would barely be room for it here," I whispered to myself, as I looked into the little room.

The cupola was round and only about seven feet in diameter. To reach it, one climbed the stairs and entered through a rectangular hole in the floor which was almost as large as the floor area itself, and once inside it, unless one unhooked and lowered the hinged trap door into place, he would have only the narrowest strip of floor around the stairwell to walk on.

I stepped up into the lantern, closed the trapdoor, and sat down on the circular wooden bench which ringed it.

"What a charming little belvedere this could have been," I remembered saying to Vivian, when she had first shown it to me, and I wondered again that afternoon why it had never been finished on the inside.

Its walls were almost entirely of glass, and as I looked out, I could see from the park, on all sides of the house directly below me, to all points on the horizon—the bay, the mountains, and the sea.

And I sat there for almost an hour looking down at the grounds of the Castle, wondering what secrets lay hidden from me there.

I finished the letter to Lord Mauldridge the next morning. I had not been able to force myself to write it the afternoon before. And anyway, after I had talked with Lord Clareham, investigated the top floor of the house, and daydreamed in the lantern, there had not been time to walk to the village and back before dinner time. So I had decided to write the letter directly after breakfast the following day, take it with me when I went to the store, and mail it at the post office.

By the time I had finished writing it, the dew had dried on the grass, and shortly afterward, I left the house and walked over the hill to the village.

It was a glorious morning for a walk. A steady breeze, cool and dry, blew from the northeast—from Norway—chasing the clouds away and leaving the sky's blue bowl bare.

On such a day it seemed a pity to go indoors even for a few minutes, and I was almost sorry when I reached my destination.

The post office had been easy to find. As Mitchell had said, it and a store occupied together half the ground floor of a large ivy-covered, stone house on the main road, beyond the church. A sign above the doorway of the building read: MILTON PENDERTON POST OFFICE, and under it a smaller sign had been fastened to the stones which said simply: STORE.

The door of the house opened to the tinkle of a bell, and I stepped into a hall which ended in a staircase rising to the second floor of the building. The walls on either side of me were pierced with two doors: the one to my left was closed, but the one to my right was open and revealed the post office and store beyond. The one-room store had four windows, and shelf-lined walls displayed the store's merchandise. At the end of the room above a small table, a shallow wooden cabinet hung on the wall. It was divided into cubbyholes in which letters lay. Nearer me stood a much larger table—long and narrow—which served as the store's counter.

A woman stood behind the long table, waiting on two girls about my age. One of the girls had bought some fabric which the proprietress was folding for her. They were so engrossed in conversation that they had not heard me enter.

"In broad daylight," one of the girls said. "Bearded and masked and with guns blazing. Lord Portland gave it to him: what else could he do?"

Then the woman behind the counter saw me, and the two girls, following her eyes, turned around.

"Please don't let me interrupt," I said. "May I look about until you are finished?"

"Certainly, my lady," the woman said. "I will be with you in just a moment."

A short murmured conversation between the three women followed, and in less than a minute the two girls left the store, scrutinizing me on their way out.

"I am sorry to have kept you waiting, my lady," the proprietress said. "May I help you?"

"I would like to buy a pair of stockings," I said.

Then she asked me what size I wore and showed me her selection.

After I had made my choice and paid for the stockings, she asked, "And how is his lordship, my lady? As I was saying to Mr. Hollycombe at dinner last evening, my lady, 'I do hope his lordship will recover. How dreadfully tiresome it must be for him—in bed the whole time, like he is, and half-paralyzed, they say.' 'Now, now, my dear,' he says to me, 'you mustn't worry about his lordship. He must be a strong man to have lived all those years in India. And if anybody will get better, he will. You can take my word on that.' That's just what he said, my lady."

"How thoughtful of you to ask, Mrs. Hollycombe," I said. "He is feeling a little better, and there seems to be some feeling in his right side. We are very hopeful that he will recover completely." I reached into my bag and drew out the letter to Lord Mauldridge. "Will you post this for me, Mrs. Hollycombe? And can you tell me when it will arrive?"

"Oh, no, my lady. It's Mr. Hollycombe that's the postmaster, my lady. He can tell you. If you could wait for just a moment, I'll go and tell him you're here."

Mrs. Hollycombe left me, crossed the hall, and opened the door beyond. I heard her say, "It's Lady Beauford from the Castle, Herbert. . . ." A mumbled exchanged followed, but I could not hear what was said.

In a few moments she returned with her husband. Mr. Hollycombe was a short man, not more than five feet tall, with thick white hair—some of which stood on end. I was sure that his wife had waked him from his afternoon nap.

"Ah, Lady Beauford," Mr. Hollycombe said, as he walked toward me, "this is a coincidence—a coincidence indeed. How very fortunate that you should arrive just as I was about to set out personally for the Castle. I owe you an apology—a very deep apology indeed. I have a letter for you. Somehow it was misplaced when sorting the mail. It should have been given to Mr. Taylor this morning, but somehow I believe it knew that your ladyship was coming and decided to wait here to be received personally, so to speak."

By this time he had walked past me to the post office portion of the room, reached into one of the cubbyholes in the cabinet on the wall, returned to me, and handed me a letter.

"I trust you will forgive the delay, my lady," he said, "but it would be only a matter of two or three hours, I believe."

"That is perfectly all right, Mr. Hollycombe. I understand. There is no harm done. Thank you."

I glanced at the letter as I took it from him. It was postmarked London, and above the return address appeared the name N. Schraw, Esq.

"Will you post this for me?" I asked, as I handed Mr. Hollycombe the letter to Lord Mauldridge. "When will it arrive at Flowerwick Hall?"

"With pleasure, my lady," he said. "It will go to Barnstaple tonight, my lady, then to Exeter, then to Bampton—tomorrow, my lady."

"Thank you Mr. Hollycombe and Mrs. Hollycombe," I said. "I must be getting back to the Castle, and it is such a lovely day that it seems a pity to stay indoors. Good-by."

"How is Lady Vivian getting on?" Mr. Hollycombe asked, before I could walk away.

"Very well, I believe, Mr. Hollycombe. It is good of you to ask. Well. . ."

"It's not an easy road," he said, shaking his head.

"I beg your pardon?" I asked.

"It's not an easy road, but a rewarding one, my lady. Nothing like it, my lady." Then with elaborate gestures he continued: " 'Where is our usual manager of mirth? What revels are in hand? Is there no play, to ease the anguish of a torturing hour?' " After he had finished this recitation, he stood still, staring at me pop-eyed with his arm raised above his head.

"That was excellent, Mr. Hollycombe," I said. "Now, I really must go."

"I toured with the Keans, my lady."

"Oh?"

"Birmingham, Liverpool, Manchester, Bristol, Newcastle, Portsmouth, Plymouth. It's not an easy road. I had to give it up—my height was against me, my lady. Will she be coming this way, do you suppose?"

"Who?"

"Lady Vivian. We've a very good theatre in Exeter, you know—the St. James's."

"I don't understand, Mr. Hollycombe," I said. "What connection could Lady Vivian have with a theatre in Exeter?"

"Oh, now you don't have to pretend with me, my lady," he said. "There's very little that can stay hid from the postmaster—that's if he's got anything up here." He tapped his head with one finger. "And though most would be shocked in this unenlightened age, my lady, you see before you a brother of the boards. Lady Vivian was born to it. As I was saying to Mrs. Hollycombe not long ago, I said, 'Lady Vivian was born for the theatre. It was what she loved—look at the theatricals she was always arranging. Why they did Tom Taylor's *Contested Election* at the Castle two years ago this summer and the *Heart Wreck* and *The Merchant Son* before that. She'll play the Drury Lane, and it won't be long either, and I'll be there to see her do it.' That's what I says to Mrs. Hollycombe."

"But Mr. Hollycombe, how could you possibly suspect that?"

"Very easy, my lady," he said, chuckling. "Very easy— a simple matter of deduction. Lady Vivian is going to marry Mr. Field, but instead she goes off, says good-by to no one, and she writes to no one and no one writes to her. 'Well, they've disowned her,' I says to Mrs. Hollycombe. 'They don't write to her because they disowned her, and she don't write because she's been disowned.' Then your ladyship arrives, being an old friend of Lady Vivian—as Mrs. Muldoon tells us. And Lady Vivian writes to your ladyship, but your ladyship doesn't write back. 'Now why don't Lady Beauford answer her friend's letter?' I ask Mrs. Hollycombe. 'Because she's not in one place long enough to receive them. She's playing the provinces—Manchester one night and Bristol the next—I know what that is,' I says to Mrs. Hollycombe. 'Newcastle the next and Portsmouth the next. . . .'"

"And *I* says to Mr. Hollycombe," Mrs. Hollycombe interrupted, "'But you can write to an actress if you've a mind to.' That's what I says to Mr. Hollycombe. 'That's nonsense,' I says. 'And Lady Vivian never ran off to the stage, you can be sure of that,' but it was odd, I must say. She was very close to her mother. Her ladyship loved her and his late, young lordship more than anything in this world.

"They're like family to us—her ladyship is like a mother to us all—so it's natural that we're concerned, my lady. 'Well,' I says to Mr. Hollycombe, 'even if she ran off with— Well, even if she ran off, as some say, her father might not write to her, being a very strict man, but her ladyship would write to her just the same. And Lady Beauford is her best friend—why they've written back and forth for years. Why didn't anyone write to Lady Vivian?' I says."

"But I did write to Lady Vivian," I said. "I answered both her letters. Weren't they posted?"

"No, my lady." Mr. Hollycombe said. "Letters to a lady in Holland, I suppose they would be to your mother, a letter to the dowager countess, and another letter to a lady in Cornwall, and a letter to Lady Withering, but no letters to Lady Vivian, my lady. I'm certain of that. We were looking for them. Oh, we're extra careful of all the letters from the Castle, you see—we give them special attention, my lady. No, there was no letter to Lady Vivian." Having finished speaking, he stood very still and gazed at me with unabashed curiosity.

Mrs. Hollycombe was equally curious.

"I— Oh, how stupid of me," I said, "I gave them both to Lord Althrop—he must have posted them in London. Thank you for the letter, Mr. Hollycombe. I really must run or I shall be late for luncheon."

And I did just that: I turned, ran from the store, hurried down the road, and did not slacken my pace until I had reached the churchyard.

I was still holding the letter from Mr. Schraw in my hand as I entered the churchyard and crossed it, to a wooden bench which leaned against the wall of the church. I sat down, examined the envelope, paused to wonder how Mr. Schraw could possibly have known I was at Castle Cloud, tore open the envelope, and read:

Dear Lady Beauford,

There is a very important matter which I wish to discuss with you, and which, believe me, you will find greatly to your benefit.

Unfortunately, my health will not permit me to journey to the country; consequently I must ask that you call at my office at the earliest opportunity.

May I suggest Monday, August 18th, at 3:00 P.M. as an appropriate time? If, for any reason, you cannot meet with me on that day, I urge you to write so informing me of that fact so that an alternate date can be arranged.

I am, my lady, your obedient and faithful servant,
                                        Nathaniel P. Schraw

28 Threadneedle Street, August 12

The letter surprised and mystified me. I sat there on the bench in the sunlight and read it over and over, learning nothing, of course, more than I had learned the first time I had read it.

It was not merely then that I decided to go to London to meet Mr. Schraw the following Monday. It was, I felt, more as though my journey had been preordained and was inevitable. I wondered, however, about the expense of it, as I had very little money. I could afford to stay a day or two in London if it became necessary, but I hoped that it would be possible to take an early morning train to the city on Monday and return to Castle Cloud late that same afternoon or evening. This would mean a long and exhausting day, but I would rather that then spend the money for a hotel room and stay overnight in London all alone.

Still, whatever was necessary would have to be done, and since it was useless to speculate about what Mr. Schraw wanted to discuss with me, I put the letter in my bag, got up from the bench, and hurried back over the hill to the Castle, where I hoped to find Colen. I wanted to talk to him, and I wanted to do so before luncheon.

Colen sat on a stool outside the tack room doorway in the stable yard, mending the strap on a harness. When he saw me approach, he rose and said, "Good morning, my lady."

"Good morning, Colen," I said. "Isn't it a lovely morning?"

"Yes, my lady. Will you be riding out on Chocolate this afternoon, my lady? If not, I would like to take the gig to the smithy in Milton Penderton to have the axle looked at."

"Do that, Colen. I think it is most important to have the carriages in repair. Colen, I have been trying to remember something. Perhaps you can help me. The letter I wrote to Lady Vivian in Greenwich— I have been trying to remember when I wrote it. What day did you post it, do you remember?"

"Oh, no, my lady, I couldn't say. I don't remember. There are always lots of letters to be taken to the post office, you know, what with his lordship's foreign correspondences."

"Do you remember posting it?"

"Well now, you asked me to post some letters, my lady,

which I did. That is, I made a point to collect them from the tray in the dining room, which I always do anyway. But I didn't look to see where the letters were going—I don't think I should do that, my lady, so I couldn't say."

"I see. I thought you might have noticed. Well, it is nothing important. Thank you, Colen."

"Have a pleasant day, my lady," he said, as I left him and began to walk toward the house.

I knew then, as I walked across the grass circle, that I would need to be in London for more than one day if I were to see Mr. Schraw and also have time to call upon the Ackermans in Greenwich.

Flora called after luncheon.

"Where is Edmond?" she asked, as soon as she saw me.

"He has gone to London, Flora. I believe he said he would not be back until Saturday or Sunday. He is staying with friends there."

"Oh, I wanted to see him. Papa and Mamma are giving a dinner party next Wednesday and, of course, you and he are invited. I wanted to tell him. You must tell him about it for me and be sure he comes. Mr. Field and his father will be there."

"I will, Flora," I said. "I am sure he will want to come, and I will look forward to it. Thank you. I should certainly be back from London by that time."

"You are going to London? When?" Flora asked.

"I don't know exactly: I haven't planned anything definite yet. I have only just learned about it. I received the most mystifying letter from Mr. Schraw, my father's solicitor, this morning asking me to be at his office on Monday afternoon and saying that he has something important to tell me. I can't imagine what it is, but of course I will go. And while I am in London, I want to look up some people in Greenwich, which I suppose I could do on Sunday. That would mean leaving on Saturday, wouldn't it?"

"May I come?" Flora asked.

"To London?"

"Yes! Oh, Mary, it would be such fun. I will have to go sometime soon, anyway. There are things that I *have* to buy. I need new gloves and shoes; and autumn is coming, and I need a good, warm cloak. 'Well, go up to London and get them,' Mamma said the other day, 'and stop complaining.' It is such a trip, though, and I hate traveling alone—well, you know, with just Emma and one of the footmen—but if we went together, it would be fun. Emma will still come along, of course, and Paul could do our errands and get the cabs. May I come?"

"Flora! That would be wonderful. I dreaded going alone."

"And I want to visit my aunt Caroline. She is my father's sister, and she lives on Lincoln's Inn Fields. She is not well and constantly complains about being neglected, but she won't come to the country. Actually she is a dear. Lewis and I are terribly fond of her. Lewis is her pet. . . ."

"But will your mother let you go?"

"Goodness, yes," Flora said. "It won't be the first time I have gone to London without her, and you and Emma and Paul will be along. I am quite old enough to take care of myself." She rested her hand on my arm. "After all, I will soon be a married woman with a family of my own. But if Mother wants to come, so much the better, don't you agree?"

"Certainly," I said.

"Let us plan to leave on the early afternoon train," Flora continued, "on Saturday, then, and I could visit Auntie on Sunday while you go to Greenwich. Paul could go there with you."

"And then," I said, "you could do your shopping on Monday. I could come with you in the morning, and then you could finish up in the afternoon while I go to see Mr. Schraw."

Thus, it was arranged. Flora said that she would call for me after luncheon on Saturday. Marsden would drive us to the station.

*   *   *

On Friday, Lady Clareham joined me for luncheon, for the first time since she had fallen ill. And afterward as we sat in the drawing room, I asked her: "Did Vivian ever think of going on the stage?"

"No!" she replied. "Oh, heavens no. She would never do a thing like that. Whatever makes you ask?"

"Well, she is so interested in plays and acting, and she does love theatricals. . . ."

"Mr. Field, my lady," Mitchell announced from the doorway.

"David!" I cried. "Oh, I am so glad."

"Good afternoon, Mary, Lady Clareham," David said. "I must apologize for calling so early, but I hoped that Mary would like to go riding this afternoon. Would you like to ride to Oakland Park, Mary, and see the farm?"

"I would love to, David," I said, "but you must give me time to change."

"That is why I came so early," he said, grinning. "Will that be all right, Lady Clareham? May I take Colen along?"

"Yes, my dear," she said, touching her forehead with her fingers.

"Are you ill?" I asked her.

"It is nothing, Mary, but I think I should go up and lie down."

"David," I said, "would you go out to the stables and tell Colen that he is to come along and ask him to saddle the horses, while I put on my habit?"

"Certainly," David replied.

"I will see Lady Clareham to her room and join you in the stable yard."

The horses were saddled, I am sure, long before I arrived in the yard. But at least there was no delay when I arrived there, and we rode off at once—over the hill and along the route that David had taken to reach the Horse Monument when we had first begun to meet there. I had not imagined then that one day I would be riding with him through those same fields and woods and lanes, and I was filled once again with joy at the way life had turned out for me.

I thought: David, this handsome man who rides by my side, will soon be my husband. Please make it soon, I prayed silently. Make us be alone together in our room as husband and wife, and make it soon.

We had hardly set out, it seemed, than the chimneys of Oakland Park rose above a grove of trees to our left, and David said, pointing to the right, "That is the new barn there. We came a more direct way this time. There, you can see the lake ahead. This is the rear wall of the stables. We will turn left at the end of it and leave the horses in the yard."

In the yard, two grooms ran toward us from different directions, eager to take the horses, and David jumped down and then helped me to dismount.

"There will be a glass of ale in the servants' hall for you, Colen," he said.

Even before Colen's "Thank you, sir," I found myself clinging to David's arm, and he pulled me toward the farm buildings. As we hurried along, I felt uncomfortably warm and began to wish I had worn Vivian's lighter, poplin habit: the day had turned hot without any breeze at all—so oppressive and still that I remember thinking it would storm later. We needed rain: everything was terribly dry and dusty. The hem of my skirt already wore an edging of dust, which rose in little clouds from our footsteps.

"The principle which we must somehow get into the heads of our farmers," David said, as we walked toward the huge new barn, "is that he who puts the most into the land gets the most out of it. Everything here is done to demonstrate this principle. Our farmers' main objective, today, is to feed their families and avoid every possible outlay of cash. It never occurs to them to spend sixpence on manure or cattle food. Modern farmers will purchase thousands of tons of fertilizers. In here," he directed.

We had come to an abrupt stop in front of a wooden building, and he opened the door of it.

"Oh, what a horrible odor," I cried, as I snatched my handkerchief and covered my nose.

"Guano from Peru—and over there is ground bones from the Pampas."

"David, it is too awful."

"We will go now. I just wanted you to see it." We left the fertilizer shed, and David continued: "It is the fertilizers and manure that will make the difference in the crops, but of course the farmer will buy large amounts of feed for his livestock to supplement his own for the winter feeding of his sheep and cattle. Now they barely survive the cold months, becoming mere bags of skin and bone.

"Here we are."

We had reached the new cow barn. It was an enormous, U-shaped, brick building. The outside of it was finished, but inside, carpenters hammered and sawed—building the stalls and finishing the paneled walls.

We entered the building, and as we did, I tripped over a

board lying on the floor. David grabbed my arm in time to keep me from sprawling, but I had gotten the palms of my hands dirty as I reached down to break my fall.

"Are you all right?" he asked.

"Yes," I answered, wiping the perspiration from my forehead with my handkerchief.

Then I cleaned my hands with it as best I could.

"See those chutes that come down from the loft just above the mangers?" David asked. "Feed will be shoveled down them from the floor above. And the trough behind, there, is for shoveling off the manure. Through here is the dairy. As I was saying—with our methods, the farmer will sell his stock to the butcher twice within the same time he now needs to prepare them once, and at the same time, triple his quantity and improve the quality of his manure. This in turn. . ."

In the dairy, David lectured on modern milk-production and sanitation. When he had finished, he took me to see the granary, piggery, and the duck and chicken houses, explaining at length their unique design. Then he showed me a self-feeding corncrib, which he had invented, and explained how it worked. We visited the kiln for drying grain and the barn that housed the farm machinery—the steam harrow, cultivator, clod-crusher, and the mowing machine and haymaker.

". . . divides it," he explained, as we stood in front of the threshing and winnowing machines, "according to quality and delivers it into sacks ready for market. The trailings go for the—I am boring you."

"No, no," I said. "It is just that I am getting a little tired, and it such an oppressive day."

"This doesn't interest you at all, does it?"

"Yes, of course it does."

"I am sorry. We had better go back to the house." He turned from me and then walked toward the doorway of the building, and I followed.

Once outside, I said, "David, please—not so fast." He slowed his pace then, and I continued: "I admire your work tremendously. I think it is incredible what you have accomplished. It is just that there is so much of it, and it is all so complicated. I don't understand it."

"And you don't like it. You think it is dirty and smelly and common. Well, perhaps it is."

"No! I don't think it is common, but it is so mechanical—it is simply not something that a lady would be interested in."

As I looked into David's face, I saw his eyebrows rise. As they did, my heart sank.

"But Vivian was interested, wasn't she?" I said.

"It fascinated her."

"Well, I am not Vivian."

We walked on in silence then. I felt wretched because I loved David so, and I knew I had hurt him by being indifferent to his work.

"You might like this," he said at last, opening a door in a long, low building.

"Oh, David!" I exclaimed, as we stepped inside. Before us stood a ewe and her lamb, not more than three days old. "It is darling—such a funny little black face."

David came to me then and put his arms around me.

"I am so sorry, David," I said.

"No, *I* am sorry," he said. "How could I expect you to love something simply because I do?"

"I love animals. I love this little lamb, and that is a start," I said. "And I love to ride, and I love plants, and flowers, and nature, and children."

"And I love you—so terribly much," he said. "That is why I wanted you to like all this as much as I do."

Then he kissed me.

"But it doesn't matter, Mary, it really doesn't," he continued. "There are so many other things. Now, let's go and see if Wakley can find us something to eat and drink."

A few minutes later, as we approached the rear of the house, David said, "I suppose you have heard about Lord Portland."

"No," I replied. "Who is Lord Portland?"

"He owns about twenty thousand acres here and in Somerset. He has a house in London and inevitably comes down to Thornton Place, his country house between King's Nympton and Barnstaple, on the day Parliament adjourns. He was robbed on Wednesday, on the high road, just after he had set out for Barnstaple."

"Oh? This is what they were talking about at the post office yesterday, then. What happened?"

"The day after he arrives, on the fourteenth, Lord Portland always takes the net proceeds of his Devon and

Somerset account days to a branch of Hale's, in Exeter, for deposit. Everyone knows he does this himself and that he carries the money in a brown-paper bag. It has become rather a joke—he is getting on in years and is a bit eccentric. Well, evidently he had no sooner turned into the high road when a man rode out of the shrubbery along the roadside holding a gun, which he pointed at the carriage, and demanded the money. He wore a long, gray beard and had tied a handkerchief across his face."

"Does that kind of thing happen often, here?"

"I don't believe it has happened at all in the last hundred years, maybe longer. That is what makes it so extraordinary. Everyone is talking about it."

"I don't wonder," I said. Then after we had walked a short distance, I asked, "Have you talked to your father since you returned? Has he said anything about us? Will he be joining us this afternoon?"

"I haven't seen him," David replied. "He left for London on Monday after luncheon. He left me a message by way of Wakley that he had urgent business there and would be staying with my brother."

"Did he say how long he would be gone?"

"No, but he hardly ever stays away for more than two or three days at one time. He has taken quite a violent dislike to the city, actually. He once said to me, 'David, if you are going to do something, do it perfectly.' And that is how he has given up the bank and his London life—cut himself off from it completely, as completely as possible."

"The waiting is dreadful. I feel as if I am standing on a trapdoor that may suddenly open and fling me down into the depths, somewhere."

"You mustn't worry. I promised you that it would be all right: now, don't think about it."

By that time, we had walked around the right wing of the house toward a side entrance of the central block of the building. David led me through rooms that I had not seen before, until we arrived in the entrance hall where Wakley stood talking to a parlormaid.

"Wakley," David said, "could you find us something cold to drink and perhaps some sandwiches?"

"Certainly, sir. I believe Mrs. Reston has anticipated your request, sir. Shall I serve it in the Rose Room?"

"Yes, thank you, Wakley. And, Hester," he said to the

maid, "would you show her ladyship where to wash her hands? Go along with Hester, Mary. I will be here when you return."

I had seen Hester before, both clothed and unclothed, and as I followed her, I remembered Alice Reade telling me about how she had seen this girl walking through the woods toward the bathing pavilion at the Castle.

But of course I said nothing about it, and when I had washed and rejoined David, he led me into the Rose Room. Two silver trays lay side by side on a low table. One held plates of tiny sandwiches and cakes, the other pitchers of ice water, lemonade, and pots of tea and coffee. Plates, glasses, cups and saucers, and napkins had been laid out for us beside the trays.

"What would you like?" I asked.

"Water!" he said, grinning.

"So would I," I said.

As soon as I had poured our water, we drank it without even bothering to sit down. Then we helped ourselves to sandwiches and sat down to eat them.

"Feeling better?" David asked.

"Yes. It is so much cooler in the house, and that breeze from the window is divine. It is going to storm, isn't it?"

"Yes, I've felt it coming all afternoon."

"Thank goodness! It will clear the air." Then after a moment I said, "I am going to London tomorrow."

"Alone? Why? Any particular reason?" David asked.

"Flora is going with me. I received a letter from Mr. Schraw yesterday—you remember, my father's solicitor. . . ." Then I told David about the letter.

And after we wondered together what it could be about, David said, "I am coming with you."

I looked at him in surprise.

Then he continued, "Well, I don't like your being alone there. Oh, I know you will be with Flora, and I suppose she will have her maid and a servant along, but I would feel better if I were there too. Do you mind?"

"Mind? I would love to have you come, and so would Flora, I am sure. Why, it will be like a party, David. That is marvelous! Thank you. But you are sure you can get away so quickly?"

"Oh, yes, there is no problem there."

"I have something else to tell you—two things."

"What?"

"Well, the coffin is not in the house. I have looked everywhere."

"You got into the wine cellar, then."

"Yes, I did. Mitchell was stealing bottles of wine, and I simply went down and looked."

"What?" David exclaimed.

Then I told him all about the incident from the beginning and about the conversation I had had with Lord Clareham afterward.

"I would have sent Ahmad to see what Mitchell was doing," I concluded, "and sacked him on the spot."

"So would I," David said.

"But Mitchell is still at the Castle. I don't believe anything happened at all. I don't believe that Lord Clareham even spoke to him about it. If he did, it doesn't seem to have affected Mitchell."

"Strange," David said.

"I think Mitchell has a hold over Lord Clareham and Edmond. Once I overheard Edmond threaten Mitchell, and Mitchell told him he wouldn't dare to call the constable. That was when Mitchell had stolen something else—a valuable box. I think that Mitchell has threatened them or let it be known that if they sacked him, he would tell what happened—to Vivian."

"Oh, now, Mary."

"Well—why haven't they sacked him then? And something else has happened. My letters to Vivian were never mailed."

Then I told David about my conversation with Mr. and Mrs. Hollycombe at the post office.

". . . so there is another reason why I am going to London. Will you take me out to Greenwich, David? I want to call on Vivian's friends, the Ackermans."

As I finished speaking, a clap of thunder crashed outside the house.

"Yes, Mary. I think it is time we did just that," David said, "but don't be surprised if Edmond mailed the letters from Barnstaple. After all, he was anxious that you write to Vivian, wasn't he? We will ask Nancy about it on Sunday, shall we?"

Huge drops of rain plopped on the drive outside the window then, and we got up and stood by the window to watch. In a moment it was raining so hard that we could not see the end of the gardens.

As we watched, David put his arm around me, as if protecting me from the storm outside.

Flora called for me after luncheon on Saturday, as we had planned.

I sat down beside her in the carriage and said hello to Emma, who sat facing us with her back to Marsden and Paul on the box. I said: "You are right on time. Your mother didn't object to your going, then?"

"No," she replied, "I think she is relieved to have me away for a bit. What a perfect day. Thank goodness the weather has turned cooler—if it were as hot as yesterday, we would have roasted on the train."

"Flora, David is coming with us. He asked if he could, and I didn't think you would mind. Is it all right?"

"Only if you take separate rooms."

"Flora!"

Flora laughed, and then she said, "No, I don't mind. Men are very handy when one travels—one should always have plenty of them on hand. I wish—I wish Edmond could have come along. Has he returned yet?"

"No. As far as I know, he is still in London."

"Wouldn't it be odd if we met him there? Then perhaps he could join the party. Well, stranger things have happened."

We did not meet Edmond during our London trip, as it turned out, but we did meet David in Braunton, as he and I had arranged. He stood waiting for us on the railway-station platform, and when we arrived, he hurried down to the carriage to help us out of it.

"Good afternoon, Mr. Field," Flora said. "Welcome to the party."

"Then you don't mind my coming?" David asked.

"The more the merrier. You are alone?"

"I prefer to take care of myself. I was going to bring one of the footmen to help out generally, but I thought *I* would do just as well: so here I am—at your service, ladies."

"Emma and Paul are coming," Flora said, "so it is just as well. I thought we would stay at the Clarington, if that is all right with you. We always do, and they know us there. Will you be staying at the hotel or with your brother?"

"I thought I would get a room at the hotel near you and Mary, so I can look after you. Do you have your tickets?"

"Paul will do that. Paul," she said to the footman, "will you get the tickets for us and get one for her ladyship, too." She opened her bag, then, and drew out some folded notes, which she handed to the footman.

"I will take care of Mary's ticket, Miss Stratton," David said, "and the rest of her expenses. I would like to get into the habit, if you don't mind."

"I can do it, David," I said.

"You are my responsibility from now on," David said.

After that, we stood on the platform chatting. We had arrived early. The train was not due for another twenty minutes, so there was plenty of time to get the tickets. David stayed and talked to us while Paul went to get tickets. And then when he returned, David excused himself and went into the booking office to buy ours.

When he came back, I said, "Oh, I want to thank the stationmaster again for helping me the day I arrived. David, what is the stationmaster's name?"

"Mr. Chute," he said.

"I will be only a minute," I said. "No—stay and talk to Flora."

In the booking office, inside the station, I found Mr. Chute standing next to his desk in the bay window looking up the railway track. When he heard me enter, he turned and walked toward me.

"Mr. Chute," I said, "I want to thank you for taking such good care of me the day I arrived. It was so kind of you to keep my luggage until Colen could call for it."

"It was my pleasure, my lady," he said. "We do offer every assistance to those at the Castle, my lady. And how is Lord Clareham these days?"

"He is in excellent spirits, thank you, Mr. Chute, and he seems to be regaining some feeling in his right side. He will be so pleased to know that you have asked about him."

"And her ladyship?"

"In good health, but you know she is terribly upset, still. James's death was a terrible loss to her."

"Yes, yes, indeed, my lady. A terrible tragedy. We were

all quite saddened by the occurrence—quite saddened. And Lady Vivian? We understand she's gone to America. Is that so, my lady?"

"Yes. She was so distraught over poor James's death, as you must know, Mr. Chute."

"Oh, yes, yes, I know, my lady. We were all most solicitous for her in her hour of sorrow."

"That is so kind, Mr. Chute. We hope a new environment will restore her. You must remember the last time she left Castle Cloud for London."

"Oh, indeed I do, my lady."

"I am her best friend, you know, Mr. Chute. We were at school together. I have really been so worried about her. How did she look?"

"Ah, poor Lady Vivian. Oh, she looked terrible—terrible in that black veil and those heavy, black clothes. She was always such a merry little thing, I can remember. She could hardly walk, my lady, she was so ill. Lord Althrop had his arm around her and she had her arm around him, and then when the train pulled in, they had such a touching farewell. Piteous it was, my lady. How she clung to him. She couldn't bear the parting."

"Yes, the family is very close. I do hope she will recover quickly now. Well, thank you again for your kindness, Mr. Chute. Now I must rejoin my friends."

"Have a pleasant trip, my lady. Will you be staying long in London, my lady?"

"Only two or three days, Mr. Chute. Thank you," I called back to him as I left the station.

"And how long will you be staying in London, my lady?" David said, mimicking Mr. Chute.

"David!" I said, but I couldn't help laughing at his imitation.

"Didn't he ask you?" David said.

"Yes, he did," I said, still laughing. "The poor man—stuck way out here all alone. It is no wonder he wants to know about things."

"He knows *everything*," Flora said. "If you don't know the local gossip, ask Stationmaster Chute."

"Which is just what I did," I said.

"About what?" David asked.

"I wanted to know how Vivian looked when she left—that last time for London. She didn't look at all well, I am afraid." We were silent for a moment, and then to change the subject and because I wanted to know, I asked, "Did your father get back from London, David?"

"No, not yet," he replied. "I will pop over to William's tomorrow or Monday and see what he is doing—if he is still there."

"No sooner does Parliament adjourn, than everyone goes to London," Flora said. "It used to be the other way around."

We laughed at that. And then when our train came, Paul found us an empty compartment. We had it to ourselves all the way to Exeter. There, we changed to the London train, where we were not so lucky. It was crowded, and by the time we reached Paddington Station, every seat in our compartment was occupied.

❧ Chapter Sixteen ❧

As soon as we stepped off the train in London, Paul ran in search of a hackney coach, and in three minutes he returned, grinning broadly. I wondered how he had managed to engage one in all the noise and confusion—hundreds of people carrying everything imaginable, scurrying in every direction—but he did.

The coach took us to the Clarington, on Piccadilly. It towered haughtily over its neighbors, an enormous pile of gray granite built in the modern style. Its square, octagonal, and oval towers; its square, arched, and Moorish windows; and its balconies, balustrades, and porticos looked across the lawns and trees toward Buckingham Palace.

The manager greeted Flora effusively and gave us a handsome, two-bedroom suite on the second floor, overlooking the park. David's room was on the floor above. Emma and Paul would, of course, sleep in the servants' rooms directly beneath the roof. We went upstairs at once to unpack and wash.

After dinner, we left the hotel and walked down Piccadilly and along Regent Street, looking in the shop windows.

"I can see the palace from my room, across the park," I said, as we walked along. "Is the Queen there, do you think?"

"I should imagine she would be at Balmoral," David said. "By the way, have you ladies decided what you are going to do tomorrow?"

"No, we haven't really discussed it, Mr. Field," Flora said. "I told Mary that I want to spend the afternoon with my Aunt Caroline. She lives on Lincoln's Inn Fields. So I will probably go there right after luncheon. And Mary said she wanted to visit some friends in Greenwich."

"She asked me to take her there," David said. "Shall we go after luncheon?" he asked me.

"Yes, that will give us enough time, don't you think," I said. "How long will it take to get to Greenwich?"

"Half, three-quarters of an hour, I should think, on a Sunday afternoon," David replied.

"You must take Paul," Flora said.

"Oh, no, Flora," I said.

"It will be quicker and pleasanter if we take a cab, Miss Stratton," David said. "Give Paul the day off, why don't you? We will not misbehave, I promise you."

"But what will your friends think?" Flora asked.

"They won't mind, Flora," I said. "It will be all right, really. What did you want to do in the morning?"

"Absolutely nothing," Flora replied. "I intend to have breakfast in bed and stay there until I cannot bear it another minute. Then I suppose I will take a walk in the park. And you?"

"Do you know what I would love to do?"

"What?" David and Flora asked in unison.

"I would like to go out to Portman Square and see our old house again and then walk to the little church that Miss Hartong used to take me to every Sunday. I would like to attend services there."

"Which one is that?" David asked.

"St. Peter on Vere Street. I would love to go there again. Do you think we could, David?"

"Anything that would give you pleasure, mademoiselle," he replied.

"Well, you may be as nostalgic as you like," Flora said. "I shall remain in bed. I hope you have a lovely morning, and I shall see you both at luncheon. And if you won't take Paul along, there is nothing I can do about it. If you like, Mary, we will tell Emma when to wake you."

The following morning then, David and I drove out to Portman Square. The house looked larger than I remembered it and alien, somehow. I wished we hadn't gone to see it. But I did enjoy the church service. As soon as we entered the building, I felt like the little girl who had sat next to Miss Hartong for all those Sunday mornings.

Then, after luncheon with Flora, David and I set out by cab for Greenwich, driving down St. James Street, around the park, down Bridge Street, past the Houses of Parliament, and out onto Westminster Bridge.

As we drove across the bridge, I said: "I don't like London. I never did, although I don't think I realized it."

"Oh?" David said. "There is St. Paul's."

"Yes, it is like a gigantic monster humped above the smoke. How filthy the air is, even on Sunday. See how the smoke lies on the city like a blanket."

"People have to eat," David said.

"And everything is so *gray*—gray granite turned gray-black from the soot. Let us go back to the country, David."

"I didn't know I was about to marry a poet."

"You are not," I said, laughing.

"You won't pester me for a house for the season, then?"

"I won't pester you about anything."

"You get a kiss for that," he said.

"And I won't forget it."

Then, after a few moments, David said: "What will you say to the Ackermans?"

"I don't know, but I don't think that will be any problem. They are old friends of Lady Clareham's—delightful people, I am sure. I want to find out all I can about Vivian, of course: whether or not she stayed with Nancy, and if she did. . ."

"You don't think she stayed there?" David asked.

"Well, my letters weren't mailed to her. Why weren't they? Was it because she wasn't there?"

"Then you don't think Edmond mailed them from Barnstaple or some other town on one of his trips?"

"That is what we will have to find out," I replied. "I feel a little like Jane Eyre at Thornfield Hall."

"Why?"

"Because people are acting strangely, and I know something is wrong, but I don't know what."

"*Jane Eyre* is just a story."

"Yes, but a very powerful one. Have you read it?"

"No, I don't care for novels. They are make-believe. I don't see how anyone can be interested in something that somebody simply dreamed up."

"But Shakespeare 'dreamed up' most of his plays, and they are fascinating."

"I am afraid I can't agree with you there. You can't even understand them."

"Well, that is because the English language was a little different then, but they are worth taking a little trouble with. Novels and plays and poetry and painting are the things that make life worth living."

"No, Mary. Life is that sky, and those trees, and this cab, and you and me. It has nothing to do with imagination. Novels and plays and paintings are unreal. I don't know why everybody makes such a fuss about them. Life would go on just as well without them, and with a lot less wasted time."

"But the pleasure, the joy they give," I replied. "The trees and the sky—yes: but,

'Hark! where my blossomed pear-tree in the hedge
Leans to the fields and scatters on the clover
Blossoms and dew drops—at the bent-spray's
    edge. . . .' "

"Poetry?" he asked.

"Robert Browning."

"Just a lot of words. Stand, sometime, in front of a *real* pear tree that is actually *in* bloom and read that—you will see that it is just a lot of words. It isn't real."

"David!"

"I am sorry. Now I have upset you. I didn't mean to." Then he laid his hand over mine for a moment and continued, "Don't be angry with me. I am only telling you how I feel about it. That doesn't mean that you can't enjoy your novels and paintings and poems as much as ever. They are for ladies anyway."

We drove on in silence then, and finally David said: "I did want to take you to the theatre while we were here. Perhaps tomorrow night. Would you like that?"

"Yes. But you wouldn't," I said.

"Well, it wouldn't make me all that miserable. We will see about it after your meeting with Mr. Schraw tomorrow, shall we?"

At about that point, our driver called down to us: "We're getting into Greenwich now, governor. What street did you say?"

"King Street," David called back. "Number thirty-nine."

"Where's it at, governor?"

"I don't know. We'll have to ask someone."

Fortunately, a parish priest walked down the street ahead of us. Our driver pulled up beside him and called: "I say, Reverend, could you tell us the way to King Street?"

"Follow the High Road down past the old market and you will see King William Walk," the rector directed. "Then turn to the left on it, and drive down toward Greenwich Pier. You will find King Street on your right, almost at the end of it, but you won't find anything open there on Sunday afternoon."

"Thank you, Reverend," our driver called, and we proceeded down Greenwich High Road.

We found the old covered market without any trouble. Beside it lay King William Walk, and we turned left as directed.

"That must be Greenwich Pier," I said to David, as we drove along between tall warehouse buildings. "Surely the Ackermans couldn't live here."

Then we turned into King Street.

"Number thirty-nine, you say, governor?" our driver cried.

King Street was one block long—a narrow, cobbled lane lined with ancient two- and three-story brick buildings. Several of these stood empty; others housed sail-makers, one a boat builder; and, at the far end of the block, a ship chandler. The shops were closed, and the street lay silent and deserted, but smelling still of hemp and pitch.

"Ain't no number thirty-nine, governor. You're sure it was thirty-nine?" the cab driver shouted, after we had driven the length of the street.

"Stop the cab a minute," David called up to him. Then he turned to me and said, "You are sure it was thirty-nine King Street, Greenwich?"

"Positive," I replied, as I opened my bag. "Here, I even wrote it down." I handed him a slip of paper on which I had written the address.

Pointing to the wall of the corner building, he said: "This is King Street—see it painted there? Over there is number twenty-four, and that is number twenty-five. There is no number twenty-six, twenty-seven, twenty-eight—or thirty-nine. So, I think we must conclude that number thirty-nine King Street does not exist.

"Then neither does Nancy Ackerman, I suppose," I said. "We can go back to London, now, can't we?"

We drove back to London via Hyde Park in order to see the crowds, and when we reached the hotel, I told David that I wanted to lie down before dinner. I didn't really, but I thought he should have some time to himself in case he had things of his own to do. I hated to give him up for a minute, but I thought it considerate to do so.

As soon as he had left me at the door to Flora's and my rooms, I was lonely for him, so much so, that I couldn't bear the thought of reading, and I knew I would not be able to sleep. So I drew a chair up to the window of our sitting room and sat looking down at the park, trying to make sense of what had happened in Greenwich that afternoon.

It was obvious that my letters had never been mailed to Greenwich because there was no such address; if they had been mailed, they would have been returned to me. But why had Edmond and his father and mother (I was more than ever sure that the entire family was involved in whatever was going on) invented a family in Greenwich whom Vivian was supposed to have stayed with? And if Vivian hadn't stayed with the fictitious Ackermans, where had she gone when she left Braunton Station? I would ask Edmond this when I returned to Castle Cloud. Until then, there was no point in thinking in circles any longer than I had already done.

But I couldn't help going over and over the strange things that had happened, as I washed and dressed for dinner. I had agreed to meet Flora in our rooms before the meal, but since it was only seven o'clock when I finished dressing, I decided to go down to the Genoese Hall (a public sitting room, just beyond the entrance hall of the hotel), where I could sit and thumb through magazines or simply watch the people. Maybe I would see David, and we could talk until dinner time.

So I threw a light shawl about my shoulders, put on my gloves, and went downstairs. In the Genoese Hall, I found a vacant sofa from which I could look through the archway into the hall and watch the hotel entrance. On the table lay copies of *The Family Journal*. I sat down and picked up a magazine with a drawing of an American Indian on its cover. He held a scalp above his head which he had just removed from an unfortunate and, I hoped, dead white girl. Is Vivian in this primitive land? I wondered, as I began to read the article. But I could not concentrate on it and soon found myself watching for David.

It was not David, however, that I saw enter the hotel twenty minutes later: as I watched, Flora walked through the entrance with a man. At first I thought it was Edmond, but it wasn't. It was Lewis. I got up at once and hurried toward them. They saw me and walked in my direction.

"Mary," Flora called, "I have brought a surprise."

"Good evening, Mary," Lewis said.

"Lewis!" I exclaimed. "How wonderful! Where did you find him, Flora?"

"At Auntie's—looking for a meal."

"I was doing no such thing, Mary," Lewis said. "I have as much right to visit my favorite aunt as my sister has, and without criticism. Don't you agree?"

"You know perfectly well," Flora said, "that if I hadn't told you Mary was here, you would be sitting down right now to one of Mrs. Humphrey's meat pies or stuffed veal."

"Duck in orange sauce and cheesecake. Umm," Lewis said. "When she dies, Mrs. Humphrey will cook for the angels. And in the meantime, I don't think a hard-working soldier could be blamed for accepting, if his aunt should ask him to stay to dinner, do you? Mary, tell your lady friend here, that if she doesn't treat me kindly, she will not be permitted to dine with us." Lewis smiled broadly.

And Flora smiled back and said: "I should not mind in the least. I should probably avoid dreadful indigestion by so doing."

I laughed and said to Lewis: "You will have dinner here with us, then?"

"If you will permit me to stay," he replied.

"That would be lovely, but I'm sure it won't be like Mrs. Humphrey's."

"I am prepared to make any sacrifice if I am allowed to remain."

"The sacrifice may be ours, my dear brother," Flora said with mock repugnance. "Goodness, it is almost time. Mary, take care of Lewis while I change. I will be as quick as I can and meet you here."

Then she rushed toward the stairs, leaving Lewis and me alone together.

"Come and sit down," I said.

We sat on the green-velvet sofa I had used earlier.

"I warn you," I said, when we were settled, "the food here *is not* like Mrs. Humphrey's. Now if Flora and I were men, there would be no problem—we could go to a club, or to a tavern, or a chop-house and have a lovely evening dining out—but just because we are ladies, we are not permitted this pleasure and are relegated to our own dining rooms, or to friends' dining rooms, or to hotel dining rooms if we happen, perish the thought, to travel. At the risk of sounding revolutionary, Lewis, one day ladies will be permitted to dine out of an evening. We will not remain underprivileged forever."

"Don't say that so loudly," Lewis said. "You may be thrown into prison, or deported, or even put in the tower."

I laughed and asked what he had been doing since he had returned to London, and he told me, which led to some amusing stories about some of his fellow officers.

But then at last he said: "And you, Mary? I understand a great deal has happened to you."

"Do you mean about David and me?"

"Yes," he replied. "I think it is wonderful. Field is a good chap. I like him. I hope you will both be very happy. I must tell you though, that if he hadn't gotten the jump on me, I might have asked you myself."

"Would you really have?" I asked, laughing. "Thank you so much, Lewis." I laid my hand on his arm for an instant. "That is very sweet of you. I am so glad we are friends—"

Then I looked up and saw David walking toward us.

I smiled up at him and called, "David! I hoped you would get here early—that is why I came down. Flora brought Lewis back with her from her aunt's. He is going to stay and have dinner with us."

Lewis stood and said: "I have just been wishing Mary happiness, and I want to wish you the same, David."

"Thank you, Lewis," David smiled, as they shook hands. "Will you be coming down to Hawthorn Hill for your mother's dinner party on Wednesday?"

"Yes, on Wednesday afternoon, but I will have to leave early Thursday morning."

"Pity you couldn't stay longer," David said.

"Well, I suppose I could. Actually, I am thinking of selling my commission. I never wanted to make a career of it—just something to do. Naturally, I will have to look after Hawthorn Hill someday."

Then Flora arrived.

"Shall we go in?" she said.

Later during dinner, David told Flora and Lewis about Suda, which led us to talking about horses. That led, somehow, to riding as children, which led the conversation to Mumford, Lewis's first pony.

"There is a drawing of Mumford at Hawthorn Hill," Lewis said to me. "I will show it to you on Wednesday."

"Speaking of Wednesday," Flora said to her brother, "Mother still hasn't heard from your friend."

"My friend's name is Charles," Lewis said. "You used to be able to remember his name quite easily."

"He doesn't deserve to have a name. How can you have him down? He practically insulted Mary."

"Lord Charles?" I asked.

After an embarrassed silence, Lewis said to me: "Charles is, I am afraid, a gullible fellow, and Flora hasn't forgiven him."

"He should have had better sense," Flora said. "Well, is he coming or isn't he?"

"Yes, he is coming. And I am sure he has let mother know."

"Don't be too hard on Lord Charles, Flora," I said. "It really doesn't matter any longer."

"And he is a gambler," Flora added. "He is always at the Berkely Club, or Brooks, or Crockfords."

"Who told you?" Lewis asked.

"Mr. Tuttle."

"Don't be absurd," Lewis said. "He goes occasionally, but what is the harm in that? At least *he* is not *addicted*."

"And what is that supposed to mean?"

"You know perfectly well what that is supposed to mean," Lewis replied. "I have told you many times: beware the man who is addicted to it—that means trouble. And speaking of Trouble, I don't suppose you know that he has become the talk of London."

"I don't know whom you are talking about."

"Edmond, Lord Althrop—Trouble. That is whom I am talking about."

"Lewis, how can you? That is not fair. What do you mean?"

"I mean that he lost £20,000 at the Berkely Club last Wednesday night and would have continued playing if some questionable friends of his hadn't insisted he stop. But he was back on Thursday, won a few pounds, and then last night he lost another £15,000, which was all the money he had. That is £35,000 he lost at the tables in three days' time. Where did he get £35,000?"

"How should I know?"

"Then you had better ask him," her brother said.

On Monday afternoon, as we drove to Mr. Schraw's office, David and I talked about our expedition that morning. David and Lewis had accompanied Flora and me (Emma and Paul were with us also) from one shop to another on Regent Street, and from there to Pall Mall, where Flora had bought some material. Lewis had been in high spirits and kept us laughing almost all morning long.

" . . . and his story about the baked-potato man and the parson was priceless," I said. "I never laughed so hard in my life. I must remember to tell it to Mrs. Muldoon. David, this is not the way to Threadneedle Street."

"I know," David said. "We are early—we have at least a half-hour to spare—and there is something we should look into."

"What? Where are we going?" I asked.

"Here," David said, pointing to a gold-lettered sign which read, 'Cunard Line.'

"To the Cunard Line office?"

"Have you forgotten? There were two definite things we knew, or thought we knew, about Vivian's last weeks in England. One was that she stayed with the Ackermans at 39 King Street, Greenwich. The other was. . ."

"The *Royal George*. Of course, David! If she was aboard it, her name would be on the passenger list, wouldn't it? Do they keep old passenger lists?"

"There is an easy way to find out if they do," David said.

He gave our driver his fare, helped me down out of the cab, and we went into the steamship office together.

A clerk got up from a desk, walked over to us, smiled, and asked, "May I help you?"

"We hope you can," David said. "We have a friend who, we believe, sailed to America on one of your ships. When was it, Mary, the middle of last month?"

"Yes," I said. "I don't remember the exact date—the fifteenth or sixteenth, perhaps."

"And the name of the ship?" the clerk said.

"The *Royal George*," I said.

"On, no, I'm afraid you must be mistaken," he said.

"I am sure that was the name," I declared.

"Yes, madam, but the *Royal George* has not been on the transatlantic run since last October," the clerk said. "She was sold by Cunard to the Collins Line at that time, and I believe she now sails between Plymouth and Naples, and to other Mediterranean ports. I could inquire about that if you wish, but I am sure that she has not sailed to America since autumn."

"No, that is quite all right," David said. "We must be mistaken. Thank you very much."

We left the Cunard office. David hailed another cab and gave the driver Mr. Schraw's address.

"Well, that is that," he said. "The thing I can't understand is—why King Street?"

"King Street, Queen Street, Regent Street, Court Street—common street names," I said. "There is one in any city of any size. Why the *Royal George* for that matter? Why not just, 'I am sailing for America tomorrow, good-by,' without a ship's name? We know Vivian left Castle Cloud. Did she go to London? Did she go to America? Did she have those letters written by someone because she couldn't do it herself? Did she make up the Ackerman's address and use another ship's name?"

"Why should she do that?" David asked.

"So she couldn't be followed."

"But you said Lady Clareham had known the Ackermans for years. Surely she would know where they live."

"Yes, but suppose Vivian *and* her family didn't want me to contact her for some reason? The Ackermans could live somewhere else, you know. But you think the Ackermans are fictitious, don't you?"

"I don't know what to think."

"Neither do I, David."

David was thoughtful for half a minute. Then he said: "Well, we still have a few minutes to spare. Would you like to see where I used to work?"

"The bank? Yes. Is it nearby?"

"Lombard Street. Go down Lombard Street, cabbie," he called, "and around Gracechurch Street to Threadneedle." Then he turned back to me and asked, "What are you looking at?"

"That woman with the gray hair and beautiful eyes, riding in the carriage, there."

"Do you know her?"

"Yes. She is Mrs. Kummann, the mother of the American author. She was Lorana Leather, before her marriage.

As we drove down the canyon of bank buildings, down Lombard Street, David said, "There it is—see the unicorn and the lion?"

The Elliot, Field & Co. building was number fifty-four—a soot-blackened granite structure fronted by a Greek, ionic portico.

"It is most impressive," I said. "But so stone-cold, somehow. I wouldn't like to work there. Those doors must weigh tons. How would you ever get inside?"

"They swing open with the push of a finger. Many's the time I have wished they *would* get stuck. No, you wouldn't like to work there. Let us go back to the country, Mary."

"Yes, let's. But after we see Mr. Schraw."

Mr. Schraw's office was on the second floor of number 28 Threadneedle Street, and after we had climbed the stairs to it, we were admitted by a clerk into a gloomy, dusty room where a row of high, slant-top desks and stools stood against the wall—each with a shaded gas lamp jutting from the wall above it. Only one lamp, however, was lit, and only the desk below it appeared to be in use.

Evidently we were expected because the clerk ushered us into Mr. Schraw's office at once.

A slim, grimy window and the heavy curtains that partially covered it rendered Mr. Schraw's office even more dusky than the room outside. The solicitor's desk stood so that one end of it almost touched the window, while the other end stretched into the gloom toward the room's fireplace, on the opposite wall. Behind the desk, facing us as we entered, sat a gaunt, white-haired man whom I did not recognize. Feeble daylight shone through the dirty window and lit one side of his face, and as he sat there gazing at me, I thought, suddenly, that it was all rather like an enormous Rembrandt painting, which needed cleaning.

"Lady Mary?" the man said. "Come sit down here." He pointed with a shaking hand to a chair in front of his desk.

I walked to it and sat down. As I looked more closely at the man before me, I recognized Mr. Schraw. But he was so changed from the way I remembered him: the vigorous man I had known had wasted away to mere bones covered with bluish-white skin.

"It is Lady Beauford now, isn't it, Mr. Schraw?" I asked.

"Yes, of course," he said. "I beg your pardon. Habit—matter of habit."

"This is Mr. Field," I said.

"Please sit down, Mr. Field," Mr. Schraw said. He smiled. Something amused him.

Then I noticed that Mr. Schraw was not alone. In the shadows, against the book-lined wall, sat David's father.

"Good afternoon, Mr. Field," I said to him.

"Good afternoon, Mary, David," Mr. Field said.

"Hello, Father," David replied.

"Well, now, Lady Beauford," Mr. Schraw said, "it has been a long time. Let me see, when did we last see each other?"

"Won't you call me Mary, as you used to? Yes, it has been a long time. It must have been ten years ago that you took me to Windsor."

"Windsor?" Mr. Schraw asked.

"To Mrs. Romilly's. Don't you remember?"

"Yes, yes. And I believe we have had no contact with each other since that time. A great deal has happened in the meantime, and we have changed—perhaps for better, perhaps for worse."

"You wrote me a birthday letter after that—the following June. I still have it." As I spoke, a chime sounded softly, three times. "Your watch! Do you remember how it fascinated me? Do you remember the story you told me about it—how the grandfather clock cried and cried when the little girl died, and it shrank and shrank until you could put it in your pocket?"

"Yes, my dear, and what did you ask me then, do you remember?"

"How it got to be round."

"That was when you were still at—what was the number on Portman Square?"

"Number twenty-two, and I remember sitting on your lap as if it were yesterday. I must have been five years old at the time."

"Yes, yes," Mr. Schraw said. "Well now, Mary, first of all, may I offer my condolences upon the death of your father. He was a fine man, and not only a client but a friend as well. And now we will proceed to matters of the estate. By the way, I am indebted to Mr. Field, here, for finding you. If it had not been for him, I should still be endeavoring to discover your whereabouts. Why did you and your mother disappear?"

"We couldn't keep the house any longer: we were quite reduced in circumstances all of a sudden, you know."

David's father stood then, and said: "If you will excuse me, Mary, Mr. Schraw, I have some business to attend to, and I do not wish to intrude. Mary, I am pleased to have been able to bring you and Mr. Schraw together. I wanted to be sure that you and he did meet, and since I had no idea where you would be staying in London, I took the liberty of waiting for you here so that I could extend my son's, William's, and his wife's, Cecilea's invitation to dine with us this evening at thirty-nine Hanover Square. David will bring you. And now I must be on my way.

"David, I would like a word with you outside, if I may. We will leave Mary and Mr. Schraw together."

"Come back as soon as you have finished, David," I said. And then, when they had left, I continued: "David has asked me to marry him, Mr. Schraw, and I have accepted. I hope you won't mind him being present. Now, what about my father's estate? I know there was nothing left; he told me so."

"That is not quite true, Mary."

"Oh?"

"No. You see, due to a—umm—misunderstanding, too involved to go into at this time, your father believed that his estates and all his possessions in England had been liquidated and transferred to his Swiss bank and then, finally, during those last tragic months, to Barclay's in The Hague. But that was not quite the case.

"You see, although your father and I were old friends, we did not always agree. I never believed that he had a right to divert the estates away from the title. Naturally, if the estates had been entailed, your father could not have alienated the property. But since there was no male heir, there was no question of primogeniture, and in your father's mind the maintenance of the family dignity was no longer of significance."

"Mr. Schraw," I said, "I do not understand these legal terms. I do not understand what you are telling me."

"Simply that your father was under no legal obligation to do so, but he *meant* you and your mother to be provided for. Unfortunately, he had no conception of the extent of his, I must say, ample capital in relation to his— umm—monumental expenditures. My warnings were to no avail. 'You are being an alarmist, Nathaniel,' he would say. 'There will be more than enough left when I am gone.' But that proved a fallacy, as I had predicted."

"Yes, I know," I said. "He was shocked and wretched when he realized; he couldn't believe it. I think he died more of shame and remorse than— There was a misunderstanding?"

"You have heard of the Sipp diamond?" Mr. Schraw asked.

"No."

"Hum— The Sipp diamond was named after Hilary Sipp, who brought it to England from India in 1704. Its history prior to that time is shrouded in mystery. It was a large rough stone of about 328 carats. Here, it was cut in brilliant at a cost of £14,000 and its weight reduced to 115 carats, its size about one inch in diameter. It was purchased by your great-great-great-grandfather, the fifth marquess, in 1723 and presented to his daughter-in-law upon the birth of his grandson. The stone was, of course, entailed and, together with the other family jewels, was to be passed to the wives of future marquesses.

"When the late lady Penbroke, your father's first wife, died, the family jewels were deposited with me. These were to await his second wife, your mother. In due course, they were delivered to her with the exception of the Sipp diamond, which has always, from the beginning, reposed in a vault in the Bank of England. It lies there still."

"Please go on," David said, as he stepped back into the room. "Don't let me interrupt." He closed the door quietly behind him then, and sat down in a chair against the wall.

"Is it so very valuable?" I asked Mr. Schraw.

"I have had it appraised at £135,000."

"One hundred and thirty-five—" I gasped.

"One hundred and thirty-five thousand pounds," Mr. Schraw repeated. "As your father's sole heir, the gem is your inheritance, Mary. I shall await your instructions as to its disposition."

"Why didn't you tell me your father was going to be there, David," I asked, as we drove back to the hotel after leaving Mr. Schraw's office.

"I didn't know he was going to be there, Mary. I was as surprised as you were."

"I suppose he was checking to see if I was genuine?"

"Yes."

"Rather the way one would investigate an investment of some kind."

"Mary, he didn't mean it that way—that is the way he *is*. It was unpardonable, of course, but— Can you keep a secret?"

"Yes, why?"

"He has given his consent."

"Oh, David!"

"He is going to announce it at dinner tonight, and you must be surprised."

"Oh, I will be. I am so happy, David. What else did he say to you outside?"

"Only that, and that dinner at William's will be at eight o'clock. That was all."

"But I have nothing to wear."

"Wear the dress you wore to dinner last night. You looked very pretty in it."

"Did I? That is very sweet of you. It is a rather poor thing, I am afraid, but I haven't anything else, and I can't refuse to go."

"Certainly *not*."

"I will hate leaving Flora alone," I murmured.

"I thought of that, and I told father she was traveling

with you. He said that she must come too—that they would need another lady to make the number even."

Then David took my hand, held it tightly, looked into my eyes in that disturbing way of his, and asked, "Happy?"

"Yes! Yes, yes, yes."

"I wish we were alone together."

"So do I," I said. I squeezed his hand and then took mine away from his. "What would your sister say if she saw us holding hands in the middle of Fleet Street?"

"Which one?"

"Either one. I don't suppose Silvia will be there tonight. Will Malessa?"

"No, you will meet her later. Just William and Cecilea, Flora and father, and you and I."

"Would your father have invited me to dinner if I had come to London alone?"

"I am sure that that was his intention—after all, he would want to look out for his future daughter-in-law, wouldn't he?"

"Only if she passed the tests. You had told your father about Mr. Schraw?"

"No. And I didn't know his trip to London had anything to do with you."

"How did he find Mr. Schraw, then?"

"That would have been easy. You told him about Gunderbury Hall. He must have known about it anyway, and it would have been a simple matter to look up the transaction and find out who managed the sale. Anyway, dozens of people must know who handled the marquess of Penbroke's affairs."

"Yes, of course. Poor Mr. Schraw—he is so changed. He saved the diamond for me, you know, on purpose. He must have been frantic when he couldn't find me. I should not have kissed him when we left, should I? One doesn't do that to one's solicitor."

"He loved it," David said. "So, now you are a lady of means with a handsome dowry."

"I am no different than I was before."

"Sure?"

"Of course I am sure. What do you mean, David?"

"Nothing. I love you so much the way you are—I don't want you to change, that is all."

Later, when we arrived at our hotel, David saw me to Flora's and my suite and stood in the doorway while I looked to see if Flora had returned.

"She hasn't come back yet," I said.

David stepped into the room then, and closed the door behind him.

"Come here," he said.

I went to him and slid my arms around his neck, as I felt his hands grip my waist and pull me to him. Then he held me tightly in his arms and kissed me for a long time.

Finally I drew back and said: "I love you, David. I can't tell you how much, but. . ."

"But you wouldn't want Miss Stratton to come flying in and find me here," he said, smiling. "And I wouldn't either. Will you extend the invitation to her for Father? I will leave you then, darling, and return for you and Miss Stratton at seven-thirty."

Flora returned about fifteen minutes after David had left me.

"Well," she said, as she entered the sitting room. "You are back early. I am exhausted! Put the packages there, Paul, and Emma, draw some water—I feel as if I had been down in a coal mine."

"Flora," I said, "David's father has asked us to dinner at William's house, this evening."

"Oh, lovely," she said. "I couldn't face another dinner here. What time, Mary? Thank you, Paul. That will be all."

The footman left the room then.

"David said he would come for us at seven-thirty."

"Dinner at Hanover Square?" Flora asked. "Is there an occasion? What did your Mr. Schraw want? I am dying to know."

I told Flora, then, what had happened at Mr. Schraw's office. ". . . so you see, things are not as bleak as I thought," I concluded.

"I have heard of it somewhere: I think it is a rather famous stone. It must be worth a fortune."

"Yes, well anything is a fortune when one has nothing."

"When you marry David Field, money will be the *least* thing you will have to worry about. How much is it worth?"

"Flora!" I cried, laughing. "Well—Mr. Schraw had it appraised at £135,000."

Flora gasped. "Let me sit down," she said. "But that is wonderful. You are an heiress now. From rags to riches in one afternoon."

"Well, it is nice to know that I am not penniless, anyway."

"What will you do with it?"

"See that it goes to my eldest son's wife and their eldest son's wife. It should be kept in the family as it has always been. Now I am going to lie down for an hour—not that I will be able to sleep, but it might help me to look my best this evening."

After my rest, I bathed and dressed. Then Emma offered to help me with my hair, and before I knew it, it was seven-thirty and David was knocking on the door.

We went downstairs with him then, and shortly William's carriage arrived to take us to his house.

It was an imposing Restoration building—seven windows wide with a center section broken forward and topped with a pediment—luxuriously furnished in a cool, formal manner, accurately reflecting the personality of its occupants.

When we met them, I couldn't help thinking that David must resemble his mother. David looked nothing like his father, but William was a young edition of him, with the same piercing eyes. And Cecilea was slim and elegant. She would, I thought, always say the perfect thing at exactly the right moment.

"We are so pleased that you could come on such short notice, Lady Beauford," she said to me when we met.

"It was so very kind of you to ask me," I replied. "But won't you call me Mary?"

"Thank you, my dear," she replied. "Then you must call me Cecilea. We are a tiny, informal party this evening— just the family," she said softly, "and since you will soon be part of it—which father is to announce later, as a surprise—you must feel completely at home."

The evening rolled by easily and has little to do with my story, with the exception of the announcement at dinner, which came at the end of dessert.

David's father stood, and when he had our attention, said: "I should like to say how pleased I am to announce that Mary and David are engaged to be married and that they have my blessing." Then, looking first at David and then at me, he continued: "I hope you will both be very happy." Then he sat down.

His pronouncement had been short and formal, but somehow I was deeply touched. How much this man loved his sons, I thought, and his family. To be welcomed into it seemed an almost unbearable compliment. His little speech had brought tears to my eyes: I don't know exactly why.

I felt foolish because of them, and I was barely able to stammer: "Thank you, Mr. Field, you have made me very happy."

"We are all terribly pleased, Mary," Cecilea said, coming to my rescue.

"Wonderful! Mary, David," William said.

Then, after Flora had added her congratulations, Cecilea rose and said, "Shall we leave the gentlemen and have our coffee in the drawing room?"

Later, when we were all together again, Cecilea played the piano for us and sang in a lovely, flutelike voice, and then it was time to say good night and return to the hotel.

And the following morning, we returned to Devonshire.

As planned, we caught the eleven-thirty train, which ended its run at Barnstaple at three-twelve in the afternoon. Flora's and David's coachmen were to meet us there with the carriages.

I hope they will be wearing their weatherproofs, I thought, as we left Exeter. The rain had started about the time we reached the city, and by the time we arrived in Barnstaple, the storm was upon us full force. The southwesterly had flung itself across the Atlantic, gathering water as it came; and now it lashed at us in fury at being impeded by our high hills and spewed its water upon us.

Through the rain-spattered windows of the railway carriage, we saw John and Marsden and a footman, whom I didn't recognize, waiting beneath the overhanging roof of the station, next to the horses. When the train stopped, David opened the compartment door for us, and we stepped out onto the covered platform.

"I see that Marsden has brought the old four-in-hand," Flora said. "Well, at least we shall be dry."

"Let me take Mary to the Castle, Miss Stratton. John

has brought the brougham. It will have a much easier time with the Castle hill than all that." He pointed to Flora's heavy carriage and the horses. "It must be a rushing river by now."

"Yes," Flora said. "If you don't mind, Mary, and I see that you don't, it is much the best thing to do. We will be lucky if we get home at all—any of us. Did you ever see it rain like this? I have enjoyed our lovely party, Mary, Mr. Field. Come along Emma, Paul." Then she waved and called over her shoulder, as she hurried toward Marsden: "We will see you tomorrow night. Don't forget. Bye-bye."

"Good-by," we called in unison.

"It has been lovely," I added. "Thank you."

The strange footman came to us and picked up our luggage then, and we darted to David's carriage.

"Wet?" he asked, when we were seated inside.

"Not quite," I replied. "Did you ever see so much water? Exciting, isn't it? Do you think they will get stuck along the way?"

"No, not really. The ground is still hard enough, probably."

Just then, as we pulled away from the station, a gust of wind rocked the carriage.

"Oh!" I cried.

"Hold on to me," David said, putting an arm around me and then taking my hand. "There, isn't that better?"

"Much," I said, looking up into his eyes.

Then he kissed me. There was no one about to see him do it: but if there had been, they could not have seen us through the sheet of water that ran down the window glass.

"David, I am so happy with you," I said later, as we drove along. "I hate to go back to the Castle. Oh, I love the place, but there is a heavy atmosphere about the house, now. And Edmond— He drags me down so. I feel as though I am fighting him all the time. We are so antagonistic toward each other. I must know what has happened to Vivian, and I must ask Edmond about it, but I don't look forward to it with pleasure."

"My poor Mary," David said. "Don't then."

"I must."

"What will you say to him?"

"I haven't decided. It is the letters—I keep coming back

to the letters all the time. I know Vivian didn't write or dictate those letters or have anything to do with them. I have always felt that way. Who wrote them, David? I wonder if Edmond wrote them himself."

"Why do you think that?"

"Well, I can't think of anyone else who might have—certainly not Lord or Lady Clareham. And who else is there? The servants? No. And why the letters at all if she didn't write them? If she went off—disappeared, why didn't they tell me so instead of making up letters?"

"As you said, they might all be trying to hide her whereabouts for some reason."

"Why?" I asked. "Because she is mad or has an incurable disease and is in an institution somewhere? I thought of that, but surely they would simply have told me—not other people, perhaps, but they would have told *me*. No, I am sure something terrible has happened to her and they don't want me to find out what it is."

"You will be lucky if you find Edmond at home," David said.

"Do you think he is still in London?"

"I doubt it. This is race week, you know."

"Race week?"

"The Barnstaple Race. It is on Saturday, but all week nearly every building on Treadmere Street is turned into a roulette or hazard house. And they have an attraction for Edmond."

"But gambling is against the law. Do you mean it happens openly?"

"Oh, yes, the houses pay huge fees for the privilege—just like the clubs in London and everywhere else. The magistrates, the constables, et cetera—all paid off. But it is only during race week, and it gives the gentry and farmers some diversion."

"Not you," I said.

"No! Gambling is one thing that never appealed to me. But we should see the race. Shall we go on Saturday afternoon? It is quite a spectacle."

"I would love to."

"And I won't wager a penny. Meanwhile, tell me what happens. Perhaps you shouldn't stay at the Castle. When are you going to let me take you away from it?"

"When shall we be married, do you mean?"

"That is up to you to decide, isn't it?" He bent then and kissed the tip of my nose.

"Could we be married in the church in Milton Penderton?"

"I approve of that," he replied.

"I would like a wedding dress, and I would like Mother to be there. Could she, David?"

"But that would take forever."

"But we have the rest of our lives, and a marriage only happens once."

"All right, my darling. If that is the way you want it, that is the way it will be. I will get your mother's and stepfather's steamship tickets, and you will send them to her. Now, ask about a dressmaker—Lady Clareham will know of one—and get her started on your dress. Tell her to send the bill to me. Anything you like, but hurry, please."

"Yes, David."

"You can't stay at the Castle that long, you know."

"Well, Edmond was very insistent that I stay until we are married, but he may change his mind when we have had our talk."

We had crossed the stone bridge by then, and began to climb the hill to the Castle.

"Oh, you were right," I said, "this is a raging torrent." And then after a moment, I asked: "When will I see you again?"

"Tomorrow night. I am afraid not before. I will call for you at six-thirty. Then, would you mind if we stopped at Oakland Park for Father on the way to Hawthorn Hill?"

"Of course not. I will miss you terribly," I said.

"And I, you. I suppose we should offer to take Edmond."

"I suppose we will have to. I wish. . ."

But I couldn't finish because David had tilted my face up to his and his mouth had come down upon mine. And he didn't release me until just before we stopped in front of the Castle. Then the footman opened the door and helped me down.

"No, don't get out, David. You will only get wet. Good-by until tomorrow night," I called, as I ran up the steps under the footman's umbrella.

He opened the entrance door for me, and I turned and waved to David.

"Just leave the bag in the vestibule here, thank you," I said.

When the footman had put my bag down and gone back to the carriage, I walked into the empty rotunda. It didn't matter that Mitchell was not there; he could bring my luggage up later.

Then I glanced into the hall chamber and the drawing room, hoping to see Lady Clareham, but the rooms were as silent and empty as the hall. Finding no one to welcome me, I climbed the stairs and walked along the gallery toward my room.

But as I passed Vivian's bedroom, I heard someone singing softly. The door to her room was ajar, and I tiptoed over to it, pushed it open a few more inches, and peeped inside. Jane Spence posed in front of the mirror wearing Vivian's yellow ball dress, as she sang:

"Her name was Jane Spence, just nineteen years old,
    with a very large fortune in silver and gold.
Ritoorali, toorali toorali da."

The dress fit her lovely figure perfectly.

How dare she parade about in Vivian's clothes, I thought. But then I wondered if I were a parlor maid if I too wouldn't dream of having beautiful dresses, and I smiled in spite of myself, and walked on to my room.

Once inside, I removed my damp clothes, put on a robe, lit the fire that had been laid for me, carried a stool to the fireplace, and sat down on it before the flames.

And as I watched them dance, I tried to decide what I would say to Edmond and Lady Clareham at dinner that night.

"If only I knew who had written those two letters," I whispered. "It *must* have been Edmond."

If I were sure of that, I would have a better idea of what to say to him. Perhaps I could tell if I had a sample of his handwriting and compared it to the writing in the letters. But how on earth could I get that? How could I recognize his writing if I saw it?

Thinking that I might find a letter that Edmond had written and never mailed, and so learn to recognize his handwriting, I put on a dress and shoes, tidied my hair, went down to the drawing room to the writing table, and looked through the drawers. But I found only blank paper and envelopes. Then I left the drawing room, walked across the rotunda (Mitchell still was not to be seen and the house was silent), and into the little writing room, to the left of the vestibule. After opening its curtains, I crossed to the desk, lifted the dustcover, and examined the contents of the drawers. I found many letters there, but they were from friends of Lord and Lady Clareham—mostly invitations and casual notes. But I found nothing that might have been written by Edmond.

Then I realized that I had had what I needed all along—Nancy Ackerman's address, which Edmond had written on a slip of paper for me the evening I arrived at Castle Cloud. It was only a small sample of his handwriting, but it might be enough. I had kept that slip of paper, and it now lay among Vivian's letters in my trunk.

So I hurried back to my room and to the trunk, brought out the packet of Vivian's letters, removed the suspicious ones from Greenwich and the sample of Edmond's handwriting, and carried these to the window.

First, I examined the address in Edmond's handwriting. Edmond's writing slanted to the right, and the formation of his letters—the eighteen that I had samples of—was not particularly unusual with the exception of his *r*'s and *d*'s. These, I noticed at once, were oddly formed; his *r*'s were made rather like tall, leaning *e*'s ($\searize$), and even stranger, his *d*'s remained separate letters—not connected to their neighbors—and wore oddly shaped, hooked stems (∂). So the word "address" in Edmond's handwriting looked like this: *address*.

I compared the handwriting in the letters from Greenwich with the address in Edmond's handwriting, and I found that they did not resemble each other at all. The handwriting in the letters slanted slightly to the left, and the *d*'s and *r*'s were quite ordinary in their formation.

But then, as I examined the two handwritings more closely, I discovered similarities between the two: the size of the letters in both handwritings was the same, and the *l*'s looked identical, except for the slant of the letters, and so did the *o*'s and the *a*'s. And here and there, several letters at a time leaned a little to the right. And toward the end of the June 27th letter, the words "to care," in the last paragraph, slanted to the right and the *r* looked like a tall, leaning *e*.

It was then that I began to feel certain that Edmond had written the letters, disguising his handwriting. And when, in the July 16th letter, I discovered both *d*'s in "Edmond," in the third paragraph, had his strangely hooked stems and that the entire word slanted to the right, I was sure of it. He had written his name as usual, without thinking, and when he had read the letter over, his signature, being so familiar, hadn't seemed out of character.

Finally I compared Vivian's signature on the letters she had written to me with the signature on Edmond's letters, and it was evident that he had forged her name and not done it particularly well. He must have thought that as long as I believed Vivian had hurt her hand, I would not be suspicious.

When I entered the drawing room before dinner that evening, I found that both Lady Clareham and Edmond were already there.

"Good evening, Mary," Edmond said.

"Good evening, Edmond," I replied. "Good evening Lady Clareham. How are you feeling?"

"Not quite well, I am afraid, Mary," Lady Clareham said. "I have a slight fever and a headache which does not leave me."

"I am so sorry," I said, as I sat down on the sofa next to her. "Shouldn't you see the doctor?"

"He is coming tomorrow, though I have little faith in doctors, particularly. . ."

"So our traveler has returned," Edmond interrupted. "And how was the trip to London, Mary?"

"We are both travelers, it seems," I replied. "Very pleasant, Edmond, thank you. And yours?"

"Enjoyable."

"What plays did you see?" I asked.

"Shakespeare. I have little patience with the popular drivel."

"Oh? I noticed that *The Merchant of Venice* was being performed at the Drury Lane. Did you see it?"

"Wonderful play—ingenious. Unquestionably one of his

greatest. And you, Mary; what provoked your sudden trip to the metropolis?"

"I went to see my father's solicitor, Edmond, and I also went out to Greenwich to call on the Ackermans.

"Dinner is served, my lady," Mitchell announced.

Both Edmond and Lady Clareham had been alarmed by my mention of the Ackermans: I had seen it in their anxious glances at one another. So, after we were seated at the dining table and had begun our soup, I simply waited quietly for their questions.

"And how did you find the Ackermans, Mary?" Edmond finally asked.

"I didn't find them at all," I replied. "They do not live on King Street in Greenwich. King Street is an alley of sail-maker's lofts and other commercial buildings near Greenwich Pier. It is not even a residential area." Then I turned to Lady Clareham and asked, "Where do the Ackermans live, Lady Clareham?"

Lady Clareham glanced up at me, then at Edmond, and then back at her plate. She did not speak, and I noticed that her hand shook uncontrollably.

"Do they exist at all, Lady Clareham?" I asked.

I looked at her, but she did not return my gaze.

Then, when I realized that she would not answer me, I turned back to Edmond and said: "Why did you make them up, Edmond?"

"Who? What do you mean?" he replied.

"The Ackermans don't exist, do they? You never mailed my letters to Greenwich, did you? And *you* wrote the letters that were supposed to have come from Vivian, and mailed them from London. Did you go to London especially to mail them?"

"What an absurd idea. What makes you think that?"

"Surely you don't think you can carry on this charade any longer? I have been to King Street in Greenwich, Edmond. I have inquired about the *Royal George*. She has not sailed to America since last autumn. I have compared your handwriting with that of the letters. Your *r*'s and *d*'s are very distinctive, and you did not bother to disguise them all. Further, the signatures were poorly forged. I could have done better myself."

"Oh, is that so?"

"Yes. Why have you done this? *Where is Vivian?* Why

won't you tell me what has happened to her? *Why?* I am her best friend. I wouldn't harm her in any way, nor would I hurt you or your parents—you must know that. Why have you made up this elaborate story? Why won't you tell me?"

Edmond looked at me in panic for a moment, and then he said: "We don't know where she is. We don't know what happened to her."

"What do you mean you don't know? Haven't you heard from her?"

"She left. I saw her to the station in Braunton and put her on the train. You can ask the stationmaster there if you don't believe me. And that is the last we heard of her."

"Well, did she say where she was going?"

"No."

"And you let her go in that condition? And you didn't know where she was going?"

Edmond didn't answer me.

"Why was it necessary to make up this ridiculous story and forge letters," I asked. "Why didn't you tell me?"

"It is not a ridiculous story at all, it is quite an ingenious one," he exclaimed. "We were trying to save you. We knew you would be upset if you knew that she had disappeared, and we wanted to save you the worry. Isn't that right, Mother?"

Lady Clareham did not answer or look up from her food.

"We have gone to great lengths to help you, Mary," Edmond continued. "We have had only your best interests at heart. We have thought only of you, and you have repaid us with doubt, and suspicion, and mistrust, and innuendos of improper conduct. You have searched our house, meddled in our affairs, and interrogated the staff. Is this the way you repay kindness?"

"Vivian is my best friend, Edmond. I am terribly worried about her. I think something has happened to her, and I want to help her. But I can't help her until I find out where she is and what kind of help she needs. I don't believe this silly business of not knowing. I don't believe a word you say. You know what happened to her, and you know where she is. I beg you to tell me."

Then, when he did not reply, I continued: "Since you

find me such an objectionable guest, I shall leave in the morning."

"And do what? Where will you go?" he asked.

"I have an inheritance from my father, which I knew nothing about until yesterday. I am no longer the poor, defenseless little girl who could be pressed into service as a governess. And I have David Field, and his father's permission to marry him, which I shall do. I shall stay with friends of the Fields until my marriage. *And* I shall find out what happened to Vivian in spite of you."

"No, that you will never do," Edmond whispered with an omniscient smile.

"Are you so sure?" I asked.

Then his smile turned unctuous, and he cajoled: "Mary, you are tired and overwrought after your journey. You know you are very dear to us. You will remain here until after your marriage, of course. Please try to understand that we have only tried to help you. Forget about Vivian. She is gone without a trace—you cannot find her."

"I shall not rest until I do, Edmond. But since you have asked me to remain at the Castle, I shall accept your hospitality for a little while longer. We shall be neighbors, and I know that I shall find an opportunity in the future to repay you for your kindness."

"Excellent, then," he said.

"Edmond, please tell me what happened to Vivian," I pleaded.

"We simply do not know, Mary, as I have told you," Edmond said. He glared at me for an instant, but then he looked back at his soup.

After that, we did not speak again until the second course had been served. We did not even look at each other. We were imprisoned at the table, while all around us our hostile thoughts continued to slash at each other. But there seemed no point in further questions.

Finally, Edmond looked up at me and said: "Say nothing about this, Mary. Do not tell anyone that Vivian has really disappeared. There is no point in encouraging idle gossip and absurd conjecture. After all, we have our reputation to consider. It is best left as it is."

"But what could be more damaging to Vivian's reputation," I asked, "than to infer that she has eloped with a groom?"

"She has," he replied.

"How do you know that?"

"Well, it is obvious. Vivian was ill—distraught over James's death. She wanted to get away from Castle Cloud, she said. She had friends in London who would look after her. She would write. She would be all right. Her 'friend' was O'Connor. She ran off to London with him once. He swore that he would have her as his wife one day: he swore that to my face. He was a very determined man. So it is perfectly obvious that she ran off to meet him again, and then they went to America. Well, they couldn't stay in England. So you see that is what really happened."

"Then why didn't you tell me that in the first place?"

"I told you—why—we didn't want you to worry."

"How could I have worried more if you had told me this at once? It is essentially the same story as you told me in the letters."

"Well," he replied, "it is obvious that you have less sensitivity than I thought you had, Mary. We wanted to soften the blow—to lessen the shock."

I did not reply to him, but I am afraid I could not disguise my look of disgust and disbelief. There was no use, however, in further pleading, or reproaching him. I would have to find out some other way. I was furious with Edmond, of course. But although there was no further conversation, dinner went quickly for me. I was lost in trying to figure out what had *really* happened and what to do next.

Later on, when we had finished dessert, I said, casually: "Flora asked me to extend her invitation to dinner at Hawthorn Hill tomorrow night, Edmond, and David suggested that you drive there with us. He is calling for me at six-thirty."

"Lady Wilton sent a footman with the invitation," he replied. "Six-thirty is a trifle early, isn't it?"

"We want to stop at Oakland Park for David's father."

"Thank him for me, but I do not plan to return to Castle Cloud afterward, so I will have Colen drive me."

Lady Clareham rose then, and she and I left Edmond and retired to the drawing room for our coffee. I sat down, and Lady Clareham sat in a chair facing me. Her hands lay folded in her lap, but her fingers stirred. She looked into my eyes, and I returned her gaze. Several times her lips quivered, but she did not speak.

"Where is Vivian, Lady Clareham?" I asked, at last.

Her mouth began to form an answer to my question, but then she evidently thought better of it and closed her lips.

"At least you can tell me if she is all right," I said. Then when she still did not speak, I asked: "Are you afraid to tell me? What are you afraid of?"

"I knew this would happen, Mary," she said, finally. "That first day when you came into this room, I knew it. I had no reason to know it, but I knew it." Tears filled her eyes and ran down her cheeks then, and she sobbed. But she did not take her eyes from mine. "Mary, stop! Stop what you are doing! You will bring it all crashing down upon us, and I couldn't bear it. I have so little left. Don't take that away from me. Please don't take that away from me."

"Lady Clareham! I wouldn't hurt you for anything in the world. Put the tray there, Mitchell, I will pour it. Thank you."

While I poured our coffee, Lady Clareham collected herself somewhat, and when I handed her a cup she was calmer.

After she had taken a sip of coffee, she said: "Mary, Vivian has gone out of our lives. She does not need your help. There is nothing you can do for her. Forget her. Don't ask any more questions. *Don't* destroy us." She began to weep again. "Or yourself: God only knows what he might do. Don't make him *angry*."

"Edmond?" I asked.

Lady Clareham did not answer. She sat staring at me, her face streaked with tears, her mouth working silently.

"That night you came to my room," I said, "and brought me the soup. You were worried about what Edmond would do. You were afraid of him, and you are afraid of him now. What has Edmond done to make you so afraid of him?"

"I am not afraid of him. He is my son," she murmured.

"Then you are afraid of what he might do. You are afraid of what he might do to me, aren't you? But why should he want to do anything to me? He wants me here now. He has asked me to stay until my marriage. Surely a few questions— What has he done to make you so frightened?"

"Please," Lady Clareham shrieked. "Stop it! Stop it!"

Then she covered her mouth with her handkerchief, jumped from her chair, dashed into the rotunda, and disappeared in the direction of the stairs.

After she had gone, I finished my coffee, went to my room, threw a cloak over my shoulders, and left the house by the entrance portico.

Edmond stood there smoking his cigar. "The rain has stopped," he said.

"Yes," I replied, "I thought I would walk in the fresh air."

I walked past him, down the steps, and strolled down the drive to the stone bridge and back. And then I went to my room and to bed. I was exhausted, and fell asleep at once.

I slept soundly all night and woke refreshed in the morning. During breakfast, Edmond told me that he would be away all day and therefore would not be present at luncheon. We spoke little after that, merely exchanging a pleasantry or two. And when I had finished eating, I went upstairs for what I think was a rather extraordinary interview with Lord Clareham.

Ahmad opened the door, and Lord Clareham called: "Come in, Mary. I have been expecting you. Sit here." When I was seated, he asked: "Now, what can I do for you?"

"How are you feeling?" I asked.

"Quite well, Mary. Quite well," he replied.

"Lord Clareham, I do not wish to upset you, but I have a question to ask." I paused, not knowing how to approach what I wanted to say, and Lord Clareham waited patiently without interruption for me to find my way. "Vivian and I are close friends, as you know. She is my best friend, and even though four years have elapsed since we last saw one another, there is a very strong bond of affection between us. So it is perfectly natural that I should be concerned about her and want to know that she is well."

"I understand that, my dear," Lord Clareham said.

"I would like to— What has happened to Vivian, Lord Clareham? You must know by now that I know all about the letters and the Ackermans and that story about her going to America. Where is she?"

"I understand your concern for your friend, Mary," Lord Clareham said. "But friendship does not entitle one to know *everything* about one's friend, does it? Even in the closest relationship there are bound to be personal things which are not, cannot be shared. We all have private matters which we wish to keep to ourselves alone. This is true between friends, between parents and children, brothers and sisters, even husbands and wives, and—forgive me—between families and outsiders, no matter how fond we are of them. In all these relationships, there exists a line of privacy which no one is permitted to cross—even those closest to us.

"In asking these questions, Mary, you have crossed that line, and we must warn you away. Here are private, family matters which we do not wish to share, and we know you will respect that wish."

"Then I will not ask you about it further, Lord Clareham," I said, getting up from my chair. "Now I shall let you rest, and next time I will tell you all about my visit to London."

Then I left him.

But as I stepped out onto the gallery, the door of Lady Clareham's room, the room next door, opened, and Dr. Norton backed out of it.

"A teaspoon every four hours, remember," he said to Cecile, "and, I should think, bed rest for a day or two. I shall come again tomorrow to see how she is."

"How is Lady Clareham?" I asked, hurrying to the doctor.

"Ah, Lady Beauford?" he asked.

"Yes."

Doctor Norton's complexion was red and puffy, and his breath smelled strongly of whiskey.

"Oh, a mild debility," he said softly, as he glanced behind him to be sure that Cecile had closed Lady Clareham's door. "Her ladyship is not growing any younger, you know. Nothing to worry about."

"Are you going in to see Lord Clareham?"

"No, I have already seen him. He is doing splendidly, splendidly."

"Then shall we walk down together?"

"Very kind of you. Very kind of you, I'm sure," he replied. "And how is Lady Vivian getting on?" he asked, as we walked toward the stairs together.

"A bit better, we think. You know, she was terribly upset by her brother's death—quite ill with grief. But of course you know all that. Was she *very* ill, doctor?"

"Ill? No, not that I know of. Concerned about her brother, certainly, but hardly ill. She had—umm—a very strong constitution."

"Oh? When did you see her last?"

"A day or two before the late Lord Althrop passed away, I think."

"Not the night he died?"

"No, I was not here the night that his young lordship died. You see I had visited him that morning, and, his condition being relatively unchanged, I had planned to return the following day. Naturally, I was prepared to come at once—at any hour of the night or day if I should be needed: I am always prepared to do so. But I was out—I was not at home—when Mr. Taylor came to fetch me that evening. He was quite insistent, according to the missus, that I come at once. Well, I have many patients, and they take me out into the countryside, sometimes for many miles.

"Actually, it was very odd—umm—that before I returned home, his present young lordship, Lord Althrop, had ridden to the house and said that I was no longer needed—that the emergency had passed and that I needn't trouble myself about it further—umm—and to come in the morning as planned. I must say, I thought it strange at the time, but it was very late when I returned, and I was tired, and since his young lordship had said specifically that I should not come, I went to bed. The next morning, I found, of course, that his late young lordship had passed away during the night. I certainly would have come at once, you understand, but—umm—well—you understand."

By the time he had finished telling me this, we had descended the stairs and walked halfway across the rotunda toward the vestibule.

"Did you see Lady Vivian the following day then?" I asked.

"No, no, I never saw her again. Everyone knows she was terribly upset by her brother's death. She was not at the funeral, you know. You say that she is feeling better? Well, I am glad of that, and when you write to her, please say that I have inquired."

"I will, doctor. Thank you."

"Yes. Well, I must be off. I'll look in again tomorrow. Good day, Lady Beauford."

When he had left me, I turned back toward the drawing room and saw Edmond leaning against the doorjamb. He must have heard the last half of our conversation.

❦ Chapter Seventeen ❦

I WORE my blue and green dress that evening. I had worn it to Hawthorn Hill before, but it was a pretty dress, and somehow I couldn't bear the thought of wearing one of Vivian's. I was dressed and waiting for David in the hall chamber well before six-thirty. I waited alone: Mitchell had disappeared. Since Lady Clareham would be having dinner in bed and Edmond and I would be dining out, he would not be needed that evening to prepare for and serve dinner. So he had probably decided to take the night off. When David rang, I went to the door myself and opened it.

"No Mitchell tonight?" he asked, stepping inside.

"I haven't seen him," I replied.

"That is fortunate," he said, as he closed the door behind him. Then he pulled me to him, wrapped his arms around me, and kissed me. Finally, he held me at arm's length and asked, "Are you all right?"

"Yes! Very happy. And I have something to tell you."

"And we must go," he replied, as he opened the door for me. "What do you have to tell me?"

"The letters—I was right. Edmond wrote them," I said.

David offered his arm, and I took it as we descended the steps to the carriage.

"Are you sure?" he asked. "How do you know that?"

"I compared the handwritings. He had tried to disguise his, rather clumsily. Then he admitted to it at dinner last night."

Peter held the door of the carriage open for me while David helped me into it.

When he was seated beside me and we had begun to move, he asked, "He did? Then where is Vivian?"

"I don't know. They won't tell me."

"What do you mean they won't tell you? Did you ask them?"

"Of course."

"Well, what did they say?"

"Edmond made up a ridiculous story about their not wanting me to worry, that Vivian just disappeared after he put her on the train, and that they don't know where she went—which is absurd. Lady Clareham wouldn't answer my questions at all, and Lord Clareham told me, in a nice way, to mind my own business."

"She can't have disappeared," he said. "Why the letters at all, then? Why not tell you she had disappeared in the first place? Or better still, why not tell you where she is? Why all the mystery?"

"I think I know why the letters," I said, as we passed the glasshouses (we were taking the shortest way to Oakland Park—toward the home-farm and Milton Penderton). "That first day, when I arrived, Edmond didn't know I had come to stay. He thought it was a casual afternoon call and that he could get rid of me simply by saying that Vivian was visiting friends. Once he had said that, he had to continue with the story or it would have looked strange. And, so, the letters were necessary.

"When he returned last Sunday, he must have been horrified to find that I had gone to London. He couldn't wait to find out what I had done there. I think the reason he has wanted me to stay in the country, preferably in an isolated house somewhere as a companion, was so that I *wouldn't* go to London where I could investigate and ask questions."

"But you are asking questions now," David said.

"Yes."

"Then he can't still want you to stay at the Castle."

"But he does. He insisted again last night that I stay."

"Why is he so insistent on that?" David asked. "And where is Vivian? She may be here in England still. This may not have anything to do with O'Connor."

"I wonder if it does," I said. "I don't know."

"But now that you have discovered their hoax, wouldn't you think they would tell you what happened. Why not?"

"Not if they had *done* something," I replied. "I have been thinking about that too, and I think that if Vivian had done something to be ashamed of, they would tell me about it, but if they had done something—if *Edmond* had done something, they would try to hide it. I keep thinking about that coffin. If I didn't know that Vivian had left the Castle— Oh, I don't know. I just don't know, and I don't know where to go from— David!" I cried, grasping his arm.

He followed my gaze and shouted, "John, get away! Fast!"

"I see him," John called back, as the horses lept forward at a gallop.

Then, as we sped down the road, David twisted around—looking back at the thicket of hemlock in which the man with the gun had stood.

"You saw him?" he asked.

"Yes, for an instant," I said. "Then you tensed forward between us, and I shut my eyes."

"He had that gun pointed right at me. What in blazes did he think he was doing? He could have killed me if he had fired it. Why didn't he, if he had wanted to kill me? You don't go about pointing guns at people and scaring them half to death for no reason."

"He wore a beard and something wrapped around his face."

"Handkerchief. Phew! I think I know how a soldier must feel in battle. I don't like people pointing guns at me."

"He wanted to rob us," I thought aloud.

"The bandit that robbed Lord Portland?" David asked. "Maybe—long gray beard and handkerchief across his face. Maybe. But why the devil didn't he do it, then? He didn't do anything. He just stood there in the bushes."

We speculated about it all the way to Oakland Park, and then when David's father joined us, we told him about it. And during the drive from Oakland Park to Hawthorn Hill, which took about ten minutes, we speculated about it some more. David's father was as baffled as we were, and he advised that we report it to the constable in Milton Penderton in the morning.

As we drove along and talked about the bandit, I watched the sun, a hazy orange disk, sink and finally vanish beyond Lord Wilton's park. I began to wonder if we might arrive too early; but as we approached the house, a carriage pulled away on its way to the stable yard, and a lone figure ascended the stairs. We were not the first, then, to arrive.

The figure was Lady Agatha Prigger. She paused to rest on the landing and stood for an instant looking down at us as our carriage came to a stop before the house. Then she waved to us and entered the building. I wondered, briefly, if she had recognized me.

When we had climbed the stairs, entered the house, and been shown to the drawing room, my misgivings about our timing were assuaged. Already, twelve or thirteen people had gathered there, and the room buzzed with talk.

"The Baroness Beauford," the butler shouted. "Mr. Thomas Field, Mr. David Field."

"Mary," Lady Wilton called, as she hurried toward us. "Oh, how lovely. Good evening, Mr. Field, David."

"Good evening, Mary, Thomas, David," said Lord Wilton, who had followed his wife to us. "Thomas, do you know the viscount Spree? Would you care to meet him? And you too, David, come along. He is very interesting. . . ."

"Mary, I think you know everyone here," Lady Wilton said, "except Lady Spree and Ruben, her son. Come and allow me to introduce you to her. Her mother and mine were the closest friends. She is staying with us for a few days." And as we walked across the room together, she continued: "Their seat is Hill House, near St. Molton in Edmond's old parish. As a matter of fact, she was largely responsible for his getting the living at Arford St. Mary. This is all rather a surprise for both of them. They haven't seen each other in ages."

Then as we approached a plain-faced woman, Lady Wilton said, "Lady Beauford, may I present Lady Spree?"

Lady Spree wore a very low-cut decolletage, displaying a full-blown bosom.

"Good evening, Lady Spree," I said.

"Lady Beauford," she replied, "how delightful. Flora has been telling us about your good fortune. I knew your father— Oh, very slightly. I had the pleasure of visiting Gunderbury Hall for a short stay together with my father and Sir Robert Pell—they were great friends, you know— but that was long ago."

"The Marchioness of Tyringford," the butler announced, "and Lady Patience Ditterly."

"Ah, here is Auntie," Lady Spree said. "Do you know Lady Tyringford? She is not my aunt at all, really. She is my godmother, and I love her dearly, but her daughter, Patience, is a prune. Prune, did I say?" She laughed. "I meant to say 'prude.' Well, 'prune' will do just as well. Let us go and say hello to them."

Lady Tyringford must have been eighty years old—a tiny, dried-leaf of a woman—and, as I realized when Lady Spree shouted, "Darling Auntie!," she was nearly deaf. Patience, tall, fiftyish, had never been married. One simply knew that at once.

"Darling Auntie," Lady Spree shouted again, "How lovely to see you. Oh, it has been so long. Good evening Patience."

"Rosanna," Lady Patience replied.

"Mary, darling," Flora cried from behind me.

I turned to see her standing beside a dark, Italian-looking young man.

And after she had kissed me on the cheek, she said, "I have been telling Ruben all about you."

"Well, I hope not everything," I replied, smiling at the young man.

Was he Italian, or Indian, I wondered. This couldn't be Lady Spree's son, could it?

"Mother says she knew your father, Lady Beauford," the young man replied. "She visited him with Sir Robert Pell, I believe."

"Mr. Paul Pridell, Mrs. Winifred Pridell," the butler announced. "Mr. Phillip Pridell and Miss Philomena Pridell."

"Yes, she was just telling me so," I replied.

"How is Lord Clareham?" he asked.

"About the same. He is partially paralyzed. His condition remains unchanged."

Mr. Pridell walked from the doorway directly to Lord Wilton, Lord Spree, and David and his father, all of whom stood in front of the fireplace. Philomena almost ran to Dierdre Swoop, who stood flirting with Lord Charles at the window. And Mrs. Pridell and Phillip walked straight toward me.

"Ruben and his mother and father are staying for the race on Saturday," Flora said.

"Mary, my dear, how lovely," Mrs. Pridell cried, as she approached. "Where is it?"

"Where is what, Mrs. Pridell?" I asked.

"Why, the diamond. I am dying to see it. Aren't you wearing it?"

"I haven't seen it myself, yet," I said.

"It is in a *vault* in the Bank of England," Flora volunteered.

"I can't wait to see it," Mrs. Pridell exclaimed. "Oh, Mary, I am so thrilled for you. . . ."

"Winifred," Lady Wilton said from behind me. "I have been telling Rosanna about the Barnstaple Race."

"Oh, how lovely," Mrs. Pridell cried, as she turned toward Lady Spree. "Excuse me, my dear," she said to me, as she did so. "I was just telling Mary, Georgiana, how thrilled I am that she will be living here in the county with us."

"And may I tell you how happy I am, too?" Phillip Pridell said.

"Sir Roger and Lady Molehill," the butler shouted.

"About what, Mr. Pridell?" I asked.

"Well—about the—diamond and everything."

Then Lewis joined us and, a moment later, so did David.

And then Lord Charles left Dierdre and Philomena, and when he reached me, he said: "Good evening, Lady Beauford. I was furious when I found that you had been in London and that Lewis hadn't told me. I would have called at your hotel, had I known."

Lewis winked at me.

"Good evening, Lord Charles," I said. "We should love to have seen you, but we were in the city for only two-and-a-half days."

"Ruben, will you take me over to the window?" Flora asked. Then she whispered to me: "I must look after Dierdre and Philomena, Mary. You understand, don't you?"

"Of course," I whispered in return, as I glanced at the two girls.

They had been staring at me as they whispered together, but they looked away when our eyes met. I may have become everyone else's darling all of a sudden, I thought, but it will be a long time before I can make friends with them.

Then I noticed that Lady Wilton stood in the doorway speaking to the butler. She seemed worried. Surely it must be time to go in to dinner, I thought. But where was Edmond? How could he be late—it was unforgivable. Then, as I watched, relief smoothed Lady Wilton's face, and Edmond appeared. As he was announced, she guided him toward us.

"Rosanna," she cried, "I have a surprise for you. How long has it been since you and Edmond have seen each other?"

"Almost three years, Georgiana," Lady Spree replied, "but the memory is vivid. As a matter of fact, the last time I saw the Reverend Ramsay. . ."

"It is Lord Althrop now, Rosanna," Edmond said.

"The last time I saw the Reverend Ramsay, Georgiana," Lady Spree continued, "he was having servant problems. Particularly the female servants seemed always troublesome to him."

Lady Spree spoke loudly and with a sharpness that caught the attention of everyone in the room. We all listened.

"On the contrary, Rosanna, servants have never presented *any* problem to me at all."

"Quite," she replied. "I would have thought to hear of your taking a living in one of the proper sections—St. Giles, perhaps—where your talent for ministering to the lower classes could reach its fullest potential."

"There would seem to be a need for Christian charity among the privileged classes as well."

"Charity begins at home, Edmond, and how well you practice the belief."

"Dinner is served, my lady," Ludley announced.

"Stewart, will you take Lady Tyringford in?" Lady Wilton said at once. "And Lord Charles will take Lady Spree. Edmond, you and Flora will be followed by Mary and Lewis. . . ."

But it was only after we had passed into the dining room and were seated at the table that I breathed a sigh of relief: Lady Wilton had seated Edmond and Lady Spree far apart, with David, Mrs. Pridell, Ruben Quenby, and Flora between them.

We were twenty-two at the table. I sat next to Lewis, who sat between me and Lady Tyringford—who sat on Lord Wilton's right. David sat between Lady Spree, who was on Lord Wilton's left, and Mrs. Pridell. David's father sat on my right, next to Patience. Lady Wilton, Lord Spree, Lord Charles, and the rest of the guests at the other end of the table seemed very far away.

When we had begun to eat, Lewis turned to me, smiling broadly, and said: "Tell me what wild adventures have befallen you since your return to the country."

"As a matter of fact, we did have a wild adventure—on our way here, Lewis. The bandit has returned. It was terrifying."

"The bandit?" Mrs. Pridell cried from across the table.

"What bandit?" Flora called to me.

"The bandit that robbed Lord Portland," I replied. "At least I think it was he. He had a long gray beard and a handkerchief tied around his face."

"Oh!" screamed Mrs. Pridell.

"What did he do? Did he hurt you? You poor dear," Lady Agatha cried.

"No, no, he—he merely stood there in the bushes," I said. By that time everyone at the table was listening. "I really didn't see him as well as David did. David, tell them about it."

"You think it is the same man, then?" Lord Wilton asked David. "Hadn't you better inform Constable Nash?"

"Yes, that was what Father suggested," David said. "I will, in the morning. It could have been the same man. He had a gun. He was standing in an evergreen thicket as we drove by him toward Milton Penderton, and when I looked, there he stood—pointing his gun straight at me. Fortunately John, our coachman, saw him at about the same time I did and drove the horses to a gallop straight away. But he could have shot me if he had wanted to."

This brought on a barrage of questions, but then the conversation divided quickly, as almost everyone had a theory about the bandit to share with his neighbor.

"Thank God he didn't shoot you," Lewis said to me.

"Yes. Well, you see, David was between him and me; so he couldn't have. But let us talk about something else. I notice that Dierdre is here all alone."

"Her parents and her brother are in Manchester. Mrs. Swoop's sister's baby daughter is being christened and Dierdre's mother is to be godmother."

" . . . fascinating," Lady Spree exclaimed to David. "You must be very strong."

"And Dierdre didn't want to go?" I asked Lewis.

"She was ill or so she said. They were fortunate to get Dr. Norton, who prescribed for her."

"Why fortunate?"

"Well, he is never at home when you need him. Confidentially, one might try the taproom of the Red Lion, but then he wouldn't be in any condition to do one any good anyway."

"Who, Dr. Norton?" Mrs. Pridell asked. "You might as well not have a doctor—you can never find him."

"We have a marvelous man," Lady Patience said to Mr. Field, "at Pendelmore. When I fell and hurt my wrist in the garden. . ."

"Well," Lady Spree said, "I think the medical profession leaves a great deal to be desired—butchers, most of them. Don't you agree, Mr. Field? Not to mention the clergy."

"I should think it would depend on the doctor or clergyman," David replied. "There are very fine men too, you know."

"Oh, I should think I might place a few small wagers," Edmond cried, from the other end of the table."

"Any particular clergyman in mind, Rosanna?" Lord Wilton asked.

"Perhaps, but he shall be nameless."

I was barely able to hear Lady Patience whisper to David's father: "Lord Althrop, of course. It was an affair—that is why she got him the living in the first place—until he started running after a servant girl. Hell hath no. . ."

"The one I have in mind was a philanderer, to say the least," Lady Spree continued. "Well, I suppose they all are. Imagine, a man of the cloth up there in the pulpit preaching on Sunday morning and on Sunday afternoon—"

"You intrigue me, Rosanna. What on Sunday afternoon?" Lord Wilton asked.

"On the study couch with the parlor maid."

"Red Pepper in the first," Edmond shouted. "You can be sure of it."

"Oh, it is so exciting," Flora cried.

"She is talking about Edmond," Lewis whispered to me, glancing at Lady Spree. "Mind if I hear this?"

"But you had always led us to believe that you had been

so fortunate in your choice of clergymen at Arford St. Mary," Lord Wilton said to Lady Spree.

"I don't believe there was ever any reason to discuss it. But now that Flora is of an age—well, I certainly would advise her to avoid the cloth."

"Quite," Lord Wilton replied.

Then, after a moment, I heard Ruben Quenby say to Flora, "But surely we shall go together on Saturday. I have looked forward to it."

Flora looked at him in astonishment and, I think, with pleasure. Edmond did not seem to notice this. He daydreamed, and his head bobbed from too much wine.

After that, the rest of dinner passed uneventfully and with a great deal of talk—much of it about the Barnstaple Race, a hunt at Sir Anthony Spicker's, the shortcomings of Parliament and Palmerston, and the war. And the bandit who had frightened us earlier in the evening.

Finally, when Lady Wilton had risen, and we had left the dining room to the men and entered the drawing room, Mrs. Pridell said to me: "Sit here with me, Mary. You must be very happy, and we are delighted for you. David Field is a fine boy, even though his father was. . ."

"You mean because his father *is* so rich," Lady Agatha said, sitting down in the chair next to Mrs. Pridell. "One should ask Mrs. Crinnings about him."

"Mrs. Crinnings?" Lady Spree asked, as she sat down next to me on the sofa.

"Agatha," Mrs. Pridell said, "he was young. The wild oats must be sown, you know."

"Well," Lady Agatha replied, "there are wild oats and *wild* oats. Dearest Lady Beauford, Mary, my child, one cannot think too carefully about these things. For a young lady of *family* with a splendid dowry—"

But she did not finish that because of Ludley's entrance with the coffee.

And then, after we had all been served coffee, Lady Wilton turned to Lady Spree and said, "But you thought the world of Edmond when he was at Arford St. Mary. I remember your telling me over and over again how fortunate you were to have chosen him."

Lady Wilton spoke loudly since the two deaf ladies, Lady Tyringford and Lady Molehill, had discovered one another and sat across the fireplace from us happily shouting at each other. Fortunately they provided a barrier of sound through which Flora, Philomena, and Dierdre, who were sitting at the end of the room beyond them, could not hear.

"I thought," Lady Wilton concluded, "that you would be happy to see each other, but apparently you were not."

"I have never mentioned it, Georgiana," Lady Spree answered, "but Stewart and I were both dreadfully disappointed in him when we found out."

"Found out what?"

"Simply that he was having an affair with the parlor maid at the rectory. Well, we simply could not have it, and when Stewart found out, they had a little talk and Edmond moved out the following week. Stewart has endowed the living there, you know, and Edmond was asked to leave. The whole tawdry affair disgusted us—it was tasteless and vulgar."

"Oh, Rosanna," Lady Wilton murmured.

"We all know he has a taste for servants," Lady Agatha declared.

"Agatha!" Lady Wilton cried.

"Well, I have seen it with my own eyes, Georgiana, and the very day after his brother's funeral."

"*What* did you see, Agatha?" Lady Wilton demanded.

"Edmond and that pretty maid at the Castle—Jane Spence, I believe her name is. He met her alone in a gig at the station in Barnstaple. She came in on the five-thirty train from Exeter. I remember because I had had my prescription refilled at Hadman's, across the street. They drove off alone together. It was all quite—intimate."

"Are you sure it was the day after James's funeral, Lady Agatha?" I asked.

"James was buried on Sunday, and this happened on Monday afternoon, the following day. I have a perfect memory, Mary."

"Yes, I am sure you have. Did you go to the funeral?"

"Of course."

"Which is more than his sister did," Mrs. Pridell said. "Forgive me, Mary, but we all thought it was peculiar, and what happened then was even more peculiar—I am afraid even scandalous. And *that* was Edmond's sister, Georgiana. And he has been almost living down there on

Treadmere Street, I hear. Really, I think you should take a hand."

"Speaking of the race," I said, hoping to change the subject, "do you think I would enjoy it? I have never actually seen a real horse race. Papa was always going to take me out to Chantilly, when we lived in Paris, but he never did."

"But you must go," Lady Agatha said. "Everyone will be there. . . ."

It was not very long after that that the men joined us, and since I had consented to play the piano, we all adjourned to the music room. Knowing that Lady Wilton was nervous about the success of her party, I played my best in order to help. And I believe my performance turned out very well, since I was obliged to play two encores. Then Lady Wilton asked me, in a whisper, if I would accompany Lady Spree. I agreed, gladly, and after her songs, Dierdre played for us, and then Lady Patience played and sang the fortunately brief 'May He Be with You When We Part."

It had all seemed to work out well: I am sure everyone enjoyed themselves. So when it was time to leave, I was able to tell Lady Wilton that it had been a most enjoyable evening.

"Did you enjoy your evening, Father?" David asked, after we had left Hawthorn Hill and drove toward Oakland Park. "You seem to have made a conquest."

"If you are referring to Lady Patience, David, I was merely being polite," he replied. "I have long since passed the age of being otherwise to ladies.

"Mary, my dear," he continued, turning to me, "I received a wire from David's sister, Malessa, this afternoon. She informs us that she will arrive on the morning train tomorrow for a short visit at Oakland Park. Malessa never plans anything in advance if she can help it. I know it is extraordinarily short notice, and you must think that I never plan anything in advance either—which I assure you is not the case—but David and I hope that you will come to dinner tomorrow night at Oakland Park to meet her. I say tomorrow night because she may have vanished by Friday."

"Thank you," I replied, "I should love to come."

"She will want to know when you and David plan to be married," Mr. Field added.

"We plan to be married in the church here in Milton Penderton," I said.

"Yes, yes, David has told me about that. How are you progressing with your wedding dress? When will it be finished? You must not spare the expense, you know."

"Thank you, Mr. Field. Lady Clareham has recommended a dressmaker who lives in Barnstaple. I hope to go in to see her tomorrow or Friday. Then I will be able to tell you an approximate date."

"Excellent," he replied. "I see no point in long engagements when two people have made up their minds. They may just as well get on with it."

Later, after we had stopped at Oakland Park, where David's father left us, and were driving toward Castle Cloud, David said: "You seem very preoccupied, darling. Is anything wrong? Where did you and Lewis go as we were about to leave? I looked everywhere for you."

"Oh, he wanted to show me the drawing of Mumford."

"Mumford?"

"His pony. Don't you remember at dinner in the hotel, he said that he would show it to me? I had forgotten all about it too, but Lewis remembered. It must have been a dear little animal."

Then after a pause, I reached for David's hand, and he took mine in both of his.

"What is it?" he asked.

"Something I heard tonight and something I saw the afternoon we returned from London. That afternoon I saw Jane Spence, the chambermaid at the Castle—"

"Yes?"

"She was trying on one of Vivian's dresses in Vivian's room. She didn't see me. The dress fit her perfectly."

"Well?"

"Tonight, Lady Agatha said that she saw Edmond meet Jane Spence in the gig at Barnstaple Station. Jane had come in on the five-thirty train from Exeter. That was on Monday, the day after James's funeral—the same afternoon that Vivian left Castle Cloud."

"Hum."

"David, I am beginning to wonder if Vivian ever left Castle Cloud at all. I wonder if it could have been Jane Spence, under that heavy veiling, whom Edmond drove to Braunton and put on the London train."

*   *   *

It took me a long time to go to sleep that night. Over and over, my conversation with David repeated itself in my mind as I lay in bed. And again, the question—why?— had remained unanswered. In the morning, I sipped my tea while Mrs. Muldoon prepared my bath, and the conversation began to repeat itself once more.

"But if she never left, where is she?" David had asked. "You say you searched the house."

"Wherever the coffin is, I think Vivian may be in it."

"In the coffin? You mean dead? Oh, Mary! What have you been reading? Where do you get these fantastic ideas?"

"Is it so fantastic to think that she died?"

"Yes! Vivian wasn't that ill. You have no *reason* to think that. I admit it is all very strange, but you have no reason to think she is dead."

"It is something I feel. I *feel* that she is no longer alive."

"That is nonsense. She may have run off on her own, secretly—in the night. You know how rash she was sometimes. But she is not dead. If she were, there would have been a funeral. The doctor would have signed a death certificate, and there would have been a funeral."

"There might not have been—funerals didn't always happen, you know. One can die and be buried without a death certificate and a funeral."

"Yes, but this is 1856. Vivian is Lord Clareham's daughter, and he is a famous and honorable man. If Vivian had died, she would have been buried properly in the mausoleum with James and all the other Ramsays."

"Yes. Why wasn't she?" I had asked.

"Why wasn't she?" I asked again, aloud, that morning.

"Did you say something, my lady?" Mrs. Muldoon said, as she set the bath down on its sheet.

"I was thinking out loud, Mrs. Muldoon," I replied.

How little I suspected, as I sat there in bed waiting for my bath, that an odd incident was about to take place which, had I but realized it, could have helped answer my question.

"Should I pour your water now, my lady?" Mrs. Muldoon asked.

"Yes, thank you," I replied.

"There," she declared, when she had finished pouring the water from the cans. "Leave everything as you always do, and while you're at breakfast, I'll be tidying it all up."

She left the room then, and I got out of bed and began to bathe. I had almost finished when I noticed the glint of a metal object that had fallen on the carpet half behind the water cans. By leaning over the edge of the bath and stretching my arm, I was able to grasp it. The object was a corkscrew. I wondered, briefly, where in the world it could have come from and then concluded that Mrs. Muldoon must have dropped it there.

My supposition proved correct. While I dressed, Mrs. Muldoon knocked on my door and, after I had asked her to come in, she said: "Begging your pardon, my lady, but there's something I might have dropped."

"Yes, I put it there on the wash-hand-stand, Mrs. Muldoon," I replied.

"Oh, thank you, my lady. Sure, I don't know where I leave things sometimes. It's more time I spend looking for them—"

"You must have dropped it by accident," I said.

"And speaking of accidents, my lady," Mrs. Muldoon said, her eyes sparkling, "did you hear about the lady-in-waiting named Pam?"

"No."

"Well it's like this:

A lady-in-waiting named Pam
Slipped on a spilled pot of jam.
'Did you fall?' the queen cried,
'Did you think,' she replied,
'I sat down for the fun of it, ma'am?'

"Ha, ha, ha. ' . . . sat down for the fun of it, ma'am?' Ha, ha, ha."

And even after she had left the room and closed the door behind her, I could hear her laughter.

But it was quite another sound that startled me three or four minutes later, as I was about ready to go down to breakfast: it was a scream. Immediately I ran out onto the gallery.

There I saw Mrs. Foley standing outside the open door to the linen closet, halfway between Vivian's and James's rooms, staring into it.

"What are you doing?" she shrieked. "Where did you get that?"

As I watched, she lunged into the closet and, at once, withdrew from it, clutching a bottle.

"Your lordship, your lordship," she cried, as she whirled around and ran toward the stairs. "I told her to take them away. She never does anything I tell her to do. I told her to take them away, the lazy slut. Oh, your lordship!"

And in a moment I saw Mrs. Foley emerge from the stairwell and dash across the hall below, toward the dining room.

"Your lordship, your lordship," she cried.

Of course I walked to the linen closet at once, and I arrived there just as Mrs. Muldoon walked out of it.

"What happened, Mrs. Muldoon?" I asked.

"I don't know, my lady," she replied.

"But what was Mrs. Foley screaming about?"

"Sure, I don't know. Why should she get so upset, my lady. Holy saints! I didn't put the bottles there, and she never told me anything about them. And what's the harm? It was a bit off, I was feeling, my lady, you see—a bit coldish, you might say. 'Well,' I says to myself, 'it's a little sip of wine you'll be needing to set you to rights again. So I opened a bottle, and it was just as I was taking a sip or two that Mrs. Foley comes screaming her head off, and then she grabs the bottle out of my hands and off she runs to his lordship."

"But—but wine in the linen closet?"

"Two bottles, my lady, way back on the upper shelf they was—tucked behind a pile of sheets," Mrs. Muldoon explained. "The one's still there. See it?"

"Is it open?"

"No, and the other one wasn't either. Here's the cork to it." Proudly, she displayed the corkscrew with the cork still impaled upon it.

"How odd," I said. "I would leave it alone if I were you, Mrs. Muldoon. Meanwhile, I will see if I can find out what all the fuss was about."

I left her standing there then, and hurried after Mrs. Foley. And when I reached the hall below, she and Edmond were leaving the dining room together. Mrs. Foley scurried away when she saw me coming, but Edmond walked toward me.

"You have finished breakfast early this morning, Edmond," I said. "What was all that about?"

"Oh, nothing, Mary. Mrs. Foley discovered that someone had stashed away some wine in the linen closet—a former servant, probably. She is old and gets upset easily. It was nothing. Well, I must be off."

"She seemed far more upset than that to me."

"Oh? How upset would you say that she seemed?"

"Well, I don't know, but one would think that discovering a bottle or two of wine in a linen closet could hardly be a matter to scream about."

"Sometimes you show an astonishing lack of understanding of others, Mary. Mrs. Foley is an old woman. One would think it obvious that a woman of her age could be upset by almost anything. I shall not be in for lunch; so you and Mother may have a quiet time together."

"And I shall not be at dinner," I said. "I am dining at Oakland Park."

But Edmond had already begun to walk away. He had heard me, however, and called back over his shoulder: "Then it would seem that we shall not see each other for the rest of the day."

That evening, after dinner at Oakland Park, Malessa and I sat in the blue drawing room drinking our coffee and waiting for David and his father to join us. As we talked, I admired her, as I had done almost continually since we had met. Malessa's huge brown eyes seemed a darker shade of brown than David's, but perhaps they only appeared darker because of the contrast between them and her palest, creamy skin—skin that blushed an exquisite shade of peach pink at her cheekbones. Her hair was the color of horse chestnuts and had their sheen. She sat opposite me in a dress of turquoise silk, and each time she gestured with her lovely hands, a necklace of emeralds and tiny sapphires flashed against the skin below her throat.

She gestured constantly as she spoke, and her hand

glided through the air now, as she spoke of her daughter: "Caroline? Oh, no. She would only hurt herself."

"But she must be six years old," I said.

"Didn't David tell you?" she asked. "Caroline is not—normal. It is not her mind. It is not her mind, no matter what the doctors say. But she cannot move the way other children can. It is really quite grotesque to watch her try to walk."

"Oh, Malessa," I said. "I am so sorry. Is there no cure?"

"None. She has been taken to all the doctors."

"How heartbreaking."

"She has her nanny."

Then casting about for something to say, I commented: "It is such a pity your husband couldn't have come down with you. I should love to have met him."

"Charles? I rarely see him anymore."

"Yes, he must be very busy. He is in the bank too. That is how you met him, isn't it? We had dinner with William and Cecilea on Monday evening, and Cecilea was saying that the bank demands so much of William's time."

"Bankers are callous people. They lust for power. There is nothing they would not do to further their ambitions. They are inhuman."

"Well, I must say that I am glad David is not in the bank. I don't think I could live in London, I mean. I can't tell you how grim London seemed. But it is exciting, isn't it? I mean the theatre, and the Queen—especially during the season."

"It is a bore," Malessa replied. "A terrible, interminable bore. Oh, I suppose it would be amusing if one were the duchess of Hartsbridge or the countess of Sterlingham—in that set—and it was all one ball after another. Tell me, Mary, why does the *baroness* Beauford wish to marry David Field, especially now?"

"What do you mean by now?" I asked.

"Well, you have a dowry now," she answered.

"Because I am in love with David, Malessa."

"And you think that love will last, and last, and never change. But it will change, providing it existed in the first place. Then will you regret?"

"Regret what, Malessa?"

"Marrying beneath your class."

"No."

"Now I have hurt your feelings," she said. "Forgive me, Mary. I didn't mean to, and I know I have no right— I just don't want you and David to make a mistake. Have you set a date for the marriage?"

"No, not yet," I replied. "I want a wedding dress, and Lady Clareham has suggested a dressmaker in Barnstaple who could make a beautiful one for me. David has offered to take me to see her tomorrow. We will be married as soon as it is finished."

"Oh, how fortunate! I am going into Barnstaple tomorrow, too, for Honiton lace. That is one of the reasons I came down. The Devon women still do the loveliest work, you know. It is what the Queen's wedding dress was made of. Had you thought of it for your own? Let us see what your dressmaker has to say about it. We will leave David here; it is no place for a man. I will call for you at two. Will that be too early?"

"No, that would be wonderful, Malessa," I was obliged to reply.

"No, wait!" she said. "That would not give us enough time. Not enough for shopping and a dressmaker, and we shouldn't hurry that. I know, come and have an early luncheon here with us. Could you do that?"

"Why, yes, but. . ."

"Good, then, I will call for you at eleven-thirty. Could you be ready by then? We will have luncheon here at noon and be off by one o'clock.

True to her word, Malessa called for me at eleven-thirty the following morning and drove me to Oakland Park, where we lunched with David and his father. Then, after luncheon—almost on the dot of one o'clock—we left the house.

And as we walked across the drive to the carriage, Malessa said: "Thank heaven we have the sun. I thought for a time this morning that we would be driving to Barnstaple through the mist."

"Yes. I love these sunny-misty days," I replied, as David helped me into the carriage, and when Malessa was seated next to me, I added, "They are so refreshing; they soften the skin."

"Yes, and encourage mildew, and mold, and decay."

As she spoke, the carriage began to move, and I waved

and said good-by to David, who stood on the drive beside us.

Then as we drove away, Malessa said: "You waved to someone when we left Castle Cloud this morning. Who were you waving to?"

"Lord Clareham," I replied. "He has a mirror arranged so that he can look down on the drive from his bed."

"And how is he?"

"About the same. He tries so hard to get well and to feel something in his right side, but I wonder if he really does."

"Speaking of decay, hasn't he let the Castle grounds go. It was unkempt the last time I was there, but now it is positively overgrown."

"I suppose it would be, if it weren't for the sheep. There are no gardeners anymore. All the gardens have gone to ruin—it is horrible." And then I told Malessa what it had been like four years before when I visited Vivian, and about that idyllic week, and how I had fallen in love with the Castle.

"You and Vivian are very close friends then?" Malessa asked.

"Yes," I answered. "I think some of our closest ties are made when we are young, don't you? There is something about the closeness of a school friend that stays with one, somehow. I suppose it is because you have gone through so much together. Vivian and I were very close at school, but of course after I left for the continent, our letters became infrequent. We had such very different lives: we were completely separated from each other then. It was bound to change. So I was surprised when she wrote, begging me to come immediately to Castle Cloud."

"She has gone to America with her groom, anyway. I am not surprised," Malessa said.

"Not surprised at her going?" I asked.

"Not surprised at her inviting you to Castle Cloud. But it would never have worked if she had stayed, and I don't suppose she knew that O'Conner or O'Connel or whatever-his-name-was would send for her."

"What wouldn't have worked?"

"Bringing you here for David."

"Bringing me here for . . . ?"

"Yes. You see, it would never have worked as long as

Vivian was here because David was so appallingly in love with her. He worshiped her. He could not have borne to be with another woman as long as Vivian was here. She infected him like a disease of some kind. Well, that is not surprising, is it? I think she is the most beautiful creature I have ever seen—almost unreal. But *she* was not in love with David. I knew that at once."

"David wasn't in love with Vivian, Malessa," I said. "He liked her enormously, and they had so many things in common; but he wasn't in love with her. He told me so."

"Of course he did, and that he is in love with you."

"Yes, and he is," I declared.

"Of course, but don't underestimate David's vast experience with women. He was extremely active in that regard at one time, and he is an expert in such matters. But, oh, my dear, if you could have seen him and Vivian together. He almost devoured her with his eyes—it was as though he couldn't assuage his thirst for looking at her. I think the more indifferent she was to him, the more his passion flamed for her."

"Why did she consent to marry him then?"

"David didn't tell you?"

"No."

"No, he wouldn't have, would he? Well, I shall have to, then—*before* your marriage. You may be one of the lucky ones. When you learn about it afterward, it is too late. Edmond arranged it."

"Against her will? Why? How could he do that?"

"You must know Edmond a great deal better than I do," she continued. "I know him only casually, but well enough to have noticed how he pushes and pushes for something: he will never give up until he has won. If you disagree with him, he will come back to it and back to it until he has beaten you into submission. Isn't that so?"

"Yes."

"Well, that is how he was with Vivian about her marrying David. She must have surrendered simply to get some peace. She was acting strangely at the time, according to David, almost as though she didn't care about anything, anyway—because of O'Connel, I think now."

"I don't understand," I said. "Why should Edmond do that? Why?"

"For money."

"Oh, no. Money from whom?" I asked.

"From my father. You see, Father has always craved one thing which he has never been able to have—a peerage. He knows Lord Palmerston, and Lord Palmerston has recommended it to Her Majesty—not once but several times, I believe. But it has never been forthcoming, and never will be. It is our Jewish blood, of course."

"Jewish blood?"

"My father's father was a Jew, Mary. Surely David has at least told you that. That was the primary reason why Grandfather Elliot objected to Father marrying Mother. And you know how the Queen feels about the Jews.

"Well, if Father couldn't have a peerage to pass on to his grandchildren, they would at least have noble blood. And who knows, David's marriage into the nobility, to Lord *Clareham's* daughter, might help his own chances with the Queen—probably not, but maybe. Anyway, it became an obsession with him. So the arrangement was made: Edmond would be loaned a considerable amount of money and, if the marriage took place, the debt would be canceled."

"I see," I said.

"And David would get Oakland Park. Oakland Park would be his, and Father would go to live on the estates in Northumberland. But you see, David, as it turned out, needed no incentive at all. But the arrangement remained: Father wasn't taking any chances."

"But Vivian couldn't do it, could she?" I mused. "And I was to be her way out of it. 'Comfort and luxury will surround you.' 'And you have the title.' "

"I beg your pardon, Mary?" Malessa said.

"Something Vivian wrote in one of her letters."

"Oh. Yes, your title. Father's first grandson will be a baron, won't he? That is much better than blood alone—almost as good as being created a peer one's self, don't you think?"

"Is there an 'arrangement' again this time?"

"Well, of course. David will get Oakland Park and all the estates in Devonshire and Cornwall, and Edmond's debt will be canceled."

"But Edmond didn't *want* me to marry David."

"Not at first, but he didn't object after David asked you,

did he? Why? Because he realized that he could make Father pay for his not spoiling it."

"How do you know that, and how could he spoil it?"

"Edmond called to see Father last night—late, after you had left—and I overheard. Evidently race-week required more money. How could he spoil it? Simply by telling you all of this."

"But you told me," I declared.

She smiled. Then she said: "Would you rather I had not?"

We did not speak again until we reached Queen Anne's Walk in Barnstaple. I had too much to think about to talk. My mind was in a turmoil and Malessa knew it. Was what she had told me true? I wondered. If so, it explained a great deal that had happened.

But when we reached Queen Anne's Walk, John drew to the side of the road, stopped the carriage, and got down from the box to look at something on the front of the carriage.

And when we straightened up, he said to Malessa, "Bit of trouble, madam."

"What is it, John?" she asked.

"Rim is coming off the front wheel, madam."

"Is it dangerous? Can you get it fixed?"

"Wouldn't drive anywhere we don't have to till we get it fixed at the smithy."

"How long will it take?"

"Oh, not long, madam."

"Well then," Malessa said, "go straight to the smithy and stop as near as you can get to Messrs. Hardy, Coldwell. We will walk from there." Then she turned to me and said, "I am sorry, Mary, but it can only be a short distance. Then we will go on to Mrs. Mummins'."

The draper's shop of Messrs. Hardy, Coldwell and Co. was large and stylish for a town the size of Barnstaple. It boasted arched glass show-windows and a dome-shaped skylight lighting the interior where bolts of cloth lined its walls—some as thin as an umbrella and some thicker and heavier, I supposed, than a rolled-up carpet. Plain and printed muslins, poplins, silks, and boreges lay among chenilles, velvets, cashmeres, and balzarines in plain colors, paisleys, tartans, stripes—quite an astonishing array. But I was not interested in the shop or its merchandise.

My mind was busy coupling things that Malessa told me in the carriage to events and conversations that had occurred since I had come to Castle Cloud. I knew it would be some time, however, before I could link them all together in my mind.

"Which do you like better?" Malessa asked, finally.

"What?" I replied. I looked down at the counter then, and saw, separated from a pile of others, two lengths of lace laid out side by side. "Oh, well—they are both lovely," I declared. "I think the smaller flowers."

"I will have the smaller flowers, then," she said to the shopman. "I am Mrs. Charles Guarnini. My father is Thomas Field. Would you put it on his account, please?"

"With pleasure, madam," the shopman replied.

"And can you direct us to Corn Street? We are looking for a Mrs. Mummins."

"If you turn to the right, madam, when you leave the shop and bear to the left past the parish church, you will cross it."

So, when the shopman had wrapped the lace and given it to Peter to carry, we left the shop, found the parish church, and walked to the left, around its churchyard. But there we stopped, puzzled by a fork in the road. Malessa suggested we take the branch to the left, as it seemed to be the wider of the two streets, and shortly we came to a crossroad.

"This must be Corn Street," she said. "What is the number of Mrs. Mummins' house?"

"Number thirty-two," I replied.

"Shall we ask that man standing there? Peter, will you ask that man where number thirty-two is?"

Peter walked ahead of us then and we followed him toward a man dressed in a frayed, ill-fitting black suit who leaned against the wall of the corner house. And as we approached him, I heard loud talking and shouts coming from inside the building.

Men's voices cried: "The caster's in for five pounds! Done! I'll bet fifteen to ten. What's the main and chance? Seven to five. I'll take on doublets!"

"Ah!" the man in the frayed suit shouted when he saw us. "The angels have descended to earth."

He pushed himself away from the wall of the house,

then, and staggered in a wide arc, avoiding Peter entirely, toward Malessa and me.

"Look out!" I cried, thinking that he was about to run into us.

But he stopped, miraculously, in front of me and stood swaying for an instant, as if at a loss. Then he removed his hat with a flourish and bowed low saying: "Ladysh! We are emenchly complemented, but the eshtablishment is not permitted to ladysh."

At this point, Peter, having returned to our side, grasped the man by his vest and would have flung him to the ground, I think, if Malessa hadn't cried: "No, Peter! I am sure the gentleman means no harm."

"No dishrespect intended, beautiful ladysh," the man said, as Peter let go of him. "For your husband or gentleman friend, my card."

With that, he handed me a small white card. Then he turned and handed one to Malessa, and then staggered back to his place against the building.

"Malessa," I said. "I don't want to see Mrs. Mummins today. Let us go back to the carriage. I am not in the mood to think about styles, and I couldn't bear being measured."

"No wedding dress?" she asked.

"Not today—I think I would like to go back to Castle Cloud."

"Of course." Then she turned to the footman and said: "Thank you, Peter. We will walk back to the smithy now, for the carriage."

As we walked along, I glanced at the card that I still held in my hand, and after I had read it, I slipped it carefully into my bag.

Then when we reached his shop, we found that the blacksmith had finished repairing the carriage wheel, and as soon as the horses were harnessed we set out for Castle Cloud. Malessa and I remarked about the landscape occasionally during the drive, but most of the time we left each other's thoughts undisturbed.

Finally as we neared the Castle, Malessa broke the long silence. "Have you changed your plans?"

"About what?" I asked.

"Your marriage."
"I don't know."
"But my dear. . ."
"I want to talk to David."

✠ Chapter Eighteen ✠

WE ARRIVED at the Castle at four o'clock, and after I had left Malessa, I went straight to my room, removed my shawl and gloves, carried my bag to the window, and took out the card the drunken man in Barnstaple had given me. It read:

Note: This house is insured against all legal inter-ruptions. Players are guaranteed free of jurisdiction at all times while within and shall be at ease—as in their own homes.

It was not on Corn Street that the man had handed it to me; I had known that as soon as I heard the shouts from inside the house. No, we had turned into Treadmere Street, and the men inside the house had been playing haz-ard. And I had wondered at the time if Edmond were among them.

I wondered if it were identical to the card I had found in that macabre book in Vivian's room. So now I went to her room, found the book lying on Vivian's bedside table, and picked it up. It fell open to pages seventy-three and seventy-four, and there, still marking the pages, lay the card.

The wording of its message was not identical to the card I had been given in Barnstaple that afternoon, but it was so nearly the same that I had no doubt that it too had come from a gambling house.

"It never belonged to Vivian," I whispered aloud. "Vivian loathed gambling of any kind. And, anyway, ladies are never permitted in such places."

Then I wondered, briefly, if the card could have been Lord Clareham's or James's. No. That was out of the question. It was Edmond's: I knew that, and I told myself

480

that there was no need to be so overconscientiously unprejudiced about it.

But why, I wondered, was that card that belonged to Edmond in that book? Was it Vivian's book which Edmond had borrowed, or was it Edmond's book that Vivian had borrowed? Had it come from the library downstairs? I glanced at its title page and read again: *One Hundred Cruel and Inhuman Murders Explained and Described in Detail.* I couldn't believe that Vivian would have been interested in such a book; that would have been contrary to everything I knew about her. And there was no way of telling when it had been published. It looked quite new. Then I glanced at the contents page, and under the chapter heading "IX CLUBBING," I noticed a story titled "The Crystal Palace Robbery." That must have taken place after 1851; so the book had probably been published in 1852 or later—rather new for the Castle Cloud library, judging from what I had seen of it. No, I decided, it was Edmond's book, though I had no idea what it was doing in Vivian's room.

Pages seventy-three and seventy-four of it, I discovered, dealt with the death of a Mrs. Armstrong in Chester on February 22, 1850. I read:

... peripheral neuritis, vomiting, high-stepping gait, diarrhea, and discoloration of the skin.

Then, on February 18th, Mrs. Armstrong lost complete use of her limbs, continued to suffer violent pains in the abdomen, and on the 22nd of February she died.

Since the first Mrs. Armstrong had died of almost identical symptoms six months before, Dr. Burton rapidly became suspicious and called in the police. The body was chemically analyzed and sufficient traces of arsenic were found to attribute death to arsenic poisoning.

Whereupon, under questioning, Mr. Armstrong quickly broke down and confessed his foul deeds. The monster had, he admitted, poisoned both the unfortunate ladies with diluted weed-killer added to Burgundy wine which he had urged upon them as a restorative (weed-killer is shown to contain fifty to seventy percent arsenic—easily soluble, and if dissolved in red wine or coffee, not detectable either by taste or color).

The culprit then showed the police the poisonous powder, bought by the pound at the local nursery. . . .

I could read no further and closed the book in disgust. No doubt those things happened, I thought, but why write about them—and with such relish? The author was as much a monster, probably, as was Mr. Armstrong.

"Well, what of it?" I murmured aloud, as I closed the book and replaced it on the table. "Detective Mary Thorpe is suspicious of everything but finds out nothing."

It was an odious book, and I thought it strange that it had found its way into Vivian's room, but it and its card held no significance for me.

The book had, however, started me thinking again about Vivian. And as I left her room and walked back to mine, I wondered, for perhaps the millionth time, where she was, what had happened to her, and what had become of the coffin. Was she dead? Had Edmond poisoned her? His own sister? No, that was too absurd. How David would laugh at me if I suggested it.

"David," I whispered, as I closed the door of my room behind me. "So, if you marry me, Oakland Park is yours. How nice for you."

I had been a business transaction after all, then, hadn't I? I could hear David's father say: "Now, David, Vivian has gone. Marry the baroness and I shall deed Oakland Park and the estates over to you."

David's beloved Oakland Park Farm, I thought, as I sat down again in the chair by the window. But I don't want to think about David or Vivian either, anymore, not today. It doesn't matter anyway because I am going away. I will not be here much longer, and I want to think about my beautiful Castle Cloud now, that placid bay, and those gulls, and that park down there. How Vivian and I used to run there after Sarah—poor Sarah. Now the lawn is a ruin, and it was so lovely once—so smooth and green. I wonder if it could ever be like that again? Gardeners could restore it, I suppose. First the weeds would have to go. Dig them up? Weed-killer? Was there weed-killer at Castle Cloud? If so, it would be on the potting bench in the greenhouse with all the other gardener's paraphernalia. Nonsense! You are tired. Lie down and try to sleep, and stop thinking.

And I did just that. I walked over to the bed, removed my shoes, and lay down, but I couldn't sleep—my mind wanted to think. It wanted to think about David. But I didn't want to think about David, and I wouldn't—it wouldn't do any good.

Was there weed-killer at Castle Cloud? If so, it would be on the potting bench in the greenhouse with all the other gardener's paraphernalia.

I got up then, put on my shoes, threw a shawl about my shoulders, walked downstairs and out to the glasshouses. I looked about as I opened the door to the conservatory and, seeing no one, stepped inside and closed the door behind me.

Then I walked to the entrance of the east greenhouse, entered, and stood just inside the doorway. Nothing had changed since my last visit: the cobwebs and dust lay undisturbed, and the air about me hung dry, and bitter-smelling, and silent.

The potting bench looked undisturbed too. And as I ambled toward it, I thought about how brown everything around me was—brown and blue. Above me, beyond the glass roof, floated the blue sky, and on all sides of me on the dusty, brown wooden benches stood dry, dead, yellow-brown plants in brown pots. Before me a bag of shriveled, dead bulbs spilled out onto the potting bench beside bags of plant tags, and bags of fertilizer, sand, compost, and grass seed. A pile of rusty trowels, hand rakes, and clippers and shears lay beside a stack of flowerpots, and yellow-brown seed packets and gardening pamphlets lay scattered on open yellow-brown newspapers—all with sun-faded lettering.

Yellow-brown is sun color, green is earth and water color, I thought, as I stood in front of the bench and picked up a paper bag from beside a rusty watering can. The bag was yellow-brown, like all the rest of the paper bags on the bench, but it had attracted my attention because it was of a much darker value and of a brighter hue than the rest; the sun had not yet had time to bleach it or dull its color. Nor, I realized at once, had it been used much: its paper was uncreased and its open end was neatly folded together. It was obviously new.

It was new and filled with pale gray powder—a powder which, as far as I was concerned, might have been anything from fertilizer to lime. I hadn't the vaguest idea what it was. But as I set the bag down again, I noticed a notation in red crayon on its side which read: "1 lb. weed." The word "weed" had been underlined several times. If "weed" meant weed-killer, I thought, the bag had surely been marked to identify its poisonous contents quickly among similar bags of other products.

But if it was weed-killer, who could have put it there recently? The gardeners had long since gone. Edmond? Why would Edmond have bought weed-killer? Certainly not for the lawns. To use as poison, then? Then why hadn't he bothered to hide it? One couldn't help noticing it where it was.

And why had Edmond been walking in the glasshouses on the day I had seen him from the top of the hill? Had he come to see if the bag of weed-killer was still there? But if he had been concerned with its safety, he would surely have hidden it in the first place. I wondered if I would ever know for sure what he had been doing that day, but I believed that Edmond had left that bag of weed-killer on the potting bench in the greenhouse. And I was going to prove it.

How? Simply by asking Mr. Wood if Edmond had bought it. By the look of things, all the gardening supplies had come from Wood's, a seedsman in Braunton—every bag, large and small, on the potting bench bore his advertisement. The new bag was no exception, except that its lettering was still black—unfaded by the sun. On each bag, below a woodcut of a sheaf of wheat and crossed scythe and fork, was printed:

W. WOOD
SEEDSMAN & NURSERYMAN
George St. corner of Newheart St., Braunton
Agent for
ARTHUR BATES & CO. CELEBRATED RELIABLE
SEEDS ETC.
and
D. HAY & SON NURSERYMEN
To serve you well, it gives him pleasure
For he always gives full Weight and Measure.

But before I could go to Braunton to see Mr. Wood—before I did anything—I needed to wash my hands. I left the greenhouse, hurried across the conservatory, and stepped outside to the edge of the lily pond behind it. There I scrubbed my hands with sand and water, and then I waved them in the air to dry as I walked along the path which led around the building to the drive.

It was five twenty-five when I reached the drive. I remember looking at my watch and thinking that it would take no longer than fifteen minutes to drive to Braunton. That would give me time to see Mr. Wood before dinner, if Colen were free to drive me there and we hurried.

I walked directly to the stable yard where I found Colen sitting on a stool outside the tack room doorway, smoking his pipe.

He rose when he saw me coming and walked toward me. "Lovely afternoon, my lady," he said.

"Yes, isn't it?" I replied. "Could you drive me to Braunton, Colen?"

"With pleasure, my lady. When would you like to go?"

"Now, if you could. Use whichever carriage would be quickest to harness the horses to. I want to go to Wood's, the seedsman. Do you know where that is?"

"Certainly, my lady. It is just as you enter Braunton. It will take a few minutes to hitch up the horse, though. We will take the cabriolet, then, my lady."

"Good! And that will give me time to fetch my gloves."

In less than ten minutes, I had collected my gloves and bag, and returned to the stable yard where Colen had the horse and carriage ready to depart. We drove off at once.

But as we sped toward Braunton, I began to wonder if I had acted hastily and perhaps foolishly, and if I had assumed too much simply because I had wanted to. That the brighter-colored paper bag in the greenhouse was new was no fancy: I was sure of that. But Lady Clareham might have purchased it, or Mrs. Foley (perhaps she gardened), or someone other than Edmond. And it might not contain weed-killer at all.

And even if the new bag did contain weed-killer and Edmond had bought it from Wood's, what would I say to Mr. Wood when I arrived at his store? I couldn't very well say: "I am afraid Lord Althrop has poisoned his sister with weed-killer. Did he buy the poison here?" Was I about to make a fool of myself? Well, I thought, I would simply have to figure out what to say as best I could, and if I did make a fool of myself, that was the way it would have to be. I would at least learn if Edmond had bought anything at Wood's, and, if so, what it had been.

All these thoughts had made the drive to Braunton seem terribly short. Colen called to me: "It is just around the curve in the road at the bottom of the hill, my lady."

He had hardly finished speaking when the town of Braunton came into view, and there on the outskirts of it, just beyond a stream below us, stood a stone house and beside it, an enormous, slate-roofed, stone barn with the words "W. Wood Seedsman and Nurseryman" painted above its wide, gaping doorway.

We drove directly to the barn and stopped in front of it. As Colen helped me out of the carriage, a heavy-set, broad man with black hair came out of the house and started toward us.

"Mr. Wood?" I asked, as he approached.

"Yes," he replied.

"I am Lady Beauford. I am staying at Castle Cloud with Lord and Lady Clareham."

"Oh, yes, my lady," he said. "And how is his lordship getting on?"

"We think he is improving, but slowly," I replied.

"Well, I am glad to hear it. We're all very concerned about him, you know, and hoping for the best. Now, what can I do for you, my lady?"

"Do you remember Lord Althrop's buying some weed-killer here recently? At least we think he said he bought it here. We would like some more of it, if he did."

"No, my lady, that wouldn't be recently. No, sometime ago, I think that would be. Let me see—yes, I remember, it was the second or third of May. Yes, Bates Patented Eureka Weed-killer—one pound."

"Oh, I don't think that sounds right, somehow," I said. "Are you sure?"

"Certain, my lady. We were waiting for a shipment of guano from Hay at the time, and I remember asking his lordship if they were about to do some work on the grounds up there, if they would be needing a gardener. I knew one who was looking for a place in the neighbor-hood at the time. But his lordship wasn't interested in hiring. Eureka Weed-killer—one pound." Then having finished speaking, Mr. Wood stood silently gazing at me.

"Well, then I would like another pound, please."

"Certainly, my lady," he said. "What are you going to use it for, my lady?" he asked.

"Well—for roses," I replied.

"And you know how to use it?"

"Oh yes, just sprinkle it about."

"In water, my lady. Dissolved in water: 16 gallons to 3 ounces. Very poisonous. I don't think for roses it would. . ."

"Poisonous?" I cried, hoping I sounded suitably surprised.

"Very poisonous, my lady."

"Oh, no!" I cried. "No! Then I don't think I would want to use it after all. I am terrified of poisonous things. Perhaps we had better do it by hand."

"That might be better, my lady."

"Yes, well I am sorry to be in such a rush, but I did hope to do some gardening in the next day or two, and I thought you might be closed tomorrow because of the races." I flicked open my watch. "Heavens, it is almost six-fifteen and I must fly."

"Yes, my lady," he said, examining me curiously.

"Colen," I called, as I turned to the carriage, "we must hurry back or I shall be late for dinner." Colen helped me into the carriage, and as we began to move, I waved and shouted: "Thank you, Mr. Wood. Thank you ever so much. I am so sorry to have troubled you."

Mr. Wood, with an expression of wonder, watched us as we left. As we drove back up the hill toward the Castle, I glanced back at the barn. He stood there yet, looking after us.

That evening Edmond did not dine at Castle Cloud with his mother and me. I was not surprised—we had seen little of him during race week. This was just as well because when he was there he had been morose, and rude, and argumentative, which had caused me to believe that he had been losing heavily on Treadmere Street.

Dinner was a simple meal that evening. The servants would all be going to the races the following afternoon, and I supposed the holiday atmosphere had already permeated the kitchens.

Later, in the drawing room, Lady Clareham excused herself after a few sips of her coffee, saying that she was tired.

I didn't mind being left alone. In fact, I welcomed it because I wanted desperately to think: so much had happened that day, and I needed to try to put what I had learned into some kind of perspective and then to see what conclusions I could draw about Vivian's disappearance. I wanted to think about that, not about David, though he came to my mind constantly. Each time he did I wanted to cry. I was determined, however, not to let myself think about him until after we had talked.

But the drawing room oppressed me; inside, the air smelled stale and the walls seemed to close in upon me. Outside, the wind had changed during the late afternoon, and the evening looked fresh, and cool, and dry. And it was, I discovered when I left the house and sat down on the top step of the west portico stairs.

I leaned against the base of a column and retraced the events of the day, trying to isolate the things I knew about Vivian from the things I merely suspected.

My day had begun, after breakfast, by continuing my search for the missing coffin. I had become obsessed by it and had begun to wonder if it could have been buried in Diana's Temple or James's grotto: both places had dirt floors where a coffin could easily have been buried without leaving a trace. So I visited them both. But when I examined the floor of Diana's Temple, it did not seem to have been disturbed. The earth inside James's grotto had obviously been dug up, but then Edmond had said that James had done it. I did not believe anything Edmond said, but James could have dug it up. How could I tell? I could not even tell how long ago it had been done.

My morning's investigations then, had yielded nothing that I had not already known. But though I hadn't found it, I felt certain that the coffin remained somewhere at Castle Cloud in spite of Lord Clareham's denial. Mr. Podock could not have invented his story. And I knew that Edmond had bought the bag of weed-killer at Wood's, and I felt certain that he had read the page about poisoning in that revolting murder book—else why should the gambling-house card, which could only be his, be marking the page? And I knew that Edmond had met Jane Spence at the railway station in Barnstaple later on the same afternoon that Vivian was supposed to have left for London. Jane could easily have impersonated Vivian, boarded the train at Braunton, gotten off at Exeter, changed clothes, thrown away the bag, and then simply have returned to Barnstaple that afternoon.

I got up and began to descend the steps to the drive. I would, I had decided, take my usual walk down to the stone bridge, and then when I returned to the house, go to bed early.

If Jane Spence had impersonated Vivian then, there was no evidence at all of Vivian's having left Castle Cloud the day after James's funeral. But what was the use of going over and over it? I really didn't know anything for sure except that Edmond had bought a bag of weed-killer.

But no, the coffin had disappeared, and Vivian had not left Castle Cloud: Edmond had poisoned her and buried her somewhere in that coffin, and I would have to prove it. I had to find out what had happened to Vivian. It was as though she were urging me to. But how could I? Only by finding the coffin and looking inside it.

As I reached the bend in the drive and began to walk down the hill, my thoughts flew to poor little Sarah. It was here, where the hedgerows began, that she would so often meet me in the evening. How horrible her death had been. Had Vivian's death been horrible too? I wondered. Why should Edmond wish to murder his own sister? He had had everything to gain by Vivian's remaining alive and marrying David. As Malessa had told me, if David and Vivian had married, Edmond would never have had to repay the money Mr. Field had loaned him—that had been the agreement.

And now, David would get Oakland Park if he married me. "Oh, David, why didn't you tell me?" I whispered to myself. "There are so many things you didn't tell me." But I would *not* let myself think about David. I would see him the following day and ask him about them then. There might be an explanation for—

Bang!

The ear-splitting crash of an explosion buffeted me, while at the same moment something struck a stone in the hedgerow to my right. Panic swept through me. To my left, in the direction of the explosion, I saw a veil of smoke. I smelled gun powder, and started to run. But I tripped almost immediately and fell headlong on the drive.

I had lain there only a moment, it seemed, when I realized that a sickening pain pounded in my head above my left temple, and when I raised myself on one elbow and felt the side of my face, it was warm and sticky with blood. This made me think that I had been shot, and that the bullet had lodged in my head. But then I looked down and saw a blood-covered stone embedded in the drive, and realized that I had struck my head on it. My hands were bleeding too, where I had scraped them. But I did not seem to be seriously hurt, and I was able to walk.

I was, however, shaken, and cold, and frightened. And after walking a few steps back up the hill, I felt that if I didn't sit down I might faint. So I sat on a rock at the edge of the drive and wiped my hands and dabbed at my face with my handkerchief. And I noticed that it had gotten nearly dark much too suddenly. Had I lain then, unconscious, on the drive? If so, how long had I lain there?

I would probably never know. But I did know that someone had shot at me. Who would want to do that? Had it been an accident, then? Or had I been mistaken for someone else? Was whoever had done it still nearby?

If he was, I might still be in danger. I knew that I should leave that place as quickly as possible, so I got up and stumbled quickly toward the house.

I don't really remember that walk up the hill, or entering the Castle, or climbing the stairs. But I do remember standing in the darkness of my room wondering why Jane Spence had not lit the lamps for me, or drawn the curtains or turned down my bed. She had forgotten me completely.

I was still too unnerved, however, to think about anything very clearly. And I kept wanting to do more than one thing at a time. I knew I should go see Lord Clareham at once and tell him what had happened: but, at the same time, I needed to take care of the wound on my head. It throbbed terribly. I poured some water into the basin and washed my hands and face. Then, with fresh water, I gently sponged away the dried blood on my cheek and temple until I was able to see the wound. At the hairline a lacerated area of skin about an inch in diameter showed red and swollen in the lamplight, but although it had bled a great deal, the cuts did not look deep or serious. The impact, I decided, had been more damaging than the abrasions.

But I still felt faint, so I made a pad of folded handkerchief, dipped it in clear water, and lay down on the bed, holding the compress against the wound for ten minutes or so before I removed it and allowed the skin to dry.

By that time it was nine-thirty, and I was beginning to feel a little better, though still terribly shaky. But regardless of how I felt, I knew I must see Lord Clareham that evening. So without changing my dress, which was dirty from the fall, I lit a candle and hurried to Lord Clareham's room.

I knocked on his door. Ahmad opened it a crack and shook his head.

"But I must see him tonight, Ahmad," I cried. "Something terrible has happened."

Then I heard Lord Clareham call something in Hindustani to Ahmad, and the door swung open. "What is it Mary?" Lord Clareham asked. He wore his nightcap and was dressed for sleeping. "Come in—it is all right. Sit here now and tell me what has prompted this late visit."

I had no sooner stepped into the room than Edmond arrived at the doorway behind me. "What is all the—" He stopped speaking the instant he saw me, but then he continued: "Mary! What on earth are you doing here at this hour of the night? Father needs his sleep. And what is the meaning of all that shouting on the gallery?"

"Someone shot at me," I said to Lord Clareham, as I sat down in the chair beside his bed. I ignored Edmond. "I was walking down the drive toward the stone bridge, and someone shot a gun at me from the top of the hedgerow."

"Are you sure?" Lord Clareham asked.

"Did you see him?" Edmond asked. He had stridden into the room, wearing a dressing gown, and stood beside my chair glaring down at me.

"I would know if someone shot at me, wouldn't I?" I said to Lord Clareham. "Of course I am sure. The bullet struck a stone just beyond my shoulder somewhere. I heard it."

"When did this happen?" Lord Clareham asked.

"Did you see him?" Edmond demanded at the same time.

"Just before dark," I replied.

"Did you *see* him?"

"No, Edmond, I didn't see him," I said.

"Someone shooting in the field beyond," Lord Clareham declared.

Then Lady Clareham appeared in the doorway that connected her room and her husband's. "Is something wrong?" she cried. She hurried across the room to us. "What has happened?"

"Nothing. Nothing, Julia," Lord Clareham said. "Somebody was shooting in the field and the bullet narrowly missed Mary. I will have a word with McComb in the morning."

"It was somebody shooting at *me*, Lord Clareham," I cried. "Someone aimed a gun directly at me and shot it. He was very near—just on top of the hedgerow. I don't know how he could have missed at such close range. He must be an abominable shot."

"You were lucky it was practically dark," Edmond observed.

"I don't know who or why," I continued. "But he was shooting at *me*. Why should anyone shoot at *me?*"

"Oh, Lord, no!" Lady Clareham cried.

"All right, all right! Try to be calm," Lord Clareham shouted.

"Reade," Edmond declared.

"I am sorry, Lord Clareham," I said. "Yes, we must be calm. I hated to come in and bother you, but I was frightened and didn't know what else to do."

"It was obviously Reade," Edmond declared. "He is crazy, that man, and he is always walking over our land with that gun of his—shooting our animals. Now he has started to shoot at *us*. I tell you he must be put away. He came up to me in Barnstaple the other day, looked at me in the strangest way, and then asked me how I felt. He is mad. He should be in an asylum, and by God. . ."

"Edmond!" Lord Clareham said. "Stop talking nonsense."

"Nonsense?" Edmond cried. "Now you take that crazy poacher's side against your own son."

"Edmond," I said, "if William Reade had shot at me at that close range, I would be dead now with a bullet through the center of my head—or the center of my heart. He is a dead shot. Don't be stupid."

"Stupid?" Edmond shrieked. "By God you have gone too far, Mary. You will be very. . ."

"Edmond!" Lord Clareham shouted. "Be quiet! I demand that you be silent."

"George, please," cried Lady Clareham. "Mary, please don't let him get excited."

"No," I replied, as calmly as I could. "But we must do something. I think it was the bearded bandit—the one who robbed Lord Portland. He is the only person I can think of. David and I saw him on Wednesday night. He pointed a gun straight at David as we drove toward the home-farm. We must tell Constable Nash about it, Lord Clareham. He will know what to do."

"Nash?" Edmond said. "Hardly! You leave it to me. I will get rid of him. . . ."

"Edmond!" Lord Clareham shouted. Then more quietly, he said: "You did the right thing to come and tell me, Mary. We will get in touch with Constable Nash in the morning. There would be nothing to be gained by doing so tonight. Now, you leave it all to me. You hurt your head, didn't you?"

"It is all right. I fell, but it will be all right."

"Good," he replied. "Now, you go to your room and go to bed. You have had a nasty experience and you should rest. Try to sleep. And you too, Julia. Edmond, I would like a further word with you."

I left them, then. I had had all I could bear for one day, and I wished to be alone, I went to my room. When I had locked my door behind me, I felt safe. But I couldn't sleep. I kept hearing that gunshot, and smelling the powder, and I kept falling down.

And when, at last, the sun had risen above the hill and had gilded the edge of the stone molding outside my window, I got out of bed, put on my robe, and went to sit by the window. In the park, the birds called to each other. The bay below lay as still as flat, blue slate in the morning air.

It was six o'clock then. I was relieved that it was morning: it had been such a long night. I hadn't slept at all. I had tossed from side to side, trying to put the attempt on my life out of my mind.

And I had thought about David. I couldn't prevent myself from thinking about him any longer. I had known, after examining it, that what Malessa had told me about him and his father was true. So David *was* still in love with Vivian. I had suspected that myself and, even after his denial, the feeling had nagged at me. I couldn't marry him, then. I couldn't marry a man who loved another woman, nor a man who wanted me for my title—for the house and land that marrying me would bring him. I loved David terribly; nothing could change that. But I loved the David I had created in my mind. I loved the David I had wanted David to be, not the real one. The real David was, evidently, quite a different kind of person. Had the kissing of girls on the nose become one of his hallmarks? I wondered. I didn't know the real David, and I didn't want to.

I wouldn't marry a man who didn't love me. I would go away instead—leave Castle Cloud—leave Devonshire. Perhaps I could go to the dowager countess: perhaps she would let me stay with her at Lewis House until I decided what I wanted to do.

But first I had to satisfy Vivian, I thought. More and more I had come to feel that she called to me to avenge her death. I examined what I knew about her disappearance, and again I came to the conclusion that I knew very little for sure. I had even begun to doubt that she was dead at all.

But as the sky outside my window began to turn gray, a plan took shape in my mind. And when it was completely formed, I went over and over it, deciding exactly what I would say to make Edmond show me where the extra coffin lay. I thought my little scheme might work. But it would work better, I decided, if I knew Constable Nash.

I was still thinking about the constable when Mrs. Muldoon knocked on my door and I got up to open it for her.

"Sure," she said, " 'Twas all locked up nice and tight, I see, my lady."

"Yes. I couldn't sleep, Mrs. Muldoon."

"And what have you done to your head?" she asked.

"I fell on the drive last evening. It will be all right. It looks a lot worse than it is. It is only a bruise, actually."

Then Mrs. Muldoon left me briefly to get my bath and its sheet. And when she returned and had begun to arrange them on the floor, I asked: "Mrs. Muldoon, do you know Constable Nash?"

"Know him?" she replied. "Sure, I know him. It's just three cottages down the lane he lives with his mother."

"What is he like?" I asked.

"Like an ass, if you want my opinion. A big fat ass. How it's a constable he ever got to be is beyond me, my lady. Och, he wouldn't know a thief if he saw one. And if he saw one, he wouldn't be able to catch him."

"Oh, dear," I murmured. "You don't think he is very smart, then?"

"Smart?" she cried. "Faith, he thinks a mandolin is a Chinese lord. Ha, ha, ha. A mandolin is a Chinese lord. Ha, ha, ha. Now, let me get these cans in here, and then I've got to hurry."

After she had poured my water and left, I bathed, dressed, combed my hair so that it hid the bruise above my temple, and went down to breakfast.

Edmond was seated at the table when I arrived.

"Just coffee, Mitchell, please," I said.

"Good morning, Mary," Edmond said. "Isn't it a perfectly splendid day? Superb for the races—couldn't ask for anything better. It is Red Pepper in the first race, Mary, if you should want to put down a little wager. He is sure to win. Positive! And the odds were twenty to one the last time I heard. Twenty to one! Try the trout. It is superb."

"I am afraid that after last night, I couldn't be very interested in horse races or food," I replied.

"Oh, yes, nasty business. The man is mad. You never know what they will do when they are that way—erratic. Just a thought on the spur of the moment, that is the way the madness works—nothing premeditated, you know. He just happened to be there and the thought went into his mind: so he shot at you—erratic behavior. He will not be back. Shoot at somebody else, most probably—complete stranger, like as not. Dangerous, but I wouldn't worry about him. You are perfectly safe until I can put. . ."

"Edmond, if you are talking about William Reade, you could not be more mistaken," I interrupted. "As I said last night, he would have killed me at that close range even if it had been dark. It was somebody else."

"Well, you know, I didn't say he meant to *kill* you. He was obviously trying to frighten you—enjoyed watching your reaction. But we can't have him wandering about the neighborhood."

"Constable Nash will know what to do," I said.

"Nash? Ha! He doesn't know how to tie his own shoe. I suppose his mother does it for him—stupid ass."

"I wouldn't be too sure about that," I declared.

"What?"

"He could be a lot smarter than you think, Edmond."

"Nonsense! You don't even know him."

"We have met."

"Don't be ridiculous, Mary," Edmond replied.

"Well, he may seem stupid to you, but he seemed rather clever to me. And he has an astonishing knowledge of crime techniques."

"Ha!"

"Oh, yes. For instance, I found it particularly interesting that he knew so much about chemical analysis. The body of the victim of a suspected poisoning, when disinterred and sent to London, can be chemically analyzed and the results received in three days. Isn't that fascinating?"

"What do you mean?" Edmond asked.

"Well, don't you think that is interesting? Constable Nash will want to have a chat with you soon, I think."

"What exactly would he want to talk to me about? What have you been up to?"

"Why, about the attempt on my life last night, of course. He will, quite naturally, want to talk to everyone about it. Is there anything *else* that he would want to talk to you about?"

Edmond glared at me, and I returned his stare for a moment.

Then I laid my fingers on my forehead and cried: "Oh, you must excuse me, Edmond. I have a violent headache from falling last night. It is becoming unbearable—I must go up and lie down. Oh, I am in such pain."

I got up from the table and, covering my eyes, stumbled (convincingly, I hope) into the rotunda. But I did not go to my room. Instead, I climbed to the second floor of the house, ran to the third floor, then to the stairway to the lantern, and up them. I closed the trapdoor behind me and crouched on the wooden bench in the cupola, panting, watching the grass and the drive below me for Edmond. I had no idea from which direction he would appear or which way he would go. My neck began to ache from twisting it constantly in every direction.

Then I saw him. He had left the house by the east portico, and he walked across the grass circle toward the rose garden, then ran down the garden steps and along the gravel path to the fountain. He paused to glance back at the house—but only for an instant—and then hurried across the garden, across the meadow, and vanished into the trees.

Had I lost him? If so, at least I knew the direction he had taken. I watched and waited, and at last he appeared near the top of the hill. Yes, he was going to the Horse Monument.

He walked directly to the pyramid and entered it. And a minute later he emerged, walked slowly around it, and then—after standing still for perhaps half a minute—he walked back to the path, down the hill, and to the house.

After what I had said to Edmond at breakfast, he would have had to be sure that Vivian was still where he had left her. Had he buried her in the horse's tomb, then? Was that why Lady Clareham had left the roses there, shortly after I had arrived at the Castle? Instead of discarding them from James's bouquet, as she had claimed, had she left them there purposely for Vivian?"

Since I had no wish to meet Edmond again that morning, I remained in the cupola until he had ridden away from the Castle. I felt certain that he would set out for Barnstaple soon after he returned to the house, and he had. I believed he would be gone for the rest of the day. But even after he had left, I remained in the lantern. I felt that being high above the world might give me perspective, and help me decide what to do next.

I would have to look inside King Charles's tomb in the Horse Monument to see if the coffin was there. But I couldn't possibly lift the marble slab myself. It became necessary, then, to decide what I could say to David to convince him to lift it for me.

I remained in the cupola, thinking, for almost an hour. Then I went to my room, and then I walked in the rose garden, as the morning dragged on interminably. Luncheon also dragged on interminably. Would it never be time for David to arrive? He was to call for me at two-thirty, but it seemed that two-thirty would never come.

Finally, I saw one of the Oakland Park carriages approaching the house, and I ran out onto the portico, and down the steps.

"Hello, darling," David said, after he had jumped down from the carriage. "Are you ready? Shouldn't you be wearing something around you?"

"I can't go to the races, David," I replied, glancing at John and a footman whom I had not seen before. "May I talk to you?"

"Of course," David said, giving me his arm. And as we walked out onto the grass away from the carriage, he continued: "Has something happened? What is wrong?"

"I have found Vivian."

"Where is she?"

"Edmond has buried her in the Horse Monument," I blurted out.

But even as I spoke, I realized that I had made a mistake. I knew he wouldn't believe me, and he didn't.

"Mary," he said, after looking down at me for a moment. "Vivian has not been buried in the Horse Monument or anywhere else. We don't know where she has gone, but making up wild fantasies won't help. I know how concerned you are, but we will simply have to wait and see. Now, Father is waiting for us. Put it out of your mind. . . ."

"David," I interrupted, "let me tell you why I think so. Will you please listen to what I have to say?"

"Very well," he murmured.

"We know that something strange or terrible has happened to Vivian—something strange or terrible enough to cause Edmond to go to all the trouble of inventing those letters, and strange or terrible enough for him and his family to refuse to tell me what has happened to her. And an extra coffin was made and left at Castle Cloud."

"But you don't *know* that," David said.

"Please let me finish. I am sure that Mr. Podock was telling the truth. I found a book in Vivian's room. . . ." Then I told David about the book, briefly, and the gambling-house card and the weed-killer. ". . . so when I asked Mr. Wood about it, he said that Edmond had bought the weed-killer. He even remembered when." Then

I described what had happened at breakfast and after. "Edmond went straight to the pyramid and looked inside it and all around it before he returned to the house and left for Barnstaple."

"That is all very interesting, Mary," David said, "but all these things could be interpreted in many different ways. You have no real proof. Just because Edmond bought weed-killer doesn't mean that he poisoned his sister. Do you realize what you are suggesting? It would be more reasonable to believe that he used it on the grass."

"David, I am *not* going to the races," I replied. "I must find out if she is there, and if you won't help me, I will do it myself. You go to the races, if they mean so much to you. I will find a hammer and smash that slab bit by bit if it takes me all afternoon."

"All right, but if she is not there—and I promise you she isn't—will you stop all of this?"

"She is there," I replied.

We walked back to the carriage then, and David told John to return to Oakland Park and take his father to the races in Barnstaple, and to tell him that there was a matter that required his attention at Castle Cloud—that it was not serious, and not to be concerned about it.

When he had finished his instructions, we walked around the house and across the grass circle. David decided that we should take an iron bar along to pry the pieces of marble loose from the top of the tomb in case he couldn't lift them off. So we walked to the stables and, after some searching, David found a crowbar in the carpenter's shed.

We hardly spoke as we walked up the hill.

When we reached the pyramid, David said: "We may as well get right to it. At least no one will see us; *they* are all at the races."

"Yes" I replied.

We entered the monument together, and David looked down at the tomb's marble lid, ran his hand across the crack that divided it in two, and then squatted and twisted his body in order to look under the overhanging edge of the slab.

"Cemented all around," he murmured. Then he stood and grasped the lid with both hands. "Well, let's see if we can— No, we will have to use the bar."

After that, he removed his coat and hat, gave them to me to hold, and rolled up his sleeves. He left the pyramid, walked to one of the building blocks that lay scattered about in the grass, and carried one back to the monument. He placed it at the foot of the tomb. Then, one by one, he carried two more blocks into the monument, placing them on top of the first one until he had built a tall enough fulcrum to rest the bar upon in order to lever the slab.

When the blocks were finally arranged and the crowbar rested in place, David asked, "Ready?" Then, straight-armed, he jerked down the end of the bar with both hands. The marble slab uttered a low, sharp cry, and one end of it flew into the air. David grabbed it and thrust it aside.

He stood motionless, looking down into the tomb. I stepped to his side and looked: in the dusky interior lay a black, polished wooden coffin. From its side a silver handle glinted in the shadows, and on its lid a silver plate bore an engraved angel above, and flowers below, but there was no name in-between.

Only part of the coffin was visible, because David had lifted only half of the broken lid of the tomb; so, without looking at me, he built his fulcrum at the other end of it, levered up the remainder of the lid, and shoved that aside too. Then he straightened up and stared across the sepulcher at me.

"I don't want to see her," I said. "I will wait outside."

Outside the monument, a fresh breeze blew in from the sea. I searched the horizon for a ship, but I knew that I couldn't run away from what was happening; so I forced myself to face the pyramid and wait for David to appear.

In a few moments he came to the doorway and stood there, wide-eyed. Then he turned and ran back through the structure, and I heard him being sick on the other side of it.

While I waited for him to recover, I sat on one of the building blocks in the grass, numb. Shortly, David came to me, flung himself down on a block nearby, and sat—hunched forward—his elbows on his knees, his chin on his chest, his eyes closed.

I waited for him to speak, but he didn't. At last I asked, "It was Vivian?"

He looked up at me then, his eyes glistening, and murmured: "That bastard! That filthy, rotten beast. Butcher! Wait until I lay these hands on him." Then in a louder voice he declared: "I'll beat the blood out of his body, Mary. I'll kill him! I'll kill that scum." He paused, questioning me with his eyes. "Why did he do it? Why? That murdering beast!"

"You did love her, didn't you?" I said.

"Yes! No! What does it matter? Do you want to see her?" he shouted, staring at me. "Her eyes are all eaten away."

Then he twisted around so that his back faced me, and he covered his face with his hands.

I didn't speak again and neither did David, until, after more than a minute, he dropped his hands and faced me. "Where is he?"

"I don't know—at the races, I suppose. He left shortly after he came up here, and I haven't seen him since."

"I am going to get him."

David leapt to his feet, and stalked off toward the path that led down to the house. I ran after him. I caught up to him and grabbed his arm. He stopped walking, and I swung around in front of him.

"David," I said, "don't! He isn't worth your getting into trouble over. Turn him over to a constable. There must be one in Barnstaple."

"Why did he do it?" David asked. "Why, Mary? She was so fragile, so vulnerable. How could he?" After a moment, he added, "I will take one of the horses. Chestnut must be there."

"But Colen has gone to the races."

"I can saddle him."

"But you are not dressed for it, David."

"Does it matter?"

He had stepped around me by then and began to stride down the path. I had to run to keep up with him."

"What will you do?" I cried.

"Get him. I will know what to do with him then. Don't worry, I won't kill him. I will leave a little life in him— just a little."

I ran after David all the way to the stables. It would have been impossible to talk as I ran: I was soon out of breath. I couldn't think of anything to say anyway, and even though I hadn't actually seen Vivian, I was still in a state of shock and couldn't think clearly. When we arrived at the stables, I did nothing but stand helplessly beside Chestnut's box while David saddled him.

Before I could object, David grabbed me, kissed me quickly, and said: "I will be back before long."

"Bring him back with you, David," I cried, as he led Chestnut out of the stables. Then I followed them into the yard. "Bring him back to his father—he will know what to do."

But before I could say anything more, David leapt into the saddle, and they flew from the yard and down the drive.

I stood watching them until they had vanished around the side of the Castle, and then I walked into the house. Inside it, the air hung silent as a tomb. It was deserted: I looked up at the gallery from the floor of the rotunda, and then I looked into the drawing room and the hall chamber, but I did not see Lady Clareham. I supposed she was lying down, as she often did in the afternoon. And of course the servants had all gone to the races. I was left alone, and I supposed I would remain alone until I saw David again. I could do nothing until I had seen him and learned what had happened. I might have gone for a walk in the park to clear my head, but after my experience the previous evening, I had no wish to leave the house alone. There was nothing to do then but sit by the window in the hall chamber and wait for David.

How can I describe my thoughts as I waited? I was confused, shocked, horrified. Even though I had suspected it for weeks, the reality of murder was unacceptable to me. And at the same time, I wondered why Edmond had done it—what Vivian could have done to have prompted so final an act. I wondered if I would ever know.

And then when I thought of Lord and Lady Clareham, my heart sank. I remembered how she had pleaded: "Don't bring it all down about our heads, Mary." Of course she knew. Everyone in the house knew about it; that was why they had wanted to get rid of me so badly. Why had the servants kept the secret? For Lord and Lady Clareham and, I supposed, for their own security. Heavens only knows, I thought, what would happen to the Castle, and their employment if there were no heir when Lord Clareham died. Was there another heir besides Edmond, a distant cousin, perhaps? Perhaps there was, but that could not help Lady Clareham. If Edmond were taken away and hanged, it would be the end of everything for her. Then I remembered her saying: "Mary, please don't let him get excited." Edmond's hanging would kill Lord Clareham. Nothing could bring Vivian back: so why must Lord and Lady Clareham suffer any more?

And I realized why Lord and Lady Clareham had so badly wanted Edmond to marry, and why grandchildren were so important to them—only Edmond's grandchildren could bring any hope back into their lives. But Edmond had refused to marry.

It was all very complicated and tragic, and in spite of myself, I began to wonder if it wouldn't be better to forget Vivian's death. What good would it do to avenge it?

It was four-thirty when I saw a horse and rider rise into view as they approached the hilltop and rounded the bend in the drive. I watched then, for a second rider to appear behind the first, but he didn't: David had returned alone. As he neared the house, however, I saw that it was not David who rode alone toward me—it was Edmond.

When I was sure that David had not also returned, I rose from my chair and walked into the rotunda. I waited for Edmond to enter the house and, when he did, I walked toward him. He looked exhausted, and I could tell that he was in a nasty humor.

"Where is David?" I asked him.

"How the devil should I know where David is? Don't you know? Have you lost him?" he sneered.

"He went to find you. Didn't you see him?"

"Is he dying?" Edmond asked at once.

"No, Edmond, your father is not dying," I replied. "David and I found Vivian."

"You don't say. And did you tell her to come home? What kind of a fool do you think I am, Mary?"

"In the Horse Monument."

"Ha! If you think she is in the Horse Monument, why don't you go and look? Don't be absurd. What kind of game do you think you are playing? All that stupid talk at breakfast. I think you are losing your mind."

"We already looked, Edmond. If you don't believe me go and see. The tomb is open. Then, for God's sake, give yourself up to the police—at least spare your mother and father the ordeal of David's coming to get you. He wants to beat you."

Edmond stood motionless for a moment, staring at me; then he spun around and ran out the door to the east portico. I walked after him and stood at the top of the steps, watching him run across the grass circle, across the rose garden, and up into the meadow toward the pyramid. I stood watching the place where the path led through the trees beyond the meadow, waiting for Edmond to reappear. I knew he would have to return that way to reach the stables, and I wanted to watch him ride away in order to see which direction he took.

But he did not go to the stables. He walked directly to the house.

And after he had climbed the stairs to the portico and stood before me, I said: "Edmond, David is hunting for you. He will come back here and. . ."

"What the bloody hell do I care where he goes?" Edmond snarled. "So you did it. So you found her. You schemed, and lied, and deceived. You used every foul trick you could think of to find out, didn't you? You cunning little bitch."

"Murderer!" I retorted. "I am going to your father."

Then I turned and fled through the open doorway back into the rotunda, but Edmond sprang after me and caught me before I could reach the stairs. He grabbed my arm and swung me around to face him.

"She killed herself," he cried.

"Let go of me!"

"She killed herself! Don't you believe me?"

"No!"

"Father will tell you. Go up to Father. She killed herself."

But he held me fast for a moment, glaring at me. I tried to wrench myself free of him, but he was too strong for me. Then he let me go, and I ran to the stairs. Edmond followed me.

"You never could face reality, could you?" I called back to him. "Have you convinced yourself that Vivian took her own life? Is that what you have done? Come out of your dream world, Edmond. All you have ever done all your life is dream—dream about winning piles of money, dream about making Castle Cloud a showplace. You dream about everything. If you can't answer a question, you dream up the answer." I was breathless; we had reached the second-floor landing and now hurried along the gallery toward Lord Clareham's room. But I continued: "You don't know the difference between what is real and what is a dream. You killed Vivian. You poisoned her—your own sister." Then I beat on Lord Clareham's door. "And you are going to have to pay the price for it."

"What is it?" Lady Clareham cried.

She had stepped out of her room onto the gallery just as Ahmad had opened Lord Clareham's door for us. As he did so, Edmond pushed the door open wide with both hands, brushed past me, and strode into his father's room. Lady Clareham and I followed him.

"Mary has found Vivian's body, Father," Edmond said. "She won't believe that Vivian killed herself. She thinks I did it."

I looked first at Lord Clareham. He lay propped up on his pillows, a closed book in his left hand, gazing at me. He did not move or speak. Then I glanced at Lady Clareham, behind me. She stood frozen still, gaping at her husband. At that moment, for just an instant, I felt as though everything in the world had stopped.

"Well, tell her what happened," Edmond demanded. "Tell her how she drank the wine and killed herself over her dear brother's death. Tell her!"

"Sit down, Mary," Lord Clareham said, laying his book aside and motioning me to sit in my usual place. "I think you had all better sit down."

I sat in the chair, Lady Clareham sank down upon the edge of Lord Clareham's bed, and Edmond sat in a chair that Ahmad hurriedly placed next to mine.

"Vivian took her own life," Lord Clareham said.

"She would never do that," I declared.

"She did, my dear," he continued, "in James's room shortly after his death. I don't think you know how much she loved her brother. His death was a violent shock to her, and she had recently suffered ... an emotional loss of another kind which had left her unstrung. She may have written to you about it. James's death was the blow that destroyed her reason. She appeared in his room—I was not there of course, but Julia and Mrs. Foley and Edmond were—carrying a bottle of wine, which she had poisoned, and a glass. She said she didn't want to live any longer, that life was too cruel, and then she poured a glass of the wine and drank it."

I glanced at Lady Clareham just as she began to speak.

"She sat down on James's bed and looked at us. She just sat there looking at us, with her hands folded in her lap," Lady Clareham said. She didn't speak to anyone, rather she seemed to describe what was happening as she relived the experience. " 'Why did you do that?' I cried. 'Vivian!' But she didn't speak—she just sat there. She was exhausted—we all were. We said she should go and lie down, but she just sat there and stared at us." Lady Clareham paused, her lips quivered. She was crying but she did not wipe the tears away.

"Then the pains began," she continued, "and she was sick. Finally we got her to her room. Mrs. Foley was there and we sent for Jane to help. She screamed with pain— how my darling screamed. We tried everything we knew. She couldn't keep anything down. She was out of her mind with the pain until Mrs. Foley got the chloroform. Thank God! Thank God for that. By nine o'clock she was so weak, and cold, and damp— She could hardly breathe. Edmond had gone for the doctor, but by eleven she was no longer conscious. She passed away shortly after eleven o'clock."

For a few moments I sat silently gazing at Vivian's mother, my mind racing.

Then I asked: "Why didn't she have a funeral?"

"A funeral?" Edmond cried. "Do you know what they used to do with suicides? They used to bury them at a crossroad with a stake in their heart. Funeral? You can't bring a suicide into a churchyard. No clergyman would have it—Canon Law forbids it. '. . . they that die unbaptized, or excommunicated, or have laid violent hands upon themselves,' " he quoted. "She would be buried in a field somewhere. And why have the coroner puttering about and the coroner's jury to go through?"

Then Lord Clareham spoke. "James had died, Mary. He had been ill for some time, as you know. That had been an ordeal, and then Vivian— Ourselves not withstanding, we decided that if Vivian was to bear the disgrace of not being allowed to lie in the mausoleum in the churchyard with her family, then she would do so without a coroner's abuse as well, or the censure of her neighbors."

"Yes, I suppose so," I murmured.

Edmond and his mother and father all studied me as I sat there looking from one to the other of them.

Finally I said: "I am so awfully sorry—I feel as though I have betrayed you and your hospitality." I was going to apologize further, but at that moment, I heard a horse approaching the house. "That must be David." I got up from my chair and crossed to the window to see if it was he. "Yes. I will go and tell him what happened."

"Must you tell him?" Lord Clareham asked. "Wouldn't it be better not to, Mary?"

"He was with me," I said. "We found her together, Lord Clareham. But I will ask him to keep the secret. I am sure he will."

"I think you had better ask him to come up here, then. I would like a word with him," he said.

"Certainly," I replied.

Then I left the room to fetch David. And by the time I had stepped out onto the east portico, David was already hurrying toward the house. I went to meet him.

"I left Chestnut; Colen is on his way," David said. "I couldn't find Edmond. There were hundreds of people at the course, and afterward I tried Treadmere Street, but he wasn't there."

"He is here—with his father," I said. At once David slipped past me and strode toward the house. "David, don't! Wait! He didn't do it. She did it herself." He stopped in his tracks when I said that. Then he turned and faced me, and I hurried to him. "Vivian killed herself. It is true, David—over James's death. She was miserable over O'Connor, and then when James died, it was too much for her."

"Are you sure?" he asked. "How?"

"Poison. Yes! Lady Clareham told me all about it. It must have been horrible—it was hours before she died."

David stood looking at me and shaking his head almost imperceptibly, but he did not speak.

Then I said, "Lord Clareham would like to speak with you."

"I don't believe it," David said, as we walked toward

the house together. "I don't think Vivian would do that, no matter how much she loved James."

"I didn't think so either, but she did."

As I said this I heard a carriage behind me. I glanced about; Colen had returned from the races with the servants in the wagonette.

I led David up the stairs and along the gallery to Lord Clareham's room.

When Ahmad had opened the door, Lord Clareham called, "Come in, David. Come in and sit down here."

David sat in the chair that Edmond had used a few minutes before, and I sat down next to him. Edmond stood near the head of his father's bed. Lady Clareham still sat beside her husband on his bed.

David nodded and said: "Lady Clareham, Lord Clareham." He ignored Edmond.

"Mary tells us," Lord Clareham said, "that you and she have discovered Vivian's body."

"Yes, sir," David replied.

"Has she told you how Vivian died?"

"Very briefly," I said.

Then Lord Clareham described again Vivian's emotional state, and how she had taken the wine without warning, and how she had suffered before she died.

At last, when he had finished, David said: "I can't believe it. For Vivian to have done such a thing is inconceivable."

"It is true, David," Lady Clareham almost whispered. "I was with her every minute." Then she sobbed, "I never left her—I stayed with her until morning."

"As I explained to Mary, David," Lord Clareham said, "we could not subject our daughter to a coroner—there would have had to be an examination and a coroner's jury, you understand—nor could we subject her to vilification, or ridicule, or the indignity of lying forever separated from her family. That is why I must ask that you say nothing about this to anyone."

David looked at Lord Clareham, plainly mystified.

"If it became known that Vivian took her own life, David," Lord Clareham explained, "she could not be buried in the churchyard: you understand that that is prohibited by church law. But if, sometime in the future, Vivian were to be returned from, say, a distant place, having supposedly died there of natural causes, she could then be buried with the proper funeral in the Ramsay mausoleum—next to James, where she would wish to be. Do you understand? We do not think that this little deception could be of any harm to anyone."

"I understand," David said. After a moment's silence, he rose from his chair and said: "This must be very painful for you both. I—you can be sure that I will say nothing. I give you my word. Now, I must go. Mary?"

"Yes, I will come with you," I said.

We left the room together, descended the stairs, and when we reached the hall below, David said: "I still can't believe it. Poor Vivian. God, how she must have suffered—she must have gone through hell."

"Yes," I replied.

"And you, Mary?" he asked. "Are you all right, my darling?"

"Yes, I am all right."

"You seem so far away."

"David, will you come into the drawing room? I want to talk to you."

"What is it?" he asked, when we had sat down together and he had taken my hand in both of his.

"I am going away," I said.

"Yes, you must. And I will take you. It will do us both good, after this. Where shall we go? Italy? France?"

"I don't mean that. I—I am going away alone."

"That wouldn't do any good. We can't run away from things. Vivian is gone. Only God knows why things like this happen, but they do, and somehow we have got to put them behind us."

Then he cupped my face between both his hands, and as his face moved toward mine, I said, "No, don't," and pulled away.

"Why?" he asked.

"Because you don't mean it."

"Why do you say that? Because I was excited this afternoon? Because I got angry? Of course I was angry—I thought Vivian had been murdered. We both thought so. What would you have thought of me if I hadn't been angry? What kind of man would I be?"

"I can't marry you," I declared.

"Yes you can, and you will, my darling," he said, taking

my hand in both of his again. He smiled down at me, then, and looked into my eyes in that thrilling way of his.

He was lying to me, blatantly, with his beautiful eyes. He made me want to cry, and I was furious with myself for being so affected by him. And I was angry because I knew he was so different from the David I loved in my mind.

"No," I replied.

"Why? What has happened? Why?"

"Why?" I cried. "Why didn't you tell me about the arrangement? Why didn't you tell me that you would get Oakland Park if you married me? You knew that Vivian brought me here to marry you, didn't you? Why didn't you tell me? You knew all about what your father was doing in London when he went to see Mr. Schraw—that he was investigating me—and you knew why. . ."

"No! I told you," he interrupted. "I didn't know anything about that."

"But you knew how much your father has always wanted a peerage, and how disappointed he was about not getting one, and how he has always wanted noble blood in the family. And you didn't suspect? You knew that that was why he wanted you to marry Vivian so badly. That was why he was willing to *pay* you to marry her by giving you Oakland Park. That was why he *paid* Edmond to pressure her into marrying you. You knew about that, didn't you?"

"I didn't know about it at first," David said, "but I did later. It wasn't *like* that. Father didn't pay Edmond to do anything. It was blackmail. Well, a kind of polite blackmail. Father didn't want to see me hurt, and he could well afford the money. And he didn't want Edmond as an enemy, so he loaned him money."

"The debt to be cancelled when you and she were married."

"Yes—but you are thinking about it in the wrong way. I have told you about it. I wanted to settle down and have a family—a son to inherit the farm. I liked Vivian enormously. We were great friends. She—she would have made a good wife."

"And have assured you and your father a more secure place in local society and just possibly influence the Queen on your father's behalf."

"It wasn't important to me whether Edmond was being paid or not, and anyway, I don't think he had that much influence upon Vivian."

"Then why do you think she insisted that I come to England?" When David didn't reply immediately, I continued, "You know that Edmond is being paid now—again by your father."

"Why?" he asked.

"So that he won't tell me all these things which I already know. Your father considers me an even bigger catch than Vivian, doesn't he? Now, he thinks, his grandson will be a baron. So he is paying you to marry me and paying Edmond not to spoil it. I suppose he would have tried to pay *me* if he had thought he could. But he knows that I am not for sale."

"Mary, the fact that my father is giving me Oakland Park has nothing to do with my love for you. It will be a perfect home for us. You said that you liked it—that it is beautiful. You should be overjoyed that it will be mine. Yes! I suspected that was why Vivian brought you here. And I will always be grateful to her for that. And I *didn't* know that father was checking your background when he was in London. He has this obsession about a peerage— about his lineage. Well, let him. It doesn't do anyone any harm. It is not doing us any harm. If he should take pleasure in having a baron for a grandson, let him—that has nothing to do with us.

"I love you, Mary, and I want you to be my wife. I want you to be my wife because I love you, and for no other reason. Not for your title—that means nothing to me. I love *you*. I would love you no matter who you were."

"No, David," I said. "You were in love with Vivian. You still are. I saw it in your face this afternoon. You are not in love with me."

"You didn't see it in my face this afternoon. Outrage, yes. Hatred of Edmond because of what I thought he had done, yes. Repulsion because of the brutality of it, yes; But not love. I *wasn't* in love with Vivian—not the way I am in love with you. You have no reason to say that. It is not true." He stared at me then, searching my face. "Don't you believe me?"

"How can I? It is not only one thing—it is so many things. It is all such an obvious plot."

"But I have explained everything to you," he said.

I looked away from him. I felt exhausted. Finally I said, "I am sorry, David."

"You have no reason to doubt my love for you, do you?" David said. Why don't you tell me the *real* reason for this? If you loved me, it wouldn't matter if my father was paying the whole country, or if he wanted to be the King of England, or if he was giving me the whole country and Scotland too, would it? I should have realized this was coming."

I looked back at him, my eyes asking what he meant.

"You have a dowry now—a title *and* a dowry," he continued. "You are not helpless anymore, are you? Now you can do better. Lewis Stratton, perhaps."

"No!" I cried.

"Who will one day be the seventh viscount Wilton. You have to stay with your own class, don't you?"

"Oh, no, David. That is not true. There is nothing between Lewis Stratton and me. There never was and never will be. That is impossible."

"You protest too much. Do you think I am blind? I saw you sitting in the hotel together that afternoon before you saw me, and I saw how you looked at each other on Wednesday night. Well, if that is what you want to do, you have every right to do it, but you might have the decency to admit it."

It was incredible that David actually believed what he was saying, but he did. I tried desperately to think of something to say to convince him that it was not true. But when I couldn't, I decided that it didn't matter.

David stood then, and said: "I will borrow Chestnut. One of the grooms will return him later."

Then he walked out of the room.

❧ Chapter Nineteen ❧

THE FOLLOWING MORNING, as Lady Clareham and I drove to church, heavy clouds hovered just above the trees, completely hiding the hilltop and Vivian's grave.

After services, we returned to the house, and I went to my room, lay down, and tried to nap. I was tired from having slept little again the night before.

I had gone to bed almost directly after dinner the previous evening and had fallen asleep immediately, but then I had wakened in the middle of the night and lain awake thinking about Vivian and David and everything that had happened that Saturday afternoon.

But I wasn't able to nap after church, and it would be more than an hour before it was time to go down to Sunday luncheon, which was always later than on weekdays. What should I do in the meantime? The grass outside was too wet for walking. And anyway, I was afraid to walk the grounds alone. Again, I wondered who had shot at me and why.

"Well, it doesn't matter," I whispered to myself. "It is time to leave Castle Cloud, and I will not walk alone outside until I do."

As I said this, I got up from my bed and walked over to the chest of drawers. I took out some folded fichus and sleeves, which I had not worn, and placed them in my trunk. But I could not bring myself to pack in earnest, though I knew I must very soon.

Yes, I would leave Castle Cloud in a day or two, and Edmond would be pleased. He had asked, during dinner the evening before, when my wedding dress would be finished and when David and I would be married. He wanted to be rid of me now. He had, however, been polite in a proper, formal way—quite a different Edmond from the one I had encountered that afternoon. I suppose his father had reprimanded him for his behavior and demanded an improvement. At any rate, I had not told Edmond or his mother that there would be no wedding. It had been the very last thing that I wished to discuss, and I had avoided a direct answer to his question.

I closed the lid of my trunk and walked to the window, gazing out at the bay. But my thoughts were interrupted by a noise outside my door—not a knock, but a scratching sound. As I turned toward the door, it was flung open wide. A man strode into the room. He wore a long gray beard, and he was dressed in a long coat and a wide brimmed hat which hid his face. It was the bearded man that had pointed his gun at David on Wednesday night. He carried no gun this time but held both his arms extended high above his head, the fingers of his hands spread wide apart and pointed down at me, as if casting an evil spell.

I screamed.

"Ha, ha, ha, ha. Sure and if you could have seen your face. Ha, ha, ha," the figure cried. "Thought it was the devil himself, didn't you? He, he, he."

"Mrs. Muldoon!" I shouted. "Oh! Oh, how could you? I have never been so frightened. I might have had a heart attack. Mrs. Muldoon, you will get into serious trouble doing these things. What are you doing here on Sunday, anyway, and where did you get that—those clothes?"

"Ha, ha, ha. Fooled you didn't I? Sure, you didn't think it was me at all. Frightened half to death you were. Ha, ha, ha. If you could have seen your face. Ha, ha. From his young lordship's room, though you mustn't tell him. 'Twas more than I could resist. . . ."

"Is there a costume party somewhere?" _ Edmond shouted at Mrs. Muldoon from the open doorway.

He had arrived without a sound, and I had no idea how many seconds he had been standing there before he had spoken.

"No, my lord," Mrs. Muldoon replied.

"What has happened?" Lady Clareham asked.

She too must have heard my scream and come to investigate.

"Then why are you wearing those ridiculous clothes?" Edmond demanded.

" 'Twas a joke, my lord," Mrs. Muldoon said.

"A joke?" he screamed. "Is that what we pay you to do—joke? Take those things off and return them to the costume trunk in the storage rooms where you got them. Then you may go to Mrs. Foley who will give you your wages to date. Tell her that we no longer require your services at the Castle."

"But it was only a little joke I was playing, my lord—a little practical joke."

"That will be all, Mrs. Muldoon," Edmond growled.

"Edmond," I said, "there is no harm done. Let Mrs. Muldoon have her joke—surely you can overlook something as harmless as that."

"Kindly allow us to manage the servants, Mary, without interference," Edmond said. "Mrs. Muldoon, that will be all."

"Yes, my lord," Mrs. Muldoon said.

She left the room and turned right toward the stairway to the third floor.

"We cannot have that sort of behavior among the staff, Mary," Edmond said. "How much time do you think it took Mrs. Muldoon to go up to the storage rooms, rummage through the costume trunk, find that ridiculous beard and those clothes, put them on, and come all the way down here for her little joke? Doubtless she had work to do, and if she would take the time to do all that, what else would she take the time to do? I cannot understand your willingness to tolerate such behavior."

Then Edmond flung himself around and strode away.

"Mary, I am so sorry," Lady Clareham said.

"Oh, there is no harm done, Lady Clareham, but I am sorry for Mrs. Muldoon. Is there something you can do?"

"I am afraid not, Mary," she replied. "I rather agree with Edmond in this instance."

"Yes," I said. "Well, don't let me detain you. I am perfectly all right. Won't it soon be time for luncheon?"

Lady Clareham left me then, and as soon as I thought she had gotten to her room, I ran out onto the gallery and up the steps.

Mrs. Muldoon stood at the top of the stairs. She had been about to descend them when I appeared. "How should I know which trunk is the costume trunk?" she said, as I approached her. "Sure, I don't go pawing through people's trunks."

"I tried to help, Mrs. Muldoon," I said, "but neither his lordship nor her ladyship would listen."

"Now, don't you worry about that, my lady. Mrs. Reston wants me up at Oakland Park. She asked me once. It's a reputation for *working* I've got, and she knows it. It's just that it was more convenient, the Castle was, that's all. But after yesterday, it's glad I am it happened."

"Yesterday?" I asked.

"Yesterday, Mrs. Foley says, 'If it's the whole day you're going to take off for the races, then you got to come tomorrow after church and make up the time. It's not for going to the races,' she says, 'that we pays your wages.' The races are *once* in the whole year, my lady, and it was only an hour in the morning and the afternoon. Faith, you'd think they could give you the afternoon off *once* in a whole year. Cheap, that's what they are, and it's glad I am I'm going."

"Well, I did want to say good-by and to thank you for taking such good care of me, Mrs. Muldoon."

"That's very nice of you, my lady, very nice I'm sure. But I'll see you at Oakland Park. Well, sometimes I may see you—it being such a big place and all."

"You put the clothes in the costume trunk, then? But you said you found them in his lordship's room."

"I did, my lady—in his wardrobe. It's these long gray hairs I see, peeping out, you see. So I opens it up, and there's this long gray beard and that coat and hat hanging under it—on a hook, they was. Well, I takes one look— ha, ha, ha. Sure I couldn't help it—I had to—ha, ha, ha."

"I was terrified, Mrs. Muldoon."

"Yes, and it's somebody else that was too, maybe, my lady, not long ago. You might ask yourself about that, my lady," Mrs. Muldoon said, looking exaggeratedly shrewd. "Now it's the good news I must go and tell Mrs. Foley. Oh, wait till I see her face—ha, ha. She won't like it—she won't like it one bit."

By the time Mrs. Muldoon had finished speaking, she was halfway down the stairs. At the bottom, she turned and waved to me, and then she vanished.

I returned to my room where I tidied my hair and put on my watch, and then I went down to the drawing room. It was one-thirty then. I was early on purpose because I hoped that Edmond might come down before Lady Clareham did: I wanted a word with him alone. As I entered the drawing room, I was surprised to see that he had already arrived. He stood with his back toward me, gazing out of the window toward the knot garden and the entrance to the hedged walk. He glanced over his shoulder at me as I entered the room, but he did not speak.

I sat down on a sofa and, after a moment, said: "Someone ought to replace the pieces of marble in the Horse Monument."

"Already done," he replied, without turning around. "My God, you don't think I would leave it open like that, do you?"

"How did you get it up there?"

"The coffin?" he asked. "Well, obviously it was too heavy for one person to carry—it weighs a ton. Mitchell helped me."

"I see," I replied. "So that is why he was not dismissed for stealing."

"Everything has its price." Edmond left the window, walked across the room, and, standing before me, continued. "We needed a man's help at the time, and we have been willing to pay the price for it. That Vivian should rest in peace means all to us—much more than a few trinkets or a few bottles of wine."

"So your father told you about that."

"Of course. Mitchell was about the house the night Vivian died, carrying messages and fetching this and that. So he knew all about her, anyway. Father had decided that Vivian would lie in the wine cellar, but that was absurd—she was apt to be discovered there. So, on Sunday night, Mitchell and I carried her to the Horse Monument. I cemented it up later."

"And then on Monday morning Jane impersonated Vivian," I added. "You drove her to the station in Braunton and then met her later that afternoon in Barnstaple."

"How do you know that?"

"Lady Agatha saw you."

"Busybody!" he scoffed. "Oh, yes, and one bit of ingenious business which I am rather proud of—until Monday morning, Vivian's meals were taken to her room by Mrs. Foley and eaten there by Jane—just soup and custards. Oh, don't worry, Vivian wasn't there. She was resting temporarily in the coffin in the wine cellar."

"Why go to so much trouble?"

"So that the rest of the staff wouldn't know she was dead. I should think that would be apparent."

"So Mrs. Foley knew, and Jane, and Mitchell," I declared.

"And Cecile—she was there—and Ahmad," he added.

"And you expect so many people to keep your secret?" Then, before he could answer me, I said: "Judging from your mother's description, it was arsenic, wasn't it?"

"Probably."

"Why did you buy the poison for her? Did Vivian ask you to?"

"What?" he demanded.

"Eureka weed-killer, one pound—from Wood's."

"I don't understand you at all."

"Fifty to seventy percent arsenic," I declared.

"That was for the lawns."

"One would never know it to look at them, would one?" I said, as his eyes met mine. "And another thing—Colen had been sent to summon the doctor to the Castle the night that Vivian and James died. But then you left word for Dr. Norton *not* to come. Does your mother know you told the doctor not to come? Didn't you want Vivian to recover—or James either?"

"James was already dead and Vivian seemed much better," he growled.

"I suppose you wore your beard," I taunted.

"Beard? Oh, that awful thing," Lady Clareham said, as she entered and walked toward me. "Vivian wore it—Shylock in *The Merchant of Venice*—and that hat too. That was carrying things too far, I thought. Most unnerving. I don't know how she could bear to wear it. Ophelia was her role—she was lovely. . . ."

"Luncheon is served, my lady," Mitchell interrupted from the doorway.

During the meal we spoke little—each of us was preoccupied. Lady Clareham thought, perhaps, about Vivian and her theatricals. Edmond stared gravely down at his food. He looked up seldom. When he did, it seemed to be to examine me. If I hadn't begun to suspect it before luncheon, his eyes would have told me then that something even more dreadful than Vivian's suicide had happened at Castle Cloud.

Later on, when the meal was over, Lady Clareham went to her room to take a nap. I strolled to the writing table in the drawing room, sat down, and toyed with the idea of writing to the dowager countess to ask if I might stay with her for a week or so at Lewis House.

But my thoughts were interrupted by Mitchell, who announced from the doorway, "Miss Stratton."

"Mary, we thought you had died," Flora cried, as she hurried toward me. "Where on earth have you been?"

"I didn't hear you arrive, Flora," I said. "My thoughts must have been miles away. Oh, the days have gone by so quickly—I don't know, really, where they have gone. I saw Edmond go upstairs after luncheon, but I don't think he has come down yet."

"Good," she replied. "I don't wish to see him—ever." Then she grasped me by the hand and began to pull me toward the other end of the room. "I want to show you something." When we arrived at one of the west windows, she gestured to her carriage outside, "Look, isn't he attractive?"

"Mr. Quenby? Don't you want to ask him in?"

"Oh, no. We are going for a drive. He insisted that we go for a drive alone. Well, with the servants, of course. So I can stay only a minute. Isn't he lovely?"

"Yes, but you and Edmond—"

"Edmond? Perish the thought. Lewis found out that he was *cashiered* from the army, and then that business at Arford St. Mary. I know all about it now, and his philandering, and his gambling. Father has forbidden it and wants to see him. He wants his money back."

"What money?" I asked.

"The money Edmond borrowed from Father—when he first began to come to Hawthorn Hill, a few weeks ago. Father wants it back. He loaned Edmond a great deal of money—well, he didn't know all about him then, and Edmond was so ingratiating. And there was the thought, just the slightest suspicion, that he might—become part of the family. Thank heaven we found out in time! Edmond will be devastated, of course, but I couldn't, Mary. I simply couldn't, knowing what I know. And Ruben has been constantly attentive. He won't let me alone for a moment. Oh, see? He is getting impatient already. But where have you been? We expected you would call and be at the races."

"We—I had planned to go," I replied, "but it didn't—I hadn't been sleeping well. . . ."

"Poor dear. Ruben took me to the races and was most attentive. We were all there of course. And we are going down to Hill House to visit Ruben and his parents for a fortnight, starting a week from Wednesday. Ruben says it will be like forever before we arrive, and it is only a week and two days away. It is such a beautiful house, and they keep it in perfect repair. And the gardens and the lawns wouldn't need a thing done to them—they are gorgeous."

"I must *go!* He is getting anxious."

"It is a pity you must go so soon, Flora," I said. "Perhaps we shall. . ."

"Mitchell!" It was Lady Clareham's voice, and it came from the rotunda. "Mitchell!" I knew by the panic in her cry that something terrible had happened.

Flora and I had already begun to walk toward the hall before Lady Clareham shouted. But when she did, I ran into the rotunda, with Flora following close behind. Lady Clareham rushed down the last few steps and out into the hall. Looking frantically about, she shouted, "Mitchell!"

"Yes, my lady?" Mitchell called, as he climbed the stairs from the floor below.

"Send Colen for Dr. Norton," Lady Clareham cried. "His lordship has had an attack. Where is Mrs. Foley? Hurry, Mitchell!"

"I'll come, Lady Clareham," I said. "I must go and help, Flora. You can see yourself out, can't you? Good-by. I will see you soon."

Then I ran to Lady Clareham, who was too distraught to acknowledge Flora's presence.

"Come quickly. He has had an attack," Lady Clareham said.

"How?" I asked, as we dashed to the stairs.

"George and Edmond—a terrible row," she cried, as we climbed them. "He tried to strike Edmond—tried to get out of bed before we could stop him. Then he—he fell to the floor with a pain in his head." And then as we ran along the gallery to Lord Clareham's door, she added, "It is bad. Oh, God, what can we do?"

By the time we entered his room, Lord Clareham had

been lifted back onto his bed by Ahmad. He lay there vomiting into a chamber pot while Ahmad held him over it, but Ahmad had not gotten the vessel quickly enough—Lord Clareham had been sick on the bed.

I realized that we would need towels, clean sheets, and blankets, and I ran to the linen closet on the gallery.

When I returned with the fresh linen, Lord Clareham lay on his back, pale, sallow, and exhausted, his eyes closed. I knew what to do for him; I was familiar with the sickroom, having nursed my father during those many months before he died. And since neither Lady Clareham nor Ahmad seemed to know what to do next, I assumed command and directed Ahmad, who understood my combination of words and sign language. Lady Clareham was far too panic-stricken to be of any assistance at all. In five minutes then, Lord Clareham lay sponged clean and dressed in a fresh nightshirt, between clean bedclothes, under several blankets.

Only after we had finished did I think about Edmond. He had stood in his father's room when we arrived there. But as I returned with the linen, he had slipped out of the room and hurried off in a direction of his own.

But I had no sooner thought about this than I forgot about it. We settled Lord Clareham in bed, I went to summon Mrs. Foley to help with the soiled linen, and then Lady Clareham and I sat down by her husband's bedside to wait for the doctor.

Ten minutes later, I said: "He looks better. His color seems to have returned." Then I got up and felt Lord Clareham's forehead. "And he is much warmer." At my touch, Lord Clareham opened his eyes. "It is all right," I said to him. "Everything is going to be fine. Are you feeling better?"

"Headache—sick," he said. He spoke slowly and with effort.

"Yes, but you are going to be better," I said. "Dr. Norton is on his way."

"It doesn't matter, Mary," he said. "Julia?"

"I am here," Lady Clareham said, as she rose and bent over the bed. "Are you better?"

"Don't try to talk. Try to sleep a little," I said to Lord Clareham. Then I whispered to Lady Clareham: "It is all right. He is much better. Let us sit down now and wait for Dr. Norton."

I hoped, desperately, that Colen would find Dr. Norton at home. We were fortunate that afternoon—he did. The doctor arrived at six o'clock, and by six-thirty, when he was ready to leave, Lord Clareham was resting comfortably. The doctor had bled him, given an enema and an emetic, and propped him up on extra pillows.

While Dr. Norton ministered to his patient, Lady Clareham and I waited in her room. When he finished, we stepped back through the connecting door to ask about him.

"Apoplexy. No need to worry," Dr. Norton said. "He will come out of it, I think. Rest—no excitement." Then he handed a bottle of medicine to Lady Clareham and added, "One teaspoon, four times a day." He also said that he would return the following morning, and soon after that he left us.

I could do nothing further for Lord Clareham, and I wanted to be alone and quiet for a few minutes, so I went to my room. It was six forty-five. I sat by the window and looked out through the rain at the misty trees, and at the bay, which blended with the sky. I was terribly lonesome sitting there, and I thought how badly everything had turned out. Three days before I had been happy—dining at Oakland Park with David and his father, talking about wedding plans. My relationship with David had ended. I felt as if an outside pressure were trying to collapse me, as would crush an empty paper bag. Crying would relieve it; but the tears wouldn't come.

And now Lord Clareham had fallen ill, raising the possibility of Lady Clareham's having to say good-by to him.

And underlying everything, lurked something ugly—something which had happened before I came to Castle Cloud. And at the heart of it stood Edmond, whom I now knew was the bearded bandit. I almost began to wish that I would never find out anything further.

What should I do next? I couldn't leave Castle Cloud and Lady Clareham until we knew for sure whether her husband would live; and if he should die, certainly not until after the funeral.

Then I glanced at my watch. It was seven-thirty, and I was late for dinner. I smoothed my hair before the mirror, dashed from the room, and ran toward the stairway. The hall was empty. Then something on the gallery across the rotunda caught my eye; it was Ahmad's long white shirt. He was coming out of Edmond's room. He didn't see me until he had closed Edmond's door behind him, but even when he knew that I watched him, he gave no sign. He hurried to Lord Clareham's room and disappeared inside.

Had Ahmad and Edmond met in Edmond's room? I didn't think so because I was sure that Ahmad hated Edmond; I had seen it in Ahmad's eyes often enough. What, then, had he been doing in Edmond's room?

When I entered the drawing room, a moment later, I knew that they had not met because Edmond was there, pacing back and forth before his mother. She sat on a sofa, her back to the doorway.

"... the way you talk," he said, "anyone would think that *I* had struck *him*. It was Father who tried to strike me. He has always had a foul temper; you can't blame me for that. If he hadn't been so stupid as to try to get out of bed to strike his own son, he wouldn't have had an attack. Don't blame me for it."

"You goaded him into it," Lady Clareham cried. "I heard you arguing."

"I did nothing of the sort, and if you must have a scene, Mother, let us have it in private and not in front of our— guest." He had pronounced the final word with unmistakable repugnance.

Lady Clareham turned and saw me then and said: "Oh, Mary. Come in."

"I am so glad you came down to dinner, Lady Clareham," I said. I walked to her and sat down beside her. "It is so important to keep up one's strength at a time like this."

"We must try," she replied.

"How is he?" I asked.

"The same," she said. "Ahmad and Mrs. Foley are with him now." Then after a moment she said. "I don't know what we would have done without you."

"I am glad I was here to help. Does his head still pain him?"

"Yes, but not so badly."

"The pain is the dreadful thing—one feels so helpless. I know—my father suffered terribly. At least when someone is sick at the stomach one can *do* something, or at least offer comfort."

"Yes."

"Will his stomach continue to be sick?" I asked.

"I don't know, Mary. How could I?"

"But James's did. Didn't you say that James was sick until the end? Did he also have head pain?"

"Must you?" Edmond asked. "Just before dinner?"

"There is illness in the house, Edmond," I replied. "One's major concern then is to understand—to know—so that one can help." Then I turned back to Lady Clareham and said: "But then, James had diarrhea. Thank heaven Lord Clareham is spared that."

"For God's sake!" Edmond cried, glaring at me. "James had valvular disease of the heart, complicated by epidemic diarrhea. Father has apoplexy. It should not be difficult to understand that they are two entirely different illnesses. Now, if you do not know what is and is not appropriate conversation while waiting for dinner, please do not talk at all. Discussions of illness come between one and one's enjoyment of his food. It is enough to turn anyone's stomach."

I did not reply because Mitchell announced dinner at just that moment.

Again, as at luncheon, we all fell preoccupied during the meal. And again, several times, I caught Edmond examining me with that strangely intent stare. But, this time, Lady Clareham examined me too.

After dinner, as we drank our coffee, Lady Clareham was just saying that she must hurry—that she must see how her husband was—when we heard shouts from the direction of the servants' hall. One of the voices sounded like Edmond's.

"Now, what has happened?" Lady Clareham cried, rising from her chair.

"I will come with you," I said.

"Thank you, Mary, but it has to do with the servants. I think it would be better if you waited here."

I felt uneasy about being left alone like that, but I sat still and listened. The voices gradually decreased in volume and then were quiet.

Five minutes later, Lady Clareham returned, sank into
er chair, and said: "Will you pour me some more coffee,
Mary?"

"What is it?" I asked, after I had poured her coffee and
anded it to her.

"Monsieur Laval is leaving. Nothing I said made any
ifference. *Now* what will we do?"

"Why?" I asked.

"He is a very sensitive man. I am afraid Edmond said
ome critical things about his cooking. Edmond's stomach
as been upset and he blamed it on Monsieur Laval.

"But the food is always excellent," I declared.

"Of course. It is not the food—it is Edmond. He is
estless and I think he has been sleeping badly. I heard
im walking on the gallery before dawn this morning. Oh,
hy does this have to happen now?"

"When will Monsieur Laval be leaving?"

"Immediately. He was terribly angry."

"He may change his mind."

"No, I don't think so."

"Then I must go too," I said. "It will be difficult enough
ithout a chef, let alone having an extra mouth to feed."

"No! Mary, please," Lady Clareham begged. "Don't
eave. Help me with George—just for a few days. That is
ot very much to ask." As she spoke she began to cry.

"Of course I will stay if you need me—I will stay as
ong as you want me to. And I will even help with the
ooking, if you think you could eat it."

"That will not be necessary," Lady Clareham tried to
mile. "We will manage. I will have a talk with Mrs.
Foley. Now, I must go up to George."

"I will come with you," I said.

When we reached his room, Lord Clareham was awake
nd sensible, but he was terribly oppressed. And when he
nswered our questions, he spoke slowly, with effort. A
ittle later, as I watched by his bedside, Mrs. Foley and
Lady Clareham stepped into Lady Clareham's room where
hey discussed how they were to manage until a new chef
ould be engaged. When Mrs. Foley had gone, Lady
Clareham returned and asked if I felt well. She said I
ooked pale and tired, that she had summoned her maid,

and that they would sit with her husband if I wished to li
down in my room for a while.

I did not feel tired, but I thought it would be wise to li
down, as I might be needed during the night. So I lef
Lord and Lady Clareham and Ahmad, asking Lady Clare
ham to call me at once if she needed me.

I hurried to my room and locked the door behind me
removed my dress and shoes, and lay down on the bed
Jane Spence had closed the curtains and lighted the lamps
and I left them burning brightly while I tried to sleep.

But I couldn't sleep. I was afraid. I was afraid because
had begun to suspect, at dinner, that it was Edmond wh
had shot at me. I had known before luncheon tha
Edmond was the masked bandit who had robbed Lor
Portland and pointed his gun at David. The realization ha
merely puzzled and disgusted me. But during dinner tha
evening, one of Edmond's remarks had reminded me o
something that I had said at Hawthorn Hill on Wednesda
night.

Edmond had said something about talk of illness com
ing between himself and his food. On Wednesday night
Lewis had said that he was glad the bandit hadn't shot a
me. And I had said: "David was between him and me; s
he couldn't." That thought made me realize that if Davi
had been sitting on my left instead of my right, Edmon
could have shot at me. And that may have been *wh*
Edmond was standing there. He had meant to shoot me
just as he had shot at me, I was sure, two nights before a
I walked down the drive toward the stone bridge.

I was able to understand then why Jane Spence had no
prepared my room for me that same evening: she had no
expected me to return. And I understood why Lord Clare
ham had not called in Constable Nash to investigate th
attempt on my life: he must have known it was Edmon
who had shot at me, and he had probably given him a lec
ture instead. I imagined I could hear him saying: "Now
Edmond, we will have no more attempts on Mary's life.
And I laughed bitterly. I wondered if that could have bee
the cause of the argument between Edmond and his fathe
that afternoon. I believed, somehow, that it was.

But why should Edmond want to kill me? I had neve
done him any harm. Was it because of what I knew, then
On Friday night, when he had shot at me, I did not kno

very much that might be harmful to Edmond. No, but I had suspected that Vivian was dead; I had been asking questions; and I knew about the coffin. Edmond realized all of this.

If Vivian had merely taken her own life, then Edmond would surely not have risked murder to keep her death hidden from me. There must have been more to it than that. And, possibly, something more than Vivian's death alone had happened at Castle Cloud—something that I knew nothing about. And Edmond was willing to kill me to keep me from discovering what it was.

Fear for my own safety, however, overpowered all these thoughts. I wondered if I should go to Constable Nash, or to the chief constable in Barnstaple, and tell him that Edmond had tried to kill me. But he would only laugh at me. I had no proof that it was Edmond who had shot at me or even that he had been the bearded bandit. After all, other artificial beards existed besides the one that now lay in the costume trunk—not to mention all the men with real beards who lived in that part of Devonshire.

It would be wise to leave Castle Cloud immediately. But I knew I must stay and help Lady Clareham with her husband. I couldn't leave her when she needed me.

I decided I would be very careful and very watchful—lock my door, stay with people, and certainly not go out of the house alone.

I had just reached this decision when someone knocked at my door. "Mary, are you awake?" Lady Clareham called. "Could you come?"

I jumped out of bed, ran to the door, unlocked and opened it. "As soon as I slip on my dress."

"What is it?" I whispered, when I had joined her in Lord Clareham's room. Her husband seemed to be asleep, and I whispered so as not to wake him.

"Is he asleep?" Lady Clareham asked.

"He seems to be. Why do you ask?"

"I don't think so." Her eyes had filled with tears, and she held a wadded handkerchief near the corner of her mouth as she spoke. "I was talking to him a few minutes ago, and he seemed to drift off—he wouldn't take his medicine."

I stepped over to the figure on the bed and called to him softly, but there was no response. Then I took his wrist and felt his pulse—his heart was beating—and I bent to listen to his breathing—it was labored and hollow sounding.

"I don't know, Lady Clareham," I said. "It may be a deep sleep or it may be a coma. It is probably a very deep sleep. After all, he must have been exhausted. But don't you think we should send for Dr. Norton, just in case?"

"Yes," she replied. "Cecile, go and ask Mitchell to send for Dr. Norton, please. Then you may go to your room. I will call you if I need you."

After her maid had gone, Lady Clareham sat with me watching her husband for a sign of conciousness, but he lay utterly still. After perhaps three-quarters of an hour, Colen returned, saying that Dr. Norton was not at home, but that he had left word for him to come to the Castle as soon as possible. I suggested then that the dowager countess would want to know that her son had had an attack, and that we telegraph her. Lady Clareham agreed, and before Colen left for the railway station to attend to it, I asked him to stop at the Red Lion in Milton Penderton on his way, to see if Dr. Norton might be there. When Colen arrived back at the Castle almost an hour later, he said that although Dr. Norton was not at the Red Lion, he had been at the railway station earlier in the evening. Stationmaster Schute had said that the doctor had telegraphed the *Times* about Lord Clareham's attack and that everyone in Milton Penderton knew about it.

I thought that it was hardly Dr. Norton's place to do this, but Lady Clareham did not seem to notice—she looked worn-out. I suggested that she go to her room and rest, but she refused. When I urged her to, however, saying that we would leave the connecting door between the two rooms open and that I would summon her at the slightest change in her husband's condition, she consented, asking that I wake her in any event at three o'clock so that she could relieve me.

So I sat alone when she had gone, except for Ahmad, who sat in his usual place by the door, waiting for some change in Lord Clareham's condition.

Half an hour later, we heard a knock on the door. Ahmad unlocked and opened it a crack. I thought it must be Dr. Norton, but it was Edmond.

"He is asleep," I whispered quickly. "There is no change."

"Well, if it isn't Florence Nightingale," Edmond sneered. His breath smelled of whiskey.

"Don't come in—you will only wake him," I pleaded. "And your mother is resting. I will sit with him for a while."

"If he dies, I want to be informed at once. Do you understand?"

"Yes. Good night, Edmond," I said, as I drew back from the door. Ahmad closed it.

When it was safely locked, I returned to Lord Clareham's bedside and sat watching him. Ahmad sat stiffly, across the room, watching me. The room lay silent except for the ticking of a clock on the mantel. The minutes dragged by, and soon I found myself nodding.

Fifteen or twenty minutes later, a knock on the door woke me with a start. I bounded out of my chair and ran to the door. Ahmad had unlocked and opened it, and was peering through the gap into the gallery outside.

Over his shoulder I saw Jane Spence standing in front of the doorway.

"Mrs. Foley thought her ladyship might like some coffee and cake," she said.

"How thoughtful, Jane," I replied softly, as I motioned for Ahmad to open the door and let her in. "As a matter of fact, I would, very much. Set it on the table there, would you please? And thank you for bringing it."

"How soon do you think he'll die?" Jane whispered, as she set the tray down.

"We hope he won't die, Jane," I replied. "He is resting now—he was very much better earlier." As I poured myself a cup of coffee, I remarked, "Those little cakes look lovely. Be sure to thank Mrs. Foley."

"Well, if there is nothing else I can do, my lady—" Jane said, beginning to walk toward the door.

"No, thank you, Jane. Good night."

And as Jane walked out of the room and Ahmad secured the door behind her, I picked up my cup and saucer and smelled the steaming coffee—a delicious fragrance. But as I lifted the cup to my lips, Ahmad sprang at me from across the room and struck it from my hand.

"Ahmad!" I cried.

He stood before me, violently shaking his head and hands. "No, no, no," he whispered, staring at me wide-eyed. Then he spat at the cup which lay on its side on the carpet.

"The coffee?" I asked, pointing to the little coffeepot on the tray. As I did so, his movements became even more frantic, and then my heart lurched as I understood what he was trying to tell me. "Poison, Ahmad? Was it poisoned?"

Without attempting to answer me, he picked up the cup from the carpet, took the saucer from me, and placed them back on the tray. Then he carried the tray across the room. Balancing it on one hand, he unlocked and opened the door with the other, motioned for me to lock it after him, and disappeared.

Immediately I ran to the door and locked it. Then I turned around and leaned against it while waves of panic swept through me. Had Edmond tried to kill me again? If I had drunk that coffee—if Ahmad hadn't stopped me—would I have been plunging toward a horrible death at that very moment? Terror rose in me. I knew that when it reached a certain pitch, I would become hysterical. And I knew that I must force myself to be calm—to realize that I was safe, and think of something else. So I walked to Lord Clareham's bedside and smoothed his covers gently. He lay still; he hadn't moved. And then I tip-toed to the open door of Lady Clareham's bedroom. A low lamp burned inside, illuminating her sleeping figure on the bed.

It was only then, after I was more composed, that I allowed myself to think about the attempt on my life. I realized that if Mrs. Foley had sent it, she would have sent enough coffee for two people, with two cups. She did not know that Lady Clareham had gone to sleep—only Edmond knew that. But what, I wondered, had made Ahmad suspect the coffee had been poisoned? Had Edmond told his father that afternoon that he was planning to get rid of me? Had that been the cause of their argument? Did this have something to do with Ahmad's visit to Edmond's room earlier?

I knew then that I would have to be very careful if I were to leave Castle Cloud alive.

Ahmad returned shortly. He knocked and when I knew who it was, I opened it for him. He carried a large coffeepot and two cups and two saucers on a tray which, after locking the door, he set down on the table near his master's bedside. Then he gestured me to my chair and, when I was seated, he poured coffee into a cup. But before he handed it to me, he poured some of the coffee out of the cup into its saucer and drank from it.

"Thank you, Ahmad," I said, after I had taken the coffee from him and sipped it.

How wrong I had been about Ahmad! I was astonished at his concern for me, and thankful for it. And even though I said no more, I knew by the look of satisfaction in Ahmad's eyes that he understood my gratitude.

We sat then, I by the bedside and Ahmad on his chair by the door, waiting. Two hours later, at about 2:00 A.M., Lord Clareham died. He had not moved. His heart must simply have stopped beating. One moment he looked as he had looked for hours. And when I looked at him again, I knew that he was dead.

✖ Chapter Twenty ✖

WHEN I WOKE the following day, it was almost noon. The sky was deep blue, and the sun shone almost directly down on a magnificent old oak tree which I could see from my bed. At first I thought what a beautiful day it was, and then I woke completely and remembered all that had happened the night before.

I had roused Lady Clareham just after Lord Clareham's death, and after she had knelt weeping by her husband's bedside for a few minutes, I had sent Ahmad to fetch Cecile and Edmond. When Edmond had finally entered the room and had seen me sitting quietly in my chair—alive and well—the look of frustration on his face had confirmed my suspicions entirely. He did not stay long with his father: he walked past me to the bedside and stood looking down at the figure lying there just long enough to be sure that he was dead. His eyes did not tear: he did not pray, nor did he attempt to comfort his mother. After a malignant glance at me, he walked from the room. Neither he nor I had spoken a word.

Shortly after Edmond had left us, I expressed my sympathy to Lady Clareham once again, asked if there were anything further I could do, and—realizing that she wanted to be alone with her husband—left her.

But as I sat in bed that following morning remembering these things, I realized that everything at the Castle was changed: Edmond was Lord Clareham now. Castle Cloud and the estates were his, and everything and everyone in the house was under his control—even his mother, who would no longer have any voice in running the Castle if Edmond wished her not to. And what were Edmond's plans for me, now? I felt sure that his first attempt on my life had been to keep me from finding out what, besides Vivian's death, had happened at Castle Cloud. His second attempt, then, must signify that he believed I was close to discovering his secret. What was it that Edmond believed I suspected?

And I wondered why Jane had not wakened me that morning and brought water. Was she loath to face me? Or, now that Edmond had succeeded to the earldom, was her status at Castle Cloud changed too? How would I get water to wash with if she didn't bring it?

And how could I eat, knowing that any morsel of food might be poisoned? I couldn't. I must leave at once. I would be a fool to stay and wait for him to murder me. How would he try to kill me next? Poison, again? Or would he lure me out-of-doors and shoot me, or would he lie in wait for me at night in the darkness of the house and strangle me? He was capable of anything.

Yes, he was capable of doing anything—to anybody. Was there anyone besides me, then, in danger of being harmed? Jane Spence knew his secret. She was probably his accomplice—she had been the night before, at any rate. Would Edmond eventually be obliged to kill her to keep his secret—to end her control of him? I had heard her threaten him one night: "Don't you ever speak to me like that again, do you hear? Don't you ever dare." And what about Mitchell, and Mrs. Foley, and even his own mother? Would he eventually have to kill them too, to silence them? I had heard that each time it was easier—that killing often became a habit.

"No," I whispered aloud, "I can't leave him at large."

I would never rest easily if I left, knowing that, at any moment, Edmond might be taking someone's life. Wouldn't some of that blood then be on my hands because I hadn't stopped him?

I knew that it was my responsibility to expose Edmond as the potential killer he was. I couldn't run away from it. Looking back, I realized that from the day I arrived at Castle Cloud, Edmond had been afraid I would discover what he had done and expose him. I had no choice but to do just that.

Having made up my mind, I got up and walked to the wash-hand-stand. Fortunately, enough water remained in the pitcher to take a sponge bath. When I had washed and dressed, I left my room, locked my door behind me, and went downstairs to find Lady Clareham.

When I looked in the drawing room for her, I saw Mitchell standing before one of the chimney pieces, examining an ivory and bronze statuette.

"Mitchell," I called. "Has her ladyship come down?"

"No, my lady," he replied, as he replaced the statuette on the mantel. Then he walked toward me saying: "I believe she is still with his late lordship."

"And his lordship?" I asked.

"His lordship has only just left, my lady."

"Do you know where he has gone, Mitchell?"

"He has gone, I believe, to telegraph the news of—his succession—to the *Times* and to meet the dowager countess, who is arriving on the one-thirty train, my lady."

"Have you seen Mrs. Foley?"

"Mrs. Foley has gone to the village in an attempt to find a temporary replacement for Monsieur Laval, my lady."

"Has Dr. Norton arrived?"

"He has arrived and departed to prepare the necessary papers."

"Thank you, Mitchell," I said, turning away from him.

But before I could leave the room, Mitchell said: "I have received no instructions about luncheon, my lady. Since there is no chef, I presume that it will not be served."

"And was breakfast not served?" I asked.

"His lordship had no appetite. He did not wish breakfast, my lady."

"Thank you, Mitchell," I repeated.

Then I went upstairs to Lord Clareham's bedroom where I found Lady Clareham still sitting by her husband's bedside. She was dazed with sorrow and exhausted from having sat up all night. She hardly seemed to recognize me. And when I asked if there was anything I could do, she said that there was nothing anyone could do. I knew then that she wished to be left to mourn alone, and as I walked from the room, I suggested to Cecile that she try to persuade Lady Clareham to lie down and rest.

I realized that Lady Clareham knew what Edmond had done—that was why she had opposed me in so many ways. And I was going to bring her still more grief. But I had no choice: Edmond must be exposed, and quickly. Could I do it? How?

But before I did anything else, I had to write to Mr. Schraw. Then I must walk to the village, mail the letter, and return to the Castle before Edmond came back from Barnstaple.

So I went directly back to the drawing room. Mitchell was no longer there. Nor, incidentally, was the ivory and bronze statuette. I had much more important things to think about than Mitchell's thievery, however, and I was glad to have the room to myself. I hurried to the desk then, and wrote:

Castle Cloud, August 25, 1856

Dear Mr. Schraw,

I enclose a letter which I should like to place in your care. I wish the envelope to remain sealed and opened only in the event of my death. In that case, I trust you will open and read the letter and, having done so, act as you think best. I have complete faith that whatever you do as a result of reading this letter will be wise and just.

Forgive me for being so mysterious, but I cannot explain more now. I will, however, be in London shortly and look forward to seeing you and discussing the matter further.

Yours most truly,
Mary

Then, on separate paper, I hurriedly wrote a letter telling all about Edmond's masquerade as the masked bandit and his two attempts on my life; Vivian's death and the whereabouts of her body; Edmond's purchase of the weed-killer from Wood's; his asking the doctor not to come to Castle Cloud the night James and Vivian died; and my suspicions that some other dreadful thing had happened at Castle Cloud before I had arrived.

This letter, I folded and sealed in a small envelope addressed to "Nathaniel P. Schraw in the event of the death of Mary Elizabeth Thorpe," and placed in a larger envelope, together with my letter of instructions, addressed to Mr. Schraw at his London office.

All this had taken a great deal more time than I had anticipated. If I were to walk to the village and walk back before Edmond returned, I knew that I would have to go quickly. So, after I had fetched my bag from my room, being careful to lock my bedroom door behind me, I rushed from the house.

And I half walked, half ran to the post office in the village. When I reached it, I gave my letter to Mr. Hollycombe and came away as quickly as I could without being rude to him and his wife. They had kept me there for almost ten minutes, asking one question after another about Lord Clareham's death and what was happening at the Castle.

I hurried back toward Castle Cloud then, but when I reached the hilltop near the Horse Monument, I stepped off the path and ran down the slope through the grass toward the glasshouses, praying as I went that Edmond had not come home from the station yet—I had one more thing to do before I could return to the safety of the house. When I reached the conservatory, I threw open the door, ran to the eastern greenhouse, and over to the potting bench. The bag of weed-killer was gone.

It took only a moment to be certain of it. Then I left the glasshouses and hurried along the drive toward the Castle. As there was no sign of Colen or a carriage, I slackened my pace a little.

And as I walked toward the house, I once again began to have doubts about my suspicions. Perhaps the weed-killer had been bought for the lawns, after all. Perhaps Vivian had not used it: she may have gotten arsenic powder for herself from a druggist, or someone. And perhaps Edmond had not poisoned my coffee the night before. Perhaps I was imagining everything.

And David—had I imagined that too? Perhaps he really did love me. No, he didn't. I couldn't think clearly: I had become muddled and weary from lack of food. I had eaten nothing since dinner the night before, and I was hungry—that was what was the matter with me.

By that time I had entered the Castle by the east vestibule. It was silent and deserted. I stood looking about for a moment, relieved to be inside the house again and to have gotten to the village and back safely. Then I walked across to the stairs which led to the servants' hall.

I paused in the doorway to look inside the room and was surprised to see Ahmad standing at the far end of it. His back was toward me. He stood, his hands clasped behind him, looking up through the high windows at the sky. I felt very sorry for him. How alone he was now that his master was dead—alone in a strange country with a strange language. What would he do now? Would Lady Clareham be able to keep him on here, or at her dower house if Edmond asked her to leave the Castle? I thought how odd it was to have been frightened of this strange man only to have him save my life.

Then and there, I made a vow that Ahmad would be taken care of—I would see to it somehow.

"Ahmad," I said, as I stepped into the room, "I don't know if you can understand this, but thank you again for what you did for me last night."

He turned around and when I had finished, he bent his body and head very low, touching his forehead with the inside of his fingers and then the floor with the back of them, three times.

"Do you think I could find something to eat in the kitchens?" I asked, trying to recover from the surprise.

I spun around and walked out into the corridor toward the rooms which I supposed were the kitchens. Ahmad followed me.

When I opened the kitchen door, a plain girl, perhaps fourteen or fifteen years old, jumped up from her chair and curtsied to me.

"Oh, my lady!" she exclaimed.

"You must be May Brooke," I said.

"Yes, my lady. I—is there something you wish, my lady?"

"I wondered, May, if I could find something to eat."

"Oh, you've had no breakfast, my lady."

"And no luncheon, either."

"Oh, you must be starved, my lady. But Monsieur Laval has gone, and I don't know what we're going to do."

Ahmad, meanwhile, had taken a pot from the stove and was filling it with water from the pump, which stood directly outside the kitchen door. He began to make coffee.

"Perhaps some bread and butter," I said.

"I could boil you an egg—I've kept the stove going," May said. "And I could make you some toast."

"That would be heaven, May," I said.

My reply pleased her. She beamed and went to work at

once, filling a pan with water and placing it on the stove beside the coffeepot.

"Please don't go to any trouble," I said. "If I may, I will eat right here on the kitchen table—that would be perfect."

"Very good, my lady," she replied. "Sit right down and I'll have a cloth laid before you can blink your eye."

In less than ten minutes May Brooke had set the table with a clean cloth, silverware, and pots of honey and strawberry jam. She served me two soft-cooked eggs and a small mountain of toast.

"Thank you, May," I said. "That looks delicious."

Ahmad poured my coffee.

I thanked him and said to May: "Won't you have a cup of coffee too, May?"

"Oh, my lady!" she cried.

"Yes, come sit down and keep me company."

"Well, I don't mind if I do, my lady. Thank you ever so much, my lady, I'm sure."

When she had poured herself a cup of coffee and sat opposite me, very straight and ill at ease on the edge of her chair but immensely flattered by my invitation, I said: "It is such a sad time, isn't it? First his late young lordship and now his father. You were employed at the Castle the night his late young lordship died, weren't you, May?"

"Oh, yes, my lady."

"Did anything peculiar happen that night, May?"

"Peculiar, my lady?"

"Yes, anything out of the ordinary."

"No, my lady," May said. "His late young lordship died—that was all, my lady. He was sick a long time."

"I see."

Then after a pause, May asked: "And her ladyship? Have you heard from her—way off there in America?"

"No, I don't believe she has written," I replied.

"She was always so nice to me," May said.

"Yes—did she have any visitors, May?"

"When? That night, do you mean? Oh, no, my lady. I'm sure I don't know who would come to call, my lady."

I parried several questions of May's about Vivian as best I could, and after we had agreed that she was a lovely person and had been too ill with grief over her brother's death to have been allowed to go off like that, May observed: "We had Monsieur Laval then. I don't know what we're going to do now."

"Mrs. Foley has gone to find someone, I understand," I said. "Perhaps you and Mrs. Foley and Jane Spence could cook a meal or two in the meantime?"

"Oh, no, my lady. She can't cook, and Jane—she wouldn't be caught dead in the kitchen. She's much too grand for that. Very hoity-toity she's become lately, if you ask me, my lady."

"Oh?" I prompted.

"Yes, my lady, why you'd think she was the mistress of the Castle herself, you would. 'Can't do anything with her,' I hear Mrs. Foley tell her ladyship. 'She won't do a stroke of work. I don't know how we can manage with her here,' she says. And her parading around in those fancy clothes the way she does. It isn't right, my lady, when the rest of us has to work."

"Well, that was marvelous, May," I said. "Nothing ever tasted so good."

"But she gave it to her good and proper the other night about the bottles," May continued. "Oh, it was lovely to hear—what a tongue-lashing it was. I never saw Mrs. Foley so mad. I thought she'd have an attack."

"The bottles?" I asked.

"His late young lordship's bottles—in the closet."

"The bottles in the linen closet?"

"Yes, my lady."

"What were they doing there, May?"

"Well, Dr. Norton said he should have *plenty* of wine with his meals, my lady, to build up his strength—so they always kept the bottles in the closet. It saved carrying them up and down the stairs, you see. Well, after he died, Mrs. Foley told Jane to bring them down, but she didn't do it. So she got what she deserved. That's why they had words, and nobody gets the better of Mrs. Foley when it comes to words, my lady."

"No, I am sure not," I said, rising from the table. "But someone must have authority or things would not work, would they? Thank you so much—that was lovely. I feel like a new person."

"Oh, I'm very pleased I'm sure, my lady."

"And don't worry, May," I said. "Everything will be all right."

As I walked toward the door, Ahmad rushed to open it for me, and I left the room.

Near the foot of the stairs, I paused. I had heard a door close. Then I saw Mitchell round a corner beyond the servants' hall and walk toward me.

I waited until he was near and then asked: "Did I hear a carriage a few minutes ago, Mitchell?"

"I had some personal things to attend to, my lady," he replied.

"Yes, of course, Mitchell. I was wondering if that was his lordship returning from the station."

"I should imagine so, my lady."

I preceded Mitchell up the stairs to the hall above, where I noticed a trunk and two bags sitting on the floor inside the vestibule doorway. Mitchell walked toward them while I entered the drawing room. There, on a table near the doorway, folded and unread, lay a copy of the day's *Times.* I carried it to a chair by the windows, from which I could look out into the rotunda and see anyone coming, sat down, and found the news article I was looking for. It was under the Court Calendar on page five, and it read:

SERIOUS ILLNESS OF LORD CLAREHAM

*

A communique on the health of Lord Clareham was received this day:—

Lord Clareham was strickened with a severe attack of apoplexy this evening, but has responded well to treatment. The symptoms have assumed a favorable character and he is resting comfortably.

HENRY NORTON, M.D.

Castle Cloud, Milton Penderton, Aug, 25.

I thought what pleasure Dr. Norton would take, now, in showing it to his companions in the taproom of the Red Lion.

But my thoughts were interrupted by Edmond. He entered the drawing room, glared at me without speaking, and then began walking about the room. He seemed to be examining the furniture and art objects.

Suddenly he strode to one of the open north windows at the far end of the room and slammed it shut.

"Must we have all of the north winds blowing through the house?" he growled at me.

"I did not open the window, Edmond," I replied.

"How could you sit with it blowing on you like that? You will catch pneumonia before your wedding day. And just when *is* the extraordinary event to take place?"

"I am not going to be married," I said. "Hasn't Mr. Field told you? Haven't you been to Oakland Park lately?"

"You are not going to marry David?"

"No."

"Oh? When did all this happen? Don't tell me you let the golden gander get away. That wasn't very smart of you, was it? Or did you think you might do better? Our clever baroness with her newly found dowry looks for more patrician pastures?"

I did not reply.

"Well, it is just as well," he said. "You will have the decency to stay at Castle Cloud until after the funeral and help Mother with the condolences. That is the least you can do."

"Certainly," I answered.

"They will be coming from all over the empire, I suppose. Letters, telegraphs—tons of them." He paced up and down the room. "And God only knows how many ghastly people will be trooping down from London for the funeral. God! The house will be crammed with them—if I can just get through that and all the weeping and mourning and the disgusting smell of flowers. Get it over and have some peace."

"And your mother and grandmother, what of them?" I asked.

"Mother has been this way since my brother died. There is nothing new about that, is there? At least Grandmamma is sensible—all tears and sobs, of course, but she will get over it. Why do women make such spectacles of themselves? One would think they could be more considerate."

Then Mitchell interrupted: "The Reverend Anderson, my lord."

Reverend Anderson strode into the room.

"My dear boy and Lady Beauford," he said. "I came as soon as I heard—from a chance encounter in the lane."

"Good of you to come, Anderson," Edmond replied, as they shook hands. "Thought everyone knew. I was just about to leave Lady Beauford to ride to the village myself, to tell you—just in case, you know. Indescribable loss—we are destitute. Terribly sorry, but there has been so much to do—the dowager countess has only just arrived."

"God will give you strength, Edmond. He is the staff that supports us in our great sorrow—through prayer. Shall we pray?"

"Very kind of you," Edmond answered, "but could you go right up? Mother and Grandmamma are with him now. They will be so grateful. Mary, would you show Reverend Anderson up? I will join you later."

So I led the rector up to Lord Clareham's room, and when he had expressed his sympathy, he offered a prayer at the bedside. I greeted the dowager countess and, in a few moments, she asked if I would slip out onto the gallery with her.

The elder Lady Clareham blotted her eyes with a handkerchief and asked: "Where is Edmond? Has Mrs. Foley returned from the village?"

"Edmond was in the drawing room a few minutes ago," I answered. "He may still be there. I don't know about Mrs. Foley."

"I am afraid Julia is completely undone," she said. "She is in no condition to think about the house or the servants. The chef has left?"

"Yes."

"And Mrs. Foley has gone to find someone?"

"That is what Mitchell told me."

"Let us see if she has returned, then, and find Edmond."

Edmond was still pacing about the drawing room when we entered, and Mrs. Foley arrived almost immediately after we did.

"I can't find nobody to come today," she said, as she walked into the room. "Mrs. Heart can't come till tomorrow for dinner. She can't come today and there ain't nobody else that I know about."

"Then you must do it yourself, Mrs. Foley," Lady Clareham said. "There must be someone down there to help you—you should be able to make something."

"Oh, no, my lady," Mrs. Foley said. "I don't know what I could do, and May couldn't make tea."

"Might I make a suggestion, Lady Clareham?" I asked. "Ahmad cooked everything for Lord Clareham, who told me that Ahmad was a superb cook. I have seen some of the food he has prepared—it was Indian, but it looked very good. He could cook for us, don't you suppose?"

"I should think he would if we asked him," Lady Clareham said. "Wouldn't he, Mrs. Foley?"

"Heathen food!" Mrs. Foley exclaimed. "Have you ever seen it?"

"Well, if you would rather make dinner yourself—" Lady Clareham said.

Mrs. Foley snapped her mouth shut then, with such force that I heard her teeth click, but she continued to stare down her long nose at Lady Clareham in disapproval.

"If you think," Edmond cried, "that I am going to eat anything that filthy Indian has thrown together, you may think again."

"Edmond!" Lady Clareham exclaimed. "And must you pace up and down like that? I know how hard all this is for you, my dear, but try to be calm. Mary is right. What else can we do?"

"Oh, for God's sake! All right—if you will eat it. What difference does it make?"

"Has the undertaker come?" Lady Clareham asked.

"I haven't sent for him."

"You haven't sent for him? Edmond, the day is practically gone! Go and ask him to come as soon as he can. If he can't come tonight, tell him he must come first thing in the morning."

"All right!" Edmond shouted.

Then he walked across the room to the door. He must have hurt his foot—I noticed that he limped.

And at the doorway, just before he left the room, he turned and cried: "I'll be glad to get away from here."

When he had gone, Lady Clareham said to Mrs. Foley, "Would you please go and find Ahmad, Mrs. Foley, and bring him to the gallery outside his—late lordship's room? I will meet you there, and will speak to him about dinner."

Lady Clareham and Mrs. Foley left the room, and I walked to the east windows to watch Edmond as he rode away from the stable yard. He galloped down the drive on

Cinnamon, toward Barnstaple. I was certain that he would not call in Mr. Podock, but would go to see Mr. Hackley, the undertaker in Bideford. How long would he be gone, I wondered? Two hours? Perhaps a little longer?

I felt an immense relief that he was gone. I was relieved, also, that I would be able to eat dinner that evening: if Ahmad cooked it and I ate what the others ate, I would be safe enough.

But as I had kept my room locked, Jane Spence would not have been able to put it in order for me, or to bring fresh water. This meant that I would have to do these things myself if I wished to be comfortable. So I went to the basement, filled a can with fresh water from the pump, and carried it up to my room. Then I made my bed and put my clothes in order.

Afterward, I sat down by the window and thought how sorry I was that Lord Clareham had died. I had liked him, even though he had not always been honest with me. But I could do nothing for him now, nor could I do anything for Lady Clareham. Later, I would help her with the funeral and the messages of sympathy.

It was my own peril, however, that worried me. Edmond was planning to kill me. He must be handed over to the authorities. And again I wondered how I could do that when I knew so little? What was it that I didn't know? Would I find a clue to it if I examined everything again?

After alternately sitting and pacing for almost an hour and going over and over what I knew, I found that I was still as ignorant as ever.

Then I thought of one other possible source of information which I had not investigated—Vivian's diary. Vivian was, after all, dead. One could not, I reasoned, trespass upon the privacy of a dead person. So I decided to go and look at it. I left my room then, locked my door behind me, dashed along the gallery to Vivian's room, hurried across to her chiffonier, pulled out the bottom drawer, and found Vivian's diary where I had replaced it weeks before. I carried it to the window and glanced at the last few entries.

They were brief thoughts jotted down hurriedly: it looked as though Vivian had lost interest in her diary after Edmond had brought her back from London the previous

January. She had written in it only seven or eight times since then, and after glancing at what little she had written, I wondered why she had bothered at all. The last few entries read:

APRIL 30, 1856

My love is coming—the world is beautiful again. I feel him drawing nearer and nearer and soon heaven will be mine. But if he doesn't come? He *will*. He said he would!!!!! I know he will.

MAY 2, 1856

Mary is coming.

MAY 6, 1856

I want to die. How could he go like that—how could he leave me? Will he return? No, not now—never, never, never. And James is ill.

MAY 20, 1856

God, if you exist, make James well!

JUNE 2, 1856

James gets worse. Cannot Dr. Norton help him? So weak, so pale. Will he be taken from me too? I am so afraid—

After reading these entries over several times, I closed Vivian's diary. But instead of returning it to the chest of drawers, I carried it back to my room with me.

Then, still holding it under my arm, I returned to the window. All of a sudden, as I looked out at the flock of sheep grazing in the park, pieces of the puzzle began to fit together. Vivian, I thought, had not gotten better the night she died, as Edmond had said—she had gotten steadily, horribly worse. If Dr. Norton, then, had come to Castle Cloud, what might she have told him? And why had the earth been disturbed in James's grotto? I thought I knew.

It had been the memory of May Brooke's face that afternoon that caused the revelation. When I asked her if

Vivian had had any visitors, I thought I had seen a momentary expression of alarm there when she had answered: "When, that night?" And this had reminded me of Mrs. Muldoon's comment, "If John O'Connor says he'll do something, he'll do it, my lady. That's the way he is." These recollections became significant after reading Vivian's diary. Her April 30th entry had been written just two or three days before Edmond had bought the weed-killer. Yes, it was financially vital to Edmond that Vivian and David marry. And I supposed that Vivian had found out what Edmond had done the same way I had—from the murder book which she had probably taken from his room.

Then, of course, she had gone to the linen closet and taken a bottle of the wine and poisoned it with the weed-killer (how ridiculous of Mrs. Foley to think that the remaining bottles were dangerous—they were still corked, and Mrs. Muldoon had suffered no ill effects from drinking from one of them). But why poison a whole bottle of wine when a glassful would do? Because Vivian was theatrical; she must have relished the drama of pouring the wine from the bottle.

Then I glanced at the clock on the mantel. It had stopped, but my watch hadn't—it said six o'clock. Edmond must have returned from Bideford by now, or shortly would. Then what I must do next have to wait until I was certain that Edmond would be away from the house again for an hour or two. In the meantime, I decided to go downstairs and see if Ahmad had agreed to cook dinner and when it would be served.

I found Mitchell arranging the table in the dining room. He told me that Ahmad was preparing the meal and that it would be served at the usual time.

When I entered the drawing room before dinner that evening, Lady Clareham, the dowager countess, and Edmond had already arrived. The ladies sat side by side on a sofa. Edmond leaned against the chimney piece, his hand to his brow.

"Does your head ache, Edmond?" the dowager countess asked.

"Yes," he replied. "It is all this damned turmoil."

"I know, my dear. Good evening, Mary."

"Good evening," I said. And when I had sat down opposite the ladies, I said to Edmond's mother. "I am so glad you have come down to dinner. Are you feeling better?"

"A little," she replied. Edmond began to walk about the room, and she looked up and said: "Edmond, must you pace up and down like that? Can't you sit down?"

"What difference does it make to you," Edmond asked, "whether I sit or stand or crawl? What difference does it make to anyone? Nobody ever thinks of me, and even that doesn't make any difference—we will all be dead and buried soon, anyway. He is lucky." Edmond pointed in the direction of his father's room. "He is done with it all."

"I wish you wouldn't say things like that," his mother said, beginning to weep.

"Edmond!" his grandmother cried. "We do think of you. You are very dear to us. You know we would do anything for you. Come," she extended her arm and hand to him, "and sit here by me. We should all be very close to each other at this time—comfort each other."

"That is no reason why we should sit on top of one another," Edmond said. "I am fine right here."

"Dinner is served, my lady," Mitchell announced.

Dinner that evening was a very simple meal. But even so, Ahmad had performed miraculously, I thought, in the short time he had had to prepare it. It consisted of a main course and dessert.

"What is this?" the dowager countess asked, as she chose a piece of chicken from a shallow serving tray which Mitchell held for her.

"I am afraid I couldn't say, my lady," Mitchell replied.

"Chicken curry—*murg kari*," Lady Clareham answered.

Then Mitchell served a saffron rice, a mixed vegetable dish made with coconut, and a plate of little, deep-fried rolls.

"Well, I must say it is all very good," Edmond's grandmother said. "Spicy though, isn't it?"

"There should be a chutney," Lady Clareham said. "Is there no chutney, Mitchell?"

"I couldn't say, my lady," Mitchell replied. "This is what I was given to serve."

"Edmond, you have taken hardly anything," the dowager countess declared.

"I am not hungry," Edmond said. "It looks and smells positively vile."

"It is very good—try just a little of the chicken," she begged.

Edmond tossed her a look of disgust and took a bite of chicken, but he spat it out at once. "Awful!" he cried. "Disgusting! Water, Mitchell—get me some water."

"On the table in front of you, my lord," Mitchell said. "If you wish me to pour a fresh glass. . ."

"No, no," Edmond said. He took a sip of water, but this he spat out too, crying: "Uh, what did you put in this? Mitchell, what is wrong with this water?"

"Nothing, my lord."

"I won't have it! I can't stand it!" Edmond cried. He jumped to his feet then and threw back his chair. "I can not stand everyone's staring at me and breathing down my neck—all huddled together in this miserable room and," he pointed to the table, "that loathesome Indian muck." He stood there, his fists clenched at his sides, staring at us as though we were diseased. "I am going out! Out of this house! Away from the lot of you, and don't wait up for me to come home." Then he stalked out of the room. In a moment we heard the door to the east portico slam.

"Poor boy," the dowager countess said. "I had no idea he would take it so hard. But he will be all right. He is very strong, actually. It is the shock. Are you all right, Julia?"

"I can't eat any more," Lady Clareham said. "I am going back upstairs."

Then Mitchell helped her with her chair and she left us.

"Poor Julia," the dowager countess said.

"Yes," I replied. "I wish I could help."

"One can't, Mary. But we must be thankful that he did not suffer."

Later, when we sat in the drawing room, Ahmad himself brought us coffee. And although he did not go through the ritual of tasting it, I knew we could drink it without fear.

It grew dark outside before we finished it. Anticipating this, Mitchell had left the dining room while we were eating dessert and had lighted the lamps in the drawing room for us. I remarked to the dowager countess, as we sat there, that it grew dark a full hour earlier than it had when I arrived at the Castle in June.

That evening I was glad of the early darkness—it would help me to slip into Edmond's room all the sooner without being seen. As soon as I could properly do so, I left the dowager countess and climbed the stairs to the gallery: but I did not go into my room. Instead, I paused at my door, looking to be sure that the rotunda was deserted, and then I stole through the gloom to Edmond's room and stepped inside it.

I felt uneasy as I stood there and looked about—not only because I trespassed in a man's bedchamber, but because the brightly lighted room was so austere. Its vivid blue plaster walls held no pictures or ornaments of any kind except for a huge mirror over the chimney piece. Opposite this, Edmond's double bed, heavily draped in deep-blue velvet, dominated the room. Tables stood on either side of the bed, and two wardrobes, a chest of drawers with lamps sitting on them, a wash-hand-stand, and two chairs completed the furnishings. That was all—no carpet; no books; no childhood mementoes or evidences of hobbies lay about. Only a dressing gown laid out, and toilet articles on the wash-hand-stand indicated that the room was occupied at all.

But there was no time to compare the personality of the occupant to the decor of the room. If I were to find what I sought and not be caught doing it, I had to begin at once.

Nothing in the wardrobes interested me, and as I tiptoed across the room toward the bureau, I heard a sound at the door and glanced toward it. The door swung open.

It was not, as I had feared, Edmond, but Jane Spence who entered the room then. She started as she saw me standing there, but she recovered quickly and closed the door quietly behind her.

"Well, Lady Beauford," she said, "I certainly didn't expect to find you here. Are you waiting to see Edmond?"

"Would it displease you if I were, Jane?" I asked. "But no, I came to find a book which his lordship offered to lend me. And you? Have *you* come to see his lordship? I must compliment you on your dress—the color becomes you. It was one of Lady Vivian's, wasn't it? I remember seeing it in her room."

"What if it was?"

"Wouldn't your uniform be more appropriate? It woul[ ]
be a shame to soil her dress."

"I shan't be wearing a uniform anymore, and all o[ ]
Lady Vivian's dresses will be mine if I like."

"Oh?"

"Yes. Edmond and I are going to be married, and [ ]
shall be mistress of Castle Cloud."

"You don't think his lordship will *marry* you?"

"And why not? He promised to."

"My dear girl, there is every reason why he will not. He[ ]
would be a laughingstock if he did. Marry the chamber[ ]
maid? I am afraid that only happens in novels. Besides, [ ]
know that Edmond does not intend to marry. Why should
he, when he finds so much entertainment at the bathing
pavilion and in countless other cottages, and barns, and
hayricks throughout the countryside? Surely you are no[ ]
deaf and blind, Jane, and I should think not a fool." [ ]
studied her for a moment and then said: "You know why
he has told you these things, don't you Jane?"

"I don't know what you're talking about, and you
weren't looking for a book either. What were you doing[ ]
searching his room?"

I considered carefully what to say; then I answered: "[ ]
will tell you what I was looking for. I was looking for the
bag of weed-killer—the poison which you and his lordship
put in my coffee last night. I know everything, Jane—ev[ ]
erything that has gone on here at the Castle."

Jane scowled at me.

"I am collecting evidence," I said. "Then I shall go to
the chief constable with it. And you will go to prison. You
are as guilty as he is."

Still she did not speak, but she continued to stare at me.

I continued: "Edmond is not going to marry you, Jane.
And, you know, it will be easier for you if you cooperate
with the authorities. There is one thing that I do not quite
understand. Perhaps you would explain it to me. *Why* did
Edmond kill him? Why was it necessary?"

"Why?" Jane cried. "Ha! If you knew anything, Lady
Know-it-all, you would know that. You can't fool *me* with
your tricks, and I'm not saying another thing until I talk
to Edmond. Just wait till I tell him about this. He'll be
very interested."

"Then you may tell him this also: I have written everything I know in a letter to be opened in case of my death. I mailed that letter while his lordship was in Barnstaple this morning. If you don't believe me ask Mr. Hollycombe. It is now well on its way to my solicitor in London."

And without another word, I turned and walked out of the room.

I went directly to my own room then, locked myself in, lit the lamps, closed the curtains, changed into my nightgown, drew on a robe, and sat down before the fireplace. And as I sat there, Jane Spence's voice repeated over and over in my mind: "If you knew anything, you would know that. If you knew anything, you would know that. If you knew anything. . ."

But I didn't know that. I didn't know why Edmond had killed John O'Connor. Surely he could have gotten rid of him without killing him—unless O'Connor had found out something about Edmond which Edmond could not afford to have known. But I hadn't the vaguest notion what that could be. I was certain, however, that O'Connor had come back for Vivian; that Edmond had killed him; and that Edmond had buried him in James's grotto.

Still I continued to hear Jane's voice repeat in my mind: "If you knew anything, you would know that." How humiliated I had felt when she laughed at me. My ruse had not worked—I had underestimated her intelligence. She was much more clever than Edmond. Edmond was not clever at all. In fact, I had long since decided that he was rather a fool, in spite of his exalted opinion of himself. Well then, could Jane Spence be responsible for what had happened? Was that why she was so sure that Edmond would marry her?

"If you knew anything, you would know that." But know what?

I also thought about the night ahead—it was going to be a long one. I considered doing one more thing—going up to the storage rooms and getting the beard out of the trunk to keep as possible evidence against Edmond—but then I decided that that must wait until daylight. So I tried to read, but after reading an entire page of a magazine and not remembering a word, I laid it aside and sat there thinking about the situation at Castle Cloud. Had Edmond returned home yet? Had he talked to Jane Spence? I was

glad I had written the letter to Mr. Schraw, but would
knowing about it deter Edmond?

And then I thought about David. I realized I had made
a mistake in not marrying him. I loved him, and I longed
for him, and it didn't make any difference why he had
wanted me. Nothing made any difference; I wanted to be
near him, regardless. And I needed his help and his protection. But I knew that it was too late.

Finally, about midnight, I blew out all the lamps except
the one at my bedside, turned it down low, and got into
bed. I knew I would not be able to sleep—I did not even
try. After lying there for what seemed an eternity, I heard
a sound outside on the gallery. I sat up and listened for it
to come again, but the house was silent. I reached for my
watch; it said two o'clock. Then I heard the noise again. It
was a scraping sound—as though two pieces of metal were
rubbing together—but it was such a stealthy sound that I
could barely hear it. Then it stopped again. It had come
from the other side of my door, I was sure of it. Quietly I
lay back the covers, slipped down from my bed, and tip-
toed barefoot to the door. As I reached it, I heard a faint
tap of metal on metal, and then the scraping sound began
again. The sound was coming from the other side of my
door.

Then, to my horror, I noticed the key waver in the lock,
and as the scraping sound became more frenzied, I saw it
shake and then slide out of the keyhole toward me.
Instantly, before it could fall to the floor, I grasped the
key, rammed it back into the lock, turned it to its locked
position, and held it there. I listened. For a moment I
heard someone breathing rapidly; then the night was still.

I must have remained standing there, holding the key
and listening, for half an hour. I soon became tired of
standing, but I had no way of telling whether the person
on the other side of the door was still there, and whether
he would try again. Did he have a key, then, that would
unlock my door? Was he still standing on the other side of
it, listening, as I was listening? He might have gone—the
thick carpet on the gallery floor would have muffled his
footsteps. Finally, I let go of the key and stood watching
it. It did not move.

But I was terrified that he would return. To go back to
bed then, and risk falling asleep was unthinkable: so I

slipped quickly into my robe, carried a straight chair to the door, sat down, and watched the key until long after the sun had risen. And only when the house had wakened and it was time to get ready for breakfast did I leave the door.

That was the beginning of a day that, more than any other, I wish I could forget.

❧ Chapter Twenty-one ❧

"GOOD MORNING, Lady Clareham," I called to the dowager countess as I walked toward her. "You are breakfasting early this morning."

"Such as it is," she said. "Good morning, Mary, my dear."

"Where is Mitchell?" I asked.

"Mitchell has declared that he is ill, and gone to his room—at least he has gone somewhere. Mary, this house is in a state of chaos. Of all times for this to happen. I don't know how Julia and Edmond could have allowed it. First of all, my room was not prepared for me in the least—Delphine has had to do it all, even carry the water. There is still a chambermaid, I understand, but Mrs. Foley says that Jane something-or-other. . ."

"Spence."

"Yes—has become very independent and is impossible to manage. 'Well,' I said, 'sack the girl, and don't give her a character.' 'Oh, no, his lordship wouldn't like that,' she said. I must have a talk with Edmond about it. Then, of course, he has sacked the chef, apparently for no reason. But I shouldn't blame the dear boy. His father's death has been a wretched blow. He is so sensitive—much too sensitive for his own good. And now this Mitchell business."

"How is Mitchell ill," I asked. "Did he say?"

"He isn't, if you ask me. He is off somewhere, pouting, like a spoiled child. I never liked that man. He is rude and thinks entirely too much of himself. He and Edmond had a quarrel. When I came down, they were arguing in the hall, and then they stepped into the hall chamber. Something about wages, and Edmond refused. Then Mitchell came to the doorway, there, and said he was ill and must go and lie down. I would have gotten rid of him long ago.

You will have to serve yourself from the sideboard, I am afraid."

"I am really not hungry."

"Neither was Edmond—no breakfast at all, poor lamb."

"Where is he now?"

"I don't know."

"Is there coffee?"

"I haven't seen any."

"Oh, dear." I got up from the table. "I will go and see if Ahmad will make some then, if I can find him."

So I ran down to the kitchen. There I found Ahmad lifting the coffee off the stove. The fragrance told me that the coffee was ready; it was as though Ahmad had read my thoughts. He followed along behind me, carrying the coffeepot to the dining room, where he poured coffee for Lady Clareham and myself. After that, he left the pot on the sideboard in case we wanted another cup, and then left us.

I helped myself to a cold, hard-cooked egg and a little, grayish-white rice cake—which Ahmad must have made, and one of which I had seen Lady Clareham eating—but I did not eat much of either. I did, however, have a second cup of coffee. Just as I was finishing it, Colen appeared in the doorway and asked if he could speak with me.

"Yes, Colen?" I asked, when I had stepped out into the hall.

"I came to say good-by, my lady," he replied.

"Good-by?"

"His lordship dismissed me this morning, my lady."

"Why, Colen?"

"He claimed I was insolent, but it was an accident. I would never have done it on purpose."

"What happened?"

"Nothing very much, my lady. I was carrying water to the horses when he comes up behind me and startles me, so that one of the pails slips out of my hand and the water splashes a bit on his trousers. He was very angry, and he sacked me then and there, and he won't give me a character, my lady. I wondered . . . if you could say a good word for me up at Oakland Park, my lady."

"I wish I could, Colen, but I am afraid I won't be seeing the Fields anymore."

"I'm sorry to hear that, my lady."

"Suppose *I* write a note for you."

"I'd appreciate that, my lady. It wouldn't be like a character, but it would help."

So while he waited in the hall, I went into the drawing room and wrote a note praising his work at Castle Cloud. But as I finished it and got up from the desk, something outside one of the north windows attracted my attention. It was Edmond walking through the knot garden toward the hedged walk. He still limped, and he seemed to be looking inquisitively into the bushes as he went.

Then I returned to the hall and gave Colen the note. "When will you be leaving?" I asked.

"His lordship told me to clear out at once, my lady. I'll get my things together and try to get something to eat in an hour or so, and then go."

"Today? But who will take care of the horses?"

"I don't know, my lady. That is up to his lordship, isn't it?"

As he spoke, the doorbell rang.

"I must see who that is," I said. "Thank you for everything, Colen, and good luck to you."

Then I left him and went to let Mr. Hackley, the undertaker, into the house. I knew as soon as he told me his name that I should tell Edmond that he had arrived, but I could think of nothing more foolish than to go alone down to the bathing pavilion to fetch him. So I showed the undertaker up to Lord Clareham's room, where I left him with the dowager countess and Lady Clareham.

Since they were occupied with Mr. Hackley, and Edmond was away from the house, it occurred to me that it was a perfect time to go up to the costume trunk in the storage rooms and get the beard that Edmond had used as his disguise. I had little difficulty finding the costume trunk—it was the third trunk I opened. The black hat and cloak still lay in it on top of the other costumes where Mrs. Muldoon had placed them. But the beard was not there. I looked for it in the other trunks and boxes and then searched the costume trunk again, thoroughly, but Edmond had come and taken the beard away with him. I should have known he wouldn't leave it there—even an idiot would have taken it away and destroyed it.

I returned to my room, bitterly disappointed. Why, I wondered, had I not taken it immediately after Mrs. Muldoon had left it in the trunk. Edmond had thwarted me again—first the weed-killer and now the beard. Was he plotting something? His dismissal of Colen made me feel uneasy and isolated. Now there would be no one to saddle a horse or hitch up a carriage if I wished to leave Castle Cloud quickly. I would have to walk. Mitchell and Ahmad were now the only men left in the house. This was hardly reassuring since I could not easily communicate with Ahmad and Mitchell could not be trusted.

But at least, I thought, I have Vivian's diary. And the safest place to keep it, I decided, was in my trunk, locked. So I took the diary from the chest of drawers where I had hidden it, and opened the trunk. I stood still, staring down into the trunk—astonished at what I saw inside it. There on the little stack of fichus and sleeves, lay a brown paper bag with the words "W. WOOD, SEEDSMAN AND NURSERYMAN" printed in large letters on its side. I recognized it at once as the bag of weed-killer from the greenhouse. Now, however, the bag was half-empty.

It took me only a moment to realize why Edmond had placed it there: if I had died from drinking the poisoned coffee, two nights before, Edmond would have claimed that I had taken my own life, and the proof of his allegation would have been this bag of poison which would have been found in my trunk. Edmond must have placed it there two days before—before I had begun locking my door.

Instantly then, I wondered if Edmond had tried to enter my room the night before in order to recover the bag of weed-killer, or to murder me, or both. I decided that the latter was the most likely. So, after placing the diary alongside the paper bag in my trunk and locking it, I left my room, locking it behind me also, and went downstairs to find Mrs. Foley.

She came out of the laundry rooms just as I reached the basement, and I hurried down the corridor toward her.

"May I have a word with you, Mrs. Foley?" I asked, as I approached her.

"Well?" she said.

"I wanted to ask you about the keys to my room. I have a key. Is there a duplicate anywhere?"

"There's only one key to each bedroom that I know about, and they're in the doors."

"Would any of the keys to any of the other bedrooms unlock my door?"

"How would I know? They might. But I've got better things to do than go playing change-the-keys-in-the-doors-and-see-if-they-work. Besides, we don't lock our doors here."

"Not even when there is a murderer loose among us?"

She started when I said that.

And I was quick to seize the advantage. "Edmond murdered him, didn't he?"

Mrs. Foley stared at me wide-eyed, but only for a moment. Then she said: "I don't know what you're talking about. If you have something to say about his lordship, say it to his face."

Without another word, she brushed past me and ran up the stairs to the rotunda. I followed her, but more slowly, and when I reached the hall above, Mrs. Foley was not there. I wondered if she had gone to find Edmond—he must have returned from the bathing pavilion by then.

But I did not stop to wonder long: I went directly to my room. And during the next half-hour, I left it several times, intending to try my key in the locks of the empty bedroom on one side of my room, and Vivian's and James's rooms on the other. But each time I did so, either the dowager countess, Lady Clareham, or Mrs. Foley were walking on the gallery, and I returned to my room hoping that the next time I would find the gallery deserted. I was not successful in this, however, and since by that time it was time to go down to luncheon, I knew that I would have to wait until later to learn if the keys to any of the bedrooms were interchangeable.

I went downstairs then, and when I reached the hall, I discovered that Mitchell had resumed his duties and was arranging the table in the dining room. I found no one else about; the drawing room stood empty—neither the dowager countess nor Lady Clareham had come down yet. Nor had Edmond arrived. I had not seen him since early that morning. But I found a copy of the day's *Times* on the table, directly inside the drawing room doorway and sat down to read Lord Clareham's obituary while I waited for them to join me. Shortly, the ladies came into the room together, and almost at once Mitchell announced that luncheon was served. Still Edmond had not arrived.

"Have you seen his lordship?" the dowager countess asked Mitchell.

"Yes, my lady," Mitchell answered.

"Well, where is he?"

"I do not know where he is, my lady."

"Where did you see him?"

"Here in the rotunda, my lady."

"When was this, Mitchell?"

"An hour ago, my lady."

"Which direction was he going?"

"Toward the stairs, my lady."

"Have you seen him since?"

"No, my lady."

"In other words, he went to his room an hour ago. Why didn't you tell me that at once, Mitchell?"

"Because you did not ask me that, my lady, and I do not know that he went to his room. There are other places upstairs that he could have gone to, my lady."

"You might have tried to be helpful, Mitchell, instead of making things difficult."

"I have a great many things to do in this house, my lady—far more things than a person in my position is usually required to do, and at a recompense lower than is appropriate. I would consider, if I may say so, my lady, my position here to be difficult."

"Go in and begin," the dowager countess said to Lady Clareham and me, ignoring Mitchell's last remarks. "I will be there as soon as I have found Edmond. I hope the dear boy is all right. He must eat, you know."

Then she walked toward the stairs, and Lady Clareham and I entered the dining room. When we were settled and Mitchell had handed a platter to Lady Clareham, we heard Edmond's voice. It sounded as though it came from the gallery.

"Not until we get some decent food in this house!" he cried.

Then a door slammed shut, and a few moments later the dowager countess joined us.

"He is much too upset to eat," she said. "I don't like it. His health will suffer if he continues like this. I have never seen him act like this before, have you Julia?"

"No," Lady Clareham answered.

"He will be better when the funeral is over. Oh, I meant to tell you that a man came from the *Times*, wanting to know about the arrangements. Mr. Hackley and I spoke to him."

Then she told me that Lord Clareham would lie in state in the hall chamber from Thursday morning until noon on Friday, and all about the arrangements for the funeral and burial, the people who would be coming down from London, and the supper afterwards, which Mrs. Heart would prepare. Mrs. Foley was, of course, to hire extra help— footmen and maids for the day.

I told them then how impressed I had been with Lord Clareham's obituary in the newspaper. I discovered that neither the dowager countess nor Lady Clareham had read it. Lady Clareham asked if I would read it to them in the drawing room after luncheon, and I agreed.

After that, we spoke little during the meal. Ahmad had prepared Indian food, and I was sure it was safe to eat, since it was served to all of us. I was uneasy, however, about Edmond's not joining us and wondered why he hadn't. He probably did have a prejudice against Indian food—he seemed to dislike anything Indian—but he must be hungry. I didn't think he had eaten since the day before. Or could it be that he was deliberately staying out of sight. If so, why?

It was after luncheon that the bombshell landed in our midst.

When we had finished eating, Lady Clareham, the dowager Lady Clareham, and I withdrew to the drawing room, where I read Lord Clareham's lengthy obituary aloud:

> . . . few statesmen have raised such expectations or attained such magnificent achievements. Lord Clareham had not only an enormous administrative faculty, but also the fortunate ability of inspiring confidence and making everyone with whom he came in contact participants in his plans and comrades in feeling. Everything he did was conducted on the principle of personal integrity and. . .

It was at that point that Mitchell interrupted me, crying: "Lady Clareham, my lady."

I looked up and saw a woman enter the room. She stopped just inside the doorway and looked about. I recognized her at once: she was the Frenchwoman with the rouged cheeks who had driven up to me on the stone bridge weeks before and asked if the drive led to Castle Cloud. This afternoon, instead of her brilliant yellow dress, she wore a black one.

"Bring in my bags," she said to Mitchell. "It is beginning to rain. And return the gig to the village."

"It is hardly my duty to do either, *my lady*." As Mitchell said the last two words, he smiled triumphantly at the dowager countess. "But I should not like to see her ladyship's bags ruined; so I shall bring them in."

"One moment, Mitchell," the dowager countess said. She rose from the sofa then, took a single step toward the doorway, and stood imperially facing the Frenchwoman. "I do not believe we have met."

"That is so, madame," the Frenchwoman said. "I am Edward's wife."

"Edward? There is no Edward here."

"I am Louise Ramsay, madame, now Lady Clareham. Edward has not told you? No, I see he has not."

She walked into the room, and as she did so, Mitchell turned and hurried away—to fetch the woman's bags, I supposed. But Edmond's wife, if she was Edmond's wife, did not sit down with us. She walked to a nearby table to examine an ivory elephant, and then to the wall alongside the chimney piece to view a painting. She seemed calm, and she moved leisurely about, inspecting the room as she talked to the dowager countess.

"My grandson's name is Edmond," the dowager countess said.

"Edmond then," the Frenchwoman replied. "What does it matter? I am still his wife."

"That is absurd. Edmond has no wife."

"Ask him, madame."

"Mitchell," the dowager countess called. "Mitchell? Oh! Very well," she exclaimed. Then she left us.

"We have met, mademoiselle," the Frenchwoman said to me. "But you said you did not live here."

"I am visiting," I said.

"Ah. It is charming, is it not?"

"Yes."

We waited silently then for the dowager countess to return.

Edmond's mother examined the Frenchwoman with a mixture of disbelief and dismay. But the Frenchwoman did not seem to notice. She continued to look about the room.

I wish I could remember what went through my mind then. I suppose I was too shocked to think about anything except to wonder whether the woman's declaration were true. I did not have long to wait, however, before finding out. Not more than three minutes after she had left, I heard the dowager countess returning with Edmond. Lady Clareham, the Frenchwoman, and I all turned to watch them enter the room. The dowager countess preceded her grandson, but she stopped and stood just inside the room, watching Edmond as he brushed past her and walked toward us.

When he saw the Frenchwoman, he stopped in his tracks.

"What do you want?" he cried.

"I want to be with my husband," the Frenchwoman said.

"Now that his father is dead. How touching." Edmond was flushed, and there was a wild expression in his eyes as he stared at her. "Very quick about it, weren't you?"

"It was in the *Times* this morning. I knew it would happen when I read that he was ill."

As they spoke, Edmond began to walk rapidly up and down the room, visibly upset. Every few seconds he stopped pacing and whirled about to glare at the Frenchwoman. She stood by the north windows, watching him calmly. Edmond carried his head in that odd position which I had noticed before—tilted to one side—almost as though he could inquire into her thoughts by holding it that way.

"Max thrown you out?" Edmond demanded.

"I am here. Does it matter?" she said.

Then a movement in the hall behind the dowager countess caught my eye. Jane Spence had arrived and stood gazing into the room. And Mitchell stood beside Jane, smiling as he watched her.

"So," Edmond shouted across the room at the French-woman, "you leave the stinking streets of London to live in luxury in the country, now that your husband has come into his inheritance. Is that the idea? Ha! Welcome to Castle Cloud, my dear, dear wife." He stopped pacing just long enough to bow and sweep the carpet with his finger-tips. "Can you cook? We need a cook. There are no ser-vants left here. There is no money to pay them with—you of all people should know that. Our chef left days ago. Our coachman-groom is gone. We have had no footmen, or housemaids, or gardeners for *years*. Welcome to the country, my dear. We hope you will enjoy it here. But there is no question of a lady's maid for you, nor even a housemaid, for that matter. You won't mind cleaning your own room, carrying your own water, dressing yourself, do-ing your own hair, will you?

"And let us hope that your wardrobe is extensive be-cause there will be no new dresses. But that won't matter since it would hardly be appropriate to call or entertain. No, we shall remain at home where you may walk in the garden, such as it is, or in the park—but be careful of the sheep dung. And there are some old magazines, I believe, scattered about which you may read. Did you say you can read? Oh, you will find life here luxurious and exciting indeed."

"But it will not be long before everyone knows that I am here," the woman said. "You wish us to say as little as possible about the past, yes?"

Edmond had reached the far end of the room as she fin-ished speaking. He flung himself around, ran across the room, and stood before her, panting with short, shallow breaths.

"Blackmail, is it?" he said. "You think that I will pay you to be silent about your disgusting past by making a comfortable nest for you here, is that it?"

"I do not think that is a very nice thing to say. It is my experience that if one is treated nicely, she is nice in return, n'est-ce pas?"

Edmond smiled at her then, but before his smile had faded, he swung his arm with all his might and struck her in the face with the back of his hand. She fell to the car-pet with the force of the blow.

"Think again, my dear," Edmond cried. "Think about

living in the same house with a man who loathes the sight of you. You want to talk? Talk your bloody mouth off then, and see what happens."

At that moment Edmond saw Jane Spence, and he ran toward her.

"I would like a word with you, Jane," he said.

"Edmond!" the dowager countess called.

But Edmond stalked out of the room, across the rotunda, and out of sight, ignoring his grandmother. Jane followed him, and a moment later, we heard the doors of the hall chamber shut.

All during this scene, Lady Clareham had been gazing at Edmond's wife with revulsion, yet there was resignation in her face as well. Now she rose from the sofa.

"Are you coming, Mary?" she asked.

Then she walked out of the room. Since her back was toward me, I could not see whether or not she signaled to the dowager countess. But after glancing at me, Edmond's grandmother followed his mother into the hall, leaving me alone with Edmond's wife.

I knew that I was expected to follow them, but I was curious about the Frenchwoman and thought I might learn something useful from her if I stayed behind.

So I remained seated while I listened to the dowager countess ask Mitchell—outside in the rotunda—to tell Edmond that she and his mother would like to talk to him in his mother's room as soon as he left the hall chamber. After that the house was quiet.

Edmond's wife had gotten up from the floor and walked to a mirror, where she stood examining her face. I glanced at her then, and as I did so, her eyes met mine in the mirror.

Without turning around, she said: "You despise me."

"I don't know you," I answered.

"You despise what you think you know."

I did not reply to this. I got up and walked quietly to the doorway to look out into the hall. If we were going to talk, I wanted to be sure that no one was listening. The dowager countess and Lady Clareham were no longer there: they must have gone upstairs. The rotunda was empty except for Mitchell, who stood with his ear against the hall chamber door.

As I returned to my seat, Edmond's wife said: "Ah—

You judge harshly about things of which you are ignorant." She spoke in French.

"You are mistaken, madame," I said, also in French.

"You could not know," she continued, "what it means to have nothing. When it is a matter of survival, one does not choose a way of life—one is grateful to live at all. But this is something that you cannot imagine.

"Can you imagine your mother beaten to death by a man who was not your father? It happened to me before my eyes in a little room where the three of us lived on the Rue Huchette. Ah, you know it."

"I lived in Paris with my father."

"Then you should know what it is like there. I was five years old. After that—I was alone. Do you know how a five-year-old child lives alone on the streets of Paris? It is not an easy life, and it was not a nice one, but I managed. Fortunately, God gave me beauty, even as a child. Well, he had to give me *something*, my dear."

"Why are you telling me so much?"

"It is not very much. I tell you because I am here, and I need, if not a friend, then someone who is at least not hostile toward me. I do not think you will be hostile."

"No. But I do not think you should stay here. How can you?"

"I am no longer young." She shrugged. "My beauty has gone. Oh, yes! In my place, what would you do?" When I did not answer, she said: "Ah, you see? No, I shall stay here."

"Are you really his wife?" I asked.

"Yes, it is recorded with the registrar. It is all perfectly legal; it had to be. But I made a mistake—I fell in love with a bad man. Well, it was natural—I did not meet any good ones."

"Was Edmond in love with you?"

"He did not even know me. Oh! No, I was not in love with Edmond. His name is Max le Rouquin. You have heard of Red Max?"

"No."

"No, you would not have heard of him—I thought not. He is a Frenchman, very attractive to women, and married to an Englishwoman."

"I don't understand."

"It was impossible for me to go back to France. Max

wished me to stay in England with him, and of course I wished to stay. To remain in this country, I must marry an Englishman and become naturalized. You begin to see?"

"Yes."

"Yes, it was a business transaction. That was in the spring of 1854. Edmond had come to London in January with some money. . . ."

"Into trade," I thought aloud.

"I beg your pardon?"

"Something his grandmother said. She lent him that money to go into trade. He gambled it away, didn't he? She would be heartbroken if she knew."

"Then do not tell her. Yes, Edmond lost it at the tables. He began to borrow heavily, and got into debt to Raymond Hooker. Do you know him?"

"No."

"He is the third son of Lord Tweedsmere—a dangerous man. Edmond owed him £50,000. Hooker is a friend of Max's. So it was arranged: Max would pay Edmond's debt to Hooker and give Edmond an additional £50,000 if he would marry me. It was advantageous to everyone. Do not forget that Edmond was Mr. Ramsay then. He had no expectations—his brother would inherit Castle Cloud and the estates. It was only later, a short time before you and I first met, that he became Lord Althrop at his brother's death."

"And that day you came to see his inheritance."

"Of course. But I had not come to see him, nor did I. I had seen him only twice before today: once at the ceremony and one other time at Max's, when he came to borrow money."

At that moment I heard the hall chamber doors thrown open with a crash. I got up and went to the doorway to see what was happening, but by the time I reached it, the rotunda was empty.

"Edmond lost the additional £50,000 I suppose," I said when I had returned to Edmond's wife.

"Yes. Now you know a little of my story and a little of his. And you?"

"I am the baroness Beauford, a friend of the family—of Lady Vivian, Edmond's sister. But I shall be leaving the Castle soon."

"Ah. It is true there are no maids?"

"There is one chambermaid, but though she remains here, Edmond has evidently seen fit to relieve her of her duties. Her name is Jane Spence."

"I see. And the rest of the servants, besides the butler?"

"Mrs. Foley, the housekeeper—she is an elderly woman; May Brooke, the kitchen maid; Ida, the laundry maid—she is a bit mad; and Edmond's mother's and grandmother's personal maids. That is all."

"Will you show me a room that is not occupied and where the linen is kept, and will you show me where one draws water? Do not worry about doing these things for me: I am legally Lady Clareham, and so I am the mistress of Castle Cloud."

"Yes, I will show you—"

"Call me Louise, I think. And if you have no objections, I will call you Mary—it will not be for very long, since you say you will soon be leaving."

"The room next to mine would be the most appropriate." I rose then and walked to one of the west windows. "It has not belonged to any of the family, and it is not occupied. It *is* raining. Your carriage!"

"It is not mine. It is a hired one."

"Those poor horses. They have pulled the carriage off into the park. They are standing in the midst of the sheep."

The animals looked so miserable standing there in the downpour that I could not bear the sight of them. I turned from the window almost at once and led Louise out of the drawing room and into the rotunda, which was deserted. Her bags sat in the vestibule. I carried the smallest one upstairs for her (why should I not help her? I felt sorry for her), and I showed her the linen closet as we passed it and then the room next to mine. I set her bag inside the door, telling her that I would be in my room. When she was ready she was to knock on my door, and I would show her where the pump was and where the water cans were kept.

I stepped into my own room then, locked my door behind me, walked again to the window overlooking the bay (my thinking window, I had begun to call it), and sat down. I knew Louise's arrival had altered the situation at the Castle enormously, but I needed to figure out exactly how, and whether it could help me in any way.

Her arrival certainly explained Edmond's negative attitude toward marriage. He had never had the least intention of marrying Flora. She had simply made it possible for him to borrow money from her father. Nor had Edmond any intention of marrying Jane Spence.

What effect would Louise's arrival have on Edmond? She had certainly brought out the beast in him in the drawing room. That had been a vicious blow he had dealt her, and I shuddered when I remembered the sadistic look in Edmond's eyes as he had struck her—he had enjoyed doing it. This made me wonder if Louise had become next after me on his murder list.

And how could Lousie stay in the same house with Edmond's mother and grandmother? I could not imagine eating a meal with Edmond, the dowager countess, Lady Clareham, and Louise all at the same table.

Then I thought I heard Louise moving about in her room. It was rather comforting to have her there; at least I knew she was not part of the conspiracy. But was there a sound in Vivian's room, next door to mine on the other side? No, probably the wind.

Or was Jane Spence next on Edmond's list?

What effect had Louise's arrival had on Jane's relationship with Edmond? No wonder Mitchell had listened at the hall chamber door. But it was more than mere curiosity that had caused him to spy on them: he was attracted to Jane. Many times, I had noticed his covetous glances toward her.

Jane Spence. How did she feel now? What would she do next?

I sat for nearly half an hour waiting for Louise and thinking about these and other things when a sound interrupted my thoughts. It was a thud, as though something had struck the wall, and it had come from Vivian's room. I jumped up, ran to my door, unlocked it, opened it a crack, and peeked out.

I didn't see anyone, but I heard Edmond shout: "Don't you tell me what to do!" Then a door slammed shut. That, however, had come from the other side of the rotunda— from the direction of Edmond's mother's room—an area of the gallery which I could not see without opening my door much wider than I wished to do. Anyway, the thud had come from Vivian's room. Her door was open, and as I looked at the open doorway, a man backed out of it. It was Mitchell carrying one end of a trunk. In a moment, Jane Spence appeared carrying the other.

At the same time Edmond ran into view. He was out of breath, and as he approached Jane and Mitchell, he cried in a low voice: "What are you doing?"

"Leaving! That's what I'm doing," Jane said.

"What are you doing with that?"

"Taking it."

"What is in it? God, you have made a wreck of that room. What were you doing in there?"

"Lady Vivian said I could have anything I wanted, and you can't prove she didn't."

"Take it—take the lot, but you say one word about what has happened here and I will have you thrown into prison as a thief—and more."

"Ha! You won't do a damned thing, you. . ."

"Jane!" Mitchell said.

"Get out!" Edmond cried. Words cannot describe the anguish those two words expressed.

I closed my door then, and pressing my ear to it, waited until it was quiet outside. Then I left my room, looking to be sure that the gallery was empty, and knocked on Louise's door. She opened it a crack and said that she would be ready in five minutes.

Those five minutes seemed to last forever. I was impatient: before Jane Spence left the Castle (and she was in a hurry) I wanted her to meet Louise face to face.

So after Louise came to my room, we quickly descended to the floor of the rotunda where I glanced about for Vivian's trunk. Since it was not in the hall or in either vestibule, we hurried down to the basement. I pretended to show Louise about while I looked for Jane. We stepped into the servants' hall, into the laundry rooms, and finally the kitchens—but we did not see Jane anywhere. We did find Vivian's trunk, however, in the kitchen next to the open door which led to the areaway and the pump.

I had no idea where Jane had gone, but I knew she would return for the trunk. I tried to find excuses to detain Louise, hoping that Jane would return at any moment. But Louise had filled her water can and, saying that she wished to wash, she left me.

My little plan had failed, but I decided to wait for Jane

for just a few more minutes. Perhaps I could learn something by talking to her.

Meanwhile, I would have a close look at the burlap bag which stood next to Vivian's trunk. Its neck was tied too securely to be opened quickly, but after I had felt the shapes of bowls, platters, and candelabra inside, and seen the glint of metal through the sacking, I knew the bag was filled with silver—probably all the Castle Cloud silver that Mitchell had not already stolen.

Was Mitchell leaving the Castle too, then? Were they going together? As I wondered about this, Jane burst into the kitchen wearing a hat and a waterproof cloak. She carried her reticule and a traveling bag, which she set down beside Vivian's trunk and the burlap bag.

"What is in the sack, Jane?" I asked.

"That is none of your business. It is Martin's," she said.

"Martin's?"

"Mr. Mitchell's."

"Judging from the look of it, I would say it was his lordship's."

Jane gazed at me sullenly, but did not answer.

"Well," I said, "it doesn't look like you will be mistress of Castle Cloud after all, does it?"

"Well, it doesn't look like you will be mistress of Oakland Park, either."

"I am sorry you were not here a few moments ago. I brought Edmond's wife down to meet you."

"Why'd you want to do that? To make me feel better?"

"I thought you might like to meet her."

"Very kind, I'm sure."

"To meet your reward."

"Reward?"

"For all your trouble—the wages of sin, so to speak."

"Ha! The wages of sin is it?" Jane pointed to the ceiling. "Look at her new ladybitch up there. There's the wages of sin if I ever saw it. She doesn't know what she's got herself into. Come just in time, didn't she? Just in time to collect *her* wages."

"Your harvest doesn't seem so bountiful."

"What do you mean?"

" 'As ye sow, so shall ye reap.' "

"Why do you look at me like that? I didn't do anything. What do you think I done?"

"You brought me the coffee for one thing."

"What if I did? He gives it to me and says to take it up to Lady Beauford. I worked here. I did what he told me to do."

"And he told you to impersonate Lady Vivian, didn't he? And what about the other things he told you to do before that?"

"What other things? I didn't know anything about it till it was all over. Nobody did. That's why she drank the poison—to prove it. She was the only one that knew."

I thought quickly and said: "She didn't have to drink it."

"She had to! They wouldn't believe her otherwise. His own brother? Who would believe a thing like that?"

"His own brother?"

Jane stared at me wide-eyed for a moment; then she smirked and said: "You didn't know, did you? You've been trying so hard to find out, and you didn't find out anything, did you? His brother! He poisoned his brother, that's what. Edmond poisoned his brother. What do you think about that?"

I was too shocked to answer. I suppose I just stood there gaping at her.

"Didn't think of that, did you? But I didn't know anything about it until I heard Lady Vivian screaming it all over the house. Her brother was dead by then. I didn't do anything wrong—I didn't know anything about it. I was just a chambermaid till after it happened.

"I didn't sow anything! Anyway, it doesn't work that way. I met a loser, that's all; *that's* how it works. He couldn't do anything right. He couldn't kill his brother without her finding out. He couldn't win tuppence at a table. All he could do was borrow and lose it, borrow and lose it. And then you came along, and that stupid business about the letters. Of course you found out about them. Why, he couldn't even shoot you from six yards away. And look what he married. I'll bet there's a story there! He was a loser. Everything he touched turned bad. It wasn't my fault. There wasn't anything I could do. If it had been anybody else—if it had been *anybody* else but him, it would have been all right."

I was astonished to see tears glistening in Jane's eyes as she finished speaking, but I saw them for only an instant before she turned to the open kitchen door and looked up into the rain. She did not look back at me.

I was astounded and horrified by what she had told me but also curious to know what she was going to do next.

So I said: "You are impatient."

"I'm not staying in this house with him—" she said, "not a minute longer than I have to."

As she finished speaking, I heard the sound of boots sloshing in the areaway. Mitchell entered the kitchen. His waterproof glistened with rain. Water ran in rivulets from it making puddles on the floor, and water dripped from the brim of his hat. Even his face and mustache were wet.

"Well, Lady Beauford," he said. "Come to see us off?" Then he examined me more closely and turned to Jane. "What have you been talking about? What have you been telling her?"

"Jane has been telling me how his lordship killed his brother," I said.

Mitchell did not take his eyes from Jane's face.

"Well, what of it?" Jane said to him. "She won't say anything. Did you bring the gig?"

"On the contrary, Jane," I said, "I am going to tell the chief constable in Barnstaple all about it."

"I doubt that, my lady," Mitchell said. He paused, gazing at me—his vindictive eyes narrowing with amusement. "And so—the most vicious, thieving, blackmailing, murdering bastard in the history of the county is never brought to justice. And the great Clareham title goes unsullied."

"What blackmail? He certainly will be!" I said. "What do you mean?"

"What do you think his lordship wanted from McComb out there, a game of cards?" Then he smiled slyly—clearly he intended to say no more.

He grasped the burlap sack and threw it over his shoulder. The silver inside it clanked, but he did not seem to care. Then he picked up one end of the trunk and Jane, carrying her bag and reticule, picked up the other. They walked out into the areaway.

I heard them shuffle along it, the trunk scraped against something, and Jane cried, "Ow!" Then they were gone, and a minute later I heard the clomp of hoofs and the grind of wheels above the pounding rain.

My one thought then was to talk to Lady Clareham. So

I left the kitchen, and when I entered the corridor, I saw two things: Ahmad hurried down it away from me, and Mrs. Foley hurried past him toward me.

"My lady," she called, as she approached. "I must speak to you at once. I have something very important to say to you. I've just been to your room and I've looked everywhere. I was beginning to be worried."

"Why should you be worried?" I said.

"Please come with me. Yes, of course I was worried."

I followed her into the servants' hall, and as soon as we were inside the room, we stopped and faced each other.

"I have something terrible to tell you," she continued. "Your life is in danger! That night that someone shot at you— It wasn't a mistake like his late lordship said. It was done deliberate. It was his lordship, my lady. His lordship tried to shoot you." She paused, staring at me with her beady, birdlike eyes, frantically trying to decide how to continue.

"How do you know that, Mrs. Foley?"

"Mr. Mitchell told me not an hour ago, my lady, right after he heard them talking in the hall chamber. But that's not all. I saw it all clearly at once—I saw where my duty lie, my lady." She squinted at me, then she continued: "You asked me if his lordship murdered him. Well, he did! His late young lordship's bottles of wine were kept in the linen closet and his lordship poisoned them—a little at first and then more and more until his brother died of it. And now he wants to do the same to you because he's afraid you'll find out. You must stop him—you must go to the constable. He's a dangerous man and must be taken away. He must be taken away at once."

"Why didn't you tell me this before?" I asked.

"Because I didn't believe it. Lady Vivian said over and over the night she died that his lordship killed his brother, but we didn't believe it. His late lordship and her ladyship told you that Lady Vivian took her own life. That's what we thought, and that was all there was to it. Of course that's what we thought. I didn't know, my lady. I didn't know."

"But you know now."

"Because he's tried to murder you too, don't you see?"

"But you didn't tell the doctor. You threw away the poisoned wine, I suppose, and buried Lady Vivian's body in secret; and yet you didn't know. I don't suppose the question of a chemical analysis of his late young lordship ever came up—to see if Lady Vivian had told the truth. Oh, no, you didn't know anything about it."

"I didn't have anything to do with her body—it was his lordship and his late lordship. You've got to have him taken away. He can't be allowed to stay here. He's ungrateful and unscrupulous! After all I've done for him and his mother. He's going to dismiss me—just like that. Mr. Mitchell told me so. And make Jane Spence the housekeeper! I'm too old, he says to Jane. 'We'll get rid of her, and you'll have her rooms and be in charge of the house and all the servants,' he says. After all I've done for him. Where would I go? I've got nobody. Where would I go? This is my home—has been for over seventy years. I came here when I was ten years old, and I gave it my life. I took care of him and Lady Vivian and his late young lordship when they were this high, and his late lordship too, God bless him, and I took care of them that came before them too. I gave everything for the Castle, and what do I get for it? Sacked like a common scullery maid. . . ."

"Mrs. Foley!" I interrupted. "Will you tell the constable everything that happened the night his young lordship died? Will you tell it in court?"

"Certainly, my lady. But it must be understood that I didn't believe it. I didn't believe a word of it, not a word of it."

"Thank you, Mrs. Foley. Then I will go into Barnstaple as soon as the rain stops and see the chief constable."

I left her after that and hurried to my room: I wanted to talk to Edmond's mother, but before I did that, I wanted to decide what I would say to her and what I would say to the constable. So I sat down by the window. Clouds pressed down upon the Castle, shutting out the light of afternoon. It was not yet four-thirty, but how dark it was. And it was raining hard.

So that was what Edmond had said to Jane in the hall chamber. I could almost hear it: "You will have Mrs. Foley's rooms and be in complete charge of Castle Cloud and all the servants and we will go on just as we have been. Nothing will be changed between us." I was sure that that was the way he had put it. But Jane wouldn't have it, of course. She could never have lived as housekeeper in the same house with Edmond's wife. It was marriage for her—mistress of Castle Cloud—or nothing. But why, after overhearing that conversation, had Mitchell told Mrs. Foley about it? So that Mrs. Foley would expose Edmond? She had no choice but to do so and, thereby, save her position at the Castle. Edmond's destruction would benefit them both: Mrs. Foley would stay on then, during the long search for a possible heir, and even after that, when the estates reverted to the crown; and Mitchell would have Jane. Mitchell had his farm and money in the bank from the proceeds of his thievery. He had been ready to leave the Castle, but he had wanted to take Jane with him. It was all very clear—except for one thing: in the kitchen Mitchell had implied that Edmond would not be brought to justice. I did not understand this. Had something happened, then, to make him say that?

But then a thought made me start. Would Mrs. Foley be so anxious to testify in court when she found out that Jane had left the Castle for good? Perhaps not—not until after the result of the chemical analysis of James's body became known. That would open her mouth.

Beneath all this, however, lay the realization that Edmond had killed James. Not O'Connor, but James. How clever I had thought myself and how wrong I had been. It terrified me once again to know that someone capable of such a thing was in that very house with me then and wanted to kill me. Perhaps he stood outside my door at that moment.

Frightened as I was of Edmond, I was relieved: the danger, I knew, would be over with the rain. But I must tell Lady Clareham what I was going to do—she had a right to know. So I got up, listened at my door before opening it, and then dashed around the gallery to Lady Clareham's room.

Cecile opened her door. "I would not disturb her ladyship now," she said.

"I am afraid I must see her," I said, glancing into the room. Lady Clareham stood in the doorway that connected her room with her husband's. "Something has happened which she should know about. Is the dowager countess with her?"

"It is all right, Cecile," Lady Clareham called. "Go and rest now. You must rest too, you know. Please come in, Mary."

Cecile left us then, closing the door quietly behind her, and Lady Clareham crossed to one of two armchairs separated by a table which stood before one of the windows and sat down.

"Come and sit here with me," she said.

The curtains had been drawn and lamps lit in both Lady Clareham's and her husband's rooms. I sat in the chair on the other side of the table. From there I could look into Lord Clareham's room and see him, so terribly white, lying on his bed.

"Are you feeling better?" I asked.

"I don't know," she said. "I think I have stopped feeling. One gets to a point beyond feeling."

"I am so terribly sorry. I wish there were something I could do."

Lady Clareham turned her head away from me as I spoke and looked through the doorway into her husband's room. For a moment I wondered if I must really tell her what I had learned and what I was going to do. Couldn't it all be forgotten? Must I cause her even more pain? I knew I must, but I didn't know how to do it.

"You have something to tell me?" she asked, finally.

"Mitchell and Jane left not quite an hour ago. I am afraid they won't be coming back."

Lady Clareham gazed at me, but she didn't reply.

"Before they left they told me about James," I said.

"James?"

"How Edmond—killed him."

"Oh."

"And then Mrs. Foley told me about it too. Mitchell had overheard Edmond offer Jane Mrs. Foley's position— Mrs. Foley was to be let go, you see. Mitchell told Mrs. Foley about it, and then Mrs. Foley told me about Edmond. How could you expect them all to keep the secret forever?"

"They would have. It would have been to their advantage," she pointed to the room that Louise had taken. "If it weren't for that woman, they would be here now."

"But why didn't you *believe* Vivian, Lady Clareham? How could she ever have made it up?"

"Believe—that one of my boys had done that to the other?"

"Then it *was* the only way she could prove it."

"Yes." A tear crept down her cheek and her lower lip quivered as she spoke. "The wine was still on James's bedside table. It was almost a full bottle. Vivian came in minutes after—he had died. I shall never forget the look on her face when she saw him: she was too late, you see. Edmond was there. 'You killed him! You killed him!' she cried. Edmond denied it. Then she poured a glass of the wine and ran to him. 'Drink this then. Drink it!' But he wouldn't. 'He poisoned the wine,' she cried to me. She held the glass out for me to see, but I didn't believe her. If only I had said, 'Yes.' Just that one little word—but how could I? If only I had believed her."

Lady Clareham closed her eyes then and sat shaking her head while she wept. And then after a minute, when she had become calmer, she looked up at me and said: "Well, we won't say anything about it. It is all in the past, now."

"But it is not in the past, Lady Clareham. He tried to kill *me*—twice, perhaps three times. That was Edmond who shot at me. He poisoned the coffee that Jane brought while I sat with Lord Clareham—while he was dying. And then last night he tried to get into my room. We can't let him go on killing people."

"No, no. He won't do it anymore. He won't do it—I promise you he won't."

"We can't take that chance."

"What do you mean?"

"I am going to the chief constable in Barnstaple."

"No. No, no, no. . . ." She sprang from her chair and ran to the door to the gallery, sobbing each word louder and louder until the last was a scream. ". . . no, no, no, *no!*" Then she flung the door open and stood in the doorway. "Edmond, Edmond," she cried. *"Ed-mon-d!"*

Her cries seemed to exhaust her, and she leaned against the doorjamb gazing across the rotunda toward her son's room.

Almost at once I heard a door thrown open, and then in a moment Edmond stood in the doorway beside his mother glaring at me.

"She knows!" Lady Clareham said to him. "She knows about James. She is going to the police."

"Police?" It was the dowager countess.

She had appeared on the gallery only a few seconds after Edmond and now stood behind him. She must have been lying down. Her hair was disarranged and she wore a robe which looked as if it had been thrown on hastily.

"It is nothing, Grandmamma," Edmond said. "Some of the silver stolen. Going to the police."

"Edmond! You *are* ill," the dowager countess said.

As she spoke, Edmond extended his arm toward Louise's door and shouted: "Go back! Go back to your room!"

"Don't shout at her, dear," the dowager countess said. "Go into Mamma's room and let me look at you. Come along, that's it. Now, sit down here."

Edmond slumped into a chair beside the door.

"Poor dear—you are exhausted," she continued, as she felt his forehead. "You have a fever—you are burning up."

"Stop it!" Edmond cried, thrusting her hand away. "So thirsty," he muttered. He threw himself out of the chair then, and began to limp rapidly, impatiently, back and forth across the room. "I am all right!"

"You are not all right. You are ill! We must send for the doctor."

"No!" he cried.

Then Edmond whirled abruptly about and walked in my direction. I could see beads of perspiration glistening all over his face, and as he glanced at me, I saw a strange, wild look in his eyes. I had once seen that look in the eyes of a rat that our gardener had cornered and was about to club to death. Then as he approached my chair my heart lurched. He coughed, and I saw that his mouth was filled with froth.

"I'm all right. I'm all right! Don't crowd in on me so— stay away! Nothing wrong. Upset, that's all. Thirsty." He seemed to have trouble breathing—after every two words he paused to take a shallow breath.

I knew at once what I must do. I leapt from my chair and darted past him to the wash-hand-stand, took a glass from it, and poured it full of water from the pitcher. Then, holding it out to Edmond, I walked toward him.

"Water, Edmond," I said. "A drink of water. Drink the water."

He whirled about to face me as I spoke and took a step

toward me. Evidently he wished to take the glass because he extended his hand hesitantly, but as I approached him, he drew back from me. And when I was almost upon him, he clutched at his throat and uttered a half-strangled cry. A convulsion shook his body. Then, still clutching his neck, he fled from the room.

After he had gone, I stood looking at the empty doorway, unable to accept the terrible thing that I knew to be true.

"What is it? Mary, what is it?" Edmond's mother asked.

"He is very ill."

"What?"

"Hydrophobia."

"No."

"Sarah did bite him."

"No, he said she didn't."

"Hydrophobia? Sarah?" the dowager countess said. "What are you talking about?"

"Sarah, Vivian's dog, had hydrophobia," I said. "She snapped at Edmond. He told us she didn't bite him—that she only caught his trousers—but she did.

"No!" Lady Clareham said.

"*Yes!*" I cried. "He was frothing at the mouth. You saw him. He was terrified of the water."

Then Lady Clareham sank into the chair that Edmond had used, bowed her head, and began, I think, to pray.

The dowager countess walked slowly to the chair across the table from me and stood looking down at it for a few moments. Then she turned to me and asked: "Are you sure?"

"I am not a doctor. How can I be?" I said.

"What will happen to him next?"

"I don't know. I don't know a great deal about it. I suppose he will go mad."

"We must send for the doctor— What is his name?"

"Dr. Norton. There isn't anyone to send. I will go."

"No, you will catch your death in this weather. We will send Ahmad."

"But he doesn't speak English."

"Surely he knows where Dr. Norton lives. It is only a small village, and he has been here with George for years. We will send him with a note."

"Ahmad," I called.

The Indian stood just outside the room in the gloom of the gallery. How long had he been standing there? I wondered. Often, since he had stopped me from drinking the poisoned coffee two nights before, I had seen him hovering nearby. I think he had decided to assume responsibility for my safety, and I wondered why. I wondered if Lord Clareham had ordered him to do so before he died.

Ahmad entered the room and salaamed.

Lady Clareham looked up and spoke to him in Hindustani.

Then she said to me: "Write the note to Dr. Norton, would you please, Mary. There is pen and ink and paper in the drawer of the little table next to George's door. Ahmad will take it to him.

Then Lady Clareham got up from her chair and went into her husband's bedroom.

And when I had finished writing the brief note to the doctor, I glanced into Lord Clareham's room and saw that Lady Clareham sat by her husband's bedside. Her lips moved silently. She was telling him what had happened and, I knew, asking for his help.

I got up from the table and handed the note to Ahmad.

"Please hurry, Ahmad," I said.

He salaamed and left us at once. I followed him out onto the gallery and, standing just outside Lady Clareham's open door, watched him until he had descended the stairs, crossed the hall below, taken a waterproof from a closet in the east vestibule, and walked out of my view toward the door. Then after looking about to see if Edmond lurked nearby, I stepped back into Lady Clareham's room, closed her door behind me, and turned the key in the lock.

"Mary, what are you doing?" the dowager-countess said, from her chair at the table by the window.

"He might try to get in," I said, as I walked toward her.

"Did you see him?"

"No."

I sat down opposite her.

"But suppose he needs us?" she said. "We can't lock him out. He won't hurt *us*."

She got up then, walked to the door, and unlocked it. Then she returned to her chair.

"How do we know what he will do?" I asked. "If he

goes mad, he is apt to do anything. When dogs go mad, they attack people, or animals, or even trees. They are vicious—they don't know what they are doing."

"But Edmond is not a dog. If he—bit one, would one get hydrophobia?"

"Of course, Lady Clareham. He is terribly dangerous! His saliva is deadly! Even one drop of it on the tiniest cut or sore anywhere on the skin and you would have the disease. And there is no cure for it."

"Nothing?"

At that moment the door flew open and Edmond stood on the threshold.

"Where did that Indian go?" he said to his grandmother.

Then he began to scuttle, limping, about the room, wiping his face and mouth with his handkerchief.

"I saw him go out," he continued. "He went for the doctor, didn't he? *Didn't he?* You sent for the doctor. You said you wouldn't. I don't need a doctor."

"But you do, my dear boy," his grandmother said. "You are ill and Dr. Norton will come soon and make you better. Now please, Edmond, go lie down and rest."

Then without looking at her, Edmond stopped pacing and pointed his finger at me.

"You are responsible for this," he said.

And without another word, he whirled about and darted from the room. The dowager countess and I sat there then, looking at each other—waiting for the other to speak.

"Isn't there something we can do?" the dowager countess asked, at last.

"I don't think so," I said. "Should we tell his wife?"

"I can't think of that woman as his wife."

"But she should know. And what about the servants and Delphine?"

"Delphine is upstairs. She uses the old nanny's room. She will be all right. What time is it?"

I flicked open the cover of my watch. "Five-fifty."

"How long will it take him?"

"At least an hour."

"What do you think Edmond is doing?"

"Pacing about the house, I suppose. He can't seem to remain still. That hideous running-limp. His stiff leg is the one Sarah bit. And his eyes—did you see his eyes?"

"Yes." The dowager countess was crying. "He is going to die?"

I nodded my head.

We sat quietly then, each engrossed in our own thoughts, but each watching the door in case Edmond should return. I don't know what Lady Clareham was thinking, but I was thinking about the look in Edmond's eyes when he had pointed at me and said I was responsible. There had been madness in them, but also a shrewd awareness. He knew that I knew everything now, and that I was going to the police. He couldn't allow me to do that.

Nor could he allow me to talk to Dr. Norton for fear of what I might say to him. I shuddered at the parallel between the situation at Castle Cloud that night and the night that Vivian had died. Both nights, I thought, the doctor was on his way to the Castle, and both nights a girl here might tell him something which would destroy Edmond. Vivian would have told Dr. Norton that Edmond had murdered James. Tonight when he arrived, I might tell Dr. Norton that Vivian was dead and how she had died. I might tell him that James did not die of heart disease, but was poisoned. I knew that Edmond could not risk the possibility of my doing this. The night that Vivian had died, he had kept his secret by keeping the doctor away. How did he plan to keep his secret tonight? Tonight he would not go out—he would not go out in the rain.

He could not know it, of course, but there was no longer any question of my going to the police or telling Dr. Norton anything. Edmond was going to die very soon. What would be the point in telling anyone about his crime? The scandal would only hurt his mother and grandmother needlessly, and perhaps if I said nothing, Vivian could, somehow, rest beside her brother.

So Jane had been right after all: I would say nothing. She must have known about Edmond's disease when I spoke to her in the kitchen, and Mitchell must have known too. He might have suspected it long before. After all, part of Mitchell's duties were to valet Edmond, and he saw more of Edmond than anyone else did.

No wonder Jane had wanted to leave the Castle so quickly. I remembered her saying: "I'm not staying in this house with him—not a minute longer than I have to," and the controlled terror in her voice when she said it. I had taken it for impatience.

And now I understood what Mitchell had meant when he said that Edmond would never be brought to justice. (Well, not by the authorities perhaps, but he was being brought to justice nevertheless.) And Mitchell had been right about the title, too. It would lie unsullied, wouldn't it?

I would say nothing about Edmond's crime, but I was terrified of him and wished that I knew something about his disease. Would Edmond go raving mad? If so, how long would his madness last? When would it happen? How long would it be before he died? Though he had been terribly agitated, he had seemed rational a few minutes before. How rational was he, and how long would he remain so?

What should I do? I decided to stay with Lady Clareham and the dowager countess. I did not think he would try to harm me in their presence. But if he should, they would help me.

"What time is it?" the dowager countess asked.

"Five fifty-five."

And again we fell silent. How had I gotten myself into such a situation? Gradually, block by block, the prison of fear that I found myself in had surrounded me, until I found myself threatened by a madman with only a few women to guard me, while a storm raged outside. It couldn't be real. It couldn't be happening to me, but it was. "David," I cried out in my mind. "David, David, David. I need you. Come to me. Please come to me!" I realized that it was foolish to call him. But even though I knew he wouldn't come, thinking about him made me feel less alone.

Concern for Louise's safety pricked at my mind. I didn't care what she was or what she had done. It was not a question of liking or disliking her. She had a right to know about Edmond's condition so that she could protect herself from him. I couldn't leave her in ignorance.

"I am going to tell Edmond's wife," I said.

The dowager countess nodded, but she did not speak.

The door to the gallery stood open, as Edmond had left it. If it was not to be locked, it might as well remain open, I had decided. At least that way we might know what

Edmond was doing. We might hear him coming and be warned.

I looked out into the rotunda, but I did not see him. Then I ran to Louise's door (it was not far—her room was just next to Lord Clareham's) and knocked repeatedly.

"Louise, it is Mary. May I come in?" I called.

The door was opened, and when I had slipped inside, I motioned for her to close it.

"It is Edmond. I think you should know. He is ill. He was bitten by a mad dog. He has the disease."

"What disease?"

"Hydrophobia."

"He is mad? Why did you not tell me this before?"

"We did not know it before. He has all the symptoms. He is frothing at the mouth and is very agitated."

"My God! Oh, my God! But I must leave. I must leave at once."

"You can't leave in this weather. Anyway, I am afraid the butler has left the Castle and taken your carriage. Louise, calm yourself. It will be all right. Stay in your room. I must go back to Lady Clareham now, but lock your door after I am gone. Stay in your room, keep your door locked, and don't come out. Do you understand? If you do that, you will be safe."

"Yes. Oh, my God! Oh, my God! Oh, my. . ."

She was still calling to Him when she closed the door after me. I heard the key in the lock, and then I ran back to Lady Clareham's room.

The dowager countess sat at the table, still, and I sat down opposite her.

"I told her," I said. "She is terribly frightened."

Edmond's grandmother glanced at me but she did not reply. What was she thinking about? Was she listening for some sound that would indicate what Edmond was doing? It would be difficult to hear him, I realized: one moment the house would be silent, and the next, the wind outside would hiss and hurl the rain against the windowpanes.

"What time is it, Mary?"

"Ten minutes past six."

Just then, as the storm smacked against the window behind us, Edmond ran into the room. With hardly a pause, he began his incessant pacing.

"I'd like a word with you, Mary," he said, panting, "in private—in the hall chamber."

"Oh?" I said. "What do you wish to speak to me about, Edmond?"

"I told you. It is a private matter. I wish to speak to you alone."

"But surely you can tell me what it is about."

"Your future plans."

"But there is nothing about my future plans that we cannot discuss in front of your grandmother. She is a member of the family. I have no secrets from any of you. What did you wish to say?"

"Come to the hall chamber with me. We will talk there."

"Surely it can wait until morning. I have a dreadful headache and I am much too ill to discuss anything now. Please let us discuss it later."

He stood still for a moment, glaring at me. Then he whirled about and ran from the room.

"He looks better," the dowager countess said.

"The same, I think."

We sat silently for several minutes. I watched Lady Clareham through the doorway of her husband's room. She sat by Lord Clareham's bedside, still, her mind far away. And I thought that I had been right to stay with the dowager countess and Lady Clareham. Edmond had wanted to get me away from them—to get me alone. Had he really thought that I would go with him? The ruse hadn't worked, but what would he try next?

"We must tell the servants," I said. "Suppose he goes down to the servants' hall?"

"Who is down there?" the dowager countess asked.

"Mrs. Foley could be, or May Brooke, or Ida."

"Ring. If someone is there, she will answer it."

I walked to the bellpull, but though I pulled it thirty times, no one came.

"They must not be there," I said, finally.

Then I returned to my chair and sat down.

"I wonder if Mrs. Heart has come?" the dowager countess thought aloud.

"I wonder."

"What time is it?"

"Six thirty-five."

"He should be coming soon."

"I hope so."

Then we heard it—a voice calling softly at first, then louder.

"Grandmamma. Grandmamma. Grandmamma!"

"It is Edmond," I said.

"He is in pain," the dowager countess cried, as she leapt from her chair. "Oh, my poor, dear boy. I am coming!" She ran across the room and out the door. "Grandmamma is coming!"

I followed her as far as the doorway and stood watching her run along the gallery toward Edmond's room.

"Grandmamma!"

Then the dowager countess entered Edmond's room and disappeared from view. I stood still, watching his partly open doorway. I could see it clearly in the gloom, though no lamplight shown through the opening; it was only two doors away from Lady Clareham's in the opposite direction from Louise's room.

A minute crawled by. Nothing happened.

Then Edmond's door opened suddenly, and the dowager countess appeared.

". . . just as soon as I can," I heard her say.

She closed his door behind her and walked rapidly along the gallery toward me. But she did not come back to Lady Clareham's room. Instead, she turned to the stairwell. As she did so, she glanced toward me.

And seeing me standing in the doorway, she called: "It is all right. He is in bed. He wants a glass of warm milk."

Then she began to descend the stairs.

I watched the floor of the rotunda below until she had come out of the stairwell, and I saw her cross the hall and pass from view in the direction of the basement. But then as I began to walk back to my chair, I stopped suddenly. That must be wrong, I thought—if Edmond was afraid of water, he would not want milk. The thought prompted me to glance back at Edmond's door. As I did so, it was thrown open, and Edmond shot out of it and dashed toward me. He wore a nightcap and a pink nightshirt, but instead of the bare shins and slippers I expected to see, he wore his trousers and boots.

His appearance was so unexpected and so bizarre that I was too astonished to move. He was almost upon me before I slammed the door shut and locked it. My heart pounded as I leaned back against the door, and I felt suddenly out of breath. But in that moment of panic, I had not thought quickly enough of the other doorway—the doorway to Lord Clareham's room. At once, I darted to the doorway that connected the two rooms, but I was too late. Edmond was already bounding across Lord Clareham's room toward me. As I shoved the door to close it, he reached it and hurled his body against the other side of it with such force that the door flew back, struck me, and knocked me to the floor.

The blow stunned me, and before I knew what had happened, I felt myself held by the armpits and dragged across the floor. A lock clicked; Edmond opened his mother's door, and he dragged me out onto the gallery toward the railing. In a flash, I realized that he planned to throw me over it to the stone floor below. But just then Lady Clareham screamed from behind me, and at that moment I pushed and punched at Edmond with all my might. He let go of me (he must have been too startled to fend off my blows effectively), and I fell to the floor. Before he could grab me again, I rolled away from him and sprang to my feet in a run.

But he was after me at once, and as I ran around the gallery, I glanced back at him and realized that in spite of his stiff leg he could run as fast as I could in my long dress and petticoats.

All I could think of then was to hide—to get away from him and hide where he wouldn't find me. And the only place I could think of quickly was in one of the trunks in the storage room in the attic. The stairway to the third floor lay directly ahead of me, beyond James's room. When I reached it, I darted into its landing and ran up the steps as fast as I could. The storage room was the first door to the right at the top of the stairs, and as soon as I reached the corridor above, I dashed into it and closed the door behind me.

Before I shut the door completely, however, I glanced back toward the stairs to see if Edmond was close behind. To my horror, I saw that Edmond's head and shoulders had already risen into view as he climbed the stairs. He must have seen me enter the storage room, or at least seen the door close.

It would be folly to climb into a trunk now, I thought. I wouldn't have time to do it anyway. What should I do then? Yes, Edmond had seen me: he had reached the landing and now I heard him running directly toward the storage room door. In a second he would throw it open and find me. In that moment I was able to throw myself flat against the wall so that I would be behind the door when it opened.

When he opened the door, Edmond was sure that he had trapped me, and therefore he did not throw it open with any violence. Rather, he opened it with assurance and stood in the doorway, still holding the doorknob, as he stared into the semidarkness. I could not see him, but I heard him cough and I heard his shallow, rapid breathing on the other side of the door.

His back toward me, Edmond darted to the center of the room and stood looking first at one trunk and then at another. And as he did so, I scurried noiselessly around the door and out into the corridor. I ran back past the stairway that I had just come up, and around the corner of the corridor to the door at the bottom of the cupola stairs. I opened it, slipped inside, and shut the door behind me.

Immediately, I turned around—though there was barely enough room for my feet to do so on the tiny triangular landing—pressed my ear to the door, and listened. I decided that I had been quick enough this time—Edmond did not know where I had gone. He had probably seen me dash to the left as I ran from the storage room, but he would certainly not imagine that I had dodged into this stairway: it was a cul-de-sac with no place to hide.

But I had gone there with good reason. As I stood behind the door in the storage room waiting for Edmond to enter, an idea had sparked in my mind. I realized that I should never have come up to the third floor, and I knew that I must get down to the ground floor. But if I were to do that, I would need a head start on Edmond, and hiding behind the door to the lantern would give it to me. I was sure that if I stood there, he would pass by me, run on down the corridor, and search for me in the Nanny's room, or nursery, or schoolroom. While he was doing that, I could slip across to the second-floor stairway and down it without his pursuing me.

So I stood behind the door to the lantern, listening. I heard nothing—how quiet the house was. Did that mean that it had stopped raining? Surely, if it were raining, I would hear it on the roof above me.

"Please, God," I prayed, silently, "don't let it have stopped raining."

But where was Edmond? I was sure that he had heard me leave the storage room. Had he not seen me turn to the left outside it? He must have gone down the corridor in the opposite direction then—toward the governess's room. No, he *had* seen me leave. He was coming. I heard him cough, and I thought I could hear his footsteps.

He seemed to be moving very slowly. I could hear him plainly now. Then I heard his breathing. He was very close—just outside the door. Instinctively I drew back, stepping up onto the first step of the stair. And as I did so, the wooden tread squeaked. It was only the squeak of a stair, but in the stillness of that house, it might as well have been the blast of a cannon. He had heard it. But I didn't wait for the door to open: I spun around, lifted my skirts above my knees, and fled up the stairs toward the lantern. And in a second or two, I heard Edmond's boots drumming on the stairs behind me.

I would be safe, I thought, if I could reach the cupola, unhook the trapdoor, let it fall, and stand or sit on it before Edmond got to the top of the stairs. If I did that, I doubted that he would be able to raise the combined weight of the door and me from below. He would have to push it straight up with his arms, and I didn't think he was strong enough to do that.

I had no idea how far ahead of Edmond I was. I desperately wanted to look back to see, but I dared not. The stairway seemed endless, and my legs ached before I reached the top. But finally the steps ended, and I threw myself behind the trapdoor, unhooked it, and thrust it down with all my strength.

It was a heavy door, and it fell with a thud. But it did not close: Edmond had been in the way. He had reached the opening in the floor and had been climbing through it at the moment the door fell. It hit him on the side of the head and threw him against the far edge of the stairwell. He lay there pinned between the door and the edge of the floorboards—his head, left arm, and shoulder protruding from the gap. He lay still. The side of his head was red with blood, and his left arm reached limply into the air. I thought I had killed him. But then his eyes came to life and he glared viciously at me. With a tremendous effort— with his whole body—he thrust the door back open and half rolled, half crawled up onto the narrow strip of flooring on the other side of the stairwell from me and lay there panting.

I should have run down the stairs as soon as he forced the trapdoor open. But I had grasped it to prevent it from striking me, and it had taken me a moment to realize that he was not dead after all.

That moment was all Edmond needed to recover a little and scramble to his feet. From around the stairwell to my left, he lunged at the trapdoor, grabbing it just as I let go, and darted to my right. For an instant, we stood at either end of that oblong hole in the floor, staring at each other. I knew that if he slammed the door shut while I stood there, I would be trapped in the cupola with him and he would kill me; but if I ran down the stairs, he would slam the door on top of me and kill me just the same.

I remember glancing down the black hole in front of me; it was too dark to see the stairs. I jumped. Desire to live gave me the courage to do it. I jumped, and slid down the stairs as one would slide down a snowy hill. And as I shot down into the darkness, the trapdoor slammed shut, narrowly missing my head.

Unlike a snowy hill, the stairway was neither smooth nor soft: as I slid down the steps, each tread scraped my legs and rammed my buttocks sending a shock up my spine. My upper body and head, however, were enveloped in skirt and petticoats and thus were protected. So, though badly bruised when I stopped falling at the first little landing, I was not seriously injured and managed to spring to my feet and run down the remaining steps and out into the corridor below.

Edmond's mother and Delphine walked toward me from the direction of the nanny's room, but I did not stop. I plunged into the stairwell and down the stairs that led to the gallery.

I could not have been halfway down them when I heard Lady Clareham cry: "Edmond! Edmond!"

I did not pause then, but when I reached the gallery

landing, I stopped to listen. Edmond was coming. I ran on—down the stairs toward the ground floor of the house. If I could reach the ground floor and the east portico before he caught me, and if it were still raining, I would run out into the rain. I knew that Edmond would not follow me out into it. I would be safe.

Suddenly I felt very tired, however, and my legs didn't seem to want to obey me anymore—they were terribly bruised from sliding down the stairs, and it was painful to run. I drove myself on.

But when I had reached the bottom of the stairs and had taken a few steps across the floor of the rotunda, I heard the sound of Edmond's boots on the marble behind me. How could he have descended the stairs so quickly? I glanced around: he was very close, and already he reached out to grab me. I tried to run faster. Just a little faster, I thought, and I will have time to open the door to the portico. I never got that far: when I reached the middle of the vestibule, I felt Edmond grab the back of my dress at the neckline. I tried to knock his arm away, but I couldn't. He held me fast. And then, in a desperate effort to free myself, I spurted forward, hoping that my dress would tear, but it didn't. Then as I felt Edmond's breath on my neck, the vestibule door flew open.

And David stood in the doorway.

"David!" I screamed.

My scream checked Edmond's attack for an instant, and I wrenched myself free of him.

"David!" I cried. "He is mad! Sarah did bite him."

But even as I warned him off, David bounded toward Edmond and me, and I was barely able to get out of the way before David struck Edmond in the face with his fist sending him staggering backward. Before Edmond could regain his balance, David sprang at him and struck him again under the jaw. The force of the blow seemed to raise Edmond into the air; then he crumpled to the floor, unconscious.

David stepped over Edmond's body and stood staring down at him. Edmond's head was bleeding; his mouth hung open, and from it frothy, stringy saliva dripped into a puddle of blood on the floor.

Then several things happened at once: David said, "I need some rope." Lady Clareham and Delphine ran into the vestibule followed by the dowager countess, holding the glass of milk she had gone to prepare for Edmond. And two men rushed through the doorway from the portico and stood gaping at us (they were grooms from Oakland Park—I recognized one of them).

"David, what have you done?" Lady Clareham cried.

"Do you have any cord or rope?" David demanded, looking from one of us to the other.

"No! What are you going to do?" Lady Clareham said.

David did not answer; he had already whirled about and was running into the rotunda.

"Don't touch him!" he shouted back at us.

"Edmond!" the dowager countess shrieked, as she darted to his side.

"Don't! Stay away!" I cried. And before she could kneel, I sprang at her, grasped her arm, and pulled her away. "He is mad! He attacked me, and he would have killed me if—Lady Clareham, don't!"

Then David dashed back into the vestibule. He carried some lengths of cord and instantly fell on his knees beside Edmond and turned him over on his stomach.

"Patrick," he said, "give me a hand here."

Patrick, one of the grooms, rushed forward, and as he did so, David tossed him a length of the cord and pointed to Edmond's feet. In an instant, David had Edmond's arms pinned behind him and was binding his wrists together and Patrick was binding his feet.

As David knotted the cord, I noticed that one end of it terminated in a tassel. He had torn the cords from the curtains in the drawing room or the hall chamber.

But then, at the same moment, I noticed something else—something that made my blood run cold. David's right knuckles and fingers were covered with Edmond's blood.

"David!" Lady Clareham cried. "What do you think you are doing? How dare you! Release him at once!"

David had finished knotting the cord by then. He straightened up briefly, and then he bent to examine Patrick's bindings. And as he did so, the dowager countess marched up to him and pointed to the cords that bound Edmond's wrists.

"Remove those," she demanded.

Only after David seemed satisfied that Edmond was tied securely did he stand up straight and face her.

"I am sorry. I can't do that," he said.

Meanwhile I had rushed to David's side. "David!" I said, "you must wash your hands. Come with me."

"And why not?" the dowager countess demanded. "You cannot leave him tied there like an animal."

I grasped David by the arm and tried to pull him toward the rotunda.

"Please!" I begged.

"All right," he said, but he did not move. "The man is mad, Lady Clareham. He is dangerous. He cannot be allowed loose. He attacked Mary, and he might attack someone else."

I jerked David's arm. "David you must wash your hands," I cried.

"I will take full responsibility," the dowager countess said.

"It is my responsibility," David said. "If I untied him and he. . ."

"David!" I shouted at him.

". . . injured someone, I could never forgive myself. He will remain tied up until the doctor arrives."

"David, please *come!*"

I was frantic. I pulled him then with all my strength, and he came with me.

"See that he remains tied, Patrick, and you too, Robert," he called back to the grooms.

"Hurry, David," I cried. Then I began to run, and he followed along behind me. "You must wash. You might get infected. Hurry, please!"

From the rotunda we ran down the stairs to the basement, past the servants' hall, and into the laundry rooms. Luckily, two of the washtubs were still filled with soapy water. I grasped David's arm, pulled him to one of the tubs, and plunged his right hand into the water. As I did so, I picked up a bar of yellow soap from the bench beside the tub.

And I would have soaped his hand—I was so anxious about it—if David hadn't reached for the soap and said: "I will do it."

After he had begun to lather his hands, I glanced up at David's face. He was looking down at me, smiling. Then my eyes fastened on his, and even in the semidarkness I was able to read their message and was thrilled by it.

But I knew how important it was for him to wash, so I looked away at once and watched to be sure he did so. When he had finished, we went into the ironing room and David dried his hands on a clean towel which I found for him. Then he lit one of the lamps, and we examined his right hand very carefully for any cut or open place.

"I don't see anything," I said.

"It is a tough farmer's skin," he said. "No, no cuts—nothing open. I think it will be all right, don't you?"

"Yes, I think so." Then I looked up at him and studied his face. "David, if you hadn't heard me—if you hadn't come—"

"If I hadn't heard you?" he asked.

"Yes, I called and called to you. Didn't you hear me?"

"How could I?"

"In your mind."

"No, Mary. I don't believe in that sort of thing."

"Then how did you know to come?"

"Your note."

"What note?"

"Your note to Dr. Norton. Ahmad came to Oakland Park."

"He went to Oakland Park?"

"Yes, and thank God he did. What could old Norton have done if he *had* gotten to the Castle in time? No, Ahmad knew it would have to be someone who could handle Edmond. Actually, I was on my way here—the horses were all saddled. Ahmad heard us in the stable yard. That is where he found me."

"You were on your way here?"

"Yes. Do you remember Hester Glenn, the parlor maid at Oakland Park who showed you where to wash your hands one day? Well, it turns out that she has been meeting Edmond down by the river. She was there with him this morning. Finally, this afternoon, she got up courage to come to me and tell me that he had acted very strangely; that she thought he might be going mad; and that she was concerned for the people at the Castle. Damned good of her, I thought. Most girls would have been afraid."

"Then you knew before you came that Edmond had hydrophobia."

"I suspected it when Hester told me, but I was sure when Ahmad. . ."

"And you hit him, knowing he had the disease? You got his blood on your hands knowing it?"

"Yes."

"Oh, *David!*"

Then David slid his arms around me and pulled me close to him and kissed my mouth and the tears that ran down my cheeks.

Then he said: "You *are* in love with me."

"Of course I am in love with you."

"And you are going to marry me."

"Yes."

"As soon as the bans are published—wedding dress or no wedding dress."

"Yes. Yes, darling, just as soon. . ."

But I couldn't continue because his mouth covered mine again, and he held me so tightly that even if my mouth had been free, I wouldn't have had the breath to speak.

David and I never finished that kiss. In the midst of it, a cry resounded through the house that froze our blood.

"My God!" David said.

He released me at once, grabbed my hand, and pulled me into the corridor at a run. Hand in hand we ran down it, up the stairs, and into the vestibule.

I shall never forget what we saw and heard there. To this day, still, it sometimes haunts me in the night. In the vestibule, Lady Clareham, the dowager countess, Delphine, and the two grooms all stood pressing themselves back against the walls and staring at Edmond. He lay, conscious now, in the center of the floor. His bonds still held fast, but he writhed and threw himself about in a frenzied effort to burst free. His wild eyes flashed and darted everywhere, and he snapped at the air with his teeth. And when his seizure seemed to have reached its climax, he opened his foaming mouth wide and uttered that ghastly cry of anguish—so like the howl of a dog in pain. Then a convulsion racked his body, and he fell back silent and still. But he did not lay quiet for long before an almost identical fit began. And during the next hour, this happened over and over again.

I stood watching him: the horror of it fascinated me,

and I was unable to remove my eyes from him. But then suddenly I found it repellent and turned away.

"What can we do?" I said to David.

"Nothing," he said. "Go into the drawing room."

I went. Shortly the ladies and David followed me, and when they had all entered the room, David closed the doors. This muffled Edmond's cries, but did not silence them.

"Patrick and Robert will see that he doesn't get loose," David said. "Some gloves would be useful."

"In the closet in the vestibule—some old ones on the shelf," Lady Clareham said.

"Ahmad will be here with the doctor soon," David said.

"He went for Dr. Norton after he left Oakland Park?" I asked.

"Yes."

Then David left the room to get the gloves for the grooms. When he had gone, Lady Clareham, the dowager countess, and I sat down. And before long, David returned and sat next to me. We sat there trying not to listen to Edmond's screams while we waited for the doctor.

Ten minutes later, the doors opened and Ahmad entered the room. His clothes were wet. He was alone. He explained to Lady Clareham that the doctor was not at home, but that he had left the note with a woman there.

"He must be in the taproom at the Red Lion, then," David said. "I will go and get him." Then he looked at me. "Ten minutes there, ten minutes back. Patrick and Robert will be here, and Colen is in the stables."

"No, Colen left this morning," I said.

"And he came back with me. He works at Oakland Park now. I will be as quick as I can. And while I am gone, you had better get some coffee made for Norton."

He left us then, and shortly I heard him ride from the stable yard toward the village. Lady Clareham asked Ahmad to make coffee after he had changed into dry clothes.

After that, Lady Clareham, the dowager countess, and I sat in the drawing room together and waited.

At last the dowager countess said: "Why did it have to be he? Such a good, sweet, kind boy—intelligent and thoughtful. Such a dear boy." She was crying. "Why did it have to be he?" Then after a moment: "I can't bear it any longer—I can't bear listening to him scream. Delphine, go up and get my cloak, please. I am going outside."

When her maid had returned with a mantle and they had left us, I opened one of the long windows and stepped out onto the portico to breathe. Though the rain had stopped, it was cold and damp out there, and I soon returned to Lady Clareham.

"It wasn't really his fault," she said, after a while. "He destroyed himself, and he destroyed us. He didn't mean to do it—it was just the way he was.'

"Yes."

"God is too cruel—too cruel to endure."

Hours seemed to pass before David returned with Dr. Norton, but it was only thirty minutes. When we heard them enter the house, Lady Clareham and I rushed into the hall to meet them. We were terribly disappointed when we saw Dr. Norton: he had been drinking heavily.

Immediately David led him away from us and downstairs, to the servants' hall.

And when they had disappeared, we returned to the drawing room and closed the doors behind us. Edmond seemed somewhat quieter, but there was nothing we could do for him, and we could not have borne watching his agony.

After several minutes had passed, Lady Clareham said: "It is quiet. I don't hear him now. What are they doing out there?"

"I think David is giving Dr. Norton coffee," I said.

I got up then, walked into the rotunda, and looked into the vestibule. Edmond no longer lay there. And when I looked up at the gallery, I saw the doctor, and David, and the groom, Patrick, coming out of Edmond's room. Patrick remained outside Edmond's door, but David and Dr. Norton turned to the stairwell and descended to the hall.

I went to meet them.

"You have taken him upstairs?" I asked.

"Yes, Lady Beauford," Dr. Norton said. "He is asking for you. If you will be so good as to go up, I will go and have a word with Lady Clareham. She is in the drawing room?"

"I would rather not," I said. Then, when Dr. Norton looked at me in surprise, I explained, "He tried to kill me before you came. I was terrified."

"Yes, well, no need for that now. The excitement stage

of the disease has past. The paralysis is becoming general, I'm afraid—affecting the face already. He will become increasingly feeble and gradually pass into a comatose state and then—"

"Still, I would rather not go up."

"Lady Beauford, Lord Althrop is going to die. In two, perhaps three hours, he will no longer be with us."

"Yes. Will you come with me David?"

David nodded, and together we climbed the stairs, walked into Edmond's room, and crossed to the bed where Edmond lay. He seemed to breathe more easily now, and the wild look had left his eyes. He looked pale and thin, and very tired.

"Have you told the police?" Edmond asked.

Because of the paralysis, he spoke with difficulty. His pronunciation was distorted, and it was difficult to understand what he said.

"Not yet," I replied.

"But you will."

"I have no choice."

"Absurd. No proof. James wanted to die—slowly, so we wouldn't know. He poisoned himself. Luck is changing now. Always was against me—always. But it's fine now. Win a fortune. I know how. Restore the Castle. Wonderful!" Then he paused and tried to smile. "You thought you'd won. Thought you'd beaten me. No."

"Beaten you?" I said. "The conflict was not between you and me, Edmond. It was what you had done that opposed you. If I hadn't found out, someone else would have. It would all have come out anyway."

"No. If you hadn't come, it never would have."

Then Edmond turned his head away from us, toward the wall.

For a moment I stood looking down at him: then I swung about, walked away from his bed, and left the room.

David followed me, and as we walked toward the stairway together, I asked him: "Was he right?"

"About what, my darling?"

"Would Lord Clareham still be alive, Edmond had lived, and the servants have kept his secret, if I had never come to Castle Cloud?"

A pulsing romantic saga

Marilyn Harris
Bleeding Sorrow

Within a magnificent, spirit-ravaged mansion, on the eerily beautiful Yorkshire moors, a lovely child-bride is kept drugged and hidden—forced to submit to her husband's strange desires . . .

Ann Bledding, young mistress of the manor, dared to escape with James, the handsome coachman; but she was destined to re-enact the tortured passions of an ancient horror too terrible to end—a love too strong to die!

"A chilling novel, centered around an ancestral estate in England, a recurring family madness, a ghastly crime in the 17th Century, reappearing spectres . . . rich prose and deftly maintained suspense."

Milwaukee Journal

AVON   31971 $1.95

SOR 5-77